To BCN from DCN, 2/90 — Just because I mentioned it.

Please return my book

bn 8/92

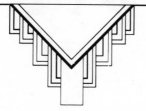

MICHAEL M. THOMAS

HANOVER PLACE

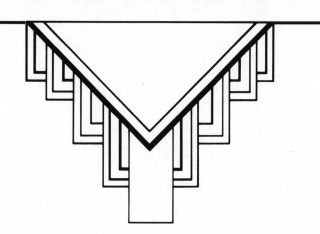

WARNER BOOKS

A Warner Communications Company

Warner Books, Inc., 666 Fifth Avenue, New York, NY 10103

 A Warner Communications Company

Printed in the United States of America
First printing: January 1990
10 9 8 7 6 5 4 3 2 1

LIBRARY OF CONGRESS CATALOGING-IN-PUBLICATION DATA

Thomas, Michael M.
    Hanover Place/Michael M. Thomas.
        p.   cm.
    ISBN 0-446-51330-X
    I. Title.
PS3570.H574H36   1990
813'.54—dc20   89-40038
                                                    CIP

Book design by Giorgetta Bell McRee

This book is for two extraordinary men,
born eighty years apart, who from opposite
ends of my life have made such a difference:
my late father, Joseph A. Thomas,
and my little son Francis.

This is a work of fiction. Apart from certain historical figures, the characters in this book are products of the author's imagination.

A man will talk about how he'd like to escape from living folks. But it's the dead folks that do him the damage. It's the dead ones that lie quiet in one place and don't try to hold him, that he can't escape from.

—FAULKNER, *Light in August*

CONTENTS

AUTHOR'S NOTE

The disclaimer in the front of the book is not entirely candid. In certain of my characters, I have attempted to memorialize—with affection and respect—a number of people I have known and admired. Lyda Warrington is in various important aspects based on my adored maternal great-aunt Miss Mary Whitney Bangs, "Polly" to her friends, and a true lady to the bone. She was the last of her branch of the family, which landed in New England in 1623 on the *Anne*, to bear the surname Bangs. It would normally have been perpetuated by her beloved nephews, Whitney and Francis, but they died in combat within weeks of each other in the spring of 1945.

In a number of other characters I have incorporated bits and pieces of the singularity and example of Albert H. Gordon (who also appears as himself), the late Edgar B. Kapp, the late Robert Lehman, the late Harold J. Szold and, of course, my own father, Joseph A. Thomas.

The last four were all associated with Lehman Brothers. In the 1960s, it was not only the best firm on the Street, but the most fun to work for. We made good money, and—as far as possible in any business predicated on money-spinning—we played by the rules. It was the people, of course, that gave One William Street its special character, and there is a lot about this book that is based on my experiences there, and the men and women with whom I worked. In a way, some of this book is theirs. It is impossible to list them all, but to them I tender a valedictory tip of the hat and tilt of the glass, along with the wish that, wherever fate may have taken them, the force is still with them.

The best a writer can hope for is that the book he produces more or less approximates the book he set out to write. For me, this objective would have been utterly beyond reach without the help of others. Laurence Kirshbaum, president of Warner Books, has been a dogged, inspired, and inspiriting friend and editor. When it comes to holding my feet to the fire and beating sense and grammar into my prose, no one has the resolution and effectiveness of my wife Barbara, especially when abetted by my son Will.

Jason Epstein, under no obligation apart from the generosity of friendship, offered advice that was both cogent and indispensable. Betty Prashker and Morton Janklow also made crucial observations.

Three times during the long and often fretful gestation of this novel, Irwin and Terry Allen Kramer uprooted me and my family, took us to the sun, spoiled us rotten with good company and good food, and gave me a chance to walk on the beach and rethink this enterprise. Without such friends, nothing gets done.

BOOK

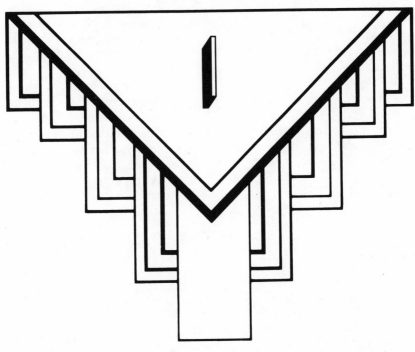

1

PARTIES OF THE FIRST PART

1924

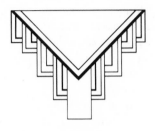

Consider the photograph.

Study it with the same care and curiosity as did many, perhaps most, New Yorkers of a certain social and economic level when it appeared in the rotogravure section of *The New York Times* on a Sunday in May 1924.

It shows four people, two couples: one quite young, in their middle to late twenties to judge by their appearance; the other—a woman about fifty, her husband a decade or so older.

The caption reads: "Miss Lyda Vanderlyn Farwell and her fiancé, Mr. Howland Micah Templeton Warrington, who are to be married in Trinity Church on November 17. The couple are photographed in the drawing room of the Stuyvesant Square residence of the parents of the groom-to-be, Mr. and Mrs. Fletcher St. G. Warrington. Mr. Warrington is the managing partner of S. L. Warrington & Son, 1 Hanover Place, which has been in business in this city since 1814. The younger Mr. Warrington is also associated with the family firm."

The little group is posed in what is clearly a large and impressive room. In the shadows, one can make out the dim shapes of important pieces of furniture. Someone studying the photograph closely, with a magnifying glass perhaps, might make out a large painting in the background. This is the famous Eastman Johnson group portrait *Erasmus Warrington and His Family*, painted in 1872, which is now in the Museum of Manhattan. In the foreground of Johnson's painting is a twelve-year-old boy with a hoop; he and the older man in the photograph are one and the same.

The two women are seated in front, in large tapestried wing chairs of the Queen Anne period. Their men stand behind and slightly off to the sides. Both the women seem tall. The younger is no conventional beauty; her features are too strong for that, although they are good and well spaced; her mouth, especially, seems generous and determined. In the fashion of young women of her day and station, she wears her medium-dark hair in a modified bob, just below the nape of her neck. Her hands, clasped in her lap, are long and graceful, and arranged to display an engagement ring with an obviously important stone.

Although well into middle age, the older woman is an undeniable beauty in the Edwardian fashion. Her dark hair is piled high in thick, lustrous coils. Her head is tilted ever so slightly to the right to present her best angle. Under her ankle-length gown can be read suggestions of a figure of ample, Junoesque proportions. Her long neck is adorned with a necklace of extraordinarily large square-cut gems. The impression is that she could step out of this photograph and into a grand Sargent portrait without missing a beat.

The younger man is fair in all respects, with the sort of blond, angular, refined good looks that many think epitomize the nation and the class at its finest. Like his mother, he is the perfection of a type. He has a prominent, sharp, sloping nose, and frank light eyes, features he shares with his father. His bearing is military. He wears his well-cut medium-dark lounge suit as if it were a uniform; indeed, the razor-ironed kerchief peeping from his breast pocket might as easily be a row of ribbons on an officer's tunic.

The older man is several inches shorter. He is obviously not altogether at ease with the camera. He inclines slightly forward, faintly combative, on the balls of his feet like a prizefighter. In the gaze he turns on the lens there is just a suspicion of mistrust. He is a vigorous man for his age, obviously very fit and aware of it, with strong square features under carefully brushed and parted gray hair. Although there is a hint, no more than a shadow really, of a second chin pressing down on his stiff collar, there are no soft bits in this man; even the dark double-breasted suit encasing the solid, compact body seems made of a material tough enough to stop a bullet; it fits like armor.

The four people regard the lens as if looking right through it to the spacious vistas of a fine and privileged existence. They display the attributes you would expect from people of this sort: pride, satisfaction, confidence. They are each in their own way impressive as individuals and specimens, yet it is to the younger woman and the older man that the eye returns. They are clearly full of self-assurance about themselves and their destinies, and yet it seems equally certain that they take very little for granted.

In the months following the announcement of their engagement, the papers would carry numerous pictures of Lyda and Howland: on the Morgan yacht *Corsair* at New London for the Harvard-Yale boat race, at Newport and Saratoga, at Cedarhurst for the Rockaway handicap, at Forest Hills for the tennis, at the international polo matches at Meadow Brook. This was, after all, the wedding of the year, at least on Wall Street, where the standing in the canyons of finance of the groom's family made the union the most consequential since Pierpont Morgan's daughter Louisa had married the Satterlee boy at the turn of the century.

Small wonder. In his 1871 memoir, *Twenty Years Among the Bulls and Bears of Wall Street*, Matthew Hale Smith listed Erasmus Warrington, the great-grandfather of the groom-to-be, among "the heavy men of the Street." By the time of Lyda and Howland's engagement, a half century after Smith wrote, a century and some since the family firm had been founded in a stabling yard just off Wall Street, the Warringtons were "heavier" than ever.

Employees of "The Firm," as S. L. Warrington & Son was known to its people, were thoroughly catechized in the key dates of its history. Founded in 1814 by a privateer captain with prize money for its initial capital, The Firm had been nurtured to greatness by the founder's son Erasmus. The latter's son Micah was killed in 1862 at Antietam, with his young wife pregnant with their first child. Thus Erasmus's infant grandson Fletcher was designated by cruel fate to be heir-apparent. His training began in early boyhood. Indeed, in his famous diary, George Templeton Strong records calling in 1870 at the Warrington family mansion, then on Union Place, and finding Erasmus Warrington in the upstairs parlor drilling his small grandson in the compound interest tables.

On March 12, 1888, Erasmus Warrington, obdurate as always, had insisted on setting out for Hanover Place in the teeth of the Great Blizzard. The old man's frozen body was later found clinging to a stanchion on the Bowery, an expression of intense vexation on his face. It was one of the few times on record that a Warrington was known to have let stubbornness overcome prudent calculation. Fletcher, then a young man of twenty-five, just three years out of Yale, now succeeded to the generalship of The Firm. In the next forty-six years, he raised 1 Hanover Place, located on a small square off Old William Slip, near Pearl and Water Streets, to an eminence beside which even his grandfather's notable achievements paled. At the time of Lyda and Howland's betrothal, "Hanover Place" was one of the best-known addresses in the square half-mile rabbit warren of down-town Manhattan in which was concentrated the greatest aggregate money power the world had ever known.

In terms of family wealth, the Warringtons hardly compared to indus-trial or transportation dynasties like the Rockefellers, Harrimans, Van-derbilts, or Du Ponts. By Wall Street standards, the family hoard was small; by comparison with the purses of the partners of the house of Morgan at 23 Wall Street and the great German-Jewish banking houses —Lehman Brothers, Goldman Sachs, and Kuhn Loeb—almost minuscule.

Influence was something else, however, and here The Firm excelled all but Morgan. Influence was based not merely on the ability to mobilize vast sums of one's own and others' capital, but on character, presence, financial ingenuity, market prescience—and a reputation mostly deserved, sometimes not, for those qualities. It helped also to have all that history —for potential "connections" to note that S. L. Warrington & Son was already about to celebrate its half-centenary at the time a bright young man named J. Pierpont Morgan struck out on his own.

Socially, the Warrington name was no less daunting. The family was not, as many thought, of Mayflower stock, but its roots were deep. The first Warrington to establish himself on this side of the Atlantic had left perfectly agreeable circumstances in the English town of Warrington, on the Mersey estuary, and crossed to the New World in 1664—in search not of religious freedom, but of fortune. By 1676, the family were recorded as ship captains and landowners in the towns of Sag Harbor and East Hampton. Their social ascent in Manhattan came later. The name "War-rington" does not appear on Mrs. John Jay's "Dinner and Supper List" of 1787, the first renowned "in list" of Manhattan society; exactly a century later, however, it could be found, between "James Varnum" and "Mr. and Mrs. James M. Waterbury" on Ward McAllister's compilation for Mrs. William Astor of the four hundred people who counted in New York. On the eve of Lyda and Howland's marriage, the Warringtons were ranked beyond question at the very top of any census of Manhattan aristocracy.

The upcoming marriage was discussed with avidity right through the summer and early fall of 1924. Indeed, only the juicy divorce of Count Salm from Millicent Rogers, the Standard Oil heiress, vied for the atten-tions of society. It was pondered over the rough linen that covered the oak and walnut tables of the Stock Exchange Luncheon Club and the Downtown Association and chatted about over the delicate lace shrouding the veneered and inlaid surfaces on which the inhabitants of exquisite

Murray Hill townhouses, grand Turtle Bay drawing rooms, and vast Sutton Place apartments poured tea and exchanged gossip.

Much of the interest lay in the prominence of the groom's family, but the bride was also deemed to be uncommonly noteworthy. She was originally from Chicago—Lake Forest, of course!—and an orphan: Her parents had perished on the *Titanic* when she was twelve. She was independent, of means to some extent, of mind without any doubt; who else but a woman with a will of steel could have prevailed on Fletcher Warrington to stage the wedding on the day of the Yale-Princeton game! Yet there was nothing "madcap" or "flapperish" about her, notwithstanding an early New York life that smacked faintly of bohemianism. Men found her alluring yet easy to talk with, women admired her instinct for style and liked the discretion with which she carried it off; her tall figure and excellent bearing showed off to perfection the Pacquin and Poiret frocks in which she was photographed for *Vogue* and *Vanity Fair*. She was bright, and she understood what becoming a Warrington wife meant.

This above all was why the groom's parents made no bones about how delighted they were with Howland's choice of a wife. She possessed the attributes necessary to serve and protect the traditions embodied in her husband-to-be, to share with him a sensible, productive stewardship of the family's advantages and obligations. Everyone counted the Warringtons lucky, but as a wise man would observe years later, luck is in most instances the residue of design.

In these times, people said, standards were exceedingly difficult to maintain. A roaring bull market was getting under way. All kinds of dubious people were starting to make large fortunes on Wall Street. Custom and tradition and society were under siege; the barbarians were at the gates, armored in their newly minted gold. It was good to know that strong hands had been found to help Howland Warrington bear the torch that must sooner or later pass to him.

For the day of the wedding, the newspapers predicted more dreary, damp weather. At midday of November 17, however, as the bells of Trinity Church tolled noon and the closing gong of the Stock Exchange bonged an end to as busy a week as the Street had known in its history, a pale and chilly scrim of haze melted away and Manhattan was bathed with the soft dull gold of late autumn sunlight.

As favorable an omen as this seemed, even more so was the behavior of the stock market. When the week ended, both the Dow-Jones average and *The New York Times* bond index had posted handsome gains for the day and week on huge trading volume. Over a million shares a day! And for four days running! A level that had not been seen for two decades. The existence of a great bull market was now surely confirmed. The previous Sunday's *Times* had bannered: BOOM DAYS COME AGAIN TO U.S. and now those words had been proven true.

Well, it was about time! Here was what the Street had expected to enjoy right after the Great War, when the success of the huge Liberty Loan syndications—in 1917–18, almost ten billion dollars had been placed with investors—had seemed to confirm the existence of an unquenchable, rabid public thirst for securities investment. But the Street had forgotten how problematical peace can be for markets; the deflationary depression of 1920–21, as the war economy ratcheted down, had sent investors to the sidelines and there they had remained for the last few years. But now, praise be to God, the rising tide of savings had brimmed its banks, overflowed levees of apprehension and prudence, and investors large and small were clamoring frantically for bonds and, praise Him again, stocks. A spirit of optimism was in the air, a feeling of economic destiny made manifest. America's God-given right to prosperity was finally being realized, and its rightful beneficiaries, the men of finance, the heavy men who knew their markets, understandably stood to profit the most. The years after the Great War had been difficult: a time of letdown, price disruption, subversion, and unrest, followed by the scandals of the Harding administration, black stains on the business and financial community. Only with the accession of Coolidge had the tide begun to turn. Just two weeks before the wedding, President Coolidge had been thumpingly returned for a second term. Wall Street could reassure itself that for at least another four years, the governance of the nation would be securely lodged with solid men who understood business, men like Andrew Mellon at Treasury and Herbert Hoover at Commerce. There was a growing feeling up and down Wall Street that America was safely launched on a New Era, an age of prosperity and growth not seen since the glorious days of William McKinley.

Thus the mood downtown on November 17, 1924. If there was a cloud on the Street's sunny horizon, it was purely social in nature. It had first been sighted some nine weeks earlier, on the Tuesday following the Labor Day weekend, when roughly five hundred double envelopes, of Tiffany's heaviest cream stock, addressed inside and out in the familiar backward-sloping Spencerian script of Miss Julia Cutting, social secretary to Manhattan's elite, were deposited at the Battery post office. This was the beginning of what one wit called "the Society Panic of 1924."

Each envelope contained an invitation to the wedding reception of Lyda

Farwell and Howland Warrington, at six o'clock in the afternoon at the Colony Club, only recently installed in its grand new premises at Park Avenue and 62nd Street. In addition, three hundred envelopes also held invitations to the wedding ceremony itself.

Although it was not true that an impromptu market in the invitations was conducted in the cloakroom of the Stock Exchange, the social ripples assumed tidal proportions. It soon became apparent that there were clearly only two acceptable alternatives for the late afternoon of November 17, 1924: to be at one or both of the Farwell-Warrington festivities, or to get out of town. The transatlantic shipping companies reported a remarkable upsurge in first-class bookings for that weekend, as did leading resort hotels from the Green Mountains south to the Smokies.

The invitation list was fairly predictable. The pews right behind the family would of course be reserved for the partners of The Firm and their families. Next would come the partners of J. P. Morgan & Co., led by Thomas Lamont, since Jack Morgan himself would be away in Berlin sorting out the latest German financial crisis. Prior to the wedding, Lamont would host a lunch at 23 Wall Street for a number of the more noteworthy out-of-town guests: a choice covey of steel magnates from Pittsburgh and Gary, automobile barons from Detroit and South Bend, railroad satraps from Chicago, St. Louis, and San Francisco, mining magnates from the West, and managers of the great Boston and Edinburgh investment trusts.

This gesture of hospitality was not the only means by which the House of Morgan chose to acknowledge its half century of close and profitable collaboration with the Warringtons. Visitors to the suite in the Colony Club in which the young couple's wedding gifts could be viewed invariably halted breathlessly before a thirty-place table service, in vermeil, crystal, and Meissen, which a small typewritten label described as having been the property of six Electors of Saxony, two kings of France, and a Russian emperor. The service was fronted by a business card on which was engraved, simply, "Compliments of the Partners of J. P. Morgan & Company."

Speculation about the guest list remained feverish right up to the moment the early arrivals' towncars deposited them at Trinity. Who on the Floor would be invited? Would there be any Jews apart from the dynasts: Otto Kahn, the Schiffs and the Lehmans, the Seligmeyers? Would there be any Irish, lowest of all on the ethnic ladder? Who from Europe? The Warringtons might rank with the Morgans and that ilk, murmured some, and the barrier Fletcher and his wife Ariadne maintained between the family's private life and its business connections, the so-called "Warrington Wall," was famous and formidable, seldom scaled and never breached, but everyone also knew Fletcher had done right well from time to time with socially questionable people in dealings over the wire or behind closed doors, people he wouldn't be caught dead with on a Sunday stroll through Murray Hill or lifting a glass within the card room of the Gorse Club. Would he use his son's wedding to acknowledge some of these relationships? The old boy might be a snob socially, but when it came to making money, there was no more committed democrat on the Street!

As the great day approached, a few nerves—mainly female—finally cracked. Coming right on top of the September visit of the Prince of Wales, this was simply too much! The stresses attendant upon even the most battle-hardened social sensibility were intense. But it was not only the fair sex that was devoured by anxiety. As the first limousines pulled to a stop on Broadway, in the shadow of the famous spire, there were men on the opposite sidewalk furtively noting, from beneath the slanting brims of down-pulled fedoras, who were there and who not. These were not journalists, nor sea-green youths, callow youngsters of the Street anxious for a glimpse of the stars of finance, but men who, on any other day on Wall Street, would have been considered heavy in their own right.

Fifty blocks uptown, on the third floor of the Warringtons' Madison Avenue mansion, Lyda Farwell examined herself in the mirror and approved of what she saw. The mirror was a fine Empire cheval glass, which Lyda had admired in Miss McMillen's smart new decorating shop and which her mother-in-law-to-be had promptly bought for her.

"I wonder what sort of life you and I are going to have together," she murmured to the looking glass.

She turned slightly, checking the drape of her Worth wedding gown, adjusting the train so it pooled just so. Around her neck, the famous Warrington pearls gleamed in the pale sunlight flooding in from the avenue. She went over to the desk between the windows and for yet another time took a pen from a silver holder, wrote "Lyda V. Farwell" on a piece of monogrammed paper, stared at the signature briefly, crossed it out, and wrote "Lyda F. Warrington" underneath.

She smiled and nodded to herself, turned and studied the room. I really must persuade Ariadne to have Eleanor McMillen come and make some suggestions about this, she reflected. The ornate appointments chosen by the Herters were all very well for the turn of the century, but life was different now.

A door opened and her aunt came in. "It's almost time, dear," said Miranda Farwell, hands nervously rotating her beaded handbag.

"Auntie Miranda, will you please relax!" said Lyda sharply in the flat, unaccented Chicago tones that four years at Wellesley and two living in New York had failed to efface entirely. "You're making me nervous! I'll be ready when the time comes, I promise!"

As her aunt remained fidgeting in the background, Lyda returned to the mirror. She was glad she was dark. Hair almost raven, eyes bright and black, possibly a touch far apart; her nose was long, but it wasn't out of proportion. Her mouth was her favorite feature: wide and strong, sensual but not forward, forceful but not snappish. She wondered what the fullness of time would do, how would she look twenty years from now?

She pursed her lips, grinned widely, then turned the corners of her mouth down in a sulk. Age goes right for the mouth, she thought. The thing to do was to keep calm and even. Don't smile too much, don't frown too much. As in all things: moderation. She held her hands up on either side of her face. If I'd had my druthers, she thought, I'd have opted for smaller hands and a bit more in the bosom department. She also thought herself a trifle bottom-heavy—although those wide hips augured well for child-bearing—but with her height and long legs there was nothing pendulous about her.

She turned back into the room. "Well, Auntie, what do you think? Very Sargent, no?"

"Very grand indeed," said Lyda's aunt with a touch of asperity, refusing to shed her socialism even in this hour of glory for her adored niece. Then the older woman's voice softened. "No, dear, you do look absolutely ravishing. Just exactly like the portrait downstairs." In the salon below hung Sargent's famous, much-exhibited full-length portrait of Ariadne Warrington.

"Why, thank you, Auntie!" exclaimed Lyda. "Such a compliment!"

Lyda crossed the room and gave her aunt a kiss. Instinctively the older woman put up a motherly hand and smoothed the tight satin cap, straightening the veil that Lyda had pushed carelessly back.

"Look, Auntie," said Lyda, "why don't you go downstairs and join the Warringtons? I need a moment to gather myself."

She was dying for a cigarette, a habit that her aunt regarded as a typical indulgence of a frenetic capitalist society and thus almost a social evil.

"Shoo, now," she cried. "I just need a minute or two by myself. To think."

"Call it anything you want," said her aunt with a wink. "Just keep an eye on the time." She looked significantly toward the gold Tiffany clock on the mantel to reinforce her instruction.

Lyda's gaze followed. Got to do something about that clock, Lyda thought; it's completely wrong. The sort of thing Howland and his father kept winning at golf tournaments and cluttering the various Warrington establishments with. There would be none of that in *her* houses!

"Auntie, the last time I was late for anything was when I was born. You know how I hate tardiness myself! Now, shoo!"

With a mock gesture of defeat and a big smile, her aunt withdrew, backing out of the room like an ambassador leaving the presence of a volatile pagan empress.

Lyda rooted in her handbag for a Chesterfield, lit it, and went over to the French windows that overlooked the corner of Madison Avenue. Across the Avenue and a bit south stood the implacable bulk of the late Pierpont Morgan's house, only recently opened to the public as a museum and library. Next to it stood his son Jack's mansion. Rumor had it that the J. P. Morgans would soon be leaving the neighborhood, now that an office building was going up across the way. An office building in the heart of Murray Hill! The idea infuriated her. Like most people who were relatively new to the city, Lyda cared for it much more passionately than its natives seemed to.

Was nothing in the city to be safe from the realtor's rapacity and the wrecker's ball, she wondered. Well, perhaps she'd be able to do something about that once she became Mrs. Howland Warrington. Change wasn't necessarily progress; real-estate profits shouldn't be the sole gauge of urban life. The thing to do was to become involved. Her husband-to-be was of a like mind.

"When we're finally properly set up in the new house," Howland had told her, "one of our first orders of business will be to get to know the powers in the city. It's a big gap in The Firm's position. We have no real public role. I don't think Father even knows who the mayor is, and that's ridiculous. People in our position have simply got to get involved with the larger affairs of life, including local politics!" Then he'd added hastily: "But for God's sake, don't tell Father. You know how he is. Politics are poison to him and public service is a form of madness!"

Puffing on her cigarette, she reviewed the coming weeks' schedule, speaking out loud to herself, as was her habit. It was one reason she needed time alone with herself. Solitude recharged her.

There would be no honeymoon, nor even a wedding trip. On Monday, Howland was traveling to Pittsburgh with his father to meet with the Bethlehem Steel people. By Tuesday evening, when he returned, Lyda would have moved them into the St. Regis, where they had taken an apartment until their new Park Avenue townhouse was finished, which wouldn't be until after the first of the year. Wednesday: she and Ariadne and Mrs. McMillen were meeting at Hanover Place to see if something could be done about the dreary partners' conference room on the fourth floor; then, after the close of business, she and Howland and the senior Warringtons were hosting a reception and buffet for the employees of The Firm and their families, an occasion she feared might prove uncomfortably feudal, with much forelock-tugging and knee-bending. Neverthe-less, there had to be some appearance by the royal newlyweds before their subjects, and this was probably as good a way as any.

Thursday the Fentons were giving a dinner in their honor. "Damn!" she muttered to herself and vexedly contemplated the prospect of a life spent in close proximity with Charles Christian Fenton III. Men did conceive the oddest friendships! Chubby had a bluff, back-slapping manner that grated on her, and as for his intellect, it was nonexistent! It wasn't that she wanted all of Howland's friends to be Menckens or Einsteins—Lyda had been a prodigious and precocious student, but she hardly con-sidered herself an egghead—yet Chubby seemed utterly determined to know *nothing*. Obviously he was fighting his own demons, which he appeared to think he could suppress by making noise or pleading stupidity. Well, other men did the same via expenditure or promiscuity, so what was the difference? For richer or poorer, better or worse, Chubby came along as part of the package; no use fighting the fact.

Her thoughts returned to their schedule. Next, the weekend: a Green-wich house party and the Yale-Harvard game. Most of the men could be counted upon to drink too much. And so on and so on. One engagement after another right through the end of the year. She and Howland had resigned themselves to the fact that it would be February before they could enjoy a proper honeymoon, a three-week sojourn in Murren and St. Moritz. Howland was determined that she learn to ski, just as he was also teaching her to fly. If everything went just right, when they got back in early March they could move into the Neo-Federal house at 68th Street and Park Avenue that Howland's parents had commissioned from McKim, Mead and White as a wedding present.

"I'm going to miss you," she whispered, thinking of her small but airy Greenwich Village apartment, the three rooms on West 9th Street she'd occupied after coming to New York following her graduation; they over-looked a single plane tree, forlorn but doughty, and she'd hung them with Sloan and Pennell etchings of city scenes. Lyda could take or leave Impres-sionism and Cubism, but she had a real passion for the art of the city. Now at least she could indulge that fancy; in fact she'd already reserved two brilliant Childe Hassam paintings of Fifth Avenue decked out in flags. They'd look wonderful in the library of the new house, and the nice man at Grand Central Galleries had been very sensible about the price when he found out she was Mr. Howland Warrington's fiancée.

Well, her Village existence was a dead chapter now, a way of life she doubted she would ever know again, mildly bohemian, pleasant, warm, populated by varied but insignificant people, open to spontaneous turnings and chance encounters. Thinking about it, she felt a rush of nostalgia as rapid and faint as a wingbeat, and then regret flew from her mind. The

Village had only been an interlude. The journey on which she was about to embark was her destiny.

If there was one thing Lyda shared with her husband and his family, it was a sense of mission. The Warringtons went about life as if they had made a just and equitable bargain with the Maker; they did their part: good works, regular church attendance, handsome tithes to virtuous causes, honored their ancestors; God did His and saw to it that the family fortune multiplied. Lyda's sense of fate was less religious, more in the spirit of the Greek plays that had so impressed her at Wellesley. The gods dealt the cards, and even hinted how best they might be played, but it was up to the individual to spot the bluff, or to finesse, or barge ahead with trumps, or play off the other man.

As to the specifics of her future, she was under no illusions. Her mission would be the mothering of greatness: in her husband and in the children she would bear him.

That Howland had the makings of an important man, one who would manifestly enlarge the great advantages he was born with, she had no doubt. Sometimes, in the middle of the night, she found herself wondering if she was less in love with the man than with his possibilities. The notion never vexed her for long. Whether she loved him for himself or for the idea of him, whether the object of her infatuation was the man or his potential, was a fine distinction she felt no urge to tax herself with.

To other people, Lyda appeared to possess a cool heart and a clear eye and a notable sense of emotional proportion. She did not laugh or cry easily, or for effect. Perhaps—it was surmised—the sudden, shocking loss of her parents had in some way cauterized her feelings and regulated her deportment. She herself knew there was something to this. It often struck her, in her relentless bouts of self-examination, that what aroused her, opened her up, made her rage and weep, were as likely to be ideas as much as people, a trait she saw in her Aunt Miranda, who hurled herself briefly and helplessly at every high-sounding noble cause and prophet that came along, provided the rich and privileged were the targets. Lyda's father used to laugh at his sister, and tease her about the obvious advantages of being "a socialist with a private income."

But there was also a vulnerable, idealistic side to Lyda, which she kept stowed out of sight. Even Howland was barely aware of it. This was a faith, both consoling and complicating, in the reality of the true and the good. She got it from her father, a great reader and declaimer of inspirational poetry, and from the books he gave her as a girl. Indeed, for the first couple of years after her parents' death, books had been Lyda's sole effective solace.

She was therefore fighting a constant inclination to expend her emotions on causes, campaigns, ideals, on the great designs and issues of which individuals, as she saw it, were but instruments. Absent self-control, each dawn might be interpreted as a summons to a new crusade, a noble quest or adventure undertaken in the name of the just, the fair, and the right. It was not, she tried to remind herself sternly, a very grown-up way to go through life in a cynical world, but it took a great deal of energy to hold in, so she was halfheartedly hopeful that the duties of marriage and motherhood would leaven her illusions.

She knew Howland shared, and was quite open about, a degree of the idealism she concealed. Thus theirs would be an honorable and true partnership to noble public and private ends, a world beyond money-grubbing.

Although she never said as much to Howland, she believed there was a certain *smallness* to The Firm's—to Fletcher's—ambitions that she had every intention of seeing transcended in her husband. She did not consider her expectations unrealistic. After all, Howland had seen the largest matters of life and death at first hand. Compared to such mortal business, how possibly could Wall Street's little game of eighths and quarters, of buying and selling pieces of paper, impress such a man? Thank God for that, Lyda told herself; in her cosmology, stockbrokers—men like Hap Carruthers or Eddie Stanforth—ranked at the very bottom of the universe.

First things first. Under the terms of The Firm's charter, it would be another two years, until Howland turned thirty in 1926, before he could be taken into the partnership, and several years after that, Lyda guessed, before he could expect to have a real voice in the affairs of Hanover Place. There would be plenty of time to lay the groundwork.

Lyda and Howland had met at his parents' house in September 1923, when she came to photograph the dining room for the house-and-home magazine for which she was then working. She was three years out of Wellesley and counted herself extremely lucky to be able to turn her enthusiasm for photography into a career that usefully supplemented the income from her inheritance.

He had come back from playing golf with his father. It was a blustery day, and he looked flushed and windblown after the ride in from Long Island in the open car. She had immediately found his appearance to her taste; she liked her men lanky, beaky, fair, and light-eyed. It was just as quickly obvious that he took an instant shine to her. He had fussed around her, made silly small talk, and insisted on lugging her heavy Graflex and tripod down to the sidewalk and flagging a taxi for her. He asked for her address and telephone when she left. He called the following week, and they made a date for lunch, but then he was suddenly called to Georgia on a business trip; it was three weeks after their meeting that they finally went out. He took her to Sunday lunch at the Plaza, where he behaved with a chaste, calculated offhandedness that she realized spoke volumes about the intensity of his interest. Then she heard nothing for a month. His silence didn't bother Lyda; she knew he'd be back.

And he was. In November, he invited her to drive to New Haven for the Yale-Dartmouth game. They picnicked outside the Bowl with some of his classmates; at halftime, they walked halfway around the Bowl and he introduced her to Eddie Stanforth, and Colmer Hardesty, who ran The Firm's Bond Department. Afterward they went into New Haven and had supper at Mory's with still other friends.

On the drive back to New York, with night settled close around them, hurtling down the Boston Post Road in his coupe, it was apparent he was in the grip of a considerable agitation. Somewhere around Darien, where the road twisted among dark fields and forests, his feelings took over. He yanked the automobile off onto a narrow side road and as it glided to a stop, embraced her violently.

She responded to his kisses and caresses, trying to make it physically easy for him to take her, although what with all their clothes and the automobile's cramped cockpit it wasn't easy. He pressed against her desperately; powerless, she felt him go off before he could enter her. He was mortified, trying between gasps to pull back to some condition of dignity. She acted as if nothing had happened. She held him, kissed and soothed him—he seemed so terribly inexperienced!—and brought him back to a state of excitement. When he was ready, she took him inside her smoothly and let him make love to her.

When they got back to the city, they went to her apartment and he spent the night. When he departed in the morning, they were as good as engaged.

It had happened as it happened. She had not calculated or engineered his arrival in her life, had not gone to any lengths at all to put herself in advantage's way. It would be idle to say she wasn't impressed by the Warringtons and who they were, most of New York was, but she had certainly not hunted him down. Whatever had come to pass was fair and square.

She let her eye range round the room again. It was a metaphor for the world she was about to enter: luxurious, costly, ponderous, self-assured. It reeked of the establishments and institutions of a buttoned-up age that was no more. Even Howland's very grand mother saw it needed lightening up. There were plans afoot to slosh on white paint, to fill some of these heady spaces with French Deco furniture, even hang a Picasso on the walls. Still, Lyda wondered, would it ever really lose that weighty aura

redolent of a state of affairs that was secure, self-satisfied, and sancti-
monious, peopled by decent, careful, substantial folk, solid patroons like
those in the Eastman Johnson portrait in the parlor on the floor below?

She stubbed out her cigarette. Her mind turned to another matter. She
felt a tremor of apprehension, mingled with a dual sort of satisfaction, a
compound of pleasure at a noble deed and the special thrill that she always
felt when she accomplished a first-class bit of mischief. Well, she thought,
let's see what happens.

The way of life into which Lyda Farwell was marrying, as well as the
role and expectations allocated her by family tradition, compelled her to
develop an understanding of The Firm and its ways. This, in the months
preceding her wedding, she set out to do with characteristic thoroughness,
or, as her father-in-law put it, "with a vengeance." At least two afternoons
a week, sometimes more, she went downtown to the handsome limestone
building that occupied ground not two hundred paces from the historic
site of the buttonwood tree where Wall Street began, where, in 1814, a
thirty-two-year-old former privateer captain had set up house and shop,
determined to try his wits and prize money at the absorbing business of
speculation. The present building had been erected in 1907, to the designs
of Kimball and Levi, whose Seligman (later Lehman Brothers) building
at 1 William Street was greatly admired by Fletcher Warrington.

Lyda absorbed it all, inside and out, lore and legend, fact and apocrypha.
She learned the history of the medieval gargoyle, brought from France
under suspicious circumstances to guard the cornice, and the history of
the carved and molded cartouche with the incised words HONOR AND
OPTIMISM, a phrase that had apparently been fancied by Fletcher as a
possible motto for The Firm at the time the building was put up, and then
discarded because it didn't render into Latin with sufficient grace.

In such matters, Lyda's principal guide and tutor was Flora Merrow,
the partners' receptionist—"our Cerberus," said Fletcher—and self-ap-
pointed historian of The Firm. She was a lanky, cadaverous woman, with
dark, rouged skin, but her vulturelike appearance belied a disposition that
was positively chirpy, a predestined spinster in her late thirties who had
mated herself to Hanover Place in lieu of a union of the flesh, and felt as
blessed as the most devout nun. Her eagerness and wish to be of service
sometimes verged on the oppressive, Howland complained, but to Lyda,
she was a godsend.

Miss Merrow sat at a large desk that barred the way to the small, barrel-vaulted passageway that connected the fourth-floor elevator foyer to the splendid room in which The Firm's dozen partners were lodged. The most notable features of the partners' room were the dozen oversized partners' desks copied from the Duncan Phyfe original that still stood, as it had for almost ninety years, on a low, raised platform at the head of the room, flanked by windows facing east. It was from "the Platform," where the managing partner was enthroned, that final decisions on matters involving S. L. Warrington & Son were handed down.

To Lyda, the spirit of the place in 1924 seemed little changed from the old days. It looked as it had in the conversation piece of *Erasmus Warrington and His Partners*, which had been painted by Eastman Johnson in 1887 as an institutional pendant to his earlier family portrait. The Firm's partners still gathered after the close of Saturday trading for sherry and biscuits. Of course, by 1924, the primitive telephones, stock indicators, and telegraphic devices shown in Johnson's painting had given way to modern tickertapes and teletype machines. But apart from such details, anyone comparing the partners' room in 1924 with the depiction of some sixty years earlier would have come away with the impression that here, still, were the same kind of men engaged in the same kind of business in the same intent fashion.

The pride of Flora Merrow's fiefdom was The Firm Archive, a small reading room tucked behind the tickertape wall that contained a couple of comfortable chairs, a shallow vault, and a fine Chippendale secretary, of rosewood, on the shelves of which were ranged books incidental to its history and reputation and the history of Wall Street. Here, too, were kept the seventy-seven morocco-bound volumes of The Firm's "Visitor's Register."

Rooting around in the Archive with Miss Merrow, Lyda realized that here was a veritable museum of American finance. It was her happy inspiration, quickly agreed to by Fletcher, who was thankful for any diversion of Miss Merrow's relentless wish to be helpful, to mount small "exhibitions" of Firm memorabilia. A pair of handsome, glass-topped walnut cases were acquired, and placed to flank the sofa on which visitors were stashed while waiting to be admitted to the *sanctum sanctorum* of the partners' room. The first such display included the log of the Founder's sloop *Ocelot*, opened to the page recording the capture of His Majesty's ship *Luton*, which had furnished the prize money that originally grubstaked The Firm; the Visitor's Register for November 1859, where in crabbed handwriting, the famous market scalawag Daniel Drew had scrawled above his signature his well-known doggerel: "He that sells what isn't his'n/Must buy it back or go to prison"; a fair copy of the Articles of Partnership, the original of which rested in the Morgan vaults beneath 23 Wall Street; a letter of condolence from President Lincoln to Erasmus

Warrington and his wife on the death of their son Micah; and a sampler confected in the mid-nineteenth century by a Warrington niece. It depicted the family enterprise in a symbolic convention of its time: as a great tree, a noble elm, as impervious to man's ax as nature's gales and downpours. The tree's roots are shown threading deep in native soil; at its base sprout a riot of thick shrubs and flowering plants. According to Miss Merrow, this thicket of crudely sewn foliage represented the true strength of Hanover Place, its "connections," as Fletcher Warrington persisted in calling The Firm's clients and anyone else with whom Hanover Place had a "meaningful," that is to say mutually lucrative, relationship.

The Warringtons had grasped from the beginning that true money power lay in the ability to convince others to back your judgment with their capital. Or, as Fletcher told Lyda with his customary directness, "to put *their* money where *your* mouth is."

By 1924, it was generally agreed on Wall Street that the capital influenced by Hanover Place was exceeded only by the resources on which the House of Morgan might call. That was just a guess; the Warringtons were notoriously discreet. Among The Firm's "connections" would be numbered old Boston capital, Pittsburgh and Denver mining and metal fortunes, San Francisco railroad money, Manhattan real-estate and merchanting fortunes, a true cross-section of American wealth. These relationships dated back to the textile dynasties of the 1830s and 1840s, as well as the railroad fortunes of the 1860s and 1870s, and the mining and oil baronies of the 1880s. In 1866, Erasmus Warrington had rescued the great London house of Lucas Brothers during the Overend, Gurney, panic, and it could be assumed The Firm thereafter could, if it needed, call on the Lucas's uncounted millions in sterling.

It was the Morgan connection that mattered most. In 1924, the relationship was almost fifty years old, dating to the time Erasmus Warrington had marked young Pierpont as a man to watch and committed The Firm to take up "fifty millions notes or specie" in the $260 million U.S. government loan being syndicated by the young financier. In later years, The Firm would make similar undertakings to Cyrus Field, the Pratts, and John D. Rockefeller, and other founding fathers of what would one day be called "the American Century." These, like the original Morgan commitment, would be gratefully memorialized in sterling by Tiffany or Shreve. By 1924, so numerous would be these gleaming souvenirs, not only engraved silver jugs and platters, but miniature barges, hopper cars, and at least one oil derrick, that they nearly filled a rank of glass-fronted shelves that had been constructed along the long wall of the large dining room on the tenth floor of Hanover Place. Naturally, the most substantial commemorations of The Firm's financing coups, however, were to be found in its books of account.

Fletcher, too, made no bones about the importance of the Morgan "connection." As he beamed his approval of Lyda's and Miss Merrow's first "exhibition," chuckling with amused approval or sighing pensively over the various items in the glass-topped cases, his eye settled on a cartoon that had been drawn by the famous Thomas Nast in the 1880s. It depicted an ichthylogical food chain, a small fish being eaten by a larger which in turn was being eaten by one still larger, and so on.

"That's my grandfather, all right," said Fletcher, pointing to a sinewy, sly-eyed pike recognizable by the unmistakable pointed Warrington nose, the next largest fish but one in the sequence. About to gobble him up was a fierce, goggling, mustachioed shark.

"Pierpont Morgan himself," said Fletcher. "There was a man. I doubt we shall see his like on the Street again. My God, my dear, I remember the 1907 Panic as if it were only yesterday: we were still in the process of moving into this building. I remember coming in that Monday, October twenty-first it was, and wondering if the world was coming to an end. We'd made it through a great many panics: 1837 and 1857, 1867—that was 'the Marston Panic'—and the Gold Crisis of 1869 when Fisk and Gould got out of hand, and there was the 1873 Crash, when Jay Cooke failed, that one was a real terror, and the slumps in 1884 and 1893. We got through those, but you always wondered: was the next one going to be the one that took you down? I can tell you, 1907 was the one that had me shaking. Most of that Sunday we'd met at Morgan's house; the old boy even skipped services at St. George's, and if Pierpont Morgan missed church, you knew it was damn serious! It seemed clear enough that the Knickerbocker Trust was past hope; the question was could we save the Lincoln and a couple of others. Well, when I came in on Monday, there was this old fellow working in the vestibule on a packing case. Benjy he was called, died a few years ago, sort of the man of all work around here. My grandfather picked him off the streets when he was just a ragamuffin and he was with us sixty-two years. He used to keep pigeons up on the roof.

" 'Well, Benjy,' I said, 'I shouldn't be too hasty with that. By tomorrow, there just might not be anything to unpack for.' And d'you know: old Benjy just tipped his busted-up old stovepipe hat, and he said to me, 'Don't you worry none, Mr. Fletcher. Mr. Morgan'll fix things. Yessir, he will.' And, by God, Morgan did!"

Morgan, Field, Edison, Rockefeller, the Macy brothers. Firm legend accredited these as "noble" connections, and the Street concurred. But there were rumored to be others less lordly. The Firm's detractors claimed that the Warringtons were every bit as quick-footed morally as they were financially. Hanover Place, they whispered, for all its high-falutin' airs and holier-than-thou pose, wasn't above consorting in pursuit of the almighty dollar with men who were less than respectable. More than one dubious operator had been reported to be seen creeping into Hanover Place. During the Civil War, it was asserted that, notwithstanding the loss of his own son to Confederate musketry, Erasmus Warrington's Liverpool agents had been active right up to Appomattox in financing the sale of English-made arms to the Confederacy. There had been rumors that The Firm had taken an invisible hand when Gould and Fisk tried to corner gold, and that Hanover Place had played both sides against the middle in the war for control of the Erie Railroad. Lyda asked Fletcher about these tales.

"Balderdash!" he told her. "Don't listen to any of it! Wall Street's as noisy a coop for gossipy old hens as the Colony Club."

For her final catechism, Lyda was sent to see "the Judge," Ferdinand Stenton, former presiding judge of the U.S. Second Court of Appeals and senior partner of Auchincloss, Wharton, Stenton and James, counsel to The Firm since the time of the Civil War. He sat her down in a conference room lined with engraved maps of Old New York, placed his pince-nez on the slim ribboned folder before him, and addressed her in the grave tone he reserved for displaying tablets to hushed multitudes. He was a tall, spare man, as high and starchy as his flawless stiff collar, with a dry, reedy voice that Lyda found out of kilter with his distinguished mien.

"You understand, Miss Farwell, that it is in the nature of founding fathers to seek to perpetuate their philosophical eccentricities and peculiarities in the institutions they establish."

Lyda nodded with, she hoped, proper deference. She was well aware that Samuel Warrington had been a man of strong convictions. The stern, bewhiskered face in the portrait painted in 1844 by G. P. A. Healy, which hung in the small partners' dining room, might have been that of a fierce Old Testament prophet.

"You are also doubtless aware," Judge Stenton continued, "that paramount among the Founder's concerns was a fierce intention that The Firm remain within the control of his family, for as long as his descendants should wish to control it." He patted the ribboned document lying on the table. "Hence the Samuel L. Warrington Survivorship Trust."

He paused reverently. Lyda said nothing. She would not have been surprised if the Judge had crossed himself. For the better part of thirty seconds, the lawyer's words hung in the room like another person, then he picked up the thread: "The Founder realized all too well the uncertainties of time and personality, especially in family firms, Miss Farwell. These have a way of making questions of governance and succession unspeakably messy."

For the next forty-five minutes he took Lyda through matters with which she was already roughly familiar. She knew that The Firm's Partnership Agreement vested control of The Firm in two "Parties of the First Part": the managing partner, by definition a family member, and—through its trustees—the Samuel L. Warrington Survivorship Trust. Thus, as amended up to 1924, the document in front of Lyda designated Fletcher Warrington and the Trust as "the Parties of the First Part," and The Firm's other eleven partners as parties of the second, and distinctly inferior, part. In the former were vested all powers of appointment, commitment, and distribution; in a word, virtual total discretion with regard to the membership of the partnership and the allocation among partners of its resources and profits, which in turn gave the Managing Partner and the Trust dictatorial control over The Firm's policies and hence its destiny.

The Partnership Agreement, the Judge pointed out, had its own quirks. Subject to amendment only under the most extenuating circumstances— as when, in 1888 on his grandfather's unexpected death, Fletcher found himself at twenty-five the only living Warrington at Hanover Place—no man was to be admitted to partnership before reaching the age of thirty. Nor was nepotism permitted outside the ruling family. "And, in my opin-ion, a good thing, too," said the Judge with finality.

"But why?" challenged Lyda politely. "Suppose one of the nonfamily partners had a very able son?"

"Miss Warrington, this is a business in which stability and consistency of practice are every bit as important as individual genius. You need only look at the continued eminence of our Morgan friends to see that. More-over, the Founder had his own reasons . . ."

He went on to explain that Samuel Warrington numbered seven daugh-ters among his nine children, and harbored a morbid fear of fortune-hunting sons-in-law; moreover, in other firms, the admission of nonfamily sons to partnership had proved an invitation to palace revolution.

"The Founder was a happy and gratified husband, Miss Farwell, with an unabashed and candid appreciation of his wife's contribution to his good fortune and general well-being. He consulted her on everything, and her counsel proved wise. By midlife, he was convinced that, as much as anything, the support and wisdom of an intelligent and committed wife was essential if the larger affairs of life were to be brought to a satisfactory and profitable conclusion. He had also observed that women tended to outlive their husbands, and thus were, at least actuarially, the vessels by which true, living continuity could be assured from one generation to the next. He thus specified that the co-trustee for life of the Survivorship Trust, along with the managing partner, be the managing partner's wife. It was an excellent decision, if I may say so. Actuarially sound, and . . ." the Judge unbent himself with a thin little smile, ". . . astutely cognizant of the fact that no one was likely to be as ferociously protective of the interests of her cubs as the mother wolf. So it has proven and so will it

again, I am certain, Miss Farwell, when in the fullness of time you succeed
Mrs. Fletcher Warrington as a Trustee."

World without end, amen, thought Lyda.

In addition to her historical tutelage from Judge Stenton, Flora Merrow,
and Howland's father, Lyda insisted on a thorough grounding on The
Firm's current business. She went through Hanover Place from top to
bottom, guided by the heads of various departments. Vinnie Grady tutored
her in the order room; Eddie Stanforth took her into the Visitors Gallery
at the Exchange, others showed her around Sales and Syndication; even
Fletcher devoted an afternoon to showing her various ways in which The
Firm committed its own and its connections' capital.

She insisted not only on seeing The Firm's glamorous departments, its
public face, as it were, but its counting-house side, the "cage" in which
the bookkeeping was done, securities received and delivered out, mail
sorted and the like. Here faceless clerks toiled to keep the glossy upstairs
types like Hap Carruthers and Chubby Fenton abreast of their accounts
and accurate in their determinations.

It was not exactly a Dickensian netherworld that Lyda was shown.
The "cage" itself was an elaborate, indeed elegant enclosure of marble
and wrought iron on the first floor, which gave the impression of an airy,
exclusive banking office; the term, however, also included a rabbit warren
of virtually airless basement offices, every bit as unappealing, even pris-
onlike, as the suffocating cloister under the roof where The Firm's telephone operators toiled on the spot where old Benjy had once slept. If not
Dickensian, however, it struck Lyda as she toured the operations, and
watched the sorting, bundling, and ledgering that were the essence of
these operations, that it was certainly Dantesque, in that all who entered
there might as well forget the prospect of higher advancement. It was,
she sensed almost immediately, a classic dead end.

It chanced that, on the day Lyda visited the "cage," the head of back-
office operations, Robert Carlucci, fell ill with an impacted wisdom tooth.
His number two was tied up with a problem on a recent syndication, and
so a young man from the Transactions Section was hastily deputed to
lead the princess-elect through the bowels of her future kingdom. Lyda
had learned that to focus closely on a person was helpful in getting the
most out of him, and so she focused closely on her guide. He was a young
man in his mid-twenties, obviously Jewish, dressed as well as a clerk's
salary afforded. As they toured the cage and the basement, she learned

that he was married, with one child and another on the way, and that he lived in Brooklyn.

All this was interesting as far as it went. In the course of her tour, however, Lyda found herself becoming interested in the young man him-self. He was extremely articulate about what he was showing her, with an impressive, instinctive grasp of the technical side of Hanover Place. Once or twice their progress was halted as he dealt with questions put to him by other men. Some of these had to do with accruals, and interest payments, and other exotic formulations, but the speed with which he calculated his responses amazed her. Lyda knew little of the specific arith-metic of Wall Street, but she had sat in enough math classes in her life to have a fair sense of what a genius for numbers sounded like. Her interview with the Judge came to mind, with his rather offhand dispar-agement of individual talent as a necessity for The Firm's continued pros-perity.

She heard something else in the young man's voice that stirred her even more. Something that spoke simultaneously of yearning and hopelessness. Of talent stuck below its capabilities. The song of a bird in a cage. The voice of her ever-vigilant social conscience suggested that here, but for background, or the luck of birthright, could be she, could be anyone. By the time she finished her tour, she had resolved to speak to Howland and his father about the young man. To tell them that, if she was any judge of ability and character, they had a young man working for them whose abilities were being cruelly wasted belowdecks, and that they really ought to do something about him—for the good of The Firm.

The young man's name was Morris Miles.

At about the same time Lyda was completing her toilette in Stuyvesant Square, two Warrington partners were completing theirs downtown, fol-lowing the celebratory lunch that the partners of The Firm had tendered to its heir apparent and his groomsmen.

Edmonds Stanforth, the younger and heavier of the two, examined his smooth, plump, ruddy face carefully in the mirror, and preened the ends of his careful little mustache. Satisfied with the result, he adjusted the knot of the gray silk tie that the man from Sulka's had just delivered.

He picked up his champagne glass and finished it off. With a pleased little belch, he patted his gray waistcoat, turned to the other man, and asked: "Think 'Paddy's Pig' will be there?"

"Who can tell, old boy; in this wedding anything's possible," drawled

Harding Carruthers. He was bent over a chair, vigorously buffing a black oxford that gleamed as bright as his watered and combed blond hair. In comparison to the beefy Stanforth, an athlete run irretrievably to fat and alcohol, the veins in his cheeks already starting to give way, Carruthers was lean and pale and unblemished, with a slim, fastidious figure tailors yearned for.

"After the flea in the ear the old man gave Mr. Kennedy after our little Hertz flutter, I should be very surprised to see him turn up at Trinity," Carruthers added, "although I must say nothing the old man does surprises me." Carruthers spoke in the accents characteristic of his upbringing and schooling: the vowels lengthened, the hard consonants softened to the point of elision so that "very" came out as "ve'y."

A careful listener would have discerned that Stanforth's accent was a hard-working imitation of what in Carruthers seemed innate and entirely natural. His vowels, too, were stretched and broadened, but in Stanforth's mouth, Carruthers's "rather" came out sounding "rawther."

"Hap" Carruthers had acquired his accent in his cradle. He was Groton and Yale, a vestryman at St. James's Church, on the house committee of the Union Club, the Brook, and the Gorse, stockbroker to the Phippses and the Frelingvilles.

He had fine, pursed Protestant features that people likened to George Whitney, the man people accounted the cleverest of the Morgan partners. The physical comparison served Carruthers well in business, and he did nothing to discourage it. Coupled with his excellent lineage, full array of social credentials and graces, together with a nimble opportunism agreeably masked by a languid disinterest in the cruder realities of getting and spending, Carruthers had assembled a lucrative coterie of brokerage clients. In the society columns, he was often tagged "the '400's favorite customers man," a term that he detested as demeaning to a partner of S. L. Warrington & Son; he preferred to describe himself as an "investment broker."

Eddie Stanforth was the principal Warrington partner on the New York Stock Exchange. The Floor was a natural venue for Stanforth, who was quick with a joke and could bully other men with a bonhomous robust humor that left his victims smiling through their discomfiture. He mingled freely with all sorts, chaffing clerk and partner alike, although out of earshot of certain of his more useful connections, in places like the bar of the Recess or the Union League club, he conducted a busy trade in jokes about "micks" and "yids" and "dagos." His bigotry was unconsidered, intended to curry favor with men he admired and to get even for the way he was treated by others. He was a frequent butt even within The Firm; a Dartmouth man set down among the flower of Harvard, Yale, and Princeton, a middle-class Catholic encircled by Episcopal and Presbyterian

aristocrats. In the face of their teasing, he kept up a jolly front. Like
Carruthers, Stanforth had taken a Whitney for his model, in this instance
George Whitney's younger brother Richard, a big man on the Floor and
the broker through whom 23 Wall Street did the preponderance of its
Exchange business.

"Paddy's Pig" was Stanforth's derisive nickname for the principal figure
in a recent market operation that had proved extremely lucrative for
Hanover Place and certain of its connections, including several of Carruthers's most blue-blooded accounts. In the spring of 1924, the Yellow
Cab Company of Chicago found itself under siege by a "bear pool," a
group of speculators (rumored to have the financial backing of Yellow's
principal rival, the Checker Cab Company) who had for some weeks been
selling Yellow Cab stock short in large quantities, driving the price down
sufficiently to cause other stockholders to rush to unload, which in turn
accentuated the decline. The object of the bear raid was to drive down
Yellow Cab shares, bankrupt the company's principals, and take it over
on the cheap.

Yellow Cab's founder and largest stockholder, John Hertz, was a fighter,
however. He also knew it took money to fight money. Through Lehman
Brothers, his brokers, he invited a select group of New York financial
interests, including Hanover Place, to subscribe to a $5 million buying
syndicate, or "bull pool," to be managed by an up-and-coming financier
in whom Hertz had absolute confidence, a brash Boston Irishman named
Joseph Kennedy.

Fletcher Warrington liked the sound of the deal. It was well thought
out, and—as he told his son—although this sort of thing was still within
the law, who could say for how long? Best to strike while the iron of
legality was still hot. So he agreed to participate to the extent of
$750,000—provided, as always, that The Firm's name was never men-
tioned.

In the following weeks, working from a suite in the Waldorf-Astoria,
Kennedy manipulated the pool's open-market purchases and sales of Yellow Cab shares with a guile that old-timers said would have done credit
to Daniel Drew or Jay Gould. He "painted the tape," buying in Chicago,
selling in San Francisco, now creating the impression that buying power
many times the pool's actual resources was rushing into Yellow Cab, at
the next instant selling large blocks of shares. Confused, uncertain of the
future direction of Yellow Cab stock, seeing their fat short-sale profits
evaporating by the minute, no longer playing a pat hand, the bears were
routed. Yellow Cab was saved; Kennedy's reputation was made; the pool's
investors earned a most handsome return.

The Firm did better than "handsome." Prior to Kennedy's launching
his counterattack, Fletcher purchased a substantial number of Yellow Cab

shares in various Firm accounts at prices in the high forties. The position was closed out at an average realization of nearly sixty dollars a share. The total profit to Hanover Place and certain connections was over a million dollars.

A few weeks later, after the smoke had cleared, "Paddy's Pig," flushed with success and ambition, called at Hanover Place and sought an audience with Fletcher Warrington. A few weeks earlier, he had appeared at 23 Wall Street asking to see J. P. Morgan. As at the House of Morgan, so at Hanover Place: Kennedy was left to cool his heels in the vestibule until it got through to him that there would be no audience with the powers upstairs. He went away incensed; it would later be conjectured by his biographers that it was on account of these snubs that he communicated to his then eight-year-old son Jack that so-called "establishment" businessmen were the worst sons of bitches of all.

"It would appear Mr. Kennedy had ambitions of becoming a connection of ours," Fletcher Warrington told his partners, "but frankly it was certain of *his* own connections which precluded that possibility."

The partners nodded. To make money off a fellow in a trading coup was one thing; to admit him as a "connection" was quite something else. Hanover Place never touched money with even the faintest whiff of dubiousness about it, at least not knowingly.

In Fletcher's mind, some of his partners recognized, Kennedy was as good as convicted by his marriage. He had married into a bootlegging family. How could he not be contaminated?

It was one of Fletcher's pet theories that the market's huge rise was being fueled with untraceable bootlegging money finding its way back into the legitimate economy through bearer bonds and shares.

As he told his son, Prohibition provided the gangster element with a vast, dependable cash flow needing to be washed clean, and where could that be done more swiftly, and in sufficient quantity, than in the booming stock and bond markets? Fletcher lectured his partners almost daily to be wary, to ascertain absolutely who it really was with whom they were asked to do business, to realize that the suavest Wall Street lawyer might well be a front for Al Capone.

Naturally, none of them was brave enough to point out to the managing partner the anomaly of the flood of commission tickets that Hanover Place was happily writing on orders from various banks in Canada, where the biggest, industrial-size bootlegging operations were centered. Well, it was the Warringtons' firm, wasn't it? That was the point of being Parties of the First Part.

Stanforth tugged at his pearl-gray vest and smoothed the wrinkles. Grinning at Carruthers, he asked: "Tell me something, Hap. Was your heart really in that eloquent toast you proposed to the blushing bride at lunch? That stuff about 'a breath of fresh air.' I never heard such bushwah! More like a hurricane, if you ask me! Hell, if it wasn't for her, we'd be at Palmer Stadium right now!"

"That's the trouble with you, Eddie, no sense of social grace. And why, may I ask, should the Yale-Princeton game concern a Dartmouth man? Shouldn't you be up in the North Woods for the homecoming game against the Iroquois or the Algonquins or whatever other tribe you're playing today? I must say, you look very dapper in your cutaway. I should have thought war paint would be more your native costume."

"Yeah," mumbled Stanforth sulkily. "Very funny." He picked up his glass from the bureau and found it empty. "Damn! You got anything left, Hap? Where's that waiter, anyway?"

Carruthers produced a hammered-silver hip flask, shook it, and handed it over. "Don't drink it all. That's Johnnie Walker Black Label, the real thing. My bootlegger made me stand and deliver for it."

"Hey, fellas, c'mon! Time for church!" Chubby Fenton's voice, the same strong baritone that had called signals at Yale before the war, rang up the stairwell.

"On our way," called Carruthers. He slipped his flask into his hip pocket, flipped the tails of his morning coat into place, and snapped open his gray topper.

At the top of the stairs, he had a thought. He put a languid hand on his colleague's sleeve and said: "Y'know, Eddie, speaking of the blushing bride, something occurs to me. I suppose you've heard she persuaded the old man to take this Miles fellow out of the cage and put him in Hardesty's care? Wouldn't it be something if we ended up working for a pack of Jews? I'll bet that's a contingency that not even a Dartmouth education prepared you for!"

As the stairs resounded with the tread of heavy young feet and the chaffing of boon companions, Fletcher and Howland, alone in the large bedroom in which they had dressed, smiled at each other. "That's a fine group of men you've chosen to see you off," said Fletcher. "I'm glad you were able to persuade Tommy Creedmore to try his luck with us."

Howland's ushers were mostly long-time friends from Exeter and Yale, old comrades of hockey rink and secret society like Chubby Fenton. Tom Creedmore, with whom Howland had served in the Army Flying Corps, was the exception. Howland had brought Creedmore with him to Hanover Place after the war, thinking he could be made into an investment man. He knew Carruthers and most of the other partners doubted his judgment; among themselves, they agreed that while the slow-spoken Midwesterner was a fine fellow, square and steady, no doubt a good man to have on your wing when the Red Baron was about to bounce you, he was woefully short on social graces, not really on the *qui-vive*, and this was, if anything, a business for gentlemen with quick minds and tongues. Still, if that was what the Warringtons wanted, all agreed, so be it. It was their firm, and they could do with it what they liked.

Fletcher poured out a finger of brandy into each of the two snifters on the table between them. "The last of the 'eighty-eight Hennessy," he said. "It was a wedding present from your grandfather, the late senator. What an old gasbag he was!" He sipped his brandy, pursed his lips, and nodded appreciatively, and raised his glass. "So, my son, here's mud in your eye. And best wishes. Your very good health, sir!"

As the old man beamed, Howland launched into a recapitulation of a learned academic's views on the economic situation. His father listened without much interest. Fletcher preferred not to swim in the great tides of theory; he preferred the sharper flows and eddies of the market. Economics bored him stiff. Take this reparations business. A lot of damn foolishness, if you asked him! America lent the Germans money to pay reparations to the British and the French, who then used the money to repay their war loans from America, which then gave it back to the Hun—and where was the end to it!

He listened patiently as Howland went on. From behind a screen of pensive nods he considered his son. As "good" a war as his son had had, it was time to get it over with and get on with Hanover Place's affairs. There was a lot to be said for war, but there was a lot of damn foolishness, too. War left a man with a taste for large issues and noble causes, especially a young man with Howland's disposition. That was to be expected.

Howland would come to like the Street, no doubt of that. The beauty of finance and speculation was that they could be different things to different men. To some: poetry or high drama; to others, physics, scientific and immutable; to still others, politics, or philosophy, even philanthropy. And to still others, war.

To most, of course, it was simply a way to make money to buy from life whatever one wanted: yachts, celebrity, influence, new friends, a comfortable existence, a way up, a way out. To Fletcher, a keen and combative sportsman, finance was simply the best game there was, requiring the calculation of chess, the judgment of poker, the steady nerves of golf, and the quick reflexes of squash and racquets.

When Howland had finished his digression, his father said mildly, "I had a word with Hardesty after lunch. It seems he's very pleased with your bride's protégé, young Mr. Miles. Hardesty sees the fellow's a demon with figures, I gather, with a decent nose for the market in the bargain. Of course, ten days upstairs is much too short a time to tell."

Howland smiled at his father. "She'll be delighted with the news."

"You can tell her for me I hope it works out for Miles. It's been a good many years since we've had a Jewish fellow upstairs. Keeps everyone on their toes."

The older man sipped his brandy pensively. "Odd, you know," he said, "there was a time when Jews and Christians bedded down happily together in this city. Your great-grandfather and old Judah Benjamin used to dine regularly at the club. Until the Civil War, of course. Not long afterward, everything changed. I suppose it had something to do with the immigrations. Too many hungry and poor yearning to be free for everyone's comfort, I expect."

"I don't think some of your partners are rooting as hard for Morris as you are, Father."

"I expect not," said Fletcher. "Nevertheless, should push come to shove, my boy, you can be certain they'll be made very much aware just whose name is on the door. In any case, it's merely an experiment at present, and like anything else, we shall just have to wait and see. For the time being, it's up to Mr. Miles. I wish him a fair wind."

Howland eyed his father with good humor. Typical of you to change the subject. The issue's reparations—damn important, but there's no money in it right now, so why bother? It was the one thing that irritated him about his father. Fletcher was content to operate on a scale that his son found constricting; he was tied to the tickertape, which Howland scarcely looked at. Fletcher seemed not to care a whit about the great possibilities available to The Firm, Morgan-style opportunities for statesmanship and leadership on a scale that the narrow money-spinning of Wall Street barely comprehended, but which he and Lyda saw clear as day.

Not the least of the reasons Howland Warrington was head over heels in love with Lyda was that he was certain that she saw in him what he saw in himself.

He was convinced he was destined to be a great man. There was little vanity in his optimistic view of himself, simply recognition of the fact that fate and nature had conspired to deliver into his hands and orbit everything that a man should possess in order to play an important and meaningful role in the world's great business. His self-appraisal was honest and objective, he thought: his strengths were both personal and derivative, part based on character and personality, part on the luck of the genetic draw. He was brave and clever; his decorations and citations testified to the first; the words *magna cum laude* appended to the bottom of his Yale degree spoke to the second. Other men liked him and seemed willing to follow him, to trust his judgment and leadership in battle or in business. He got along well with all sorts, old and young, humble and powerful, male and female, officers and enlisted men. The successful prosecution of any form of strife or competition required the contributions of all sorts.

Of course, the real difference between him and his father was that he'd been to war and the old man hadn't. Fletcher talked about the Street in the same terms men described combat, and in fact, there were similarities. Like dogfights, trading coups were won with reflexes and luck and training—in more or less equal measure. Aerial combat was to some extent like playing squash with bullets. There could be no denying that instinct and reaction won more skirmishes and saved more lives than all the field marshals plotting in their bunkers, but the winning of *wars* required generalship.

The self-perceived paradox of Howland Warrington was that his greatest achievement—his heroic record in aerial combat—had come through the exercise of talents that he valued most lightly in himself and others. Howland considered himself a long thinker. Not that he lacked appreciation of pragmatic individuals like his father, men who were alert for the quick chance and knew how to act on it when they saw it. Fletcher Warrington had a certain capacity for the long view, to be sure, but it seemed to Howland that his father reserved that angle of vision principally for retrospection, for long looks back into the past of the family and The Firm from which he seemed to gain a certain strength and renewal.

The bottom line was, Howland thought, that he knew—as his father understandably did not—where the teachings of combat legitimately applied in civilian life, and where they didn't. To some extent—but only *some*—Wall Street resembled a dogfight. The business demanded open eyes, wits about you, and the assumption that even the silkiest cloud contained enemy fighters waiting to pounce. But there any real similarity ended. People on the Street liked to employ the language of combat, but money was one thing; bullets quite another. The amount of coolness and nerve required to stand firm in a market panic was a pale fraction of what it took to get through a minute of combat in the trenches or in the air.

Which did not mean that Howland disparaged the Street, or had the slightest notion of turning his back on The Firm for some "loftier" calling like politics or philanthropy. Hanover Place, like God and country, expected every Warrington to do his duty. Perhaps if he'd had a brother it might be different, but he had only his sisters, and his obligation was clear.

"By the way," said Fletcher, "I don't know if you saw what Roger Babson had to say in this morning's *Times*, but he thinks stocks should triple in the next few years. Good man, Babson. Solid."

"Really," said Howland without much interest. His mind was off in Germany with Jack Morgan, remaking the very structure of an entire nation.

Fletcher let his son's uninterest pass.

"That was a damn good party last night, wasn't it? Everyone says

Sherry's gone downhill as a restaurant, but if you ask me, they can still serve as good a dinner as anyone. I certainly overdid it!" Fletcher stood up and patted his stomach. At sixty-five, he was stockier than his son, and long since gone to gray, but extremely fit. He nursed a powerful belief in the value of strenuous exercise. Apart from his matches with his son, he boxed three times a week with a trainer in the small gym he had built on the eleventh floor at Hanover Place, in the garret in which Old Benjy had lived until the influenza epidemic of 1918 got him.

He played and won at his rich men's games—racquets, court tennis, and polo—and he played and won at others more plebeian with equal ferocity. In the end, his son knew, they were just pale substitutes for the real war that the timetables of history had crudely denied Fletcher Warrington.

He watched quietly as his father pulled an engraved gold watch from his handkerchief pocket.

"Almost time for the last mile, my boy. I'll just have a pee, and then I think we'd best be getting up to Trinity."

Howland watched his father move across the room with bouncy, assertive little steps. What a bundle of energy, he thought affectionately. How odd life is: Father's got all the combativeness and I'm the war hero. Probably a good thing. Someone like Father would have been shot down on his first patrol. Always going for the knockout punch or the impossible angle.

In a way, Howland felt sorry for his father. These freewheeling, to-the-death set-tos on the golf links or trading floor must be dishwater compared to the real battles he craved to fight and never got to. Born too late for the Civil War and too old and saddled with responsibilities for the Rough Riders.

Well, thought Howland, we each of us have our particular strengths and virtues, don't we? It's the combination of these that counts. He and his bride were an ideal combination, which meant that today, with flags flying and trumpets blaring, they would take the first steps together on what would surely be an utterly triumphant progress through life.

By a quarter past four, when Lyda was completing her final tucks and twirls, Trinity Church was already half full. The lofty interior was ablaze with candles, the choir stalls were banked in African fern and stephanotis.

Howland's ushers were already hard put to keep up with the sorting and proper disposing of the brilliant crowd flowing in. Outside, the fading afternoon light was punctuated by the popping flashes of photographers' flashbulbs as one after another luminary of society or finance descended from a towncar and made his or her way under the garlanded white satin awning that shaded the path running the length of the churchyard, from the Broadway curb to Richard Morris Hunt's splendid bronze doorway.

Among the crowd waiting patiently at the head of the aisle to be seated was a young man in a considerable and visible state of agitation: a short, blocky man in his middle twenties, with a roundish, clever face, normally very pale but now flushed with nervousness, bright, attentive dark eyes, a broad fleshy nose, and a full-lipped mouth with a permanent hint of frown. His wirelike black hair receded back in crinkled ranks from a bold and brainy forehead. He was sweating profusely; under his rented cutaway his shirt was soaked through. He was convinced that a hundred hostile, questioning gazes were boring into him from behind.

Morris Miles felt guilty just being here. Given the week's volume, his colleagues—*ex-colleagues*—in the cage would have to work right into the evening to plow through the snowdrifts of paperwork. It was hard to believe: four two-million share days in one week! Over nineteen million shares traded since Coolidge's election and that didn't count the Curb and the Consolidated Exchange! The old hands said there were tickets coming through on accounts that hadn't bought a single share of common stock since Teddy Roosevelt was President.

His celluloid collar felt like it had sawed halfway through his neck. He shouldn't have let Miriam make him come without her, he thought, shouldn't have let her march him over to Rockaway Avenue to rent this monkey suit. He had no business being here.

But the Warringtons had invited him, so what choice did he have?

The arrival of the heavy cream-colored envelope had been the talk of the Pitkin Avenue gossips within minutes after its arrival at the four-story, four-family sandstone building where Morris and his expectant wife Miriam lived, along with their three-year-old son Benjamin. At first, Morris had wondered if it might not be a joke played by one of the boys in the cage, but—as Miriam pointed out—so formidably impressive and expensive a feat of stationery had to be genuine. Besides, he couldn't deny the satisfaction he got from seeing people like his cousin-in-law Berger squirm with envy. Berger was such a mouth. He worked as a customers man at Kuhn Loeb, where he sold utility bonds in small lots to rich dentists in Crown Heights, but to hear him boast in the *shvitz* on Eastern Parkway, Mr. Otto Kahn never made a move without personally consulting him. Then there was Miriam's Uncle Friedl, a Bushwick court stenographer with dreams of faraway places. Just think, said Friedl: little Moshe moving "upstairs" at Hanover Place. And now invited to the Warrington wedding! Friedl said this made Morris an anthropological curiosity, and he was going to write a letter about him to *The National Geographic*.

"Upstairs"—it had a ring, didn't it? Before he was just a machine: bundling certificates and checking adding-machine tapes. Then, three weeks after he'd shown Miss Farwell around, he'd been sent for by Mr. Carlucci, who was in charge of the cage and the administration, and told that he was being transferred to Mr. Hardesty's Bond Department on the seventh floor!

Upstairs! That was where the real business was done, where a man could make a career. It was a wonderment. Berger, who claimed to know Wall Street history from A to Z, said as far as he knew there had never been a Jew upstairs at Hanover Place.

Amid all the satisfaction and excitement, there was only one small consolation for the local gossips, who by vocation reserved their greatest relish for the disappointments of others. The invitation was addressed to "Mr. Morris Miles" only. It had to be a mistake, said Morris, and he begged his wife to accompany him, but she said no, these people were very precise about such things. Serves her right, buzzed the grandmothers on the stoops. Too ambitious by half, that Miriam! Well, what did you expect from the Irish, eh? From a woman who got her husband to go into court to change his name from Moshe Miloshvitz to Morris Miles! Nice to see her get her just deserts!

If Miriam Miles was upset at the slight, she didn't let the neighbors see it. She showed no resentment, just dragged her husband off to Rockaway Avenue to rent a wedding suit, and at home rehearsed Morris in the mysterious ways of an Episcopal wedding. It never ceased to surprise him that she knew about such things, but Catholic and Episcopal weren't supposed to be all that different, after all. Now here he was.

"Bride's side—or the groom's?"

Morris could see Mr. Fenton didn't even recognize him. He was one of those men who had no eyes for people below his station. Like Mr. Carruthers.

"Bride, please—or the groom?"

Morris found himself tongue-tied. He became aware of people shifting impatiently behind him.

"Bride or groom, please? There are people waiting." Morris, helpless, saw Fenton examine him. Was that a flicker of recognition?

"Groom," he stammered. He feared he sounded like a second banana in a Yiddish music hall. He followed the husky Fenton down the aisle, cursing himself for being such a klutz.

He took a seat about a third of the way down the nave and looked around. A bit further on, he saw Mr. Carruthers standing languidly in the aisle, chatting with a pretty, well-dressed woman. Carruthers looked like he was posing for an illustration for a men's magazine. Morris couldn't stand Carruthers. The man was arrogant, but for what reason! He never got his tickets and account balances right, and was always having to come to the cage to fix things, where he behaved as if it was the clerks' fault.

A lot of them were that way, Morris reflected. Fenton just now looked at me as if I was no more than a shrub or a stone. He put the ugly thought out of his mind and tried to catch the conversations around him. Berger said a man could become rich tuning in on the idle chatter of the right people.

"Will you look at those flowers," muttered the woman directly in front of him. "Like a gangster's funeral! They must have bought out Wadleigh and Smythe!"

". . . had a nice turn last week in Anaconda . . ."

". . . gave ten thousand dollars to this fellow Mizner down in Florida to invest in land, and he says . . ."

". . . bootlegger demanded five hundred dollars a case, and what can you do . . ."

". . . take a look at Montgomery Ward in here. My man at Clark, Dodge says . . ."

"Baruch may *say* he's out of the market, but personally I think the old fox is . . ."

"Fellow I know's made some money on the Curb and paid forty-five thousand dollars for one of those new cooperative apartments at Eight hundred Park. Can you imagine! Doesn't money mean *anything* to these new people . . ."

As Morris listened, he watched the parade down the aisle. He recognized old Judge Stenton, the Warringtons' lawyer, faultless in morning coat. And right behind the Judge was another man it took him a moment to place—could it be! yes it was!—Otto Kahn, no less. As the great financier, his wife, and their son and daughter were led to a ribboned-off pew just a few rows from the very front, Morris felt himself shiver with awe. In his personal mythology, the lords of finance were gods and heroes, stars on the order of Barrymore or Tom Mix or even Douglas Fairbanks.

A florid, cheerful man passed; wasn't that Charles Schwab, the head of U.S. Steel? Then here—walking behind his parents—came young John Schiff, the Kuhn Loeb heir, a Yale senior handsome as a god, with whom Miriam said Howland Warrington played polo.

A tall, sharp-eyed woman passed and the lady in the pew ahead forward hissed to her companion: "Isn't that Edith Wharton?" "No," came the hushed reply. "I think that's one of the Schermerhorns. Mrs. Wharton never leaves France these days."

Edith Wharton! Now wouldn't that have been something to tell Miriam! Miriam was Edith Wharton's biggest fan. She read all her books. Her Uncle Friedl said the rabbis should know their Talmud as thoroughly as Miriam Miles knew her Edith Wharton—or her *Vogue* and *Smart Set*, for that matter. When the rooms at the Colony Club had been kept open late one night so that people from the The Firm could view the wedding gifts, Miriam had come over from Brooklyn on the subway, and she and Morris had gone uptown to have a look. Everybody was oohing and aahing about the silver and the crystal and the gold, but all Miriam could look at was these four little leather books, which she told Morris were parts of a new novel called *Old New York*, which Mrs. Wharton had specially bound and autographed for the young couple.

The traffic in the aisle continued. An elegant middle-aged man strolled down the aisle, nodding or waving a languid hand to acquaintances as he passed. Morris knew him: Piers Lucas, Baron Lucas, the managing director of Lucas Brothers, 33 Cheapside, London EC2, The Firm's big City connection. "Cheapside"—Morris thought that was a very odd address for a great English banking house.

Morris loved the story of how old Erasmus Warrington had saved the Lucases. It was a better story than Joshua at Jericho or David and Goliath. When it came to high finance, Morris was a true romantic. To Morris, the transactions hatched at Hanover Place were more exciting than anything in a movie. Of course, he didn't let his hero worship confuse his brain. As Miriam said: don't confuse the tingling with the thinking.

He watched the Lehmans go by, Mr. Philip and his son Robert with their cousin Herbert. Close behind came a couple of the Harriman partners and their wives. Then two handsome young ladies came down the aisle, causing a murmur. Morris knew them: the groom's two sisters: Miss Florence, the elder and darker, who was married to a coming man at the Guaranty Trust, but he'd have to come pretty fast to keep up with the way she spent money, or so the boys in Family Accounts said; then Miss Alice, who was fair like Mr. Howland, widowed in the war right after her marriage, but now engaged to a partner in the Auchincloss firm. And now at last here came Mrs. Warrington, Mr. Fletcher's wife, very much the great lady, sweeping by on Fenton's sturdy arm; and finally—taken to a front-row pew by Mr. Creedmore—a pleasant-faced square-bodied woman he didn't know. She seemed as awkward in her big hat and long frock as Morris was in his morning clothes, but she had Miss Farwell's nice smile and firm carriage. This must be the aunt, the bride's only living kin.

Just at that moment the organ gave a mighty bleat, and everyone looked back up the aisle where the bridal party was forming up, so he looked, too. The organ started to play stately processional music. Then there was movement at the front, near the altar, and everyone's eyes went there.

From a side door, Morris saw Mr. Howland, with Mr. Fletcher beside him, both of them smiling. Then from behind the altar appeared the groom's maternal uncle, the Right Reverend Henry Temple, the Suffragan Bishop, accompanied by Trinity's rector, Dr. Caleb Stetson; in their vestments, they were as splendid as kings. The music seemed to grow louder. As Morris watched the bridal procession approach down the aisle, he felt that just to be here was nothing less than a miracle.

Exactly thirty-three minutes after the Trinity organist launched into *Lohengrin*, Lyda and her new husband stood on the church porch posing for pictures.

The damp chill of evening had driven off most of the crowd across the way. Wall Street was deserted except for a few late-working clerks scuttling under the street lamps on the way to the subway. Outside the churchyard gate, the darkness was cut by the headlights of waiting limousines, stretching like a brilliant necklace down Broadway practically to the Battery. In the distance, the Statue of Liberty shone vague and ethereal, looming above the slow lights of the harbor's shipping. A foghorn sounded. The dark hulks of the surrounding buildings seemed to press in on the churchyard.

"One thing you can say about my uncle Henry," muttered Howland out of the side of his mouth as the photographers' flashbulbs popped, "for a bishop, he does get on with it. Are you cold? Are you happy?"

Lyda shivered under the white fox cape that the woman from the bridal department at Saks had thrown over her shoulders. She smiled for the cameras, but she felt a distinct chill. She looked around her and it seemed for an instant that Trinity's graves had opened and Howland's ancestors were perched on their moldering headstones, pointing at her and grinning cynically, challenging her right to be there.

She clutched the cape around her and looked up at her husband. "I'm freezing," she said. "Can we go now, darling?"

Howland made a time-out sign with his hands. "Okay, boys," he told the knot of photographers. "Mrs. Warrington is cold and we've got a party to go to."

As they made their way through the churchyard to the automobile that would bear them uptown to the Colony Club, Lyda's apprehensions fell away and her normal iron self-confidence returned. She looked about her fiercely, routing the ghosts that a moment earlier had seemed so real, sending them gibbering back into the earth. You don't scare me, she said to them silently as her new husband handed her into his parents' big Simplex towncar. I am someone for whom time holds no terrors, not past, not present, not future.

Uptown, it took well over an hour before the bride and groom could terminate the receiving line and make their way out to the center of the Colony ballroom for their first official performance as man and wife. Emil Coleman's band struck up the title air from *Rose Marie*, the first hit of the new Broadway season.

Amid murmurs of approval—how beautiful she looked, how well they moved together—Lyda and Howland Warrington began to dance. Even though she hated dancing, Lyda felt divinely happy. Howland was the only man she'd ever enjoyed dancing with. He held himself erect, gave a firm lead, and didn't pump his left arm the way Chubby Fenton and the rest of those never-to-grow-up college boys did.

"Ev'ry mornin', ev'ry evenin', ain't we got fun, until my father gets ahold of you," he sang softly into her hair, moving her through a gentle spin.

"I saw Miles in church," he said next. "That was very naughty of you. Do you have the slightest idea what a nuisance it'll be if it gets around The Firm? Don't you know how delicate and Byzantine the pecking order is at Hanover Place?"

"Don't be ridiculous," Lyda said through a bright, public-consumption smile. "Your father didn't even quiver when Morris came through the reception line." As opposed to you, she thought; when Howland had caught sight of Morris Miles in the reception line his hand—holding hers—had clenched involuntarily, so tight that it had made her gasp.

"But don't worry, my love," she murmured. One, and two, and three, and twirl, she thought, and followed him into another graceful maneuver. The band switched to "It Had to Be You."

She spoke very rapidly. "It's all for The Firm. To do the things you want to do, it has to be more than a one-man shop built around your sly fox of a father. And you're not going to do it with overgrown college boys like Chubby and Hap Carruthers, not if you want Hanover Place to become more than a nice family business clipping an eighth here, a quarter there. That Hertz business your father's so proud of: d'you call that 'finance'? Do you think J. P. Morgan would? To be a true financier, my sweet, you need truly big ideas of your own. You can't go on borrowing them from Twenty-three Wall Street."

Over her husband's shoulder, she saw Fletcher Warrington detach himself from the encircling crowd and move toward them to cut in. To her relief, she noted that the old man was smiling warmly. She added quickly: "Unless I miss my guess, Morris Miles has that kind of mind. It's like yours, darling, only just enough different to be complementary. Morris is smart and ingenious; he works hard; those are qualities that can be put to much better use than simply tying bonds into bundles. Besides, it's not as if we're going to be friends! I'm not asking you to put him up for the Gorse or take him shooting at Mashomack! But it won't do any harm if we help him learn which fork to use."

"You may be right," Howland said, but he sounded doubtful. He added, "We'll just have to see. Oil and water, you know. By the way, I'm surprised Miles's wife isn't with him. Bobby Carlucci says she's very forward."

"That is precisely why I didn't invite her," said Lyda lightly, just as she felt her father-in-law's hand on her shoulder.

After much deliberation, Morris had decided there could be no harm in a second glass of champagne. He was beginning to calm down after the ordeal of the reception line. Not that Mr. Fletcher had been a problem. He'd taken Morris's hand, looked at him with a trace of amusement, and said, "Ah, Miles, nice to see you," in that way he had of being both curt and courtly.

Morris hadn't partaken of the lavish buffet. He was hungry enough, but he simply couldn't face the prospect of having to have to sit down and explain himself to some stranger. He hung about the corner of the room and took it all in, storing details to report to Miriam.

Around him people talked of the events of the day: the Teapot Dome indictments and the Dawes Plan and the outlook for the market with the discount rate now at three percent; of the Leopold-Loeb murder and the gangland killings in Chicago; of the books they were reading, *The Plastic Age* and *A Passage to India*, and the forthcoming Scott Fitzgerald novel —which was said to be about all these dreadful people who were making money in the stock market; of the sensations of society: the Rhinelander elopement and the Winthrop girls carrying on with the family chauffeurs and how dreadful it was of the *Times* to publish how much or how little people had paid in income tax. They chattered of D. W. Griffith's *America*, which they'd seen at the Plaza, and the new *Ziegfeld Follies*, the best ever, and *Desire Under the Elms*, which had just opened but was too long; of Ralph Barton's *The Man Nobody Knows*, which portrayed Jesus Christ as a profit-seeking businessman and was selling like hotcakes; of the new Baldwin government in London and the uprisings in China, and Red

Grange's four touchdowns against Michigan and the Giants losing the World Series to Washington and Babe Ruth and the "Four Horsemen" of Notre Dame.

Much of it was Greek to Morris; it would have been helpful to have Miriam here to interpret, especially what he gathered was society chatter: about people whose names meant nothing to him, and places he vaguely thought he'd heard of but wasn't sure, and golf and clothes and bootleg liquor and speakeasies and the ridiculous cost of servants and life's other indulgences. The closeness of the room and the second glass of wine made him giddy. The scene seemed to levitate, to float before his eyes on a cloud; he felt adrift in this world of entitlement and privilege, as if making his way in a fog.

He watched Chubby Fenton whirling around the dance floor, pumping away like a man churning butter, humming in his dance partners' ears, foulard askew; obviously tipsy. He supposed this was the gentile "charm" that Berger—who spent most of his commissions with the same smart Fifth Avenue haberdashers people like Carruthers favored—was always talking about and trying to emulate.

Here and there, Morris could spot pockets of heavy business. At the head table, Fletcher Warrington sat and conversed earnestly with B. C. Forbes and Alexander Dana Noyes, the distinguished financial editor of *The New York Times*; at another Schwab and Thomas Lamont had their heads together.

He took it all in the spirit of a grave yet skeptical child observing a bunch of intoxicated grownups. So these were the lords and ladies of creation, the genteel elect, the gentile elect, the rarest, most privileged, decentest, most heroic and perfect people on the face of the earth. The people who were, in all respects, "upstairs."

And wasn't "upstairs" where he craved to be? But yet, as he watched and listened, Morris began to feel unsure. He didn't quite know why; he hadn't time to organize his thoughts, but he sensed from the bottom of his being that this was not for him the way it was for Berger, or for Miriam. If things worked out, if he proved bright and productive and useful, it might be that he would get to know these people, move freely among them, possibly make friends with some of them—good friends, lasting friends, trusting friends. That he might in time have as much as they of the world's material goods. And yet, and yet . . . he knew he would never want to be numbered as one of them. He might try, for Miriam's sake, say, or his children's, if that should seem proper, to belong. To feel the same concerns. To join the clubs they prized so highly, agonize over the invitations over which they grew flustered and desperate. All well and good. But in his heart he knew this was a world that didn't

want him on the terms it accepted its own and that was something with
which, not necessarily for his own sake, he might someday have to deal.

Since the happy couple were voyaging no further on their wedding night
than back downtown to the Warrington mansion, the reception was
allowed to drag on. By nine o'clock the bonhomie began visibly to fray
with drink and boredom and familiarity. All the requisite toasts had been
drunk: the bride to the groom, the groom to the bride, groom's father to
bride's aunt—and so on, and so on. Two engagements were tipsily, spon-
taneously proclaimed. The glamorous décor had degenerated into plates
stained with scrapes of icing, bits of chicken, cigarette butts, stale coffee,
and half-filled glasses of champagne from which the bubbles had long since
gone. At least three people had been carted off insensible and there had
been one near-fight in the men's room. Someone had vomited in an upstairs
sitting room and a vase had been smashed in the members' library.

"My love," said Howland, "I think the time has come."

She nodded, and they rose. In the background the band sawed doggedly
at "How Come You Do Me Like You Do." A few tired dancers fox-
trotted gamely. Even the orchestra was sounding weary.

Lyda started for the stairs, to throw her bouquet. She had decided
to aim for Aunt Miranda. People rose as she went by. Then, suddenly,
there was an anxious hammering of a spoon against a glass, and everyone's eyes shot to the head table. Chubby Fenton had lurched to his
feet. Again he banged his glass. The room fell silent; the band stopped
in mid-bar.

"There's one toast left's gotta be made," Fenton declared. It was obvious
that Charles Christian Fenton III, chief usher, Yale All-American (twice
in football, once in hockey), polo seven-goaler, was thoroughly drunk.
Only his enormous physical vitality was keeping him erect.

As Chubby eyed the room blearily, Howland smiled reassuringly at
Lyda and then at Chubby. True friendship required patience along with
everything else.

Fenton steadied himself on the table and lifted his glass.

"I want us to drink to why we are all here together," he declaimed,
slurring his words. He paused for an instant to gather sense. When he
next spoke, it was almost a shout: "To The Firm!"

He bashed the tabletop with a heavy-wristed paw for emphasis. "To
The Firm!"

Glasses clinked; voices murmured "The Firm" in response. The air seemed still. All frivolity vanished. Like Glendower, Fenton had summoned a spirit from the vasty deep, had urged into being an individual presence as specific and commanding as any personage in that crowded room.

BOOK
II

MONEY
MEN

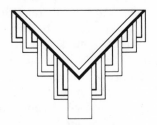

1929

AUGUST

On Friday, August 29, 1929, Morris Miles telephoned Miss Merrow, the partners' receptionist, and asked if Mr. Fletcher and Mr. Howland might have a few minutes to spare before lunch. It was quite urgent.

When Miles appeared, Fletcher got to his feet and shook his hand: "That was a damn nice piece of analysis on those Western Utilities equipment trust certificates, Miles. We certainly missed a bullet on that one. Don't know what's going on on the Street these days. People think they can sell anything, as long as they can find a printer who can run up a prospectus. Damn foolish of Lee Higginson to get caught like that, though. That's what happens when a bunch of johnny-come-latelies take over a good old house. Colonel Higginson must be spinning in his grave. I hear the syndicate's stuck with over three million in unsold bonds!"

"Closer to three and a half, sir."

The two men went on to discuss the intricacies of the issue. Howland could barely stifle a yawn. This sort of talk bored him stiff. Perhaps he *should* have left The Firm and gone with Global Airways, the new airline Tom Creedmore had started two years earlier with The Firm's backing. Global was going great guns. Next month it would add New York-Chicago to its routes and Creedmore was now talking about buying new airliners that could make it across the Atlantic and Pacific in as few as four or five stops. Global was the stuff of true adventure, thought Howland, as he heard his father say: "In any case, Morris, you can pretty much count on a very handsome piece of the profit on our Western Utilities short position showing up in your bonus envelope come Christmas. By the way, have you had a look at that water company issue City Securities is doing?"

Fletcher didn't miss his son's mood. He was well aware that Howland was impatient with the kind of work The Firm did, but damn it! the work was determined by the kind of market they were living in. It was all very well for Howland to dream of putting together and financing grandiose from-the-ground-up schemes like Global, new ventures through which men, money, and machines braved new business frontiers, but this was basically a speculators' market, a market of margin men, get-rich-quick stuff, no holds barred and the hell with the little fellow.

On the other hand, he reflected, Lyda's instinct about young Miles's ability had been confirmed a dozen times over. Colmer Hardesty, the crusty New Englander who ran the Bond Department, had taken Miles on grudgingly. Now he'd be the first to admit he couldn't get on without him. Five years earlier, Hardesty's scrupulous spreadsheets and bond comparisons were regarded as little more than lip service to credit discussions; everyone knew that credit quality was really a matter of character, based on assurances given each other by honorable Christian gentlemen, exactly as Pierpont Morgan had declared it to be fifteen years earlier, testifying to Congress about the causes of the 1907 Panic. Now, with Wall Street in the grip of a speculative frenzy, The Firm had several times diverged most profitably from the conventional wisdom, stood back from the herd and missed being trampled, thanks principally to the hard work and careful attention to detail of Morris Miles.

There were still people, like Carruthers, who dismissed Miles's painstaking analyses as small-minded bean counting. Such men "played" the market; to them, investment was as much dash and old acquaintance as hard-eyed calculation. "Invest and then investigate," they declared, grinning over their martinis.

In Morris Miles's view, the numbers, and the numbers alone, governed investment judgment. To dismiss them was as futile as for a stock trader to fight the tickertape. He had made his point quickly. Just months after he joined Hardesty's department, The Firm—on his urging—declined to participate in the syndication of the Chile Mortgage Bank "Gold" 6½s. The decision at the time appeared precipitate and contrary. The Chile Golds were a hot issue; the sponsors were Kuhn, Loeb and the Guaranty Company.

Morris Miles, however, had made exhaustive calculations with respect to the South American nation's economic situation, the quality of its pledges and collateral, as well as close, lawyerly readings of the security provisions of the instrument. He concluded that here was a real can of worms, likely to default before the first interest payment came due. He went to Hardesty, whose native shrewdness compelled him to agree. Hardesty was a fair man, a believer in giving credit where due, and he insisted that Morris Miles present his case to Fletcher face-to-face. Together they went downstairs to see Fletcher, judge and jury in Hanover Place's court of final decision.

Over the objections of his partners, Fletcher stuck by Morris Miles's guns. Otto Kahn personally called Fletcher Warrington to ask him to change his position, but Fletcher, convinced by Morris Miles's analysis, remained obdurate. His decision was much derided, not least because it quickly got around certain fashionable club bars that he had listened to the advice of a young Jew with practically no experience "upstairs." When—just as Miles had foreseen—Chile defaulted, those same gossips sought to lay all the credit at Hardesty's feet, but the department head was man enough to know where it belonged, and he praised Miles's work unstintingly around the partners' lunch table.

As a result, in January 1929, Morris Miles had been named an assistant manager of S. L. Warrington & Son. His promotion was signaled in a "tombstone" advertisement in the financial pages.

"The ad in the Journal announcing Morris's promotion has apparently caused Chubby and Eddie Stanforth all sorts of grief at the Brook Club," Howland reported to Lyda.

She was delighted. "I can well imagine. What do you expect from those two numbskulls and the bastions of blockheadedness they frequent? Why in the world you keep up your membership in a club that won't take your future partners . . ."

Morris Miles was unconcerned by this issue. The money and position were what counted. Still, he couldn't dismiss a growing uneasiness. The more he saw, the more he was struck by how little real brainpower and hard work seemed to count on the Street. This was not to disparage luck. Anyone in his right mind would rather be lucky than smart. It was the other factors that troubled him. Take The Firm's "connections." It had been one thing to watch a bunch of half-drunk gentiles disport at Mr. Fletcher's wedding reception, another to realize that such people monopolized an entire important sector of business life; that business was based on who a man knew rather than what he knew. When he mentioned this to Miriam, she turned it immediately into a social thing, as if he were talking about something on the ladies' pages. Miriam's head was full of society dreams. If Uncle Friedl wanted to get to Pago-Pago, Miriam's idea of paradise was Park Avenue.

Well, they were moving closer. Practically the minute he'd been taken into The Firm bonus pool, she'd insisted they move away from Pitkin

Avenue to a two-family house on Berkeley Place. So much was new. Sometimes it seemed to Morris that they had nothing but new people in their life—not so much real friends as people who made the noises of friends but who had something to sell: the people at Miriam's new beauty parlor, the woman at Loeser's who helped her pick out dresses.

Miriam was also talking about wanting a third child, as if two weren't enough. The way she made it sound, their infancy in the old neighborhood had tainted Benjy and little Selma. She wanted a child with a clean start in life.

While Howland sat stiffly silent, his father and Morris began to discuss the general market. It was a subject of keen interest to Fletcher. He knew his, and Hanover Place's, reputation for stock-market genius was based as much on bullets missed as coups realized. If you could hold on to what you had, it was always possible to make more. Lose your capital, however, and the game was very likely up. Now, as the summer of 1929 drew to a frenetic close, Fletcher's instincts were troubled.

Bright "New Era," though its adherents might proclaim it, the years since Coolidge's reelection hadn't been all that easy. The Firm had snap-rolled away from the 1926 Florida land crash just in time, but the ensuing stock-market dive had nicked a few of the slower-responding connections pretty badly. In '27, the general business news had looked to be turning sour and Fletcher had been too cautious, missing a good part of a nice rally that had bailed out the perpetual bulls like Carruthers. At the end of 1928, with Hoover elected, Fletcher had read the economic entrails— farm bankruptcies, exploding broker loans, the world awash in debt— with a pessimism that seemed entirely rational, and The Firm had been a hundred points late getting back into what was every day looking like the lustiest wave yet in the greatest bull market in history. Even though the summer of 1929 was certain to go down as one of the market's most golden chapters, Fletcher couldn't help feeling cautious.

His attitude irritated a number of people around The Firm. Hanover Place's men on the front line, Stanforth and "Dolly" Jergens at the Big Board and Bobby Henderson over on the Curb, were catching it regularly. Not to mention Chubby Fenton, who had to listen to his fellow Bond Clubbers and syndicate managers. The refrain was the same: When in Christ's name was Warrington going to get off its duff and get back hell for leather into a market that was making everyone richer by the minute? If they waited too long, the choicest cuts would all be gone.

Fletcher's stance had caused other problems. Apart from a limited num-ber of high-grade bonds, he wasn't buying new offerings for The Firm's account and he wasn't letting his partners put them in the connections' accounts.

Which meant Hanover Place was on the sidelines for the hottest game on the Street: the pyramided investment trust: an upside-down paper ziggurat of highly-indebted companies balanced on a pinpoint of equity. Everyone was caught up in the mania. The trusts were eloquently promoted, elegantly brochured, and, above all, hugely lucrative to their promoters and syndicators, which now included the best Wall Street names. Even J. P. Morgan & Co. had floated a series of investment trusts, United Corporation, Allegheny, and Standard Brands. For the sake of the Morgan relationship, Fletcher had made an exception and grudgingly taken participations, but as soon as he deemed decent after the offerings, he had sold them out. Now the shares of all three issues stood many points above their offering prices, and Fletcher was looking like a stodgy old fool.

The Morgan trusts seemed ultraconservative by comparison with what the rest of the street was shoveling into its customers' portfolios. Goldman, Sachs was practically melting the presses turning out circulars for its glamorous pyramids: Blue Ridge, Shenandoah, Goldman Sachs Trading Corporation. Halsey Stuart had opened a nationwide wire system. Mike Meehan had put brokers on ocean liners to let his big customers trade their way right across the Atlantic; shouldn't The Firm do the same for its connections? This was a once-in-a-lifetime no-risk opportunity to cash in!

Fletcher knew the litany of his partners' complaints by heart now. Why should Hanover Place be the only house to decline a participation in Insull Utilities Investment Inc.? Hell, Carruthers pointed out, Insull was so big that Halsey Stuart had set up a separate company just to underwrite Insull bonds! All the banks now had "securities affiliates" peddling stocks and bonds; mightn't it not be time for The Firm to fight fire with fire and start taking deposits again, and making loans, which it hadn't done since 1838? How long could Hanover Place sit still!

All these assertions added up to a confident siren song hard to resist —even for those older partners who had felt the claw of the bear in 1907 and before. For the younger men, the sharp market break of 1920–21, their only brush with calamity, might as well have never happened. On the Street, a short memory was a prerequisite for facing each new day, which had to be considered whole and entire unto itself. It was no good preaching the lessons of history because history, as Mr. Henry Ford had said, was bunk!

"Well now, Miles," said Fletcher finally, "you obviously didn't come down just to palaver with us about the bond market. Miss Merrow says she detected a certain urgency in your voice. What's on your mind?"

"Sir," said Morris, taking a small notebook from his pocket, "something's come up that might represent a pretty special trading opportunity."

He looked from one Warrington to the other. "On the short side," he added.

As Morris studied his notes, Howland found himself struck by how much sleeker and slicker the young man had become in the five years since leaving the cage; he seemed rounded, buffed, polished, manicured. The main change was in his expression. The former darting, rodentlike nervousness was gone. He now had the look about him of a confident man who knew what he was talking about: who had the facts and the measure of the facts and saw things other men didn't and knew exactly how to convert this special perception into financial advantage.

"I was at Babson's the other day," Miles was saying. He paused to look at Howland and—in an edifying voice—added, "Roger Babson."

"Sure," said Howland with some irritation. Of course, he knew who Babson was. The economist and market soothsayer who, practically on the eve of Howland's wedding in 1924, had predicted the start of the glorious Coolidge bull market. The Street listened to Babson: he had been right often enough, and moreover he had been right in the way the Street preferred to honor its prophets—on the upside. He put great store in economic data, which was why Fletcher had more or less appointed Miles to be Hanover Place's liaison with Babson, as he now was with other Street theoreticians like Benjamin Graham.

"Well," said Morris Miles, "next week Babson's having his 'Annual National Business Conference' up in Wellesley, Massachusetts. I happened to see a confidential draft of the speech he's planning to make. It's pretty strong stuff. I thought it might make for a good trading opportunity if the stock market reacts the way I think it will."

Miles began to read aloud. This was indeed strong stuff, thought Howland:

" 'Sooner or later a crash is coming and it may be terrific . . . a drop in the Dow-Jones of sixty to eighty points, a fall of almost a third . . . closed factories . . . high unemployment . . .' " and so on. A checklist of catastrophe.

As Miles read on, Howland watched his father close his eyes and steeple his fingers, then begin to nod, as if in time to inner music.

When Miles finished, there was a moment's reflective silence in the room. Then Fletcher said: "That's quite something, Miles. Do you mind if I asked how it happens Babson let you see that? It's most unlike him."

Morris hesitated. He wasn't an unethical man. He certainly would never have gone through Roger Babson's desk drawers, not in a million years. On the other hand, left alone for an instant while the economist was called out of his office on some urgent matter, could he be blamed for letting his eye range over the desktop, where it was transfixed by a document, a few paper-clipped sheets of hand-corrected typescript, obviously fresh from Babson's own machine? Across the top of the first sheet the word "Confidential" was printed in large handwritten letters, underlined with two bold slashes. Such a document was asking to be read. It was the matter of a few seconds to slide the pages over, scan them quickly for gist, commit a few choice phrases to memory. Then a matter of a few moments more to pause downstairs in the lobby and jot these phrases in his notebook.

"I happened to see it when Babson was obliged to step out of his office," said Morris. "It was lying on his desk," he added helpfully.

"I see," said Fletcher. He resteepled his fingers. Then a broad smile crossed his face.

"Very interesting, I must say," he commented. "Now, Morris," he asked—it was the first time he had ever called the young man other than by his surname—"if it were up to you, what would you do with this?"

Miles was ready with his answer. "I'd go short across the board," he declared.

The ensuing conversation infuriated Howland. One of the things he had come to hate about Wall Street was the way cheating was so casually countenanced. Anything short of outright felony seemed acceptable. As played by the heavy men, the game's rules were unwritten and subject to undisclosed change. Famous speculators like Duranty and Raskob, Meehan and Livermore, seemed to view the Exchange's rules as little more than come-ons designed to draw in the public's savings—the way a skillfully dressed window at Lord & Taylor might entice shoppers.

Still, Howland could tell himself The Firm was different. Hardly a day went by when The Firm wasn't invited to participate in a pool operation of some sort, but Fletcher turned them all down. It was one thing to have done what they'd done in Hertz, back five years earlier. That sort of exercise had a legitimate industrial point, a kind of virtue, if you will.

His father had once said to him: "I don't see much wrong with a fellow's coming by information the best way he can—short of stealing it outright, of course. My grandfather once said he'd made as much money from what he'd read upside down on other fellows' desks as what he'd read right side up on his own. And he wasn't alone, I can tell you." At the time, he'd thought his father was joking. Now he knew the truth.

As Howland sat there steaming, Morris addressed Fletcher: "Frankly, sir, some of these prices look insane to me. Radio's over ninety dollars; Telephone passed three hundred this morning, and eighteen months ago it was one eighty and change. The business news isn't all that positive and there's an awful lot of call money pouring into the market just begging to plunge into margin loans willy-nilly, and there's certainly no shortage of borrowers looking to play the market on credit. The treasurer of the Euclid and Monongahela called Carlucci this morning and offered fifteen million of call money at ten percent, no strings attached. The thing that really bothers me, sir, is that the value of the market is half as great again as the total value of the economy. That just doesn't make sense."

"It certainly doesn't," said Fletcher. "The time to start watching out is when there's more money than sense in a market."

People who bought without thinking sold without thinking. Markets dominated by overeager latecomers were invariably nervous; what had struck Morris struck his employer: something like this speech of Babson's—coming on top of the recent collapse in Britain of the Clarence Hatry pyramid, which had caused the London markets a nasty tumble— could trigger a sharp spike on the downside.

"Babson's making this speech when?" he asked Miles.

"Next Thursday. September fifth. At lunchtime. Five trading days from now."

Fletcher nodded to himself, warmly commended Morris for his enter-prise, and dismissed the two young men, waving off Howland's obvious wish to discuss the matter. Returning to his private office, he got on the phone to Vincent Grady, the manager of Hanover Place's order room, and unreeled a series of extremely precise instructions. His mind was at ease. If he turned out to be wrong, if the market ignored Babson's dire prophecies and sailed blithely on upward, all that would be lost would be a few hundred thousand dollars and, within The Firm—since word would soon spread from floor to floor that the old man was shorting the market—another iota of his reputation for omniscience. These were the risks one took.

He was not surprised when, at the end of the day, his son asked to see him alone in his office. "Don't tell me," he said before Howland could open his mouth, "I know what you're going to say: gentlemen don't read each other's mail, right?"

Howland looked glumly at his father and nodded.

"The way you see it, my boy," continued Fletcher, "is that our loyal employee Miles has purloined a valuable confidential document on which we have no right to act?"

"Something like that. What about the fellow who buys the stock you short? Would he be a buyer if he knew Babson was going to be making this speech?"

"He might; he might not." Then, seeing that this hardly mollified his son, Fletcher added: "My dear boy, Wall Street is not something out of King Arthur and his Knights. Have you considered, by the bye, that perhaps Babson left the paper on his desk deliberately, expecting that Miles would see it, and probably read it and tell me about it?"

"I would hope Babson would have a higher opinion of us than that."

"Mr. Babson is in the market, too. I'm sure he also feels that discussions of character are best left until after the close of trading."

"What if this gets out?"

"It won't," said Fletcher with calm assurance. "You're entitled to in-terpret this any way you wish, my boy, but you must understand that the reputation of this Firm is like any other lens through which people see something; it's only glass, subject to distortion, and it may or may not reflect the realities of how we go about our business. Beauty after all is said to be in the eye of the beholder, a proposition with which I have little disagreement."

"May I say that strikes me as totally hypocritical!"

"And so it should if we were living in the best of all possible worlds, which, despite the pleadings of some of our colleagues on the Street, I fear we are not. Nevertheless it's the reality, and reality is what, in the end, this business is about. Let me ask you an ethical question, since that seems to be what we're about at the moment. Who in your opinion is the greatest baseball manager in the world? Connie Mack? Huggins? McGraw?"

"McGraw, I guess."

"Now, what is Mr. McGraw's job?"

Howland hated it when his father talked to him like this. "To win the pennant, I guess," he said sulkily.

"Indeed. Now, do you think, if it will help him beat the other team, that Mr. McGraw is above stealing the other team's signals?"

"Oh, for God's sakes, Father, that's baseball! It's just a game."

"And what may I ask do you think this is?"

For an instant, Fletcher's question hung in the air between the two men. The father watched his son try to find a satisfactory answer. Finally, Howland shook his head and shrugged his shoulders in capitulation. "I must say," he murmured feebly, "I am disappointed in Morris."

"Are you now?" asked his father. "May I ask why? Morris Miles isn't Otto Kahn, you know. He's a fine ambitious Jewish lad from the slums who knows his duty when he sees it. Surely we can't ask more of our employees than that, can we?"

"I suppose not," replied Howland.

Fletcher grinned. He got up and patted his son firmly on the shoulder, pleased to have shown the young man the light, pleased that his son had sense enough to see it.

If Howland was disappointed, it was only in part due to having been bested by his father's ineluctable pragmatism. He could live with that. What troubled him was the sense, a feeling he could not rationalize his way around, or otherwise suppress, that between his father and Morris

Miles there was an important core of understanding of which he was simply incapable of being part, a mutuality from which he, by his own nature, was excluded.

It was a feeling that embarrassed him, and so he did not discuss it with Lyda, for fear of seeming petty.

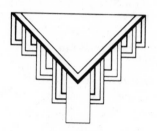

1929

SEPTEMBER

Lyda satisfied herself that Fraulein Erdmann had the twins settled for the night in good order and returned to the library to find Howland busy with the cocktail shaker. She could tell from his voice it had been a hard, exasperating day. She went over and kissed him lightly on the cheek and stroked his hair.

"Another hard one, eh?"

"More of the same. Hap Carruthers is, naturally, the leader of the insurrection. I think Father's being remarkably patient."

Lyda grinned and accepted a martini. "I should think," she said, "that, if anything, your father would derive great confidence from the very fact that it's Hap who's making the most noise. Hap is a fool. He may dress smartly, but once you get beneath the Weatherill tailoring, there's nothing there."

"Ah well," sighed her husband. "Tomorrow will tell the tale. Mr. Babson speaks at noon. What time are we meeting the Frelingvilles?"

"Eight-thirty, and I hate to tell you, it's black tie."

"How was the boys' day?"

"As usual, rambunctious. I think Fraulein Erdmann's Prussian reserve's showing a few cracks although she's not ready yet for the Hartford Retreat. They're very disappointed, naturally, that you didn't show up to rough-house with them this evening."

"It couldn't be helped. I had to help Father quell an impromptu revolt. The firm's own short positions are over a million dollars to the bad, and some of the larger connections are hurting, too, and asking embarrassing questions. Coming up in the car, Father said that if we can send the Marines to Nicaragua, perhaps President Hoover can spare a few to help keep the peace at Hanover Place."

It was the evening of Wednesday, September 4, 1929, six days after Morris Miles had conveyed his knowledge of Roger Babson's speech, and five days after Fletcher Warrington had laid down a drastic redirection of The Firm's new-term investment strategy. The markets had been closed Monday for Labor Day, but Tuesday and Wednesday had done painful damage to The Firm's short positions and, as he had predicted, its managing partner's reputation.

Howland used the word *revolt* advisedly. By the closing bell, the partners' room at Hanover Place was seething. The partners milled around, exchanging dreadful stories of connections' angry phone calls to protest missed profits, which translated into missed commissions for The Firm, and of how far under water were The Firm's positions in Telephone, shorted at $300, now $310, New York Central, shorted at $240, now $260, and Carbide, shorted at $140, now $150. Their mood was not helped by the knowledge that the managing partner, at this moment of crisis, was upstairs in the small gym on the eleventh floor, having his customary afternoon massage.

At his corner desk, Howland fiddled with paperwork and tried to shut his ears to some of the things that were being said.

Halfway down the room, Hap Carruthers lounged against his desk, displaying a perfectly aligned Sulka clockwork sock between a razor-pressed cuff and a gleaming bench-made shoe. Speaking in an unnaturally loud voice, obviously for Howland's benefit, and pounding the desk with a rolled-up newspaper for emphasis, he asked: "For Christ's sweet sake, what the hell am I going to tell old man Frelingville? Or Louis Stoddard! We shorted forty-two hundred Monkey Ward at four sixty and change! How the hell can we stay in business with trades like that! Do any of you idiots know what this is going to mean to our reputation!"

In counterpoint, Eddie Stanforth, back from the Floor, could be heard complaining to Colmer Hardesty and Charlie Runnels—who looked after corporate finance—about what Mike Meehan had said when Stanforth had chugged up to the specialist's post, in the very teeth of a bull gale, and offered twenty thousand short. Meehan had taken fifteen thousand shares at $99 for his own book, Fenton reported, then closed the stock at par, which was $505 on the old stock, and grinned while doing it like a crocodile eying a bather. Words to the same effect burbled like a wood-wind obligato from the partners who worked the smaller, more speculative markets where the fever burned even hotter: the Curb, the Consolidated exchange, and the unlisted markets where the investment trusts were traded. Apparently at a couple of the tonier lunch clubs, there had been some stick from Goldman, Sachs people who'd heard Fletcher was shorting Blue Ridge and Shenandoah. All in all, a discomfiting day for the proud citizens of Hanover Place.

Howland listened but said nothing. Chubby Fenton, sitting across from him, also held his peace, doubtless as a courtesy to their longstanding friendship. The unmistakable scent of gin wafted across the two yards of walnut that separated the two men. Chubby had obviously made a detour to the ninth-floor dining room for a stiffener. He had followed Fletcher blindly and placed a heavy shortside bet with his brand-new wife's Cuban sugar fortune, and he was nervous.

Howland could add and subtract. There was no getting around the fact that these two days had been disastrous. The market strategy his father had described on Saturday as "a finger in the wind" had cost The Firm and its connections well over a million dollars in paper losses. The way the market was roaring ahead, it seemed unthinkable that a lunchtime speech given by even as well-known an economist as Babson could have any effect at all. His father's record as a market reader was nothing short of spectacular, but pedigrees weren't something Wall Street paused to consider when a market had the bit in its teeth. He pushed his face lower in his papers and tried not to hear the grousing around him.

At a little after four thirty, Fletcher Warrington strode briskly into the partners' room, freshly barbered and shaved, giving off a faint aroma of witch hazel. His blunt, strong features seemed lit up with health and confidence. He went right to the Platform, examined his messages briefly, stepped down, and marched over to the glass-globed tickertape machine and unspooled a yard or so of the tape from the bracket on which Miss Merrow kept it neatly hung. He examined the symbols coolly, then devoted a moment's notice to the clipboards that held the "broad tapes," the wide paper tracks from Reuters and Dow-Jones on which news bulletins were printed. At last, he turned back to the room and his partners. "Goodness," he said cheerfully, "it's been quite a day, hasn't it?" He smiled around the room. "Although as a disaster I'm bound to say I wouldn't rate it with 'aught-seven.'"

There was a noticeable easing of tension around the room as the managing partner's confident tone flowed into the backbones of his partners. "Wall Street lives by the minute, gentlemen, and two bad days can seem like an eternity, as we all know. I urge you to be patient. I have seen nothing to alter the thinking I outlined to you last Saturday. I am unalterably convinced that we may find ourselves on the edge of a financial abyss. I expressed that concern to you earlier in the year, when things in

Europe began to go badly after Hatry failed and then the Boche market fell apart. Some of my judgment is instinctive; much of it is based on hard experience; some of it you might call 'house wisdom,' things I learned from my grandfather that he learned from his father. Some of it, I am embarrassed to say, might even be called 'analytical.' " He grinned at the room.

"My grandfather often talked to me of financial crises, of which in his long lifetime he saw a great many. He used to speak with particular feeling about 1837 and 1873, when what first appeared to be short-range panics turned out to be merely the door-openers for nothing less than economic cataclysm. Some things—many things—suggest to me that 1929 may turn out to be the same. There are times when the structures and institutions of our financial markets, and, in particular, the individuals who find themselves in control of those institutions and structures, comport themselves in such a way that what under normal conditions would be a more or less orderly retreat from an overblown bull market turns into a general crash. I believe this may be such a time, and have therefore decided that we are going to act with a prudence that some of you at the moment doubtless find akin to idiocy, based on what's happened these last two days. Well, so be it. Normally we arrive at our policies through consensus. Sometimes, however, that isn't possible. At such times, you gentlemen are faced with the less alluring aspect of working in a family business. After all, gentlemen, it is my family's name which is on the door of this establishment and not yours. Generally speaking, my family happily cedes to you whatever good notice The Firm may earn in flush times; in return for that, I think we are at least entitled to reduce our exposure to blame when clouds appear. Is that fair enough?"

Most of the room murmured relieved assent. Out of the corner of his eye, Howland saw that Carruthers's neck was flushed under his shiny, pinned collar. For an instant, the good-looking man held his tongue, but then he spoke up in a sharp voice. "I know it's not my place to say anything, Fletcher, except just this: do you intend to continue in this foolishness, because if you do . . ."

" 'If I do'—what, Hap?"

The managing partner's smile was patient and dangerous. Carruthers started to interrupt, but Fletcher held up a neat, square hand. "Hap, I just want you to consider this. You came here the day after you left New Haven with little more than a 'Y' in crew and a Bones pin to recommend you, along with the fact that I knew your Uncle Johnny when he was still at the Chelsea Trust Company. You seem to have prospered with us. You have risen in society, by which you place great store and which has done well by you in business arrangements. You have become a member of the best clubs and you are seen in enviable company at the theater and the racetrack. Enviable company which directs enviable business to you and through you. Thanks to your own charm and ability, of course, but also because The Firm's name on your business card means something."

After a pause to let the point sink in, the managing partner continued: "Now obviously you are free to make whatever professional arrangements you feel are suitable, Hap. You may be relieved to know that I am going to let matters rest here. We have built up the short positions I specified in Radio, Carbide, and in certain other issues for which there currently appears to be a mania, to wit, the Goldman Sachs investment trusts, and equally tenuous pyramids. Now we are going to wait and see."

"See what?" demanded Carruthers in a surly tone.

Before Fletcher could reply, Charlie Runnels, always a peacemaker, intervened. "Why the rush, sir? It sounds like you're expecting a sign from heaven, like the Star in the East."

His comparison drew a chuckle from the partners.

"Charlie, I like the way you put that," said Fletcher, lighting up the cavernous room with one of his famous smiles. "That's really quite apt. Anyway, gentlemen, there we are."

He turned his gaze to the other men, looking into each of their faces in turn, measuring—Howland knew—individual levels of doubt and dis-content. Finally, he came back to Carruthers. "Hap, you still seem un-convinced. You may be right and I may be wrong. But sadly, there's only one football here at Hanover Place, and it's mine, at least for the time being. I recognize the extent of your dissatisfaction. However, I hope you'll sleep on it, and come around. But if you still feel strongly in the morning, it'll be short work to have Bobby Carlucci downstairs calculate the value of your partnership interest and get a check to you before the opening bell tomorrow. There are a dozen firms on the Street, I'm sure, who would die to get you. You would of course go with my blessing."

Fletcher smiled at Carruthers. Howland looked at the floor. Nothing like this had ever happened, not right out in front of everyone. One of the partners got up and hastened to shut the door leading to the partnership lavatory and typing pool, sealing off the proceedings from the gossipy ears down the corridor. When Fletcher spoke again, it was clear that a point of no return had been passed. "Some of the rest of you may share Hap's concerns. If so, now's the time to speak out. If I'm going to have to pay the Judge his ridiculous hourly fees to amend the partnership agreement for one man's withdrawal, I'd prefer to deal with any others at the same time."

No one said anything. Fletcher made a fist of his right hand and smacked it briskly into his left.

"In that case, gentlemen, let us be of stout heart! Can I give anyone a lift uptown? Come on, Hap. Don't look so gloomy. We'll stop off at the Racquet Club and I'll buy you a sarsaparilla."

The next morning, Fletcher canceled his regular weekly golf date at Blind Brook—a sure sign, said Miss Merrow to her colleagues around the coffee samovar, that something big was up.

By noon, after a sandwich upstairs, he was in the partners' room, moving nervously between his desk on the Platform and the stock tickers. Now and then he went to the window that looked across Hanover Place and Water Street to the East River, and stood gazing fiercely out, hands balled pugnaciously on his hips, as if physically willing a special wish to come true.

At just after one, Howland joined his father, having cut short his meeting at Lehman Brothers, which had recently moved into the old Seligman building a block and a half south at 1 William Street. As the lunch hour wore on, in the mysterious way that men are drawn together, other partners began to drift into the big room. By one thirty, all but the floor partners and one or two others out of town on business were gathered by the tickers.

They made a pretense of business as usual: talking on the phone, checking the tape, making small talk among themselves. The tickers chattered measuredly away. Every five minutes or so, as was her routine, Miss Merrow would come in from her station in the vestibule, snip off the news and quote tapes, peek to see how her fifty shares of Carbide were faring, and affix them to clips on the ticker pedestals.

The market was holding steady; the historic highs set by Tuesday's monster rally were being maintained.

Finally, at a little after two, a summary of Roger Babson's speech at his conference began to come over the Dow-Jones newswire. Fletcher hovered over the clacking printer, watching the words unspool, scarcely reading them; Howland stood at his shoulder, watching, too. Watching and waiting. Behind them, the other partners, sensing an intensification of the Warringtons' mood, fell silent.

The newswire finished its summary of Babson's speech and began to recapitulate the day's closing prices on the Vienna Exchange; the stock ticker tat-tatted away at its normal busy but steady tempo.

Then, without warning, this racket shifted to a frenzied pace. Howland would swear to his dying day that the machine's voice literally changed, that it seemed to go into hysterics. The next instant, all three telephones on Fletcher's desk began to ring, then all the phones in the room, and Miss Merrow appeared in the doorway.

"Vinnie Grady on your house wire, Mr. Fletcher. He says it's urgent." Grady was The Firm's chief order clerk.

Howland's father snatched up the phone, nodding to his son to pick up the earpiece extension and listen in. "Yes, Vinnie?"

"All hell's broken loose down on the floor, Mr. Fletcher. Some guy gave a speech somewhere and . . . well, Steel was up a fraction, now it's off six points, no, make that six and a half, make it three-quarters, make it seven. And in size, too, sir! Sainted Mary Mother of God! I think I just saw Radio go by at under par! Yessir, Radio's at ninety-seven! Let's see where Carbide's selling."

Howland heard Grady shout to the order room at large. "Anybody see Carbide? Who has Carbide? What! No! Jaysus! Sorry about the language, Mr. Fletcher, but Carbide's off eight; it was one thirty-six and change, Stanforth says we can buy all we want at twenty-eight, no, there it goes by at twenty-seven and three-quarters, twenty-seven, now six and three-quarters, six and a quarter; you want me to cover any of the shorts in here, sir?"

"No, Vinnie, just sit back and watch for a while. I want to sit tight, at least until near the close."

Fletcher Warrington was grinning as if he'd found a pearl in his oyster. He hopped down from the Platform, amazingly nimble for a man in his sixties, and clobbered the air with a brisk left jab followed by a snappy right cross.

"By God in heaven, we've got 'em," he exulted to his partners. He turned to Howland. "Come on, son, let's go downstairs and watch the Trans-Lux in the order room. If you're on the right side of a panic, these things can be a hell of a lot of fun to watch, but these damn tickertapes move too fast for my old eyes. Hell, my boy, if you thought the Meuse-Argonne was something, wait'll you see this!"

That evening, Fletcher called his partners together before dispersing for the day. "Gentlemen, this afternoon a tiny pebble almost derailed the Broadway Limited, so to speak. The next one is going to pitch the whole caboodle off the tracks and into the abyss, but we're not going to be aboard. At all!"

"Which means what?" asked Carruthers, sounding sullen, looking worried. Just after the close, Howland and his father had been informed by Carlucci, The Firm's administrative manager, that not all of Carruthers's stock positions had been brought into line with the managing partner's earlier directives. Some of his choice accounts had been buyers on Tuesday and Wednesday, and had now suffered extremely unpleasant setbacks.

"Which means, Hap, that we're going to sell everything in the shop, and then some, in as orderly a manner as we can, taking what prices we get, and then we're just going to sit and wait and try not to smirk when the time comes. And believe me, my friends, come it will!"

On the way uptown, he remarked to Howland: "To tell the truth, all I expected was a faint crack on Humpty-Dumpty's forehead, but I think the old boy had better see his physician as soon as possible. He looks to me as if he's terminally ill."

At Howland's, Fletcher came upstairs to see his grandsons. He let the twins crawl all over him, then, when they had him out of breath, he bought a moment's rest with a pair of shiny half-dollars that Fraulein promptly appropriated with a prim expression of disapproval.

Lyda poured them a glass of champagne.

"Well, my children," he said, raising his glass, "to joy and sorrow and the morrow. I do love to be right, because there's money in it, but it's a mournful thing to see a bull market die. And dead this one is, of that I'm certain. It'll take some time, a month or so perhaps, but I'll lay any amount you please that by year-end the *Times* index will have lost close to half its value. Fortunes will be lost—and a few made or added to, including our own—and many innocent, undeserving hearts will be broken. Sadly, a crash takes no prisoners."

"But if you've guessed right, Fletcher, The Firm is going to come out of this sounder and richer than ever," Lyda said.

"Very possibly, but if things get really bad, it's hard to say how much satisfaction we'll be able to take from our own good fortune. I emphasize the word *fortune*, because that's what makes the difference, my dear. The Street's not the most intellectually demanding business, you know. All it really takes is a bit of capital, and a lot of luck."

"Or vice versa," rejoined his daughter-in-law.

"Or vice versa," Fletcher admitted. Then, looking up sharply, he asked: "I suppose Howland's told you of young Miles's part in all this?"

"A bit."

"I think you were right about Miles, my dear. I think he has what it takes."

"Apparently," Lyda said coolly.

Fletcher looked at his son. "I know Howland has his doubts, but that's the beauty of finance, it's all things to all men. In some it brings out the Newton, in others Beethoven, in still others Napoleon. Old Morgan was a proper Napoleon. Miles is more in the Newton vein."

"And how do you see your son?" Lyda asked mischievously.

Fletcher chuckled. "How about Sir Galahad?"

"And is that a bad thing?"

"Not at all. A good deal of the time, character ranks right up there, after luck, but before most other things, including genius. It does help to have a good and faithful and well-mounted squire riding beside you."

"Lest Sir Galahad turn into Don Quixote?"

"Very well put, my dear. Oh dear God in heaven, here they come again!"

With a rush of noise and laughter, two identical little boys, blond as butter, bowled into the room followed by their starched and remonstrative governess.

"Aha," said Fletcher, putting his glass down hastily. "The future is upon us. But isn't it always?"

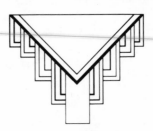

1929

OCTOBER

The future seems to be taking its time, thought Howland. Father's ebullient toast back in September might better have been drunk in wormwood than in Veuve Clicquot.

"The Babson Break" had been a one-day wonder. The market regrouped the next day, and promptly took off again. On September 19 the *Times* stock index was higher than on the eve of Babson's speech. The hot favorites had regained their zip and were routinely making new highs. Investors who had taken to the sidelines now feared to miss the next hundred upside points in this greatest of all bull markets, and rushed to commit.

It was a difficult time for Howland. No one said anything directly to his face, but he knew what some of his partners—and others lower down in The Firm—were muttering about his father's judgment. The old man might have been right for a day, but that was all. The derision wasn't restricted to Hanover Place. At the Monday partners' lunch three weeks after the Babson Break, Hap Carruthers had conspicuously and contemptuously passed around the latest *Barrons*: the chief editorialist, an unreconstructed cheerleader for the Great Bull Market, had referred to "the sad spectacle of a venerable and once brave firm turned panic-monger."

The Firm lost some business along the way. Fletcher exercised his prerogative as managing partner and overruled the majority decision of the Commitment Committee—Hardesty, Fenton, Ed Stanforth, Charlie Runnels, and Howland himself—to participate in the offerings of two new Insull Trusts being promoted by Halsey Stuart. Everyone in the Bond Club knew that Chubby Fenton had been dressed down drill-sergeant-style by old man Stuart in the dining room of the Downtown Association. Samuel Insull was the greatest financial genius since old Morgan, Fenton was told in no uncertain terms, and if Hanover Place was too stupid to see that, it would only cost them and their customers millions.

At the end of September, when the word came down from the managing partner that "all margined accounts, *including partners' debit accounts*, are forthwith to be paid up, sold out, or moved elsewhere," Hap Carruthers finally picked up the gauntlet that Fletcher had earlier thrown at his feet and resigned to take a desk at Lee Higginson. He needed a more go-ahead house, he told one and all, and he said some other things, too —about how a "real firm didn't dance to the tunes of untested Hebrew pied pipers."

Carruthers was the first partner in The Firm's 115-year history to resign of his own accord, and the simple fact of his departure reverberated through Hanover Place and up and down the Street.

"It's times like these that try the souls of the sons and heirs of crusty old bastards like me," Fletcher told Howland consolingly. The two were sitting in the steam room of the Union Club after a midweek squash match.

His son shook his head supportively as Fletcher continued: "Frankly, the only thing I feel bad about is that Miles seems to have taken some short positions himself which are pretty badly under water. We'll carry him, as we'll carry all our good people. Will you have a word with Carlucci?"

Howland said he would, but he didn't like it. Once again he experienced that embarrassing tremor of unease. He tried to put it out of mind with small talk.

"By the bye," he told his father, "there's fresh news from the Carruthers front. Apparently he boasted to all and sundry at Piping Rock last Sunday that he ignored your orders to sell, and that he's accordingly made millions for his connections, and that he fully expects the Phippses and Frelingvilles to take all their business to Lee Higg."

"Hap is free to say anything he wants. The Phipps women are very fond of him; he's the sort of fellow who goes far in good times because he amuses people, and the rich must always have their jesters, provided they don't cost too much. Actually, I shouldn't be surprised if, after the sun goes down, Hap didn't prove to be a bit of a nancy boy, notwithstanding that he was in Bones. He certainly looks like one, and rich New York women have always liked a pansy or two to dress up the scene.

Anyway, that's neither here nor there. If you'll take a close look at the daily sheets you'll notice that the big Phipps accounts, not the chickenfeed they let Hap play with but the ones on which H.C. himself calls the tune, are in exact conformity with our own. Not only that, but Max Kramer, that fellow who advises them on real estate, has moved some of his own accounts here—I've asked Miles to keep herd on them—and I think that's a pretty solid vote for the way we see things. As for Toddy Frelingville, what can I say? The boy's a fool. I always told his father he should have tied that kind of money up in trust, but there you are."

The old man shrugged and ran his hands back through his damp hair. "What really worries me is that ten years ago you'd never have taken that fifth game off me, damn it! Anyway, my boy, just shut your ears to all this palaver. I've heard it before, but markets can only run so long on sheer talk, and this one's about over. I hear the earth creaking underfoot and it's a sound I recognize from long experience."

Howland must have looked dubious, because his father's voice softened and, in a gesture so rare that Howland felt almost shocked by it, he put his hand on his son's bare shoulder.

"I know how you feel, because if I'm crazy, or I'm wrong, well, then you're marked for life with my failure. But that's what families in business are about, for better or worse. It's not easy being the son and heir. Can you imagine how I felt when your great-grandfather died suddenly, and I had to get up on the Platform? A mere boy with only five years on the Street? You can well imagine how keenly I felt what the other men in the room—older men, wiser men—were thinking. But you see, I had to follow the stars the way I read 'em, and so I did, from day one. Howland, this Firm belongs to us. That's the whole point of it."

As they moved into October, Howland began to relax. The market was finally beginning to look shaky again. What had passed in September for robust good health now seemed to be no more than a suntan on a critically ill patient. The bulls kept trying to talk reality away, but the hearty laughter in the clubs had acquired a distinctly nervous edge.

The mood in the partners' room was shifting. The short positions had edged back into the black. Fenton and the rest no longer arrived at work like condemned men.

Reviewing the trading sheets with Carlucci, Howland was interested to see some large new names. "These here," said Carlucci, "are new connections. Some of the Rockefeller charitable trusts. Strictly small stuff for them, but a start. Mr. Fletcher sent Miles over to the family office to talk to them and he got the ball rolling."

Howland was interested to note that Morris Miles had doubled his own shorts. He asked him about it. "For one thing, stocks are starting to fall pretty conclusively," Miles observed. "For another, the latest Federal Reserve numbers on brokers' loans are frightening. The banks seem to be in some kind of a lending frenzy. The foreign loan picture looks just awful. When Morgan gave up lending overseas, that spoke volumes. I heard that Mr. Sloan's told General Motors to pull in its horns—both in business and in the call money market."

"What about the seven billion in new bank money the papers have been full of? Mightn't that mean the public's still coming in?"

Miles shrugged. "Who cares? The public's always wrong anyway. If it wasn't, there wouldn't be a Wall Street. Personally, I think the Street's borrowing all this money to prop itself up. I hear Kidder, Peabody won't last another week if it keeps up like this. And they're not the only one."

He sounded highly confident, but his stomach was churning. He was in deep, well over his head. Fletcher Warrington's implicit endorsement of Morris's reading of the market had emboldened the young man to plunge further. His exposure, on the short side, was at least three times what anyone except himself knew it to be—not Miriam, not the Warringtons or Carlucci or anyone within the four walls of Hanover Place.

On Monday, October 21, what Fletcher had perceived months earlier as a dim and monstrous apparition struggling to be born burst into the open tooth and claw. All the previous weekend, margin calls had been going out from Wall Street; long into Sunday night, the financial district was ablaze with lighted windows. The air seemed full of awful portents; breath seemed choked in the throat; the unspoken prayer seemed to be: please God, don't let the market open Monday; let clocks and calendars be halted here and now.

God proved deaf. The market sold off steadily through Monday and Tuesday on terrific volume. Once again office windows stayed lit right through to the next morning's opening. Wednesday was a real charnel house: the *Times* stock index was off eighteen points; the ticker ran an hour and a half late, so that an order sent to the Floor was in effect dispatched into the great unknown. Trading volume exceeded six million shares!

By noon of Thursday, the 24th, when Miss Merrow hurried to Fletcher's desk to tell him that Mr. Thomas Lamont of Morgan's was on the line, the market was in total, headlong, disorderly retreat. Vinnie Grady reported that stocks were being thrown at the specialists by the basketful, and that the specialists, their capital long since gone, were letting them find whatever level they could.

At The Firm, as everywhere else on the Street save the trading floors and order rooms, motion was suspended as the partners left their desks and gathered around the tape machines, watching the parade of numbers with a fixed and helpless gaze, unaware that clerks and secretaries had drifted into the *sanctum sanctorum* to join the vigil. Hearing Miss Merrow's message to Fletcher, a few detached themselves and gathered by the Platform.

"Hello, Tom," Fletcher said into the telephone, "what can I do for you?"

His tone was measured. He listened for a minute, then replied without hesitation. "Tom, that's a noble idea, but also a foolish one. If you want to send good money after bad, that's your prerogative."

Another pause.

"No," Fletcher replied calmly. "I regret to say I do not agree. This is not 1907 all over again. That crisis was institutional; this is a general public hysteria and in my judgment there isn't enough money in the world to put the brakes on what's happening down there. I'm afraid I have to say to you that the long-term interests of this firm, my family, and our own connections oblige me to pass."

After the usual courtesies, Fletcher hung up.

He turned to his partners. "Well, gentlemen, I think you have probably gotten the idea. Morgan's putting together a group to go into the market and buy stocks. Baker at First National and Prosser at the Bankers Trust are going along, and Wiggin at the Chase, of course, largely to save his own neck, from what I hear. They may have some momentary success, but not for long, in my opinion, and not in any meaningful way. They're naturally disappointed at our position, and so am I at having to take it. Many's the time we've stood shoulder-to-shoulder with 23 Wall. Now, I think I'll go take my massage."

His audience drifted back to the tickertape, which continued to hammer out its numerical tales of woe. Price reports were now almost two hours behind the even worse realities. There had never been a day like this.

As they watched the tape, Chubby Fenton said to Charlie Runnels, who had played across the line from him when Yale beat Harvard in Fenton's final game, "Do you really think it's as bad as the old man says?"

Runnels let the tape slip through his fingers. He watched as Radio lost two points in the space of half an inch. "How would I know?" he replied.

"He's the only one here who knows what one of these things really looks like."

When the butler announced that Mr. Fenton was downstairs, Lyda and her husband had finished an early dinner with the twins and were in the library listening to a radio report of the day's disaster. The room was painted a deep, dark green and furnished with large, reassuringly solid pieces covered in unobtrusive fabrics, a good, calming room to be in at a time like this.

Chubby, arriving without warning in a city that still set some store by formality, even among close friends, was obviously keyed up, too restless to sit at home, needing to share his high excitement with someone else. Three quick cocktails did little to subdue his agitation.

He bounced up and down on the burgundy leather chesterfield, which groaned ominously under his bulk. He snatched at the proffered martini like a large seal taking a mackerel from its keeper, and gulped at it as if it were the last ounce of gin left on earth.

"Golly," he exclaimed, "you two should have been there! It was magnificent!"

"What was magnificent?" asked Lyda.

He looked at her with narrowed, disbelieving eyes, as if she had asked the most foolish question of all time.

"Why, Whitney, of course. Dick Whitney. He was absolutely magnificent, damn it!"

"*C'est magnifique, mais ce n'est pas la guerre*," said Lyda, smiling at her husband.

"What's that supposed to mean?" asked Fenton.

"Oh, nothing, Chubby," said Lyda. "It's just something someone said about the Charge of the Light Brigade. Now—tell us all about Richard Whitney."

"Well, I tell you, it was fantastic! Just like Horatio at the bridge!"

"Horat*ius*," said Lyda. "Horatius at the Bridge. Thomas Babington Macaulay." Her father had been a great one for parlor poetry, and left her with a head full of the stuff. Howland said she was the only woman in Christendom who could recite "Casey at the Bat" straight through.

"Well, maybe more like LeBaron," said Chubby doubtfully.

"Who's LeBaron?" asked Lyda.

"Oh, come on, Lyda: you know! In *Stover at Yale*, the part about Tap

Day, when he sweeps through the crowd to tap Dink Stover? Well, Dick was just like that! When things started to get sticky, I hustled over to the Exchange and Eddie Stanforth got me a Floor pass, and by God, I was right there in the Steel crowd when Dick walked in, just as cool as ever you please, and bid old General Bridgeman two hundred and five for ten thousand Steel. I've never seen anything like it! And then off he went to the Carbide post, same thing, and to Radio and right on around the floor, and by jingo that did it! The market turned right around!"

"So I heard," said Howland. "It must have been bedlam down there. What'd they end up doing on the day: thirteen million shares?"

"All of that at least," said Fenton. "The big thing is the Dow cut its loss to thirty-nine points and change. That's half of what it was before Dick went out on the floor! The talk is that tomorrow'll see Morgan bringing in more buying power. They'll lift this thing clear out of the woods. This bull ain't dead yet! And don't you think our name isn't mud for not going in with Morgan! How about another one of those excellent martoonis?"

Hope talking, thought Howland; as his father said, banks didn't cash checks drawn on hope. He knew Chubby had reversed his nervous shorts and gone long in the market. Chubby was a bull at heart; most men were.

Anyway, Chubby to the contrary, the Dow was hardly the story; Grady had called just before he left the office to report that in the other markets, where the investment pyramids were traded and margin borrowing was highest, the damage had run uncontained. There were no buyers; only calls going out to speculators large and small to cough up more margin.

"Yessir, they've turned it right 'round," Chubby repeated, sipping hard, "I hear Morgan's got a quarter billion more lined up to support the market. But it probably won't be needed."

More like fifty million if that, thought Howland. It was his father's guess that the Morgan syndicate would sell out its support positions in the morning, when the strength of the previous close would still be in the market. They had done what they could. Anything more would be foolish—and there were damn few fools at 23 Wall.

His father had a different slant. "Damn foolishness to do anything, if you ask me," the old man had declared as they stood at the end of the day watching the tape. "Makes it look as if 23 Wall and the rest of us are responsible. Lamont should have turned his back: if there's going to be a rescue, let the guilty parties foot the bill: Wiggin and Mitchell and Meehan and the rest of them. They're the ones who turned this into a casino, let them be the heroes. If this thing gets worse, and I think it's going to, there'll be hell to pay, including a hunt for scapegoats and, just you watch, now it'll be Morgan that bears the brunt."

As Fletcher predicted, the market steadied just long enough to let the Morgan syndicate get its money out, but by Friday noon it was clear there were going to be no more gallant charges into the cannon's mouth. By the close, the Street wore mourning.

For the first time since the war, the market was shut on Saturday: to let the Street catch up with the avalanche of paperwork. The following Monday was a horror; Tuesday proved immortal in the chronicle of financial carnage: "Black Tuesday," October 29, 1929.

By the time the market closed, some sixteen million shares had changed hands; the *Times* index was off forty points.

At noon on Black Tuesday, Fletcher, his fortune intact but obviously shaken by events, advised his partners to go home to their families. In such a storm, he declared, it was a man's duty to be by the side of his loved ones. He put on his homburg and walked over to Howland's desk. "Get your hat and come with me."

They went down, out the heavy wrought-iron doors, crossed Hanover Place and went up the narrow alley that led to Wall Street. It seemed to Howland that the very air was sulfurous. They turned west at the Brown Brothers building, which stood directly across Wall Street from the spot where the buttonwood tree had flourished back when Samuel Warrington had first set up in business. At the corner of Wall and William they paused; Fletcher gestured back toward the narrow bulk of the National City Bank.

"I hear Charlie Mitchell's in the soup with his personal margin accounts," he said. "Just like Al Wiggin at Chase. It boggles the mind, doesn't it? Bankers: the good gray men of finance. Hmph!"

Three-quarters up the next block, in front of the headquarters of J. P. Morgan and Co., Fletcher halted again. He pointed to the scars left in the building's façade by the 1920 bombing.

"Damn fools, these anarchists, trying to make an end to Wall Street by blowing its head off. All you end up doing is killing the clerks. Much better to leave the job to the Street itself. When the fit's on us, we can make a quicker, cleaner, and more thorough end to capitalism than any Bolshevik!"

Another few paces brought them to the old Sub-Treasury building. The steps of the neoclassical temple, on which George Washington had taken the oath of office, were packed with men. They stood there in a weird calm, staring across the intersection of Broad and Wall at the Stock Exchange as if seeking divination. Their faces were stunned, made blank by shock, confusion, and disbelief. For all that Howland knew, the hopes if not the very lives of most of them were being shredded at that very moment within the Stock Exchange building on the other side of Wall Street. A strange sound filled his ears; a low unbroken murmur, like the humming of a hive, rising from the men on the steps.

"It was like this when your great-grandfather brought me down here in 'seventy-three," Fletcher said. "Like something out of Dante. Do you still read *The Divine Comedy* at Yale?" He didn't wait for an answer. "I never wanted you to see this, my son. The death of an era. Not like any other kind of death, is it? I never forgot it, and I daresay you won't. But realize this: all the remembering in the world's never kept the Street out of trouble."

On that acrid day, as the New Era convulsed in its death agonies, here and there were pockets of emotions other than chagrin and despair: one man's loss, after all, usually is another man's profit, although in cataclysmic times not necessarily.

On the night of Black Tuesday, in a quiet family house lying behind a small lawn abutting on a peaceful Brooklyn street, Morris Miles was seized by a sexual passion born of inexpressible relief, mixed up with a no less virile and intense feeling of omnipotence. Both had their earthly origin in a clear $35,000 profit on Morris's short positions. Trembling with excitement and a sense of power, Morris possessed his wife that night with a violence and creativity that took her utterly aback.

Two months later, when stock prices had settled at what would prove to be close to their 1929 lows, when the market had lost some thirty billion of the eighty billion it had been worth on the eve of the Babson Break and it was becoming clear that the world's economic difficulties went much deeper than even the market disaster suggested, Miriam Miles advised her husband that—barring misadventure—some time in July 1930, he could look forward to becoming a father for the third time.

BOOK III

FAMILY CONCERNS

1931

DECEMBER

ow utterly like Father this is, Howland thought with amused exasperation as the big Pierce-Arrow towncar carried them down Madison Avenue.

It was December 15, 1931, approximately three weeks before Howland and Lyda's fourth child was due to be delivered at Doctors Hospital. They were hoping for a girl this time, but Lyda was certain it was another boy.

Howland and his father were bound for Brooklyn on an errand that Fletcher Warrington regarded with insufferable relish. They were on their way to advise Morris Miles that he was being admitted, as of January 1, 1932, to partnership in S. L. Warrington & Son.

Howland found the performance ridiculously theatrical, right out of *A Christmas Carol!* How much easier and more comfortable it would have been just to summon Morris to Fletcher's office and give him the good news.

It wasn't a large partnership interest he was being offered. Indeed, in strict money terms, he probably wouldn't make much more than he was now, if one included his bonus. But a partnership in The Firm meant infinitely more than money.

Lord knows, Howland reflected, the fellow deserves it; it was largely to Miles's credit that Hanover Place was going to show a decent profit for 1931, a miracle by the Street's standards—and almost an embarrassment, considering how badly most other people were doing. Even Miles's great friend, Benjamin Graham, the brilliant investment theoretician, was in trouble; Graham, too, had pulled out in '29, but he'd gotten suckered back in when everyone thought shares had made their lows.

Fletcher hadn't.

"It's the second wave, the one just over the horizon, that really swamps the boats," he'd said back in the spring of 1930, when prices had recouped most of their Black Tuesday losses. Miles's analytical work suggested that corporate profits were not simply lagging, they were disappearing. A few months later, Miles's interpretation of the effect of the Smoot-Hawley tariffs on the world economic situation convinced Fletcher to triple his short positions.

By mid-1931, prime securities were selling for roughly a tenth of where they had stood at the apex of Mr. Coolidge's "New Era." Wherever the eye looked, it found default, credit collapse, and bank failure. "Free-Market" capitalism and the Republican Party were in headlong political retreat. Hoover was certain to be defeated at the next election, no matter who the Democrats nominated; this was an election even Al Smith could win.

"Hard to believe they might put up Roosevelt, isn't it?" said Fletcher, interrupting Howland's train of thought. "A Groton man who's a Democrat!"

The older man chuckled. Howland shifted irritably in his seat. His father's high spirits seemed singularly inappropriate today. Couldn't he have waited until tomorrow to see Miles? He stared disconsolately down the gray, uninviting river as the car nudged onto the Brooklyn Bridge.

"Hap was Groton, too, wasn't he?" asked Fletcher.

"St. Mark's."

"Well, no difference when you're dead, I imagine."

They had left for Brooklyn directly from Carruthers's funeral, a sparsely-attended, impersonal ceremony in an obscure East Side church whose rector had been persuaded to bless the soul of a suicide in return for a $1,000 contribution to his grossly understaffed and undercapitalized soup kitchen. Two weeks after Thanksgiving, his money and credit gone—including $10,000 Howland had loaned him—his acquaintanceships used up or alienated, and his prospects nil, Harding Carruthers had jumped into Vanderbilt Avenue from his dingy little room at the Yale Club.

Poor, poor Hap, thought Howland. He had found the service a sad, shabby, yet oddly moving occasion. To rush off on an errand of business seemed distasteful and disrespectful, but as he knew only too well by now, the sovereign creed of men like his father was that if time was money, then there was never a time like the present. Certainly no time to spare agonizing over the past, in the remembrance of other human beings whom life had overrun. It was the rise and fall of markets by which men like Fletcher marked their calendars.

Still, as he told Lyda later, recounting the day's events, it was hard to separate himself from that small crowd that gathered to mourn Hap. By right, the ceremony should have been at the Gorse, with its Romney portraits of British admirals and cases full of shining trophies, but it had seemed indelicate to stage a service at a club from which Hap had been forced to resign. Looking around him in the church, Howland had reflected that these were men not only like Hap, but like himself, at least in terms of upbringing and education, men raised to believe their futures were every bit as custom-fitted and shiny bright as the polished Peal shoes in which Hap Carruthers had been buried. There they sat, listening to friends and classmates speaking better of the deceased than he probably deserved—but what harm in that? Most of them, with their trust funds on the ropes, their Exchange sinecures obliterated, looked poleaxed by circumstances. What distinguished him from them? A piece of paper spied by Morris Miles on another man's desk? Was that it? Was that all there was?

As the car sped across the bridge, it was difficult for Howland to concentrate on what his father was saying: something about looking into some defaulted railroad bonds that Uncle Sam might be talked into making good if things got bad enough.

On the other hand, thought Howland, to be fair, the word on Miles's partnership would get out as soon as Auchincloss, Wharton got to work on new partnership papers. It might already be. You couldn't keep these things quiet, so why wait? Indeed, while his father was putting Ariadne into her car, Toddy Frelingville had drawn Howland aside. "Saw poor old Hap in the bar at the Brook a couple of days before he did the deed," said Frelingville. "Guest of some Johnnie I never saw before. Of course, these days they'll take anyone with the price of the dues."

Frelingville looked ruddy and confident, unscathed by the Crash, but then Toddy Frelingville could have lost $50 million and still be able to banco the house at Monte Carlo as casually as another man might spend a nickel for a newspaper. Howland knew that Frelingville had turned Hap down cold when asked for a loan of $5,000.

"Pretty drunk he was," Frelingville continued. "Said he'd heard your old man was going to take that clever Jewboy into The Firm. That true?"

"You know we never discuss things like that, Toddy," replied Howland with a smile.

"Course not," said Frelingville. "Anyway, I hope you know what you're doing. Suppose you do. Bunny Ducretil told me the fellow made him a bundle last year; think he could do the same for me? These shylocks can be regular old slyboots when it comes to the market. Still, you'll do well to keep an eye on him. Blink and that sort'll make off with your wallet in three shakes of a lamb's tail."

Morris's partnership had not been a matter that Fletcher chose to discuss with his partners, including Howland. It was simply to be presented to them as a *fait accompli*. Let them make of it what they would.

He had told his own family over Thanksgiving dinner. There had been just the five of them at table: Fletcher, Lyda and Howland, the twins. The ten-month-old baby, Andrew, had been left at Park Avenue in the care of M'amselle, who had succeeded Fraulein. Howland's mother had gone South to see her ailing sister in Charleston.

"Frankly," he said, "I rather like the prospect of publishing to the Street that we're taking a Jewish fellow in. And Morris certainly deserves it."

The old man paused to drain the last dregs of his sherry while a maid cleared his soup plate away. "Of course," he said to Lyda, "the timing couldn't be better. When you and Howland persuaded me to move Miles upstairs, my dear, I swore to myself that, from that point on, events would have to take their own course and Miles be judged entirely on his own merits. All very well, but I also knew that the Jewish thing would rear its ugly head absent an act of God, and that is what He, by giving us the Crash, has provided. Miles saved our bacon. Because of that, even the Neanderthals in our midst, like Eddie Stanforth, have no choice but to forever hold their peace, if you will pardon the split infinitive, or to start selling apples from a pushcart, and I fear that line of work is getting pretty crowded, especially for a chap of Eddie's rather limited abilities."

"You've never had a Jewish partner, have you?" interrupted Lyda. She was very pleased with herself over this news, but she tried not to show it. She was out of sorts with Fletcher. Why in hell couldn't he have discussed Morris's partnership with Howland, with his own son!

"Quite right," Fletcher replied, "but there is a good reason for that. There was in fact a young Jew in whom my grandfather had taken a great interest, just as we have taken an interest in young Miles, but the lad went off to war in 1861, just as my own father did. My father, whom I never really knew, died at Antietam; the other young man perished of dysentery in a Confederate prison camp. Andersonville, as I recall. In the event, talented young men are never easy to come by, not the genuine article, and don't forget that in those days, family came first, for Lehmans and Goldmans and Schiffs and Seligmans every bit as much as for Warringtons and Drexels. Perhaps we should have exchanged scions. Perhaps we should now. Howland could go to Lehman Brothers and Phillip Lehman could send young Bobby to work with us.

"Anyway, that was the way it was when I was a boy. How it got to be the way it is now I'm frankly not quite sure. It does appear, from what little I know of history, that whenever there's a big change which results in wealth leaving one group and lodging with another, the change is invariably ascribed by those on the way out to the gross and crass money-spinning of those on the way in, and never to their own ineptitude or decadence."

"In other words, envy?" asked Lyda.

"Envy, frustration, bad sportsmanship, a need for scapegoats: I could think of a dozen words and so could you, my dear. Every human frustration requires another human to blame it on. I have to say, however, that I don't think it's only money. There have been times when the Jews have given a pretty unattractive account of themselves—stereotypes don't just arise out of thin air—and the immigrations of the 1870s hardly dumped the flower of mankind on our fair shores, and if you don't take my word for it, go ask our German-Jewish friends up on Fifth Avenue. Whatever the cause, it's a prejudice as old as time and when something's survived that long, the chances are it's going to survive quite a bit longer. Still, it puts the Jews in a very difficult position. Damned if they do, damned if they don't."

"What do you mean by that?" asked Lyda.

"If they do well, sooner or later they catch hell. If they don't, what's the point of living in a free country? The worst is when they try to tread a middle ground with a very soft and unostentatious step. Then it's the worst of both worlds for them. They catch hell from their own for being cowards or bootlickers, while the non-Jews don't appreciate their self-restraint. Fortunately, when it comes to that sort of thing, we're amateurs compared to Europe, except for the Ku Klux Klan fellows.

"Anyway," the old man continued, "this particular 'New Era' is over and we'd better get ready for another one. The day is past when someone like poor old Hap Carruthers can carry all before him on the strength of a Groton accent, a Bones pin, and membership in the Gorse. The Street likes to say brains are cheap—"

"Probably because there're so many dummies on it," interjected Lyda. She shifted uncomfortably on her seat. The baby she was carrying was very active. It had to be another boy.

Fletcher had smiled at her approvingly.

"Possibly so, my dear. In any event, brains *aren't* cheap, and we're going to need all of them we can lay our hands on over the next few years."

Howland stared out the car window. They were coming off the bridge now, into Atlantic Avenue. His father, next to him, looked up from his paper.

"Ah, Louis," he said to the driver, "I think this is it. Take a right on DeKalb."

When they got back from Brooklyn that evening, Howland found his wife stretched out feet-up on the library chesterfield, vainly trying to interest Lex and Dee in *The Wind in the Willows* while the baby, Andrew, slept peacefully in a cradle next to the sofa. To the twins, their father's arrival was a welcome reprieve from enlightenment. They bounced off the sofa and went for him.

Howland roughhoused with them briefly, then shooed them into the hall and made himself a cocktail. He went over to the sofa, bent and kissed Lyda first on the lips and then on the great mound of her stomach; he rocked the cradle absentmindedly with his toe.

"That is the quietest child ever born," he said. "Where do you suppose he came from, compared to these other two brutes?"

"Listen, we should count ourselves lucky. The twins are bad enough, but as for this thing I've got thrashing around inside me now . . . anyway, how'd it go?"

"Hap's service, or Morris Miles's investiture?"

"Both. Either."

"Hap's was very depressing for all. With Morris, it went fine. I still can't understand why Father didn't take me into his confidence."

"He probably couldn't tell you why himself. Fathers are that way."

"You're probably right. Anyway, *du côte de chez* Miles, I think I can safely say we made at least two people very happy, three if you count the little boy. I must say, he's an engaging little beggar."

"I thought there were three children. A boy and a girl."

"I never saw the other two. They may have been off studying some-where. The little boy's a nice-looking lad, though. You'd hardly know he was . . ."

Lyda interrupted: "I thought we had an agreement about that sort of thing! If you start talking like Chubby Fenton, I'll be in Reno as fast as the Broadway Limited can get me there!"

"Be loyal, my darling," said Howland. "Don't forget you can now fly Global to sunny Nevada."

"In eighteen excruciating hours, thank you very much. Tom called, by the way. I told him where you were and what you were up to . . ."

"Did you tell him about Miles?" interrupted Howland.

"I did. Why? Shouldn't I have?" Lyda made a long face while she pondered her own question. Then she looked candidly at her husband. "No, I guess I shouldn't have."

"Don't look so glum. It's just that I haven't figured out how to break the news to a number of the connections."

"I must say, from the way Tom sounded, he seemed upset. Has he got a thing about Jews?"

"You know Tom. There can't have been many Jewish people where Tom came from in Kansas, and we certainly didn't have any in the Flying Corps. Moving Global to Los Angeles and living in Pasadena hasn't broadened his point of view either, I can tell you."

"Be that as it may," Lyda said, "you and I have better things to discuss than Tom Creedmore's brand of bigotry. What'd the Mileses call their little boy? I should remember, I suppose, if only as a good Firm wife. We did send flowers?"

"Someone did. I'm sure Miss Merrow took care of it. He's named S— something Maximilian Miles," said Howland. "Samuel? Solomon? Anyway, they're going to call him Max."

Maximilian? S. Maximilian Miles. Lyda considered that briefly. How very imperial, she thought, how very imperial indeed. Well, it was every mother's right to dream, wasn't it? Wasn't that the American way?

"And the wife?" she asked next. "How was she? You know, I've never met her?"

Her question was rhetorical. She had a very clear picture in her mind, one that she was certain had to be accurate. Short, plump, shrewish, whiny.

"Ah," said Howland, his pause causing Lyda an instant on edge, "well now, I'm bound to say that she was a surprise. For one thing, she's quite tall. For another, she's a redhead. She looks very Irish. Got a face like a camel. A very tough camel, however. There's no doubt where Morris gets his marching orders once he's home."

"And how was your father? I can just hear him: 'Rise, Sir Miles.' Or was it: 'Ho, ho, ho, my dear Cratchit?' "

"Mostly the latter. Much chuckling and rubbing of hands together."

Howland paused thoughtfully and took a sip of his drink. "You know," he said, "I've never told you this, but there are times I feel that Father's found a real soulmate in Morris. They seem to see things the same way, all this hunting around in dark corners of the market for bargains, and cackling like banshees when they beat the Dow or get the best of someone else. It makes me feel like an outsider. I can't help thinking sometimes that what's the right business for Morris Miles can't be the right business for me."

"Well, then," said Lyda, "we shall either have to change Morris or change the business."

1932

FEBRUARY

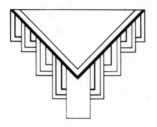

The sunny room overlooking Carl Schurz Park and the East River was perfumed by a score of bouquets from the city's most fashionable florists, along with a faint carbolic hospital smell and the sweet milky fragrance of the baby boy who had minutes earlier been returned to the nursery. Someone with a keen nose for human sentiments might have detected another, acrid aroma: the unmistakable odor of antipathy. It was given off by the two women in the room, who within minutes of first meeting had realized that they would never be friends.

Propped up in bed in an elegant silk and maribou jacket from Henri Bendel, a present from her mother-in-law that was altogether too fancy for her taste, Lyda put on her sweetest, most interested smile—using it as a screen from behind which she could study Miriam Miles. She guessed that the other woman, behind her studied chatter, was doing the same.

That Miriam should have appeared at Lyda's bedside was surprising. Firm protocol limited unannounced visits by partners and their wives to occasions of bereavement. Good manners decreed that Miriam should have telephoned, which would have permitted Lyda to put her off, at least until she could regain the fastness of the Park Avenue house. Outside Hanover Place, the partners did not, on the whole, mix. If they did, it was usually not because of friendships evolved in the course of working under the same roof, but because they shared older ties—schooling, a common passion for golf, or marriage to sisters.

Still, here the woman was, and so Lyda told herself to make the best of it. It would only be for a half hour or so, at the worst.

The woman who sat in the armchair a few feet away was rather raw-boned, and overdressed for her size and the occasion. The feather-trimmed floppy beret was just too much, Lyda thought, as was the fox stole trimmed in animal heads, and the matching muff. Otherwise she was just as Howland had described her. Tall, no more than an inch or two shorter than Lyda, with thick upswept auburn hair and a complexion of Celtic ruddiness, and certainly no beauty. Her jaw was large and her eyes were set close together. Her nose was flat and square, with a hint of the horsy, flaring look about the nostrils and cheekbones that Lyda had observed in a great many Jewish women, notwithstanding that Miriam Miles was Irish. If the woman's features weren't comely, however, there was in her face an unmistakable quality of determination and ambition that was peculiarly compelling; a face that bespoke inner qualities which, once fastened on an objective, would see the struggle through to completion.

Still, Lyda wasn't the sort to take an instant dislike to someone solely because of her looks. Nor was it the woman's conversation that had put her off. Like anyone whose husband had risen rapidly in the world and was now making good money at a time when a dollar went further than it had in living memory, Miriam Miles was full of money chatter. In little more than ten minutes, she had already mentioned the names of five fashionable stores, beginning with DePinna, the source of the embarrassingly expensive cashmere crib blanket that she had brought for Lyda's new son.

Well, what was wrong with that? Wasn't it natural for his family to enjoy Morris's new fortune? Lyda wasn't like a lot of people she and Howland knew who complained about the threat posed by "new money." It was hard for Lyda to judge what exactly it was that old money feared to lose. Social position? The affections of headwaiters and shopkeepers? Lyda's father-in-law was pretty succinct on the subject. "Never for an instant heed all this balderdash about old money and new money," Fletcher had told her. "The only money really threatened by new money is *no* money!" Then he grinned in that naughty way he had and added: "Of course, my dear, let us never forget that old money has a natural tendency to turn into no money if we don't watch out. Those who inherit it tend to become careless about it."

No, it wasn't that which troubled Lyda. What bothered her was a feeling that this visit was part of an agenda in which she had been assigned a calculated part, a role, a specific utility.

She considered herself to have done her part by first pleading Morris

Miles's case. That had been for the good of The Firm, which in turn would be for the good of her family. New blood had been needed; in a world without Fletcher, which one had to anticipate, what had been on hand in the way of drive and brainpower back in 1924 simply hadn't been up to the job. Morris had shown the prowess she had sensed in him; the money he was piling up seemed a more than fair *quid pro quo*. To ask more of me is unfair, thought Lyda.

As if reading her thoughts, Miriam shifted the subject from Lord & Taylor. "Your Andrew must be just about a year old now?" she asked.

She had a hard, cutting voice. Lyda's ear picked up only the faintest trace, a mere palimpsest, of a "borough" accent. A lot of study and practice went into that voice, she thought; there was none of that exaggerated broadening of the vowels that New Yorkers on the rise adopted in an effort to pass for Knickerbocker gentry.

"Just a bit more," Lyda replied. "He was born on January 14, 1931. And your little boy—Maximilian, is it? He'd be how old now? A year and a half?"

"Two come next July fourth."

"What an auspicious birthday! I was born with the century, you know. New Year's Day, 1900." Lyda laughed, shook her head, and added, "I hope Maximilian's stars prove as lucky for him as they have for me, knock on wood." She tapped the side of the bed.

"Well," said Miriam, "they're not that far apart, then. Perhaps they'll be friends."

Lyda smiled at this, but said nothing.

"Provided I can ever get Morris to leave Brooklyn," said Miriam. "I think he's almost convinced. I'll call you, if I may, for the name of a good real-estate person."

Again Lyda smiled, more thinly this time, and nodded without speaking and without much enthusiasm. Miriam gripped her crocodile bag with her large hands and looked down, as if suddenly realizing she'd overstepped. There was an awkward moment's silence while each woman took stock, seeking to negotiate their way back to a standoff, a difficult business when the essential chemistry was lacking.

"Yes, that would be nice, wouldn't it?" said Lyda finally, trying to keep any hint of encouragement out of her voice. "To move to Manhattan, I mean."

She wished Miriam Miles would leave. She wished the woman had never come. Her feelings were now both personal and institutional. The last thing she wanted to be saddled with was the social sponsorship of the Miles family. There was the Jewish thing, for one. Schools, buildings, an entire new structure of relationships, all would have to be coaxed into being whether the newcomers' names were Stuyvesant or Ginsberg, and whether they came to dwell on Park Avenue or Main Street. Still, the name *did* make a difference, like it or not. Lyda despised anti-Semitism, at least she despised it institutionally, which was the only form in which she'd experienced it, but there were her four sons to think of, whose lives were ordered in certain directions from birth, and she could see all sorts of problems if she had to cope with the Mileses. Well, if she had to, it was something she could discuss frankly with her friend Belle Seligsohn; maybe Belle would help with the Temple Emanu-El crowd, but for the moment Lyda was suddenly too tired to face thinking about it. No good deed goes unpunished, she thought resignedly. Now, Mrs. Miles, be off with you!

She sighed in a manner that would have done Camille credit, passed a languid hand across her forehead, let her shoulders slope in exhaustion, and closed her eyes.

Miriam took the hint. A moment later, feigning the level breathing of sleep, Lyda heard her visitor depart.

It was chilly out, but Miriam had her stole and muff, and the sun was shining brightly, so she gestured to the chauffeur to wait and walked across to the park. She took a seat on a bench and looked across East End Avenue at the hospital, calculating which was Lyda's window.

Not exactly a smashing success, this first meeting, she thought. Well, it couldn't be helped. She needed to see the other woman plain to have any idea of what she might, and might not, expect to get from Lyda Warrington.

Not much, if Lyda had her way, thought Miriam. Too bad—but she mustn't let it set her back. It would have been nice if they'd fallen into each other's arms right off, but they hadn't. Sisters under the skin they weren't. Yes, it would make things much easier if Lyda had volunteered to help, but she hadn't, and in any case there would be other ways, on other days, to get her involved.

So, thought Miriam, onward and upward. You took what you could get, step by step, but that shouldn't for an instant deter a body from always pushing forward to get the most you could. Always go after the most you can, the most you can afford. There weren't many positive lessons Miriam Miles had learned from her mother, but that was one of them. Of course, her mother's definition of "most" was a limited one, while Miriam's dream for herself and her family knew no limits.

Well, one or two, actually. Obviously they could spend only as much as her husband's money-making brain could earn, but Miriam was starting to believe that the sky was now the limit in that regard. The realization of her dreams of society and fashion would be more problematical. For one thing, Morris not only didn't share them, he thought them foolish.

"You quote that stuff you read in those women's magazines like the letter of the law," he said, and then smiled shyly at his jest. He was not by nature a humorous or witty man and was ill at ease with jokes and quips.

Who could have expected that there would be someone in the precincts of Pitkin Avenue who would have known at once that the firm, sharply angled script in which Morris's wedding invitation was engraved was not that of Miss Julia Cutting? But Miriam knew, because she had read an article on "How to have a proper wedding" in *Bazaar*. Two years later, after her twins were born, Lyda sent a gracious thank-you note for Miriam's flowers; Miriam was able to compare the handwriting on Lyda's note with the handwriting on the invitation and confirm suspicions formed years earlier.

Miriam was not one to confuse information with expectation. She was under few illusions about her own social prospects. She knew herself to lack the brilliance and wit and talent and style it took to transform a Brooklyn housewife into a leader of Manhattan society. In the eyes of the world she coveted, no matter how well Morris did, they would always be marked with the world from which they'd risen.

It might be different, she thought now and then, if Morris had possessed social ambitions of his own. But his universe was entirely circumscribed by the four walls of Hanover Place, his sole longing was for the approbation of the Warringtons. He seemed oblivious to the possibility that he might, as others before him had, rise in wealth and esteem high enough to bask in the company of the great German-Jewish families: play golf at Century or Sands Point, nod to men of his ilk on Saturdays at Temple Emanu-El, serve on the board of Mt. Sinai Hospital, live on Fifth Avenue, and see his sons educated at St. Bernard's and his daughter at Brearley.

This last scenario, grand as it could be, was not where Miriam's plans ended. She was the daughter of a mixed marriage, and though having a Jewish mother made her "technically" Jewish, it was from her paternal, Irish side that she took her maiden name and her point of view. Low as the Irish stood in the scheme of things, they could still go where Jews could not—once they got enough money to buy a toehold on the social ladder. Provided he could come up with the entry fee, the crudest Killarney braggart could disport himself in precincts and purlieus barred to the most cosmopolitan, civilized Jew.

Yet the paradox of Miriam's life was that the only way out of what she saw as a confining, untenable future presented itself in the unlikely shape of the former Moishe Milovitz, met by accident at a cotton candy stand on the boardwalk at Coney Island back in 1922, when he was nineteen and she a year older.

In November 1901, when Senta Buchsberg, four months pregnant, married handsome Billy Halloran, both sets of in-laws hung their heads in disgrace and their windows in black crepe. In time, the groom's parents forgave, after Senta converted to Catholicism and the baby daughter was baptized at the altar of St. Agnes R. C. Church. The bride's family never relented, however—not even when, in a halfhearted gesture of reconciliation, the new mother turned aside her in-laws' pleas to name the baby Moira and chose instead to call her Miriam, after the child's maternal grandmother.

Senta Buchsberg's seduction and subsequent shotgun capture of Billy Halloran, a trolley-car driver ten years her senior, was a calculated move on her part. He was curious to discover if it was true about Jewish girls, that they were wilder in the primal act than even the darkies were said to be; Senta satisfied his curiosity on the matter, although she never afterward asked him what his conclusion was; more important from her point of view, the consequence of their heated, hasty couplings made it possible for her to escape from the suffocating uncertainties of Brownsville ghetto life to a two-family house in Windsor Terrace. There, five months later, Miriam was born, to a way of life in which the husband's Saturday night whiskey and his frequent use of fists to make his point on domestic issues were rendered tolerable by the prospect of a secure city pension, which glowed perpetually in Senta's dreams like the pot of gold at the end of the rainbow.

Perhaps it was the confusion in her genes, but Miriam Halloran detested the world into which she was born almost from earliest awareness. It must have been that her Jewish blood gave her a taste for brains that made the bluff existence of Windsor Terrace insufferably dumb, even without the drinking. Her mother's dream for her—the be-all and the end-all of life—was the same safe haven for which Senta herself had opted: marriage to a hard-working Mick with a good, safe city job, a cop or fireman or trolleyman.

But Miriam was not her mother. As she came into womanhood and entered high school, she saw that, for her mother, the vision of the pension was like staring into the sun: it blinded one to all of life's other deformities, the red-veined, crusty faces, the slurred and drunken talk, the coarseness of mind, the sheer dumbness of it all!

There were many things that her boardwalk swain left to be desired, but intelligence was not among them. Miriam recognized a brain when she met one. After an hour's conversation with Moishe Milovitz, the two of them sitting on the edge of the boardwalk, legs dangling, hearing at their back the happy shrieks and rumbles from Luna and Steeplechase parks, now and then pausing in their talk just to sit and watch the gray Atlantic roll smoothly toward the crowded beach, she knew she had found a mind which, with a break or two, could be her meal ticket out of Windsor Terrace. Out indeed of Brooklyn, and into the Sunday rotogravure world of which she had dreamed.

And Moishe not only had a brain, he had a job—at S. L. Warrington & Son on Wall Street. A clerk's job, sure, but it was a start.

It would have been nice, in the alternative Miriam's daydreams some-times proposed to her, if a young Phipps or Frelingville, slumming at Coney Island, had chanced upon her, been smitten by her, and had borne her off to *The Social Register*, and Piping Rock and the Colony Club and her photograph in *Smart Set*, but that wasn't going to happen. Moishe at least was in a place where, in theory, he might come to the attention of Phippses and Frelingvilles; he was therefore as promising a prospect as was likely ever to come her way.

And so Miriam married back into the world her mother had fled; she was reclaimed for the faith of her maternal ancestors who, in taking back their lost lamb, were more than willing to overlook the fact that the bride was somewhat older than the groom and that their courtship had been by any standards rapid. She settled into the house on Pacific Street off Pitkin Avenue, was a good and supportive wife to her husband, and quickly bore him two children, Benjamin and Selma. She kept house, studied, and dreamed, and waited for his break—if it came.

When it did, she was more ready than he.

Now they had come a long way, but this was just the beginning, she thought. Already Morris was worth several hundred thousand, but for every dollar he had made for himself and his family, he'd made five or ten for the Warringtons, the difference between the earning power of brains and capital. Still, the Warringtons were fair people. Over time justice would be done and Morris would be very, very rich.

Just to make money wasn't the point, however. Wealth brought enti-tlements in its wake, and it was upon these that Miriam principally fas-tened. She was too old and homely to claim them, she felt; the reek of the ghetto would be with her forever; after so many years it was too ingrained to be expunged. There was a certain way Lyda had looked at her; other women would always look at her that way. She was resigned to that. So she would live through her children.

Or would she? It wasn't something she'd ever say out loud to Morris, but Benjamin and Selma . . . well, even this early she could see they had too much Brooklyn in them. Too much time spent in the company of her husband's family had made them . . . well . . . too Jewish. Benjamin was set on becoming a doctor and Selma was a serious spectacled seven-year-old who would rather read than go shopping with her mother. They were, she had to admit, unpromising material, in other words, for her ambitions—brilliant children, but like little rabbis, studious and serious with plain, narrow faces. In their voices Miriam could pick out the unmistakable, derided accents of the streets of Brooklyn.

Not so her baby Max. Here was the pillar on which to found a fresh new existence. There would be no Brownsville about him; no Pitkin Avenue in his bones. No childhood memories of dark old men in beards and skullcaps chanting endlessly at the backside of his memories. Max was clean, pure material from which Miriam might mold, as in the Greek myth, the embodiment of her own dreams. She and Morris might never, nor Benjy and Selma, but her Max would be a part of the pure and perfect world occupied by people like the woman whose bedside she had just left.

A chilly gust blew off the river. Miriam pulled the stole tighter about her, absently fingering the foxes' heads. She looked up toward Lyda's window and thought she saw the faint movement of a shadow.

Lyda had crossed to the window. A half hour a day out of bed on the fifth day, Ralph Damon had instructed. Funny, she'd thought, in many parts of the world women gave birth in the morning and were back in the fields by afternoon.

She looked down. The sight of Miriam Miles looking up made her gasp and draw back. She watched the other woman stand up, cross to a large car, and get in, ducking low to keep the extravagant pheasant's tail in her hat out of harm's way.

Ridiculous, thought Lyda. The big car pulled away from the curb. Lyda lifted her gaze. Across the river, beyond Astoria, a stately row of clouds was making its lavalike way northeast above the Sound.

I can't wait to get out of here, she thought. She had the new house to pull together, a rambling thirty-room "cottage" on the East Hampton seafront. It had always been Lyda's dream to have a house on the sea, and Howland had finally indulged her. His parents liked the Adirondacks, but Lyda couldn't stand the mountains. They pressed in, and what little sun they let through, the high forests took care of, and of course the water in the lake was frigid right through the summer, so one couldn't swim.

Lyda had insisted on the seashore. They'd considered a number of places: Watch Hill, Newport, Nantucket, Fishers Island, even Northeast Harbor in Maine, where Howland's sister Floss and her husband summered, but for one reason or another—more freezing water, too many rocks, place too distant or inescapable, people too stuffy or monotone—none had suited. Then Double Dune (the name came from the singular fold in the East Hampton sandhills on which the house was situated) had come on the market when the speculator who owned it went bust in the '31 collapse. She and Howland practically stole it, but that was life. Someone else's loss was your gain.

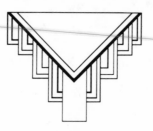

1936

AUGUST

It was a hot day. The menfolk, practically jumping out of their skins with anticipation, had gone off to the Reich Sports Field, the Olympic stadium. This afternoon, Jesse Owens was expected to anchor the U.S. team to victory in the 4×100 meters relay and claim a fourth gold medal for himself.

Lyda saw them off gladly. She hated all sports, an ironic attitude for the mother of two boys who at ten were already being spoken of by their elders in the same breath as the immortal Hobey Baker or Clint Frank and Larry Kelley, Yale's invincible quarterback and end.

The irony caused Lyda no concern. Her responsibility for the twins was pretty well reduced to scheduling doctors' visits and seeing that they were outfitted at Rogers Peet with proper school clothes. She was also expected to take the lead in the disciplinary front, but on the whole Lex and Dee minded their manners and schoolwork as thoroughly as they laid waste to their athletic opponents. In return, Lyda was spared long afternoons on the hard plank seats of the Yale Bowl.

Father and grandfather had taken over the twins' education in the great businesses of life. At this point, the principal temples of learning were the great sporting venues of the city: Yankee Stadium, the Polo Grounds, Madison Square Garden, with an occasional voyage across the East River to see Bill Terry's mighty Giants dismember the hapless Dodgers at Ebbets

Field. Thanks to their grandfather's limitless connections, by the time they set sail for Hamburg and Berlin in the summer of 1936, they had shadow-boxed with Joe Louis, played catch with Bill Terry and Lou Gehrig, been taught to slapshoot a hockey puck by Eddie Shore, and to swing a mashie niblick by Bobby Jones. They were as well known to the ticket-takers at the Yale Bowl as such living legends as Pudge Heffelfinger and Winslow Lovejoy.

In the morning of one Saturday each month, Louis, their grandfather's driver, would pick them up and take them downtown to Hanover Place, where the order clerks let them punch the telephone buttons and dispatch pneumatic order canisters to the Floor. After the Exchange closed down for the week, they would all go uptown for lunch. Thanks to Fletcher, they were better known by the age of ten at "21" and Jack Dempsey's than half the tycoons on Wall Street.

They were bluff, charming boys, hugely poised for their age, quick and strong, with grown-up, sporty personalities—the sort of boy in whom every older man likes to think he sees his own young self.

Though Fletcher indulged them shamelessly, Lyda said nothing. Princes should be trained to rule, and properly so—otherwise—she thought—you ended up with a vacant, irresponsible little man like the King of England who that summer of '36 was making a perfect jackass of himself over a much-traveled divorcée from Baltimore.

Better, thought Lyda, that Lex and Dee be perched on the throne early, to let them see how the world looks from that lofty height, get used to the altitude. Now and then Fletcher *did* get carried away: the previous Christmas Eve a cabinetmaker's van had arrived at the Park Avenue townhouse and disgorged a three-quarters-scale replica of the partners' desk that Howland and his father shared on the Platform. That—thought Lyda—was really a bit much, but she held her tongue. Practice for the real thing, she thought; toy indentures and tiny prospectuses from Hanover Place instead of tin helmets and wooden swords from F.A.O. Schwarz.

This trip to Berlin for the Olympic Games had been especially for the twins. Howland and Lyda made annual summer excursions to Europe, usually to London and Paris, combining "diplomacy" on behalf of The Firm with private interests and indulgences. He called on his opposite numbers in the financial capitals of Europe; she went for fittings at Molyneux or Chanel. The last two years they'd brought the twins, Lyda thinking it was high time a jolt of culture was administered, but her efforts to mother-hen them down the long corridors of the Louvre and Uffizi had been an unmixed failure. The boys fixed the long walls of masterpieces with the dull gaze of the bored and loudly demanded in unison, "What're we gonna do next?"

This year, as a tenth birthday treat, they had come to Berlin for the

Olympics and Fletcher, who normally spent the second half of August in the south of France, had insisted on coming along, leaving his wife in Cap d'Antibes, as he put it, "with her bridge and pansies."

Having her father-in-law along was a mixed blessing. He curried the adoration of his grandsons by trying to be twice as mischievous as they. Most of it was silly, but Lyda didn't like it when he said things like, "Wow, that darkie showed his heels to the lot of them, didn't he!" Or when, on the terrace of the Adlon, Fletcher had cast his eye upon a table of uniformed S.S. men sitting well within earshot and loudly declared, "There was a pansy uncle of your mother's, Howland, who told me I wouldn't know what Valhalla was like until I'd been buggered by a Uhlan!"

Still, she thought, thumbing through her Berlin Baedeker to get her bearings, it could be worse. While her menfolk gloried in the licking that Owens, John Woodruff, and the others were giving the Master Race, she roamed Berlin. She visited the mandatory high spots, but mostly, as she did in every city, wandered freely and without a plan, letting her feet take her where they would.

Her guidebook informed her she had found her way into the quarter of the city near the famous zoo. Turning a corner into a narrow, prom-isingly medieval-looking street, she saw a crowd gathered down the block. This was something no New Yorker could resist, and she found herself hurrying down the street to see what the commotion was.

Lyda had never seen a street fight before, if that was what this could be called. Two young men—large, bareheaded goons in leather overcoats adorned with swastika armbands, characters right off a poster glorifying Führer and Fatherland—were beating up an elderly man. They had knocked him to the ground and were now kicking at him vigorously, pausing to spit and shout at him.

The man on the ground Lyda guessed to be in his sixties; blood from a cut under his bruised eye stained his bearded face. The fright in his eyes was something Lyda had never before seen in a human being: beyond extreme physical pain, it was a look of sheer terror. A skullcap was lying on the pavement amid fragments of glass from the shattered shopfront before which the little drama was being enacted.

Lyda stood there transfixed. All at once, the confrontation ended. With a last kick, the two young men turned abruptly away, grinned broadly at the small knot of onlookers, and walked briskly down the street. One of the spectators hurried forward to help the old man up and led him into the recesses of his shop.

Lyda found herself shaking with horror and confusion. The man stand-ing next to her saw her condition, smiled reassuringly, and touched his hatbrim. "*War garnichts,*" he said in a helpful voice. "*Nur eine Jude.*"

"I beg your pardon."

"It was nothing," said the man in careful English, each syllable proudly enunciated. "He is just a Jew." He smiled again, pleased to be of service, turned, and went on his way. The rest of the crowd dispersed, leaving Lyda standing there trembling, staring at the shattered window.

After a few moments she made her way across a wide avenue to a small park, found a bench, and sat down heavily. She clasped her hands to steady her pulse and took three or four deep breaths. There was nothing she could do about the way her mind was racing.

It was not just the episode itself, shocking though it was, that had produced this reaction. It was more personal than that. For an instant, before they had moved off, heavy shoes clomping on the cobblestones, Lyda had looked right into the faces of the two young men.

They could be my own sons, she realized. Strong, square of jaw and shoulder, with bright blue eyes and thatches of thick blond hair. Take away the cruel and stupid leer, she thought, and there were Lex and Dee ten or fifteen years from now.

Is this what it can come to? she thought suddenly. Is this where the casual locker-room joke leads, the reflexive, unthinking slur peddled by the Eddie Stanforths of this world? And what about the more deep-rooted bias, tinged with viciousness, that one heard in a Tom Creedmore or a Chubby Fenton?

If you took such seemingly innocuous things to the limit, was this where it ended?

From the zoo came the blast of an elephant trumpeting, and some great cat responded with a roar, and Lyda heard children shriek with laughter in a nearby playground. Not a hundred yards from where an old man had been savagely beaten—beaten!—presumably for no other reason than that he was Jewish.

Sitting there, Lyda realized that she had never really thought seriously about anti-Semitism. All I have to go on, she reflected, is a collection of amorphous, well-meant reactions to incidents and remarks, mostly gleaned at second- or third-hand, from gossip and the newspapers: so refracted that they seemed disembodied, remote, abstract.

Well, not quite. There *had* been the unpleasant business at the East-water Club. The Warringtons had belonged to the Eastwater from its founding. It was a club that practiced highly restrictive policies: no Jews, no Italians, no Irish, no one who wasn't (or couldn't pass for) Plymouth Rock or old Murray Hill—and that went not just for members but for guests brought to the club. The place was run by committees of elderly, disappointed men and women whose trust funds had been eroded by the Crash and, with them, their influence in the wider society of Manhattan. Lyda didn't like the club; she thought the members by and large abominable, and had told her husband so; she had in fact once or twice considered pressing Howland to resign, but it had an excellent children's weekend program, good tennis and squash courts, and a fine swimming pool. Most of the children's classmates' parents were members, and in addition Howland had a regular Thursday evening tennis game there with men he'd known long before he met Lyda. The time had never seemed quite right for Lyda to push on the issue.

The Eastwater had been the natural place to hold Andrew's fifth birthday party back in January. Without thinking, Lyda had invited Max Miles. Although she resented Miriam Miles's implacable determination to entwine her son Max's social life with that of the two younger Warrington boys, all-out resistance was against the interests of peace at Hanover Place, or so she was told by Fletcher when she complained of the deluge of invitations that Miriam rained on her children. His position irritated Lyda. It seemed that "the Warrington Wall" between business and social life was only for adults. Children could be "sacrificed" for the greater good of Hanover Place.

On the other hand, Max was only a child, too, and to visit on any child the mindless prejudices of his elders seemed unfair. Nevertheless, Lyda realized afterward that she should have given more thought to Andrew's party. A clown at home might have done just as well, or a film followed by supper at Hamburger Heaven, but Andrew's heart was set on a swimming party, and the fact was that Lyda was getting used to Max, so she really didn't give it a thought when she went ahead and booked the Eastwater. It was only after Miriam phoned to accept for her boy that Lyda realized what she'd done.

To disinvite Max was unthinkable. So Lyda did something foolish: she changed Max's last name on the list that the club required in advance of any such affair, a list which, she knew, would be scrutinized by the Gorgons on the club's House Committee. It seemed a harmless ruse, done for the best and most decent of reasons, and nine times out of ten would have gone off without incident. This was the tenth time, however; instead of, as had been agreed, the Warrington chauffeur dropping Max off at the end of the day, a last-minute change in the Mileses' schedule led to Miriam herself appearing at the club, to be told by an obdurate head porter that there was no Master M. Miles listed in the Warrington group. Miriam was made to wait outside under the club awning while Lyda was summoned from poolside.

Lyda had tried to set things right with a bland fib about confusion in the club office, but she saw at once that Miriam—whose knowledge of Manhattan mores was encyclopedic—knew she was lying. There was nothing for either woman to do but continue in the falsehood, but Lyda had never in her life felt so filled with self-disgust.

She had always hated prejudice. She hated anti-Semitism and she hated Jim Crow and at Wellesley she had marched outside the Boston state house screaming for justice for Sacco and Vanzetti. And yet, to be totally honest with herself, it was impossible to summon up real anger over someone's exclusion from Maidstone, to feel the fire in the marrow that the "Scottsboro Boys" had aroused.

She could guess how Miriam had felt. But that was as a mother. Lyda had really never thought what it must really be like to be Jewish. Lyda and people like her tended to make a useful distinction between the nice Jewish people one knew, the individuals and families one liked, saw in society, did business with, even fell in love with, sometimes even married, and "Jews" considered as a race, as a tribe, the word pronounced, at best, with uneasiness.

Was it like being a Negro? Almost but not quite, she supposed. Jews were white; they didn't have the added burden of the color of their skin to contend with. In twentieth-century America, they weren't caged by law, weren't slaughtered by Cossacks, weren't shut up in ghettos in privation and filth, weren't beaten up in the streets. As far as Lyda knew, it principally came down to small-minded private exclusions: from clubs, schools, from minor aspects of upper-class life that probably weren't worth bothering about in the first place. How much was really at stake? As long as Miriam and her family had the run of Morris's money, was there, in the end, much to choose between a Century Country Club or a Meadow Brook? Such had been the reasoning Lyda employed to make peace within herself on the subject. Now, on a Berlin park bench, she wondered.

Yet in the next thought she could not help asking: what about my own children? They're innocent, too. Can I, for the sake of abstract ideals, ideals not even practiced by many of the Jews she and Howland knew, can I yank *my* children out of the life they've known, out of clubs over whose policies they and their parents had little or no control, out of schools universally judged to be excellent, and particularly excellent at training young men to serve class and country in a certain way?

Moral theory said she should, but life, God knows, wasn't theory.

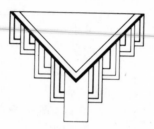

1938

NEW YEAR'S EVE

El Morocco was packed, but the crowd cramming the vestibule parted magically for Lyda's party. Carino, the nightclub's imperious maître d', led them through the smoky, noisy room to a choice table. "Will this be all right, Mrs. Warrington?"

"Just fine, Carino, thank you."

Like a genie, a waiter appeared with a magnum of champagne. "Compliments of Mr. Perona, ma'am. He'll be coming by to extend his good wishes for the New Year personally. He's with the Duke and Duchess just now."

Carino lowered his voice and bent closer to Lyda. "And we all wish you a most happy birthday, Mrs. Warrington," he added.

"That's all right, Carino," laughed Lyda. "You don't have to whisper. Not for the next fifty minutes, at least."

Carino now turned his attention to Howland. Bending over, he said in low tones: "Your father was in here last week, Mr. Warrington. He says it's a good time to invest now. He said that if there's a war in Europe, it will be tremendous for business in this country and for the stock market. He told me to look at CBS. What do you think?"

Howland smiled. "Why don't you ask Mr. Paley." He gestured over his shoulder at a handsome, dark man seated at a corner banquette. "He looks very pleased with the way things are going."

He placed a comradely hand on the maître d's shoulder, very much the officer sending his platoon over the top, and said heartily: "Carino, if there's one thing we all should have learned by now, it's not to disagree with my father when he says 'buy' or 'sell.' Honestly, though, we do think things are looking much, much better in the market. Of course, my father is right: a great deal depends on Herr Hitler."

"Well, thank you, sir." Carino bowed, started to move away, then paused and said: "And may I just say how sorry we all are to have heard the bad news of Mrs. Warrington Senior."

"Thank you, Carino. About all I can say is she's doing as well as can be expected."

Just after Labor Day, Ariadne Warrington had suffered the first of a series of strokes that had left her a gasping, bedridden wraith tended round the clock by nurses. Fletcher Warrington was one of those men who couldn't grasp the fact of physical disability in himself or anyone else, and was having a hard time dealing with it. Lyda was helping out as best she could, given her own rambunctious household. Fortunately, all four boys were at school all day now, which left her days free to supervise the maintenance of her in-laws' cavernous Fifth Avenue apartment.

Lyda surveyed her table. I should be able to do better than this, she thought. Originally, they had intended to be six: themselves, Howland's partner Charlie Runnels and his wife Bess and Charlie's cousin Corky, who was slated to be the next president of the Corn Exchange Bank, and his wife. At the last moment, it had been enlarged by the addition, not entirely welcome, of Howland's sister Alice and her new, fourth husband Milo Mitchell, who was a jewelry salesman Alice had found in Palm Beach and married on the rebound. Perched uneasily at the end of the table were some people named Bimswill who Lyda vaguely knew from Maidstone, and who seemed to have attached themselves to Lyda's group at La Rue, where they'd stopped in after dining at "21."

Ah well, she thought, looking around. On the tiny dance floor a moist tangle of humanity banged elbows vigorously to the strains of "My Heart Belongs to Daddy," Cole Porter's newest hit, which had made an overnight star of a cute Texas girl named Mary Martin.

Things *are* better, she thought. Everyone was dressed to the nines, and working hard at having fun, but that had been true at El Morocco right through the worst months of the Depression, ever since society had convinced itself that going out and being photographed and written about was somehow a patriotic function—"It distracts the masses from their plight, and gives 'em something to aspire to, don't you know." Lyda didn't approve of "Café Society"; she wasn't comfortable drinking champagne in public while millions were deprived, and she saw to it that the ubiquitous gossip columns left her and Howland's names out of their rapturous accounts.

And yet, as recently as Columbus Day, she had been ready to write 1938 off as the worst year yet. There had been her mother-in-law's stroke, the September hurricane that had blown off half of Double Dune's roof, the general condition of business, and on top of it all, the blowup between Chubby Fenton and Morris Miles.

By mid-1938, stocks had fallen to just about half their 1937 highs, and the financial district really resembled a ghost town. Men who had made it through since 1929 were forced to throw in the towel and take whatever work they could find; Howland had even gone into Tripler's to buy a tie and found himself dealing with a man he'd known in the Bond Club. Next, as if the dismal market wasn't enough, came the revelation that Richard Whitney had embezzled from the Stock Exchange Trust Fund; this had been the blackest eye yet for the old regime.

But suddenly, for no discernible reason, the rain stopped, the sun came out, and the stock market took off, so that the Dow-Jones Average—and Lyda's mood—finished the year up almost eighty percent from the bottom.

The thing between Chubby and Morris had been the worst. Perhaps Fletcher and Howland, or Lyda, should have seen it coming. It had all begun with the decision to transform what had been a fundamentally casual corporate finance effort into a full-fledged, aggressive Corporations Department.

The conception had been Lyda's, although she took no credit for it; it was simply a matter of building on what she knew to be in her husband's mind.

"If trading and stock investing bores you, why not open a second front?" Lyda had asked one evening early in 1937. She was becoming bored by Howland's nightly diatribes on the subject of his father's short-range thinking.

"The Firm's got a lot of capital now," she observed. "Relative to the rest of the Street, it's probably richer than it's ever been. Why not put some of it to work where it can make a long-term difference? Do some more Globals. There must be other Tom Creedmores out there. Go out and find them. There must be people who need capital—to whom an investment by you now might make all the difference between going under or living to fight another day, with The Firm sharing in *all* the spoils of victory."

Fletcher was agreeable to Howland's idea about putting together a real corporate finance department. With things as they were on the Street, he said, growing more enthusiastic by the sentence, they could go out and get some first-class people from Morgan's and Lehman, places like that.

"I like the idea," said Fletcher. "You'll have to be careful, of course, to distinguish between bad money—which only fools throw good money after—and good money that is merely temporarily inconvenienced. If you can do that, and it'll take a sharp mind, we'll do very well indeed."

After a moment's pause, Fletcher added: "Of course, speaking of sharp minds, you know there's none sharper than Brother Miles's?"

"I rather thought Charlie ought to take it on," said Howland. "It's been his bailiwick."

"Bailiwicks don't make money," said Fletcher sharply, "deals do. Charlie's a capital fellow, but you and I know that his idea of a new business effort is eighteen holes at the Links."

"Actually, Father, I thought I'd sort of co-run it with Charlie."

"I think not. For one thing, I need you up here next to me. We've got an entire firm to run, lest we forget, m'boy."

Fletcher studiously ignored his son's disappointment. He pressed his fingertips together and said: "My boy, there's no point in starting a Corporations Department, as I think we'll call it, unless it's a crackerjack operation that'll set us apart from the rest of the Street. Do you want me to speak to Morris?"

Howland shook his head. He liked Morris, and he'd gotten used to the business intimacy that had grown up between the man and Howland's father, so that he no longer felt those twinges of jealousy. But Miles was, well, a trader, a money man—not the sort one sent to call on major corporations or deal knowledgeably with new industries or technologies. Money men were a different breed. To them, like other predators, it was all the same, fresh meat or carrion. They prowled the market licking their chops at the prospect of overdiscounted defaulted bonds; out-of-the-money preferred stocks, like those of textile companies, which might recoup if Hitler went into Austria and war came.

Fletcher saw all of that going through his son's head and conceded. "All right, all right, we'll give Charlie his shot. He's been a loyal soldier."

As Howland got up to leave, his father added: "But by the bye, do tell Charlie to call on Morris if he can help. The market's a little slow and the fellow's a regular demon when it comes to separating the wheat from the chaff in a balance sheet."

And so the Corporations Department began life in the summer of 1937. Within a year, it had established itself as the crowning glory of Hanover Place. Credit for that was mainly due to Howland. His father's objections notwithstanding, the fact that Hanover Place's traditional business was in the doldrums left him able to concentrate on Corporations without seriously impinging on his responsibilities on the Platform. More important, the desperate condition of the financial world presented nothing but opportunities. The Street was dazed and confused by new government regulation that had taken the banks out of corporate underwriting. The disappearance of a number of once-prominent houses threw up for grabs a large number of potentially lucrative corporate connections. Howland and Charlie Runnels moved on these with a high degree of success. It helped that they were grand, clubable fellows, but it was more important that The Firm had the money.

But not so much money that they could buy every piece of business they wanted. Fletcher had been right. Brains were needed as much as capital. As the months went by, Morris Miles began to establish himself as an invaluable part of the effort. He was still very much involved with Fletcher, still accompanied the managing partner on what Howland described to Lyda as "father's ragpicking expeditions" through moldering heaps of distressed securities. By mid-1938, it was clear to all concerned that Morris's heart, like Howland's, was in using the tools and resources of finance to build, and not merely buy.

By now, Howland knew how to use Morris, or as he—sensitive to his colleague's feelings—put it, "how we can best work together." Prospective corporate connections liked to be able to talk to a man like Howland and Charlie: smooth Christian gentlemen who also knew a thing or two. But it was equally reassuring to top company executives that their figures were being analyzed by a really smart Jew.

This was something that both Howland and Morris had come to terms with.

"They think I can't multiply beyond ten times ten, Morris, but they know I won't steal the silver," Howland put it, as jocularly as he could. "With you, it's the other way around."

It was an uncomfortable situation. Apart from retailing, the motion picture and broadcasting industry and distilling, the men who occupied the chairs behind the largest desks in the nation's executive suites didn't want their business handled at the top Street level by Jews. That was why Bobby Lehman and the Schiffs had loaded up their firms with smooth, personable gentiles.

"It simply will not go away, this Jewish thing," Howland told Lyda. "I don't dare ask Morris to go out to Pittsburgh, say, to call on Duquesne Trust or Three Rivers Power, because I know what'll happen and I'm not going to expose him to that. On the other hand, if he starts to feel that he's little more than a high-priced coolie with an abacus, that's no good either."

It didn't seem to bother Morris. He seemed more than content with his life. He and Miriam had moved in 1936 to a Park Avenue apartment a few blocks north of the Warringtons' townhouse. It was a fine building, even if Miriam bridled that it was known as "the best *Jewish* building in the city." The children were in good schools. In tune with his rising reputation, he had been invited to join both the Harmonie Club and the

Century Country Club. He and Miriam took a nice house during the summer at Atlantic Beach. In terms of Jewish society, the Miles family was thriving.

Then came the business with Chubby Fenton.

Of course, everyone said after the episode was closed, Charles Christian Fenton III was a damn fool to begin with. The fellow just hadn't used his head.

Lyda, turning the matter over in her mind afterward, wasn't so sure it was as simple as that. She was sure Chubby had thought he knew exactly what he was doing. He had bulled forward on the assumption that the world worked pretty much the same way it had back when he was playing tackle for Yale. And what could one expect? Sealed off year after year from reality by assumptions and prejudices reinforced by a network of friendships and institutions which themselves had a vested interest in keeping things the way they had been, insulated by his wife's money, could one expect a dim creature like Chubby Fenton to do any differently?

He obviously resented Morris's rising influence, especially after Hanover Place took on American Spirits and Distilling as a client, and it became obvious what Fletcher was about and that Howland had roundly opposed his father before being overruled.

Fletcher himself was under no illusions about Sid Ascheim, AS&D's founder. He was an ex-bootlegger who'd sat out Prohibition in Canada, and after Repeal, recrossed the border and converted his previously illegal business into a major distiller and marketer of alcoholic beverages. AS&D owned or controlled three distilleries, two national distribution systems, a dozen premium brands, choice vineyards in Bordeaux, and bonded ware-houses holding several million gallons of premium whiskey.

"Sidney was a pillar of the community then," said Fletcher naughtily, "and he's a pillar of the community now. It's only the law that's changed."

Fletcher had bought a lot of liquor from Ascheim in the old days, including the spirits for his son's wedding celebration. When Ascheim approached The Firm for financing to set up his own glassmaking and bottling facilities, Morris Miles was promptly called in.

The old man had a private agenda about which he had taken his son and daughter-in-law into his confidence. "Of course, Sid Ascheim's a lowlife who'd sell his mother into slavery to make an extra dollar. But he's also a director of First Interstate Stores and Borough U.S. Bank, not to mention a leading light of Westchester and Palm Beach society.

"The Jews hang together," Fletcher continued, "and well they might, after what happened to them when the Bank of the United States failed, not to mention what's going on in Germany. They're mistrustful of our sort. Sid'll help us infiltrate that business. There's nothing these people like better than to be able to boast they use Morgan as their banker, but

Morgan'll never touch 'em for fear of upsetting right-wingers like the Du Ponts. We're the next best thing. And by the bye, my boy, tell Brother Fenton to put a sock in it about Ascheim in the bar of the Brook Club."

Morris devised a brilliant financing package, which yielded two hundred thousand very cheap AS&D shares to The Firm. Raising the money was a feat most of the Street likened to the financial equivalent of drawing water from a stone, given the shape the market was in. Overnight, AS&D became the only truly integrated liquor producer and packager in the world. Ascheim insisted that Morris join his board.

Perhaps, Lyda reflected later, that's what drove Chubby, as a gesture of contempt and defiance, to join the Committee for German-American Amity, a group described by one New York paper as "a semi-secret cabal engaged in financing every conceivable form of organized American anti-Semitism, in particular Father Charles Coughlin's Christian Front Organization."

Coughlin was a rogue priest who preached every Sunday night to a radio audience of three and a half million people; what he preached was not very different from what, on the far side of the Atlantic, the author of *Mein Kampf* was telling *his* howling audiences.

On the morning of November 18, 1938, Morris asked to see Howland privately. Howland expected that he wanted to talk about a new AS&D financing. Ascheim and his people had been at Hanover Place the previous afternoon to discuss raising $10 million for an expansion of AS&D's Lexington distilling and warehousing facility.

When Morris entered his office, however, Howland could see at once that the other man was agitated.

"Well, Morris," Howland said in a carefully genial voice, "how'd it go with Sid yesterday? Everything on track?"

For a moment there was no reply. Then, in a choked voice, Morris Miles said: "Howland, I'm submitting my resignation."

From behind an easy smile, Howland tried to digest what had just been said. Resign? Partners of S. L. Warrington left Hanover Place only on their shields. The late Hap Carruthers had been the only Warrington partner ever to resign voluntarily.

"I'm a little confused," said Howland calmly. "I think you'd better explain."

Morris leaped forward from the sofa, fumbled in his jacket pocket for a newspaper clipping, and thrust it at Howland.

"Have you seen this?" said Morris.

The clipping was a sidebar to a *Times* article on avowedly anti-Semitic organizations; it named a number of them, and identified their more prominent contributors and directors. Among them was "The Committee for German-American Amity," and among the organization's directors appeared the name of Charles C. Fenton III, identified as a general partner of S. L. Warrington & Son.

Howland read the clipping a second time and handed it wordlessly back to Morris. He blew out a little, sharp breath, a quick sort of sigh, laced his fingers behind his head, and grinned ruefully. Then he leaned forward, placed his clasped hands on the desk, and said: "I shouldn't get excited if I were you, Morris. This is just another of Chubby's crackpot fads. Remember the Liberty League? He was in that one, too. It'll last about a month and then, poof! Nothing to get excited about."

"Howland," said Morris, in a pleading voice, "the Committee for German-American Amity is a Nazi front. It's worse than the Bund. It gives money to Merwin Hart and the National Economic Council! It supports Father Coughlin. Do you know what Hitler's doing to us! Haven't you read what happened in Germany two weeks ago . . ."

"Of course I read it," Howland interrupted. How the hell could you miss it, he thought. It was a terrible thing, but what could you do in New York about something that happened in Germany? Hell, the family had stood up and been counted. Just the other day, Fletcher had sent $25,000 over to old man Warburg at Kuhn Loeb, to be used for Jewish relief.

Morris said nothing for a moment. He took a dazzlingly white handkerchief from the breast pocket of his dark suit and patted his forehead.

"So . . ." said Howland, deliberately letting his voice trail off to give Morris an opening.

"Well, you see, it's just . . . well, obviously, as a Jew, I cannot work in a place with people who are Nazis."

Howland grinned. Morris experienced a rush of resentment that surprised him. Easy for you to sit there, Mr. Howland Warrington, he found himself thinking, with nothing more on your mind than a squash game and a rubdown and a martini at one of your clubs, while at this very moment Jews are probably being beaten to death in the streets of Frankfurt. Morris had seen photographs of the *Ubermenschen.* Big blond beasts with dumb faces and huge heads. Just like Fenton.

He started to give words to these thoughts, but then his mind told him to keep still. This wasn't Fenton he was talking to. This was a man to whom he owed his and his family's life and prosperity. Without Howland and Lyda Warrington, he thought, Morris Miles would not even be sitting here having this discussion. It was a point he'd tried to make without success to his wife. Not that Miriam didn't appreciate how generous the Warringtons had been, what decent people they were.

"Well, maybe you're right," said Morris. He spread out his hands and examined their backs reflectively. He wasn't about to back off altogether. "Still, you see how it is," he said. "I don't see I have any choice. I'm a human being, too, you know."

Of course you are, thought Howland. You've got hands, organs, dimensions, senses, and I forget the rest. The reflexive flipness of the thought made him feel foolish.

"So, Morris, where are we going with this? My inclination, not that I've had much chance to use it, is when a fellow threatens to quit because of what someone else says or does outside of this building, which is beyond Father's or my control, why then, probably the best thing to do is to let him have his way. Is that what you want? I don't know what *you* do with your spare time, but I do know you don't clear it with Fenton, and yet it strikes me that's exactly what you're asking him to do with you. I urge you to think this over, Morris, because fond as Father may be of you, he takes very badly to anything that smacks of blackmail."

Howland's tone was firm, but his words were utter hogwash, and he knew it. He was trying to buy himself some time and room to maneuver so he could talk it over with his father and his wife.

Fortunately, Morris took him off the spot. "Howland, we're old friends. You're right. Let me sleep on it. Maybe it's not so bad as I thought."

They shook hands and, after Morris had left, Howland buzzed Miss Merrow and told her to find his father pronto.

The men at the table nodded and one said: "Well, Jesus Christ, Chub, you gotta hold the line somewhere!"

Those were the very words Dinny Himmington had used on the night at Fishers Island when he signed Chubby up for the Committee for German-American Amity.

Gotta show these yids who's who! Himmington had smirked. What's more, Chubby's recruiter had murmured, it's not just the St. Thomas's and St. Bartholomew's crowd that we're getting our money from, but some big names at Century and Harmonie and Emanu-El, who're also damned if they want these goddamn Zionists to get us into something that isn't any of our damn business, not if this market starts to dance to Mr. Hitler's tune.

The men at the club bar felt strongly about what had happened and Chubby was being hailed as a hero. Another round was called for.

It was a goddamn disgrace what had happened to good old Chub, yes it was! Of course, the Warringtons had always been a little pink. Not the old man, of course, but that Lyda, she was a goddamn suffragette, she was, who'd turned into a middle-aged Jew-lover just like "Mrs. Rosenfelt." Hell, back in '31, when a bunch of niggers raped some white girls down in Alabama, Lyda'd run all over town raising money to pay a couple of Jew lawyers to take the case. As if the Street didn't have enough trouble of its own! Hear, hear!

Yeah, and then there was all that fuss she'd kicked up just last year about Spain! If Franco needed the Germans' help to beat the goddamn Bolsheviks, what the hell business was it of Lyda Warrington's! That was the trouble with these goddamn Wellesley girls, always trying to make the world a better place for a few people and screwing it up for everyone else!

The glistening heads at the table in the Gorse bar bobbed in time to these sentiments. Finally, since it was Chubby's quarrel, it was fitting that he be given the last word. "What really surprised me," he said, shaking his enormous head so hard his jowls shook, "seeing how most of the really big Jews on the Street are sitting on their hands about Hitler, where'd this kike get the balls to go to Howland to complain?"

Chubby had asked Howland the very same question, in just those words, the night before in the very same bar. It had been after midnight, at the end of a long evening.

"I expect he got them the same place you got yours," said Howland. He was tired and impatient and a little drunk—and this was going nowhere. They'd gone over the same ground again and again, but Chubby simply didn't get it. Now Howland was starting to lose his patience.

Up to now, everything had gone according to plan, just as they'd foreseen. Fletcher had insisted on including Lyda in the council of war. For one thing, Miles was her baby. For another, it was—or soon would be—her legal right. Ariadne Warrington would be incapacitated for as much of her life as remained to her; Fletcher had made it known to the partners that as of January 1, 1939, Howland would be designated Joint Managing Partner. Under the terms of the Trust, Lyda would become a trustee and *de facto* Party of the First Part.

They met at the younger Warringtons' apartment. "Well, now," said Fletcher off the bat, "what do you two think Br'er Miles would consider a suitable pound of flesh?"

He cast a mischievous grin at Lyda. She met it with a serene smile off which Fletcher's naughty little barb pinged harmlessly.

"I really ought to leave this mess up to you two," Fletcher continued. "You're the responsible parties. Anyway, as I see it, Miles's alternatives are, reading from easiest to most drastic, to ask simply that Fenton get quietly out of this damn fool Committee or whatever-it-is, and leave everything otherwise as it was before. If necessary, we can give each of them an additional quarter-point carried interest for the insult."

"I doubt Chubby'd accept that," said Howland.

"I doubt Morris would," said Lyda quietly.

She looked from one to the other, and said, "Chubby has to go."

Both men looked at her in surprise.

Before either could say anything, she added: "You cannot, for any number of reasons ranging from good business sense to sheer self-respect, afford to keep a publicly identified anti-Semite at Hanover Place."

"Oh, cut it out, Ly," said her husband. "You're just using this Jewish thing as a lever. You've never liked old Chub."

"That has nothing to do with it," replied Lyda evenly.

Howland looked at his father helplessly. "Ly's had this Jewish bee in her bonnet since we were in Germany a couple of years ago."

"I know," said Fletcher. He looked around the room, at the ceiling, the pictures of his grandsons. A horn hooted outside on Park Avenue. "We have to be practical, you know," he said. "We have a Firm to think of. This isn't the Maidstone Club."

"Which makes it all the more important," Lyda responded.

"I'll take your point as offered, Lyda. Now, if we follow your thinking, which I daresay is more reflex than reflection, and give Brother Fenton the sack, we might as well close up, because we'll never again get the sort of people we want at Hanover Place."

Lyda nodded. His point was undeniable.

"I also feel, much as I prefer it, that a public recantation is out of the question. Fenton's no Martin Luther, but even fools have their pride. The perfect solution would be to negotiate an armistice. Pretend the whole thing never happened, even if it costs us an extra fifty thousand a year to the two of them, but I gather you think that's out of the question?" He looked at Lyda, who nodded. "In which case, we have a Hobson's choice. I'm damned if I'm going to lose Miles."

"Are you saying you're going to let Chubby go?" asked Howland.

"If all else fails, yes. Oh, I'll be gentle about it. I'm sure I can work something out with young Al Gordon at Kidder; he owes us a favor or two. Or Clarence Dillon—you might have a word with young Doug, Howland, if it comes to that."

The old man paused and shook his head violently. "Damn, damn, damn! I should have known this was going to happen from the beginning. That's the trouble with the Chosen People. They have this tribal thing. You never get into trouble with them man-to-man. Look at one sideways and the whole damn crowd's on your neck! I'm disappointed in Miles, I'm bound to say. Here we took the fellow up, scrubbed the stink of the ghetto off him, set him up on Park Avenue like a scarlet woman, and what thanks do we get! And don't you look at me that way, young lady! I ran into Harry Luce last night at the opera and he told me they ran a poll right after this 'Crystal' whatever they call it in Germany two weeks ago. You know what they found?"

"No."

"They found that while nearly ninety percent of those polled thought what the Nazis had done was terrible, almost sixty percent thought the Jews had somehow brought it on themselves!"

"My hunch is," said Howland, speaking up for the first time, "that you're both wrong about our problem. I think Morris feels embarrassed at having stirred up such a commotion. My guess is that he'll be satisfied to let the dust settle if Chub gets off this idiotic committee. Provided we act quickly, before this gets around The Firm, and opinions harden into factions and we find ourselves in a real civil war."

"And how do you propose to do that?" asked Fletcher.

"Divide and conquer, Father. Take Morris out on the town. Boys' night out. Take him to '21' and El Morocco and leave it to the mediating wisdom of alcohol."

"I don't think Morris drinks a great deal," said Lyda.

"All right," he said, "if that's the case, why don't we have the Mileses to dinner. . . ."

Lyda shook her head violently. "Out of the question, absolutely out of the question." She turned to her father-in-law. "Fletcher, you've always been the first one to say that business and pleasure don't, and mustn't, mix. If ever an occasion proved your point, this is it! This is between Morris and Chubby and the two of you. Introduce Miriam Miles into this equation, and you change everything. I have a feeling she's involved enough as it is, but let's for God's sake keep her off the stage!"

Lyda prevailed. Two nights after the council of war, Howland invited Morris Miles to dinner, just the two of them, to discuss the situation.

It had all the makings of a glum, unproductive evening and indeed was so for much of its duration. Morris Miles drank very little of the wine at "21," a noble Château Latour from Fletcher Warrington's private stock, and participated without noticeable enthusiasm in their East Side night-club crawl. The two men's conversation skirted what was on both their minds. Instead, they chewed over financing alternatives for the ten new DC-4 airliners Tom Creedmore wanted to buy for Global; it was amazing, they agreed, Global wasn't ten years old yet, and already into its fifth generation of aircraft! If the capital markets ever sprang back to life, Hanover Place could practically live off a Global, especially if the future of air transportation was one-tenth as bright as Tom Creedmore promised. They talked about Sid Ascheim's plan to acquire a second Louisville distillery and Morris's evidently successful courtship of Hyman Gessel, the difficult, autocratic head of a major Hollywood studio. They flirted with politics, world affairs, the market. They pointedly did not mention Germany.

Howland kept looking for the propitious moment, but it never seemed to arrive. It began to get late. Finally, he suggested a nightcap at the Gorse Club.

The club was deserted except for a scarlet-jacketed night porter nodding at his counter and the barman and a waiter upstairs. A couple of Scotches were ordered, poured, and brought to the table. Instinctively, Howland cocked his glass at Morris.

"Well, Morris, here's to the future."

Morris raised his glass and looked around the small room, taking in the splendid silver mugs and ewers in the lighted cabinets that flanked the bar, the vermeil sconces that had come from a Vanderbilt mansion, the Copley portrait of an early Adams, the Ferneley hunting scenes.

So here is where the past gets even with the present, thought Morris Miles.

Howland watched his guest survey the room. It occurred to him that every jot and tittle of these surroundings, the crystal, the heavy drapes, the old leather, the snooty patroon faces staring down from the heavily-varnished portraits, must suggest "Fenton" to Miles. This was the epitome of Chubby's world; of his own, too, come to think of it. Miles must be feeling like a Kiowa invited to parlay in the heart of Sioux territory.

"This is a very old club, isn't it?" asked Miles. It was clear his mind wasn't focused on the Fenton business.

"Around 1870, I think. Another stepchild of the Union Club."

"I see."

"Morris," said Howland, "we have got to resolve this business between Chubby Fenton and yourself. I think you know how Father and I feel about you."

Morris looked at him carefully and slowly, then said: "You want to know my price, right?"

"If we thought you had a price, we wouldn't be bothering to talk with you. Nor, may I add, would you be a partner of ours."

Morris made no comment. He flushed and studied the surface of the table.

"You have to understand," said Howland, "someone like Chubby—well, he's just a babe in the woods, politically, that is."

Miles's eyes narrowed. "It's always the babies that break things isn't it? First the cradle, then the concentration camp."

"I'm sorry, I don't think I . . ."

"It's nothing," said Morris. He examined his well-groomed hands and ran an appreciative finger along the rich, gleaming wood of the tabletop.

"It's not about clubs, you know," he said. "Fenton probably thinks it's about clubs. I'm happy at the Harmonie. It doesn't bother me that you play squash at the Racquet Club, and I can't. How many squash courts can a man play on?"

He interrupted himself and smiled. "My goodness," he said with a nervous little smile, "such a talker. Anyway, such things may affect my children, or their children, but I know my place. In fact, I count myself very lucky to be where I am, and I know that it's thanks to you and Lyda that I am. Social position I can do without, Howland. Breathing, I can't!"

"I think that's a bit of an overstatement, Morris. This isn't Germany."

"Maybe not yet!"

Both men sat still. Then Morris waved a hand in the air, as if chasing off his last exclamation.

"I'm sorry, Howland. You probably think I'm paranoiac and possibly I am. We Jews have had many centuries to become skillful at paranoia. By now, it's in our bones."

"Maybe that's part of the problem, Morris."

"Of course it is. Everything feeds on everything else. Take yourselves. People like you can't help the way you feel about Jews. You go as children to Sunday schools, blond, innocent, scrubbed little boys and girls, where you're taught that the Jews killed Christ. Something like that has to stick with a person, no matter how far back in his mind it gets pushed. The next thing you know: *Kristallnacht!*"

"I really think that's an oversimplification, Morris. And untrue. Everyone knows Christ was a Jew."

"And so he was," said Morris heatedly. "Right up to the moment he was dead, but in that instant he became a Christian! With a capital letter! Maybe that's what Hitler wants; maybe that's what Fenton wants! To make Christians of us by killing us! Then we can all lie down together, the lion and the lamb!"

Howland said nothing. He had never seen Morris so agitated. The man was practically sputtering.

After a moment, Morris calmed down. "Someone like you, Howland, you understand, I think. But you're special. For one thing, you're smart, which people your sort aren't supposed to be, especially on Wall Street. People like you are supposed to get on by where you went to college or what your last name is. But that's not your way. More importantly, you're a just man, Howland. Both you and Charlie are. I know you felt guilty about that business with Jones and Laughlin. It was my idea, I wrote the proposal, did all the work, but you went to Pittsburgh, you made the presentation, because Jews aren't welcome in the Duquesne Club. I understand. I don't like it, but I understand. Warrington's is a business, after all, not a human-rights organization. Did it make it better for me that I knew you felt bad? I think so. But it is such a waste that things have to be that way, Howland! Such a mistake! This country was founded by you *Mayflower* people, and it's grown up around you. You settled here first, you wrote the Declaration of Independence, wrote the Constitution, the Bill of Rights. But not just for you! For anyone else who happened in. Jews, Italians, Poles! You opened the door for us; we didn't break it down, did we? So if you don't honor those guarantees, not only do you lose whatever the rest of us have to offer, you lose your moral authority, and when you lose that, sooner or later someone you've excluded will come and take away your power—unless you kill him first—and that's not your style, not yet! Tell me, when you were in Germany, did you go to see places like Dachau, Buchenwald?"

"The detention camps?"

"That's what they call them. They are just the beginning. Have you read *Mein Kampf*?"

"I'm afraid I haven't."

"He doesn't say it in so many words, but if Hitler ever gets his way, he will try to kill every Jew on earth. Fenton's committee wants to help Hitler. I think you can complete the equation. That's my speech."

Morris sat back. Howland felt immensely relieved. Miles had made his declaration. Now they could get down to cases, do a deal.

He was not so lucky with Chubby.

It might have been wiser, Howland later conceded to Lyda, if he'd followed her advice and sat Chubby down sober in one of the partners' dining rooms and talked turkey, and not waited until after a long and admittedly bibulous dinner at the Union Club, a look-in at Elmo's followed by a drink at a couple of jazz joints on 52nd Street before repairing to the Gorse for the moment of truth.

Wiser perhaps, Lyda consoled him, but the result probably wouldn't have been much different.

After all, Howland had simply requested that Chubby terminate his formal, public affiliation with the Committee for German-American Amity. That was all that Morris Miles wanted—beyond that, Chubby was free to do whatever he wanted.

But Chubby wasn't buying. First he tried to bring Howland around to his thinking. Someone had to keep "Rosenfelt" and the Jews from getting us into a war, he argued. Why didn't Howland talk to Lindbergh, or to Tommy Creedmore?

Howland heard his old friend out. He smiled and nodded and tried to smooth the proceedings. But as the brandy in the crystal decanter disappeared, so did Chubby's hold on logic. He began to mutter ominously about "kikes," to say things like "if you're going to go this far, maybe you can get a nigger to run Syndicate."

And so, in the end, during Thanksgiving week of 1938, six weeks before Lyda found herself in the smoky New Year's Eve bedlam of El Morocco, Charles Christian Fenton III formally resigned from S. L. Warrington & Son, received a check for $632,000 in payment of his capital and accumulated free interest, and left Hanover Place for the last time.

Lyda looked at her watch. Another twenty minutes to midnight. At that moment, a man with a camera hurried up to their table.

"C'mon now, Warringtons," he cried, "don't be a bunch of old poops! Look at the birdie, Alice. Okay now, everyone ready? Say 'cheese'!"

For an instant the table froze and smiled for Jerome Zerbe's camera; the flashbulb popped.

"Thanks loads, dears," said Zerbe. He bent over and kissed Lyda on the cheek. "Not to worry, dear," he whispered. "It's just for my personal scrapbook! Won't be published to incite the starving masses!" He waved gaily and fluttered off in search of other El Morocco prey.

"How about a dance?" asked Howland. In the background the band finished up with "Ain't We Got Fun" and shifted to "Falling in Love with Love."

Lyda turned to her husband.

The New Year was almost upon them. If Howland was right, the squawk of noisemakers would soon be followed by the roar of artillery. He regularly met to discuss such matters at a clandestine world-affairs forum Vincent Astor had convened in an apartment on 62nd Street which its habitués simply called "the Room." Just two weeks earlier, Siegmund Warburg, the youngest and in most people's opinion the brightest of the European Warburgs, had told "the Room" that Hitler needed war, wanted war, and was determined to get it. Forget the "peace in our time" that Mr. Chamberlain had proclaimed back in late September. In Warburg's opinion, Poland would follow Austria and Czechoslovakia into Hitler's maw, and after that, France and the Low Countries and then England, and then, with the Western hand, it must surely be Russia's turn.

Howland and Warburg had become good friends. They were men of a common kidney, idealistic about finance. Warburg had this conception he called "haute banque," which cast the financier in a role that transcended money-spinning, made him a hinge upon which turned the world's greatest issues and largest affairs, no longer a mere orchestrator of markets and deals but a shaper of policy. It was, as Fletcher said to Lyda, a fine and harmless fantasy, a small indulgence to which the father happily paid lip service as the price of keeping his son's mind on the real business of Hanover Place.

The band now plunged feverishly into a medley from *Snow White and the Seven Dwarfs.*

"Heigh-ho, heigh-ho," Howland hummed. With his right hand he gestured toward the dance floor and turned away. Lyda shook her head. She hated this song. Just before Christmas she had taken the boys to see *Snow White* at the Radio City Music Hall, and Jay now sang the song approximately a hundred times a day, over and over and over.

Over her husband's shoulder, she looked at her watch. Seven minutes now. She felt tired. The smoke and the noise were bringing on a headache. They returned to the table. Howland began to chat with Bob Benchley, sitting at the next table with Linda and Cole Porter.

Nineteen thirty-nine: Fletcher was predicting a banner year for the market. He'd told Morris to get his people in Corporations to make up lists of companies that the likely combatants in a European war might have to sell to raise money.

Howland turned back and leaned across to Lyda. "Benchley says we really ought to go see this Lincoln play of Bob Sherwood's. Let's take the boys. I'll get Miss Merrow . . ."

He stopped in midsentence and Lyda saw him stiffen, his eyes fixed on someone behind her. She turned and followed his gaze.

Carino was leading a party through the crowd. They were dressed in full evening clothes. Lyda recognized Randolph Scott and Rocky and Gary Cooper; was that Barbara Stanwyck with them? Next came a sallow little man with a large, bald head; on his arm was a tall blonde, whose face was well past the prime her bosom still enjoyed; finally an extravagantly got-up woman with flashy, Latin looks whose arm was gripped tightly by a familiar blocky figure, now definitely more suet than granite: Charles Christian Fenton III.

Chubby was busy working the room, smiling, winking, waving with his free hand, and it was a moment or two before his bright little blue eyes lit on Howland and Lyda. He stopped in his tracks and muttered something to his wife, who looked around and put on her best company smile. There was a moment's awkward hesitation, while both sides calculated how best to handle the situation. It had been six weeks since Howland and Chubby, who had hardly been out of each other's sight for the best part of thirty years, had seen or spoken with each other.

For no good reason, Lyda looked at her watch: three minutes to midnight. She sensed rather than saw her husband get up, nervously adjust the tails of his evening jacket, and beckon the Fentons to the table. As Chubby advanced on them, Howland reached down and squeezed Lyda's hand; she wasn't sure whether to reassure her or draw courage for himself.

"Well, Merry Christmas!" Chubby exclaimed. He shook Howland's hand vigorously and planted a kiss on Lyda. It was apparent that he had had a good deal to drink.

"My goodness, Chubby," said Lyda, "what in the world are you two doing here? We thought you were in Havana."

Fenton plumped himself down in the place recently vacated by Charlie Runnels, who had gone off to dance with Alice Mitchell. "Were," he said. "Hadda come back on business. Left the son and heir down there —sun and sea and sand, y'know. Gotta big thing going . . ."

He stopped in midsentence. The orchestra had started to count out the final seconds of the old year. The crowd picked up the cadence: "four . . . three . . . two . . . one!" The place erupted in a din of noisemakers and shouted greetings. The band launched into "Old Acquaintance." On the dance floor, couples embraced. At a nearby table a striking young man in a tailcoat and his equally handsome lady appeared ready to slide to the floor and consummate their happiness under the table.

"Excuse me," shouted Howland. He leaned over and kissed Lyda quickly on the lips. "Happy New Year, my love!"

He broke out in a big, self-satisfied grin, and Lyda knew the worst had happened. Behind her she heard the band strike up "Happy Birthday to You," and when she turned around, here came Carino leading a waiter carrying a cake decorated in the nightclub's zebra stripes followed by another with a jeroboam of champagne in a silver cooler. If looks could kill, she thought, smiling lovingly at her husband, as he took up the refrain in his enthusiastic, ill-tuned baritone and was joined by the rest of the room.

"Ha-a-ap-py Birthday, dear Lyda!" Next to her, Chubby practically shouted in her ear, and she looked away to get out of range of his gin-and-smoke breath.

"This is too much!" she called to Howland above the din. She hated this sort of thing. Already once tonight she'd been through it, at "21," when Jack Kriendler, who'd obviously been tipped off, had produced a cake decorated in Wall Street motifs and then everyone had sung "Happy Birthday" with such gusto that the little plane and truck models hanging from the ceiling had quivered in the smoky air. She hated having a private, personal moment spread out for the delectation of a roomful of strangers. She saw Jerome Zerbe nudge his way through the crowd, shove a bulb into his flashgun, and memorialize the moment.

Within a few minutes, however, their commotion had died away, and the attention of those who weren't dancing was now focused on the kewpie face of Brenda Frazier, the celebrated debutante who had just swept in with a tableful of chair-pushing, lighter-clicking escorts.

Chubby turned serious. He gravely proffered a thick hand to Howland

and Lyda in turn. His wife seemed to have vanished. The two sets of Runnelses had departed and Milo was upstairs seeing after Alice, who had been sick in the ladies room. The three of them were alone at the table.

"No hard feelings?" Chubby asked.

He sounded so forlorn that Howland and Lyda shook their heads simultaneously. What's the point, she thought.

"Hey," he said in a thick voice, "you wanna join us? Gotta helluva group. Got Rocky and Coop, and Randy Scott and Missy Stanwyck."

"My goodness, how very Hollywood," said Lyda. "Who're the other couple?"

"The little guy's my meal ticket. Hy Gessel—you know: Gesell-Imperial-Galaxy? Met him over Thanksgiving at the polo matches at Boca Raton. Just before . . . well, you know. The blonde with the big bazooms's his date. Miss Southern California Tits of 1935." He chuckled. "Ah, 1925 would be closer if you ask me."

Fenton paused, obviously gathering himself to say something important, then reached in his pocket and pulled out a card case. With some awkwardness, his large hands weren't made for such a task, he extracted two business cards, which he shoved at Howland and Lyda. She noted that the back of his hand was heavily speckled. The gin's starting to show up, she thought.

Lyda's practiced eye registered the card as expensive stuff: vellum stock, deep-cut engraving, probably Tiffany or Van Cleef or Mrs. John Strong.

FENTON & CO./INVESTMENT BROKERS, it read. CHARLES C. FENTON III/ CHAIRMAN AND GENERAL MANAGER. There was an address on Flower Street in Los Angeles and a telephone number with a FIgueroa exchange.

Chubby picked up Lyda's quizzical look.

"That's right, Ly. California—here we come! Good-bye, New York and amen! Going out in June, jus'a soon's the son and heir's school ends. Gotta house in Pasadena just up the road from Tommy Creedmore."

"You're moving to California?" Lyda said. "You're giving up East Hampton?" Andrew would be heartbroken, she thought. For him a summer without Chickie Fenton down the road would be a season without the sun.

"Givin' it all up," said Chubby in a satisfied way that stirred a pulse of anger in Lyda. "Goin' to the land o' milk 'n honey."

He leaned forward, and as Lyda watched, attempted to compose his big, open features into a sly, conspiratorial smirk. The effect was of daunting stupidity.

"You know, you two, you were right and I was wrong. The Jews're gonna own the goddamn world, so why fight it? You think Gessel's gonna underwrite my business 'cause I'm a great investment thinker? Hah! What he wants is my eight-goal polo handicap, and brother is he willin' to pay for it! I saw Tommy Hitchcock the other night at the Bleeckers. I said 'Tommy, even if you weren't married to a Mellon, you're pissin' it away. Tommy,' I said, 'you're workin' for the wrong Jews! You oughta get outa Lehman Brothers and head for the Coast. I don't know what Bobby's payin' you, but it isn't enough! Hell, with you at number two and me at back, goddamn Gessel'd win the world championship and whaddya think he'd pay for that!' "

"And what did Tommy say?" asked Howland.

"Well, hell, Howdy, you know, hell, he doesn't need the dough!" Chubby looked around nervously. "Hey," he said, "gotta be rejoining my table. My man gets nervous if I don't lick his boots every hour on the hour. Anyway, I'm glad I saw you guys. No hard feelin's, huh? I mean, I really gotta thank you two for helpin' me see the light! Come and see us in Hollywood. By the way, Lyda, the son and heir said to say hello to Drew if we saw you."

Lyda watched him make his unsteady way back to his party.

"Well," she said to her husband, "Happy New Year!"

BOOK

IV

THE OLD LIE

1941

JULY

The sizzling day was clear but for a faint steamy haze. Good enough for flying, but Howland's Beech floatplane had developed some exotic form of magneto trouble, so its owner, who normally made the flight from 23rd Street to Georgica Pond in an hour, had to endure a three-hour steambath on the Long Island Railroad.

A lousy way to begin a three-day weekend, thought Lyda, watching the train lumber into the East Hampton station.

She expected Howland to be in a foul mood, but when he bounced down the steps of the parlor car, he was beaming. Lyda found his cheerful expression irritating. Her own week had been perfectly awful.

"Good trip?" she asked when he got to the car.

"Not so hot. By Speonk, we'd run out of ice and by Westhampton, all there was left to drink was Lord Calvert, and you know how I hate rye!"

He was carrying a large package from Weatherill's under his arm. A new white dinner jacket, she guessed. Well, about time. The old one was practically green with age and hard use, and—even though Howland had kept his figure better than most of his contemporaries—undeniably snug around the middle.

He tossed the package through the window onto the back seat and ran a finger over the woodwork of the big Buick station wagon. "We better get this revarnished," he said, sliding behind the wheel and kissing her perfunctorily. "And how was your week, my beloved?" he asked in a voice that struck Lyda as unnecessarily jolly.

"Lousy," she answered. "Yours?"

He did sound odd. Was something up? But what? She and Howland talked at least twice a day. During the summer, while she presided over Double Dune, and he stayed in town working, she always knew where to find him. After the office, he went to the Racquet or the Union Club for a game of squash, no matter how hot it got, then a rubdown and a drink with some of the boys, and then home, stopping off at Giovanni's or the Esplanade or now and then the Gorse for a quick dinner. He was always home by ten, not off chasing women like Charlie Runnels, although who could blame Charlie; everybody from Westport to Wilmington knew Bess Runnels was sleeping with the young butcher at Docherty's.

Howland threw the car in gear and backed out rapidly, screeching to a halt before he ran over Teddy Pimberson, who was standing forlornly in the parking lot peering right and left. Poor Teddy; there was another sad case. Maisie Pimberson was at it again with one of the assistant pros at Maidstone: poor oversexed Maisie—tennis instructors in the summer and ski teachers in the winter.

"Father all right?" asked Howland as they pulled into Newton Lane.

"Fine. He ought to stay down here the whole summer. He's no trouble at all."

Which was true. Fletcher was no problem for her. Of course, they'd all been living more or less together for over two years now and had learned each other's quirks and made the necessary adjustments after Ariadne Warrington finally gave up the ghost in the spring of 1940. Lyda had been apprehensive about moving out of the Park Avenue townhouse and into Fletcher's old apartment on Fifth Avenue. But with the twins off at Exeter, the house seemed like a mausoleum, and the old man had seemed so lost and lonely, and been so insistent, that in the end she had no choice.

The "consolidation" of the two households had worked out better than she had a right to expect. Fletcher had bought a smaller apartment on the floor above, and had the two joined by a staircase. Earlier in the year, he had sold off the Adirondacks "camp," and Lyda had offered him the guest cottage at Double Dune. Apart from a large moose head he'd insisted on installing in the cottage as a monument to happy times on Antler Lake, he had been as easy as pie.

In fact, relations at the moment were better between father and daughter-in-law than between father and son. From the day war had broken out in Europe in 1939 right up to the present, rational discussion on the subject between the two had become difficult; now that Hitler had invaded

Russia three weeks earlier, it was next to impossible, and dinner-table conversations were largely reduced to glum, resentful pauses with Lyda and the children watching fitfully from the edges of the quarrel.

The paradox was that both men wanted war: Fletcher because it was good for business, Howland because America had to take a stand. At one point, Howland had even considered running for Congress from Suffolk County, challenging the isolationist who held the seat, but at the last moment, his inbred distaste for elective politics prevailed, and he pulled back.

"And a damn good thing, too," said Fletcher. "Our sort shouldn't get into politics. Roosevelt was an anomaly; both Roosevelts! Our sort's incapable of thinking and acting in a low way, and a low way is what politics is all about! We don't really understand what the man looking in from the street wants from life."

Fletcher by now had become irrational on the subject of the President. He had not forgiven FDR for the exchange-rate fiasco of 1939; Fletcher had gone short sterling against the dollar—any damn fool could see the pound was hopelessly overvalued, he announced at the time—but Roosevelt's ill-judged currency intervention had caused Hanover Place a substantial loss.

"Damn criminal foolishness!" he grumped to anyone he could buttonhole. "Who ever heard of such a damn fool thing! Imagine, a government talking down the value of its own currency!"

Such was the price of having voted for Roosevelt in '32 and '36, he announced, and swore he would never vote for the rogue again. He was going to vote for Wendell Willkie, he told one and all in 1940; Willkie understood Wall Street. Fletcher sported a Willkie button and refused to face the fact that FDR was a shoo-in for a third term. That October matters came to a head, and Lyda as usual found herself in the middle. Willkie came to East Hampton to campaign, and Howland took himself off shooting in Connecticut—the idea of an "appeaser" like Willkie in East Hampton made him too sick to stick around, he claimed.

Without Lyda's really being aware of what he was up to, Fletcher kitted Andy and Jay in a full line of Willkie regalia—buttons, sashes, pennants, boaters—and the two little boys marched beside their grandfather in the torchlight parade up Main Street. A photograph appeared the following week in the local paper, and war broke out in the Warrington household.

Howland promptly announced that he would not attend his father's upcoming birthday celebration. At Hanover Place, he spent practically no time on the Platform, preferring to closet himself in his private office. Fletcher's back went up in turn. Each now outdid the other in finding excuses to cancel such traditional rites as their regular golf match, and they arranged to sit with their respective classes in separate sections at the Yale Bowl for the Harvard game.

As usual, they chose not to confront each other directly, but through Lyda.

"I never thought I'd be able to say this," Howland complained, "but I'm beginning to be ashamed of being a Warrington. Father can't see what's happening in Europe beyond what's in it for The Firm! I can't tell you how it makes me feel, sitting on my duff downtown watching Father and your protégé Mr. Miles gleefully calculating how much money The Firm can spin off the latest Nazi triumph!"

She understood how her husband felt. His mind was supposed to be at Hanover Place, but his heart was at the front. Other men were off to war. Bob Lovett had left Brown Brothers to join the War Department, Jim Forrestal was on leave of absence from Dillon, Read at the Navy Department; Tommy Hitchcock was in the RAF; even Chubby Fenton had cadged an Air Force commission, but Howland was chained by family duty to The Firm.

This was what Fletcher really feared, Lyda guessed: that Howland might take off and leave him alone to run The Firm at his age. On more than one occasion he had confessed to her that as he approached his fourth score of years on earth, even he now and then heard the whisper of the scythe.

"So," said Howland, turning the Buick into Lee Avenue, "what else went wrong that could?"

He caught Lyda's expression in the mirror, hastily added that he was just teasing, and then began to hum merrily.

Something *is* up, thought Lyda.

"Miriam dumped Max on our doorstep again," she said.

" 'Dumped'?"

"Oh, you know what I mean! I just can't leave them sitting over there on Lily Pond Lane cooling their heels, can I? I can't take them to the Club, so . . ."

"So you invited them over. Good for you! It certainly makes my life easier around The Firm, I can tell you."

"I just don't want you to think for a minute that this cancels out our deal."

Earlier in the year, they had reached a compromise about the Mileses. Aside from the partners dance, the Christmas party, and the annual Firm clambake, there would be one evening at the theater, they would take a table at Miriam's hospital charity, and Lyda would have the Miles family all to lunch one Sunday during their sojourn in East Hampton.

Still, it hadn't seemed fair to let Max, who was only a child of eleven, sit by himself in that big gloomy rented house, so she'd made Andrew telephone and invite him to come and play. It irritated Lyda that Miriam hadn't sent her son off to camp—Miriam knew what kind of a place East Hampton was.

Inviting Max meant Maidstone was out of the question for the day, but Andrew was, thank God, almost pathologically unselfish and never went to the club much, anyway. She thought of enlisting Jay to back up his older brother, but he was in a tennis round-robin, so it wasn't fair to make him miss that. And, with Jay, trouble was always just around the corner, so it was also likely to prove a blessing for him to be off at Maidstone for most of the day. That, at least, had been her theory.

She decided to resist the temptation to shove a cloud across her husband's sunny mood. I'll wait until he has his martini before making my report, she told herself.

But where, oh where, she wondered, did Jay pick up such a dreadful ditty? Overheard locker-room palaver, most likely. She resolved to have a word with the committee.

They rounded a curve, there was the sea, and Double Dune sitting solidly atop its bluff. Lyda could never see it without feeling glad.

Howland jerked the car to a stop in the drive and scrambled out, mumbling about needing to go to the bathroom; he snatched his parcel from the back seat and ran up the steps into the house.

The first thing Lyda heard indoors was raucous laughter and squealing from the living room. She went to the door and looked in. Just as she did, she heard Fletcher hoot loudly: "Two hundred fifty dollars for the use of a thousand for just two rolls of the dice! Why you miserable little shylock! Wherever did you learn such a thing? All right, here! But expect no further mercy, sir!"

Fletcher, Lex, and Jay were playing Monopoly on the floor. The old man had doffed his jacket and loosened the bright silk tie below his stiff collar. He was obviously having the time of his life. Andrew was sprawled on a window seat, reading, as usual; like his mother, he hated board games. Over the rushing sound of the ocean Lyda could make out the sound of a tennis ball being thwocked against the garage, which accounted for Dee's whereabouts.

Jay was on the point of retorting to his grandfather when he caught sight of Lyda in the doorway. His devilish dark eyebrows shot up in surprise, and his thin little mouth curled down in a guilty grimace.

"I thought you were supposed to be in your room, young man," said Lyda.

Jay looked helplessly at Fletcher.

"Howland arrive all right?" asked the old man.

"He's in the little boy's room," said Lyda, "but don't try to change the subject."

She fixed Jay with a glare. "Your father will want a word with you, young man. That was a very wicked thing you did! You cannot go around hurting people's feelings that way."

"C'mon, Ma," Jay pleaded, "Slapsie Maxie didn't even get it. Did he, Drew, did he? C'mon, Ma, he *never* gets anything. You know that!"

From across the room, she saw Andrew shrug in halfhearted support of his brother's position. That's duty talking, she thought, and nothing but. Andrew and Jay weren't particularly close; they seldom stuck together even in the face of the overwhelming fact of their twin brothers.

"The lads tell me the Miles boy has some very strange ideas about money," said Fletcher, still trying to ride to his grandson's rescue. "Talks about nothing but, I gather," he added helpfully, and was rewarded for his pains with a very sharp look from Lyda.

Lyda started to tell Jay to go to his room when, behind her, she heard "Ta-rah-ta-rah!"

She wheeled. Howland was standing in the doorway, incandescent with pride. Oh my God, she murmured.

He was dressed in khaki, silver wings on his tunic collar, on the breast two rows of ribbons; on his epaulets gleamed the silver "chickens" of an Air Force colonel.

He looked mighty handsome in his tailored suntans, no doubt of that, but that wasn't the point. He grinned broadly and snapped a sharp salute to the room at large. The three Monopoly players gaped; Andrew straightened up on the window seat. In the silence, the sound of Dee's tennis ball—thwock-thump-thwock-thump—seemed to drown out the sea like a giant heartbeat.

Howland's moment of triumph was brief. As Lyda watched, struck wordless, she saw his grin fade and his eyes lose their light as he looked past her. She heard him say apologetically, as if he were no older than Jay: "It's just a reserve commission, Father . . . I mean, just two days a week in Washington . . . Father, there's going to be a war! I had to get in now! Father, it's our *country*, damn it!"

"So it was just you and Andrew?"

"That's right," said Max.

At about the instant when Howland materialized before his family in his warrior garb, Miriam Miles was bringing her second interrogation of her son Max to its end. She made him repeat everything about his day at Double Dune, who came and went, from Lyda's masseuse to various deliverymen, and what everyone had said and done.

"And when you got there, Jay was at the Maidstone?"

"Yes."

Miriam corrected herself mentally: not "*the* Maidstone," just "Maid-stone."

Maidstone. Once, when she and Max were returning from an excursion to Montauk, and the chauffeur had taken the back road from Amagansett so they could see some of the big houses nestled in the hills and near the sea, she had ordered the driver to pull the big Packard over on the shoulder of Further Lane. It was early evening. The lighted clubhouse shimmered beyond the fairways like a mirage, the way Manhattan did back when she used to go by herself to Brooklyn Heights and stare across the river at the golden city. She and Max were gazing at the club when a car swept by them, a smart convertible with the top down, with Lyda at the wheel, her dark hair blown back over her shoulders, Andy next to her in front, and little Jay standing upright on the back seat between the two blond twins. Instinctively, Miriam had shrunk back and put a hand up, watching from the shadows as the Warrington car disappeared up the club driveway, taillights winking in the gloaming.

"So now tell me again what happened when Jay got home," said Miriam.

"Well," said Max, "it was something about Harvard being run by something I don't remember, and Yale being run by booze, and Cornell being run by farmers or something that sounded like that, and Columbia being run by Jews."

He had a loud, orotund voice, surprising in a boy of eleven unless one knew of the elocution lessons he was given by a genteel old lady on East 93rd Street. The big voice was in keeping with Max's appearance, how-ever. Max Miles was tall for his age; his large hands, feet, and head assured that he would grow taller still; already he had physical and vocal "pres-ence."

You *knew* when Max was in a room, his brother Ben said, you couldn't get away from the fact. He had very dark brown hair, thick and shaggy, luminous dark eyes and oversized features, most notably a large, square jawline inherited from his mother. Miriam described him to herself as "Byronic" or "Lincolnesque." He was very pale, and the slightest exposure to the sun parboiled him stingingly red.

It had been Miriam's expectation that Max would be a sublime genetic mixture, with manly, dramatic Irish lineaments complemented by a seeth-ingly brilliant Jewish intellect. This double endowment would enable Max to take the world as he pleased.

Alas, it was by now clear that destiny had bestowed on the boy no better than an average mind. By the time he was three, Miriam concluded that her son, this boy through whom her fondest dreams were to be realized, was "Irish dumb": dense and stubborn, opaque of perception, deficient of insight, in logic crude, in feeling coarse. In other words: as thick-headed and insensitive as his maternal grandfather.

Her harsh evaluation of her son's intellect was not quite fair to Max, as Morris tried to tell her. The boy might not be "a brain," he might lack his brother Benjamin's intellectual flair and grasp, or his sister Selma's crystalline powers of reasoning, but he was no dunce. A C+ student at Collegiate, and that was better than an "A" at Buckley, where the Warrington boys went. Miriam paid her husband no attention. She would compensate for his shortcomings, and so she spread her protective wings over her son's life. By the time he was seven, Max had utterly lost any capacity for self-doubt; instead, he possessed a view of life, authenticated by his protective, solicitous mother, which broke existence down into three simple parts: his own entitlements, the responsibility of others to see that those entitlements were fulfilled, and the just and efficient power of his father's money to make good on every desire his heart might entertain.

Unfortunately, Miriam realized as she finished grilling Max about his day at Double Dune, there were some dangers from which no amount of money could buy protection.

What had happened, it seemed, was that Max and Andrew and Jay, who had just gotten home, had been sitting on the dunes, talking the way young boys will, and somehow the subject of colleges came up, which with the Warringtons always meant Yale: the grandfather had gone there and the father and the twins would too, after prep school, and later probably Andrew and Jay.

Boys have their own pride, and Max had chafed hearing all this Yale talk—Miriam made a note to tutor her son that among these people it wasn't "Yale" you said, but "New Haven"—so he broke in and said something about his father having gone to Columbia.

Now this wasn't strictly speaking true, not in the context Max meant. Morris had taken a couple of night courses up on Morningside Heights when Benjamin Graham was teaching there, but he wasn't what you'd call "a Columbia man."

Anyway, Max had said his little piece, and out of the blue Jay had piped up with a ditty.

> *"Oh, Harvard's run by millionaires,*
> *And Yale is run by booze,*

Cornell is run by farmers' sons,
Columbia's run by Jews."

When Jay finished the second stanza, he howled with laughter, looked around maliciously, and then, as was his habit with anything that annoyed or irritated other people, he began to repeat it. Unfortunately for him, at that moment, Lyda came up behind the three boys. They hadn't even noticed she was there, not until Jay stopped in mid-verse when she swatted him on the head so hard he went flat out on the ground.

"I'm sorry, Max," she said quietly. "I apologize for my vile-mannered son."

Then she reached down and jerked Jay to his feet by the collar of his shirt, almost lifting him off the ground, the way one picks up a puppy by its scruff.

"You go to your room!" Then she'd gathered up Max and driven him home. A few times she started to say something, Max told his mother, but then she stopped and just drove on.

When Max finished his debriefing, he stood silently while Miriam considered the implications of the episode. He shifted from one foot to the other. Finally, he just had to ask. "Momma, is there something funny about being a Jew?"

Miriam weighed her answer. "Not really," she said.

Her voice was unusually soft, which was such a change from her usual direct, assertive tone that even Max noticed it, but the gentleness immediately disappeared from her voice, and her large features, which an instant before had threatened to dissolve, firmed and narrowed in an expression that would have put the fiercest demon to flight.

Howland's appearance in uniform convinced Lyda to go forward with a project she had been considering for some time: a large family portrait. She knew exactly who she wanted to paint the picture. She had seen a number of works by Jocelyn Barrow, a British artist who had been stranded in New York by the Blitz. He was good at likenesses, and had what Lyda considered a special talent for atmosphere, a distinctive gift for capturing the special way sunlight spilled through an apartment window on a winter afternoon or pervaded a bedroom on a hot July morning. Like John Koch, another young painter she admired, Barrow's style seemed a good modern approximation of Vermeer, whom Lyda considered the greatest of painters.

The painting, on which the artist worked for most of August of that last summer before Pearl Harbor, now hangs in the Museum of Manhattan, in the circular second floor gallery, across from Eastman Johnson's family portrait of 1875.

The overall impression that first strikes a viewer entering the gallery is of the pervasive presence of sun and sea. Radiant light suffuses the scene; the sea is felt just offstage. Through the windows of the big drawing room at Double Dune, thrown open onto a broad shaded veranda, one catches a glimpse of greeny-brown dune grass, a blaze of pale blue sky, a thin line of grayish-green ocean, a very satisfactory replication of the feeling of a peaceful early August afternoon.

The viewer looks down into the room from a slight elevation, about stepladder height. To the viewer's left, Howland—who insisted on being painted in his new uniform—bends over a table on which is spread a map, presumably of some theater of the European war. He is flanked by the twins, good-looking, blondish boys of fifteen as tall as their father; they are dressed in tennis clothes and Lex is holding a racquet: wooden-framed with bright yellow strings. The center of the picture is organized around the fireplace in the background. On the mantel stands an array of silver trophies. A low basket of summer flowers has been placed in the grate in front of the firescreen.

Projecting into the room from either side of the hearth are two sofas. On the left-hand one, Lyda, dressed in wide-legged cream-colored slacks and a white tennis shirt, works at her needlepoint. She is wearing her dark hair shoulder-length. On the right-hand couch, Andy is scrunched up against a careless stack of cushions, reading intently from a book with a pale cover that almost matches his mother's trousers. His brown hair, darker than the twins', is uncombed; he is wearing a red-and-white striped T-shirt, white shorts, and blue sneakers. In the right foreground, at a card table, young Jay and old Fletcher, dressed in a rumpled, discolored white suit, high collar, and a green Gorse tie patterned with white club insignia, study each other with wary affection across a backgammon board. Jay's hand is on the doubling cube; from the expression on his face it is clear he is about to give his grandfather the business.

The painting is fleshed out with details appropriate to the life it depicts: the what-not Lyda found in the Portobello Road; an Oriental rug Tom Creedmore brought back from Shanghai; a golf putter leans against a huge black urn that once stood in the vestibule of the old Warrington town-house near Stuyvesant Square. There are photographs on most of the side tables. A model sailboat, quite an elaborate one, has been abandoned on the window seat. Through an open door, on the left of the fireplace, beyond the backgammon game, one catches a glimpse of the blue-and-white figured wallpaper of the dining room.

Lyda loved the way the painting turned out: it got her family "right" and, best of all, in the instant she would always want to think of them —that last placid interval of peace and normalcy.

She thought the artist had done the boys especially well; the likenesses were expert and she thought she could see in Barrow's renderings the men her sons would become.

Except for Andrew. She was closest to him and yet he was the one whose future she had the greatest difficulty predicting. As Fletcher put it, her third son was "*adagio moderato*: a gentle interval between two riotous outer movements." The other three seemed to have been born with "Seize the Day" engraved in their souls; Andrew was less aggressive. He felt, as his brothers emphatically did not, that life consisted to some extent in making allowances. He was the lone reader of the lot, voracious but no bookworm. When he wanted, he could be as cruel-tongued as his brother Jay or his friend Chickie Fenton, but his wit was never careless, like Jay's, or bitchy, like Chickie's.

Perhaps, Lyda thought, I feel closer to Andrew because I've had more of him. There had been a period back during the early years of the Depression when, restless for reasons she never discovered, she'd gotten in the habit of taking long, aimless rambles through the city. Andrew, in his carriage, became her companion.

That had been an odd time in the city. The streets were strangely deserted, as if people, shamed by poverty or unemployment, were afraid to show themselves. All around was the racket of construction. Even in the slump, Manhattan refused to pause in its perpetual headlong rush into the future. Rockefeller Center rose in midtown, along with the Empire State Building and the new Waldorf-Astoria. Lyda could remember sitting in her in-laws' Fifth Avenue apartment, looking all the way across Central Park to the unsheathed iron skeletons of the towers that now lined the park's western perimeter. Luxury buildings being erected in the midst of rampant poverty and joblessness. It seemed somehow cruel, but that was the city's way.

It was about this time that Lyda began to collect images of the city, to buy pictures and photographs by artists of already established fame like Stieglitz and Sloan and Marin and Childe Hassam, and by rising stars like Edward Hopper and young Georgia O'Keeffe; a great many were by unknown artists who would remain nonentities—Cucuel, Greacen, Mosca—but who in a single canvas or drawing had caught a particular aspect of New York to good effect. By 1941, she had accumulated over two hundred works, too many for Fifth Avenue and Double Dune; they were kept on racks at a Manhattan Storage Co. warehouse, where she visited them the way one surreptitiously visits a relative of whom the rest of one's family is ashamed. Often she took Andrew with her, although he showed little enthusiasm for what she showed him; he seemed as "dead of eye" as her other menfolk.

The only person who showed the slightest real interest was her godson Chickie, Andrew's bosom pal—at least until the Fentons had emigrated west.

It was Lyda who had given Charles Christian Fenton IV his nickname. "Why he looks just like a baby chick!" exclaimed Lyda to Conchita Fenton in Doctors Hospital, and "Chickie" it was thereafter.

Chickie was growing up to be a perfect little old maid. He was extremely observant, had a terrific feeling for shapes and colors, and would rather read *House & Garden* than *Superman*. He was a born gossip, full of naughty tales about the great movie stars, which he picked up at the family dinner table. Like everyone else in the world, Lyda relished Hollywood gossip, even if she told herself she was far, far above that sort of thing. He could be mischievous, too. Perhaps it had been Chickie, who'd just gone back to California, who'd coached Jay in that Jew-baiting ditty; Chickie would have picked it up from his father; it was just the sort of thing Chubby and his California Club crowd would find hilarious.

Chickie and Andrew made an odd couple. Perhaps that was why they were such good friends. Chickie constantly gave off little sparks of nervous energy, while Andrew was so easygoing that Lyda sometimes wondered if his thyroid was all right. He was a supremely patient youth, so much so that his serene confidence in his ability to mediate or outlast any difficult situation often seemed arrogant. It troubled both his father and grandfather. Too much tolerance, they chorused, too much willingness to suffer fools, would be a sign of weakness!

Well, thought Lyda, it's a blessing to have one quiet soul out of all these men of action.

On the whole, she was satisfied with the boys. She prided herself that she had taught them to be sensible about money. Howland tended to be high-hat on the subject, and that, Lyda strongly believed, was as self-defeating as avarice. One could hardly pretend the money wasn't there, as did the Rockefellers, who were famous for being miserly with their children.

You didn't have to worship the stuff, to be sure, but in the position the Warringtons were in, you couldn't play possum about the family fortune.

It was hard to strike a balance. For most of the Depression, Lyda had felt, somewhat guiltily, that the family money was like a fragile sheet of ice over a black, torrential river. One could never be sure that it wouldn't give way. She took a chance and enlisted Fletcher's help. He proved surprisingly effective with his grandsons.

"Since you're never going to be short of money," she overheard him telling Andrew and Jay one day, "you'll be inclined not to respect it. Well, don't take it for granted, or talk it down, the way these country-club types around here do, or you'll soon have none! And then you'll be in a proper mess!"

Afterward, he added, to Lyda: "Damn foolishness! The only thing that got people like us where we are is our money, and then we spend half our time teaching our children not to respect it! Not that we want them turning out like the Miles boy. That lad's got to learn that there are some things in life—few, to be sure—that even old John D. can't write a check out for."

Then Fletcher scratched his head, winked at Lyda with his familiar, naughty grin, and added: "Although I'm damned if I can think of what those few things might be."

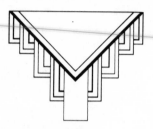

1941

DECEMBER

This particular Sunday morning, Fletcher awoke feeling exhausted. His sleep had been troubled and fitful, beset by nightmares. He hadn't really slept well all week, probably due to his exertions the previous weekend when he'd helped Lyda close Double Dune for the winter. Usually she kept the house open through New Year's, but what with the nation shifting to a state of readiness—the situation in the Pacific seemed critical—it had somehow seemed unpatriotic to use all that fuel to heat an empty house. Howland was off playing his damn fool soldier-boy games in Washington, which left Fletcher and the younger boys to help Lyda cope. As usual, he'd overdone it.

It took him several minutes to get his bearings. The disorientation made him uneasy. This wasn't the first time in recent months he'd had to take a few moments to know where he was.

For a time, he lay back, rememorizing the room, the pictures, the furnishings, getting time and place back in focus. When that was done, he swung his legs over the edge of the bed. He felt old and fragile, and hated himself for it.

By the time he got himself dressed and made his way downstairs, Andy and Jay were almost out the door, bound for Sunday School at St. James's. The day's plans were discussed. Howland and Lyda were weekending in Far Hills with the Comstocks. The boys were indentured for lunch to his daughter Florence and her children, a prospect they viewed with unmixed disgust. Fortunately, Fletcher was spared. He liked Floss and her family well enough, but as everyone knew, Sunday lunch was strictly off-limits for him.

When Andy poked his head in to say "We're off, Gramps" a brief study of the *Times* movie pages was made, and Fletcher proposed that he meet the boys back here at four o'clock. They would all then go over to Times Square to see Spencer Tracy in *Dr. Jekyll and Mr. Hyde*, after which he'd treat them to supper at the Automat. The plan was adopted to universal acclamation.

Listening to the lads clatter off toward the elevator, the old man smiled to himself. They were quite a pair. Sad, he thought, that I can't be around to see how they'll turn out. If I had to guess, he reflected, Andy'll probably be a doctor, a surgeon: he has the bedside manner to go with the brains.

The boy was certainly the brainiest of the lot—perhaps he'd become something like an editor, what with his compulsive book-reading. The thought of one of his grandsons achieving a high intellectual estate cheered Fletcher.

He held out no such grand hopes for Jay, of whom he was, among his grandchildren, secretly fondest. The youngest was salt and spice, the one who leavened the mix. Jay had style and panache, if not much concentration. He measured his days in machine-gun bursts of infatuation and absorption. He was a good-looking little bugger, though; you could already tell he'd have quite a way with the ladies. He seemed in fact to be making an early start in that department; too early his mother said, when she told Fletcher about the latest summons to Buckley. It seemed that at a recent fifth-grade tea dance in the school gym Jay had somehow induced several girls from Miss Hewitt's classes to lower their bloomers for a "heinie-judging" contest.

He scanned the papers, thumping his breastbone lightly as he read. His chest felt slightly congested; he should have shut the damn window. It had turned quite cold overnight. Well, tonight he would.

The *Times* reported that the Japanese would be calling on Secretary of State Hull this morning in Washington. Things still looked bad in the Pacific, according to Tommy Creedmore, who'd been in earlier in the week to talk about financing some more new airplanes. The way these airlines went through planes was really something! Still, raising finance for Global certainly helped pay the bills at Hanover Place.

Fletcher swung his legs over the edge of the bed and stood unsteadily. God, it was awful to grow old!

As he made his way slowly toward the bathroom, his mind went back to Japan. Untrustworthy little yellow bastards: you never knew what they were thinking. Of course, The Firm had made good money back in '05 when Kuhn Loeb had floated $75 million of Japanese war bonds to help the Mikado pay for his war against the Russians. Funny how life worked, wasn't it? If things went the way people like Creedmore foresaw, and Hirohito lined up with Hitler, they might soon be floating Russian bonds to pay for war against the Japanese.

"Might"? Hell: "Would." War was all but certain. A chilling thought struck Fletcher. In '44, his grandsons would be eighteen, draft age. Of course the war might not go on that long, but you never could tell. He made a mental note to write to Stimson on Monday about the boys. The Secretary of War owed Fletcher a favor for the times he'd gotten Winthrop, Stimson named as counsel on bond issues. Better safe than sorry.

He felt better after a few minutes on his feet, and better still after a bath and a shave. When he came out of his dressing room, breakfast was on the table near the window. He went to the radio, listened as always to William L. Shirer from Berlin, and went downstairs. Precisely at noon, as on every Sunday morning when he was in the city, rain or shine, he got into the elevator. Louis was waiting with the car. They would drive to Brooklyn, where Fletcher would visit his wife's grave in Greenwood Cemetery, and they then would go on to Tappen's, on Sheepshead Bay, where he and Louis, who had been his driver and factotum for twenty-five years, would share a shore dinner.

The day was mild for December, under broken clouds, when they arrived at the cemetery. Fletcher left Louis at the gate and climbed up toward the Temple family plot, which was located on a slight rise. It was one of Fletcher's favorite spots; with a decent pair of field glasses, you could look right over to Wall Street on a good day, and, if you squinted just so, pick out the gargoyle on the gable of Hanover Place. As he climbed, his breath grew short. For some reason, the slope seemed like Everest today, and the dark granite obelisk in whose shadow six generations of his late wife's family were buried looked a mile off. The small bouquet Louis had picked up the evening before at Constance Spry's seemed to weigh a ton. He was forced to pause several times, leaning on his stick while he got his breath. Under his heavy chesterfield he felt feverish, and he tipped back his homburg to let the cool midday air play on his forehead.

When he reached the top, he was drained. He sat down heavily on the low bench in front of the monument and gulped for breath.

After a while, he felt his pulse steady. He looked around him. It was easy to understand why the Temples had chosen this spot. The knoll was only thirty feet above sea level, but from where he sat, Fletcher could take in the whole sweep of Upper New York Bay: Governors Island, Bedloes Island surmounted by the Statue of Liberty, the grove of skyscrapers at the tip of Manhattan, and further north, to his right, the Empire

State Building glistening in the sunlight, and the edge of midtown. To the south and west lay Staten Island and the smoke-wreathed bays and piers of the Jersey waterfront.

He was savoring the view when the first wave of pain rose up through his midsection and knocked him from the bench. Fighting for breath, against the pain, he struggled to his knees and got a grip on the bench. Don't quit, he told himself, gasping, don't let that old son of a bitch with the sickle get you!

He struggled to get up, but the waves of pain kept knocking him down, and then he realized that he was making no progress, that for all his energy and stoutness of heart he was being swept away. The thought filled him with chagrin, but only briefly, because another wave came crashing in, and with a terrible sigh of resignation Fletcher Warrington fell heavily to the earth and was gathered to his ancestors.

It was just after one o'clock. Six thousand miles to the west, in a dull Pacific dawn, the first explosive gales of the Divine Wind were within an hour of lashing Pearl Harbor. Four thousand miles to the east, in a cleared, muddy place not far from the Polish city of Lodz, where a complex of low-lying buildings had been constructed by forced labor, the winter evening was trembling with the noise of heavy trucks being backed into position, and the shouts of German officers supervising the attachment of the trucks' exhaust pipes to hoses leading to a cluster of low, gloomy buildings set apart from the rest. The place was called Chelmno and it was a facility representing a new departure in industrial engineering. It had been designed and constructed specifically for the efficient extermination of human life.

Four days after his death, Fletcher was tendered a funeral service at Trinity Church with full commercial honors. All the princes and potentates of Wall Street were in attendance.

Lyda was amazed how many of them were already in uniform. Many, like Lewie Comstock in his Navy dress blues, looked like children at a masquerade, big military blossoms of khaki and navy blue threaded with gold. This is the fun part, Lyda thought, the dressing-up part, with the try-ons at Sulka and Weatherill and Saks and Brooks Brothers, the articles in *Life* on "Wall Street Goes to War." The other part, the serious work, was out there somewhere beyond the ocean, but the war was still too new and distant to be serious, even though MacArthur was encircling the Philippines, Hong Kong had fallen and Singapore and Malaya soon must, and the British had lost the *Repulse* and *Prince of Wales* to Japanese dive bombers.

As the family was shown into the front pews by the ushers, Lyda patted Morris Miles's shoulder gravely, then smiled, less in acknowledgment of his careful words of condolence than at his stylish appearance; his morning coat and striped trousers were impeccably cut—it was something of a joke around The Firm how vain and careful Morris had gotten about his grooming—but she couldn't help thinking that he looked more like a floorwalker at Saks than a man whose judgment was sought by great men of industry and finance.

Watching Morris hand the Schiffs into a pew, Lyda marveled at what a master stroke of Howland's it had been to invite him to be a pallbearer.

Two days after Fletcher died, Morris had come to Howland to ask for an indefinite leave of absence. He had been asked to go to Washington to oversee procurement for the Department of the Navy. He apologized for his timing, but he was being pressed for an answer by the Secretary. It was his only chance to do something for the war effort, he told Howland, even if it was only a civilian job. Combat duty was out of the question for out-of-shape forty-three-year-old men with incipient asthma.

The violence—there was no other word for it—of Howland's reaction took him aback. Morris put it down to grief, but it was in fact aggravated impatience. Howland was out of sorts to begin with. His father's unexpected death had severely crimped his plans to wangle a top staff job in Washington. He was caught between his sense of duty to Hanover Place and an almost erotic compulsion to get close to the war.

"Out of the question!" he exploded while Morris was still halfway through his explanation. "Absolutely out of the question! Morris, your place is here!"

Damn you, he thought. The day before, Howland had heard of a choice job—senior liaison between H. H. "Hap" Arnold, the new Commanding General of the U.S. Army Air Corps, and the brand-new Office of Strategic Services, the intelligence outfit that Bill Donovan, an old Wall Street chum, was setting up. It was his—if he could sway.

The prospect was thrilling: a lot of overseas duty; direct access to General Marshall and the Joint Chiefs of Staff; top-level security clearance; guaranteed advancement in grade—if the war went on as long as it appeared it would, he should come out of it with at least one, maybe two stars on his shoulder. He and Bunny Ducretil from Chelsea Trust—who had latched onto a nice job with General Marshall—had rented a little house on P Street in Georgetown. Now this!

"Look, Morris," he said reasonably, "a lot of people think the Street's going to be very busy financing the war. Remember the Liberty Loans back in the last show? Well, multiply that by a hundred, maybe a thousand, and you can see the job that's going to have to be done. We want to be certain The Firm does its bit—and gets its share—which means we're going to need our best manpower right here."

The other man seemed unconvinced. "Howland," Morris said, "it's important to me to do something. The Firm's been good to me, God knows, but so has this country. Now I have a way to pay that back, even if all I can do is give orders to a regiment of accountants. That's what people like me do in a war. People like you: you'll be on the front line; you'll come away with medals, photographs with the President."

As Morris spoke, his confidence ebbed. He felt ill at ease with this kind of conversation. He thought he sounded ineffectual. "I just want to do what I can," he finished lamely. "Besides, Charlie's 4-F, too, so he'll be here to keep an eye on things."

Howland listened calmly. It had occurred to him as Morris spoke that if push came to shove, he could always have a word with Jim Forrestal. Forrestal would understand. For the moment, however, he decided to try the velvet-glove treatment.

"Morris," he said calmly, "you and I are old friends. And, as friends do, we've done a lot for each other and we complement each other. I think it's safe to say that between us we make up the white-hot core of what The Firm's all about—especially now that Father's gone."

He let that sink in.

"In a way," he continued, "The Firm's like one of Tommy Creedmore's DC-3s. Tough as nails. Capable of flying on just one engine, but not on none. And none is what it'll be if both you and I take off—and we wouldn't want that, would we?"

Morris shook his head glumly.

"Look, Morris," Howland said with a comradely grin that he hoped wouldn't seem condescending, "normally I'd stay on board but, well, frankly, this job I've been handed by Hap Arnold is, if you'll forgive me, of utmost, even critical importance to the war effort. It requires a certain set of qualifications, not to mention experience in official combat. On the other hand, while I'm sure the job Navy's trolling under your nose counts, too, I'm also sure that it could be adequately handled by a half-dozen men from the Street that you and I know. Not that I think for a minute any of them could do half the job you could, but then again, none of them have a tenth of the critical importance to their firms that you have to ours."

As he spoke, he watched the other man carefully. I'm halfway there, he thought. Then he had his final inspiration. "Besides," he said, "Father was counting on you, Morris, I think that ought to mean something. You'd become sort of a second son to him. You know, of course, he specifically named you to be a pallbearer at his funeral?"

This was untrue. Fletcher's will was a model of exactitude and specificity, a finely-crafted document that had taken many hours for a team of top Auchincloss, Wharton trusts-and-estates lawyers to prepare. It embodied a considerable sensitivity on the part of the testator to the character and expectations of his heirs, and great ingenuity on the part of his attorneys with respect to the nuances of the latest revision of the Internal Revenue Code. A letter to his executors gave very specific instructions respecting any burial and memorial services, their liturgical content and manning. The omissions, Howland saw at once, were calculated. Fletcher had grasped that in death one could be insulting in a way that was impractical in life.

Morris Miles was not on the list. This was one case, however, thought Howland, looking at Morris, where not only did the end justify the means, but he knew his father would have felt the same way.

Morris seemed stunned at Howland's statement. No, he had no idea. Why, he was honored.

"Well, he did," said Howland, pressing his advantage. "And you should see who he left out!"

As Howland told Lyda over martinis that evening, he was sure Auchincloss, Wharton would see the light. If they didn't, there were plenty of lawyers around who'd jump at getting Hanover Place's legal business.

"Hell," he said, "if Father had known this was going to come up, you can be damn sure he *would* have put Morris on the list!"

Indeed, Fritz Stenton, who had succeeded his father as managing partner of Auchincloss, Wharton, readily agreed with Howland that a tiny posthumous white lie was an insignificant price to pay for peace and continuity at Hanover Place.

Lyda supposed she agreed. Still, she couldn't escape a thought that came to her while Howland was proudly telling his story. It was everyone's war, true, but it was *Howland's* firm.

1942

NOVEMBER

Lyda waited until Jay finished showing his father his maps and models—he was doing a school project on Rommel's African campaign—and then shooed him off to bed. She let Howland mix a second cocktail for himself, and then she said in a low voice: "I have some interesting news for you. It seems we're going to have another baby."

Howland's eyebrows lifted briefly in surprise, then his face broke out in a big grin, and he bounded across the room to hug her. "That is just wonderful!" he exclaimed. He stood back and appraised his wife. "I'll be damned if you show an inch! When?"

"Ralph thinks sometime in May. I'm afraid I may have gotten a weensy bit careless when you were here over Labor Day." She felt hugely relieved. All her apprehensions and guilt were consumed by the glow of his satisfactions. He passed his right arm in front of himself and vigorously patted his left shoulder.

"Well, damn!" he exulted. "Who'd've thought I had it in me?" He turned sheepish. "Us, I mean. Two old farts like us!" He screwed up his face, looking for an instant like a serious little boy. "There won't be any problem? I mean, at your age . . ."

"None at all, if you believe Ralph. He says I'm fit as a debutante."

"I think it's fantastic, darling!" he said and hugged her again. "You can use the company, I'm sure, what with me in Washington and the brood away at school. I don't want to alarm you, but it looks as if this whole thing's going to take longer than any of us thought it would. Anyway, your news certainly calls for champagne. Can you remember whether there's any of that Veuve Clicquot of Father's left?"

"Two or three bottles, I think."

"Well, let's drink one now, and keep the others for the duration."

He pivoted smartly, made for the doorway, then stopped to pull an envelope out of his jacket pocket. "This'll give you a chuckle," he said, tossing it to her. "Lewie Comstock came through D.C. on his way to London. He's going to be liaising for Admiral King with the Brits. Anyway, he left this souvenir of the Fentons' high life in Coronado."

Howland vanished down the hall. The envelope contained an eight-by-ten glossy photograph in a cardboard souvenir frame. It showed a line of people high-kicking in a nightclub somewhere. One was a three-stripe admiral; on his arm, kicking highest of all, was Mrs. Charles Christian Fenton III. It was obvious she was not wearing underpants.

My God, thought Lyda. Thank heavens Chickie's away from all that! He and Andrew had gone off to St. Paul's in September. Twelve seemed awfully young, but when they'd talked it over with the Fentons, the Germans had recently landed saboteurs not five hundred yards from Double Dune. People were expecting the Luftwaffe to appear over Manhattan and the Japanese over Santa Monica, so the New Hampshire wilds seemed safe. Besides, the boys were loving it, and since Howland seemed able to call on an inexhaustible supply of ration points and train tickets, Andrew and Chickie were assured of getting to New York for their Thanksgiving and Christmas vacations.

She heard the phone ring twice, then stop, and guessed Howland had picked it up in the kitchen. When he returned to the library a few minutes later, his face was thoughtful.

"That was Bunny calling from the Pentagon. Good news and bad news, I'm afraid. It looks as if the Japs have given up on Guadalcanal; they broke off the engagement this morning and we've broken out from Henderson Field."

Then his face darkened, he shook his head, and added softly: "The *Preston* was sunk. Corky Runnels was her exec. He's listed as . . ."

"Oh no," said Lyda. "Poor Mary."

Reflexively, as she had already done a half-dozen times in the last year, she got out of her chair and started for the coat closet.

"I'll go," said Howland. "I'm sure Charlie's there already."

Poor, poor Corky, thought Lyda. She sank back down. She had a picture in her mind of him in a silly paper hat at El Morocco. When was that? 1937? 1938? Whenever it was, it was a million years ago!

"You don't mind if we give the champagne a pass, do you?" he asked. "Under the circumstances . . ."

"Don't be silly. I'll wait up for you."

It was after midnight when he returned. Lyda had been drowsing in her chair when she heard the elevator and then the sound of Howland putting his coat away. She shook her head and picked up the book she'd been reading from where it had fallen. It was a new novel, *The Song of Bernadette*, and it was an awful bore. What could have gotten into the woman at Brentano's to have recommended it? She was usually so reliable.

She looked up when he came into the room. "How was it?" she asked.

"All right. Charlie got there ahead of the telegram, thank God. Mary's okay. Bess and Charlie are taking her up to Connecticut tomorrow. There'll be a memorial service sometime next week at St. James's. I probably won't be able to get back up, but maybe you'll feel up to it."

"I'm fine. I'll be there."

He went across the room, poured himself a brandy, and drank it quickly. "Bed?" he asked. "I don't suppose . . . ?"

"You've just made it under the wire. Let's go."

After they made love, they lay on top of the bed, talking. Lyda had just lit her second cigarette when Howland said, suddenly, "Oh my God, there was something else I meant to tell you!"

"Not more bad news, I hope?"

"Well, yes, I'm afraid. Do you remember that fellow named Laszlo, Eric Laszlo? The one whom Piers Lucas sent to see us last summer?"

Lyda drew on her cigarette, and asked: "That little Swiss man, right? With the funny hair?"

"That's the one. I must say when Piers told us to take care of him, I thought he was just another Swiss banker looking to scavenge some business."

"You mean he wasn't?"

"Absolutely not! The fellow was risking his life helping Jews get out of Germany. Anyway, I was talking to one of Bill Donovan's people last week and it seems Brother Laszlo overstayed his welcome *auf Deutschland*."

"I'm not sure I follow you."

"The Gestapo got him. Picked him up near Dusseldorf and apparently his Swiss passport didn't do the trick. Berne's beating the bushes—official protests to the Wilhelmstrasse, that sort of thing—but so far, nothing."

Lyda didn't answer. Howland turned on his side to look at her. Her eyes were wet. Damn, he thought. I should have thought before I opened my trap, you know how pregnant women are.

The August day three months earlier had been a scorcher. The Lexington Avenue subway had broken down and Lyda had been forced to walk the fifty blocks home from the refugee office where she worked the afternoon shift two days a week. The streets were jammed, mostly with men and women in uniform. There were days when it seemed to Lyda that the entire population of the city was in the armed services, although America had been at war barely nine months.

When she got home, it was close to seven. The maid told her that a Mr. Laszlo had called; he would be there at eight sharp. Laszlo was a young Swiss banker to whom Piers Lucas had given a warm letter of introduction to Howland, who was coming up from Washington so he and Lyda could take the visitor out for dinner. Howland's train was due in at Pennsylvania Station at seven thirty.

Then the maid said: "Oh, and ma'am, Colonel Warrington just called. He has to stay in Washington. Some kind of emergency, he said. He asks would you take care of Mr. Laszlo."

The young man arrived on the dot of eight. When Lyda came into the drawing room, he snapped upright and she could swear she heard his heels click. He was hardly prepossessing physically and yet there was something attractive about him. He looked to be in his early thirties. He was on the small side, an inch or two shorter than she and delicately built, but the hand that took hers was like steel. He had curious foxy features, with quizzical gray eyes; he was going bald, although odd little wisps of crinkly blond hair sprouted above his ears.

"Mr. Laszlo."

"Madame Warrington."

His voice was soft; Lyda thought she detected a trace of Britishness that marked the speech of a certain kind of educated, upper-class Continental.

"I'm afraid Colonel Warrington's been detained in Washington," she said. "You'll have to make do with me."

She took him to "21" and afterward he dropped her home. He was good company and an interesting young man. He was candid about what he did.

"Banking bores me," he told her, "but it's a very useful way to help people." He spoke in a practiced low voice. One of Manhattan's most accomplished eavesdroppers and gossips chanced to be at the next table; it amused Lyda to see him straining vainly to catch the drift of Laszlo's conversation. By the next noon, it would be all over town that Lyda Warrington had a new admirer.

As Laszlo talked, Lyda found herself speculating idly about what this young man would be like as a lover. Not that the slightest possibility of *doing* anything crossed her mind. She didn't consider herself to be highly sexed and therefore she didn't consider herself particularly sexy. Men flirted with her, but they hardly ever made passes. There had been that one time at Saratoga when Johnny Gambodge, who was by then pretty far gone, had taken her hand and placed it under the table on what proved to be a naked and—amazing, considering his condition—obviously erect penis, which instantaneously detumesced when Lyda gave it a painful pinch.

She was certain Howland had been faithful, too. He'd probably had more opportunities. Two summers back, when Ginny Ducretil was having a hard time with Bunny, she'd practically flung herself at Howland at a Meadow Club dance. Of course, everyone talked about how much trouble men could get up to in Washington these days, but if she got started worrying about that, she'd never stop.

There was no doubt that Eric Laszlo was more interesting than most of the men one ran into these days. By the time coffee came, she had most of his biography: scion of a famous Zurich banking family, educated at Le Rosey, the University of Basel, followed by two years at Oxford, then a year in Spain fighting on the Republican side. Then back to Zurich, and in 1941 to Berlin to open a liaison office which, he made clear, was both a banking office and the first stop on an underground railway to get Jews out of Germany. The way he described his activities reminded Lyda of herself as a young woman. There was a purity of involvement, an intensity and recklessness of concern that recalled her own passions, when a single injustice seemed to cancel out mankind's entire virtue. His voice was calm, his words measured, but she could sense a real ferocity of feeling at work. It seemed devoid of personal agenda, without self-interest, or calculation, or political intent. She understood how he felt, because she had once felt that way herself, and for the first time in years she found herself wondering whether she'd done the right thing with her life.

She enjoyed his company. When he dropped her off at Fifth Avenue, she was therefore not entirely surprised to hear herself say that if he had nothing in particular to do the next day, he might enjoy seeing Long Island. She had to drive down to Double Dune to pick up some things the boys, who were in Maine at camp, needed for the fall, and she would be very glad to have company.

That, he said, sounded like a capital idea.

On the way down, he told her more about Germany. The Nazi ugliness she had seen there back in '36 was now multiplied to an exponential degree of horror. There had been a meeting in a Berlin suburb earlier in the year, he told her, at which a decision had been taken to eliminate every single last Jew in Europe and the Soviet Union.

"And on earth, if they can," he said.

With characteristic efficiency, he told her, the Nazis were building factories for killing. The most advanced yet was under construction at Birkenau, near the concentration camp at the Polish town of Oswiecim —in German, Auschwitz.

"I have seen the engineering drawings," he told Lyda. "It is a blueprint for Hell. Worse than Dachau."

"Can't something be done?"

"Nothing, I fear. Washington doesn't believe it is actually happening. Even if they did, the only solution now is to bomb the place, and until the Luftwaffe is cleared from the skies, that can't happen."

"And the Jews themselves? Can they do anything?"

"I fear not. There aren't enough of us. There never are."

They were passing the new airport on Flushing Bay. A couple of big Boeing flying boats were bobbing easily at anchor. In a week's time, Laszlo told her, he would be emplaning in one of those for Lisbon. Then through Spain and across Vichy and occupied France into Germany, shielded by his Swiss passport.

"I was in Dachau last month," he told her. "On Red Cross papers. It was a show. All prettied up for the visitors but they couldn't hide the smell of death. What the Nazis are doing is one of the worst things ever. As bad, I think, as your slavery, maybe worse."

In East Hampton, he helped her load the station wagon. They lunched at the local greasy spoon and then took a long walk along the beach. Here and there the line of the dunes was broken by concrete gun emplacements. In Laszlo's opinion, they'd never be used.

When it came time to go, with three hours on the road ahead of them, the day was fading.

"One last look at the ocean, may I?" he asked.

They went onto the veranda and stood side by side, like two people at the rail of an ocean liner watching a shoreline full of fond memories disappear.

Then he turned and said "Lyda" in a choked voice.

Before she knew what she was doing, she had bent to him, was kissing him, pulling him against her, wanting to smother him. Against her leg she could feel his erection. It seemed enormous. She felt suddenly feverish.

Hopping awkwardly on one leg, she managed to get one leg out of her panty-girdle. While she did, she watched him undo his own trousers and shove them down. She had a very limited experience of men's organs, but his seemed enormous. The sight of it made her still more excited.

There was nothing but the hard, splintery wood of the porch—the matting had all been taken up and stored—to lie on, so she went quickly to the rail, her useless undergarment dragging foolishly from her ankle. She reached back and pulled her slip and skirt up and forward over her back. She grasped the rail with both hands, parted her feet in a wide stance, knees slightly bent, and presented herself like a mare.

She felt him try to push into her. She could tell she was tight and dry in spite of her excitement.

She started to say something when she felt him drop to his knees behind her and she felt him kissing and licking her. No man had ever done this to her. Seconds later, he rose and entered her, and after that, she was aware only of the concentration of sensation, a narrowing focus of exquisite, almost painful pleasure measured by his long interminable slidings, in, drawing the breath out of her, then out, making her suck in air as if by that she could prevent him from leaving a hole in the center of her. She could faintly hear him grunting, and she became aware of a heightened urgency and rhythm to his thrusts, but by then she was centering tighter and tighter on a single point of excitement, on and on and on and on until at last, finally, when there could be no possible degree of further compression, with a final piercing drive, he lanced the tight little ball of absolute excitation into which she was now gathered and it burst, and Lyda's knees went weak and she let herself melt in the sweet, overpowering warmth that flooded her from within.

Two weeks later, she missed her period, and again in October, and again in early November, and knew soon after, that at forty-six and forty-two respectively, Howland and she were about to become parents for the fifth time.

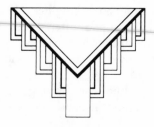

1944

JUNE

"ut do you *both* have to go!"

Lyda spoke so sharply that diners at nearby tables turned around. Lex and Dee looked at each other, shrugged, and then turned to their father.

"Why *now*?" she demanded. "The war *has* to be over soon!"

That morning, in a ceremony whose brevity was dictated by the exigencies of wartime, the twins had graduated from Exeter. Afterward, the family had motored down to Boston, for a celebratory lunch at the Ritz-Carlton. The baby wasn't with them, of course; at fifteen months, little Miranda was much too small to travel.

Lyda turned on her husband. "You set me up for this!" she said angrily.

All she could think of were the names carved on the marble memorial tablets in the Academy Building. Young men whose precious lives had been given in a dozen wars.

She should have prepared herself for the worst. She had taken too much for granted. Her war had gone too smoothly so far.

"I repeat," she said, "why *both* of you?"

She looked at each of them in turn. They are such babies still, she thought. You Warringtons and your wars! she thought fiercely. For an instant, it seemed to her that familiar ghosts were hovering about the table, Fletcher in his homburg, old Erasmus in his stovepipe hat, other figures dimmer and less recognizable. She blinked and they flashed away.

"Now, for the third time: why *both* of you?"

She tried to keep any hint of pleading out of her voice. Her question was rhetorical, she knew; the answer was in their cells.

"Aw, c'mon, Ma." It was Dee; he looked bigger and fairer than ever. He reached over and covered her hand with his. It looked terribly adult, a grown man's hand.

"You know we have to. Everyone else has. They're short of pilots, and don't forget, we've both got our licenses."

It was true, goddamn it! she thought. Howland had insisted. He'd taught them himself. They'd soloed at fifteen. Still, they were only eighteen! Couldn't someone else go?

She looked at the tablecloth, then at Howland, then back at the table-cloth. It's hopeless asking *you*, she thought. She could feel, literally *feel*, the warmth of his pride in his sons. She would have hated him if she could, but that would be pointless and she had been born unable to waste herself on pointless causes; there was no space for St. Jude on her private calendar of saints.

"Look, Ma," said Lex. He was the twinklier and more glib of the two. Dee usually delivered the set speeches when they were going two-on-one on her in search of some cherished objective; it was left to Lex to handle the *ad hoc* rebuttal. "The way we've got it figured, we'd probably have to go anyway."

"But you're only eighteen."

"Eighteen and almost a half," said Jay, earning himself a rebukeful glare from his mother.

How much more like his father is Lex, thought Lyda. Dee's more like his grandfather. One a bulldog, the other a hawk.

"So they'd snap us up at nineteen, anyway," Lex was saying.

Not if your father made one or two telephone calls, thought Lyda, but she knew two things as the thought rested with her: Howland would never do it—and she knew she wouldn't want him to.

"The way we've worked it out," Dee was saying, "we lengthen the odds to practically zero. As Gramps would say: 'M'dear, consider yourself hedged.' Lexy goes to Pensacola and Navy Air, so he'll probably end up in the Pacific. Dad's got me fixed up at Wright-Patterson. I want to fly P-47s, Thunderbolts; remember we used to go watch them at Westhampton? Uncle Tom says they're the hottest thing going, and they're used strictly in the European theater."

"Yeah," added Lex, "besides: Pythagoras says, just because twins are born under the same star doesn't mean they have the same destiny."

Lyda laughed. "And where, may I ask, did you learn that?"

"From Mr. Phillips in Greek Two. Anyway, Ma, the sooner we get this over, the sooner Dee and me can get back to Yale. We can't play football anyway, until this is over. Until the war ends, Gramps up there won't get to see us play in the Bowl."

"Dee and *I*," said Lyda. She looked at Howland. "Imagine! Eight hundred dollars a year for tuition and board, and he stills says 'Dee and me!' "

What's the use, she thought. Lion cubs are born to roam and play rough. So go, my children, she thought, go. Be off with you into that wild blue yonder you seem born to revel in. Go, go—and please, please come back. She wanted to lift her glass and make a spirited toast to her warriors, but she couldn't.

She glared at Howland. "I'm holding you accountable! I don't want these two anywhere near each other in this war, do you understand? I'm not going to be like that poor woman who lost all five sons on one ship! Now, if you'll excuse me, I'm going to the loo to tear my hair out!"

She made her way awkwardly among the tables toward the ladies' room, her eyes brimming.

It took a few weeks, but Lyda finally managed to subdue her apprehensions. She made herself visit the twins' room every day. It was a regular museum of military aviation. From the ceiling dangled the black Bakelite spotter models that Tommy Creedmore had procured for them: miniature Zekes and Bettys, ME-109s and FW-190s, Heinkels and Dorniers and Stirlings and Hurricanes; plump little Wildcats and burly Hellcats and exotic Corsairs like the one Lex was flying; Air Cobras, Black Widows, and Thunderbolts, and one of the new Mustangs that Howland had borrowed at Floyd Bennett and taken her joyriding in last month. The bookshelves contained dog-eared volumes of *Jane's All the World's Aircraft* dating back to 1935. On top of the bookcase were mock control panels; Dee had made one at camp, the other had been gotten for Wheaties boxtops. Other boys make pen holders in "shop," thought Lyda, but not mine. The walls were covered with posters, aircraft charts, and photographs of aces, half of them dead, like Colin Kelly, who'd flown down the funnel of a Japanese cruiser the very day of Fletcher's memorial service; here were Douglas Bader and "Sailor" Malan, the RAF aces, and the respective ace-idols of Dee and Lex, Francis Gabreski of the Army Air Force and Butch O'Hare of the Navy.

It was when she thought of them aloft that her heart fluttered. She could remember the day the twins soloed for the first time. Bright and sunny, but enough of a fresh wind coming in off the ocean, the wind sock straight in the breeze, pointing north, a crosswind, enough to vex a mother's heart, especially with the East Hampton strip looking the size of a postcard. Lex had come in first: the Cub's wings had waggled, the nose had for an instant drifted, then all was settled and he was safely down, and an hour later so was Dee and her sons had made their rite of passage and were birdmen now, just like their father.

They came home on leave for Thanksgiving, 1944; Andy and Chickie came down from St. Paul's, and the fact that the whole family could still be together gave her courage.

Lex and Dee were full of themselves, as bright and brassy as the wings on their blouses. They joshed each other unmercifully about their respective services; it was obvious, she thought—with a fearful inner shudder of apprehension—that they were raring to get up and into combat. Flying had come so easy to them that it was hard to be serious about war.

Well, if they were lucky, they'd make it through. People were starting to talk about the war as if it were over. Paris had been retaken and the Russian counteroffensive had penetrated into central Europe. In the Pacific, the new B-29 bombers had made a daytime raid on Tokyo, the first since Jimmy Dolittle's hit-and-run raid back in 1942.

Even Howland seemed ready for peacetime. Part of it was his concern for his sons. Part of it was that the thrill was ebbing. He'd had a "good war," but now he saw new challenges to be met and opportunities to be seized. Earlier in the year, he had moved out of his original job to help organize a Strategic Bombing Survey, many of whose members were drawn from the cream of corporate America. But he talked of the work less in terms of warfare than business. He intended to turn his new connections to account for The Firm as soon as this was over, he told Lyda.

Hanover Place was purring along smoothly under Morris's and Charlie Runnels's stewardship. Peace, when it came, must surely prove the bonanza of all time. Morris foresaw the unleashing of huge pent-up demand. Of course, said Howland, everyone had thought the same thing back in 1918, and look what had happened! It took the Street nearly four years to get moving again.

It was a wonderful five days they had together. She wangled tickets to *Oklahoma!;* Jack Kriendler at "21" got them some steaks; they did the town. By the last day of their leave, the war had become a remote abstraction of newspaper headlines and radio broadcasts. Then, the last evening, there were their flight bags in the foyer, and them in their service caps and overcoats, and after all too hasty a farewell embrace, they were gone. The next morning, when Lyda awoke to find the apartment quiet, all her momentarily suppressed forebodings returned.

1945

MAY

Outside the honking and shout-
ing let up for a moment. Lyda put down her pen, blew out a long, tired
breath and stretched her hands above her head. For the first time in her
life, she felt like an old woman.

The windows were thrown open to the spring evening, but the air in
the room was stale from all the cigarettes she'd smoked. That morning,
Jay, who now spoke a language consisting mainly of quotations from
magazine advertisements and radio commercials, had rebuked her for not
taking care of her "T-Zone." She had a splitting headache, which surprised
her since she would have thought herself completely numb to pain by
now. A sound broke her self-absorption. She got up and went to the
hallway door. Had she heard Miranda crying? There was only silence.
Must have been her nerves.

She recrossed the room and went to the window. The usually black
bowl of night was pale violet and blue; every light in the city must be
lit, she thought. Below, Fifth Avenue and the side streets were coalesced
into a crush of traffic and people. Joyful noises filtered up.

She had never felt so alone. She should have made Howland stay, but
in wartime you carried on, didn't you?

War. The "old lie." She couldn't get the phrase out of her head. Piers
Lucas had quoted it in his letter about Lex, lines from Wilfred Owen, a

153

poet who had died in the First World War: ". . . One should not tell with such high zest/To children ardent for some desperate glory/The old lie: Dulce et decorum est/Pro patria mori." How sweet and proper it is to die for one's country.

She returned to the desk and picked up the next letter. She had been writing since eight in the morning and now the stack was down to an inch or so, although tomorrow's post would surely bring more.

She hardly read the letters by now; the phrases had become achingly familiar, so she merely noted the name and address of the writer, before starting in on her reply. In a way she felt as sorry for these people as for herself: poor things, having to write all over again what they had already written once to her, as well as God knows how many times to others. Trying to find inventive words to express sorrows that war had made trite even for those original enough to find a second way of saying what she felt.

Perhaps she should have taken Howland's advice and ordered up engraved cards of appreciation from Tiffany's this time, but that just wasn't her style—to mail out her feelings in the impersonal way Saks mailed out notices of a lingerie sale. She returned to her work, now and then setting aside a note or letter that struck her as worth saving. Outside, the roars and shouts and honkings of the great city intoxicated with the jubilation of V-E Day continued, promising to last right through the night. She only hoped she could.

The first angel of death to come calling had arrived in the vestibule in February. He was a full Navy captain, no less, resplendent and dignified in dress blue; the light from the chandelier danced in the gleaming braid of the four gold stripes on his sleeve and the glistening oak leaves on the shiny black brim of the cap tucked under his arm.

The maid led him into the drawing room. He came to attention before Lyda, coughed nervously, then held out his hopeless telegram. "The Secretary of the Navy regrets . . ."

Lyda sighed and placed it carefully on the glass table, wanting to find the right thing to say, thinking, in the odd way one so often did on sad occasions, more of the messenger than the message. The officer took two letters from his black leather briefcase and held them out. "From the Secretary, ma'am, and from the President."

She took them and thanked the captain again for his courtesy. When he was gone, she looked at them curiously. She needed Howland, but he was somewhere over the Atlantic, she knew.

She put the letters and telegram aside. Later, when she read them, she learned that Lex had been flying cover for a dive-bombing attack on Iwo Jima. One of the Avengers had gone into the Philippine Sea on the way back to the *Essex*. Lex had sent his wingman on home and stayed at the scene. Stayed too long, according to one of the Avenger crewmen plucked from the water by the Naval rescue PBY the *Essex* sent to recover its stray children. Before the PBY could get there, the Corsair had shot down one and drove off two marauding Zeros looking for stragglers and cripples, but then his fuel and his luck had evidently run out. The Corsair had tried to ditch, but caught a wingtip coming in and had cartwheeled below the surface and never been seen again. According to the Secretary's letter, Lieutenant (JG) Alexander Fletcher Warrington was being recommended for a posthumous Navy Cross.

A second angel came just five weeks later, not ten days after Lex's memorial service. This fell messenger wore khaki and the wings of the Army Air Force. On his shoulder shone the bright single star of a new brigadier general and his chest bloomed with gaudy service ribbons. He brought no letter from President Roosevelt, who was himself dead by then, nor was he obliged to stand and shift on the doorstep while the maid went for her mistress. He let himself in with his own key and found Lyda in their daughter's bedroom, where she was reading a book to Miranda.

"What are you doing here?" exclaimed Lyda. "I thought you were on your way to . . ."

Then she saw his expression. She took a deep breath, to hold herself together, and put down the book. She rose carefully, as if any sudden exertion might cause her to shatter like crystal, took the child by the hand, and went to the hall where she called the governess to come and take the little girl to the park.

She stood in the hall until the elevator doors closed. Then she went into the library.

Howland was looking up at the family portrait Jocelyn Barrow had painted during the summer of '41. Lyda had brought it into town from Double Dune. She had planned to take it back when they reopened the house this June.

"Please, don't say it," Lyda said. "Please, don't."

She went to the window and pushed it open. Spring was late this year; the trees in the park were still mostly bare. What had become of spring? When she'd first come to the city, spring was always well in hand by mid-March. She filled her lungs with cool air for courage, pulled the window shut, and turned back to Howland.

"Dee?" she breathed. Her voice was tiny and frightened, a mouse's whisper.

All he could do was nod. She could see he was having trouble holding himself together.

"Where?" she asked. "How?"

"Hannover. A routine strafing run on a railyard. There wasn't any flak.

It must have been a lucky hit from a machine gun. His engine started to smoke and he went straight into the ground. I can't believe it. Seven kills and he gets it from ground fire!"

He sat down heavily. The look on his face was so forlorn it was terrifying. He suddenly looked his age. What time had been unable to do, sorrow had: his features looked thicker, coarser. He might have been drinking.

Lyda wanted to go off by herself, and let herself go, but her husband needed her worse than she did, so she took a deep breath and pulled herself together. Reflexively, she went to the bar and made him a cocktail. He took it without saying anything. For a long time he just sat there, looking into space, seeing something she didn't, now and then taking a sip.

At length, he said, in a vague kind of way: "All Father and I ever wanted was to be able to see them in the Bowl, you know."

She said nothing.

"That's all we wanted. Was it so much to ask?" He shook his head in puzzlement. For all the wear and tear of grief, he was still a very good-looking man. "Father and I were there when it opened, you know. In nineteen fourteen, or was it 'fifteen. Nineteen fifteen, I think. It doesn't matter, though, does it?"

She said nothing. She just sat there with her own thoughts, and as she watched, she saw him begin to wander off among his hopes and memories. It was almost physical. She saw him begin to disappear into them, as if among the cool and leafy bowers and alleys of a peaceful summer garden, where the noise and trouble of the world were held at bay, where hope could be reborn and time frozen.

"That would have been something," he said, but he wasn't speaking to her. "We used to talk about it, Father and I. How we would go in at Portal Sixteen and through the tunnel and then suddenly come out into the sunlight with the field down there, all green and clean, and seventy thousand people cheering. You remember?"

"I remember." She was answering for the whole of his life, she thought.

"Father and I used to talk about that. How great it would be to come out into the sunshine and look down and see Lex and Dee on the field warming up with the team."

For an instant, he was silent, and then Lyda saw, or thought she did, the damndest thing happen. She imagined that Fletcher appeared on one side of Howland, and Lex and Dee on the other. They murmured among themselves for an instant, and then, as she watched, they got up, locked arms in the old way they always did, and with confident steps moved away from her, while time and memory settled around them like mist, until, at last, he, and they, were hidden from her.

And so she'd had to write an entire new series of letters. At least there could be no more. She had given what she could. She looked at the clock. It was well after midnight, but the noise in the streets had barely abated. Let them celebrate, she thought; victory's been a long time coming.

Poor, poor darling Dee, she thought, licking the flap of an envelope: you came so close, didn't you? Just a few more weeks and you'd be coming home.

She was very tired, replowing this ground was so much harder than the first time. Once again there had been the letters from Lewis Perry and Wells Kerr at Exeter, from President Seymour of Yale, from scores of people who wrote, many whose names she barely recognized; whose sympathies, she couldn't help thinking, were more a gesture of respect and fealty to Hanover Place than an expression of personal loss.

Dorothy Bush had written. Dorothy and Prescott had been lucky. Their son George was a flyer, too, but he'd been pulled out of the Pacific. Lyda remembered the Bush boy: nice-looking, with a crooked smile. They called him "Poppy." He'd played baseball for Andover against the twins.

She supposed she should feel some animus, some envy for the lucky ones. But she liked the Bushes, and now she knew better than they ever could how lucky they were. Even if she hadn't liked them, she could never have begrudged them their luck. That ghastly Joe Kennedy's son had also been rescued, but was it his fault who his father was? All that war taught was that death was just as unfair as life.

There had been other touching gestures. Lex's wingman on the *Essex*, a nice boy from Texas, somehow had made it to New York for Lex's memorial service, "deadheading" all the way from Honolulu, almost twenty-four hours without sleep. He'd come back to the apartment after Trinity, and for a while she and Andrew had sat and talked with him in the darkened library. When it came time for him to go—he had a plane to catch at Floyd Bennett, he had to get back to the war—Lyda had told him: Come and see us when this is over, and we'll try to heal together. She hoped he would.

She looked at the stack. God, she thought, how many such letters must have been written since Pearl Harbor, a great cloud of mail crisscrossing America, darkening the sky the way the migrating flocks of passenger pigeons once had.

Others had lost children. Here was a note from Herbert Lehman. Just over a year ago she'd written him about the loss of his son Peter. Hanover Place had lost a few of its own: Hardesty's promising nephew at Anzio; a boy in the bookkeeping department over Schweinfurt; that nice George from the afternoon elevator shift on the beach at Tarawa. Flora Merrow had lost a great-nephew in a preflight accident at Pensacola. This wasn't a war limited to any class. Clerks and messengers fell next to partners' sons. Frank and Catherine Bangs had lost both their boys in Germany within a month.

She was too tired to write any more. She lit another cigarette, winced at the foul taste, and stubbed it out. She looked at her watch. 12:46 A.M. Peace in Europe was one day old. She put her hands on her thighs and massaged them.

From outside the honking of horns continued. Soon the ships would be coming home, carrying soldiers from the land, sailors from the sea, airmen from the skies, filling up holes in lives, healing the wounds of absence. Easy for them, she thought bitterly, and for an instant wished the night would collapse on the city, extinguishing all its lights, stopping its howls of celebration in its throat, burying forever the joy that rose obscenely from the street.

Don't be silly, she thought. What's done is done. We must start anew, all of us. The window rattled and she got up to latch it. A fresh breeze cooled her face; a wind had risen suddenly in the night. Its muffled high whistle penetrated Lyda's thoughts. For a moment, before she turned out the light and went to bed, she found herself wondering if that was really the wind she heard—and not the return of those ghosts she had faced down so many years ago in the courtyard of Trinity Church.

BOOK

V

FOR GOD,
FOR
COUNTRY

1950

APRIL

I n the courtyard below, a couple of freshmen were leisurely tossing a lacrosse ball back and forth. The late afternoon sunlight dappled the traceries of ivy and rendered deep sienna the weathered red stone of Wright Hall. A perfect spring day—like life itself in April 1950 for those who were fortunate enough to be young, white, moneyed, and sons of Mother Yale.

On a second-floor window seat, Chickie Fenton sat cross-legged, like a chubby Buddha, half-attentive to the latest *House and Garden* while he kept track out of the corner of his eye of the traffic beneath the window. Across the room, Andy was curled half-off, half-on a ratty time-worn sofa; his face was furrowed with that mixture of vexation, skepticism, and outright bafflement generally found on an undergraduate attempting to get through Kant's *Critique of Pure Reason*.

"Uh, oh," said Chickie suddenly, "general quarters! Here comes our fighting leatherneck."

"Fightin' Mad Max?"

"The very same. Why the hell doesn't he stay over in Silliman, where he belongs?"

Downstairs they heard the entry door slam loudly, then heavy footsteps tumbling up the rutted stone stairs. The door to the room was thrown open and Max Miles stood there, resplendent in the elaborate and colorful uniform of a member of the Marine Corps unit of the Yale Naval Reserve Officers Training Corps.

"What ho, chaps!" he boomed. At six foot four, Max seemed to fill the door.

"My God," exclaimed Andy, "it's Superman!"

Max was kitted out in a long, braid-trimmed boat cape, even though the day was seasonable.

"Except instead of Clark Kent, the caped crusader's played by Robert Cohn," Chickie added.

Max looked puzzled.

"Who's Robert Cohn?" he asked.

Chickie ignored Andy's warning glance. "Robert Cohn was once middleweight boxing champion of Princeton," he said evenly.

There was a pause while Max deliberated this. Finally, he smacked his lips, indicating that he found the matter inscrutable and thus not worth pursuing. From an inner pocket of his cape he extracted a rolled-up magazine and tossed it to Andy.

"Seen this yet, Andrew?" he asked in his stentorian way.

"I have," said Andy.

"And . . . ?"

"And all I can say is my old man must be shitting in his pants."

"Let me see that," said Chickie. Andy flipped the magazine up to the window seat. It was the latest issue of *Fortune*, which fell open to a much-thumbed article entitled: "Warrington Takes the Lead on Wall Street."

Chickie smoothed out the page and studied the photograph accompanying the article. The caption read, "The Executive Committee of Warrington & Co., photographed in Managing Partner Howland T. Warrington's office in the firm's historic building at One Hanover Place." Posed on a flowered sofa—perfectly ghastly chintz, thought Chickie—Howland Warrington and Morris Miles looked confidently at the camera; behind them stood two other men identified in the caption as "Charles L. Runnels, co-head of Warrington & Company's famous Corporations Department, and Lewis C. Comstock, head of Sales and Syndication."

"Nice photograph," Chickie said. "I gather your old man's considering a career in undertaking."

Max looked puzzled. Chickie studied the photograph some more. Morris Miles looks like a blood pudding, he thought, a shiny black sausage in his dark mohair suits; he wore them winter, spring, summer, and fall, and according to Max, to whom clothes were life, had twenty of them, made by Tripler's in three different weights.

"How about a spot of tiffin, Andy? My treat?" asked Max. The invitation clearly did not include Chickie.

Max spoke in plummy tones he'd acquired at the posh Swiss boarding school where he'd spent his twelfth-grade year. That had been a splendid time for Max. Americans had all the money in the world, and he was welcome everywhere. He had passed one vacation as a guest of the Lucases in London, where he had been received warmly by families listed in Debrett and had dined off the very same porcelain and silver from which kings and queens had eaten. He had come away deeply impressed with English ways. In his heart he dreamed of "going up" to Oxford or Cambridge, but his parents wouldn't hear of it—there was his future to think of—and so he had "gone up to New Haven," the next best thing.

Andy looked helplessly at Chickie. "Why not?" he replied. It was near the end of the month and he was broke and even Max's company was preferable to what they served at Freshman Commons.

"Fine," said Max. "The Old Heidelberg? Say, seven o'clock?"

"As you will."

Max turned smartly on his heel and left. Andy and Chickie sat looking at each other, listening to their departed guest's heavy feet thumping down the stairs.

"Chickie, don't say it," said Andy.

"Oh, for Christ's sakes, Drew, c'mon."

"C'mon yourself. And cut out that Robert Cohn stuff! We have to live with these people, you know."

"*You* have to live with them. Besides, a little Hemingway's good for a blighted soul like Max. And in case you've forgotten, it was Morris Miles who got my dear papa exiled to Cloud Cuckooland."

"Cut it out, you love it out there!"

"My old man does, because he can go down to the California Club and do silent battle with the International Communist Conspiracy. I hate it! Well, most of it. Do you know what a houseful of rattan furniture can do to an aesthetic soul?"

Andy grinned and unlimbered himself from the sofa. "I guess I better take a shower," he said.

"I should think you'd want to be fumigated. Strictly as a precaution, of course. Dollars to doughnuts he springs Himelman on you again."

Andy stopped with one arm out of a yellow button-down shirt. "He wouldn't dare."

"You don't get it, do you? Himelman's got Max's number. He's playing him like a ukulele. Leo Himelman: Svengali in a yarmulke, or should it be Iago? Wise up, Drew: Leo wants to get to you through Max. How come Max is over here all the time? Why not with his own class? How come he doesn't hang around with 'fifty-two?"

"Get *at* me sounds more like it," said Andy, finishing shrugging out of the shirt. He slipped his trousers down and stood there in the rumpled blue boxer shorts he'd worn for five straight days. "Besides, what would you do if you were Max? We're about his only friends."

"*You* are his only . . ."

"You get my point. We're people he's known forever, and I guess he was pretty hurt at not getting into a fraternity."

"He should have taken Phi Gam when they came knocking."

"Well, he didn't." Andy grabbed a clean towel of Chickie's from a half-open laundry parcel.

"Of course he didn't," said Chickie. "And you know why as well as I do. Leo's got him convinced that somehow next year you're going to get him into Fence. For the greater glory of Hanover Place!"

Andy shook his head impatiently and disappeared out the door. Chickie picked up *Fortune*. He skimmed the article, reading out loud, ". . . new power in Wall Street . . . blah, blah, blah . . . Warrington and Miles the greatest outside-inside threat since Davis and Blanchard . . . blah, blah, blah . . ." None of this was very interesting to Chickie, but he read on. ". . . first time in its history, Warrington & Co., the name to which S. L. Warrington & Son changed in 1945, may be forced to go outside the family blah, blah, blah . . . anointed successors killed near the end of the war, leaving Andrew Warrington, nineteen, a Yale undergraduate whose interests are said to be literary, and Junius "Jay" Warrington, eighteen, who has terminated his formal education and is presently clerking on the floor of the New York Stock Exchange for the odd-lot firm of De Coppet & Doremus, to carry on . . . blah, blah, blah . . ."

Literary! thought Chickie. Just because Drew was a great reader. The fact was, Drew didn't have the slightest idea about what he wanted to do with his life, and the family wasn't pressuring him; Lyda was far too clever for that.

The Warringtons were the only family Chickie considered himself to have. He loathed his father and he hadn't seen his mother in five years. In July 1945, in San Diego, with the family all packed for the move back to Pasadena, Conchita Fenton had gone out on a last-minute errand to Walgreen's, she said—and had never come back. She had turned up nine months later in Kenya, as the mistress and later the wife of a dashing Royal Navy officer whom she had met in Coronado. She and her husband were central figures in the fast-drinking, hard-playing "Happy Valley" set.

Lyda took Chickie in. He was already spending the Christmas and spring holidays with the Warringtons; by 1947 he had virtually his own rooms at both Fifth Avenue and Double Dune, and visited his father for two weeks each summer. Chickie thought his father was becoming a caricature. The New York Stock Exchange closed at noon California time, and within a half-hour, Chubby Fenton was guaranteed to be found at a certain table at the California Club, playing dominoes with men exactly like himself, indulging in gin-drenched diatribes against anyone unlucky enough not to enjoy a solid Protestant birthright or schooling.

Fortunately for Chickie, Chubby's business dealings with Hyman Gessel had led to a wide Hollywood acquaintance that extended beyond the studio executive suites, and many of these men and women were kind to Chickie; his precocity amused them, they took him up, and took him around. Thanks to the generosity of his Uncle Jorge, whose astute management of the family sugar and tobacco plantations paid Chickie's school fees and remitted a generous allowance each month, he could pay his own way at the Brown Derby and Dave Chasen's.

"Sure you don't want to come? It's a free meal." Andy had returned from the shower. He stood naked and dripping in the middle of the room, casually toweling his private parts.

"For God's sakes," said Chickie, "do you have to make such a mess? And no, I will not be beholden to Max, even if he'd have me."

Andy went into the bedroom. He came out a few minutes later in a pink Brooks Brothers shirt, one of six that made up what Chickie called his "circulating library," a ratty "Old Hundred" tie from St. Paul's, unpressed khaki pants, and a blue blazer that Chickie claimed to have last experienced the kiss of an iron during the administration of President Coolidge.

"Ah. Come on," he urged.

Chickie shook his head. "A man must have his pride," he said.

When Andy had left, Chickie began to straighten the room. He fussed briefly with the curtains, the only proper curtains in the whole of Wright Hall, and moved about the room, neatening, picking up, often making small adjustments of no more than a fraction of an inch. On the mantelpiece he'd made a little still life of "freshman mistakes": initialed beer mugs with the Yale seal, twice-smoked pipes, and canisters of "Bulldog Mixture" from the Owl Shop. What could have possessed us to buy this stuff? A photograph on the mantel had been tipped over. Chickie picked it up and looked at it. It had been taken two summers ago on the veranda steps at Double Dune. The Warringtons: Lyda, Howland, Drew, Jay— Mephistopheles as he would have been at sixteen—and "Merry Miranda." That was Chickie's nickname for a child who was in fact the dourest little girl he'd ever seen. Except for her blond hair, so fine that it stirred if someone waved a hand in a room, Miranda was utterly unlike the rest of her robust clan: she was small-boned, with strange gray eyes that seldom blinked and a little cruel slit of a mouth. Jay teased Miranda unmercifully, so perhaps you couldn't blame her for looking sour, but still there was something troubling about her.

He put the photograph back and continued with the housework. There were two stacks of records ranged vertically on either side of the Webcor record changer; on the messier side, Andy had typically left out of its jacket, *Andre Kostelanetz Favorites*. The thick black plastic was scratched deeply across two bands. Didn't Andy realize what these new long-playing records cost? He replaced it in its jacket, stood up, and straightened the Miro reproduction over the sofa that they'd gone Dutch on at Raymond & Raymond on 53rd Street.

He only fussed like this when no one—and that included Drew—was around to see him do it. Not that Drew would have minded, Chickie guessed, but this way it was easier. By the time Chickie had made certain of his sexual identity, their friendship was far advanced and well seasoned and of course Chickie would never think of coming on to Drew.

That didn't mean he never felt the urge. "Pansies"—or "fruitcakes" or "fruits" or "queers" or "homos"—weren't supposed to actually *do* anything, but Chickie knew differently, and he knew how and where to placate the rage in his hormones.

Of course if his father knew, he'd kill him, which was another reason Chickie hated his parent. With a couple of gins in him, Chubby still liked to reminisce about his own schooldays and the beating he'd given a couple of "pansies" he caught jerking each other off under the Groton football stand. Pansies were in the same category as Jews, Negroes, and Communists.

There were times Chickie imagined his father might unknowingly have a point. Being homosexual was in a way like being a Jew or a Negro or a Communist. More like a Communist, he guessed. Jews and Negroes might have a rough time of it, but at least they were whatever they were above ground. Like Red spies, homosexuals could do business only through a linkage of underground cells.

He looked out the window. Evening was settling on the Freshman Campus, the quadrangle surrounded by the oldest buildings at Yale. Male singing floated up through the deepening light: ". . . with pleasure rife/ The shortest gladdest years of life . . ." The baritone's got an especially good voice, thought Chickie. Another of the college's innumerable singing groups on their way to commons for dinner, or rehearsal, he guessed. The voices faded, but the strong yet gentle male tones had aroused something inside him. All of a sudden he felt in a terrible uproar. When that happened, there was nothing to do but scratch the itch.

He took a New Haven Railroad schedule from the top drawer of his desk; there was a train leaving for Grand Central in twenty-five minutes. Hell, he figured, I can cut Saturday art history; it would be too bad to miss Vince Scully, but what could possibly be said about Frank Lloyd Wright that the old charlatan hadn't already said about himself? He jammed some clothes, his Proust (he was halfway through *Albertine* for the second time), and a Wells Fargo checkbook into the snazzy green leather Mark Cross duffel that Lyda had given him for his last birthday. Lyda always gave the best presents!

He scribbled a note to Andy, slammed the door behind him, and clat-tered down the stairs as fast as his short little legs could take him, almost colliding at the bottom of the stairwell with one of the jocks who lived on the third floor. He could tell with one sniff that the muscular weenie was already well-advanced on an epically vomitous weekend.

There was a taxi parked outside the Yale post office. Chickie jumped into it. He was in a state of high excitement. He had a card to a new club in a basement on West 22nd Street; a friend from Santa Monica had called to tell him there was the most extraordinary Negro working there, a fellow the color of coffee grounds. Cutting his Saturday morning art history lecture meant he could stay over on Sunday. He'd call Lyda and see if she'd take him to lunch.

Max wanted to ask Leo Himelman why Chickie had called him "Robert Cohn" but somehow he felt he wouldn't get the answer he was looking for, so instead he asked: "Hey, Leo, did you ever hear of a Princeton guy named Robert Cohn?"

Leo Himelman looked up from *Fortune*. "Why do you ask?"

Max waffled. "I don't know. It's a name somebody brought up."

"I see," said Himelman. He regarded Max with his lifeless dark eyes and intoned pedantically, "The only Robert Cohn I can think of is a character in a novel by Ernest Hemingway entitled *The Sun Also Rises*."

He had a flat, nasal New York voice.

"It is the sort of hair-on-its-chest fiction that Fraternity Row types like your friend Warrington consider all the rage. It was published, I believe, in 1925 or 1926, the same year in which your father made several million dollars for the Warringtons with his analytical work on the Chilean gold bonds, a fact which this silly article does not choose to disclose. It is mostly about rich gentile expatriates getting drunk in Spain. The Cohn character is a stereotypical Jew, treated with mockery and condescension, as you might expect from an anti-Semite like Hemingway. I suggest you read the book some time. It should furnish you valuable insights into what is really going on in the minds and hearts of those people whose good opinion you so obviously covet and who are only too happy to trade their crumbs for your cake."

"I might just do that," said Max. "And if by that you're trying to say that Andy's freeloading off me, you can just forget it! Hell, Leo, you know how rich the Warringtons are!"

He was used to Leo talking this way. It wasn't as if it was coming from a friend. Leo wasn't a friend. Friends were people you opened your life to, and Max wasn't about to do that—at least no more than necessary to keep Leo on a string.

Leo was simply a functional acquaintance; theirs was a relationship based on mutual need and advantage. He and Max had known each other for nearly two years now. They had met in September 1948, during Freshman Week, when Leo had sought to recruit Max for Hillel at Yale, the organization formed to help Jewish students cope with life amid the alien corn.

Himelman was himself new to Yale. Four years older than Max, he was beginning his first year at the Law School on a scholarship, which he had arranged to supplement by working as a grader in freshman Sociology, and with a few dollars of bursary aid from Hillel in return for serving as a counselor. It promised to be a narrow existence. As Chickie put it, Leo Himelman was "as poor as the proverbial templemouse."

His poverty grated on Himelman. It was undeserved and he knew exactly who to blame for it. His family, like many others, had been bankrupted by the failure, in December 1930, of the Bank of the United States, an ill-named institution which, when it collapsed, took with it the savings, ranging from fortunes to modest pittances, of thousands of depositors. Many of these, like Leo Himelman's family, were from Manhattan's garment district; they had placed their faith and resources in a bank whose appeal was that it was managed and promoted by hard-working Jews like themselves.

The subsequent trial and conviction of the bank's senior officers established a record of gross mismanagement that bordered on misappropriation. Over the subsequent decade, however, the myth was promoted over a thousand kitchen tables, including that of the Himelman family, that the real culprits in the situation were the Federal Reserve Bank and Wall Street, which could have helped but didn't. As the myth took hold, it acquired a subtext: that the Bank of the United States had been allowed to fail as a way for "the establishment" to punish a bunch of pushy, upstart Eastern European Jews. The list of villains was enlarged to include the swank "Park Avenue" Jews, the Germans and Sephardics, the Temple Emanu-El–Century-Country-Club–Harmonie-Club–Sands-Point set. It was this lot that had precipitated the Himelmans out of their Riverside Drive apartment and, so to speak, into the gutter, along with the boy Leo's hopes for a brilliant future that would lead from Horace Mann to Harvard to Harvard Law to a great Wall Street law firm and perhaps someday to the Supreme Court. Instead, he found himself condemned to public schools where his ugliness, his diligence, and his arrogance were singled out, not his brilliance, and he was regularly thrashed. More of the same followed at City College. By the time he arrived in New Haven, his disgruntlement and alienation had festered into a cancer of vindictiveness.

The view of life he had evolved counted virtue and merit as beside the point in the pursuit of success. Men got what they wanted because of other men. Leo needed a meal ticket, an "angel," someone who would be his passport out of his dreary life. In the amiably pompous and affected young man who, unthinkingly quite rudely, dismissed Leo's earnest urgings on behalf of Hillel, he sensed he might have found the connection he was seeking.

Max was obviously not very bright; he had, as Leo saw at once, a remarkably high opinion of himself and his prospects, tempered by anxiety about the strange intellectual and social environment in which he now found himself. His mother's attentiveness was no longer at hand; his father's ample purse might not dominate; Leo sensed Max felt unprotected.

So Leo courted Max carefully; he didn't press; he made himself helpful in one small way, then another, until all these odds and ends of usefulness accreted to indispensability. He understood how to exploit Max's faith in the power of money. It didn't trouble Leo to borrow from Max. The deeper he sank into Max's pocket, the deeper he burrowed into the very fabric of the younger man's existence. Leo insisted on repaying, if not in cash, then in what he could offer. By the spring term of freshman year, Leo was writing Max's papers and drilling him for examinations of which he had obtained copies in advance.

Gradually, the relationship evolved from purely tutorial—"define Pope's philosophy of wit"; "name the three geological ages following the Pleistocene"—to something more nearly approaching mentorship—in which Leo undertook to design Max's future with his own interests in mind. To do this properly, he calculated, it would ultimately be necessary to include Hanover Place; the essential prelude to that would be to ingratiate himself with his tutee's family.

This did not prove easy. Morris Miles and Leo disliked each other on sight. In response to a casual inquiry from Howland as to how Max was enjoying New Haven, Morris let his hair down on the subject. "Fine, I think," he told Howland, "except he's picked up a fellow called Himelman who, to tell you the truth, is exactly the kind of person who makes me ashamed to be a Jew!"

To Leo, on the other hand, Morris Miles was the pluperfect *Hofjude*, the favor-courting, deferential "court Jew," a type who for centuries, from Aaron of Lincoln through Bismarck's banker Bleichroeder to Otto Kahn, had with great astuteness and fidelity managed the financial affairs of Christian kings and princes, only to be ostracized or bankrupted for their troubles.

Still, the game was worth the candle, and Leo persevered. Every five or six weeks, he managed an invitation to Sunday lunch at the Mileses' Park Avenue apartment. If the day was fair, lunch would be preceded by a stately perambulation south on Park Avenue, then over to Fifth, and back up to the apartment. Along the way, like small clusters of ships making up into a convoy, the Miles party would join up with other families headed by men of Morris's rank at Goldman Sachs or Bear, Stearns or Wertheim. The men all seemed to be the same shape and they dressed identically, in heavy navy-blue mohair overcoats, bluish-black homburgs, and black wingtips so brightly shined that you could see reflected in them the great encroaching apartment buildings and houses of worship.

Like ponderous, dignified beetles they would pick their way down the avenue, rapt in Wall Street conversation, their wives a yard or so behind, with the younger family members and their guests and swains bringing up the rear. Morris was still in his mid-forties, but his lugubrious gravity made him seem much older.

Leo fared better with Miriam. She was disposed to open her heart to anyone who served her Max loyally and usefully. Such revulsion as Leo stirred in her was purely physical. His skin was psoriatic and acne-pitted, and oddly pulpy, as if the flesh beneath had worked loose from the bone. He exuded a pungent, inescapable body odor that no amount of the cheap drugstore colognes and aftershaves his meager resources afforded seemed to mitigate.

But there was no doubt he had a mind. Moreover, he spoke privately to Miriam of ambitions for Max that she scarcely dared to dream herself. He was shrewd enough not to disclose to her the one item on his own agenda that seemed to him to be essential for the furthering of his own purposes, which was to restore to his protégé precisely what it was Miriam's fondest wish to extirpate: a heightened sense of Max's identity as a Jew.

Here, sadly, Max had so far proven an indifferent pupil. The dreadful facts of the Holocaust were coming to light, but he was unmoved by them. On one occasion, he had come back from a history class perplexed by a comparison the professor had made between the Holocaust and American slavery. Leo had very reasonably explained that the Holocaust had been a crime against mankind, while slavery, although heinous and regrettable, had really been an unfortunate economic experiment. That was why, he pointed out, the Christian world properly should be less concerned with the Negro question than with recompensing the earth's Jewry for the horrors of 1939–1945; the guaranteed security of Israel was to be but the first installment on that debt.

Later in the year, when Max sought enlightenment as to what the Yale football captain, a colored man named Levi Jackson, had meant by his remark that he would probably not have been offered membership in Skull & Bones if his name had been Jackson Levi, Leo went through the whole thing again. It did not seem appropriate to pass on the wisdom of another Negro, beside whom Leo had worked in a meat-packing plant one summer. He had observed, in a voice as deep and liqueous as a swamp: "Leo, mah fren', you always talkin' 'bout how what them Nazi folks do to Jews was special, but I tell you what the real specialness is: puttin' chains on a nigger's one thing, but what happens to you Jews is done *to* white folks *by* white folks, and that's what really counts when it comes to *you* makin' *them* feel guilty!"

This Robert Cohn business was yet another example that seemed to run off Max's back like water and shouldn't. Leo decided to have another go at it. "Who brought up Robert Cohn, Max? Andrew Warrington?"

"Nope. C'mon, Leo, just forget it. It wasn't anything."

"Hah," exclaimed Leo, "Fenton! It was Fenton, wasn't it? Just the sort of thing he'd say."

Max didn't answer. He edged around in his armchair and stared hard at his magazine.

"You know, Max, I really do think it would profit you to look into *The Sun Also Rises*."

"I'll do that, Leo."

Max sounded sulky. Leo decided to change course. "You know, I quite enjoyed your friend Warrington this evening. He's better than most of that lot. Of course, like the rest of them, he takes too much for granted, about himself and other people, if you ask me. They have no idea of want, for instance, and I don't like the way he talks down to you."

"He doesn't talk down to me. He's my oldest friend."

"As you will," Himelman said wearily. He leaned over and opened his scuffed black briefcase. "Here," he said. "You can take this to the typist tomorrow. It should be good for at least a B."

"Just stick it on the desk," said Max. "You need anything?"

"I could use twenty dollars. Just until I get my bursary money."

"Sure," said Max. He dug in the pocket of his well-crafted flannels and produced a couple of bills.

"And thanks for dinner," said Leo, rising. "I have to get going. Moot court on Monday."

Max's intentions the next morning were good. He rose with a clear head to find a splendid April morning awaiting him. Going to the window, he sniffed a breath of chill in the air, a good opportunity to wear his new nubby purple Shetland sweater. It was his plan, in the course of his errands, to stop by the Co-op and pick up a copy of Hemingway's novel.

By the time he'd made his York Street rounds, which involved thorough investigation at Barrie Ltd. of a pair of Scotch-grain buckled brogues, and discourse with Moe Decker at Fenn-Feinstein on the comparative merits of doeskin and cavalry twill, as well as the purchase of a pink-striped button-down at J. Press, it was getting on for noon. He crossed Broadway rapidly and headed for Cutler's to see if the new George Feyer record was in. It was, so he bought it, chatted briefly with Mrs. Cutler at the cash register, and started back toward the campus. He looked in at Liggett's for some Lavoris, then backtracked a few doors to inspect a display of athletic gear in the window of the Co-op. There was something else he meant to buy there, he vaguely recalled, studying the Jack Kramer model tennis racquet in the window. He decided it would be better to buy it at Century and have the pro string it.

His stomach reminded him he hadn't had breakfast. He abandoned his contemplation of the Co-op's windows, recrossed Broadway and went into the Yankee Doodle, where he ordered up two "pigs in a blanket," a side of french fries, and a container of milk. A "pig in a blanket" was a hot dog, sliced and stuffed with processed cheese, then wrapped in bacon and fried in lard. Pork swathed within pork, cooked in pork. Even Leo Himelman's eyes might have widened at the sight of Max devouring such a meal. Himelman's Judaism was, however, strictly concentrated in the area of what economists called "comparative advantage." On matters of religious usage, such as dietary laws, he held no strong opinions.

Max ate happily and contemplated the traffic moving outside. Any thought of Hemingway had long since been swallowed up in the unplumbable abysses of forgetfulness. He examined his watch, a fine gold Le Coultre timepiece his mother had gotten for him at Yard, which was where the Warringtons had their jewelry made. He was due at Vassar around four for a mixer. He had plenty of time. His soul trilling like a bluebird, Max Miles beamed at the counterman and, in his most mellifluous genteel voice, ordered another pig in a blanket.

As Lyda warned her husband to expect, the article in *Fortune* caused a considerable stir at Hanover Place, much of it bickering and grousing of the sort that seems inevitable when some people in a group are singled out for publicity and others are not.

Lyda hadn't liked the idea of letting *Fortune* have the run of Hanover Place. It wasn't that she shared her late father-in-law's detestation of personal publicity. She simply recognized, as turned out to be the case, that the article would provide an excuse for some people to deplore all that had changed at Hanover Place since the war, which would be more nuisance than the publicity was worth.

Howland didn't agree. He was proud of The Firm, proud of the changes he had wrought there since 1945. He was immensely pleased with the article and ordered several thousand offprints to use as a new business tool.

For better or worse, The Firm was certainly different from the one the old-timers—the veterans of the twenties boom and crash and the Depression—had known, but so was the world, as Howland was obliged to point out several times a week to one or the other of them.

Hanover Place no longer comported itself as a dictatorially paternalistic family enterprise. The change was symbolized by its new name: Warrington & Co. The vision to which Hanover Place was now indentured called for a breadth of energy and leadership that no one family could provide. The Firm's strategy no longer emphasized affairs of the stock market. Howland's war had left him with an unregenerate faith in technology. The industrial might and ingenuity that had won a world war could surely be rejiggered to create a peacetime prosperity unmatched in history. It was America's opportunity—more than that, it was its responsibility—to put to work its abundant capital and skilled labor, its genius, enterprise, determination, and community ethic in the service of the revitalization of a world in ruins. It was only natural to expect that the rewards for fulfilling this task would be commensurate with its enormity.

Morris shared his partner's optimism and commitment. A great many people expected history to repeat itself: that as in 1919, once wartime demand ended, the economy would sink into depression while it sorted out the economic mysteries of peace. In Morris's opinion, one form of demand would simply be replaced by another; the pent-up craving and need of a huge, long-deprived population (nearly 150 million people!) for homes and automobiles and every conceivable sort of good would surge. Swords would be refashioned into plowshares. It would be Wall Street's job, and opportunity, to finance all this.

"We will continue to participate in our traditional investment and Stock Exchange business," Howland wrote in a memorandum to his partners at Christmas 1945, "but the present state of the world and the nation offers us an unmatched opportunity. With our connections, and our reputation, we should be able to build a position in investment-banking originations every bit as satisfying and profitable as we enjoy elsewhere in the world of finance. As an old dog who will be fifty in the coming year, I look forward to learning new tricks, and I know you do as well."

New people were brought in at all levels. During the last months of the war, despite his personal tragedy, Howland had thought deeply about The Firm. He would need new people, he saw. A few of the old hands had a good working knowledge of corporate finance and underwriting, but the industrial and statistical know-how wasn't there. For the first time in its 131-year history, therefore, The Firm recruited outsiders at the partnership level.

Where he could, Howland sought men who had the right kind of social and educational background. He was also keen to find men who had experienced command and understood the relationship between an officer and his troops. The war had been a leveler; the "ruptured duck" discharge button that Howland wore in his Weatherill-tailored buttonhole was also sported by Mike the elevator starter and Bruno in the mailroom and a hundred others around Hanover Place.

The new men were a mixed bag. Dick Bosworth, for example, whom Howland met in Washington in 1944, came from a good old New Orleans family; he had worked for Creole Petroleum at Lake Maracaibo and knew his way around the oil business. Along with air transportation, oil was an industry in which Howland most ardently wished to gain a foothold. Petroleum had won the war; petroleum would drive the engine of peace-time prosperity.

Wartime networks yielded most of the manpower Howland needed. The Street supplied others. Wall Street lived by a gentleman's agreement that proscribed recruiting from other firms, but if Howland demurred at going after anyone at Morgan Stanley, or Harriman, Ripley, or Glore, Forgan, he was not so scrupulous about other, smaller houses. He found his new head of Syndicate at Union Securities, and the right man to take over municipal bonds at Drexel & Co.

The introduction of outsiders at high levels was bound to create problems, but these couldn't be helped. The new partners might not have "a sense of The Firm," but that could be acquired. Moreover, the family was hardly abdicating. As Howland told *Fortune*, "In a few years my sons Andrew and Jay will be ready to join us, so that even if something should happen to me tomorrow, our control for the long term is secure."

It was not merely the partnership that expanded. Between 1945 and 1950, The Firm had grown from two hundred–odd employees to nearly twice that number. Fortunately there was space to house them, thanks to a prescient decision by Morris Miles who, on the eve of V-J Day, had negotiated the purchase of the seven-story building at 35 Old William Slip that backed up to Hanover Place. A series of ingenious architectural grafts were performed in the early postwar years, effectively doubling The Firm's working quarters.

Morris had spent *his* war building important bridges, too—notably to men who controlled vast pools of other people's savings, like Harry Hagerty at Metropolitan Life and Barney Berenson at Cosmopolitan Life and Fire. Thanks to these relationships, The Firm was able in 1949 to steal its first substantial piece of business from a blue-chip competitor, a $25 million "private placement" for United Ash and Chemical, a longtime and valued client of another house.

Howland pitched the idea member-to-member to a UAC director in the dining room of the Gorse Club, where business was notionally forbidden to be discussed, but where in fact, little else was. Two days later, Morris Miles made a detailed presentation to United Ash's board in Chicago. Six weeks after that, an advertisement in the *Wall Street Journal* announced, "as a matter of record only," that Warrington and Co. had acted as the agent in "the private placement"—a relatively new coinage—of $25 million in twenty-year Senior Notes of United Ash and Chemical, Inc.

Knowledgeable Wall Streeters, who read these "tombstone" ads with the same avid mixture of malice and envy as their wives read the gossip columns of Dorothy Kilgallen and Cholly Knickerbocker, noted the announcement with interest. The advertisement was also noticed widely in corporate treasurers' offices across the land; one thing led to another, and the United Ash placement became the first in a series of ingenious financings that would lead a year later to the *Fortune* article.

By then, things were really humming at Warrington & Co. Accompanying the *Fortune* piece was a cutaway drawing of Hanover Place depicting the various activities of a typical morning at Warrington & Co. On the various floors of the main building and the annex, jolly little stick figures packaged bonds, met in conference, reviewed documents, prepared the partners' lunch, conducted briefings, huddled by tickers, met with connections, and carried out as many of the tasks of the day as the artist's ingenuity and the space available could include.

Whatever misgivings they had about the article, people around Hanover Place greatly enjoyed the cartoon. Popular consensus maintained, however, that only one of the little stick men bore a real resemblance to its model, the figure captioned ". . . (11) In his tenth-floor office, Corporations Department Administrator Foster Klopp meets with a group of associates to review an analytical presentation to be made to . . ."

If one person could be said to represent the values and ethic of Hanover Place in those postwar days, what anthropologists, studying The Firm like a tribal village, would call its "culture," it was Foster Klopp.

He had arrived at The Firm in 1947, brought in by new partner Fred Hamer, for whom Klopp, by profession an accountant, had administered a unit of the Air Force's Statistical Control Group.

He was a meticulous belt-and-suspenders sparrow of a man, about the same age as Morris, neat to a fault, impeccably combed and brushed and redolent of Aqua-Velva, and never without a shirt pocket full of pencils and a slide rule in a scabbard at his waist. Words fizzed from him like bubbles, and when excited, he spluttered uncontrollably while his listeners ducked for cover.

The Firm was Foster Klopp's life, passion, and sole interest. The walls of Hanover Place enclosed everything that he considered worthwhile in existence. He was a bachelor, who lived with an unmarried niece on Morningside Heights. He arrived six mornings a week within a minute or two of seven thirty, and it would not be until almost twelve hours later that he would transfer from shirtfront to vest pockets his armament of pencils, clip his slide rule to his belt, don his vest and suit jacket and a carefully brushed wide-brimmed gray felt fedora and make his way to the elevator, generally leaving behind him a cadre of cursing associates slaving away at their adding machines as they revised, yet again, the spreadsheets that were their mentor's pride and their despair.

He was not a mean man, but he was a demanding one, with a persnicketiness about his work that lazier, younger men thought tantamount to sadism. It was his task, as he saw it, to fashion rude squires into knights, and he was dead serious about this responsibility.

Under his direction were prepared the comparative ratios and financial analyses from which always crucial, sometimes creative judgments on price and value, ways and means, would be distilled. By 1950, Hanover Place had attained an enviable reputation in Corporate America for the thoroughness and accuracy of its work and presentations. It could fairly be said that Foster Klopp's browbeating perfectionism had to a great extent replaced Fletcher Warrington's mythic market instinct as the source of The Firm's reputation for financial wizardry.

By 1950, he had become a legend outside Hanover Place and "to be Kloppered" had entered the lexicon of the Street. The verb had been coined in 1948, when Foster Klopp put a Global Airways bond comparison through thirty revisions. The associate assigned to prepare it, a much-decorated ex-Marine who just four years earlier had been left for dead on a beach at Bougainville, had broken down and wept in the ninth-floor men's room. From that point forward, associates of The Firm took a certain masochistic pride in being "Kloppered" and the Klopper's victims tended to compare, boastfully, the relative ignominies they'd suffered at his hands.

As always, there would be detractors, who claimed the Klopper's perfectionism was just an old man's way of getting even for being denied a partnership.

Some of this talk reached Howland's ears, and he took the matter up with Morris. Maybe we ought to make Foster a partner, he suggested. Morris strongly disagreed. "Foster's too limited. Partners have to spend most of their time outside the building, where the connections are, and you and I know they flee when they see Foster coming."

The fact was, Foster Klopp was very much at peace with himself about his assigned role. He was eternally grateful to God for bringing him to Hanover Place. He had no wish to go "outside." He'd seen enough of the great men of industry to conclude that for every bright one, there were two idiots, and even the bright ones tended to be technically unsound and slapdash. He knew where he stood. He was in the same boat as Carlucci, the firm administrator who would never make partner because he knew too much about each partner's finances, who cheated on his income taxes, who tried to charge his mistress or his wife's fur coat off to departmental overhead. Klopp considered himself extravagantly well paid; he was a member in full standing of the Capital Commitments Committee; he attended the partners' "review and outlook" lunch on the first Monday of each month.

The heart of The Firm remained the fourth-floor partners' room, where Flora Merrow, in 1950 within a year of retirement, still guarded the portals. The walnut cabinets still flanked the entryway; Lex's and Dee's decorations and citations had been placed next to the memorials of their great-grandfather, another gleaming youth whom war had prevented from fulfilling a splendid destiny at Hanover Place.

Not much had changed physically at the old building. In the partners' conference room there now hung a portrait of Fletcher Warrington commissioned after his death. It wasn't a bad likeness, but like most portraits painted from photographs, it did scant justice to its subject's lively personality.

The partners' room itself was, in all but one important detail, as it had always been. The coromandel screen still concealed the newswires; the Currier and Ives prints and old maps of New York hung on the long wall, and the portraits of Samuel and Erasmus over the mantels.

But the Platform was gone.

Five years earlier, on his first day back at work, Howland had come downtown with Lyda. A small welcoming party headed by Morris and Charlie Runnels waited out front.

"Christ," Howland said to Lyda as their towncar glided to a halt, "I feel like the goddamn lord of the manor returning from a crusade."

"Well," said Lyda, "wasn't that what you told me it was? I think it's a nice gesture—it isn't as if they're tugging their forelocks."

After shaking hands and slapping backs and kissing cheeks all around, they made their way to the third floor. Miss Merrow was waiting for them. When she caught Lyda's eye, her smile of greeting collapsed and her eyes filled with tears.

"Oh, poor Flora," said Lyda, going to her. "Here," she said, taking two slender boxes from beneath her arm. "You can help me arrange the boys' medals in the cases."

Inside the partners' room, Howland looked around, Morris at his side. "We're thinking of putting up one of the new Trans-Lux quote screens," Morris said.

"Let's hold off," said Howland firmly. "Quote boards are for stock-brokers. We're not going to think of ourselves as stockbrokers any longer."

He looked around the room. It was all as he remembered it. Finally his eye lit on the Platform. He studied it for a minute, then said: "The Platform."

"Yes?" said Morris at his elbow. "What about it?"

"Get rid of it," said Howland. "We're going to be doing things differently around here from now on."

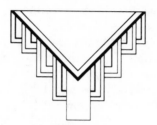

1950

DECEMBER

The shops were crowded, Miranda was becoming difficult, and Lyda's feet were killing her. They had done F.A.O. Schwarz and Abercrombie's, but there were still a couple of stops to make. A cup of tea in the Palm Court at the Plaza seemed like a good idea.

It's so strange to see uniforms everywhere again, thought Lyda, as she and her daughter were led to a table. It's too soon to have another war.

Tea was brought. Lyda eased her shoes half-off and flexed her feet. Christmas really is the most dehumanizing season, she thought. She found her mind turning to her son Andrew; her early anger at what he'd done had long since turned into concern for his safety; she was worried sick. The fighting was reported to be fierce, now that the Chinese had come in, and it had been weeks since she'd heard anything. For all she knew, Andrew might be in the thick of it, he might be . . . she refused even to *think* the word.

"Well, hello, Aunt Lyda," a familiar voice boomed in her ear.

She looked up to find Max Miles standing there, tall and stylish in a new polo coat. "Fighting the Christmas confusion, I see," he said. He smiled at Lyda, then turned toward a pretty girl standing at the entrance and gestured to her to wait for him.

"How are you, Max?" said Lyda. Miranda got to her feet, took his hand, and curtsied.

"Very well, I'm pleased to say. You're looking *très chic*, Miranda. And Andrew? What news of the happy warrior?"

"None, I'm afraid. Apparently, his unit is up there where the fighting is."

"Ah, the Reservoir, yes, indeed. Well, knowing Andrew, I'm sure he'll come out of it with flying colors. These things are always less perilous than they're cracked up to be, you know. Well, I must be going."

He grinned and made a slight bow. Miranda stared at him and then asked, "Max, someday can I see you fly?"

He looked perplexed, turned to Lyda for elucidation, got none, and smiled down at the little girl. In a bluff way, he said, "Of course, my dear, anytime. Well, have a very Merry Christmas. It's a pity about the party, Lyda, but I'm sure everyone quite understands."

Lyda watched him thump off toward his date. She tried to recall whether she'd ever invited Max to call her "aunt." As for the party, well, she hadn't wanted it in the first place, but Howland had insisted. Fifty, he said, was the only birthday really worth making a fuss about. In Lyda's view, no birthday between thirty and eighty deserved to be celebrated at all. No party, she said—absolutely not! Well, he'd gone and booked the St. Regis Roof anyway, and the invitations were practically at the printers' when she found out. But when Andrew did this damn fool thing, it suddenly seemed as foolish to him as to her, and he canceled it.

She signaled the waiter for the check.

"What did you mean," she asked Miranda, as they waited, "asking Max if you could watch him fly?"

"Jay told me he could," her daughter replied. Lyda felt a quick adrenal chill. Nothing Jay told Miranda bore repeating. He used his little sister as a mouthpiece for his mischief.

"I still don't understand," said Lyda.

"Jay says Max is a stupid kite, Mummy," said the little girl. "Kites fly, don't they?"

"Hey, wake up, sport. Don't go to sleep. Fall asleep and you'll freeze to death. C'mon, sport, up 'n at 'em! They'll be coming soon!"

Lex was shaking Andy, hissing urgently in his ear. Get up, fight, get up, fight. As on most nights, the twins slept on either side of him, right in his sleeping bag, keeping him warm, keeping him alive. Last night they'd fought almost until dawn before the bastards withdrew. It had been after five when the company stood down to catch some sleep.

It felt like it was warmer, Andy thought, stretching. Maybe it was a trend. One of the guys said it had only gotten down to nine below the night before. So cold, some of the guys had tried to thaw out the actions of their carbines by pissing on them, but if you did that, you took a chance the piss'd freeze solid in your dick and it would snap off like an icicle.

"Stay with it, sport. We're with you all the way." Dee was shouting in his other ear.

And you goddamn well ought to be, he mumbled to himself, working the action of the carbine, trying to get some looseness into frost-numb fingers, you two sons of bitches got me into this.

Six months earlier, he'd been sitting in his room at Double Dune listening to the radio when the announcer broke in to report that President Truman was responding to the invasion of South Korea by committing American forces.

For some reason, when Andy heard that, his eye fell on the photographs of the twins in a double leather frame on his desk. Suddenly it seemed the photos came alive, and Andy heard Lex say: "Well, sport, what about it?"

What about what?

"You know." Now Dee spoke. "Duty, honor, country. Us."

What do you mean, *you?* He put his book down and squinted at the photographs.

"You too, sport. All of us. It's what people like us do, isn't it, sport? Isn't it?"

Then they went away and left him to think it over, but that night they returned, waking him up at what the luminous hands of his alarm clock said was seven past three.

"You're not going to just lie there, are you, sport?"

They both had big grins, standing there at the foot of his bed, turned out in Air Force khaki and Navy blue. He blinked and suddenly they were in flight gear; Lex in coveralls with a bright yellow Mae West, the flaps and radio connections of his skull-tight cloth helmet hanging loose, opaque green goggles pushed back; Dee in a fur-collared dark leather flying suit, wearing a helmet like Lex's, his eyes hidden behind large reflective sunglasses.

You guys know I hate heights.

"Hey, c'mon," said Dee, "that's no excuse. What about the Leathernecks, the Halls of Montezuma?" Lex nodded vigorously in agreement.

He wanted to turn over, turn his back to them, but he knew that wouldn't do any good. They'd just keep after him, the way they always used to when they had nothing better to do. They'd storm his room, where he'd be reading quietly, and poke and tease and tickle him until some other diversion occurred to them.

In the morning they were back in the frame, looking at him reproach-fully. He tried moving around the room, practically flattening himself against the wall in which the fireplace was cut, but their eyes pursued him wherever he went. That afternoon he'd jumped into the little Dodge convertible he'd been given after freshman year, and drove an hour inland, to Patchogue, where there was a Marine recruiting station, and where he figured they wouldn't recognize his name.

He was given seventy-two hours before reporting to Grand Central to entrain for Camp Pendleton, north of Los Angeles, where the 5th and 7th Marine regiments were reconstituting for combat. He didn't tell his parents what he'd done until the Sunday night before he left. His father took it well, Andy could tell he was proud, but the way his mother reacted scared him. She just sat there and shook, speechless. He was suddenly full of doubt at what he'd done, but it was too late.

So now here he was, pinned down on a hillside in North Korea, frozen half to death—his left foot about to fall off—and hungry—their last real meal had been almost a week earlier, before the big Chinese offensive, before the order to pull out. C-rations, which they had to stow in the cracks of their asses to keep from freezing into cement. Out there in the ravines were about a million goddamn Chinese, every single one intent on killing Andrew Warrington, and all he had to fight back with was his rifle and a couple of ghosts on his flanks.

Thanks a lot, you two, he thought.

But still, they kept him warm, slept with him at night, walked with him by day, and huddled next to him when the Chinks started in with the mortars. They never stopped talking to him, cajoling, exhorting. They kept him going.

"C'mon, sport!" "Sport, you gotta make it!"

Most of the time since they'd started back from Yudam-ni, on the west side of the Chosin Reservoir, they fought at night. The thing was, to keep on the move. Better a Chinese bullet or grenade than to freeze to death. It went better in the daytime, when the air support took over, with the Corsairs operating out of Hungnam, laying cover, pinning down the Chinks, who were never more than a couple of hundred yards away. The Corsairs would come ripping in over the ridgetops, sometimes no more than a few hundred feet above ground, and blow the Chinks and the North Koreans away, and then the Marines would clear the ridges and ravines above the winding road. Below, the endless serpent of the retreat stretched from horizon to horizon.

Other guys in the outfit kept themselves warm with hatred: hatred of the enemy, hatred of the stinking country, above all, hatred of that fucking MacArthur who'd sent them chasing up here right into a trap.

Everyone hated this stinking country, and it stunk all right. It stunk of shit and death and Koreans. The other night, after they'd cleared the Toktong Pass and reopened the Main Supply Road to Hugaru, Andy's outfit ran into a unit of Royal Marines who'd also gotten trapped up at the Reservoir. One Brit claimed he first smelled the stinking country a full day before they landed.

They had been fighting their way for three days now and they were still a mile or so from Hugaru. Three days to cover less than fifteen miles. Three days fighting their way up hillsides and down ravines, driving off the Chinese regulars at night, keeping open the road that wound below them, along which the straggling line of trucks bore the Marine and Army wounded and dead, the only passengers on the trip.

The Chinese kept coming at them. They were tough, tougher than the Koreans, and fought until their corpses were stacked up like cordwood. When they came at night, it was like Indians in a western; you heard them skittering up the hillside in the brush, and then they hit you, shriek-ing and whooping and banging pails and shaking rattles, and all you could do was stand there and shoot at spectral figures darting in and out of pools of flareburst. Only when daylight came could you get an idea how your side had done. Most dawns it seemed no better than ever, but still the Marines kept moving toward the sea, ravine by ravine, ridge by ridge. The word from the company down the line was that Washington was passing out Congressional Medals of Honor like Crackerjack favors, but was anyone going to live through this to collect them?

The cold was worse than the Chinese. Andy had joined his new unit, a company in the 7th Marine Regiment, in early October, when he had been a Marine for just three months. For those first ten easy, misleading days, the division lay off the south coast while Wonsan Harbor was swept for mines. By the time they got ashore, Bob Hope had been there to do a show for the Air Force, and was gone, which made them all feel like assholes.

They headed north toward the Chosin Reservoir. By the first of No-vember, they had reached Hamhung. Fighting had been sporadic, mostly background noise. Andy began to wonder what the point was.

His doubts ended on November 3, when they were hit by the Chinese for the first time. The attack came so quickly that there was no time to do anything except load, fire, and try to stay collected. It helped not to be able to see the enemy, not until the next morning, when the system had digested the shock. The next morning, when they moved up toward the next ridge, past the bodies of dead Chinese, Andy felt nothing; so completely remote was all of this from anything in his experience or contemplation. So this was war. The unit hadn't come together, which added to the stress. Fellows in arms were not yet comrades trusting each other; veterans of Okinawa called back for a second go-round found them-selves fighting next to eager boys from city and countryside who wanted a taste of whatever it was that their fathers, older brothers, and cousins had boasted.

At mid-November, the Chinese faded away. Then, on the 27th, two days after Thanksgiving, winter blew down from the Manchurian steppes and all the givens changed. At twenty below zero, breath all but froze in the throat. The earth was like steel to the shovel. Weapons and machinery seized up. The weather became an enemy every bit as implacable and fierce as whoever lay out there lodged in the ridgetops between Koto-ri and the Reservoir.

With the cold, the Chinese returned. They hit after dark, with drums and whistles and sirens; Andy was sure he was going to die. Then, sud-denly, the twins appeared at his side. They were bluff and optimistic as ever. They threw their arms around him and called him "sport" and chafed his frigid limbs and helped him keep firing.

There were times he thought he was verging on delirium; other times, he sat comatose, too tired to do anything but stare with dead eyes down on the main supply route, watching the long erratic centipede of trucks and ordnance and walking wounded inch its way along the twisting, pocked road.

And then Lex or Dee would say in a quiet, commanding voice: "Time to get ready, sport. Time to move along." And they'd help him up, help him check his carbine, blow on his freezing hands, and get him ready to walk and fight and duck and fight some more.

They fought night and day back from Yudam-ni to Hugaru, and then from Hugaru to Koto-ri and, finally, from Koto-ri to Hungnam. Somewhere along the way—during the last big fight near Chinhung-ni—the twins left him on his own, just before he went out to get the sergeant who was screaming somewhere in the blackness, when in a terrible searing flare of agony the whole world blew up.

1951

JUNE

At first the pain was like a series of line squalls blowing across a lagoon. Gradually, longer spaces of calm between convulsions signaled the storm was wearing itself out, the intervals of awareness and memory expanded. He remembered nothing of the first few weeks, of the MASH unit, or the hospital ship, or the time they said he'd spent in a field hospital in Guam. He vaguely recalled the dull pain of the flight from Guam to Honolulu, and the leg after that, from Hawaii to San Francisco was clearer still. But it wasn't until the morning, eleven weeks after he was shot up at Chinhung-ni, a year to the day after he'd sat joking with Chickie in their rooms at Yale, when Andy awoke from a codeine-drenched sleep to find the sun shining through an open window, and the unmistakable smell of eucalyptus in the air, that he could be sure he was still alive. He tried to move his hand, but someone was holding it; when he looked up, he saw it was his mother.

"Hi, Mother," he said, and they both started to cry.

Then he felt another hand, on his shoulder, and there was his father.

"Hello, Son," said Howland. "Well done."

Andy remained in San Francisco, at Letterman Military Hospital in the Presidio, for three weeks after that. The medics and Navy surgeons had done a great job of putting Humpty-Dumpty together again. He would carry bits of shrapnel around as long as he lived, the doctor told him, and now and then a fragment might work its way through the skin, but his vital organs were okay. His left arm would always be a little stiff, and he might feel changes in the weather more acutely than most people, but that was about it. Apart from a nasty scar just over his rib cage, the only visible evidence was a streak of white hair running back from his left temple along the scar left by the quarter-inch-deep trench a red-hot shrapnel fragment had torn in his scalp.

His parents installed themselves in a suite at the Clift Hotel. Howland came to the hospital in the mornings for an hour or so, then went off to prowl Montgomery Street, or to lunch at the Pacific Union Club or for a round at the San Francisco Golf Club. Andy's convalescence was proving a useful opportunity to advance the interests of The Firm in San Francisco.

Each morning, Howland would report on the previous day's activity to Andy, but he could see his son wasn't really interested in the greater glory of Hanover Place.

"I can't blame you," he said at length, deciding to bite the bullet. "I felt the same way myself after my war."

He was enormously proud of his son. Not long after they'd arrived at Letterman, a three-star general dispatched from Camp Pendleton by the Corps Commandant had pinned two medals on Lance Corporal Andrew Farwell Warrington's pajamas: the Navy Cross, for extreme valor, and the Purple Heart.

"Can't blame you at all," Howland repeated. "Once you've seen the real thing, our Wall Street wars look like small change, don't they?"

Andy shrugged.

"Of course," said his father, "one *can* take a different view. In your grandfather's day, it was all buy and sell, sell and buy. No god but the tape, and speculators and traders were its prophets. Not any longer, you can take my word for that. Wall Street helps *build* things now. The old fat cats' game is over and done with. We're all in this together. It's important that every man feels he's part of the effort, which is why I thank God for those seventy million small stockholders out there."

"That's a hell of a speech, Father. You ought to run for office."

"Don't say that to your mother. She prefers to think of me as 'the Clausewitz of Wall Street,' as she puts it. She claims I think finance is the extension of politics by other means. Anyway, you know what I'm getting at."

"Speaking of speculators and traders, Mother says Jay's been up to no good again."

"What can I say? You know how he is. If life isn't a continual series of thrills and chills, it isn't fun. I must also say that when it comes to interpersonal relations with older men, Jay leaves a great deal to be desired.

Everyone says he reminds them of your grandfather, and in certain ways I suppose that's true physically, but I can assure you that my father, impatient as he was, never referred to a prominent broker on the Curb, granting that that's a bit of a contradiction in terms, as . . ."—Howland lowered his voice— ". . . 'Fuckface.' "

Two days before Lyda was due to return to New York, she appeared at the hospital, Chickie in tow. Andy's old friend was outlandishly dapper, turned out in a pinkish tropical-weight suit. The four-button jacket was wide-skirted, with tiny abbreviated lapels, and was so closely fitted to Chickie's plump pullet's body that he seemed at pains to move. The effect, all in all, was most peculiar.

Chickie had big news of his own. He was dropping out of Yale to attend the Parsons School of Design in New York.

"Your ma worked it out for me. I've decided I want to be an interior decorator."

"I thought you wanted to be a novelist of manners, an American Proust."

"Don't be silly, Drew. That takes talent."

"What does your old man think?"

"As you all too well know, CCF Third doesn't think. Not anymore. He reacts, but mostly he drinks. When he got too old for polo, Gessel cut the cord. Well, all but a few threads; he still puts enough commission business through Pater to pay the basic bills. And those are mainly for martinis and the California Club, where he hangs out the long day through, soaking up the gin with a group of like-minded troglodytes, and blaming assorted minorities for his life's low estate. But enough of that. Did Lyda bring you up to speed about poor old Max?"

Andy shook his head.

"Social disaster with a capital D. No fraternity and no spook house. On the final rush, Phi Gam gave him a bid again, but he held out for Fence, but the white-shoe boys didn't come through. Then this spring, the same thing vis à vis the tombs. Tap Day came and went: zero. Even after Miriam called your pop and asked him to put in a good word at Keys."

"She didn't!"

"Cross my heart and hope to die. Lyda didn't tell you?"

He looked at Lyda and waggled a finger. "You naughty old woman, you!"

Andy turned to his mother. "What'd Father say? Christ, you know how he is about such things. I'll bet he needed a new pair of drawers."

"Your father was, as always, the soul of courtesy. Said he couldn't see any harm in a mother looking out for her son's best interests."

"But did he actually get on the horn to Keys?"

"Of course not. *Noblesse oblige* is all well and good, provided you don't cut your own throat with it."

Chickie stayed on for two days before returning to Pasadena. Andy was glad of his company, and sad he wouldn't be around to enliven life at Yale.

Andy was released a week later. He decided to spend a couple of days on his own in San Francisco, just to decompress.

His father suggested that he put up at the Pacific Union Club, but the P.U. tended to become a tomb after seven, and Andy hated the clacking noise of dominoes, so he went instead to the Mark Hopkins.

His second night there, feeling itchy and horny, he decided to go out on the town and take pot luck. As he finished dressing, he happened to glance down at the narrow leatherette case lying on the bureau, and he opened it. A swell-looking medal, he thought. It was a bronze St. George cross; on the face, a tiny carved ship crested the waves, with crossed anchors and "USN" on the reverse. The navy-blue ribbon was bisected by a white stripe. Enjoy it while you can, he thought. It wouldn't be his much longer, he guessed, because his mother would surely appropriate it for the walnut cases that housed his brothers' medals.

He rode up to the Top O' the Mark. It was one of those indecently beautiful San Francisco nights, the bay a bowl of inky velvet encircled by the sparkling diadems of the two great bridges and the lights of the Belvedere—winking in the distance like spilled diamonds.

The bar was crowded with good-looking men and women, many in uniform, obviously coming from and going to the distant war. Andy found a place at the bar. The next stool was occupied by a bulky Navy lieutenant-commander exchanging ribaldries with the bartender in a twangy southern accent. He was a bear of a man, with a broad, friendly, weather-roughened face under a pepper-and-salt crewcut, and shrewd, pale eyes. The chest of his blue dress tunic was a riot of ribbons, five or six rows of them under the silver aviator's wings, a mass of color about six inches wide by five inches high. Andy recognized a few of them: a Navy Cross like his own, the blue strip embellished with a small metal star that signified it had been won twice; a Silver Star, various campaign and theater ribbons.

Andy ordered a Scotch and water and studied the naval officer's face in the mirror. He knew that face. He tapped the other man's arm and said: "Excuse me, sir, aren't you Lieutenant-Commander Marryat?"

The officer turned and grinned at him. "That's me," he said, "J-for-nothin', B-for-nothin' Marryat, United States Naval Reserve. Do I know you?"

"I'm Andrew Warrington. Lex Warrington's brother. We met when you came to New York for his memorial service."

The officer regarded Andy with shrewd brown eyes. Then he exploded: "Well I'll be a son of a bitch! Of course you are!"

He seized Andy's hand, pumped it, then drained his glass and pounded it on the bar for a refill.

More drinks followed; dinner was proposed. By then, Andy had learned all about J.B. Marryat: he was from Fort Worth, where his father had "a chickenshit l'il ol' exploration and development company"; he had in fact been baptized plain "J.B." and the initials stood for nothing; he was an Annapolis graduate, Class of '43, "it was that or be a Horned Frog, which I wasn't about to be"; he'd been called back for Korea, "me 'n old Ted Williams, and let me tell you, that ol' sumbitch can fly damn near as good as he can hit a baseball!"; he'd flown low-level air support for the Chosin Reservoir breakout, probably over Andy—"Shit, boy, the way my eyes are now, you're flat lucky I didn't shoot *your* ass off!" but when the new Sabrejets came in, his usefulness was over; when he mustered out in six weeks, he'd be back in the family "awl bidness."

The rest of Andy's evening faded into a dim patchwork of fragmentary memories. They dined at Amelio's and then, conveyed by a patient Chinese cabdriver, crisscrossed the city looking for trouble. Andy remembered an interval at the Fairmont, where they looked in on Dorothy Shay's "Park Avenue Hillbilly" act and a crawl up and down North Beach, refueling at various bars, but disdaining the strip-club hawkers. At one point they found themselves in a flashy nightclub filled with nothing but men.

At Trader Vic's on Cosmo Place, they ran into a brother officer of Marryat's, and then it was off to Barnaby Conrad's Matador, and finally out to a party at quite a fine house on Pacific Avenue presided over by a vivacious woman whom everyone called "Snowball." A lot of the guests seemed to know Andy's family and made a fuss over him.

He awoke the next morning with a mouth tasting like the outskirts of Hungnam. Next to him in bed was a pretty young woman, breathing as softly as a child. It took him a moment to sort out that she was in the road company of *Call Me Madam* at the Geary Theater, who had been at Trader Vic's.

He inspected her carefully. The sheet had slid down, to reveal a small, pale breast that seemed the essence of perfection and the most arousing thing he had ever seen. It seemed clear that he was no longer a virgin. An hour later, he reestablished this beyond any doubt. By then, he was also in love.

He remained in love for at least another six hours, until the white-tipped Rockies had receded under the wing of the Global Superconstellation, and the checkerboard of Nebraska was spread out below. He and the actress had exchanged addresses and promised to see each other—she would be coming east in the fall to go into rehearsals for a new musical called *Paint Your Wagon*—but somehow he knew they wouldn't: by then their paths would be routed elsewhere, he caught up in college and his old ways, she following her ambition. Anyway, at twenty-seven, she was far too old for him, especially with all of life waiting to be explored.

He looked out the window, thinking momentarily of the war, and the men he'd fought with, some, like him, home and safe, others left behind, out beyond the Rockies, out across the Pacific. He felt a twinge of real loss. He remembered his father telling him of the "hole" war made in the soul; even if a man came out of it whole, it was as if some part of him had been amputated, or left behind on the battlefield.

He shivered and opened his book, a new novel Chickie had raved about called *The Catcher in the Rye*. Chickie claimed it might as well be about Jay.

His throat felt dry. He reached into his jacket pocket for a Life Saver and his hand encountered the envelope that the desk clerk had handed him when he checked out. He had forgotten all about it in his rush to get to the airport.

It contained a battered but still functional military-issue wristwatch, a Hamilton with a radium dial. The band had been hammered out of aluminum; it was dulled and scarred with age and use. Two sets of initials had been carefully but somewhat crudely etched on it: J.B.M—A.F.W, along with a date: 11 JAN 45.

The watch had come wrapped in a sheet of notepaper on which was scrawled: "There used to be two of these, but one is where nobody can get at it. We had the bands made from a Betty that we shot down in Saipan harbor." J.B. Marryat had written down his Fort Worth telephone number.

Andy studied the watch. Well, he thought, why not? He slipped the watch on his wrist and was surprised to see how perfectly it fit.

BOOK

VI

HALCYON DAYS

JUNE

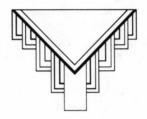

In the slatted moonlight, the girl seemed as blond and unattainable as Guinevere. They were in a small cabin she had somehow discovered, he wasn't exactly sure where in the ship it was; deck chairs were stacked against one bulkhead; a pale spill of moonlight faintly illuminated the interior.

"Kiss me again," she said. She took his hand in hers and guided it under her skirt.

"Ummm, yes, there." Her legs parted. He felt busy fingers at his trouser buttons. "Help me," she muttered, "we only have two good hands between us." Why had he worn trousers with buttons? Wasn't this what zippers were for? What did it matter? He helped her unbutton himself, then his hand returned to where it had been.

"Oh, yes, oh, yes," she gasped between kisses, "just keep doing that. Oh, yes."

Now she had hold of him. Please don't come, he prayed, oh, please don't, not yet, God.

"Ummm."

"Ummm. Oooh, yes." A long sigh.

For a minute or so they went on this way. Kissing and touching. Moaning. Ravenous.

"Now." The girl suddenly got to her feet. "Just relax." She gestured that he was to put his feet up on the deck chair. "That's right." She bent over and stroked his cock, then rose above him, gathering her skirt and petticoats above her waist. Above her stocking tops, the ivory bulge of her inner thighs swelled to meet the pale patch at their conjunction. Apart from a garter belt, she was wearing no underwear.

"Now, my lover," she murmured. She moved slightly forward, and lowered herself slowly. He felt himself sink upward into her, sensation rushed upon sensation.

She began to move steadily and he tried to follow her, half aware, half instinctively. As she moved, her breathing deepened, exhalations became sighs, became something like sobs. Ummm. Ummmm. Ummmmm. Sweet, sweet rhythms. He tried to move with her, listening to his own breath. Worrying at the back of his mind. Even as he felt what he was feeling, still . . .

She read his mind. "Don't worry, love." A massive panting, up and down. "Ummmmm, oooh, just, ummmm, *ummmm*, leave . . . leave everything to me, *ummm!*, to me . . ."

He could feel her hand reach for him, fingers circling the base of his cock, riding up and down, unendurable, excruciating, beautiful, with her own rising and falling. He felt the rush at the root, the slow, agonizing rise to the tip, the familiar exquisite pleasure, the point of everything. He heard his breath hitch.

She heard it, too. She rose and subsided onto him one last time, then shifted so smoothly he was hardly aware of her movement, letting him slide out, taking him in her long fingers, keeping the rhythm going.

"Now," she murmured, "now, now, now, now . . ."

He couldn't hold it anymore. He began to go into spasm. A cupped hand to trap his ejaculation. He heard his breath harsh in his throat. Ungh. Ungh. I sound like a goddamn animal, he thought.

"Uuugh," he moaned loudly, then realized where he was, and trapped the sound in his throat. He writhed against his pillow, caught in the subsiding excitement of the dream. His hand at his groin.

A few feet away, in the other bed, Miranda shifted in her sleep and whimpered. Andy slowly levered himself up in bed, trying to make no noise. He crossed the stateroom quietly to the bathroom. When he finished cleaning himself, he went to the porthole and looked out at the sea. For thirty-six hours, the Atlantic had been like glass and now a full moon had come out, spreading a widening white-gold swath across the surface of the ocean, a shimmering path narrowing to the horizon. From the deck below, music rose in the night; the band in the first-class lounge was playing a medley from *South Pacific:* "Bali H'ai," "Some Enchanted Evening," "Younger Than Springtime." He felt stupid. Jesus—a guy of his age and experience having a wet dream!

The music floated toward Andy, "And when your youth and joy invade my heart . . ." and again he ached for love of Laurel Hopewell, and his gut twisted at the thought that at this very moment, somewhere in a darkened cabin, in the deep shadows of a lifeboat, Max Miles might be sliding his hand into the bosom of Laurel's dress, reaching under her skirt, his clumsy, hairy fingers inching beneath her brassiere, parting her crinolines. The thought made Andy groan, and in the stateroom he heard his little sister mew in her sleep before her breathing resumed its level rhythm.

He stole back into bed. Tomorrow, he thought, I will make my move. Laurel *can't* be serious about Max Miles! But time was running out. In only two days they would dock at Algeciras, where the Hopewells would be disembarking.

Ordinarily, Lyda would have crossed on the Italian Line—the very idea of a liner that was American designed and staffed repelled her—but The Firm came first. Partners and their families flew Global if Global served a route, no matter whether other airlines offered more convenient scheduling. It was no different when it came to ocean travel. Morris Miles had practically invented American Constellation Lines, so when Lyda decided to take Andrew and Miranda to see Italy, her choice was reduced to either the *Orion* or her sister ship *Ursa Major*.

When the "VIP List" for the June 10 sailing of the *Orion* arrived at the apartment, and Lyda saw that the Mileses were on it, she briefly considered rejiggering the whole trip, doing France and the Low Countries instead, and making a North Atlantic crossing. But everything was booked, even the brand new *United States*, and she had promised the children a voyage, so she was stuck.

Still, it could have been worse. Morris was chairman of the line's executive committee, so the Miles party was placed at the captain's table, in Lyda's experience the dreariest seating on most ships, while she and Andrew and Miranda were put at the chief purser's table, which was invariably much gayer.

She could not of course completely avoid the others. A routine had been established their first night out whereby, after dinner, the two families would convene in the lounge for coffee. On the second night, they had been joined by the Hopewells.

Lyda had seen at once that the Hopewell girl could be trouble. Her looks were a striking combination of opposites. She was very pale and fine-boned, with good high color in the cheeks, eyes that were almost black under severely-cut fine blond hair that was almost white. It was a sharp, calculating little face backlit by confident self-awareness.

Laurel dressed "old" for her age, a black evening sweater, ornamented with glistening dark beading over an ankle-length black skirt, with quite decent pearls at her ears and her throat. It was difficult to tell about her figure. Her left arm was in a black voile sling.

Lyda had known the Hopewells vaguely. They were famous for being boring, as by Lyda's lights, most people from Pittsburgh were. They lived in Sewickley or Fox Chapel, Lyda couldn't remember which, and summered at Northeast Harbor, in Maine, where they were neighbors of Howland's sister Florence. Elspeth Hopewell was richer than Croesus. She was a Bayard from Lloyd Neck, and people said she came into eight million when she turned twenty-one, and that was peanuts compared to what she'd get on the death of her mother, Evangeline Bayard, the chatelaine of Windfall, the largest house on Long Island's North Shore.

Thad Hopewell did something at the Monongahela Trust and spent most of his days at the Duquesne Club and Rolling Rock. He had been at New Haven around Howland's time, where he was considered a stuffed shirt even as a young man, but he was good at administering a grand household, and that seemed to be the sort of talent girls in Elspeth's circumstances were drawn to. Laurel would be the girl who was at Foxcroft with Alice's child Annette, which would make her sixteen or seventeen.

When the Hopewells approached the table, Lyda felt Andrew and Max come to instant, aroused attention. She looked at Andrew, who was gaping like Lot's wife, as was Max, natty in a white dinner jacket and a matching madras bowtie and cummerbund.

Until he met Laurel, Andrew had been plotting a calculated assault on a covey of young southern women in cabin class, a sixteen-strong Martha Barlow Tour from Nashville. Jay, who had accompanied his mother the previous year on her annual jaunt, claimed to have had carnal knowledge of the entire complement of a Barlow Tour from Greenville, South Carolina. According to Jay, there was no surer thing on earth than a southern girl of good family making her initial visit to Europe. It was precisely against such a contingency that Jay's bon voyage gift to his brother had been a dozen Ramses-brand prophylactics, and a copy of *This Is My Beloved*. According to Jay, Walter Benton's throbbing poetry was more effective than Spanish fly. As a backup, he recommended A. E. Housman, and so Andy's luggage contained a tired copy of *A Shropshire Lad* which Jay had discovered in a stairwell bookshelf at Double Dune and appreciated at once for its seductive properties. Jay particularly recommended the poem beginning, "Wake, the silver dusk returning, up the beach of darkness brims." Recited soulfully, he swore, with a full moon mounting the South Atlantic night toward its solstitial rendezvous, with the sea afire with gold, it should be good for "bare tit" at the minimum.

Andy had been prepared to include Max in his nefarious carnal scheme for Martha Barlow Tour #6—"An Italian Midsummer Night's Fantasy," but the arrival of Laurel changed all that. Thoughts of sly adventure belowdecks fled his mind. As the steward appeared at the table with coffee and liqueurs, the band in the ballroom segued into "Who Stole My Heart Away," and Andy felt himself tumbling down the endless aching confusing corridors of absolute infatuation or, as he would have put it at that moment, love.

At the time the Hopewells joined Lyda's table on the *Orion*, Howland and Jay were just sitting down to cocktails in the bar of the Gorse Club. Surprisingly, it was Jay who had asked for the meeting, although it happened that the father had one or two things he wanted to get off his chest.

Jay had been moved "upstairs" at Hanover Place. His ascent had hardly been a well-deserved promotion, however. He had left the Big Board under a cloud, just as a year earlier, The Firm had been advised to take him off the Curb. His progress through the exchanges resembled his prep-school career. He had no regard for rules, written or unwritten, except as they were necessary to fair and honest dealing. He saw no need for manners in business, since all that really counted was what was on the tape.

Moreover, beginning with his first apprenticeship, at the "odd-lot" firm of DeCoppet and Doremus, one of two houses that monopolized the execution of Floor orders for less than a hundred shares, Jay had decided the exchanges were populated by idiots. Howland himself found it hard to disagree, and was thus only mildly embarrassed by these escapades.

"Vinnie Grady says men who don't suffer fools gladly are bound to be unhappy on the Floor," he explained to Lyda, after the episode that closed Jay's career as a floor broker.

This was a fight at the bar of Eberlin's Restaurant. All agreed that Jay's opponent, a beefy, forty-year-old Irishman who was both an important specialist and a Stock Exchange governor, had thrown the first punch. The matter at issue hardly seemed to justify fisticuffs. Jay claimed the specialist had clipped an extra eighth on a block of Superior Carbon that Warrington & Co. was selling for an important connection. He put forward his case in language that was surprisingly inventive and allusive for one who had not attended college. The other man answered with a swing. Jay countered with a swift and savage kick to his opponent's groin that left him fish-white and gasping on the linoleum.

Upstairs, Jay was reborn. He found his calling.

As Vinnie Grady told Howland, "He may only be twenty years old, but that son of yours can paint the tape as good as any man alive."

Coming from Vinnie, that was like Ted Williams praising a rookie's hitting.

Vinnie was Jay's principal tutor, along with Byron Casey, who made markets in the over-the-counter stocks in which The Firm dealt. Their tutelage extended beyond the order room. At the close of business, they would take Jay along to the Olde Ale House, where a klatsch of traders gathered every evening to rehash the day's events and boast to each other of the day's trading coups. Jay realized at once that he was different from the Ale House crowd. They were mostly still clerks at heart; he had a larger vision. It was this vision that he proposed to sell to his father.

"You see, Pop," waving off the waiter's attempt to pour his beer into a glass, "the Street's gonna change. It's gotta. You talk to guys like Gus Levy and Cy Lewis, and they'll tell you that the Floor's not where the trading action's gonna be."

Howland smiled and listened patiently. The Floor was always said to be dying, but it had more lives than a cat. The members knew how to protect their franchise. He could understand his son's enthusiasm. Young men were impatient; Jay was too young to command the ears of the middle-aged industrialists and financiers with whom Howland and Morris did business. Jay talked of the people he "knew" on various bank and Street trading desks, but how could a boy his age be expected to have developed "relationships"?

"Look, Dad," Jay continued, "now that we've gotten the Exchange into letting us 'cross' these institutional orders on the tape, so we get both sides . . ."

"As long as the specialist gets his free ride," interrupted Howland.

"Yeah, okay, Pop, but who gives a crap about that! It's the institutions we've gotta be working on. If Chelsea Trust wants to sell fifteen thousand Carbide, they don't want to sit there all day and watch the floor jew 'em down an eighth a hundred. If we get set up right, we can do the whole trade here. Make 'em a bid, even if we don't have a buyer right then!"

"I think you're right in theory, and will be proven wrong in fact," said his father. "The Floor will protect itself as it always has. And don't forget: it's the small investor who's the backbone of our business, and a very good thing, too."

"Yeah, yeah, yeah," said Jay. "Come back in a few years, and tell me all about those small investors, Pop."

Howland studied his glass. He loved the idea of a "people's capitalism" of millions of small, stable, individual stockholders, men and women who followed the exhortation developed by the Exchange's advertising agency

and "owned their share of America." It was a vision that played to his
own notion of his and The Firm's heritage and destiny. Jay was quite
right, however, Hanover Place wasn't really set up to service the small
investor; it wasn't The Firm's style. Then there was the paradox Lyda
had unkindly introduced one night at the dinner table.

"Tell me," she asked, "why is it that you people speak of the small
investor as if he was Jesus Christ Himself, but then when you look at the
market, the first thing you always say is: 'The public is always wrong.'
Aren't *they* buying what *you're* selling them? I seem to remember your
father telling me that people don't buy stocks, they're sold them. He seemed
to find that terribly amusing."

Howland shook his head. Lyda would never grasp the essence of Hanover Place's business. He smiled at his son across the table, and wondered
how the family's crossing was going.

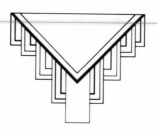

1952

JULY

By the time they got to Venice, it seemed to Lyda that Andrew was quite himself again. He had ceased to blather about the beauty of the countryside, to utter doleful sighs in the shadows of *duomos* and *campaniles* and discourse feelingly on the play of sun on old marble and the moon on the gently flowing Tiber.

And not a moment too soon, she thought. He had really become quite tiresome, with his muttered bits of Ruskin and Dante gleaned from pocket editions he'd found in Naples. As they moved north up the spine of Italy, the symptoms of infatuation—like measles spots—paled and faded away; by Milan, it was obvious the worst of the fever had passed, and as they stood on the quay of the Piazzale Roma, watching the Gritti launch being loaded with their luggage, she could tell from her son's face that he was more or less "over" Laurel Hopewell.

It was difficult to say whether Lyda was more amazed or irritated at the way the girl had thrown herself at Max Miles. She wouldn't have minded so much if Andrew, refusing to act like a man of his upbringing and experience, hadn't scavenged so pitifully on the edges of the affair, and it hadn't helped, of course, to have to watch Miriam gloat!

Lyda knew about shipboard romances, how unlikely could be the pairings they produced, but this was ridiculous! The girl was clearly up to something, probably just doing it to scandalize the sticks-in-the-mud she had for parents.

Certainly Thad Hopewell was shocked. Once or twice, out of earshot of the others, he'd bent to Lyda's ear and slyly whispered the most awful, bigoted nonsense about Morris and his son. She managed to maintain a blank, unsmiling expression that made her own feelings clear. All she could think of was something her late father-in-law claimed Otto Kahn had once said to him: "A kike is a Jewish gentleman who has just left the room." Well, everyone knew how people in Pittsburgh were on the subject, which was one reason Lyda detested the place.

She could see how a girl like Laurel, brought up in a certain fashion, might find someone like Max exotic; he was flamboyant, if a little obvious, in manner and speech; he talked about and spent his father's money freely; quite apart from the Jewish matter, he represented norms of behavior people like the Hopewells couldn't understand and therefore despised.

It was obvious Elspeth and Thad Hopewell were relieved to leave the ship at Algeciras. Laurel waved bravely from the launch bearing them toward the hump of Gibraltar, but her parents resolutely turned away, and Lyda, watching from the rail, swore to Andrew she could see Hope-well *père*'s shoulders slump with relief.

The Mileses disembarked at Genoa, Miriam still savoring her son's triumph, talking as if she fully expected to spend fine crisp weekends the following autumn chasing the Hopewell beagles over the rolling hills of western Pennsylvania.

The Miles family was part of a large Wall Street contingent bound for the Holy Land. Morris had enjoyed his crossing. Hardly had the *Orion* cleared the Ambrose lightship when he had settled into a comfortable routine with three other men who looked and sounded exactly like him. In the mornings, uneasily clad in flashy "resort wear," they soberly circumambulated the promenade deck discussing finance and Eisenhower's chances; afternoons were devoted to bridge in the lounge, whoever was dummy being responsible for checking the Reuters and Dow-Jones bulletins posted outside the chief purser's office; after dinner, they played gin rummy in the lounge. Lyda expected the same routine would somehow be pursued all the way across the top of Italy, out into the Adriatic, and across the Mediterranean to Israel.

The hotel launch was finally loaded. The steersman helped Lyda board, then Miranda. Andy jumped in lightly after them. As the launch made for the Grand Canal, he felt no less relieved than his mother.

Of course, there was no doubt he'd made a goddamn fool of himself! To think of it made him wriggle inside his skin with embarrassment. Still, any girl who could fall for an asshole like Max had to have something psychologically wrong with her! He must have been temporarily insane.

He looked at his sister.

"Hey, Miranda," he said gaily, "how about a few churches before supper?"

The girl glared at him.

"I don't want to see any more stupid old churches."

"How can you say such a thing? Do you want to grow up a Philistine?" Andy teased. He was feeling very merry.

"I hate Italy!" came the answer.

That night, Lyda, who had the soul of a tour guide, took Miranda off to a Vivaldi concert in San Marco. Andy begged off. He dined early at the Gritti, and afterward ambled down to the Piazza San Marco, where he took a seat at Florian's and ordered coffee and a brandy. The band was bouncily sawing away at a medley of Italian popular tunes. The night was clear; the façade of San Marco and the Campanile were lit up; everyone in the world seemed to be in the giant piazza.

Behind him, he picked out American voices, soft, unarguably southern voices, the voices of girls giggling with excitement at being in this strange and glamorous place. Barlow voices.

It was in fact a cohort of Barlow Belles from the ship. Talk about luck! Andy fortunately had a copy of the *Paris Herald* tucked in his jacket pocket; he ostentatiously unfolded it and began to read. The girls behind him soon noticed. Small talk was struck up, and soon, bonded by the loneliness all Americans feel in foreign lands, they were fast friends.

Like a cutting horse working a herd of calves, Andy quickly separated out the object of his choice, a Randolph-Macon sophomore with breasts that seemed astonishing in proportion to her lissome build. The next night, having cleared his credentials with the group's chaperone, he presented himself at the Bauer Grunwald.

He followed Jay's "script" to the letter: dinner—with wine—on the roof garden of the Danieli followed by a drink in the Piazza, followed by a gondola ride.

The night was warm and perfumed with romance. Casually he draped an arm around her shoulders, while behind them the gondolier moaned of Venetian nights.

"It must have been just awful in Korea," she said softly. He had managed to bring the conversation around to the retreat from Yudam-ni.

"Terrible," he said, "but we didn't have much choice. In my family, that's what we do—yours, too, I expect." He had ascertained there was a distant Robert E. Lee connection.

"Do you know the poem by A. E. Housman?" he asked. "The one that goes: 'Here dead lie we, because we did not choose to live, and shame the land from whence we sprung. Life, to be sure, is nothing much to lose. But young men think it is, and we were young.' "

Shortly thereafter, in a narrow *viale* near Camp San Moise, overcome by the magic of the night and the place, almost frantic with desire, she yielded, at least to the extent that their upright position and her complicated undergarments would permit. For the rest of his life, even though his passion had been technically unconsummated, Andy would remember this night as one of the few purely romantic moments in his experience. At the end of the evening, with early streaks of light appearing beyond the Lido, they clung to each other in farewell, and promised to rendezvous in Paris or Brussels or Amsterdam. Andy guessed that wouldn't happen, but they had given each other Venice as it should be for the first time, when one is still young enough to harbor life's better illusions, and in that they shared something that life would never again deliver. In the power of the moment, he scarcely noticed that Laurel Hopewell was utterly out of his mind.

Ten days later, the Warringtons arrived in Paris. They entered the city early in the evening, at the hour when daylight had faded but night was not yet in full possession of the city. The weather was cool for late June; the plane trees along the Seine seemed barely to have come into leaf. As Andy maneuvered the heavy black car across the Rond point toward the Avenue Matignon, it began to drizzle, and the cobblestones glistened in the yellow light thrown off by the street lamps.

Sitting in the front seat, Lyda was surprised and deeply happy to see Paris looking so well. Like her, the war had put the old city through a lot, but like her, it seemed to have overcome the ravages.

Next to New York, Lyda loved Paris best. New York had great energy and variety, but Paris had beauty and style. It apportioned being and becoming; valued the old along with the new, and admired both on their own terms.

She turned to the back seat and tapped her daughter on the forearm. "Look, darling!" She pointed up the Champs-Elysées, where the great neon signs were coming alight. "Isn't it wonderful?"

"When are we going to get to the hotel?" the child asked. "I feel sick. I hated that lunch!"

"Hush!" said Lyda. "How do you think Monsieur Point would feel if he heard you? The Pyramide is probably the best restaurant in the world!"

Andy braked to avoid a little Renault "Deux Chevaux" darting across their path, then swung into the rue du Faubourg St. Honoré, heading for the Hotel Lotti in the rue Castiglione.

Lyda couldn't help thinking that it was a fine time to be an American in Europe. The dollar was almighty. Her room at the Gritti had cost ten dollars a night—at the black-market rate, of course—and the suite at the Lotti would be about half again as much, but then Paris was always more expensive than Venice.

She intended to buy her French francs at the unofficial rate. Howland had instructed her to call the manager of Chelsea Trust's resident office on the Place Vendôme, who would take care of her, but at the official rate, which only a fool would pay. She was sure the concierge at the Lotti could see to her requirements.

From the back seat, Miranda watched the buildings go by. She was bored. She knew this trip was mostly on her account—Mama said it was important to know foreign cultures—but whose fault was that? Europe was a big fat stupid bore, just like Jay said it would be. Why couldn't they just have stayed at Double Dune?

She stared at the back of Andy's neck while her mother blabbed on and on about places called "the Velodrome" and "the Trocka-something," none of which, Miranda speculated, could be half as awful as the stupid Doges' Palace—which had about sixteen hundred million rooms, each one dumber than the one before. She studied Andy's head, which was kind of like a light bulb if you thought about it, and decided she loved him a lot, even if not as much as Jay, because Jay played tricks and made you laugh. She wished Jay had been on the boat, 'cause that really would have been fun, especially with Max. Jay didn't care what he did or who saw him do it, which was really neat. Jay would have taken care of Max Miles for Andy, that was for sure.

She also considered how much she hated Laurel Hopewell. Enough to kill her? Well, maybe not kill her—but something awful.

When they arrived at the Lotti, Andy saw about the luggage and steered Miranda upstairs to their suite. After dealing with the *réception*, Lyda walked over to the concierge's station.

"So nice to see you again, Henri," she said quietly, and regally extended her hand, in which a twenty-dollar bill was folded. The concierge smiled and bobbed his head.

"Do you suppose I could arrange to change five thousand U.S.?" she asked in a low voice.

She had calculated that $5,000 at a decent rate would see them through their week in Paris and let her buy what she needed at Balenciaga and Fath.

"Of course, madame." Henri nodded gravely. "I will have a man come tomorrow."

"*Entendu.* Now, I should also like to place a call to my husband in New York."

"I am afraid there will be a delay of at least three hours, madame."

"Whatever."

"And, madame, this arrived for your son."

He held out a postcard.

In the lift, Lyda examined it. It had been mailed ten days earlier from

Avignon and was addressed to "A. Warrington Esq." in the blocklike hand in which most young women of a certain background and education wrote. There was no message as such: just the phrase, "*Rich* III, 1, iii, 229–30."

Avignon, thought Lyda. That was where the Hopewells were headed after Barcelona. She turned the card over and over. Not just when Andrew's back on top of the world, she reflected, and tucked the card into her purse.

The next morning, a warm front swept in, pushing the damp and drizzle north toward the Low Countries. Sunlight danced in the green ranks of the Tuileries. In the sitting room of the suite, Andy settled down with the sports page of the *Paris Herald*. The Yankees were now six games ahead in the American League. In the Wimbledon finals, the Australian Sedgman had beaten Drobny, the Czech; "Little Mo" Connolly had won the women's end. He flipped through the rest of the paper. The big news was that the liner *United States* had set a new record for a transatlantic crossing.

His study of the paper was interrupted by a sharp knock.

"Would you get that, darling," Lyda called from her bedroom. "I'm sure it's the man with our francs."

The man at the door was short and gaunt, the sort of hard-used type central casting might send over to play a black-market money changer. His skin was sallow and unhealthy. Except for patchy wisps and sprouts of whitish-blond hair, he was bald. An angry scar described a jagged track above one ear. The man's nose had obviously been broken and clumsily set and under his left eye the skin was puckered and reddened, as if it had been seared. Clearly here was someone whom life, most likely the war, had used pretty hard. But his crooked mouth was shaped in a smile of undeniable warmth and his eyes, light gray, like Miranda's, were alight with good humor.

In his right hand he held a pigskin attaché case emblazoned with remnants of bright paper labels: FIRST CLASS—CUNARD, HOTEL RITZ/MADRID, HOTEL ADLON/BERLIN, OESTERREICHES ZOLL-SCHAAN, CLARIDGES/BROOK STREET/LONDON.

"Madame Warrington?" the new arrival asked. His voice was high and harsh, as if recovering from a severe bout with laryngitis, but his English, though precise, bore no trace of a European accent.

"Come in, please," said Andy, gesturing the visitor into the sitting room. "I'm Andrew Warrington, Mrs. Warrington's son."

The hand that shook his had a distinct tremor. The man preceded Andy into the room. He carried himself carefully, as if in some pain.

"Good morning," Lyda said brightly from the bedroom door. She breezed into the room, vigorously brushing the tight helmet of curls in which she had had her hair done for the trip. She looked at the stranger and stopped in her tracks; her hand flew to her mouth and she gasped. "Oh, my God . . ."

"Hello, Lyda," the man said before she could finish her sentence. He nodded. "Yes, yes, it is I."

"Oh, my God," Lyda repeated. She looked to Andy as if she might faint, and he reached out to take her arm. "We, I mean Howland, I mean I, well, we thought, we heard, oh my God . . . oh, Eric, Eric!" She sat down heavily on the sofa.

"Eric, Eric, can it really be you?"

The man nodded and smiled. "You were expecting perhaps Harry Lime?" he said.

Lyda sprang up, crossed the room quickly, and threw her arms around him. "Oh, Eric, Eric," she began again: "We thought . . . Howland said . . . we thought . . ."

The man stepped back and held her at arms' length.

"I know," he said, "there were times when I did also . . ."

He broke off, looked at Andy, and bowed slightly.

"Eric Laszlo, Andrew. An old friend of your parents. I think you were at school when I was in New York, so I don't think we ever met."

Laszlo smiled and turned to Lyda. "Permit me to apologize for my appearance, my dear. The result of having made the acquaintance of certain of Dr. Mengele's more creative disciples."

At that moment the door to the suite resounded with the impatient hammering of small fists. Miranda had evidently tired of scouting the lobby. Andy let her in.

"This is Miranda, Eric," Lyda said. "The last of my brood."

She watched as her daughter made a polite curtsy to the stranger.

"You look like your father, Miranda," said Laszlo. "And your beautiful mother, too." He smiled at Lyda. "And how *is* Howland?"

"He's just fine. He'll be thrilled to hear you're alive."

She turned to Andy. "Why don't you take Miranda and walk up to Charvet in the Place Vendôme and pick out a dressing gown for your father's birthday? Just have them send it here and the hotel will put it on our bill. I'll meet you downstairs at eleven and we can take a leisurely walk over to the Left Bank. Perhaps I can persuade Eric to join us."

When the door closed behind them, Laszlo came over to her, embraced her, and kissed her lightly on the lips. She disengaged herself and said gently: "Dear, dear Eric, I'm afraid all that's behind me now. I'm an old woman now."

"Fifty-two is not so old." He laughed and shook his head at some inner joke. "The century with which you were born looks to me to be in much worse shape than you are. As for the kiss, ah, Lyda, that for my part was also just for old times' sake. If you begged me to take you, I could not. I regret to report that not only did I contribute one rib and a kidney to the cause of the Thousand Year Reich's noble experiments in genetics, but they also removed certain other valuable parts of me. May I?"

He sat down on the sofa.

"I don't suppose you'd mind indulging me in some of the Lotti's excellent coffee?"

The floor waiter brought a fresh pot. Laszlo told her about his life since 1943. He had been caught trying to bribe an official of the Wilhelmstrasse to secure the release of five thousand Jews held for extermination. A coalition of major Jewish interests around the world was prepared to commit almost a billion dollars to purchase their release. Laszlo, with his Swiss passport, had gone into Germany, even though he knew the Gestapo wanted him, to meet secretly with certain Nazi officials. There had been a betrayal; the Germans were shot; Laszlo was sent to a concentration camp.

"With your Swiss passport?" Lyda asked incredulously.

"I'm afraid my countrymen turned their backs on me," he said. "It was 1943, don't forget. The more astute among the Germans could see it was only a matter of time, once the Russian front collapsed, until the war would end. It was obvious that to have a Swiss nest egg would be a good thing. Nazi treasure, much of it stolen, began to pour across the border and into the vaults of Zurich by the boxcar."

The camp to which Laszlo was sent was a small, specialized operation, conducting research in various exotic branches of eugenics. In 1945, of no more medical use, he was on the transit rota for Auschwitz when the British liberated the camp.

It took him a year in a Lausanne hospital to become ambulatory again. After that, he had returned briefly to his mother's family's bank in Zurich, but things hadn't worked out, so in 1947 he came to Paris, and was very happy.

"I don't believe you," Lyda said when he finished. "You're happy doing this? Selling black-market francs to American tourists! Why didn't you get in touch with Howland? Or Piers Lucas, or any other of your friends in the City? What about your own family?"

He grinned crookedly. "Lyda, my dear, I'm not selling francs, although it does sound an amusing idea. Paris is expensive, and though I enjoy the French, they are very peculiar about money, so every bit helps. But my circumstances, believe me, are comfortable."

"I'm not sure I follow you."

"As a good Swiss and a man of conscience, I found the wartime behavior of my countrymen to be rather demeaning. The treasure that the Nazis moved across the Alps to the Zurich banks in 1944 and 1945 was mainly stolen, including gold from the teeth of Jews exterminated in the death camps. It was my position, as a director of our family bank, that if the Jews from whom the treasure had been appropriated could not be found or accounted for, then it should be restored to the government of Israel. My cousin Jürg, the executive director, took an opposite position, more consistent with official Swiss policy."

"Which was . . . ?"

"To admit nothing. You may not be aware of it, but Washington has literally had to blackmail Berne into releasing some small part of the Nazi hoard, and only then by threatening to freeze all Swiss assets in the United States. In any event, I did the same with my cousin Jürg. He is more a man of the world than I. Unless a franc, or a dollar, or a scudo has another man's name indelibly written on it, he regards it as his own. When I was unable to prevail on him to do the right thing voluntarily, I furnished Weizmann's people in Vienna with certain of our bank's records, which they were then able to reconcile with their own. So far, some fifty million Swiss francs' worth of assets have been restored to Jews, many of them now in Israel.

"This made Jürg extremely unhappy. I think he would have turned me in to the authorities, in which case I should not be sitting here talking to you. Switzerland regards a breach of fiscal confidentiality a malfeasance considerably more serious than murder. On the other hand, Jürg saw that if he denounced me, I might speak out, and the bank's position would be gravely affected. And so we came to an agreement.

"A handsome stipend—what you Americans call 'hush money'—is deposited each month to my account in the Banque Rothschild. I could easily live out my days as a boulevardier, a *flaneur*, but for a man of thirty-eight . . ." Laszlo's voice momentarily took on a dreamy quality, then sharpened again. "So, in my quiet way, I have been working with Tel Aviv on the restitution problem, and I've recently been having conversations with my Rothschild friends about joining their enterprise."

"I wish you'd talk to Howland," Lyda interrupted. "He wants to open a European representative office. You'd be perfect! Promise me you will!"

"I promise. Howland is right to establish a beachhead here. Europe will one day be very interesting commercially, but one must be willing to take a ten- or fifteen-year view. Howland is one of the few Americans willing to do that. Yes, indeed, I *shall* call Howland."

"I intend to hold you to that promise, Eric."

"Enough of me, though. How is the rest of your fine family? What nice children these two seem to be. Andrew's a fine young man."

"We're very proud of him. He went off to Korea without telling anyone—I could have killed him!—but he came back covered with medals."

"Would you have expected a son of yours and Howland's to have done otherwise, dear Lyda?" said Laszlo with a quiet little smile. "He comes, after all, from a family of warriors. The little girl's enchanting. How old is she—eight, nine? She looks mischievous. Is she? I expect she's what you Americans call 'a handful.' And how are the twins? Let's see—they must be at Hanover Place by now. Are they making a great success?"

He looked up and what he saw in her face stopped him cold.

"Oh, my goodness," he said. "Oh my poor dearest Lyda. I am so sorry."

"It's all right, Eric. You couldn't have known. We all had to give something to the war, didn't we? You gave a large part of yourself. I gave my sons."

He reached over and patted her hand.

"Not all your sons," he said; "not all of myself. Perhaps that's how we should think of it."

He looked at his watch. "It's eleven. I shall join you, if I may. We'll go to Brasserie Lipp as my treat."

He reached into his breast pocket for a handkerchief. As he did, his left cuff slid back and Lyda saw, clumsily tattooed on the inside of his wrist, in rough purplish numerals, the number 40547.

He saw her looking at it.

"Is that what I think it is?" she asked.

He smiled. "A little souvenir of war. You could say that it's a kind of Purple Heart."

Laszlo shepherded them through Paris for the five days of their sojourn. He appeared to know everyone and was able to get anything done; at his insistence, shuttered galleries in the Louvre were thrown open and restaurants produced bottles for which men would die. He and Andy became fast friends.

It was a jolly time. Only now and then, at the end of an evening, over a last coffee and cognac, would Laszlo turn at all serious.

What do people think about Israel, he wanted to know. Was it true that Truman had been reluctant to recognize the new state? If Eisenhower was drafted and won, what would that mean?

Israel wasn't something to which Lyda had given much thought. After what the Nazis had done to the Jews, it seemed only fair that there be some meaningful restitution, and Israel appeared to be what world Jewry wanted in recompense. It troubled her that hundreds of thousands, or was it millions, of Palestinians had been turned out, and so many children among them. She had seen the UNRRA posters of Arab children starving in the desert.

"I think people at home are by and large for Israel," she told Laszlo. "Of course this Rosenberg spy thing hasn't helped. It would have been nice—I don't imagine that's the right word, but I can't for the life of me think of another—if there could have been an Irishman among the atom spies. All those Jewish names! And I do wish that the Arab children could be spared."

"There were children at Auschwitz, too," said Laszlo quietly, looking out the window. "In these affairs, there are always children."

Finally it came time to leave. Laszlo came by to make his farewells. They talked a while, and then Lyda saw him downstairs. He would come to New York perhaps later in the year, he promised.

"If you do," Lyda insisted, "you must come down to Double Dune for a weekend." She smiled. "You remember Double Dune?"

"Of course."

For an instant she thought he was going to say something, but if he was, he thought better of it. He bent and kissed her hand.

"*Adieu* then, or rather, *à bientôt*," he said.

He tipped his hat, pressed a folded note on the *huissier*, and an instant later was lost in the throng on the rue de Rivoli.

Lyda looked at her watch. Another half hour yet before leaving for Orly. Suddenly she remembered something she wanted to do. She walked quickly out of the lobby and down the street to Galignani's bookstore, and purchased an inexpensive edition of Shakespeare.

Back in her room, she raced through *Richard III* until she found the section she was seeking. Here it was: act one, scene three. She ran a finger down the page to the lines she wanted, and read: "Was ever a woman in this humor woo'd/Was ever woman in this humor won?/I'll have her, but I will not keep her long."

You too-clever-by-half little bitch, she thought. She heard noises in the outside hall. Andrew and Miranda were returning from their last-minute shopping. As she heard Andrew's key in the lock, Lyda tore the card into shreds, trotted into her bedroom, and threw them in the wastebasket.

1953

JUNE

t's a most beautiful evening, isn't it? Really most fortunate for the Hopewells. Of course, I shouldn't care to be in God's shoes if it rains and He has to answer to Granny Bayard."

"Amen to that," said Andy. He took a deep drag on his Lucky Strike and pretended to study the tide swirling at the pilings. He and Max were standing at the end of a pier that extended some twenty feet into Breadloaf Cove; behind them a wide, well-tended lawn ran up to the stone terrace of the big Georgian house to which Andy's aunt and uncle had moved just after the war.

Across the narrow inlet the dark hump of Breadloaf Point was bathed in the fading light of sunset. The forested grounds were in shadow, but the last orange-and-pink rays picked out the roof and chimneys of Windfall, Evangeline Bayard's mammoth limestone mansion, with a singular clarity. The great house that would be the site of tonight's party sat on Breadloaf Point's highest elevation, overlooking to the west a narrow cove and to the north, the expanse of Long Island Sound. On a clear night like this, the lights on the distant Connecticut shore would be visible.

Andy had several reasons for not looking forward to the evening. He hated big parties; no matter how "wonderfully well done" they were—Jay had announced with relish that the evening was going to be a big production, "fifty Gs minimum," which was real big time, even by Jay's elevated Wall Street standards—they seldom lived up to expectations. It was all just so much social flailing. "Good show about Hillary, what?" said Max.

"Hillary?"

"Everest, old boy. What a grand coronation present for a young queen, eh?"

Andy looked up at Max, who was as always carefully posed, one hand in his jacket pocket, feet set just so, as if Cecil Beaton might pop out of the trees at any moment and snap his picture for *Gentry*.

As he spoke, Max's hand squeezed tight around the small, square velvet box. He felt very nervous. It wasn't every night a man proposed. He also felt resentful, because he couldn't understand why he hadn't been bade to the dinner old Mrs. Bayard was giving at Windfall before the dance. As Laurel's beau, now to be her betrothed, he should have been invited. It was all very well for Laurel to say that the dinner was "strictly family," but wasn't he almost family? Hadn't he stayed with them for ten days this last spring vacation at Boca Grande?

Boca was kind of a scrubby place. Leo said you could smell the old Episcopal money; in such places, it was as pervasive, and corrosive, as the salt Gulf air. What did Leo know? Everyone had been very cordial to Max; it seemed to him he was treated in a manner appropriate to his relationship with Laurel. So much for Leo Himelman's prediction that Max would feel out of place on Boca, or his assertion that a Jew wouldn't be welcome in the wider world of the Hopewells.

Max was onto Leo's game: because Leo was the way he was, everything bad that happened to him was naturally only *because* Leo was a Jew.

That was silly, Max thought. As long as you weren't pushy or crass or money-grabbing, and didn't look and sound like some Delancey Street ragpicker, everything was okay.

He had even tried to explain this to Leo, one afternoon in Cambridge. Leo was helping get his B-School "case" put together properly. It was useful to have Leo around, especially since Max could never quite get "present value" straight.

Anyway, Leo had been spouting off about how he'd been slighted by the Law Review, and Max had said, "Well, maybe if you didn't come across all the time like a Bronx shyster, they'd take you!" Which was true, for all Max knew, because smart as Leo was, his lack of couth was really awful.

Leo had blown his stack at that! He got so mad he couldn't even speak; he threw down Max's notes and just sat there with his pocked, sour face getting redder by the second—you could almost see the steam coming out of his ears—and his dead little eyes almost glittering with rage.

Of course, Max apologized. Leo was very useful, and there was no point in losing him by pissing him off. As Max's mother said, what one did with the Leos of the world was to keep them in a certain place. You had different people in different boxes for different purposes. She and Max's father didn't have Lou Bernstein, the family accountant, home to dinner, but that didn't mean he wasn't a good accountant. And Leo, after all, was welcome in the Miles home.

Max squeezed the ring box again and glanced nervously out of the corner of his eye at Andy. Did Andy suspect anything, sense what a momentous night it was? An evening of triumph for Max. And Laurel, too. And his mother—when she knew. This was what his mother had always dreamed of for him; he couldn't wait to surprise her with the news. If he'd told her before, she would have butted in, probably insisted on going with him to choose the ring, that sort of stuff. Well, he had plenty of money of his own, so he went to Yard, and got a very pretty diamond surrounded by little sapphires.

Originally, when he thought he was included at Granny Bayard's dinner before the dance, he'd planned to find a quiet moment to take Laurel aside and pop the question. Then she could tell her family, and maybe later, at the dance itself, after a little fanfare from Lester Lanin and a call for silence, Thaddeus Hopewell would take the floor and propose a toast to the health and happiness of his beloved daughter, and Laurel's future husband, his and Elspeth's future son-in-law, Maximilian, the Hopewells always called him "Maximilian," and everyone would be beside themselves with delight and good wishes and the satin tents would ring with cheers. Of course, it would be nice if his parents could be here tonight, but some things couldn't be helped. After all, they didn't really know the Hopewells.

In his mind, he began to go over his little speech.

"Eight fifteen, Max," said Andy. "I guess we ought to be on the way. We're supposed to be at Piping Rock no later than eight thirty. They want us fed and on the road by eleven."

"How about a last gasper?" asked Max.

He extracted a square leather Brooks Brothers cigarette case from a pocket, offered it to Andy, who declined, and lit up a Tareyton. From across the water came a faint sound of music, the band tuning up.

"Go ahead and enjoy your last butt," said Andy with a smile. "There's no rush—these things never go off on time."

His grin belied his mood. Andy had been ordered by his mother to come tonight, so here he was, but he was damned if he was going to babysit Max! If he'd had his druthers, he'd be on his way to Texas now to take up his job at Marryat Oil, but Mrs. Hopewell had apparently made a big thing to his mother about his coming. He thought that very odd, considering how Laurel had dumped on him, and besides, Max seemed to think that he and Laurel were practically engaged.

Which made it especially weird that Max hadn't gotten the bid to Granny Bayard's dinner. Maybe it *was* the Jewish thing; the old bitch made Chickie's old man look like Eleanor Roosevelt; she was a big supporter of people like Gerald L. K. Smith, and now this lunatic McCarthy!

Earlier that evening, Andy and Jay and their father had watched a kinescope on the television news of one of McCarthy's press conferences. McCarthy had a lawyer named Cohn whispering in his ear who reminded Andy of Leo Himelman.

Himelman—what a loser! According to Howland, Morris had at Max's urging arranged an interview for Leo Himelman at Auchincloss, Wharton, and it had been an absolute disaster.

Andy checked his watch. "You want to ride with me? I know the way and these roads can be pretty tricky at night."

"I think I'd better take my own car," said Max as they strolled up the lawn. "You know how these Piping dinners tend to drag on, and I have to be at Windfall at ten thirty sharp. For the first dance, you know."

"Whatever you like," Andy replied. "Would you like me to make you a map?"

"No need, old boy. I know the way to Windfall like the back of my hand."

Fifteen minutes later, Max flipped his tenth cigarette of the evening over the side of his brand-new MG, double-clutched smartly, and followed Andy off Chicken Valley Road into the back entrance of the Piping Rock Club.

Andy was a friend, he thought. A real friend, no matter what Leo said. Leo said Andy was always putting Max down without Max seeing it. Like at the "Comanche" dinners at "21." Bob Kriendler, who owned the restaurant, was a high-ranking Marine reserve officer himself, and once a year he got a lot of Yale Marines together for a blowout. If Andy wore his Navy Cross ribbon, what the hell was he supposed to do? He'd won the damn medal, hadn't he? Leo said Andy just did it to make Max look bad because Max hadn't gone to Korea. Well, damn it, practically none of the Yale USMROTC unit had gone to Korea! Look at what a sport Andy'd been about Laurel. He'd had a crush on her, too, but when the best man won, he'd taken it like a gentleman, the way you expected of a Warrington! Leo said that, with these people, sports-manship was usually a coverup for weakness, but Max thought it was pretty classy.

Sure, maybe Andy's father could have done more about Scroll and Keys for Max. Maybe the Warringtons could get a bootblack into Keys if they really wanted to, the way Leo said, but look at Andy: he'd turned down Keys himself, which had really burned his father's ass. Of course, to Leo, that was just a grandstand play.

He slowed down as they joined a line of cars snaking up the clubhouse driveway. It was a delightful evening, fragrant and pleasant, with just a hint of lush summer nights to come. As Max slipped the MG into neutral, he kicked the accelerator pedal, just to hear the satisfying high-performance whine of the engine, then sat for a minute with the engine idling, savoring the night, the car, and himself.

An attendant waved him up to the door. He got out, shot his cuffs, and leaned down to check himself in the rearview mirror. He smoothed back his thick hair, and approvingly considered his confident features. From within the club, he could pick out the beat of "Hernando's Hide-away." He reached into his pocket and gave the jewel box a last squeeze for luck.

As Andy expected, dinner was a bore. He drew Susie Newton, a faintly wall-eyed brunette he'd known for most of his life. Her husband Nugget, who'd worked alongside Jay at DeCoppet once upon a time, was at the next table, one away from Max. Newton was a braying jackass, typical of the Piping Rock crowd in Andy's eyes, a stocky, bovine man with a military crewcut. In his youth he had been famous for peeing in potted palms; now, in his thirties, he had achieved a certain notoriety for picking fights with doormen. According to Jay, his won-lost so far was about fifty-fifty.

Andy could see that Newton was by now thoroughly desensitized by alcohol. For some reason, this troubled Andy.

His apprehension was soon justified. Halfway through dinner, Newton began, in a voice that would have carried to Manhasset, to tell a com-plicated Stock Exchange anecdote, shutting down all other conversation at his table and the surrounding area.

Andy picked up the tale in mid-sentence: ". . . A big fucking order in Congoleum, so I go to the specialist and ask him how the stock is, and this little sheenie tells me it's three to a quarter, with stock ahead, and he asks me do I wanna do something in here? And I say, 'Hymie, here's what I wanna do in here . . .' "

Andy felt himself growing embarrassed. He shifted around, wanting to see how Max was taking this. Newton barged on.

". . . so I say, Hymie, try this on for size, you fucking rag merchant!

No fucking sheenie's gonna do a number on me! Bid you three-eighths for a thousand, a quarter for a thousand, and *this* for the fuckin' balance!"

To make his point, Newton jabbed the air with a fat, spatulate middle finger and looked around the table with a bully, complicitous smirk. Andy saw Max look down then pick up his wineglass and drink it at a gulp. Oh shit, he thought.

After dinner, people rose from the table and made for the club's broad back porch, which looked out over the great expanse of the golf practice range. Andy thought he should seek out Max. He felt as if he had wandered into someone else's nightmare. He looked around. Max was nowhere to be seen.

By the time Max finally pulled between the high stone gates of Windfall, his anger had subsided, and his mind was fumbling for a face-saving explanation of his tardiness.

It was almost a quarter to midnight. The driveway that twisted up to Windfall was still backed up almost to the front gate, where the Pinkertons were checking off arriving guests. The reception line must surely have broken up by now! The first fox-trot, "From This Moment On," Laurel's and his favorite, would have already been danced.

Ruined, he thought angrily! The evening was ruined! Stuck between fury and a frustration so acute he felt like weeping, he stomped the ac-celerator. What was he going to say to Laurel, to her parents, to Mrs. Bayard?

He'd blame it on Jay. He'd have to. His mistake had been to double-check his directions with Jay. Max had been too concerned with getting out of Piping Rock. He should have seen that Jay was a little loaded, and everyone knew that when Jay had one too many, his propensity for mischief got totally out of control. Plus Max knew Jay didn't like him.

He should have gone and found Andy. Well, he hadn't, and now look what had happened! Anyway, Jay had been downright friendly, and eager to be of assistance. No, hell, he'd said, there's a back way you can save ten minutes. He'd taken out a gold pen and drawn a map for Max on the back of a club envelope, emphasizing that Max should be sure to take a right on 25A and then the first right, and to keep a sharp eye out for the signs to Oyster Mill Road. Shouldn't take more than fifteen minutes. In gratitude for the tip, Max had even given Jay a smart, affectionate nougie on the bicep.

That had been over an hour ago. For a while it had seemed okay. He'd found 25A all right, but he never found "Oyster Mill Road." Figuring he'd overshot, or maybe heard wrong, it was hard to read Jay's map by the dashboard light, he'd retraced his path, then tried following his instincts. He found himself traveling along the water, which he seemed to remember made sense, but after another fifteen minutes, he didn't seem to be anywhere he'd ever seen before. He backtracked about a mile, then on desperate impulse took a right and immediately found himself alone in a maze of unlabeled country roads. Finally he emerged at a crossroads and found an open diner; when he asked the counterman for directions and showed him Jay's map, the man had looked at him incredulously, but at length he understood the new directions, and after another twenty minutes here he was. As he inched up the driveway, he could make out the sound of music, bright and gay, and the excited noise of a party now in full swing. He cursed and felt himself close to tears.

In the meanwhile, Andy, sitting at a table on the terrace with his parents, kept looking around for Max. There had been no sign of him since dinner. Jay hadn't seen him leave Piping Rock, either.

"Why don't you go do your duty dance with Laurel?" Lyda said for the fourth time.

"In a minute." He gestured to a passing waiter for another glass of champagne.

He wasn't keen to take Laurel in his arms. When he'd gone through the reception line, the sight of her sent ominous little shivers through him.

In the tent below, the orchestra finished "You're The Top," and began to play the song from *Moulin Rouge*. Andy looked at his mother. She looks very elegant and distinguished with her hair swept up, he thought. She was wearing the ruby-and-diamond necklace that had belonged to Andy's paternal grandmother. She and Laurel have a lot in common, he thought, they have that same kind of scary determination and they know how to keep you off balance.

He took in the wide sweep of the scene. Jay had been right: there was at least $50,000 of expenditure on exhibition tonight, probably more. Two tents, one for dancing, one for food and drink, had been erected on the terraced lawns below the lee of the house. There had to be at least five bars scattered about the grounds. A small army of waiters labored in support. Beyond the two tents the "great lawn," a virtual meadow of meticulously groomed bent grass, fanned down between two perfect alleys of elms to a pond fed by an illuminated fountain. On the pond's surface a half-dozen swanboats were being aggressively peddled like bumper cars, harmlessly colliding while the couples in them chirped with laughter. A stitching of Japanese lanterns had been hung among the evergreens that marked the far border of the lawn.

Ah, well, he thought, no time like the present. He excused himself and made his way down to the tent where the orchestra was playing. From the edge of the dance floor, a low wooden platform that had been laid on the grass, he surveyed the scene. Girls in party frocks and their mothers' pearls and earrings were being twirled by young men whose smooth, confident faces bespoke a life without problems. No Korea, no draft, just school, college, and the Yellow Brick Road that was Wall Street. Peace, calm, and eternal prosperity, in the comforting shade of Dwight David Eisenhower. Born too late for Depression, too young to fight in the World War, too privileged to be called to Korea, and by now surely too old for whatever might come next, here was a generation destined to bask in an endless summer afternoon of ease and entitlement.

He worked his way through the stags gathered in the middle of the dance floor until he spotted Laurel, being pumped in relentless small circles by a gawky blond boy with a crewcut and a red plaid bowtie. He started toward her, thought better of it, hesitated, and she disappeared among the dancers. For an instant his attention was caught by two small figures—Miranda and the little Creedmore boy who was staying with them—methodically tracing dancing-school patterns with an engaging carefulness that was at once somehow both awkward and stately. Andy smiled at the sight—Miranda was obviously doing the leading—then looked around again for Laurel.

The kaleidoscopic activity on the dance floor shifted again, and he saw Laurel dancing with a wispy guy in a madras jacket. He made his way through the dancers.

"May I?"

Her partner released Laurel with a supercilious smile and sauntered away.

"Well," Andy said, "happy coming-out."

"Well yourself," she replied, "where have you been?" Her eyes narrowed. "I need to talk to you," she said. "Come on!"

She led him from the dance floor. From the way she moved, Andy wondered if she might be a bit tipsy.

"Let's get something to drink," she said, but when he made to head for the nearest bar, she screwed her face up. "The hell with that. Here, quick!"

She swerved abruptly and dragged him through an opening in the tent.

"Grab a bottle of champagne out of that tub! Hell, grab two! We don't need glasses."

He did as he was told.

"This way now, and be quick about it!"

She darted through an arched notch in a privet and set off briskly into the evergreens. In the moonlight, in her Mainbocher dress, she looked unbelievably glamorous. Andy hastened meekly after her. Behind them, the commotion of the pond and the swanboats faded. Laurel took off along a flagstone path that had been laid among the evergreens. Enough light spilled down from a westering half moon to let them make their way without stumbling. A few paces into the trees, she stopped suddenly and put out a hand to halt Andy.

"Well, my goodness gracious," she breathed. "Shocking! Absolutely shocking!"

She pointed. About ten yards ahead of them and another few yards back in among the pines, a small clearing opened up. On the far side of it, Jay leaned insouciantly against a tree, smoking a cigarette and sipping from a brandy snifter. A girl knelt before him, her dress pushed down to her waist, her fat, pale shoulders bobbing busily.

"Imagine!" hissed Laurel. "She was at Foxcroft with me. Whatever would Miss Charlotte think!"

They tiptoed down the path another fifty yards. The woods suddenly ended in a small, circular patio looking down on Breadloaf Cove.

"When he was alive, Grandpa used to come out here with his big telescope and star-gaze," Laurel said. "Open one of those bottles, will you?" She suddenly reached up and pulled Andy's head down and kissed him quickly on the mouth. "You never came to see me at school," she said.

"You were taken," he replied. The bottle popped open and the champagne fizzed over his hands and onto the flagstone.

"Careful," said Laurel. "That's 'thirty-seven Dom Perignon. Granny claims to have bought it from Ribbentrop. Did you know he was a champagne salesman?"

"I didn't."

Laurel took a swig from the bottle and handed it to Andy. "Do you want to make love to me?" she asked suddenly, almost fiercely. "Right here! It'll be a little messy—I'm just getting over my period—but if you don't mind, I don't."

"I don't think it's a good idea," he said.

"You wanted to badly enough on the boat!"

"That was then."

"And now is now? Is there someone else?"

"Perhaps you'd better speak to that for yourself."

She took another swig, looked at him, and a smile spread across her face. "You mean *Max*? You must be joking!"

"I don't think he thinks so. I think he thinks the two of you are practically engaged. I think his family thinks so, too."

Laurel's smile disappeared. She turned away impatiently, went to the edge of the patio, and looked out over the dark Sound; in the far distance, lights twinkled. Then she whirled around. "Why didn't you answer my postcard?"

"What postcard?"

"The one I sent you in Paris. To the Lotti!"

"I never got a postcard from you. What did it say?"

"Oh, nothing!" Laurel kicked angrily at a pebble. "The goddamn French post office!"

They were both silent for a moment, then she said, in a calmer voice: "You don't actually think I could be in love with someone like Max Miles, do you?"

"I don't know. You've been giving a pretty good imitation."

"Drew, Drew, that was just for fun. It made Mummy so upset, and you should hear Granny on the subject! All right, all right, maybe I did prolong the joke a bit long."

"A bit!"

"Oh, Drew, don't be such a stick! I mean, how can a woman consider herself modern these days without having had at least one Jewish boyfriend? Especially at Radcliffe! I mean, Harvard is simply teeming with them. It's like going to school in Jerusalem."

She giggled nervously. Andy said nothing.

"Oh, come on, Drew! Everyone says you have such a good sense of humor! Besides, there's something wonderfully exotic about Jewish men, at least until you get to know them. I was just sowing my wild matzohs."

Laurel giggled at her joke.

"I bet you were," said Andy.

"Don't be a jerk. I'm not going to talk about *that*! Ugh!"

She made a shivering movement with her arms.

"I don't think I like this conversation," said Andy. "We better get back. You're going to be missed."

"How can you be such a goody-goody! What do you think I was for Max?"

"I know what I think you *are* for him."

"Well, that's his problem. All I am is a trophy, another pretty Christian girl in a white dress. Do you know what he collects?"

"I didn't know he collected anything. Except clothes, of course. And you."

"Don't be facetious. He collects little paintings of girls in white dresses! Nineteenth-century things, by people like Benson and Chase and Childe Hassam. He must have a dozen of them in his apartment at Cambridge. Golden girls, slim girls on summer beaches, or with parasols on lawns, pale, blond, Anglo-Saxon Christian girls in white dresses! I'll tell you something else, Andrew Warrington. I saw the two of you tonight while I was getting dressed. I saw the two of you over there on the Archibalds' dock, and all I could think of was Gatsby staring across the water to where Daisy Buchanan lived. Then it was Jay Gatsby, *nee* Gatz. Now it is Max Miles *nee* whatever it was."

"I think we ought to get back."

She moved over to Andy and put her hands alongside his face. "You're sure you don't love me still?"

"I'm not sure I ever did. Right now, I'm not sure what I think about anything."

"Well, you fascinate me. You always have. Of course, I never knew about you Warrington men until Mummy told me . . ."

"Told you what?"

"That the women you marry are chosen like Valkyries or whatever. To be the mothers of kings, to preserve the dynasty. I think it's the most exciting thing I ever heard of."

"It may be exciting, Laurel, but it's also work. Just ask Mother. I really do think . . ."

She interrupted him with a kiss. He felt her tongue on his lips. He began to get hard, but he didn't see where this could go, not here, not now, so he stepped back.

"I think it's the *idea* of me you're after, sweetheart, just like you say it was the idea of Max that excited you, not *me*, but what you think I am, whatever that is."

There was a moment's pause, a silence that was almost tangible. Andy tried to lighten the moment. "Look, if you're serious, if it's Wall Street bloodstock you're after, I think you'd be better advised to check out Jay. He's Mr. Hanover Place. I'm heading to Texas next week to work in the oil fields. Wall Street's not for me."

"We'll see," Laurel said. She lifted the bottle to her lips and found it empty.

"Damn!" she exclaimed. "Damn, damn, damn!" She tossed the bottle off into the woods.

She leaned over and kissed Andy again. "A lot of help you are," she said, laughing. She seized him by the hand, gathered her full skirt with the other, and ran off up the path, towing Andy behind her.

Max looked at his watch, which seemed to say it was only one o'clock. Was that possible? It felt like five in the morning. The figures on the dial blurred and swam away.

He was standing beside the pool, swaying slightly, now completely muddled with liquor and irritation. His mind seemed to be working by fits and starts, like an automobile with its engine misfiring. One instant he was sharply aware of everything, saw truth plain, the next, it all seemed a hopeless mess. He concentrated hard on disguising his condition, on maintaining a faint smile, on looking with a careful expression of amused interest at the swanboats on the pond. Then a new wave of intoxication would sweep over him, and it was all he could do to stay upright. All he needed, he knew, was ten winks, just to lay his head down on one of the tables surrounding the pond for a minute, and he'd be as good as brand new.

He saw two figures emerge from the woods at the foot of the lawn and walk toward him. He shifted and screwed his vision into focus. It took a moment to register. One of them was Laurel.

He knew at once that action was required. Assertion of male primacy. With the awful hallucinatory clarity that is the privilege and power of the deeply, truly drunk, he saw at once what he must do.

"M'dear!" he boomed with a great smile as they came up to him. With a great sweep of his arm, he bowed low, like a motion-picture musketeer. It didn't quite come off; he swayed at the bottom of the movement, and was forced to steady himself with his fingertips on the wet grass.

With an effort, he straightened up and looked at Laurel, then at Andy, then back at Laurel. His mind was utterly concentrated on what he was about to say, so it eluded him that Laurel herself was not altogether sober and that her reactions, therefore, might not be entirely predictable.

"My dearest Laurel," he began, then stopped. In his brain, a cylinder missed, then caught, and he plunged jerkily on. "M'dearest Laurel, you and I, well, we, you know . . ." He heard his voice trailing off into incomprehension. Better actions than words, said a wicked little voice from within.

From his jacket pocket he produced the ring, at the same time clumsily taking Laurel's left hand. For an instant or two, he attempted to thread it onto her ring finger, then lost interest in having to pursue so complicated a task, and then simply placed the ring in her palm and squeezed her small hand around it.

"My dearest love," seemed to be called for, so he said the words—with deep and sincere emotion, or so it seemed. Every scintilla of concentration he could muster was focused on Laurel.

For an instant she held her fist closed, then opened it slowly and inspected the ring. She studied $4,000 worth of the art and taste of one of Manhattan's most fashionable jewelers for what seemed an eternity. By now Jay had joined them, bottle in hand. He refilled all their glasses, including Max's.

Laurel took an uninterested sip of her champagne. She examined Max's offering one more time, then raised her eyes to his face and scrutinized it with a disdainful expression. Max suddenly felt terribly hot. He gulped his glass at one swallow and pushed it at Jay for a refill.

"May I ask what this means?" asked Laurel in a dangerous voice.

Max missed her tone entirely. "You know," he said, all at once full of bravado, "well, you and I, darling . . . what we've discussed . . . you know . . . I thought . . ." He began to lose it.

"You thought what?" said Laurel in a chilly way. The champagne was working on her like gasoline on a fire.

Max started to mumble something, but she cut right through his words.

"You thought what!" Her voice rose.

It was obvious she was really quite tipsy. At one or two of the surrounding tables heads turned at her outburst. Max swayed and smiled. His intelligence had temporarily suspended operations.

"I'll tell you what you thought," hissed Laurel. "You thought you could marry me." Her voice dripped with a grand, theatrical contempt.

"You . . ." she hissed again, drawing out the word. Andy and Jay looked at each other; their eyebrows rose simultaneously.

Miranda edged closer, keen, like most children, to be in on what she could see was going to be a humdinger of a scene even if, like most children her age, she wasn't quite sure what it was about.

"You . . . you! . . . are . . . asking . . . me . . . to . . . marry . . . you!"

Laurel spaced the words carefully; with each, her voice gained in volume and scorn.

Max wanted to reply in a sophisticated, cosmopolitan fashion, but the words wouldn't come. "Well . . . that is . . . I mean . . ."

"Marry you?" Laurel practically shouted the question. "You! A man I won't even sleep with!"

She looked around at Andy and Jay. "How d'you like that! I won't even sleep with him, and he wants me to marry him! Ha! Ha, ha, ha, ha, ha!"

Max's world wavered like Jell-O. This was not going well.

Laurel turned back to him. When she next spoke, her voice was soft but steely, all the more cruel for being pitying. "Oh, Max," she said, "you really are dense as everyone says. Really you are. I *can't* marry you, don't you see? Do I have to spell out the reason?"

She flipped the ring at Max. He sought to grab it, missed, and it bounced harmlessly off his chest and fell to the grass. In the effort, the last drops of wine in Max's glass speckled the perfect white of his dinner jacket.

For an instant Max stood numb and puzzled. Then he reached for his beloved. This was all a silly misunderstanding, easy enough to put to rights with a hug and a kiss.

When he touched her arm, she slapped his hand away as if it was leprous. He reached again and caught the top of her dress.

"Hey, easy there, sport," said Jay, stepping forward. He took Max by the upper arm. "Hey, Maxie, fun's fun, but . . ."

A terrible burst of clarity overwhelmed Max.

"Fuck you, Jay Warrington! Fuck all of you!" he grunted savagely.

He swiveled fiercely to tear himself from Jay's grasp. The smooth soles of his patent-leather evening pumps lost their marginal purchase on the slick, damp greensward and he tottered sideways. His now enfeebled internal gyroscope failed. Whatever powers within him were left to fight against the disabling powers of drink now, too, gave up the unequal struggle and retired from the field. As if imbued with a life of their own, his legs started off down the mild incline toward the pond. Like a cartoon cat, the rest of Max followed. Down the little slope he went, arms akimbo, lurching, swiveling, windmilling. He bounced off one of the pondside tables, caught a gleaming toe on the raised stone rim of the pond, and swooped face down into the water, making a great splash that entirely engulfed the whitewashed wooden swan on which eighty-one-year-old Evangeline Bayard was being energetically pedaled to shore by a thirteen-year-old great-grand-nephew.

Max surfaced, shook himself like a spaniel, saw the drenched dowager, and promptly threw up all over himself.

Andy slept soundly and awoke early, before anyone else in the house was about. When he went downstairs, he looked in the driveway for Max's car. It wasn't there.

According to Frances, the downstairs maid, the Brookville Police had brought Mr. Max home about four thirty. He'd been picked up on the side of Wolver Hollow Road, his MG nudged gently into a mossy bank, evidently in no condition to continue.

"I trust Nick squared the cops?" asked Andy.

"I believe he did, sir," said Frances in her sharp Galway brogue. "He sent Eddie and Dennis to pick up Mr. Max's car. When they got back, about six thirty, Mr. Max was all showered and packed, and he was gone! He left this for you."

She handed over two cream envelopes marked with Aunt Floss's crest, one addressed to Andy, the other to Laurel.

Frances reappeared in the dining room. "Mrs. Bayard's man just brought this over. For Mr. Max." Another envelope, heavy, ominous dark blue stock this time, with WINDFALL, LLOYD NECK, NEW YORK on the flap.

As he pondered the situation, Andy heard Jay singing loudly in the hall. "Gee, but it's great after eating your date, brushing your teeth with a co-o-mb!"

His brother swept in, looking very dashing in beltless khakis, a pink button-down shirt, and loafers that were within a thread of falling apart completely. He drained the orange juice at his place, went to the sideboard, and inspected the breakfast laid out there. Andy could tell his brother was still a quarter drunk.

"How about our Max? Now that was a route-going performance!" Jay asked in a cheery voice. Before Andy could answer, Jay went to the kitchen door and shouted, "Got a beer out there, Frances?"

Andy opened Max's note. It was about what he expected. In somewhat pompous language, Max asked Andy to make his apologies to all concerned. He would of course be writing Mrs. Bayard himself.

Andy reread the note. It concluded by saying, ". . . sorry that I proved myself unfit to associate with your set."

Now what the hell did that mean? Max sounded like he blamed everyone but himself, but it wasn't Andy's "set" who'd puked in Granny Bayard's carp pond.

"Hmmm." Jay grinned, watching his brother's face, "What a tale that must tell. Hey, wait'll Mother Miles gets wind of what happened. The Dragon Lady'll flip her wig! I'd like to be a fly on the gefilte fish when that discussion takes place. And Laurel . . . hey, what's with you and Laurel, anyway. Off in the bushes! Is there something I should know?"

"Nothing is with me and Laurel."

Jay eyed his brother skeptically. "Then you must be really stupid," he said.

"As a matter of fact," said Andy, "I put in a good word for you. She fancies herself as a mother of kings, Hanover Place variety."

Jay shook his head. "Too classy for me, although I have to say, the way she looked last night gave me a hard-on a cat couldn't scratch. Usually those blond Foxcroft types don't come with hogans of that quality. Plus, there's what, about fifteen big ones coming her way when Granny Bayard croaks?"

He saw Andy's face and put up both hands: "Okay, okay, I know, I know. Money is the root et cetera and so on, right? Why are you such a fucking boy scout, Drew?"

"I'm not a boy scout. I'm just tired of the lot of you. Living with you people is like being plopped into a Waring Blender. Now leave me alone to finish my breakfast and get out of town. If you want Laurel, be my guest!"

1955

AUGUST

The glistening dark pipe stacked overhead reminded Andy of ordnance and momentarily brought back thoughts of Korea. Kneeling in the shadow of the arrayed lengths of production casing, he shielded his eyes against the shimmering glare and peered down the dirt road that ran from the drilling site out to the paved farm road. Could that be a cloud of dust in the distance, he wondered, a flash of sunlight on a scarlet truck body? They had been waiting for twenty hours on a cement crew from Halliburton. As J.B. said, "There's only three things you need in the 'awl bidness': money, luck, and time for sittin' around."

Andy liked the sitting-around part best. It gave him time to relish this new life he was leading. Like Korea there was a physical reality to it, sometimes harsh, like when the dusty gusts of the High Plains howled and eddied on the rig floor, and the crew had to fight both the wind and a balky rotary table. It was a kind of simple, fundamental existence that no amount of money or privilege could soften, not during working hours.

How different it would be in New York, he reflected. Some trusts had kicked in on his twenty-first birthday two years earlier, so he had an annual income of nearly $40,000, more than enough to pay for a glossy East Side existence. Even down here, where oilmen in eighty-dollar hand-tooled boots stomped carelessly through muddy pastures speckled with cow pies, it was a "whole bunch of money." And there would be more to come in five years, and in ten.

Yet somehow it lacked reality, didn't seem to matter. Andy tried dutifully to interest himself in the subject. Twice a year, he flew north to review his stuff with his father and Irv Nachman, who supervised the "family" stock portfolios at Hanover Place, and with the trust people at Chelsea Guaranty Trust who clipped the coupons and doled out the income from the bond holdings. These men discussed investments with the reverent enthusiasm of a connoisseur analyzing a Rembrandt, and Andy did his best to be interested, but like as not his attention would wander and he'd end up gazing out the window.

Naturally, lacking any special feeling about money, he found it hard to get excited about working at Hanover Place. His father and mother saw this, and left the matter alone. Jay was more aggressive, and he came at his brother with a different slant. Forget the money, Jay argued, it was the action that was the allure, the speed and cleverness required to play the game.

The "game" didn't intrigue Andy. There were a couple of things they were doing at The Firm that sounded okay, like the consortium his father had put together to back a bunch of guys who had visions of building a peacetime empire based on wartime technologies. If most of the people he'd met at The Firm seemed intelligent and committed, and many of them likable, the appeal just wasn't there.

Wall Street was for people like Max, who was apprenticing at Hanover Place. This went against The Firm's antinepotism policy, and Andy knew it had been the cause of a sharp quarrel between his parents—his mother, when informed, had apparently slammed down her knife and fork and stomped from the dining room, pausing only to observe sarcastically that now "the camel's nose was under the tent." When Miranda told Andy about the argument, he was surprised. That didn't sound like his mother at all. Still, as Jay said, apparently it was important to Morris, and as the price of peace, it was no big deal. Max was being Klopperized, which was a good thing. You put in your time under the Klopper, and you came out knowing which side was up, and then the necessary calls would be made and Max would move on to Abraham or Loeb Rhoades, someplace where he could cut a swath.

Besides, Jay added, Max needed all the help he could get. His old mentor Himelman was out of his life. Leo hadn't been able to catch on in New York, so he'd joined a law firm in Philadelphia. Boy, Jay snickered, wait 'til they got a load of Leo in the City of Brotherly Love; there was a guy who'd give new meaning to the term "Philadelphia lawyer"!

Andy was happy to be away from all that. He might not be "gladder'n shit to be in Texas" in every way—there was a bumptious quality to the local discourse, and the inescapable feeling that physical violence was never more than a hair's breadth away—but he was happier than he had ever been, at least outside of school.

The process that had brought Andy to Texas had commenced some two years earlier, in April of 1953.

J.B. Marryat had come north to "find me some mullets," individuals with money to invest in drilling, although the way he put it to Howland was not as picturesque as that. Howland, impressed with Marryat's can, dor, had secured Marryat an audience with Dick Bosworth, The Firm's "oil person."

The night before the Texan's appointment at Hanover Place, Lyda and Howland took him out to dinner; Andy drove down from New Haven to round out the party. After an excellent dinner at Le Pavillon, they went on to El Morocco, and when the senior Warringtons called it a night, Andy and J.B. looked in at the bar of Marryat's hotel for a nightcap. After a couple more drinks, and a lot of boastful small talk about old battles and future conquests, Marryat asked whether Andy, if he had no special plans after Yale, might like to give the "awl bidness" a whirl.

The idea appealed to Andy. When he broached the idea to his father, Howland reacted enthusiastically. In mid-June, two days after Max's fall, Andy boarded a Global DC-7C at Idlewild, bound for Amon Carter Field and, at least temporarily, a brand new life. By the time he landed, a drilling crew was within seventeen hundred feet of the discovery that would establish Marryat Oil as a Hanover Place "connection" in the fullest sense of the word.

When Marryat came down the morning after he and Andy talked into the night, he was greeted by Howland on the fourth floor and taken upstairs to a conference room plastered with geologists' maps. There were three men seated at the table: Dick Bosworth; his assistant, a young petroleum engineer recently hired away from a Houston bank; and Lewis Comstock, now cochairman with Morris Miles of The Firm's Commit, ments Committee.

Bosworth sought to put his fellow southerner at ease. "Son," he said, gesturing at J.B.'s round leather map case, "if you want me to buy your deal, just don't make me look at your goddamn maps."

Marryat chuckled nervously. He'd never pitched a deal to this kind of audience. These folks knew what they were doing.

He got right into his spiel. He needed $750,000 to take over some leases Humble Oil was about to walk away from. He'd seen some of the Humble workups, and he'd talked to some of Humble's lower-down geologists, and the way they all figured it, Humble had just plain missed the boat on this one. It sure as hell looked prospective. It might not be an "elephant," but if it worked out, it could mean several hundred barrels a day.

When he finished, the men around the table asked a few questions, then Bosworth told him that Hanover Place would do its homework and get back to him pronto.

When the young man left, Bosworth looked at Howland. "Y'all understand what he's got, don't you?"

Howland shrugged. Bosworth went on. "What he's shopping is several thousand dollars of Humble geology. Happens all the time. Those big companies are just too damn big. Anything less than a million barrels just doesn't impress the bigshots on the top floor. To a geologist, it's the punching holes in the ground that's a thrill. They couldn't give less of a shit about the annual report, and they don't get to ride in the company plane, either. It's the structure, the geologic beauty, and the proof of their judgment that they get their jollies from. This boy may have something here. Of course I'll want to talk to Jim Sherriff down at Ringling Geophysical, see what he thinks."

Howland smacked his lips and shook his head pensively. "If I read you correctly, Richard, you're implying that some of this information may have been, well, 'originated elsewhere'?"

Bosworth nodded. "If that's the way you like to put it," he said with a big grin.

"But if it checks out, you think we should go ahead?"

"Hell, Howland, that's how the West was won. If we didn't have independent oil men like Marryat drilling plays the majors consider chickenfeed, we'd be freezing in the dark or burnin' coal."

The Dallas consultant was enthusiastic. Foster Klopp's slide rule fairly smoked to devise an equitable deal; the Lyda W. number-one well was spudded July 4, 1953, and two Sundays later Dick Bosworth telephoned Howland at Double Dune to report that the well had come in at seventy-six hundred feet and was making close to a hundred barrels a day. By the end of the summer, it had been established that Marryat Production Corporation was sitting on top of a very nice pool of oil.

"Well," said Howland to Lyda, "so much for my sainted father's oft-quoted opinion that the oil business was all good news and no money."

Watching that well come in had been Andy's first real sight of money at work. Without capital, there would have been no well, no platform, nothing but empty fields and worn-out fences penning screwing heifers. For the first time, he had seen money change from a paper abstraction to something real.

Ironically, however, it made The Firm and Wall Street seem seedy by comparison. Texas was alive, gritty, full-hearted, with dirt under its fingernails and a boundless optimism. Distances meant nothing. Marryat thought little of hopping in his fat maroon Buick Roadmaster convertible and driving four hours from Fort Worth to his fishing camp over on Lake Cherokee in East Texas. Mostly he liked to fly. He had bought a surplus Navy SNJ, a hot advanced trainer he painted firehouse red. One minute Andy and J-for-nothing B-for-nothing would be sitting in the nineteenth hole at River Crest, and the next Marryat'd get a hankering to look at some acreage up in the Panhandle or over near El Paso, and away they'd go.

But the biggest difference was the work. After a few months, Andy began to realize he'd really never known what work was. Real work, that is, performed by people for their own fulfillment. Until Texas, all he'd seen were people doing things for other people: butlers, waiters, filling-station attendants, grocery clerks, bellhops, bank tellers, stockbrokers.

Here it was different. People used their hands. They made things. What men did on the floor of an oil rig might not have been all that different from what they did on the floor of a stock exchange, but somehow to Andy it seemed worthier, better. Up on the façade of Hanover Place was a cartouche carved with the words, HONOR AND OPTIMISM. Here in Texas, those words truly came alive for Andy; the commercial life here seemed to embody them. Everyone was full to the brim with the promise of tomorrow, and would sooner die than disavow a handshake. There were times Andy found it all a touch coarse, but that, he told himself, was his buttoned-up, buttoned-down, cosmopolitan sensibility talking.

J.B. in particular was full of Texas-size dreams, but he was also practical. One time, on their way from Fort Worth to Dallas to talk to the Republic Bank about financing an ABC deal on some production, Marryat had pulled the Buick off on a side road, near one of the longest, most spacious buildings Andy had ever seen. Set off behind high barbed-wire fencing, it was obviously deserted.

"This here's where Consolidated Vultee built the B-24," said Marryat. "They must've had two thousand people here. Maybe it'll start up again, maybe it won't. That ain't the point. What I'm going to show you is."

A bit farther on they passed another, much smaller cluster of buildings.

"Look there. That's Texas Instruments," said Marryat. "I bought me a bunch of stock th'other day. Makes geophysical equipment but that ain't the excitin' part. They got these itty-bitty doodads they call transistors. Science, boy, that's where it's at! We got to get with it. We do enough science in this country, ain't nobody goin' t' have to work with their hands again!"

Well, here he was two years later, settled in, on his way to becoming a true-blue Texan. He glanced at the road, saw nothing, and returned to his work. The heat of the day made him drowsy. He lay back and pulled his straw Stetson down over his eyes.

"Hey, Andrew!"

Andy felt someone kick his foot. He opened his eyes. A squat, backlit shadow loomed over him.

"There's a call for you on the shortwave."

Andy got to his feet.

"What is it, Bobby? J.B. got the red ass about how come this well isn't moving along?"

"Hunh-uh." Bobby Marryat squinted at Andy through half-inch-thick glasses. In the large straw hat he wore to keep the sun from blistering his pale skin, the youngest Marryat looked like a frog dressed as a cowboy. "Something 'bout you needin' to call New York," he said.

Andy made for the truck, Bobby shambling behind. He was J.B.'s half-brother, by their father's fifth marriage. He had recently turned sixteen, and was tubby and coarse-featured, with bulbous eyes, pale, freckled skin, and bristly, intractable hair mown short by a barber with a heavy hand.

He was working for the summer at Marryat before going north to a lily-white military academy somewhere in Wisconsin, a prospect that he roundly hated, but which spared him the dire fate recently decreed by the Supreme Court: to go to school "with a bunch of niggers, not that I don't respect 'em, y'all understand," as J.B. and Bobby's daddy put it.

What most intrigued—and repelled—Andy about Bobby was that the boy had absolutely no feeling for the romance of the oil business. Bobby Marryat rated the adventure of geology and exploration at less than zero, not to mention the boon, profane companionship and teamwork on the rig floor. He hated the outdoors; he despised manual labor; he loathed the down-and-dirty business of drilling.

Yet he had an undoubted flair for the business, but it was that of the lawyer and bookkeeper. Most oilmen dwelt on "anticlines," "structures," and "logs"; Bobby was fascinated by "delay rentals," "production payments," and "back-in overrides." On the long drive up from Fort Worth, as the road ran on flat and endless between fields burned to dirt by a cloudless summer, he had treated Andy to a disquisition on a Supreme Court decision, affecting the price of natural gas at the wellhead, which Bobby found infinitely more meaningful for his future than *Brown v. Board of Education.*

Andy couldn't help being amazed at the nature and degree of Bobby's knowledge. The youngest Marryat possessed a native aptitude for numbers; he knew the income statements and balance sheets of the major oil companies to the last decimal. He had little interest in the things sixteen-year-old boys normally fastened on, although Andy had caught him furtively peeking at the copy of *Playboy* that the roughnecks had thumbed so thoroughly that the owner of the store at the crossroads had finally made them ante up four bits and buy the damn thing.

When Andy raised Fort Worth, the Marryat Oil dispatcher told him he was to call New York, a Mr. Morris Miles at HAnover 1-1000. It was urgent.

Jesus, he thought, what can it be? His parents were in Africa on safari.

The nearest phone was a few miles away at the crossroads store, a combination greasy spoon and gas pump that serviced a "town" consisting of a feed store, a tool-supply shop, and a half dozen weedy houses and rust-blown trailers.

"Come on, Bobby," he said, "got a treat for you. Trip to the big city."

They drove back down the service road to the highway, past sparse herds of skinny white-faced Herefords. It took a minute or so to get the operator to free up the party line, get the New York routing from Wichita Falls, and connect him with Hanover Place. Morris Miles's voice was grave.

"Andrew, I'm extremely pleased we were able to reach you. I'm afraid I have some very sad news. Charles Fenton is dead."

Dead? Chickie dead? No, Morris was talking about Chickie's father. Apparently Chubby Fenton had been killed in some kind of a shooting accident in Los Angeles.

"Your father and mother are out of radio range in Kenya," Morris was saying. "It will be at least a day before we can reach them, and several more before they can possibly get back. I've discussed this with your brother and he feels it would be appropriate if you could represent your family, and by implication, The Firm, at the funeral. It's scheduled to be held in Pasadena the day after tomorrow. Do you think you can get there?"

"I'll get there," Andy said.

It was about five in the morning, Los Angeles time, when J.B. throttled back the twin Bonanza that had replaced the SNJ and began the descent through a heavy night mist that lay on the San Fernando Valley like thick gray padding; in the distance, Andy could see the Pacific gleaming like pale brass.

Tom Creedmore was waiting for them inside the terminal at Burbank. On the way to Los Angeles, he filled them in. Chubby Fenton's death had been the kind of stupid accident you read about in the tabloids. A gun, thought to be unloaded, had discharged while Chubby was clean-ing it.

"I hate to say this, Andrew," said Creedmore, "but Chubby was prob-ably drunk at the time. He'd been hitting it pretty hard recently."

"Where was Chickie?"

"Upstairs, I gather. He heard the shot, came downstairs, and found his father. Poor kid. I gather the only reason he was out here at all was that he was worried about Chub."

They descended through the mountains, drove west on Sunset, for a mile or so, and turned up a white gravel driveway that curled between an alley of eucalyptus. The trees' scent was strong in the morning air. Ahead was a sprawling yellow stucco mansion. Andy looked at his watch. It was just after six, but the sun was already up as bright and glaring as midday.

As the big beige Cadillac drew to a halt, the front door opened and the familiar figure of Jessica Creedmore appeared, a flame-haired plump little hen in a quilted housecoat with a marabou collar. Her red hair was obviously dyed; Andy remembered the time he and Jay had peeped at her through a chink in the poolhouse at Double Dune. She had a bright orange bush then, he remembered, like a patch of gaily-colored cotton glued to the base of her round little belly.

"You guys go upstairs and get some rest," said Creedmore when they were inside. "J.B., I have to warn you that my boy Jerry's beside himself that you're here. He is an absolute freak when it comes to flying, and I think he's memorized the name of every American fighter ace from Andy's dad forward. All he wants to be is a fighter pilot, although I'm not sure what he's going to do for a war. Anyway, if you're smart, you'll lock your door. Andrew, I told Chickie Fenton to expect us around eleven. There's nothing for us to do. Chubby's Hollywood friends seem to have everything under control."

"Typical!" Jessica Creedmore exclaimed angrily. "First they dumped Chubby when he got too old to play polo for them, and now look at them and their crocodile tears! That's what you get for trusting these people! Well, what do you expect: they wouldn't help their own during the war!"

She swung round in response to a movement in the shadows behind her and asked sharply: "May I ask what you're doing up?"

An angelic little boy had appeared beside her; he was staring raptly at J.B.

"Hi, Jerry," said Andy. "May I introduce J.B. Marryat?"

The boy took J.B.'s hand shyly.

"Hey, Jerry," said J.B. "How about you and me go talk about dog-fighting? Andrew, you get you some sleep. I'll fly cover with ol' Jerry here."

They drove out to Pasadena around noon. From the moment he first saw Chickie, Andy knew that something wasn't quite right about the whole scene, that it was all invented. Chickie awaited them in the front hall, carefully posed to catch, just right, the sunlight filtering pallidly through tall stained-glass windows. The varicolored sunbeams made Chickie seem to emerge from a multicolored halo.

He held out his arms. It had been at least a year since Andy had seen him. He looked like a little old Pekinese, precious with spoiling, swollen and gouty with sweetmeats.

"Drew, Tom. Do come in. Wonderful of you to come."

His normally high, cultivated voice seemed rough, as though it had been napped up with a file. Chickie's eyes, sunken and dark-rimmed, seemed full of something that wasn't quite sorrow; his skin was blotchy with weeping. To Andy, this dearest friend of boyhood seemed full of puzzles, suddenly unknowable, at least in the old way.

The funeral was held in Pasadena's most prominent Episcopal church. The ten surviving members of Chubby Fenton's Skull & Bones delegation materialized from various parts of the country and acted as pallbearers. The turnout was good; a territorial compromise seemed to have been reached—as Tom Creedmore explained it—"between the Old Money/Hancock Park/Pasadena crowd which pronounces 'Los Angeles' with a hard g"—as Tom himself did—"and the Hollywood/Santa Monica/Beverly Hills Jews." The seats on the left of the aisle were occupied by a complement headed by Hyman Gessel. On the right, where Andy sat with the Creedmores, starched faces peeked sideways over starched collars. Here and there were crossovers. Randolph Scott, the Fred Astaires, and the Gary Coopers sat on the Old Money side, in the same front pew as Rex Raines, the cowboy star who had been Chubby's closest Hollywood chum, who snuffled noisily through the service.

The minister dealt out fire and brimstone with a fervor J.B. declared "would have done a Del Rio radio padre right proud." The little Creedmore boy seemed transfixed by the sermon. His mother had dressed him in white, to set off his fair beauty, and he indeed looked like an angel.

After the funeral, most people went back and paid their respects at the

Fenton house; by the time the last captain and king departed, Chickie had turned utterly manic, breaking into other people's conversation with outbursts of near-hysterical cackling and giggling. In the course of the afternoon, he had made enough trips to the pantry to kill an entire fifth of vodka, but there was something about his intoxication that didn't seem quite right to Andy. Alcohol usually made Chickie moody and morbid, sent him into long, deprecatory silences.

He begged Andy to stay the night. "Lot to talk about," he muttered, hugging himself and then giggling. Andy looked at Tom Creedmore helplessly and shrugged. Tom said he'd get a couple of the boys from Global to run Andy's things over with a spare company car.

Chickie insisted they go out to dinner, all the way across the city to Chasen's. It was after midnight when they got home. Andy was exhausted. Chickie was muddled—he had drunk heavily right through dinner—so the giggling had subsided. Now he wanted to talk. He slumped on the sofa in the small library and looked around at the shelves.

"Looka that," he said, waving a hand. Some of the gin sloshed out of his glass and slopped on the rug. "Margaret Mitchell. Pearl Buck. Norman Vincent Peale—lotta Norman Vincent Peale. The literary taste of Charles Christian Fenton Third, late of Yale, late of life!"

Andy said nothing. Chickie turned and looked slyly at him with small, glittering eyes. "Y'know 'bout me, huh, Drew?"

"Know what?"

"Y'know. About me. Y'know: what I am?"

Andy shook his head. He wished he was a thousand miles away.

"Y'know what I mean. That I'm a queer. A fruit. A homo. A fairy, a faggot, a pansy, a queen. C'mon, Drew, y'know: the love that dares not speak its name?"

Andy made a helpless little shrug.

"And, hey, y'know who else is, huh? Hey, Drew, how about Rex Raines? How 'bout America's number two at the box office five years running? How 'bout what he likes best isn't his horse but the weewees of young white boys?"

Chickie's face went slack; for a moment he seemed to collapse before the picture he was staring at in his mind, then he pulled himself together.

"Y'wanna know wha' happened?"

"Not especially."

"Well, y' gotta, 'cause I gotta tell someone, and you're my best frien'. Hey, y'know wha' Ford Madox Ford said?"

"No. What *did* Ford Madox Ford say?"

"He said: 'The oddnesses of friendship are a frequent guarantee of their lasting texture.' " Chickie looked lovingly at Andy. "Hey, Drew, thass you 'n me, huh?"

"That's us."

It took a while for Chickie to get the story out. He had been seduced by Rex Raines back during the war, when Chickie was twelve and the Fentons were stationed in Coronado. Raines came to San Diego to make a training film and stayed with them. The relationship had gone on, intermittently and secretly, in the dozen years since.

" 'Course it hadda be secret, y'unnerstan', Drew, 'cause old Gessel's got about ten mil tied up in Rex's contract, but if everyone finds out that ol' Mr. Face Like Mount Rushmore likes the action in the closet better'n in the OK Corral, it's 'sayonara' big box office, get it?"

The night he died, Chubby Fenton was supposed to have been spending the night in La Jolla with friends, but apparently his ritual "elevenses" at the bar of the California Club had left him in no condition to make the drive. Instead, he had stumbled into the club library and snoozed away the day.

"So there I was, Drew, right there on the living-room sofa, 'cause desire won't wait, doncha know, heh, heh, sucking away on what ninety percent of the women in 'merica dream about—'n not a few of the men either, I wot, heh, heh—when who should come busting in—I guess if Rex wasn't deafer'n a post or if he hadn't been holding me by the ears in his agony of passion, heh, heh, *we'd've* heard, but we did'n', so there you are. Anyway, here comes ol' Charles Christian Fenton Third, Yale bachelor of arts of the year of our Lord one thousand nine hundred sixteen, DKE and Skull & Bones and twice honorable-mention All-America by Walter Camp, a he-man to the bone, heh, heh, and he was upset, oh, was he upset! to find his son whom he never could stand anyway, sucking away on his best chest-thumping, drinking-hunting-and-polo-playing-Jew-hating-buddy's thing!"

"Hey, Chick . . ."

"No, Drew, no, you lemme finish! Thass' wha' friens're for! Well, Papa'd obviously stopped off along the way for the odd Ramos Gin Fizz or six, and so he starts shouting how he's gonna call Louella and Hedda and Jimmy Fidler and Winchell, and wha's more, wait'll those Hollywood kikes find out their hottest meal ticket's queerer'n a three-dollar bill!"

Chickie paused to catch his breath, sighed, and went on. "Well, Rex reasons with him, y'know, hey, Chubby, it isn't what it seems, ha!, and old Papa seems to quiet down, an' he goes off to get a drink, but all of a sudden he's back wavin' this forty-five he had from the war and Rex jumps him, and there's the usual struggle, an' then bang bang!

jus' like in the *P'lice Gazette*, an' that was all she wrote for dear old Papa!"

Chickie started to sob. Andy sat there like a post, not knowing what he should do. What he wanted to do was get out of there. Drive straight back to the Creedmores, roust J.B., and hightail it to Burbank and back to Texas. Obviously, as Chickie's oldest, perhaps only, friend, he couldn't do that. While he sorted things out, Chickie continued.

"Y'know who Herman Vivian is?" Before Andy could answer, he shook his head heavily. "Head of studio security at G-I-G. Out here, if you're big in the industry, or under contract, an' you get in trouble, you don't call the cops, you don't call a lawyer, you don't call *anyone* until after you call your studio's security and they tell you what to do. Vivian's more important than ol' man Gessel. Name wasn't always 'Vivian,' it was somethin' Italian. People I know say Vivian gets mob money into the movie industry and Vegas. Say he's the guy put the kiss o' death on Bugsy Siegel, that the studio security thing's jus' a front. Anyway, Rex gets hold of Vivian and within an hour everything's hunky-dor . . ."

Something inside Chickie cut the rush of words short. He began to weep softly. Andy let him cry. He was tempted to reach out and touch Chickie's shoulder, but he held back.

After about five minutes, Chickie lifted his wet gaze to Andy and smiled wanly. "Sorry, Drew. Jus' started to think of Papa. He wasn't much, but the Charles Christian Fentons of the world, whatever their roman numeral is, don't deserve to go down like this, do they? Oh, Jesus, get me out of this place!" Chickie looked down at his watch, scrinching his eyes to make out the dial. "God awmighty, looka that!" He rose unsteadily. "Beddy-byes." He grinned at Andy. "Sleep tight," he said, "don' let the bedbugs bite."

Andy, disoriented, fought his way out of sleep like a diver ascending to the surface. The mattress had definitely shifted. There was someone in the room.

Someone was sitting on the edge of the bed. Andy felt a hand moving under the sheet, stroking his leg, heading for his groin.

"Jesus," he said softly. "Jesus! Hey, Chick, cut it out!"

He blinked to clear his night vision and looked up, seeing moonlight on blond hair.

"Shhh!"

A blond head bent to his and kissed him. Soft lips, faint sexy-sour reminiscence of wine, a tongue in his mouth; at the same time, under the sheets, a hand enclosed him. Next to him, a slender body slid under the sheet and stretched against him. He felt his hand taken, and guided between long legs.

"Oh yes, oh yes," the apparition gasped. He tried to say her name but she covered his mouth with a hand.

There was no turning back then. He entered her; a moment later, at the very last instant before he was about to come, and knew she was, too, when he realized how patiently, how shrewdly, he had been stalked and captured, she breathed huskily in his ear, more of a grunt, really: "Oh, you fucking wonder, you! Oh, now, now, make me a fucking mother of kings, you fucking fucker you! Oh God, oh God!"

Afterward, they fell asleep, not waking until dawn, to make love again. By then, in the interval, her spies had stolen into his soul and dismantled the defenses of his heart. They made love once, twice, and he told her he loved her and Laurel told him the same thing, and it all seemed the most right and natural fact in the whole history of the world.

Chickie said as much over coffee, when Andy accused him of having set him up.

"Of course I did. The two of you are made for each other. I couldn't resist, could I? Dear boy, you don't think I just arrange people's furniture? Drew, when people suit each other the way you and Laurel do, they simply have to be brought together!"

It was barely ten in the morning, but the day was a scorcher; the air was heavy with the smell of camphor from the trees in the back of the house; in the heat, it was like musk.

"Anyway, Drew, don't tell me you're not pleased. It's written all over you. I know you two always had a sneaker for each other, but neither of you would admit it, at least you wouldn't! So when Laurel called about Papa—I guess she saw it in the Santa Barbara paper—it seemed the least I could do was put two and two together. Isn't that supposed to make five, as you Wall Street types say?"

Andy's soul was on wings. He smiled and stuck out a hand.

"No hard feelings, eh, pardner?" said Chickie, taking it. "Just hard something else, eh?"

That night Chickie took them to a party in a house on a side street off La Cienega. For the first time in his life, he saw drugs used as casually as cocktails, smelled the acrid odor of marijuana, watched as Chickie and his friends huddled around a glass-top table and snorted hungrily at the small mounds of white powder. Looking for the bathroom, he opened the wrong door and his lingering schoolboy wondering as to what pansies actually *did* was resolved once and for all by the sight of one man buggering another.

The sight didn't make him angry, not the way the very idea of homo-
sexuality seemed to enrage some people, but it filled him with distaste; it
was an underworld he wanted no part of. He went and found Laurel and
they left.

She suggested they drive all the way out Sunset to the ocean. They
walked along the water, then Andy spread his shirt on the sand and they
made love. Later, as the sky became streaked with the first fiery fingers
of dawn and the Pacific turned into a blazing mirror stretching from
horizon to horizon, they crept into the back of the car and made love
again, and again.

Two days later they parted, Laurel to return to Santa Barbara,
where Thad Hopewell was recuperating from a mild coronary, Andy
to Fort Worth. Nothing had been said about where they might go from
here.

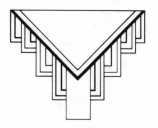

1955

NOVEMBER

Andy got home that Saturday night to find the little house off Camp Bowie empty. A note on the screen door informed him that his housemate had been summoned to Louisiana to pray over a ten-thousand-foot well Pan American was drilling near Lake Charles. It would probably take all weekend. If Andy wanted the geologist's tickets to the TCU-SMU game, they were on the kitchen table.

Andy was as exhausted as he could ever remember, including Korea. He and J.B. had been on the road since Monday, zigzagging back and forth, ending up in Midland, where a one-hour meeting had run on through lunch, by which time a front was blowing in, and J.B.'s Bonanza was grounded. Fatigued, out of shirts and underwear, Andy was determined to sleep in his own bed, so he'd rented a car and driven the six hours south.

As he walked into the house, the phone in the kitchen was ringing, but by the time he got to it, it stopped.

That might have been Laurel, he thought. Since Los Angeles they'd fallen into the habit of talking once or twice a week on the telephone. She was back in Cambridge now for her last year at Radcliffe. They agreed it was better to stay just friends for the time being, see how the passions of California survived distance and absence. Andy could tell from her voice that she was starting to feel the same doubts as he: California had been wild and perfect madness, utterly unreal. As the days without each other went by, their affair seemed to have been from another era, in another galaxy.

Not that there weren't times he craved her. Sometimes, on waking, he could see her moving naked across the room in the morning half light to the bathroom. The memory excited him, but some vital aspect of feeling was ebbing away, perhaps had never been there.

He went into the kitchen, got out some ice, and poured himself a short Scotch. On the table were the football tickets; the day's mail had been neatly stacked atop the local newspapers and the *Wall Street Journal* to which his mother insisted he subscribe. Picking up the mail, he looked idly at the headlines on the front page of the *Star-Telegram*. Friday, November 11, 1955, seemed to have been a day like any other. The big news was that President Eisenhower was back in Washington, having completed his convalescence from his September heart attack. Otherwise the world went on in its usual tangled way: a coup in Brazil, floods here, wrecks there. The SMU Mustangs were heavily favored over the TCU Horned Frogs. Sipping his drink, he examined the mail: a phone bill, a come-on for an oil and gas lease evaluation service, a letter from Chase Manhattan Bank about a mislaid dividend check. Chase Manhattan, he thought; it sounds strange. Earlier in the year, the old Chase National had merged with the Bank of the Manhattan Company. Before that, the National City Bank with the First National Bank of New York to become First National City Bank. Andy's father claimed that if this kept up, there wouldn't be more than a dozen big banks left in the city, and that might not be the good thing people were cracking it up to be.

Well, thought Andy, life is change, banks change, cities change, people change, but life goes on while memory lingers to complain. When the Third Avenue El was torn down, to hear his mother talk it was as if they'd knocked down the Statue of Liberty, but as Andy remembered, the El had been noisy and sooty, and he doubted if his mother had ridden it once in her life.

There was a blue envelope on the bottom of the pile; he saw it was a letter from Laurel. He opened it. When he got to the part where she had written, "I don't know how to tell you this, but I've missed three periods in a row, and I'm not talking about Fine Arts 34," the ceiling seemed to fall in.

He read the lines a half dozen times and made himself another, stiffer whiskey.

So this is how grown-up life gets started, he thought. He did the mental arithmetic: they had been together in July, so, August-September, September-October, October-November. Three months. Say fifteen weeks. What was the point of no return? All he had to go on were Fraternity

Row's old wives' tales: anything before three months was safe, *if* you could get it done. That was some big "if," bigger than Texas. Maybe he should call Jay. Jay was an operator; he'd know how and where to procure an abortion.

Of course, what if something happened? At Yale you heard stories, none of them nice. About back-floor flats in seedy Lower East Side brown-stones, and booze-raddled doctors in stained surgical gowns operating with bloody coathangers. Sometimes you heard about gleaming Swiss and Puerto Rican clinics, more antiseptic than Lenox Hill, manned by top specialists. If these existed, Jay would know. Or Chickie. This sort of thing happened in Hollywood all the time.

The first thing was to find out what Laurel wanted to do. He picked up the letter and looked at the date. Over a week since it was mailed. Jesus, she must be going crazy not to hear from him.

She said she wanted to get rid of it. Andy said he'd get it fixed. Something held him back from talking to either Jay or Chickie, so he went to J.B. with the problem. Marryat made some calls to people he knew in Mexico City, and Andy was given the name of a "reliable and safe" clinic in Juarez.

Laurel flew into Amon Carter Airport two nights before the scheduled operation. She looked pale with apprehension and doubt, but as beautiful as ever. "This is a sweet little house," she said when Andy showed her in. Mercifully, his housemate was back in East Texas and the "betrothed" couple was alone.

That night they went over to Mexican Town and gorged themselves on enchiladas and margaritas. Andy awoke in the middle of the night; Laurel was sleeping. There was just enough light coming in from the street to outline her features. She looked unforgivably young and vulnerable.

For some time afterward he would tease her that a mischievous angel had put in his mouth the question he now whispered in her ear, but he asked it, and when she answered "Yes, I will" sleepily, there was nothing left after that but to hold each other and try to stop shaking with relief and presentiment, and then try to get some sleep.

J.B. was delighted with the change of plan. Of course, he knew just whom to call, and just how to get this fixed and that. And so it was, on the afternoon of November 17, 1955, in judge's chambers in the Tarrant County Courthouse, Laurel Evangeline Hopewell and Andrew Farwell Warrington were married. Both being of age, parental consent was not required, nor indeed was either set of parents aware of the proceedings. The wedding ring did not come from Tiffany or Raymond Yard, but from Haltom's, the most prominent local jeweler.

When a public notice of the wedding was printed in the local papers, no one gave it much thought. The names Hopewell and Warrington were of no account in Fort Worth; it wasn't as if the little Windfohr girl had run off with some Easterner.

After the ceremony, the couple, young and glowing with happiness and health, repaired to a private room in the Fort Worth Club, where their future fecundity and prosperity—both of which had already been well taken in hand by the gods—were warmly toasted by the staff of Marryat Oil & Gas, such of Andy's few acquaintances from Fort Worth as could be rounded up on no notice, the judge and his wife, and, to give the occasion the institutional dignity it deserved, the Fort Worth city man-ager. It was a cheerful, gala occasion, with real French champagne im-ported from Dallas. Amid such high spirits, the newlyweds' apprehensions about how to tell their respective families fell by the wayside, as did a piece of news enthusiastically circulated by young Bobby Marryat. Ac-cording to Bobby, the Dow-Jones Industrial Average had that day regained the last smidgen of the ground it had lost following the President's heart attack, and had securely consolidated well above the historic highs of 1929. After the most turbulent and disorderly quarter-century economic man had ever known, the new era seemed safely in hand.

1960

DECEMBER

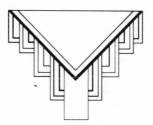

On the East River below, the lights of a vessel making its way south toward the harbor caught Lyda's eye. Colored bulbs had been strung along its funnel and superstructure and twined in its rigging. All done up for the holidays like me, she thought, watching the disembodied festoons of light twinkle slowly down the waterway. On the Manhattan side, the headlights of cars flowed steadily north on the East River Drive; in the distance glowed the beaded arcs of the bridges. Across the river, a neon sign for the American Wicker Company added its garish note.

Of the places she'd lived in the city, her old flat in the Village, the Park Avenue townhouse, the sprawling Fifth Avenue apartment, Lyda liked this one the most. They'd bought the Sutton Place duplex the year before, almost on impulse. One day the Fifth Avenue apartment had suddenly struck both of them as too gloomy, too full of sad memories, too big for just the three of them.

Miranda was the only one left at home now, and she would be off to college the following year. Laurel and Andrew had an apartment on 79th Street. Jay lived, if that was the word, in a hotel off Madison Avenue.

At the time, $100,000 seemed a lot to pay—even for two floors overlooking the river and the wide lawn that the building shared with the low townhouses of Sutton Square—especially when you added in Chickie

Fenton's decorating bill, but the Fifth Avenue apartment had fetched a pretty penny, and after all, what was the point of letting all their money pile up in stocks and bonds and equity in The Firm?

She looked at herself in the dressing-table mirror. Not bad for an old dame on the cusp of sixty, she thought. She touched her hair, ran her hand along her cheekbone, pulled down the skin beneath an eye, held up both hands and examined nails and cuticles. Not bad at all. She lifted an imaginary glass in the direction of the mirror. Well done, Lyda, she murmured, and well done, Elizabeth Arden, and well done, Rene, Pablo, and Estelle, and the masseuse at the Colony Club, and Jo Hughes, who shopped for her clothes. She leaned forward to take a closer look. Do to me what you will, God, she thought, but never never never will I have my face "done." Look at poor Floss: she'd had a facelift and now she could barely open her mouth.

On the victrola in the background, Edith Piaf was singing "Je ne Regrette Rien." The new hit seemed wonderfully appropriate to Lyda's frame of mind. Lyda reminded herself she mustn't call it a "victrola." This splendid machine was called a "hi-fi." Howland had bought it at that new Korvette store, a place he haunted at least one afternoon a week, always coming home with some amazing gadget that he swore would improve the way they lived, and which Louise in the kitchen promptly exiled to a closet.

Howland was still a boy in many ways, she thought, and thank God for that! He'd kept his looks and his figure. At sixty-five he was every inch the patrician and patriarch his father had been, but his heart was youthful. His enthusiasm for games and gimmicks remained irrepressible.

"*Rien, rien de rien, rien, je ne regrette rien*": the singer's passionate vibrato filled the room. I too, Lyda thought. On balance, we have little enough to regret, Howland and I. We have each other and our good health; God has left us three of our children. They may give us fits, but we love them and they love us. Our life is privileged, yet productive and discreet. We have been spared further death and illness. Life seems orderly.

Of course, now with young Kennedy coming to the White House, what could one know of the future? So much depended on his character. God help us if he inherits his father's, thought Lyda. Joseph Kennedy was one of those people who wanted to live through his children, and there was very little to be said for him. He'd been flagrantly unfaithful to his wife for much of their marriage, and as for his business dealings, well, to hear Howland talk, the man had been little better than a crook. Still, three decades of wealth could make a difference, although not so much as people like to think. People who didn't know their Boston mentioned the Kennedys in the same breath with the Cabots and Forbeses, and that was ridiculous.

Well, at least the Kennedy boy had looks and charm and style, which was more than you could say for that smarmy Nixon. Lyda had voted for the younger man, although she hadn't confessed the fact to her husband. The new First Lady might be a bit of a social climber, all those Bouviers were, but she had style, too, and while the benign dowdiness of the Eisenhowers had had its day, the White House could certainly use some spit and polish.

She looked around her dressing room. All in order, everything in its place. The little Darrell Austin painting of a lion cub Howland had bought her on her last birthday; the sketch René Bouché had made of Lyda for *Vogue*; the Vertes screen that had been a present from Howland's partners; an enchanting wildlife fantasy by Charlie Baskerville; and all the photographs, a catalogue of shared lives and mourned deaths.

On balance, nothing to regret. Life went on, the passing marked by small dependable occurrences: a new Ian Fleming thriller sent over by that nice woman at the British Book Centre, a new Cole Porter musical, the old rota of birthdays and anniversaries. So much seemed so little changed. They all still ate at the same restaurants, went to the same nightclubs, observed the same etiquette. New faces guarded the velvet ropes—at the Colony, a nice young man named Sirio was now in charge of the dining room, at "21" the Kriendlers' nephew Sheldon had taken over, and at El Morocco, Angelo had succeeded the legendary Carino—but the ropes still came deferentially down for Mr. and Mrs. Warrington.

There were times it seemed quite unreal, this continuing unaltered order of things. Life wasn't supposed to be stable. Life was supposed to be change, new men rising, old ones sinking. On Wall Street, there were times when it even seemed that the Crash and Depression had never happened. That after the war the music had started up again, men of a certain kind—not many of them bright, not many of them vital—took in the world as their oyster, settled into the tempo of a languid minuet that took them from home to the Floor to the club and then home again, like a procession of figures on a vase.

On the corner of her dressing table was a slim parcel Howland had laid there just before he disappeared downstairs to have his talk with Jay. A premature Christmas present, she guessed. She recognized the wrapping paper. Yet another bracelet from Yard, she surmised; men were such predictable ninnies when it came to shopping. They hunted by habit, in the same haunts, from which they always came home with the same bone.

Raymond Yard was the jeweler who'd made the gold-and-sapphire cuff links and studs she'd given Howland on his sixtieth birthday four years earlier, the year after Laurel and Andrew got married. Nineteen fifty-six had been "The Year of Ford," the year when the automaker decided to put its shares on the market for the first time, and every important investment banker in America had been out to get a piece of the under-writing. Howland had even rushed out and bought a Ford car, and he wasn't the only one; the snazziest parking lots from Oyster Bay to Burlingame, normally replete with Cadillacs and Jaguars, were for a brief time filled with Fords and Mercurys. In the end, Charley Blyth's firm had won the managership of the underwriting, but Warrington & Co. had made a proud appearance high up in the tombstone that advertised the offering, so perhaps buying the car had worked.

Lyda was looking forward to this evening. They were going to meet the children at the Colony at eight and then go to El Morocco for some champagne and dancing. At the end of the evening, if they both felt up to it, she and Howland might drop by the Drake—just the two of them—to hear Cy Walter on the piano and have a quiet nightcap.

She lit a cigarette with her heavy gold Zippo. She remained deaf to her doctor's stern lectures about the dangers of tobacco. Ben Miles might be considered the top young internist at Columbia-Presbyterian, the heir-apparent to Dana Atchley as physician to *le tout New York*, but she was damned if she was going to give up smoking! She dragged hard at the cigarette; these new Kents, with their so-called "Micronite filters," took an awful lot of energy to smoke; maybe she should go back to Chesterfields.

She made a final pass with her powder puff, looked at herself this way and that, and got up from the dressing table. She looked through her closet and decided to top off her costume with a black beaded evening shawl that Jo Hughes had also picked out for her. As she twisted to make sure the stole fell properly, her glance lighted on the three-quarter-lifesize pastel portrait of Miranda.

Lyda halted her fashion deliberations and studied the picture. Miranda had been ten when the portrait was done. It was a good resemblance, Lyda thought. Miranda looked like a sinister little angel, with her mother's dark skin set off strikingly by light hair and pale gray eyes. She had posed in a party dress from Rowes in Bond Street that Lyda had bought from the nice woman who twice a year set up shop at the Commodore. From the portrait, it would have been hard to guess that, as Chickie put it, "Miranda runs on trouble the way cars run on gasoline."

Miranda was seventeen now, finishing at Chapin and bound for Vassar in the fall of 1961. She would have preferred the University of California or Barnard, but Lyda felt that the combination of Miranda and Berkeley was potentially too combustible—Stanford would have been all right, but Miranda had flatly rejected Palo Alto, "It's full of the same sort of people as Chapin, Mummy." As for her remaining in New York, well, no, her parents thought. They needed a rest. Vassar seemed a reasonable compromise.

Life with Miranda was a series of arduously negotiated compromises.

Two nights earlier, she'd reluctantly made her debut at the Junior Assembly and even that small effort—the girls did no more than curtsy once and waltz at midnight with their fathers—she'd turned into a trial. She'd been hopelessly rude to the woman at Bendel's about her dress and practically had to be dragged kicking and screaming to Bachrach to have her "official" debut picture taken. She insisted on having Jay and young Jerry Creedmore, who was at Columbia preparing for Union Theological Seminary, to be her escorts. Jerry was crazy about Miranda, who treated him with cool indifference unless she wanted him to do something; he would have jumped in the East River if Miranda had asked him to.

Lyda abandoned her contemplation of Miranda's portrait. A silver-framed photograph of Laurel and Andrew stood on a side table. She picked it up, sighed, and shook her head. It was her sense that things were not going as well as they might, even though neither of them ever said anything.

Poor Laurel, she thought. If only the girl could give up this hopeless obsession about bearing a child. It would be so easy to adopt. Lyda had talked to the people at Spence-Chapin; Andrew and Laurel had only to say the word, and a fine baby would be theirs.

It was tragic to see things work out this way. Laurel would be such a good mother. She was a strong person, and warm, and kind; one could still see this through the growing bleakness that her situation was beginning to impose on her personality. It had been a terrible piece of bad luck that her first pregnancy had been ectopic. A bare month after she and Andrew had gotten married, he'd come home to find her bleeding all over the kitchen floor. They'd had to tie off her tubes, and that was that.

Afterward, Laurel got it into her head that it was the Fort Worth doctor's fault, even though the people at Presbyterian had assured Howland the man was absolutely tops, and that had been the end of Texas as far as Laurel was concerned. Six months later, she and Andrew had moved back to New York.

They had a nice life there. All the money you could ever need, and a nice apartment; in the summer they rented a farmhouse in Wainscott just across Georgica Pond from Double Dune. They had nice friends and busy lives; Laurel worked three mornings a week as a researcher at Knoedler's on 57th Street, and she had joined a couple of Lyda's charity committees. They went to Giovanni's, and "21" and the Stork Club and Madeleine's. All that was missing was a child, but day by day—Lyda feared—that "all" was becoming everything.

If there was a bright side, it was that Laurel's misadventures had brought Andrew to Hanover Place. Not that Lyda had ever doubted he would end up there; it was in his bones.

Andrew and Jay complemented each other so perfectly temperamentally and intellectually. They might not have much time for each other away from Hanover Place, but in business they made a very effective team.

Andrew was the steady one. Like his father, he took the long view, thought in terms of connections and relationships, causes and consequences. His work showed an innate flair for the business that surprised even him. Well, he *was* born to it. If Andrew had a glaring deficiency, Lyda felt, it was that he had too high an opinion of others, men who were neither as principled nor as reasonable as he might think. It was all very well to declare, as she had heard her son do, that "a good deal is one that is good for everyone involved," but as Jay said, if Andrew was right, then there had never ever been such a thing as a good deal, and certainly not on Wall Street!

Jay was so different. He thought and acted in quick, snappy, discrete flashes. According to his father, his mind was a mirror image of the tickertape, the quintessential trader's mentality. Andrew said that watching his brother think was the intellectual equivalent of "follow the bouncing ball" at a movie singalong.

Well, thought Lyda, there was room for all at Hanover Place. The Firm had to be many things to many men, capable of cultivating prospective connections in whatever fashion those prospects might be most productively cultivated. Sometimes all it took was an easy manner in the Gorse Club bar, or a strong head for the booze that flowed in Louisiana duck camps and New Brunswick fishing lodges. Sometimes what was needed was the ability to spout figures like an accountant or indenture provisions like a lawyer. Whatever it was, by 1960 The Firm could find someone in its ranks who could deliver the goods.

Lyda looked at the clock on the bedroom mantel. Heavens! She wondered how it was going downstairs. Well, Jay simply had to grow up. Year after next he would be thirty, and would become a partner. It was time he started behaving like one.

Still, it did seem ridiculous for Howland to have to talk to Jay about his language; that was what you did with seven-year-old boys, not a man of twenty-eight!

Well, Miriam had left them no choice. Last week, when she'd run into Miriam at a Kips Bay community meeting, Miriam had practically taken her ear off on the subject of the language her grandson Arthur Lubloff was picking up from Jay.

Arthur Lubloff—"Artie" to everyone except Miriam—was the only child of Miriam and Morris's daughter Selma and her husband Burton Lubloff. The boy was now fourteen, a student at Horace Mann. He was a brilliant boy, with a special gift for physics and mathematics, who had skipped a grade at Collegiate School. He was taking special tutoring in calculus, and—if his parents had their way—was bound for MIT. According to Ben Miles, his sister had already penciled Artie in for the 1981 Nobel Prize in physics.

Lyda liked Artie. He had an engaging, modest way about him, although people said the boy was a relentless, cutthroat competitor in everything from studies to sports. He was very tall for fourteen, over six feet already, with huge hands and feet, but not the least bit gawky. Jay said he was the best basketball player his age in the city: black, white, or brown. It vexed Selma and Burt Lubloff that of their son's two prodigious gifts, for mathematics and basketball, it was the latter Artie pursued most avidly. Naturally, it was basketball in which he was most rabidly encouraged by Jay.

When Jay spoke, Artie Lubloff listened. He had a crush on Jay. It was understandable. For one thing, Jay treated him like an equal. For another, Artie, as any boy his age would have been, was a sucker for the grand gestures in which Jay dealt as easily and glibly as he traded blocks of shares. For Jay Warrington, velvet ropes parted, box-office lines vanished, the best tables in the most difficult restaurants, or seats at ringside, automatically appeared. It was, Lyda believed, a special power he had over people; she had seen it in other men. It wasn't just tips, although Lord knows Jay threw dollar bills around like confetti; it was something Lyda could only describe to herself as "presence," a way with people.

Jay seemed to know everyone's name. Not just the Kriendlers and Perons, but the cashiers and telephone operators and restroom attendants. The waiters at the Madison Square Garden Club. The men who swept up at the Gorse. At Hanover Place, he knew them all: the porters and the elevator operators, the clerks in P&S and the telephone girls, the cooks and accounting-machine operators, the mailroom boys in the basement of the Annex. It was a gift.

To hear some people, Miriam Miles among them, Jay was utterly without qualities, redeeming or otherwise. Miriam truly *hated* Jay for the way he treated Max.

Of course, if Max had been *her* son, Lyda might have hated Jay herself. There was something about Max that Jay couldn't leave alone. Part of it had to do with Max's situation at The Firm. He wasn't going anywhere at Hanover Place; even absent the proscriptions of the Trust, it was clear that Max didn't have what it took. Howland felt that it was up to Morris to place his son with another house, but Morris behaved as if the situation didn't exist. As a result, an uneasy status quo, which everyone pretended not to see, had developed. Morris protected Max by seeing that he was assigned to business that Morris controlled; Foster Klopp, who couldn't stand to see inferior work coming out under The Firm's name, did Max's homework for him and cleaned up after him, as if Max was a large, unhousebroken dog.

Lyda's phone buzzed twice.

"We're all done," said Howland.

"I'll be right down . . . and, darling . . ."

"Yes?"

"The bracelet from Yard's absolutely beautiful. However did you know?"

She turned off the dressing-table lamp. Out the window the lights of the city gleamed dully on the eddies of the current as it swept toward the sea. From its perch above the darkened sheds and toolshops of Long Island City, AMERICAN WICKER AND HAMPER winked at her. She took a last look at Miranda's pretty, childish face up on the wall, and thought of the obstinate, cold young woman her daughter was becoming. A feeling so poignant that it was almost painful brushed through her bosom. Must be the time of year, she thought, or old age.

An hour earlier, Howland had waited fretfully for Jay. He hated to have this kind of conversation, especially so close to Christmas, but there was no way getting around it.

His eye drifted around the library. He was glad they'd moved; he liked this place; it reminded him of their first house. Fifth Avenue had never really suited them: too big, too dark.

Pacing the room, he paused at a round table in front of dark green lacquered bookshelves, where a collection of silver-framed photographs were grouped around a vase of yellow roses. Friends and family; earnests of prestige: a picture of Lyda and Howland with President Eisenhower, inscribed by Ike; another with General Marshall, flanked by his flags of office. Social mementos: Howland and Bing Crosby on the first tee at Cypress Point. Intersections of business and pleasure: Howland and Tom Creedmore at Boeing back in '58, watching the rollout of Global's first 707; Tooey Spaatz and Howland in England in 1944, posed under the wing of a B-24 at an airbase somewhere in Somerset. Here too, yellowing with age, was Chubby Fenton, forever boyish in his letter sweater, confidently leaning on the photographer's prop fence as captain of Yale football, holding a football marked "19 Y 16."

Damn, said Howland to himself, I miss you, pal, for all your faults. Where the hell was Jay!

As if in response, the doorbell rang; he heard the butler answer it, a brief exchange, then the clatter of hasty feet down the marble hall.

"Hey, Pop, sorry to be late." Jay stopped in his tracks and looked at his father. "How come the long face? Why the doom and gloom? God's in His heaven, and unless the world falls out of bed, the Dow's still gonna finish 1960 closer to seven hundred than six hundred, and you will owe me five more beautiful green portraits of Benjamin Franklin."

It was obvious he'd had a couple of drinks somewhere along the way, yet Howland felt his irritation ebb. He was too fond of the boy, and too appreciative of his abilities. This was the third straight year Jay'd called the market within ten percent.

Nevertheless, he had to launch this conversation on a properly stern basis. "I don't suppose you'd care to say what's kept you?" he asked.

Jay grinned. His thirtieth birthday was still more than two years off, but his hair was flecked with gray.

"Hell, no, Pop! Cosmo Life had a ratfuck at the Bankers Club, so I looked in just to show the flag, and piss Morris off, because he thinks the Cosmo connection is his personal property. Jesus, just 'cause he goes up to Twenty-fifth Street once a quarter and has lunch with Barney Berenson, and the two of them scratch their grizzled chins and mumble about 'leading indicators.' " Jay imitated the gesture.

"Naturally," he continued, "Morris had old Max in tow, even though this particular blowout was mostly for the Floor and the upstairs trading crowd, so it was like he was shopping a marriageable daughter. Anyway, I hung out for a while, then I ankled up to the Numbers and bought a few pops for a couple of guys from Fidelity who were enjoying boys' night out in the big town. I got Sheldon to give them a good table, and I made a couple of calls and fixed them up . . ."

"I wish you wouldn't . . ."

"Hey, Pop, this is where it's coming from. You know how many tickets we wrote with Fidelity this year? Compared to last? Don't worry. I'll run the hookers through the suspense account. Carlucci'll never catch it. So keep calm, keep cool."

It wasn't easy for Howland to do so. This was the sort of thing one heard about other firms: call girls, nights on the town, all expenses paid. Howland was no prude. What bothered him was his growing awareness that the kind of business Jay was doing was the wave of the future. Not the call-girl part; *that* kind of business had been done since the buttonwood tree was in flower.

No one could still doubt that the investment institutions were where the Street's future lay. The big mutual-fund groups owned ten times the amount of common stock they had ten years earlier. A big institutional clientele was hugely profitable—one got the same commission per share on ten thousand shares as on a hundred. One couldn't fight progress, Howland knew, but he also recalled from 1929 that a concentration of investment power hadn't proved to be the best thing for the market—or the country.

"Anyway, after the Numbers," Jay continued, "and Pete Kriendler says where have you and Ma been, incidentally, I had to drop some tickets for the Groton-St. Marks dance off for this clown who follows the airlines at Chelsea Trust. The guy's good for twenty-five thousand shares on the next Global go-round, provided we get his pimply kid in among the quality prep-school crowd. Then, as I was in the neighborhood, I figured I'd look into Clarke's, and . . ."

Howland put up his hands.

"Enough! It sounds like you're warming up for Friday's office party. May I add we are to have no repetition of last year's performance."

"I'm going to plead extenuating circumstances on that, Pop. Any broad that wears a dress cut that way to an office party not only deserves exactly what happens to her but wants it. Anyway, how was I to know she was giving it to Bosworth on the side?"

"Let's drop the subject. Now, your mother has asked me to speak to you about Artie Lubloff. But before I get to that, may I also request for the umpteenth time that you get off Max Miles's case?"

Before his son could answer, Howland added: "As a matter of fact, I'm going to amend that statement. I'm not going to request you to do that, I'm going to order you."

Jay grinned impishly. "Is the condemned man allowed a word in his own behalf?"

"Just be serious for a minute," said Howland patiently.

"I thought that was Drew's job."

"It is both of your jobs. In time, it will be your Firm to lead—Andrew's and yours. To lead responsibly, which, I need hardly add, means humanely. You can start by treating Max Miles like a human being."

"You're not gonna cork off and stick us with Slapsie Maxie! Hey, Pop, Max is a schmuck. He's been here six years now, and he hasn't learned shit from Shinola about this business. If he didn't have Morris wiping his ass for him, with the Klopper close behind with mop and bucket, he'd be out the door. If you don't believe me, ask Drew!"

"I agree Max's technique may be . . ."

" 'Technique'!" Jay interrupted his father with a snort. "You know what 'technique' is? I'll tell you: addition, subtraction, multiplication, division. And a few B-school buzzwords. Technique, my ass! You sound like the goddamn Klopper, Pop! Come on, get with it! If it was technique that counted, the Klopper'd be running Morgan Stanley. What counts is knowing markets, and people, because markets are people."

"Jay, there is no point in continuing in this vein. It is our Firm; our name is on the door. Are you familiar with the phrase 'noblesse oblige'?"

Jay smiled. "Pop, let me ask you something. You think Max'd noblesse oblige us if he was in our position?"

Howland couldn't answer that. He got to the main point. "Now, about the Lubloff boy, your mother . . ."

"I know, I know," said Jay. He shrugged his shoulders exaggeratedly and completed Howland's sentence, "clean up the language or you'll wash my mouth out with soap and water."

He grinned at his father. "Hey, Pop, you shoulda come up to Riverdale with me last week. Artie is something! He got thirty points and he might as well have been playing alone. I'll tell you one thing, Pop. When Artie gets to his senior season, Selma and Burt may be thinking MIT and Cal Tech, but there're gonna be guys in the stands from Ohio State and UCLA. A hotshot I know in L.A. told me Coach Wooden's even thinking about coming East to catch Artie's act in the private schools tournament, plus check out that big spade in the Bronx at the same time. You know: Lew Alcindor?"

"Don't change the subject, Jay. Language. Artie's grandmother is very upset. Do we have a deal on that?"

"Mrs. Miles shits her bloomers every time it rains on her little boy, Pop. Okay, okay, I surrender. I'll watch my tongue and mind my manners in front of the kid. I won't say 'fuck' in front of the b-a-b-y."

He repeated the joke, to make sure his father got it, then grinned and said, "I guess you can tell Ma the smoke and shot have cleared and it's okay to come down."

Across town, on the pavement in front of a fine 1920s apartment building on West 67th Street, the Boston Celtics were playing the National Basketball Association All-Stars. Bob Cousy drove the lane, pulled up, and fired the ball to Tom Heinsohn in the corner. The beefy Celtics rookie forward, who looked more like a bricklayer than a shot maker, planted his black-sneakered feet, jumped, and as Elgin Baylor lunged helplessly, sent the ball basketward in a high, surprisingly delicate arc. The ball kissed off the square carved plaque of an Art-Deco griffon, the center of a frieze that decorated the façade of the building. Swish! Celtics by two! The crowd went apeshit.

Phew! Artie Lubloff wiped his forehead. It was cold outside, only a few degrees above freezing, with dirty snow congealed in the gutters and heaped around parked automobiles, trapping them. Frosty rings circled the street lamps.

Artie shook the sweat from his hand and watched the drops hiss on the icy, soot-smudged pavement. It was hot work for one guy to be the ten best basketball players in the world. Especially if you couldn't help playing as hard for one side as the other. Most kids instinctively favored one side or another, but Artie couldn't make himself do that when it was just him out there representing both teams. Artie hated the Celtics, for instance, *hated* them, but even so he had 'em up by two and there wasn't much left on the clock: just seven minutes before he had to go up for dinner. Normally, he'd play afterward, but he had a ton of homework and then there was his science project to work on. Miss Prosser said that if he went three-for-three in the Westinghouse Talent Search, the first time any American teenager had done it, Horace Mann might name a laboratory in his honor without his grandfather even having to make a fat donation.

He looked down. His tall, skinny silhouette had combined weirdly with the shadow of the lamppost so that it looked like a giant spider standing there. He liked the image. "Like a spider, man," that's what Willie Naulls had told him the afternoon when Jay had fixed it up for him to go to the Garden after classes to practice with the Knickerbockers. Coach hadn't liked the idea of Artie's missing practice, but even Coach couldn't argue when he heard what it was for: an hour of "tutoring" with Richie Guerin and Naulls, the Knicks' best players. Now Jay was talking about setting up a one-on-one against Lew Alcindor, the big skinny kid up at Power Memorial. Jay could set up anything.

Well, back to work. Six points down, seven minutes on the clock. It could be done. Goddamn shit, he *hated* the fucking Celtics! Okay, fellows, he muttered, let's get those assholes! He clapped his hands and went back out on the court.

Oscar Robertson brought it upcourt, Hal Lear trotting easily to his right and a little ahead, two fingers signaling a play.

At the top of the circle, the action accelerated. The Big O tossed in a little loop pass to Wilt in the key, who faked left, faked right, and then kicked it out to Baylor in the corner, and everyone cleared it out. Now Baylor, isolated on Sharman, backed in, dribbling, his head making its patented herky-jerk, looking for his opening. Sharman had him on the inside, so Baylor suddenly faked outside, dropped off, whirled, and as he fell away, sent up a soft jumper from twelve feet.

Shit fuck piss! The shot was too high. It struck the place at which the griffon plaque was inset in the limestone, bounded high in the air—no basket!—arced over Artie's head, bounced off the hood of a snowbound DeSoto, and rolled into the street. Celtics' ball.

Shit fuck piss! cursed Artie, as he went to retrieve it.

At that very moment, another rabid sports fan entered West 67th Street, a cabdriver who'd overbet the Giants against the Eagles. If the Giants didn't come through, and with that fucking Van Brocklin you could never tell, his old lady was gonna eat his nuts for breakfast, lunch, and dinner, plus where was he gonna get the dough for the bookie, plus the vigorish? These troubles were complicated by his rage at the greaseball he'd just dropped off on Central Park West; the guy had stiffed him with a dime tip on an eighty-cent fare from Grand Central.

His brain was roiling when he made the turn into 67th Street; in a gesture of rage and frustration he gunned the cab, so intent on his own problems that he never even saw the tall kid come running out from between two cars chasing a basketball.

BOOK

VII

POWERS OF APPOINTMENT

AUGUST

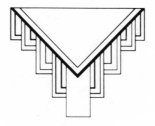

A series of afternoon thunder-
storms broke the blistering spine of the hot spell that had plagued the city
for almost two weeks. By early evening, the skies had cleared and the
temperature was pleasant.

On the steps of Hanover Place, Foster Klopp checked the tilt of his
fedora and patted himself in various places to make sure that his arsenal
of pens and pencils, slide rule, pocket notebook, and billfold was securely
in place. He decided to stroll down to Battery Park to sit and harbor
watch for a spell before catching a cab uptown. He was in no hurry. His
evening was organized. At seven, the little French restaurant on the corner
of 88th Street would have his customary table waiting. In his briefcase
were stowed the *Wall Street Journal* and a sheaf of investment reports,
as well as a draft of the financing proposal the Mileses were to present
next week to Western Factors and Finance. After dinner, before turning
in, Klopp would watch this new TV show he liked, the one with Robert
Young as a wise old doctor. It was the role Klopp thought of himself as
playing within The Firm.

Marcus Welby reminded him of the values he'd grown up with out
in South Dakota, values you didn't seem to see around much anymore,
the kind of values epitomized by the *Saturday Evening Post*, which had
stopped publishing a couple of months earlier. Another good thing swept

away by change. People blamed the shutting-up of the magazine on bad management at Curtis Publishing, but Klopp thought they didn't know what they were talking about. It was the country that had changed; the kind of country that wanted a *Saturday Evening Post* no longer existed.

At the corner of Water Street, Klopp paused and looked back at Hanover Place. The old building glowed almost golden in the early twilight. Well, it hasn't changed, he reflected, at least not in its essence; tradition still counted for something there. The name Warrington & Co. still stood for ingenious, high-quality work; for discretion; for first-class business with first-class people conducted in a first-class way.

Naturally, there had been adjustments. The roaring bull market of the last decade had its own distinctive character; to keep on top of things, to make money, any Wall Street house had to some extent make an accommodation with the spirit of the age, but changes in style and emphasis did not necessarily mean sacrifices of character. In the end, Klopp knew, all big bull markets came to an end. When that happened, houses that held fast to ancestral standards would survive, while the modish and the reckless disappeared. Hanover Place still rejected more business than it took on; it had not become involved in the hot fashions of the decade: no conglomerates, no trick financings, none of the "hot issue" business that was reaching the point of downright craziness.

How people could be made to part with good money for unseasoned stocks called "National Student Marketing" or "Four Seasons Nursing Centers" or "Gramco," or casino stocks like this "Parvin-Dohrmann," simply astonished Foster Klopp. He had it on good authority that some of these outfits were controlled by the kind of people he was reading about in *The Godfather*, the new novel Andy Warrington had given him for his birthday.

Klopp was fairly sure the bull market was already over. The *Journal* might be thick with tombstones for hot new issues, but the business lacked a good tone and had for some time now.

Funny, at the beginning of 1968, nothing had seemed impossible. The volume on the Exchange had been terrific—on April Fool's Day, 1968, they'd traded *eighteen million* shares, which broke the '29 record, and five months later, twenty-one million—which was all well and good, provided you could handle it, but most firms couldn't. You began to have the paradox of firms going broke on prosperity. The Exchange had been forced to shut down on Wednesdays just to battle the paperwork, and word on the Street was that Lehman Brothers had almost gone belly up on its "fails."

Hanover Place had been prepared. Thanks to his faith in technology, Howland had called in the IBM people back in '67. A year later, young

Lubloff came on board, with his Wharton computer tricks, so now The Firm had a system that was making darn near as much money processing other people's paperwork as its own. That was where history came in. Back in 1837, after the Ohio National failed, The Firm had gotten into trouble over protested bills of exchange because it had tried to save money by employing too few clerks and Erasmus Warrington had sworn never again. Clerks then, computers now.

Now the Lubloff lad was trying to get The Firm's computers to adapt to corporate finance. This very moment, Klopp knew, he was in the fifth-floor computer room, working like a demon at revising the terms on which Marryat Oil proposed to pay for its acquisition of Acacia Petrochemical. It was not a deal Klopp liked; it involved too much debt to be sound, but nowadays the customer was always right. Well, credit quality was declining up and down the Street. His not to reason why, however, since Marryat's banks had agreed to lend half the purchase price. Artie's job was to make his machine spit out debt ratios and cash flows that would cover the rest of the financing.

Foster Klopp was deeply proud of Artie Lubloff. He wouldn't have used the word, but everyone else at Hanover Place could see that he regarded Artie as a son, more than just a kindred soul, or a protégé. Klopp wasn't given to boasting, but in an unguarded moment he'd let slip to Howland that he had a hunch that young Lubloff was going to turn out to be the best of all the men he'd trained in his twenty-five years at The Firm. Time alone would tell, of course. Arthur was only twenty-three; he'd taken his B.S. *summa cum laude* from Wharton at twenty, even after he'd lost the better part of his tenth-grade year when he was hit by the taxi, and he'd gotten his M.B.A. just a year later.

The lad certainly threw himself into anything he took an interest in. Klopp had never seen such a bear for work. In a way, it was understandable. It must have been a terrible thing to come out of the anesthetic and be told by your doctor that you could never again play basketball, which you loved almost as much as life itself. To Arthur's credit, though, he'd picked himself up from where fate had thrown him without so much as a whimper.

Klopp liked to think that he'd played a key part in persuading Arthur to shift his sights from the laboratory to Wall Street, but he recognized it probably never would have come about if Selma and Burt Lubloff hadn't been killed in a plane crash in 1963, and Artie'd gone to live with his grandparents and his uncle Max.

Klopp started down Water Street. At Broad Street, he paused to regard the construction across the way; the building was going to be called "One New York Plaza." Klopp tried to recall what had stood there before. It all went by too quickly for memory.

Klopp didn't see that this necessarily added up to progress, but he didn't feel as strongly about it as did Lyda Warrington. She hated all real-estate development, particularly the Pan-Am Building, which had risen behind Grand Central in 1963.

"It's like boarding up the grandest picture window in the city," she'd complained.

He looked up at the steel-and-concrete skeleton rising above Broad Street. This must be where Salomon Brothers was moving. According to Jay Warrington, Salomon Brothers was planning to build a huge new trading room—"the size of Madison Square Garden," Jay said enviously.

Klopp thought that was mighty ambitious of Salomon. He still thought of them as a medium-size, medium-class bond house, but to hear Jay Warrington talk, Salomon was *the* house to keep your eyes on.

Klopp liked Jay; he liked both the Warrington boys. Andy was decent, smart, and industrious, good with people, an investment banker in the old tradition, to the manner born. The only problem Klopp saw with Andy was: was the lad hard-hearted enough to take over when the time came? Fair yet firm, that was what it took, and Andy seemed more fair than firm. Jay was more daring and aggressive, perhaps too much so. He liked to fly close to the sun, to work without a net. That was what it took, apparently, in the flamboyant, cinematic world of institutional brokerage and trading.

Klopp crossed Bowling Green and entered Battery Park. In the lee of the subway station, a small group of young people loitered. They were unkempt, to Klopp's eyes filthy, dressed like bandits, the boys' hair as long as the girls'. What was wrong with young people nowadays! Even Miranda Warrington. Why, the last time she'd shown up at Hanover Place for a review of her trust account, she'd looked like something the cat dragged in. Now that girl was a handful! She'd been arrested in the Paris riots—Eric Laszlo had to fly over to Paris to get her out of jail—and then last fall she'd gotten into trouble in Chicago. Klopp recalled reading somewhere that back in 1848, when Europe had been swept by a half dozen revolutions, there were young people that just traveled around from riot to riot, rebels looking for causes. Miranda sounded like one of those.

An acrid smell floated toward him. Darn dope-smoking hippies. They ought to be locked up. Maybe this movie actor who was governor of California had the right idea: kick the troublemakers off the nation's campuses, and put 'em in the Army and send them to Vietnam with all the other agitators.

Crazy world, wasn't it? These young people had known only good times. Maybe that was it; they were spoiled, which was why they wouldn't fight for their country and left the war to poor black kids who couldn't buy their way out of it. The whole world was topsy-turvy, thought Foster

Klopp. The best-selling book in the country was about a Jewish fellow masturbating, for Lord's sake; Klopp could remember when Edna Ferber was considered racy.

He leaned on the iron fence along the Admiral Dewey Promenade and gazed at the harbor. The late sun's rays lent a blazing halo to the Statue of Liberty. A big ship was moving out just beyond Bedloes Island, which they now called Liberty Island, another darn fool pointless name change, like changing Idlewild to "JFK," or Sixth Avenue to "Avenue of the Americas." Busywork produced by idle hands and empty minds.

He made out the red, white, and blue stripes on the departing liner's funnel and recognized the ship. It was the *United States.* The great liner was being taken out of service; the steamships had finally been done in by the jet airliner. It seemed to Klopp that it had been only yesterday that she'd set the transatlantic record on her maiden voyage. Let's see, that had been 1952, the year he and Morris Miles created the Standard Coupling income debentures. Was that all the mortality allowed these days for a great achievement like the *United States?* Just seventeen years from birth to death?

The happy innocence of 1952 seemed a long, long time distant. The country was going to hell in an economic handbasket, thought Klopp, although things might go better under Nixon than under Johnson. Nixon had Art Burns advising him, and Art was sound. The Fed was tightening—the prime rate had already moved up to eight and a half percent, a rate Klopp, for one, had never expected to see in his lifetime —but there was no choice.

The stock market was on the way down. The Dow had begun the year within breathing distance of one thousand; but already it had slipped down to the mid-eight hundreds and Klopp was prepared to bet it was going lower.

He watched the *United States* until it was almost out of sight. The evening felt unduly warm. He put a tentative hand to his temple, feeling a slight twinge. Seconds later, two large vessels in Foster Klopp's brain ruptured. The instant of conscious pain was momentary; in that fraction of time, he wished he had told Arthur Lubloff to rework the Marryat-Acacia ratios with a higher conversion premium. Then Foster Klopp's world turned black, then scarlet, then black again.

From her seat along the side wall of the auditorium, Lyda surveyed the scene and decided she had made the best of unpromising materials. There was nothing you could really do to dress up the dreary room. She'd arranged for two tall vases of lilies at the head of the room, and an American flag—Foster Klopp had been a veteran—behind the podium.

It had been Howland's decision to hold a memorial service for Foster Klopp in the small auditorium on the ground floor of the Old William Slip annex. After all, the decedent had often jocularly referred to Hanover Place as "my church."

The Klopper had died in Beekman Downtown Hospital three days after being stricken in Battery Park. He left an estate of three-quarters of a million dollars, mainly in savings accounts and Treasury bills. Most, apart from a few small bequests to charity, went to a cousin; to Arthur Lubloff he left the battered black leather notebook in which, for twenty-three years, Klopp had kept a record of deals in progress and jotted down his inspirations.

Lyda studied the people rapidly filling up the rows of wooden chairs. Describing the scene afterward to Chickie Fenton, she said, "It was like being at one of those movies where the camera pans from face to face and you're shown what each person's thinking."

Andy, in the front row, was thinking about his wife, who was seated along the side wall next to his mother. Things were pretty bad, and seemed to have gotten worse since Laurel had changed psychiatrists. He wondered if the shrink was using him as a whipping boy; he wouldn't be the first husband a psychiatrist had done that to. Laurel had turned sarcastic and full of complaints, and the white wine seemed to be uncorked and flowing by the time he got home each evening.

Still, he didn't know for certain, did he? So he remained determined to be supportive, but it wasn't always easy.

Perhaps they should move; sometimes that helped. The other day, just after Chickie's people had finished putting up a few thousand dollars' worth of new curtains in the library, Laurel had announced that she found the apartment about as cheerful and cozy as Antarctica. No, he thought, that would just be another stopgap, another new enthusiasm that would die as quickly as it arose.

Laurel had given up her art research job a few years earlier. She decided to become more purely creative and enrolled in piano and writing courses at the New School. Then she'd switched to psychology courses at Columbia. A few months later, without warning, it had suddenly been all *mens sana in corpore sano*: jogging, calisthenics, massage, no booze, no tobacco, no pot. Wheat germ and vitamin pills. That had lasted three months. Now it was white wine and gossip with Chickie.

The state of his marriage was not Andy's largest concern, however. The Firm had a lot on the fire, and it was his job to keep on top of each deal.

Most of the current stuff played itself. The InterNorthern stock offering was almost out of the SEC; it looked like they could bring it in in a week, assuming the "no comment" letter came through on Tuesday as the law-yers promised. The Bedford Tech–Gormont merger was also awaiting SEC clearance, but if the price of Bedford common didn't hold at these levels, they would be back to square one. The Western Factors financing memo was finally finished, so with luck, Jay's people could be out soliciting the institutions on Monday.

What else was there? They were being paid to run a screen of merger candidates for GIC Communications, which was what Gessel-Imperial-Constellation now called itself. Andy made a mental note to check with Larry Swint, who covered GIC out of the Los Angeles office, to talk to Howard Stark, the station broker, and find out if the Cowleses might be willing to do a deal on their Phoenix radio-TV properties. Then there was a $100 million Global sale-leaseback. They were over the hump on that one now that Jim Mitchell had committed the Chase to take $40 million on the short end.

Finally, there was Marryat Oil–Acacia Petrochemical. Marryat was buying Acacia from a consortium of chemical companies. It was a $175 million deal, and Marryat proposed to borrow $150 million of the purchase price. Artie and Bobby Marryat had worked it out. The Street had god-damn near fallen over backward when the deal was announced; talk about the minnow swallowing the whale! The deal went through; Marryat Oil would be catapulted into the energy big leagues overnight. It had taken twenty years to build up Acacia. Bobby's philosophy was that you got where you wanted to be faster by writing checks than by drilling wells or building chemical plants.

Bobby was now talking about rejiggering the terms of the convertible preferred that Marryat proposed to sell to the public to finance the equity in the deal. Bobby felt that the deal had passed its "point of no return," the stage in the process where the compulsion to close overwhelmed all other considerations, and so he could hang tough, betting that everyone involved had too much time, energy, patience, and emotion invested to walk away now. It was Andy's plan to let Bobby "hang tough" for another couple of days, and then have a quiet word with J.B.

Andy returned his attention to the podium. In the row behind him, Max Miles extracted a large handkerchief from his sleeve, while sur-reptitiously checking the drape of his new Savile Row trousers and the gleam of his Lobb shoes, mopped his eyes and forehead, blew his splendid nose in a loud, liquescent salute to the deceased, and thanked his lucky stars.

Under his aristocratic tailoring he was sweating like a pig from sheer relief. Not that it had been his fault. It was Leo who got me embroiled with Lester Vivian, he told himself.

Leo's theory was that Max needed an "angel": that was exactly the word Leo used, and Lester Vivian was supposed to be it.

Some angel! Max had never met a less angelic person.

Vivian was a slim, sharp-faced man of medium height, rather swarthy, with dull brown eyes and fine dark hair. Max figured him to be about five or six years younger than himself, which would have made him in his early to mid-thirties. He was soft-spoken and conservatively dressed; unassuming as he seemed, Max found him compelling. According to Leo, Vivian was the son of a Hollywood motion-picture executive who had moved east to look after a family company, a Philadelphia commercial finance outfit that specialized in factoring small businesses. Vivian's father had died not long after his son had graduated from Wharton and the son had taken over the operation with the intention of building it into something much, much larger. Himelman and Vivian had gotten to know each other through Wharton, where Leo taught a course in stockholder rights.

Leo had made quite a name for himself, too. According to Max's father, Leo was nothing more than a corporate ambulance chaser. The Lotus Street law firm he had started with was famous, or notorious, for bringing successful suits against blue-chip corporations, their directors, not to mention the greatest names in investment banking and accountancy, on behalf of notionally wronged stockholders.

After Himelman became Vivian's attorney, he broke off from the Philadelphia firm and set up shop in New York as Himelman, Plaskow and Gold. It was in the new firm's new offices in a somewhat disheveled building on West 41st Street that Leo Himelman introduced Max Miles to Lester Vivian. Until the appearance of Lester Vivian, the business Leo directed to Max had been small stuff: valuation jobs, the disposal of a block of stock for an estate, the sale of a tiny electronics distributor. This was obviously going to be on a much larger scale.

"Quite apart from the specific deal that Lester wishes to discuss with you," Leo told Max, "I think there can be the basis for a mutually beneficial relationship over the longer term."

Vivian was ambitious, Leo said, and had the resources to bring them to fruition. First Penn's factoring and commercial operations were growing rapidly; the company's cash flow and credit lines were abundant to insure its expansion.

"Still, everyone needs an investment banker, and you, Max, need someone like Lester. Sooner or later, you're going to have to make your own move at Hanover Place."

"My move?"

"Make yourself so indispensable they have to make you a partner, and there's only one way to do that: bring in big business and produce important revenues. Otherwise, you'll be out in the cold the minute something happens to Howland Warrington or your father. And then what? Without a Lester Vivian or someone like him, you'll drift from one place to another, to smaller firms with diminishing responsibility, just another wandering Jew, until one day you find yourself living off your father's money and calling yourself a consultant."

The deal Lester Vivian had in mind was an unfriendly takeover bid for United Brooklyn Savings. It was a sitting duck, according to Vivian, ruled by a tyrannical, aging chairman who had no friends on Wall Street and only controlled seven percent of the voting stock. United Brooklyn's shares were foundering in the market at a price significantly below what its liquid assets were worth. Vivian wanted Warrington & Co. to act for him.

Max listened with interest. Nothing in Vivian's presentation interested him more than the estimate that the investment banking fees could add up to as much as $2 million!

Max also knew that there was no way The Firm was going to get involved with an unfriendly takeover. No first-class house did that kind of dirty business. It was the quickest way in the world to get ostracized by the Fortune 500, who were Wall Street's bread and butter.

Still, the magic words "$2 million" held him back from speaking his piece there and then.

"Well, let me look into it," he said, "run some numbers and get back to you."

Although he had but a scant idea of the Dickens character, Max was a great believer in Mr. Micawber's theory that "something is bound to turn up." Unfortunately, events cascaded; they swept over Max. He got Artie to run some spreadsheets on an "XYZ" basis, met again with Vivian and Himelman, and then again. For appearances sake, he'd sworn Artie to secrecy and brought him along; that had been a good idea. Vivian and Artie volleyed figures and ratios and accumulation stratagems back and forth with unmistakable gusto. Much of it went right by Max, but he was happy to be there to preside. Then one day he realized with a chill exactly how far out on a limb he'd gotten himself. No one could say he'd lied to Vivian, or intentionally deceived the man, but he had certainly intimated that he was within an ace of having everything in shape to go to Hanover Place's Commitments Committee and that the Committee's green light was all but a mere formality.

To seriously discuss the matter with the Committee would be to ask for trouble. Then it began to seem to him that even disgrace was preferable to what Lester Vivian might do if he found out he'd been strung along. Something told Max that Vivian was a dangerous man to fool with.

Then, this very morning, Max had been called out of a meeting to take a call from "Mr. Harris," the code name for Vivian. Fearing the worst, he'd picked up the phone, but Vivian had told him that he'd reconsidered the United Brooklyn deal and had decided not to go ahead after all. Vivian thanked Max for his efforts and told him that, although no fee was due, he had directed a Philadelphia bank to give The Firm a market order for twenty thousand shares of IBM.

But how close a call it had been! Max straightened up in his seat, tucked away his handkerchief, and pretended keen interest in the proceedings.

He found himself thinking: The fact is, I handled Vivian about as well as anyone could have. It was a disgrace, he thought next, for him to be sitting here, after nearly fourteen years at Hanover Place, and still not a partner in a firm to which his own father had made the greatest contributions of anyone.

As he did when vexed or anxious, his hand went to his skull and tentatively felt the area on top where his hair, once so thick and shaggy, was definitely thinning. The prospect of a bald spot seemed worse to Max than the mark of Cain.

He thought he would miss the Klopper. The fellow had been a damn solid technician, first rate at things like "present value," and "regression analysis" and "least-squares depreciation," all the arithmetical acrobatics that so mightily impressed the small minds of corporate treasurers. That was what technicians like the Klopper and Artie were for. You needed good technicians to take care of the details while the deals were cut with the men at the top, to whom the details of a bond spread were mere incidentals in the grand design of things.

It would have been helpful if the Klopper could have waited to die until after the work-up on the Fogash estate had been finished. Max knew what people were whispering behind his back, that he'd dropped the ball on that one. Well, how the hell would any of them have handled it! How was Max supposed to anticipate that some young go-getter at First Boston would smooth-talk old Lurline Fogash into selling the estate's thirteen percent interest of UniMedia? As for the estate valuation and the IRS letter, where the hell had The Firm's Los Angeles office been? What was Max supposed to know about Palm Desert real estate?

He found himself studying the back of Jay Warrington's head in the row in front of him. Pow! Pow! Pow! He fired three right into the base of his skull; he could just see the blood and brains busting out of the ludicrous Prince Valiant haircut, smearing the flashy striped collar and the equally ridiculous Mr. Fish tie. Take that, Mr. Go-Go Years, Mr. Cover Boy, Mr. Public, Glamorous Figure. Jay cut a swath in all the choice spots of the day: the Palm Bay Club in Miami, the Daisy and The Bistro in Beverly Hills, and the Manhattan rota frequented by the big hitters: "21," The Palm and Christ Cella's, Il Vagabondo, where the jock-and-model crowd hung out. Jay had a chauffeur now, a swaggering Italian kid everyone called "Billy T." "T. as in torpedo," Jay liked to say, and of course it was as plain as the nose on Max's face that Billy T. was nothing but a gangster, but naturally Jay, despite all the genteel airs the Warringtons gave themselves, could get away with it. The last straw had been when *Institutional Investor*, a glossy new magazine that celebrated the swinging big-ticket institutional market, had devoted an entire article to Jay.

Leo told Max not to let it bug him. "These people have their little ways of distracting you," Leo said. "To keep you off balance, make sure you're not a threat to them."

"A typical WASP ploy." That had been Leo's reaction when Max complained about how the Warringtons seemed to know even the lowest employees' names. "Don't give it a thought. That's what those sort of people call '*noblesse oblige*' so they can pretend it isn't just gross social condescension. Wall Street is about making money, not popularity contests with the help. People like the Warringtons don't see that. Having been born with money, they don't respect it enough, so they waste their time trying to find more seemly ways of proving themselves to themselves."

WASP was Leo's pet new buzzword. It was like a stock symbol; it stood for "White Anglo-Saxon Protestant."

Leo got the term out of a book called *The Protestant Establishment*; according to him, it was "the *Mein Kampf* of people like the Warringtons." He'd pressed Max to read it, but it had bored Max after twenty pages, so he'd put it aside and told Leo he'd found it "very interesting."

Leo must have read it a dozen times; he knew it better than the Talmud. At Leo's urging, Max's mother had read it, too. She and Leo seemed keenly interested in stuff like that. In 1966, they spent hours one Sunday after lunch poring over the guest list for Truman Capote's Black and White Ball at the St. Regis. Between them they seemed to have memorized "Dilatory Domiciles," the section of *The Social Register* that recorded what Leo called "the WASP eschatology": births, deaths, marriages, divorces of non-Jewish society.

Max's neck suddenly felt warm, as if a ray gun had been beamed on it. Laurel was back there somewhere, sitting with Lyda. Would he never get his disgrace at Granny Bayard's out of his memory!

Laurel had turned into a real bitch, he thought with satisfaction. Everyone said she was giving Andy a hard time.

Just the other night, he'd run into Laurel and Andy at Le Club; they were out on the town with Jay. He'd sat down for a second, and out of nowhere Laurel, who had obviously been doing a major job on the champagne, said in a tipsy but bell-clear voice that no one within thirty feet could have missed: "You know, Maxie, I should have married you after all."

He'd smiled and made a magnanimous little gesture.

"Yep," she continued, "I should have married you, because then I wouldn't have had all these empty nights, waiting up for Drew while he's working late, or when he's out of town. How much easier to do what you do, to be spared the responsibility of partnership, and have the Klopper and Artie take care of what little work you get assigned. No wonder you can be such a gadabout."

What a thing to say!

"And so, in conclusion, I can just hear my old friend Foster telling the Good Lord, 'Now, Richard, about these terms and provisions . . .' "

Dick Bosworth's drawl interrupted Max's woolgathering. Once again, he focused on the podium and tried to look attentive.

As Bosworth's voice drifted over the auditorium, Arthur Lubloff watched with amusement as his uncle's hand again crept reflexively to the back of his head. He watched the long fingers probe tentatively. No, Uncle Max, he thought, it hasn't grown any larger in the last five minutes.

He returned to his original thought, which—given the circumstances —would have come as a surprise to most of the people seated around him. For some time now, Artie had been pondering the fact that he was probably the only person in the auditorium crowd who was genuinely pleased that Foster Klopp was dead.

At first, he'd felt badly about the Klopper, but then as always he thought it through. Artie listened as carefully to what his intelligence told him about his own feelings as he did to its insights into the material world. Feelings were facts, just like anything else. Like his accident: that was a fact. There was no way around it. When he woke up in the hospital and got the word that he'd never be going to the hoop again, that was that. The thing was, as his father told him, to take what God gave you and use it wisely.

The loss of his parents was simply a fact to be dealt with. Maybe it *was* like Miranda Warrington had told him when she took him aside after the service: part of God's grand design. Maybe so, although everyone knew that Miranda had gone from being a wild one to a prize Christer, thanks to her boyfriend. But maybe it was something else; maybe it was just one of those things, he missed Mom and Dad, missed them terribly sometimes, remembering all the things they'd done together, imagining the stuff they could have done together. But you couldn't live on might-have-beens.

Now the Klopper was out of the picture, thank God. Klopp hadn't been a bad old guy and Artie would be the first to admit he'd picked up a few tricks from him. But Klopp had a real stick up his ass when it came to finance, as if credit was more about words than numbers, and finance as much a function of attitude as of arithmetic. He was always talking about how long X Company had "been with" Warrington & Co., not how much The Firm had made off X Company over the years. It sounded great, but the numbers simply didn't bear it out. Relationships weren't profit-effective. If you added up all the hours spent bullshitting some corporate treasurer in the hopes of getting a piece of financing, the return per minute was lousy.

Compare that to Jay's end of the business. Jay would take some mutual-fund guy from Kansas City out on the town, get him drunk and laid, and the next day it would pay off with an order for a hundred thousand shares or ten million bonds.

It was ridiculous, the way the Klopper talked about "value," as if value was something other than how much you could raise to pay for whatever it was you were out to buy. When it came to financing, the Klopper had been strictly a meat-and-potatoes man. Stocks and bonds: that was about it, along with convertibles and warrants. Model-T stuff in the age of rocket vehicles. Artie remembered the time the Klopper'd kept him going forty-eight hours straight trying to get the numbers to come out right on the merger between Rocky Mountain Molybdnum and American Cosmos Mining. The only way it was going to work was to use some senior debt, and some subordinated debentures with a kicker, which was conventional shit. But to hold the price in the after-market, he'd had to come up with a new piece of paper, an exchangeable pre-ferred with a conversion option payable in stock or cash. He'd run it through the computer a half dozen times using all kinds of variables until the son of a bitch finally came up roses, but when he presented the Klopper with the printout, the old guy had thrown his head back and let out one of those big, spluttering, wet guffaws of his, and wiped his glasses and blinked and said: "Arthur, that's not a capital structure, that's a *pousse café*, hah, hah, hah!" which turned out, when Artie looked it up in a dictionary, to be some kind of a drink using a dozen different liqueurs: each with its own specific gravity so that they never blended and what you got looked like one of those kids' toys with dif-ferent-colored rings stacked on a post. So Artie's idea had been trashed, and the deal hadn't gotten done.

Most of the work they cranked out in Corporations could have been done by anyone with an eighty IQ, Artie thought. Everybody insisted on doing stuff the way they'd been doing it at Hanover Place for a fucking hundred years!

Even Andy Warrington had told Artie: "Nothing's less profitable on Wall Street than an idea whose time hasn't come."

Andy was kind of a creative type, Artie thought, but he was also kind of a fucking bleeding heart. One time they'd been sitting in a cab together and out of nowhere Andy had said: "You know, Artie, I sometimes wonder if what we do has ever fed a starving child or bought an hour of peace for the world."

Anyway, Artie thought, I'm only twenty-three, which means I can look forward to another forty years, minimum, on the Street unless the whole goddamn system goes down the tubes.

There was time. If his ideas wouldn't fly in '69, maybe they would in '89, but in the meantime he wasn't about to sit around the fucking Corporations Department with his thumb up his ass for the next twenty years! The trouble was, as long as the Klopper was around, Artie was going to be slack there. With Klopp dead, he could make his move.

And what a place to make it! The Firm was an unbelievable franchise because it was squeaky clean. No Mickey Mouse, no tainted deals; they hadn't touched Bernie Cornfeld and IOS, like practically every other house on the Street, or Gramco, or King Resources or Westec. This wasn't Shearson Hammill, for Christ's sake, this was Warrington & Co.! The thing to do was to build on that.

The trouble was, only Jay Warrington seemed to get the big picture, which was why Artie was determined to break out of Corporations and into Distribution and Trading. The guys in Corporations made a big deal out of their corporate "connections," but what they didn't realize was that the relationships and connections that were really going to count in the future weren't with the guys who ran the Fortune 500, but with the guys who voted the stock, the money managers, hedge-fund operators, trust officers, the guys who knew where the shares were socked away, who could take a hand in a table-stakes game because they were playing with other people's money. The way Artie saw it: if they could cross ten thousand shares of XYZ, why couldn't they cross an entire fucking company?

Artie worshiped Jay. When he was in the hospital, after he got hit by the cab, Jay came to see him every day.

"This fan's got shit on it," Jay told him. "So we got to find a new one. If it's no more hoops, let's play something else. How about our kind of one-on-one? I think you'll go for it."

Artie had gotten out of the hospital in the spring of 1961, too late in the school year to go back to Horace Mann. He came instead to Hanover

Place, worked through the summer, and came back the next summer and the next. Jay had been right. Artie loved the game and he plunged into trading with every bit of intelligence and competitive instinct he'd shown on the basketball court. The fact that his left leg dragged and his mouth was permanently set in a crooked little grin didn't matter. In his second summer, Jay let him take over a couple of institutional wires on his own; by the end of that summer, he had completely mastered a "game" he found utterly absorbing and infinitely challenging.

Jay became his mentor and model. It wasn't just that Jay had all the moves, saw the whole court, could work five phones at once. Jay had style. One time, Artie remembered, when he was hanging around the trading room watching Jay work a block of 372,000 American Photocopy, one of the guys on the convertible desk had screamed: "Hey, Jay, the Chinaman's on six; he says we screwed him on the Bessie and we either reprint at a better price or he DKs the trade and cold-storages us forever!"

"Hey," Jay told Kansas City, "hold on a second, huh?" He'd picked up the Manhattan Fund wire. "Hey, guy, on that sixty-thousand Bessie? The guys tell me you got a kvetch?"

Pause.

Jay: "Well, shit, pal, you know how it is, the best I can do is give you an evasive answer. Go fuck yourself!"

Click, Jay hung up. Then he saw Artie staring at him in disbelief— The Firm did a couple of million a year in commissions with Howard Kueng, the head trader at Union Investment Trust—and he winked and said, "Hey, be cool, pal. Who's he gonna trade with? Where's he gonna have any fun? He'll be back." And he was.

That was style, that was cool, and what's more it worked. Jay was a player. Artie's grandfather had been a player once, too; everyone said so, and look at the deals Morris had done. Still, Artie didn't want to turn out like his grandfather: ponderous, gloomy, and conservative, whose point of view was a piece with the black overcoat and black homburg he favored for his grave, discursive Sunday promenades down Park Avenue. Jay liked to wing it, but even when he was kidding, a lot of things he said rang true. Like when he told Max, "You know, Max, I'll say this, you and me, we've faked the Street out of its goddamn jockstrap, 'cause there're two things the guys down here think don't exist: a smart Protestant and a dumb Jew."

Max had gotten redder than a baboon's ass. Jay really had his number, so Jay never let up—that was the way he was. It was almost as if he was trying to run Max off, which Artie himself thought was what Max should've had the common sense to do for himself. Max could be a big hitter at a place like Burnham. Here, he was going nowhere.

On the other hand, Jay bent over backward to encourage Artie. It should have been no surprise, therefore, that when it came time to go off to college, Artie brushed aside MIT and Cal Tech, where his parents would have wanted him to go, and opted instead for Wharton, which had an undergraduate business program. Indeed, it never occurred to him to consider what his mother and father would have wished for him. The dead were to be honored, but given no vote.

In both cases the truth was in the numbers. The tape was no different from Einstein's unified field, although you could make a hell of a better case for it. The truth, all truth, was in the print. In the numbers up there on the tape, APL 24½, X 83, BR 7, COM 14⅜, IBM 112¼. Symbols followed by integers followed by fractions. Like the equations of physics or calculus, they expressed the sum total of complex situations; they embraced knowledge, opinion, expectation; time past, present, and future; people, places, and things; abstraction and essence, universal and particular, comparative and specific. With a reach and scope and diversity of application and effect greater than any scientific formulation. Nothing else that Artie knew of seemed to comprehend so many dimensions of fact and possibility.

But the tape was in the province of the traders, and when Artie got out of Wharton in 1967 he was immediately shanghaied into the Corporations Department. Corporations, he was told, was where the coming men of The Firm worked, everyone else were lowlifes; the salesmen and traders were tolerated because they pushed the merchandise out the door, but it was the investment bankers who were the class act.

The more he saw, the more certain Artie became that the presumption of the investment bankers' superiority was bullshit. The name of the game was money, and Trading and Distribution was Hanover Place's umbilical cord to where the money was.

Come to think of it, Artie's grandfather didn't owe his career to schmoozing with corporate big-hitters, he owed it to his special relationships with guys like Barney Berenson at Cosmo Life and Fruits Plager at Chelsea Trust, the guys who wrote the checks that bought the securities that financed the deals that produced the fees. The guys who bought your deals; they were the guys who really counted, like the guys in the pension funds, money managers with quick trigger fingers. Money was the gun, and as the saying went: the man with the gun was the dangerous one. Like this guy Vivian whom Max was fooling around with. Here was a guy who was talking real numbers. Max wasn't going to go anywhere with Vivian, though, you could see that after five minutes in the room with them. The two times he'd been with them, Artie couldn't escape the feeling that Vivian and Max's buddy Leo were just jerking Max's chain. Himelman had to know that there was no way

Hanover Place would touch an unfriendly deal, especially via Max, from Leo Himelman, on behalf of some guy nobody knew. So what were they up to?

Max would probably try to keep him in Corporations, Artie figured, because he needed someone to do his sums, but nobody at Hanover Place gave a shit what Max wanted. With the Klopper it would have been different, people at The Firm had listened to the Klopper; but now Foster Klopp was six feet under, so hail and farewell and away we go.

That evening, Eric Laszlo, who had flown in to attend the memorial service, came to dinner at the Warringtons'.

Waiting in the library for their guest to arrive, Howland said to his wife: "I think we did Foster proud, don't you? To use the overworked phrase, I think he would have been very pleased—not that Foster was ever truly satisfied with anything."

"I thought it went fine, dear. I didn't even mind that you insisted on reading 'Crossing the Bar' at the end."

"Coming from someone well-versed as you in cheap poetry, I regard that as high praise. How'd our daughter sound?"

Miranda was in Honolulu, where Jerry Creedmore had a week's R&R.

"She's fine. Larry Rockefeller fixed it up for them at Mauna Kea."

"Tom and Jessica must be damn proud of their boy!" said Howland emphatically. "It's nice to see one of our sort off and fighting. It makes me sick to think how this war's been left to the black kids and the professionals. People don't seem to realize this is a real war."

Jerry Creedmore was one of the heroes of the day. "The Flying Chaplain," as *Life* had nicknamed him, had taken a leave of absence from his Los Angeles parish and volunteered for Vietnam as a noncombatant. He was out there doing double duty, flying a medical helicopter and tending to the spiritual needs of young men fighting a war that the rest of the nation was trying its darnedest to pretend didn't exist. Of course, Tom Creedmore was disappointed that Jerry had chosen God over Global, but his son's heroism assuaged his regrets.

Jerry was a remarkable young man, thought Lyda. He'd managed to calm Miranda down. Wouldn't it be wonderful if things worked out between them? They certainly seemed serious about each other. They wrote every day and Miranda was now talking about going to divinity school. If there had been anyone in the universe with whom Lyda would have thought God didn't stand a chance, it would have been her daughter.

"I sent Miriam Miles some flowers," she said. "I gather she's not doing too well. I must say Morris looked awfully glum at the service. My God, he looks about a hundred, but he can't be much over sixty, can he?"

Miriam Miles was in Mount Sinai with congestive heart failure; Morris had intimated that her condition was grave.

"I suppose we should have him over some night," said Lyda. "It must be terribly lonely in that huge apartment, what with Miriam in and out of the hospital, and Max out every night gadding about town."

"I think you probably have a point. We will have Morris over, but tonight's certainly not the night. You know how he and Laszlo are about each other."

As if reading their thoughts, the doorbell rang, followed by voices in the hall, and Eric Laszlo was shown into the library.

Since taking over The Firm's European operations in 1954, Laszlo had built the business into a major presence in the uppermost circles of world finance. He was recognized, like Siegmund Warburg in London, as a wise and skilled financial diplomat whose opinion and undertaking were worth their weight in gold.

It was Laszlo's passionate Zionism that was the principal bone of contention with Morris, who had been much taken with Israel right after the war, but whose enthusiasm had waned with the passing of time. Large checks that had once gone to Israeli interests now went to local Jewish charities.

This had clearly disappointed Laszlo—he had said as much to Lyda—but it was, after all, Morris's business what he did with his money. The quarrel had come to a boil, however, with Morris's insistence, in the mid-sixties, that The Firm act for a West German chemical company's U.S. subsidiary in an acquisition. Laszlo had protested vigorously; Germany and all things German were anathema to him, it was a matter of personal honor. Howland had engineered a compromise; one could not, after all, penalize The Firm because of any one partner's personal politics; on the other hand, a decent respect for individual sensitivities was important. The German company was taken on as a one-time, one-deal client, but not a connection.

"After all, Eric," Howland had told his friend and partner, "Lyda and I have every reason for not wanting to deal with either the Germans or the Japanese. They killed two of our sons, but there has to be a point at which bygones become bygones."

"Does there?" Laszlo had replied.

Laszlo had by then become as indispensable to Hanover Place as Morris. His intelligence sources were remarkable. He had an extraordinary aptitude for anticipating events—so much so that Howland sometimes wondered if Laszlo wasn't getting some of his information from Israeli intelligence. That he should have a call on the resources of Tel Aviv was hardly surprising. It was said he had raised close to $250 million around the world in the wake of the '67 war.

Laszlo's politics were neither here nor there to Howland, so long as they didn't interfere with business. Some of The Firm's most lucrative Swiss connections, in fact established and tended by Laszlo and his London people, were private banks that everyone knew to be major repositories of Arab capital. When there had been a sterling crisis in the early sixties, and the Arabs had suddenly soured on the pound and moved vast sums out of the City and into Zurich and Geneva, Eric Laszlo had played a key role in abating the British predicament. Shuttling by limousine along the shore of Lake Geneva among the Hotel President, where the sheikhs stayed, the Banque Suisse des Ventes, and the British Consulate, he had orchestrated a series of financial maneuvers whereby the Swiss banks had reloaned the Arab deposits to London. It was taken as gospel that LONdon Wall 1000 was the first number the Saudi Arabian and Israeli finance ministers dialed whenever they came to London.

"A very nice memorial service, I thought," Laszlo said after he'd been given a drink. "We shall miss Foster. He was a great artisan, like a skilled gunsmith or cuckoo-clock maker. Thank heavens we have Arthur Lubloff to take his place."

"Amen to that!" said Howland. "Artie's far and away the brightest young man we've had at Hanover Place since I've been downtown, present company excepted, of course."

What Howland might have added was that he was so taken with the young man that he'd asked Archer Cleverley at Auchincloss, Wharton to look into the possibility of amending to the Survivorship Trust to permit the possible future admission of nonfamily partners in a case-by-case basis. It paid to be prepared, he thought, but he said nothing to anyone—not even Lyda.

"He's certainly a hard worker," said Laszlo. "After the service, I stopped on the tenth floor to pick up a prospectus, and there he was, grinding away at his spreadsheets while everyone else was downstairs in the dining room having a drink."

Over dinner, the talk was mostly of the Street and the markets.

"We had a visitor from the Chase Manhattan the other day," Laszlo reported. "He seemed very concerned about the condition of some of the larger brokerages here."

"No doubt about it," said Howland. "The Exchange is starting to worry, I can tell you. The wire houses like Merrill Lynch and Goodbody and Hayden Stone have geared their overhead up to where, if daily volume on the Exchange falls much below eight or nine million shares, one or two of them will be in real trouble."

"How do you feel about interest rates?"

"Totally at sea. Three years ago you could have knocked me over with a stick when a triple-A credit like Standard Oil of Indiana had to pay six percent for long money. Now Morgan's talking close to nine percent on the next Telephone go-round. These are rates that a pawnbroker would have been ashamed to charge when I started on the Street. Now, what's your news? All quiet on the Middle Eastern front?"

Laszlo smiled. "It's never really quiet there, you know. What frankly concerns a number of us is that if it takes war, and only war, to rejuvenate good sentiments about Israel in America, feelings that can be turned into hard cash, how far can we go from here? Peace and prosperity have a way of anesthetizing memory. Einstein once wrote—I think I can remember it exactly—'The intellectual decline brought on by a shallow materialism is a far greater menace to the survival of Jewry than the numerous external foes who threaten its existence with violence.' "

"Too fat and happy, and then one day: ka-boom, eh?"

"Something like that," said Laszlo. "So it would seem we need war to keep our overseas friends eternally vigilant. Speaking of which, what about your own recent Six-Day War?"

"I'm not sure I follow you."

"Young Mr. Saul Steinberg's attempt to take over the Chemical Bank. There seems to be considerable resentment in quarters I frequent as to his treatment at the hands of the so-called establishment. It does seem to me that a great deal of very heavy artillery was brought to bear on what realistically was about as threatening to the bank's management as a gnat to an elephant. Do you think Steinberg's being Jewish had much to do with the reaction to his bid?"

"Not really," said Howland. "You know how these things go. Bill Renchard and his people simply didn't see why they should be forced out, and no one, including me, thinks much of the idea of a large bank being bought with borrowed money. It just wasn't on, as the Brits say. My guess is, the Jewish thing had very little to do with it."

"You must admit, dear," Lyda interjected, "that the forces rallied behind the incumbents read rather like the membership list of the Gorse Club."

Howland chuckled. "I suppose so."

Lyda turned to Laszlo. "Are you suggesting, Eric, that something like this might backfire?"

Laszlo shrugged. "Who can say? How would you feel?"

For a moment there was silence, then Laszlo brightened and said: "Anyway, enough of business. How are the children? Andrew and Jay I've seen, of course, but what news of Miranda? I must say, getting her out of jail last year was the most exciting adventure I've had since the war.

I think her jailers were as relieved as she was when the gates of the Sante closed behind her."

Lyda shook her head. "With Miranda, as they say, *plus c'est la même chose, plus ça change*. Right now she's what people call 'born-again'; her beau's a minister, Tom Creedmore's boy. But with her, one never knows. One moment an angel, the next . . . well, I hate to think!"

"Ah," said Laszlo, savoring the red wine, "but that is what permits the eternal feminine, as Goethe put it, to lead us ever onward."

1971

MAY

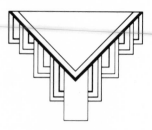

Would you repeat that?" Howland asked. He looked down at his left hand, resting on the back of his right wrist, and saw that it was trembling slightly.

The physician couldn't help shaking his head before pronouncing the words again. "Technically, we call it an adenocarcinoma." He managed a wan little grin. "Cancer of the pancreas. The prognos . . ."

"Say no more, Ben, I think I take your point. No magic bullet, eh, Doctor?"

"I'm afraid not, Howland. Not yet, at any rate."

When Howland next spoke, he seemed to have shaken off the momentary shock of disbelief and his voice was strong again. "What odds would you put on my making it to my next birthday, Ben? Fifty-fifty? Better? Worse? Hell, Ben, that's only six months away!"

Benjamin Miles pursed his lips and shook his head. "I'd like to be reassuring, but when it's this far along, no one seems to know. We could be talking a year or two, we could be talking . . ."

Howland smiled as he interrupted. "Doctor, the bad news is all I can stand for the moment, so spare me the good news."

He got up and held out his hand. "I'd like to make seventy-five if I can."

"We'll do our best; you know that."

"Of course I do. And Ben—mum's the word."

"Naturally. Of course, if you want me to talk with any of the family . . ."

"We'll see."

Howland shrugged into his overcoat. The day was warm and sunny, but nowadays he always seemed to feel cold. The damn thing feels like a tent, he thought. That should have been the tipoff. Everything had seemed a little loose all of a sudden. Of course he'd put it down to going on the wagon for Lent. That was always good for a few pounds.

In the doorway, he stopped and asked: "How's Miriam, by the way? Rude of me not to have asked."

Ben Miles shook his head. "Not well, I'm afraid. Mother's a very sick person."

Thank you for not saying "too," thought Howland. It occurred to him to ask Ben for a guess as to whether he or Miriam was likely to hit the final tape first. Instead he nodded in sympathy and said: "Give her my best, will you? And thanks, Ben, for playing straight with me."

On Fifth Avenue, the air was as soft as cotton. Spring had been late in arriving but was now here with a gentle vengeance. Over the weekend, the buds had burst; beyond the dark stone wall, Central Park was decked out in a patchy but sprightly coat of green, like a shy little girl parading her first Easter finery. He went down the steps at 63rd Street and into the park.

So now he knew. The pain in his gut had started last fall. At first, it had been an on-and-off thing—a couple of aspirin or a splash of Pepto-Bismol and he'd been right as rain—but then, after Christmas, there began to be damn few hours in the waking day when he didn't feel some discomfort. In February, when he and Lyda went to Round Hill in Jamaica, the discomfort changed; it sharpened down to something he could tell was drastic, and he began to feel light-headed. He put off consulting Ben Miles, got through Easter, but finally he couldn't duck the reality any longer, and so he went to see his doctor. Ben sent him to a laboratory for some tests, and then called him and told him he wanted to have a biopsy done pronto. Fortunately, Lyda was off to Charleston visiting friends, so Howland signed into the hospital over-night and now here he was, walking down Fifth Avenue, destined for the firing squad.

There were a lot of things he should have been thinking about at such a moment, he guessed, but he found himself trying just to embrace the day: the afternoon light on the leaves, the smells of the zoo, the faces on the ratty green benches, old, young, sad-happy, calm, distracted, some crazy. Above and outside the park wall, the city pressed in; the towers of Fifth loomed beyond Grand Army Plaza, pickets of concrete and stone and steel staked out against the easy April sky. Now he understood how

Lyda felt. She soaked up the world like a sponge. He never had; he wasn't much of one for nature. He and Andrew had that in common. He dwelt in a world from which the forcing hand of man was never absent, was the central fact of the divine scheme of things. It was the checkerboarded earth under a bright metal wingtip, the green swath of a fairway blasted by the sound of a mower, the whir of a bird flushed from a field of winter stubble to meet the shotgun.

Well, as that silly Doris Day song went, "What will be, will be." It could just as easily have been an ulcer—that would have been under-standable. Last year had been a terrible year for the securities business; by May 1970, the Dow had dropped over three hundred points in six months and was hanging above 700 by a fingernail and he'd lost another hundred dollars to Jay.

Fortunately, The Firm had made a bundle, because Jay was short what he called "the big stocks," the companies that made up the Dow. At the turn of the year, Jay scented a shift in the wind, covered and started to go long. Even as Howland stood on the corner of Fifth and 57th, idly watching the traffic, the market continued to move up strongly; Jay claimed the Dow was on its way back to 1,000.

The Street seemed to be shaking off its troubles. Back offices were catching up with the paper jam. It looked as though the Exchange had made a deal with this fellow Perot to take over DuPont-Walston. Every-one said Perot was a genius, and apparently he was willing to sink $75 million into DuPont-Walston, although according to Andy and Jay, the brokerage firm was being picked clean of its few good men even as the Exchange negotiated the bailout.

All made, it had been a rotten eighteen months. Not as bad as the thirties, but close. All one seemed to do was attend "crisis" meetings; each new day brought news of another firm collapsing. McDonnell went under, despite its ties to the Fords—one of the McDonnell girls had been married to Henry Ford II. Hayden Stone and Goodbody had been "saved" by the rest of the Street, in the name of "investor confidence," but in fact they were as good as dead.

Men could talk all they wanted of "confidence," Howland thought, but what got capitalism through its crises was money. Back in June of '70, when Penn Central had gone bust and thrown the commercial paper market into $40 billion worth of turmoil, Art Burns had opened the sluicegates at the Fed and saved the day, and Goldman Sachs had stood up to be counted. Now the Street was trying to cajole Uncle Sam into setting up a kind of FDIC for stocks and bonds, what Lewie Comstock sarcastically described as "a lifeboat for the customers' yachts." Uncle Sam would probably come through; if Washington could be talked into bailing out Lockheed, it could be talked into anything. Socialism for the men in silk top hats, Howland thought.

He crossed to the east side of Fifth Avenue, and went south, passing Tiffany's and Bonwit Teller. Bonwit's was reported to being doing badly, and its owner, this Genesco outfit headquartered in Nashville, even worse, and rumor had it the Tiffany building might be up for sale. Something else would probably be built here someday, he thought, and he was just as glad he probably wouldn't be around to see it.

How the avenue had changed from his own boyhood, when lower Fifth Avenue was known as "the Ladies' Mile" for the great shops that lined it. Most of them were gone now, hell! So were the shops at which Lyda had bought their children's clothes: Peck and Peck, Best's, Rogers Peet, DePinna. Would those names mean anything once his generation and its particular memories were gone? Nothing, he guessed, no more than Lee Higginson or Glore Forgan, also great names in their time. You only lasted in memory if you gave your name to a battle or a calamity.

He walked over to Park Avenue. Well, at least Ben sounded as if it was likely to be over with quickly. Like Ferdy Stenton. He remembered Ferdy saying over cards at the Links, "Fellows, my blood count's dropping faster than the Dow, and it hurts even worse," and he was gone within three months.

He turned into the reassuring Renaissance bulk of the Racquet Club and went up to the second floor. The head porter greeted him. "The usual, Mr. Warrington?"

"No thanks, Frank, just using the telephone."

He had urgent business to do. He called his secretary and told her to make his excuses to the Exchange for missing the meeting to discuss this damn fool idea of listed options trading. Any excuse for a pyramid, he thought; the Street went for leverage like an Irishman for whiskey. Why not leave well enough alone? If you wanted an option on a stock, you called one of the two big put-and-call houses, and they would shop around until they found someone willing to sell you what you wanted.

His secretary reminded him he was due at four thirty on West 77th Street to pose for Aaron Shikler; the partners had commissioned a portrait in honor of his upcoming seventy-fifth birthday—as a surprise for Lyda. See if I can come tomorrow, he told her, then recanted: no, hell, I'll be there. Every day counted now, didn't it?

His business with Hanover Place concluded, he dialed the number of Auchincloss, Wharton and asked for Archer Cleverley. When Cleverley came on the line, Howland asked if he might drop in at Auchincloss's offices in the Bankers Trust building a few blocks away. Something had come up, Howland told the lawyer, and it probably needed to be resolved quickly.

He got home a little after six. As he was putting his hat on the coat closet shelf, Howland heard a familiar precious voice float out of the drawing room.

"My dear, if that's the effect you're after, why not *wear* the curtains and hang an evening gown on the windows!"

Damn, he thought.

He went into the library and poured himself a finger of whiskey, neat. It's always that way, isn't it, he reflected. You have something that needs to be talked about immediately, but first you have to wait for someone like Chickie Fenton to finish blabbing about curtains.

"Is that you, darling?" Lyda called.

"It is."

"Come in here. I want your opinion on this fabric. Chickie likes it; I don't."

He went into the library and pronounced judgment. Twenty minutes later, Chickie left, leaving puffs of small talk hanging in the air. Howland sat his wife down and without mincing words broke the news that, barring a miracle, Lyda could expect to become a widow by Christmas.

Two nights after that, after Cleverley and his people had completed their preliminary drafts, Howland and Lyda told the children.

He waited until the dinner things had been cleared away and the maid dismissed. An uncorked bottle of the '47 Cheval Blanc sat on the sideboard and Andy got up to pour it. That'll be about the end of that year, Howland thought, watching the bubbling purplish-crimson liquid splash into his glass.

He took a thoughtful sip, chewing the rich wine, and nodded approvingly. He set his glass down, cleared his throat, and winked reassuringly at Lyda at the far end of the table. She winked back.

Inside, she was still numb with confusion. How dare Death walk into her house this way, insist on sitting with them at the dinner table, on going to bed with them at night, on being at the end of the bed, grinning vilely, when they awoke! When Howland had told her, she'd felt as much betrayal as horror and burst out in vexation: "Oh, you're such a dope! Why didn't you tell me earlier? Maybe we could have done something."

Then she reached out and put one hand on the back of his, and the other on his cheek and looked at him and almost started to cry. But she managed to stifle the tears and said: "Oh, you poor thing . . . oh, darling . . ."

They embraced then, and after that, their conversation became almost businesslike—what was left of life had to be got on with, after all—in much the same tone as she now listened to her husband telling their three children about his illness and his plans.

When Howland finished, he looked at each of them in turn. Miranda was the first to speak. She fixed him with her large gray eyes. "Oh, Daddy," she said in a firm voice, "may the Lord be merciful upon you." She bowed her head; it was obvious she was praying silently.

Lyda watched her husband's face take on an expression of disbelief. Miranda was so overbearingly pious these days. Well, get yourself engaged to a preacher, and it's likely you become a bit of one yourself.

Of course, she thought with her next breath, they'd have to move the wedding up now. The news about Howland would be all over New York in a day or so.

Andrew looked across the table at Jay, then put down his glass, made an importuning gesture to his father, and said, "Damn it, Father, I don't know what . . ."

"Look," Howland replied, "what's done is done. I think we ought to make the most of what's left. There're a lot of things to take care of. You're simply going to assume command a bit sooner than any of us had planned. What I've done is to fix things up with Archer to make the transition easier, and—from an estate point of view—better for your mother."

He proceeded then to outline the forthcoming reorganization of The Firm. Andrew and Jay were intent; Miranda, who couldn't care less about Hanover Place—she'd donated fifty percent of her substantial trust income to her fiancé's "New Christian Mission"—continued to murmur in the background, eyes fixed on the tablecloth.

Fortunately, thought Lyda, Jerry Creedmore had a sense of proportion. His "crusade" wasn't his whole life; there was Global, where he was a member of the board, a "hands on" director who, according to Howland, was extremely popular with everyone at the airline. He was a licensed commercial pilot, who liked to test-fly the new aircraft, and he took a special interest in maintenance and safety. About the only point where Jerry's ministry influenced his role at Global, Lyda knew, was his insistence that Global hire and train black pilots.

Jerry had a thing about colored people. Miranda said it came from his experience in Vietnam, and his violent reaction to the injustice of poor, black young men sent to fight and die so that rich white Americans could get on with their fat lives. Jerry collected hundreds of thousands in contributions from his wealthy Orange County congregation and redistributed the money to the poor and hopeless through an outpost in the Watts district of Los Angeles. The irony was that Jerry's parishioners mostly came from the extreme right wing, but they were blinded by their blazing young minister's medals and deafened by a trumpeting patriotism no less intense than their own.

"So—there it is," said Howland. "Any questions? Andrew?"

Andy looked at his father and shook his head. It all made perfect sense. The usual suspects would bitch, but as his father was fond of saying, that was the risk in working for a family firm.

"And you, Jay?"

"No, no." Jay shook his head vigorously.

"Well then," said Howland, "there's just one more thing." He saw a puzzled look on Lyda's face. "Don't worry, dear, it's something that just came up. I thought it better to tell the four of you together—since in a way it's more of a family matter than anything else."

His voice sounded unsure and for an instant he looked at his hands.

"I had a call from Ben Miles this morning," said Howland. He grinned: "I hoped he was going to tell me my tests got mixed up with someone else's, but no such luck."

He looked at his hands again.

"I could tell Ben wasn't exactly happy to have to make the call, but I also knew he wouldn't have done so unless it was really important." He hesitated.

"Go on," said Lyda quietly.

"Well, he asked me if I could stop by Mt. Sinai . . . to, um, see his mother, um, you know, Miriam. She's dying—too—and she asked to see me."

"And you went?" asked Lyda. Somehow she knew what was coming.

"I didn't see how I could refuse. Well, I couldn't, damn it! The woman's dying, and that's something I understand a great deal better than I did a few days ago. Anyway, you should see her. Tubes everywhere, and I thought I was in bad shape. Ben said in another day or two they'll have to put her on a respirator and then it's probably only a matter of weeks. Anyway . . ."

"Anyway . . ." Lyda murmured. She looked at her two sons, then back at her husband. She couldn't help what she said next: "Anyway, you went to see her. And with her dying breath—one of as many, I think we can safely presume, as it will take to accomplish her purpose—she begged you to grant her just one last wish. To let her go to meet her maker, or whoever it is those people meet, secure and happy in the knowledge that Max has been made a partner, or whatever you're going to call them in the new setup. Am I right?"

She hadn't meant to sound harsh.

"I'm sorry, darling," she added, seeing in his face that her suspicions had been right on the money, "but I've known the woman for forty years.

I'm sure she *is* desperately ill. I'm sure she feels that this is Max's last chance, that she can't count on Morris, and if anything happened to you . . ."

She stopped in midsentence and looked at her sons, then at Howland. "Am I right?" she asked.

For a moment, he said nothing. Then: "Does it really matter?"

She could see he wanted to sound impatient, but even the brief effort at impatience wore him down, and to his chagrin the words came out merely plaintive.

"No, I suppose it doesn't," she said softly. It really didn't, did it. And under the circumstances, she had no right to interfere. This is between Miriam and death and you, she thought. Like that Bergman movie: the three of you dicing for Max's future happiness. With you gone, leaving Max to Andrew and Jay would be like throwing him to the wolves, that's what Miriam fears. So of course you said yes. Probably even gave your word. Oh, you're such a softy, my love, that's your strength!

She saw Jay start to open his mouth and shot him a sharp glance. Andy also looked over and shook his head imperceptibly in a motion that said: later.

"Besides," said Howland, "it's not the same as a partnership, really it isn't."

How weak he looks and sounds, thought Andy, gray and tired right through. How in hell could I have missed it? And as for Max: so what? Sooner or later they were going to have to take Artie Lubloff into The Firm anyway, or see a good chunk of their horsepower take a walk. The way the new scheme was going to work, as he understood it, nothing would really change from the family's point of view.

The important thing was that his father be allowed to do it his way. He was a decent and sentimental man. It might be, thought Andy, that we're no longer living in a decent, sentimental world, especially not on the Street, but why shouldn't someone like Father be indulged a few illusions if they were going to be his last? Sure, having Max as a partner would be a pain, but he could be handled, and if he screwed up, he'd be gone so fast his head'd spin!

At the head of the table, Howland got up wearily. "I'm sort of beat," he said. "Don't the rest of you leave. Just let me shuffle off quietly."

The others got up. Lyda went quickly to her husband's side. "Come on," she said brightly. Then she turned to her children. "Go on into the library and have your coffee. I'll be back as soon as I get your father settled."

As soon as she was out the door, Jay jumped up. "Gotta pee," he exclaimed and rushed from the room.

"Max will pay for this," Miranda said darkly. "It's not fair!"

"May I ask how it affects you?" asked Andy. She didn't reply, just stared at him as if he were crazy.

Jay returned. Andy looked at him; his brother's pupils were like shiny little glass beads.

"You know, Jay," said Andy sarcastically, "maybe *you* better go see Ben Miles. Something wrong with your bladder? You hit the can every five minutes."

Of course Jay's problem had nothing to do with his bladder and everything to do with cocaine. Andy had even taken Jay's driver aside on the subject. "So I guess maybe he does a little blow now and then, Andy," Billy T. admitted. "The 'doocey pooder blanche,' as the Frogs say, is all over the Street. Hey, but he don't do no more'n a couple a lines maybe two, three times a week, no more. No big problem."

What do you mean: no big problem? To have a hophead for a brother was a family problem. To have a cokehead running stock-and-bond positions in the high tens of millions was a business problem. And now this with Father, and the transition to be faced.

He got up and followed his sister and brother into the library, where they were soon afterward joined by their mother.

"Well," she said, "I don't know about the rest of you, but I think I need a brandy. See if there's some of that old Hennessy in the bar, will you, Andrew?"

"So," she said, after Andy gave her a snifter, "here's to Warrington and Company, *Incorporated*."

Andy knew what was on his mother's mind. When she had married his father, she had also married The Firm, a partnership that was nearly a hundred twenty years old as they sat there drinking brandy. The change of structure might seem forbidding. Andy himself wasn't so sure. How much difference could those three small letters, "I-n-c," make as long as the family maintained its grip? Incorporating hadn't in and of itself blown firms apart, it took people to do that. It didn't have to cost them a dime's worth of business; look at Morgan Stanley.

Lyda studied her son as he pondered the matter.

There was still something boyish about him. He was forty, but he looked far too young to be taking over. Howland had been forty-five when his father died, and he had matured in a much slower-moving world. On the other hand, Fletcher had been scarcely out of college. Other men about Andrew's age were moving into positions of influence on the Street: at Morgan Stanley, young Parker Gilbert, that clever Gutfreund boy at Salomon Brothers, Sidney Weinberg's son John at Goldman Sachs and Jimmy Brady's son Nicholas at Dillon, Read.

Physically, Andrew's like his grandfather, she thought, square-jawed and stockily built, but he lacks that clenched quality of Fletcher's, that coiled combative tenseness. Did that mean he wasn't tough mentally? No—he had to be. He'd gotten through Korea; he could handle this.

It would have been better if there could have been a few more years for father and son to work together, she thought, but you only had what life designed to give you. Andy had the brains, and was good with people, and treated them fairly.

On the Street, an inclination to play fair, to deal rationally, tended to be interpreted as weakness. Sharks schooled more readily in gentle lagoons than in turbulent seas.

Certainly he wasn't as dewy-eyed as he'd been ten years earlier. Tough times at home probably helped in the annealing process, Lyda guessed, although now was the time when, if ever in a man's life, a supportive wife was a necessity. Well, perhaps when Laurel got back from Santa Barbara, the news would jolt her into making some sense.

Andrew could handle tough situations and difficult people, that much he'd proved. He was the self-proclaimed chief of The Firm's "Shit Patrol," the partners and associates who had to deal with the really difficult connections like Nils Persson of Persson Shipping and Arthur Sanborn of Second Dallas Bank. But it wasn't the hard cases that might prove the most troublesome. A wide, forgiving spirit like Andrew's could prove an alluring haven for the second-rate, which worried his father, but what concerned Howland most of all was his suspicion that Andrew's heart was less and less in the business, which on Wall Street, as anywhere else, was the kiss of death.

Sometimes, he told Lyda, they'd be in the middle of an important meeting, and out of the corner of his eye he'd see Andrew staring out the window, woolgathering. The irritation in Howland's voice when he told her this had been plain. You didn't have to eat, drink, and breathe Hanover Place the way Jay and Artie Lubloff did, he'd added, but still . . . !

Well, at least doing this for Max should ensure Morris's loyalty. Not that Morris had pushed Max's candidacy with any intensity; when Miriam had first gotten sick, he'd hinted to Howland that a partnership for the son would be the quickest cure for the mother, but when nothing happened, the subject had been dropped.

Lyda drained the snifter, kissed each of her children goodnight, and went off to bed.

As soon as they heard her door close down the hall, Jay looked fiercely at Andy. "The old man's fuckin' crazy," he hissed.

Andy put up both hands. "Down, boy! It's not as if we're making his Slapsiness a partner in the true sense. You know how the old man is: he cries at movies. Miriam set him up with a major deathbed scene."

"You don't know she's actually dying," interjected Miranda. "Those people will do anything to make an extra dime."

"Okay, I don't *know* she's dying," Andy said, "but I'm going to give her the benefit of the doubt. Besides, if you're the angel of divine mercy, you ought to be praying for her."

Miranda glared at him scornfully. "For what? *They* don't go to heaven."

Andy got up and regarded his sister with exasperation. "You're not going to start with that crap again, are you?"

Miranda's eyes glittered. She glanced quickly at Jay. "You will do well to remember what they did to our Lord, Drew," she said. "You mark my words, we're all going to pay for what Daddy's done!"

Howland's announcement that Warrington & Co. was going to incorporate caused little surprise up and down Wall Street but consternation at Hanover Place.

By then, so many inviolate partnerships had incorporated that the phenomenon had lost its novelty. Kidder Peabody had incorporated back in 1964; the real push had come in 1970, in the wake of the Penn Central bankruptcy, when "Inc." was added to such prestigious names as Morgan Stanley, White Weld, and Lehman Brothers.

Once it became fashionable, great claims were made for the fiscal and administrative superwriters of the corporate form as against the old-fashioned partnership, especially the incalculable advantage of insulating from liability or tort the personal fortunes of the men at the top. Overnight, the venerated selling point that partnerships committed the fortunes of their members to their dealings ceased to apply.

Incorporation was also claimed to offer boundless operating flexibility, organizational neatness, and so on. As the market recovered, Wall Street returned to its great and principal business of confecting new games for public investors; these perforce opened new avenues of liability; trading and dealing positions also enlarged, supported by heavy overnight borrowings; in some cases, soft assets were carried by hard liabilities. In all of this, the risks were assumed to be completely mitigated by the magical incantation "Inc."

Such considerations did not apply to Hanover Place. It was family and organizational convenience pure and simple that was the principal motivation for Howland's announcement at the May partners meeting that, as of October 1, 1971, the business of Warrington & Co. would henceforth be carried on by Warrington & Co., *Inc.*

When Howland had finished outlining the ways in which the Partnership Agreement would be translated into corporate by-laws and articles, as well as the basis on which existing and future financial interests were going to be converted into shares of "Inc." common stock, he said, almost casually: "As we are going to be a corporation, we are going to organize as a corporation, observe a corporate hierarchy, and we are going to use corporate nomenclature."

At that point, Archer Cleverley, present to deal with any legal questions that might be raised, passed around a sheaf of organization charts. When they saw it, the worst fears of a number of people in the room were realized.

The partners of Hanover Place knew that much thought at other places had been given to thinking up titles with as self-elevating a ring on the tongue or business card as the old usage of "partner." Corporations could not have "partners." Most other firms settled on "managing director" as a replacement. The term had a nice, executive sound; furthermore, it was soon discovered to possess a subtly inferential social twist—simply by dropping the preposition "a" on a wedding announcement in the *Times*, for instance, a man could describe himself thus: "the bride's father is *managing director* of Such-and-Such," notwithstanding that he might rank at the very bottom of a pecking order of two-score or more managing directors.

"Vice president" was not quite the same thing, but as Howland informed his partners, *Inc.* was going to have a chairman and chief executive, Howland; two vice chairmen, Lewis Comstock and Morris Miles; a president and chief operating officer, Andrew Warrington; and one executive vice president, Jay Warrington. These five would constitute the Executive Committee. Everyone else would be a vice president.

As for the Survivorship Trust, it would cease to be a "Party of the First Part" and become instead The Firm's largest stockholder, so that the family would retain virtually absolute powers to propose, dispose, ratify, replace, and appoint.

On the last business day of September 1971, the incorporation papers were signed; on the following day, readers of the financial pages were advised by a tombstone advertisement that Warrington & Co., Inc., had succeeded to the business of Warrington & Co., founded 1814. The new officers were listed; those not on the Executive Committee were not ranked alphabetically, but by seniority. Thus, at the bottom of the roster of vice presidents, appeared the name of S. Maximilian Miles.

It had been arduous work, and it took its toll on Howland. He kept his chin up and tried to give the lie to his condition, but by midsummer it was evident that the managing partner was not well. There was scant trace left of his old youthful ruddiness; his vigorous bearing had become gingerly; now and then his hand would press against his abdomen, or his voice would catch in the middle of a sentence, in obvious pain.

When the Stock Exchange raised objections to the Trust becoming the largest "Inc." stockholder, Howland's threat to quit the Exchange after 156 years was delivered in a wavering voice, and it was more out of pity than anything else, some later said, that the Exchange had given in to an old, sick man's honorable whim.

When the transaction was finally completed, when the last signature had been affixed to a stack of documents two feet high, Lyda took Howland to Double Dune for a rest.

The sea air seemed to do him a world of good. He took it easy at first, but by early October could summon the energy for brief walks on the dunes.

The children divided up the weekends. Miranda's visits were the most exhausting. She insisted on long Bible readings, and praying out loud for her father's soul.

"Frankly," Lyda told Chickie gloomily, "it's a godsend she can only fly in from Los Angeles once a month."

Chickie came down every other weekend or so, to keep Lyda company during the long silences when Howland dozed fitfully under the influence of an ever-more-powerful series of painkillers.

When Laurel visited with Andrew, she made an effort. She was wonderful with Howland; her old bonny intelligence and wondrous smile flashed through the gray mask of depression; Lyda could see her husband's mood lift; it was as if the presence of his dazzling daughter-in-law transported Howland to the glades and meadows of a sunny past. Lyda began to believe that there was still hope for Andrew's marriage, and she could see the same wish glowing in his eyes.

Friends came, too. One weekend Tom and Jessica Creedmore flew in with Miranda. Morris came down for lunch; Miriam continued to hang on at Mt. Sinai, but he told Lyda it was a certainty now that she would never leave the hospital. Eric Laszlo flew in and spent three days at Double Dune.

By and by, Howland seemed to grow stronger. After lunch one day, he insisted they go out on the boardwalk across the dunes and look at the sea.

The day was crisp and bright; Lyda was pleased with the way her husband looked. After his last visit, Ben Miles had told her the end might not come for several months.

It was a peaceful Monday afternoon. Andrew had flown off Sunday night to Frankfurt; Chickie and Laurel had left early that morning. As he did every morning at eleven thirty, Howland talked to the office, to Morris in Andrew's absence, and then to Irv Nachman about his sister Floss's estate. When he got off, he seemed in good spirits. Business was improving, the tone of the market was better.

After twenty minutes, Howland began to feel the chill and Lyda took him inside.

Over dinner, he seemed stronger again, and had some agreeably rude things to say about "that idiotic Lindsay," the New York mayor who'd gone over to the Democrats. After the meal, she read to him from *Gatsby*. When she saw his attention begin to drift, she took him up to bed.

She made him comfortable and gave him the pills Ben Miles had prescribed. He looked terribly shrunken in the old Charoot pajamas he insisted on wearing, even though the color was faded and the piping worn through. She remembered buying them in Paris not long after the war.

She undressed and slid under the covers. Lyda had not slept apart from her husband for fifty-one years and wasn't about to start now, even though his groans and shiftings often left her sleepless. She was sad; she was tired; she was seventy-one years old—and she soon drifted off.

Howland lay beside her, listening to the gentle regular beat of his heart. He didn't feel particularly sleepy; a residue of pain lingered; it always took the pills a little while to convert the knife in his belly into something kinder. He began to think of his life and how much he loved Lyda, and how little they really had left undone, when he felt something stir in the room and knew that Death had come for him.

All his pain had disappeared. He peered through the dimness and at the foot of his bed he saw his father and mother, and the twins, all smiling, because their long wait for him was over, and the time had come. He tried to reach out and touch Lyda's arm, just to say good-bye, but his hand wouldn't move. He felt time roll backward; he tried to say something, but all he could feel was a cough rising within him, pushing his life before it like a snowplow.

Lyda heard her husband cough and came instantly awake. She thought she heard him say: "Let's go dancing. Ted Straeter's at La Rue," and then he gave another cough, a terrible deep bark, as if he was throwing up his very soul, and she knew he was gone.

She knew, but she still reached over and put her fingers gently against his throat, seeking a pulse she knew she wouldn't find. She couldn't make herself turn on the light, nor could she bring herself to sit up and get a grip on things.

She lay still, thinking. There was no urgency now. What difference could another hour or so make? There would be time later for doctors and undertakers, people to notify, tears to be shed. Time to consider the options of widowhood. A last hour together could do no harm.

"You knew it would be today, didn't you?" she murmured. You lucky man, she thought. You were getting your things in order, that was why you were so wrapped up all day, and then when you knew it was time to go, you left. Oh how I envy you! Please work it out for me up there or wherever you are that when it's my turn I'll know, too. She tried to piece together the great happenings of their shared life, but to her surprise, she couldn't concentrate on the big things. Instead she found her mind full of small thoughts; tiny points of recollection like motes in a sunbeam. Faces and places, many dead, gone away, shuttered, scraps of old tunes, fragments of time, now came alive and chattering, joyful with noise and youth. Down they drifted, tiny piece by tiny piece, arranging themselves into a mosaic that glittered new and bright, and seemed to light up the gloom, even as her sight became blurred by tears and she felt herself begin to shudder with the chilly ague of grief.

As he would have wished, Howland Micah Temple Warrington was buried from Trinity Church with suitable military and commercial honors. The managing directors of The Firm sat in the pews behind the family, just as they had at Howland's wedding. Then, the guests had included the flower of Wall Street youth; now it was the cream of the Street's gerontocracy. Fifty years before, Morris Miles had edged nervously into a pew; now he walked confidently behind the flag-draped casket, first among a group of pallbearers that included not only giants of the Street, but a retired five-star general and a former Cabinet Secretary.

The service was simple: a proper service of thanksgiving for the life of Howland Warrington. The prayers and responses of burial were led by Trinity's rector and the Reverend Jerry Creedmore. Morris Miles, Eric Laszlo, Lewis Comstock, and the Secretary of Defense delivered brief eulogies. Andy, Jay, and Miranda read their father's favorite psalms.

As she listened to the Secretary eulogize Howland, reminiscing about their time together in the Air Force and the Strategic Bombing Survey, Lyda thought of people who had long before made the journey Howland must have by now completed: her two sons, Howland's parents. Hap Carruthers; Chubby Fenton; Eddie Stanforth, who'd dropped dead in '63 on the sixth green at Piping Rock; Howland's sister Flossie; Burt and Selma Lubloff; Foster Klopp; old Colmer Hardesty; her Auntie Miranda.

She wondered if Howland's life had satisfied him. That was the sort of thing he would never discuss with anyone, but would he have been happier to have done what others had: leave Hanover Place in 1941 on "temporary wartime duty" and never return? Devote his life and fortune to the service of his country, to advising Presidents, to heading Cabinet departments and embassies?

Earlier that morning, Lyda had stood in the gallery of the Stock Exchange and watched as the Floor observed a minute of silence before the bell. A moment of reverence for a man who, as Al Gordon had written her, "represented qualities which this business of ours is only rarely ca-pable of bringing out in people."

The Warringtons had intelligence, decency, dedication, and the money to be able to use these talents in any way they wished. Was this the best way?

Listening to Andy read the Twenty-third Psalm, she thought he looked tired. The work wore a man down. It was more than "the work," of course. The Warringtons sent their sons down to Hanover Place for the same reasons that they sent them to Tippecanoe and Shiloh, to the Leyte Gulf and the North Sea and Korea and Vietnam. To defend something that others didn't appreciate in the same way, and that must have an extra cost.

What lay ahead? Everyone agreed that the next few years would be difficult. Eric Laszlo had come for dinner the night before and expressed his opinion "that the postwar world is ending faster than you Americans think. Indeed, it may already have ended."

Sick as he was, Howland had spent hours on the phone with people like his wartime colleague George Ball, talking about the future, analyzing Nixon's decision to take the country off the gold standard. Everyone seemed to agree it was an historic decision, and an historic moment; the market had thought so, it had leaped a record thirty-two points on a record thirty-two million shares.

The world would change, but The Firm would go on. So would the family. It might be that the kind of people the Warringtons symbolized, to others and to themselves, were no longer in the ascendant. That through misuse or loss of respect, their sun was sinking.

From 1815 to 1971 had been a very long road, paved with greatly more satisfaction than regret, vastly more profit than loss. No reason to say: This is now the end of the trail. Still, as the voices rose around her in "Onward Christian Soldiers," Lyda found it difficult to put aside a fore-boding that it was her family's destiny to sacrifice their own children at the altars of a universal indifference, as keepers of flames about which no one else seemed to care very much.

BOOK

VIII

THE PURSUIT
OF HAPPINESS

1974

JUNE

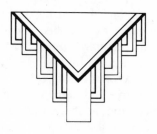

On a pleasant evening in late June of 1974, in an elegant suite in the Hotel Pierre, eight people sat down to dine. The host for the evening was Leo Himelman, although the dinner was paid for by First Penn Holdings Inc., the largest client of Himelman, Plaskow and Gold, and the lessee of the apartment.

By then, First Penn had grown from a smallish family factoring business to something much more complex. Had its shares been publicly traded, it might have been characterized in Wall Street analysese as "a rapidly growing finance, food service, and specialty retailing conglomerate." Its operations included supermarket chains in Georgia and Tennessee and several of the Plains states; a discount filling-station complex in Michigan and Illinois; fast-food operations in Southern California, Colorado, and the Pacific Northwest; check-cashing and small-loan companies in five states. The only published information on First Penn was what Dun & Bradstreet furnished prospective suppliers of goods and credit; this information was highly encouraging: First Penn's subsidiaries paid their bills promptly and took their discounts. The company was to all appearances a mishmash of small-to-medium-size retail and service businesses not untypical of the time. There was nothing in the prosaic credit reports to indicate that First Penn was also the final—and only aboveground—link in a chain of trusts and holding companies that had their roots deep in

the impenetrable schism of accommodating legal domiciles stretching from
Liberia to Lichtenstein, or that all those reported to Lester Vivian, who
sat at the opposite end of the table from Himelman.

Close scrutiny by a very shrewd eye might have suggested that what
GudValu Markets, Buy 'n Bye, Power Octane, Senor Jose's Tacorias, The
Flying Filet, and Elmer Fudd's 69¢ Emporiums had in common was that
the business they transacted was conducted almost entirely in cash. Even
closer scrutiny, were this possible, might have shown that only about
seventy percent of First Penn's units' weekly bank deposits, and the company's consolidated income, on which it happily paid taxes, had actually
been paid across the counter by customers. A comparison of the register
tapes from First Penn's three hundred units and the register tapes shown
to First Penn's accountants and the Internal Revenue Service would have
shown that, somewhere between the cash register and the teller's window,
First Penn was picking up large additional amounts of cash. By 1974, this
mysterious increment was running at the rate of $150 million a year.

This sum, however substantial it was for the time, was chickenfeed in
terms of Lester Vivian's expectations, which was the reason for the dinner
at the Pierre.

Although nominally the chief executive of First Penn, Lester Vivian
had larger responsibilities that were known only to him and another dozen
men. He was the cash flow manager for a group of closely controlled
multinational enterprises with offices and manufacturing facilities from
Palermo to Bogotá to Saigon. They were forecasting dramatic growth in
certain new markets and from certain new products, which would require
very little in the way of net new capital investment. As a result, a considerable free cash flow was projected to be generated; indeed, by the mid-
1980s, the group's more optimistic forecasts, taking into account the
sociology and demographics of its principal markets, projected profits at
a level of several billion dollars a year.

Such torrents of cash would require new investment outlets and strat-
egies. Vivian was given the task of coming up with a plan and a program,
hence the evening's dinner.

Apart from Leo Himelman, the other guests at dinner were all in their
late twenties and early thirties, and had in common that they had been
at the University of Pennsylvania's Wharton School, either as under-
graduates or graduates, between 1963 and 1970, when Himelman was
teaching there. Himelman's mandate from Vivian, who represented that
he might like to commit between $50 million and $100 million of First
Penn's surplus cash to innovative financing concepts, was to organize a
cadre of people capable of conceiving and developing such ideas.

Vivian had told Himelman he wanted fresh, ambitious young people,
men and women, whose thinking wouldn't be tied down by tradition and

whose ambition wouldn't be hampered by loyalty. Outsiders—but presentable ones.

"What I don't want, Leo," he told his lawyer, "are guys who couldn't make it, or guys with grudges. No retreads, if you please."

" 'Grudges'? 'Retreads'?"

"People like you, Leo. Guys with axes to sharpen tend to cut their own heads off. That's bad enough, but I don't want mine chopped off in the bargain. Don't show me hicks, and don't show me wiseguys who think they've been worked over by the white-shoe boys. Smart but unscarred, Leo, that's what I want. Fresh talent, Leo, fresh talent."

Vivian knew Himelman hated being talked to this way. He knew Leo had it in mind to dovetail his own thirst for revenge with Vivian's organizational requirements. Up to a point, this was okay; it added spice to the stew, and imparted a little extra, which was fine until it got in the way of objectivity.

"One other thing, Leo," Vivian added. "No poor boys. Poor boys get too caught up in the money angle, they get greedy. Find me some kids who were brought up just close enough to the real thing to know what it tastes like, who don't wear brown shoes with a blue suit. Kids whose families may have belonged to the wrong clubs, but didn't live on the wrong side of the tracks."

Of the cast assembled for dinner, only Arthur Lubloff was known to Vivian. In fact, Vivian had asked for Artie. He had been mightily impressed by Artie's work on the abortive pass at United Brooklyn. That brief foray had really been an exploratory probe of Warrington & Co. Neither Artie nor Leo knew it, but Vivian intended to make Artie the point man for the network he intended to start building tonight.

Artie had suggested that Bobby Marryat be included at dinner. At thirty-five, Bobby was older than the others—he'd left Wharton a year or so before Himelman began teaching there—but he was an unconventional thinker, and it was essential in Artie's eyes to have someone well placed in the energy business, especially now that the Arabs were playing games with the price of crude. Vivian, who knew something about the structure of the economics of wholesale and retail fuel distribution, readily agreed.

Himelman looked around the table with satisfaction. His objective had been to select a brilliant group whose talents and ambitions lay in diverse but potentially complementary directions. He was certain he had succeeded, and it swelled him with pride to reflect that it was his genius that had turned Lester Vivian's concepts into vibrant human form.

Take Kevin Kerry, the flame-haired imp he'd placed at Vivian's left. Kerry was from outside Boston; he'd grown up in Roxbury, where his father was a regional manager for Stop 'n Shop, but Kerry's interest wasn't in retailing, it was in real estate. For one thing, to hear Kerry talk, retailing *was* real estate; location was everything. For another, it turned out that one of Kerry's uncles was a monsignor who had worked for a long time in the New York diocese under Francis Cardinal Spellman.

According to Kerry, his uncle was fond of talking about his old boss.

"His Eminence used to say," the monsignor would relate, over his third glass of Sunday sherry, "that while he might be sound on matters of theology, when it came to Manhattan real estate he was infallible!" The monsignor's tone left no doubt that he, like the cardinal, shared the view that between God and the zoning laws, there was little doubt as to which more profoundly affected the affairs of mankind.

When Kerry left Wharton, his uncle found him a place in the diocesan office, where he learned all one needed to know about zoning laws and building codes. A feisty, egocentric young man, he bridled at working for the Church, at working for anyone. To indenture himself to another developer held even less appeal, however. To do what he thought he could do, Kerry had to be able to write a check on something more tangible than his boundless self-confidence and inspirational grasp of the possibilities inherent in the depressed Manhattan realty market; he needed hard cash, which was something Lester Vivian could provide.

Listening to Kerry sketch out his big ideas, Vivian realized that there was something else besides money that he could apply to Kerry's ambitions. Vivian knew people who could see to it that Kerry's union problems would be minimal, his overtime all but negligible, and that his materials would arrive in a timely fashion at a favorable price, all of which would keep his construction costs in line and his profits exceptional.

On Vivian's other side sat Norton Herzkow. Like many another mathematical genius, Herzkow belied his abnormal clarity of mind with physical unkemptness; this was ironic, for he was quite vain about his appearance and spent more on his clothes than he could afford, but to appallingly little effect. Physically, he might appear to consist of odd bulges and loose ends, but he was endowed with the ability to keep several number sets in his mind at the same time, which made him a genius at options and arbitrage, and which was already gaining him a reputation among a coterie of professional investors.

On the far side of Herzkow sat Irene Gessel, the niece of the late Hyman Gessel of GRC Communications. When she graduated from Wharton in 1966, she had joined a major Los Angeles talent agency, but that had soon palled. Compared to the Swinging Sixties on Wall Street, Hollywood seemed dull; after a year and a half, she quit, and took her talent for image-building to a New York financial public-relations firm, where she'd been responsible for manufacturing some of the most notable investment cover-boys of the late sixties. Like the other bright young people in the room, Irene believed that most everyone else in life was a dummy, and that it was her tragedy to be a genius shackled to the mediocrity of others.

Across from Irene, next to Bobby Marryat, sat Nick Palinga, a tough Vietnam veteran and fitness addict from Queens. He had graying cropped hair and a face no one wanted to meet in a dark alley. Like Kerry, he had a useful uncle, in this case an Astoria attorney who'd fixed it up for Palinga to work for the pension office of two city construction locals. Two years later, he'd moved over to the New York City comptroller's office, where he was now deputy administrator for equities and equity equivalents in the city pension funds; he had close to a billion dollars under his "supervision." More important, he could wander around City Hall as he pleased and find out what he wanted to know.

Roger Riskind, across from Palinga, had decided from the first moment he entered the Pierre apartment that he was the class act of the group. He was a frizzy-haired young man from a prosperous, middle-class Cleveland suburb, with a slight simian cast to his features. He had begun life after Wharton by riding Norton Herzkow's coattails. They had worked together briefly at Drexel Firestone in Philadelphia; then Riskind came up to New York in 1971 to join Morgan Stanley as a government bond salesman.

Riskind believed—he had convinced himself—that the venerable investment banking firm had lured him to Manhattan under false pretenses. He claimed that he had been hired with the firm understanding that he could move into Morgan's Buying (Corporate Finance) Department as soon as he proved himself in Governments.

Riskind had chafed in Morgan's bond department for three years. It galled him no end that men with half his intelligence were out calling on the Exxons and the Du Ponts; with no qualifications apart from where they'd gone to school, virtual idiots were poring over spreadsheets in paneled offices with the top officers of the nation's largest companies. Of Himelman's recruits, Riskind had been selected as much for his psychological as for his intellectual qualities. He and the lawyer were in a sense kindred spirits, in whom resentment, alienation, and a desire for vindication fueled an obsession with prominence and success.

As he sat there, listening to Irene Gessel talking about the publicity campaign she'd orchestrated in a recent proxy contest, Riskind reflected on a piece of information concerning his current employer that had come to him quite by accident. It was golden stuff, no doubt of that, and Leo had cautioned him to save it until the end of the evening.

Actually, little of consequence was said by anyone over dinner. The talk was mostly of the Street, of the shriveling equity market, the Loew's-CNA dogfight, the effects of OPEC's latest pricing pronouncement, and the fact that a seat on the Exchange, which had sold five years earlier for over half a million dollars, could now be had for under a hundred thousand. The consensus was that the Floor had at long last lost its power, which meant that negotiated transaction-by-transaction commissions were a sure thing. There was also some discussion of the expanded role that options and futures were likely to have, now that such instruments had attained total acceptance as ways to play the market.

When the coffee had been served, and the waiters gone, Leo Himelman tapped his glass. "I'm glad we could get together this way," he said. "I hope this will be the first of many such occasions. Busy schedules permitting, perhaps we should think about trying to meet every month or so just to exchange ideas.

"Now: to business. I think if there's one thing we all share, it's an understanding that the world has changed tremendously over the last year or so. Watergate, Vietnam, OPEC, what's happening on Wall Street: it's all been terribly disruptive, and from disruption—it's been my experience —come great opportunities."

"Amen to that," said Irene Gessel. "Bring back the go-go years!"

Coiled on her chair, she resembled a python, an effect heightened by her narrow untrusting features and a dress whose sequins shifted like scales in the candlelight. She seemed capable of flicking out a tongue and ingesting whole anyone at the table.

"There are very big changes coming," said Roger Riskind in a voice full of theatrical foreboding.

Even though it was a hot night, he was dressed in a black mohair suit cut from cloth that looked thick enough to stop a bullet. There was something about Riskind that reminded Artie of his uncle Max. When he talked, he ran a hand over his slicked-down, lank hair; when silent, he folded thick lips inward upon his splendid teeth as if to polish them.

"You can say that in spades," offered Palinga. "The City's broke. If you clowns wanna make some money, short New York paper up, down, and sideways. Things keep going the way they are, City Hall's gonna have to take a bankruptcy chapter by the middle of next year, no later. When Beame says he's got a study going, all they're studying is what they're gonna tell the banks next. The funny thing is, Beame and Goldin are scared shitless of telling the banks, but what they don't know is the banks are getting ready to pull the chain on them."

Down the table, Kevin Kerry's perky Irish face lit up, and his pouty round mouth widened into an expression that mingled rapaciousness and pleasant incredulity. Himelman, observing, knew what Kerry was thinking. Whenever the city got in trouble, it spread its legs for the real-estate boys. All the better to have Vivian's money on tap.

"Y'all think it's bad now," Bobby Marryat interrupted, "jus' y'all wait until them A-rabs get going. Y'all think crude's high now, at twelve dollars a barrel, man, y'all ain't seen nothin'! Them A-rabs got the smell of blood and they can read our import numbers. These ain't just a bunch of niggers wearing sheets! I'm guessin' you might see oil at twenty dollars a barrel!"

Bobby cocked his large head and stared owlishly around the table. He had put on about twenty pounds since his marriage and looked more than ever like a large, squat toad.

" 'Course," Bobby continued, ticking off his points on the thick fingers of his left hand, "where there's distress, they's opportun'ty. We never had price increases like this, and Uncle Sam don't know what to do, so they've set up this real dumb deal which sets diff'rent control prices for old oil, for new oil, for stripper oil, hell, damn near for olive oil! On top o' that, you got these refinery entitlements which I got sixteen lawyers from Vinson Elkins tryin' to figure out, so right now the fastest way to make money in the oil business is to steal it."

"The oil or the money?" asked someone.

"Hell," Bobby exclaimed, "both! What you do is buy you a barrel of old oil at the control price of six dollars, and you get you a Magic Marker, and you print 'new oil' on a barrel of old oil, and sell that barrel upstream to one of them crude-poor sumbitches like Ashland or Sohio. It's like any ol' daisy chain, you can keep the sumbitch goin' as long as there's daisies. I buy a barrel of old oil from ol' Lester here for six dollars, and he can sell it to Leo at eight dollars, and Leo can pass it on to Norton for ten dollars, and so on and such, and by the time we're through that six-dollar old oil has turned into twelve-dollar new oil an' ever'body's made money! Makes you ask yourself: why bother to drill?"

Vivian found this interesting. He made a mental note to study its applicability to the way residual fuel oils and gasolines were sold.

"Anything else?" asked Himelman. "It's getting late, and most of us have to be at our desks early."

Herzkow spoke up. There was a guy he used to know at Drexel, a kid named Milken, who was doing some interesting work on high-yield bonds. Maybe they ought to ask him to sit in on one of these dinners. Artie, always on the lookout for new talent for The Firm, made a note to check up on the guy. The word on the Street was that Drexel was probably going to be bought by Tubby Burnham, and since Burnham was a real chickenshit firm, maybe this guy might want to move to a place where he could really play.

"Very interesting, Norton," said Himelman. He looked around the table. "Well then, if that's it, perhaps Arthur would be good enough to give us his view from the Street."

"Sure, Leo. Nothing's new. Guys running around in circles trying to figure what it's gonna mean when we go to negotiated commissions next year. Mind you, I said, 'when,' not 'if.' You want to know what it's gonna mean? The rich are gonna get richer; the smart guys are gonna get richer; the Racquet Club types are gonna go out of business, and the little guy is gonna get fucked as usual. The guys who're gonna really get hit are the houses who've hung it out to dry on a roomful of registered reps selling tax shelters to dentists in Flushing."

As always, making a speech of more than two sentences abashed Artie, and he broke off abruptly, glanced quickly at each of his dining compan-ions, and stared down at his plate.

"Well," said Himelman, "that should do it then. Any last gems of wisdom?"

Roger Riskind's moment had arrived. He thrust his hand in the air and began gesticulating frantically, like a child in a classroom signaling for attention.

"You're not going to believe this," he said, his voice rising with ex-citement. "I've just learned that Morgan Stanley is about to do a hostile takeover!"

He paused to relish his companions' expressions of disbelief. He knew what they were thinking: sooner the Pope become Jewish than Morgan Stanley undertake an unfriendly bid.

"I'm not kidding!" Riskind exclaimed. "International Nickel's going after Electric Storage Battery, and Morgan Stanley's going to handle the bid for Inco! Not only that, it's a cash offer and it's all being done with bank debt; Inco figures it can borrow three-quarters of the money up to forty-two dollars a share."

"And the banks are gonna give it to them?" asked Palinga.

"Why not?" commented Himelman. "Business is slow, and slow busi-ness is what makes the greatest opportunities. You should all remember that."

After the others left, Himelman remained behind with Vivian. "What do you think?" he asked.

"Bright group. You really think we need a P.R. type like the girl?"

"Lester, we're planning nothing less than a revolution, we'll need to establish an ideolog . . ."

Vivian shut him off with a gesture. He smiled and said patiently: "Leo, *you* seem to be planning a revolution. I'm dealing with an investment problem; I'm not fomenting a damn Gunpowder Plot. Speaking of which, what was that crap about regular meetings? There are going to be no regular meetings, at least while I'm in the picture. Do you recall Apalachin, Leo, mob guys spilling out of the windows and scattering into the trees? Your guy Herzkow doesn't look like he could go a hundred yards without having a heart attack."

Himelman ignored Vivian's comments. "Let me put it another way, Lester," he said. "You heard Arthur. Things are changing. We plan to be on the cutting edge of that change, because it's with that very edge the most advantageous deals are cut. There is always resistance to change, however, and not all of it will succumb to sheer financial muscle. Public relations is an important part of my strategy: and not merely with the financial press, but in Washington."

Vivian nodded slowly. He held up his long pale fingers and examined his glistening nails.

"Okay, I'll buy that. One other thing bothers me . . ." His voice trailed off, and there was a pause; then he said, "Too many Jewish kids."

"I beg your pardon."

"Come on, Leo, you know how it is. Five of your recruits are Jews. Couldn't you find me a nice, smart Episcopalian? Or maybe a really clever spade?"

He chuckled, and added, "Of course, maybe there's no such thing."

Himelman didn't seem to care for the joke. "You are looking for certain abilities, Lester," he said stiffly. "These are young people who brilliantly embody them. That they happen to be Jewish is beside the point."

Vivian shrugged dubiously, and said: "You know what I mean, Leo. You know how people are. I don't want anyone to get the idea, if anything should go wrong, that—well—this was *organized*. This thing's got to be kosher from the word *go*, if you get my meaning."

1978

OCTOBER

The meeting in Chicago at Harris Trust had gone badly, and had broken up early with the usual promises from both sides to reconsider their positions.

The CEO of Palatine Oil took Andy aside after the fruitless session and vented his displeasure with The Firm's handling of the deal. He hinted that unless it got squared away, he might bring in Salomon Brothers, not only on this deal but to co-manage all future Palatine financings. Andy had sat patiently and listened. Both of them knew that if the CEO hadn't pressed the other guys at just the wrong psychological moment, they might well have a deal by now, and would be breaking out champagne instead of recriminations.

Ah well, thought Andy, we also serve who sit and are abused. It goes with the territory, and if it makes the other guy feel better, then my apologetic patience becomes just another service artfully provided by Warrington & Co., Inc. Of course, if Dick Bosworth hadn't had a gallstone attack, I wouldn't have had to fill in for him on Palatine and find myself in the middle of this mess.

When the executive finished his tirade, the two men promised each other to think things over and talk further in the course of the weekend. Andy went out to tell his associates that they were going to have to remain in Chicago to take another crack at the figures with the Palatine financial people. He hated to do this, but they had to show the flag; the situation was critical. Maybe the refinery runs could be massaged to eke out another two bits a share, he suggested, at the same time thinking, Christ, I sound just like the Klopper!

Two bits a share! Twenty-five cents a share on a sixty-dollar-a-share deal! Did that make sense? It didn't. It was strictly chest-beating. People didn't seem happy any longer unless there was blood all over the floor by the time they shook hands. It was the trading mentality at work. Since May Day three years earlier, when the Street had gone to negotiated commissions, the traders had been in the driver's seat. Relationships were out. Nickle-and-dime head-butting was in. That's what was making him sick of the business.

The associates took the news glumly. What choice did they have? Jobs were hard to come by on the Street in 1978. As they headed for the fleet of limousines that would take them back to Palatine's lakefront head-quarters, one of them handed Andy a note to call Bobby Forstman in Seattle, urgent.

Shit, he thought, what now? Bobby had been sent west trying to keep the Amalgamated Supermarkets deal on the track. Over the phone Andy learned that an abrasive young house lawyer for Cosmo Life, Amalga-mated's traditional lead lender, was taking a hard line on loan agreement provisions. For thirty years, such problems had been solved by a phone call from Morris Miles to Barney Berenson, but Barney had retired. Still, Morris would normally have to deal with this, but Morris was in Paris. These days Morris was always in Paris! A year earlier, a few months after Miriam finally breathed her last—she'd outlived Andy's father by almost six years!—Morris had taken a new young wife. Or maybe she had taken him. Anyway, "the vivacious Sunny Miles," as she was known to readers of the city's gossip columns, was keeping her husband busy.

In a way, that was good. After the death of Andy's father, Morris increasingly began to exhibit irritating symptoms Andy had seen in other men of a certain age. Lyda understood; Morris, she said, was merely attempting to fill up the emptiness of his professional decline with self-importance, the way one pumps up a leaky tire. The fact was, he had begun to be a bit of a nuisance, prone to interfere in situations and relationships where his usefulness had long since ended. There was no way Morris was going to retire, so in a way it was convenient to have him trailing after Sunny through the antique shops and couture salons of Paris. Who cared if Sunny was a fortune hunter? Whose business was it? So what if J.B. Marryat had told Jay that Sunny's reputation at the Love Field Admirals Club was that "she could suck the chrome off a trailer hitch"? Morris was having the time of his old life.

As long as she keeps Morris happy and distracted, the more power to her, Andy thought, especially since she had to put up with Max. It was like a *ménage à trois*; Morris refused to sell the Mileses' old apartment and move to a more stylish address—it was too windy over on Fifth Avenue, he told Andy, he couldn't keep his hat on his head, and anyway what possible difference could five blocks make? Park Avenue wasn't exactly Bedford-Stuyvesant! Nevertheless, Max remained at home. Weird, thought Andy, to be approaching fifty and still at home. Maybe Jay was right; maybe Max took care of certain of his glamorous stepmother's needs, ones that Morris, at his age, could no longer fulfill.

Anyway, that was neither here nor there with the problem at hand. It would have been helpful to have Morris around to pour oil on troubled waters, but he was out of pocket. Andy got himself transferred to Artie Lubloff, told him about the problem, and left it to the young man to haul the Cosmo back into line. He didn't even bother to touch base with his brother. These days Jay wasn't much help after lunch.

By the time he hung up, it was obvious he was going to miss his four o'clock flight at O'Hare. For an instant he debated staying over in Chicago—there was little enough to go home to, God knew!—but there wasn't anyone in Chicago whom he felt like seeing, so he headed for the airport.

In the back of the limousine, he stretched out his legs. Catching sight of his face in the driver's mirror, he was pleased to see he didn't look all that much worse for wear. His hair was gray at the sides and temples now, the shadows under his eyes seemed darker; there was no doubt his face had lost some of the merriness he'd always seen in it, and its square lines seemed slightly puffy, but that was the temporary effect of too much airline food, too many hotel nights. For all that, the light hasn't completely gone out, he thought.

He closed his eyes and began to review the problems he still had to deal with. They stretched around him on all sides, like an endless vista of quicksand.

For one thing, Hanover Place's ranks were thinning. Suddenly it seemed that his frontline troops were under fire. Bosworth's gall bladder. Irv Nachman's kidneys. Morris Miles's remarriage. That left a lot of flanks exposed to predatory competitors.

And now Laszlo was talking about retiring. That would leave an entire theater open to enemy encroachment. Eric had good people in London and Paris, but there was only one Eric Laszlo. He had become a legend for his acumen and access. Kings and premiers sought his astute advice, which had paid off in The Firm's being under retainer to a round dozen foreign governments and agencies. It wasn't just the business being put at risk that troubled Andy. When his father died, Laszlo had stepped in as a kind of wise uncle. Andy depended on Laszlo; he was about the last person left at Hanover Place with whom Andy felt able to talk frankly, and from whom he could get an honest, objective, unself-serving answer.

Well, this one would just have to be played by ear. Laszlo was flying into New York next week to discuss the matter, and Andy planned to wheel up his heaviest artillery, namely his mother.

Of course, thought Andy, it wasn't all doom and gloom. There were a few blessings to be counted. For one thing, Max Miles was under control, or at least delivered to where he could do no harm. It had been Andy's inspired insight that Max's defects as a banker might be transmuted into the virtues of a public man, that his bluster could pay as much for bullshit as for truth.

Three years earlier, in the autumn of 1975, when the city went to the brink of insolvency, The Firm had been asked to put its shoulder to the wheel, and it struck Andy that here was a heaven-sent opportunity to make use of Max. To everyone's surprise, Max had performed admirably. To be certain, it was tiresome for The Firm's other managing directors to endure his bumptious lunchtime recitals of "I told Felix . . . ," "Vic Gotbaum and I . . . ," "as I said to Pat Patterson of Morgan Guaranty . . . ," "George Gould and Jack Bigel share my view on . . . ," "the Mayor and I . . ." and so on.

The winter of '74–'75 had been the worst time Andy and people his age on the Street had ever known, so it was worth it not to have to worry about Max Miles screwing up when the ice was as thin as it was.

Hard on the heels of the city bailout came another call for Hanover Place's symbolic involvement, when Lewie Comstock, one of Hanover Place's sturdiest links with its pre-Crash past, dropped dead on the squash court, and The Firm was no longer represented on the board of governors of the New York Stock Exchange. Not long afterward, the chairman of the Exchange came to ask Andy if The Firm would consider putting one of its managing directors on the NYSE board.

Andy had mixed feelings on the subject. To name a partner would be to raise The Firm's banner behind the new, negotiated commission structure, which to him seemed like turning Hanover Place's back on old friends. The new arrangement was going to put once respected houses like Clark Dodge and Bill Hutton's firm out of business. In the end, however, he'd volunteered Max and it had worked out just fine.

Max had now attained a certain status as a spokesman for Wall Street; he was regularly contacted by newspapers and television stations for comment on large Street developments. He photographed well and he had mastered a form of generalizing blather that the media seemed to lap up.

Best of all, Max's new visibility kept him out of the office. His latest assignment, as chairman of a Securities Industry Association Committee on Regulation and Registration, kept him on the road three or four days a week "meeting and greeting and chin-scratching," as Jay put it. Who could tell: it might produce some business. Max had never been much of a "rainmaker" or producer of new fee-paying business. Mostly he continued to look after Morris's old connections. Now, Andy hoped, there might be some chance Max's new prominence might bear fruit.

"We're here, sir."

Andy thanked the driver, tipped him, and headed for the Admirals Club. The place was crowded—a big storm in the Plains states had shut down everything to the west from Minneapolis to Denver—but he was in luck. There was one first-class seat open on the six thirty to LaGuardia. He gradually gathered up a bunch of Chicago newspapers. He was starved for newsprint. The New York dailies had been out on strike since August, and he'd had to get by with the *Journal* and, when he could get it, *The Washington Post*.

There was a seat over by the Reuters machine; he checked the news tape. The market's close had left it off sixty points on the week. The dollar was down to 175 yen. Christ!

He settled into the chair, ordered a drink, closed his eyes again, and realized that there was absolutely no way he could face going home.

Laurel was out when he called, so he left word with the housekeeper that he'd been held over in Chicago. He'd call again later, he said. It was one of those lies, he figured, that could do no one any harm. Then he called the office and spoke to Louise Healy, who had succeeded Flora Merrow on the fourth floor. The motherly receptionist confirmed that the suite in the Waldorf Towers was vacant that evening; Andy had her put a hold on it. He could tell from Louise's tone that his request didn't particularly surprise her; it must be all over The Firm, he thought, that there's trouble at home *chez* Warrington.

As he hung up, he felt a glow of anticipation; for the first time in months, he could spend a quiet unvexing evening without a quarrel or silent barrage of recriminatory stares. He'd order up a couple of drinks, a steak, and a half-bottle of wine, watch a little television, and try to crack this *Garp* book he'd been carrying around. The next day he'd go to the office, then go home, and no one would be the wiser.

We really ought to cut the cord, he found himself thinking. We're just fooling ourselves, Laurel and I. This marriage can't be saved. When Laurel had turned forty, and the child issue had to be buried forever, everything just went blah! Overnight, she and Andy found themselves completely out of sync. Every question was answered the wrong way. Every criticism, however mild, was taken as an opening volley, and so every skirmish became a pitched battle. It was as much his fault as hers, but he was helpless to deal with it. Every now and then he could get her out of the apartment, usually with Chickie along for moral support, but the evenings always began with too much to drink and then one of them would say the wrong thing and it would end badly, with loud words, a scene, everyone in the restaurant turning around. It was hopeless. They ought to be calling in the lawyers. He decided to have a word with Cleverley about seeing someone who handled this kind of thing.

On the flight home, he tried to read, but he couldn't concentrate. What the hell was he going to do about his brother? Jay was out of hand. Turning forty had blown his mind, too, and, like the doors in Bluebeard's castle, each of the five succeeding birthdays had inaugurated a new stage of outrageousness. Maybe it wasn't just age. Maybe Jay could feel Artie's hot breath at his back. Artie was careful not to upstage Jay, Andy knew, or at least he tried, which was hard for someone as smart and competitive as Artie. The Street's tunes were beginning to be piped by a whole new cast of players, guys who seemed to have come out of nowhere, so it was tough for the younger man to stay in the background. Especially when four afternoons out of five, Jay was loaded or stoned or freaked out.

It put Andy in a terrible position. Jay was clearly spinning out of control; on an absolute basis, the things Jay had said to people, the foul language, the incidents like the one with the girl in Purchases & Sales, he had become a walking embarrassment marked "Warrington." The real problem, in Andy's thinking, would come if he disavowed Jay, forced him to take a leave of absence, say. This would be perceived as a family split, a sign of weakness, an invitation to insurrection. Andy was under no illusions; Hanover Place wasn't as closely knit as it had been. Times had changed, it was hard to sustain tradition and still keep competitive. By his estimate, seventy to eighty percent of the houses with whom his father had done business were gone or under radical new management. Because of the Trust, he didn't, strictly speaking, have to worry about the family Bastille being stormed, but he knew that if he, with his mother, should have to use *that* club, the result might be a hemorrhage of people that could leave Hanover Place fatally weakened.

It was exhausting work, this tightrope walking, especially if home offered no rest for the weary.

When he landed at LaGuardia, it was almost ten. The evening was crisp and so clear that only the pale band of luminescence thrown up by the city made it possible to distinguish the topmost lights of the skyline and the lowest stars.

He arrived at the Waldorf, picked up the key at the front desk in the Towers lobby, and went upstairs. When he entered the suite, the first thing he noticed was that the living-room lights were on. As he dumped his briefcase and coat over a chair, he became aware of an acrid smell in the air, and that the television was on in the bedroom. Without thinking, he went in.

The room was lit by the television screen and by a single low-watt lamp on a table. Two figures were on the bed, a blond woman, body facing the door, astride a recumbent man; she was impaled on him, grinding away joylessly. Her head was lowered, her face averted, but Andy recognized Laurel at once; she seemed to be concentrating fixedly on the thick, flushed stalk that vanished into the patch of pale hair at her crotch, as if it was the sole knowable point of her universe.

Andy stood there, frozen, helpless, unable not to watch. Finally, the light admitted by the open door caught Laurel's attention. Still pumping up and down, she raised her face and saw Andy. Even then, for an instant that seemed infinite, Laurel continued to move with a desperate determination; she stared at Andy, at first dull-eyed with contempt, and then with an ugly, slack expression; she grunted loudly, as if feeling the onset of an orgasm, but then she saw in his face his knowledge that she was merely faking it, and all of a sudden she fell still and silent and hung her head.

"Hey, c'mon, Jesus, oh Jesus, I'm almost there," grunted the man beneath her. Then he went tense, obviously aware that something was wrong, and shrugged her off him. He raised himself on his elbows and stared dumbly at Andy.

"Oh shit!" he exclaimed. "Oh shit, oh shit, oh shit!"

And with that, Jay flopped over backward and began to pound the mattress with both fists.

Waiting for Eric Laszlo and Andrew to arrive, Lyda absently rearranged a vase of flowers. Stepping back to admire her handiwork, she reflected how sensible of her it was to have moved to the Carlyle. Life was so much easier here. The new apartment, two small suites knocked together, was much more convenient for an elderly, solitary woman than Sutton Place. She missed the curving stretch of the river, although here she was on a high enough floor to look south and west across the sweep of Central Park to the concrete forests of midtown and the far shore of the Hudson.

She moved across the room and squared the pretty little Boudin beach scene that Howland had bought her. It brought back memories of Deauville; 1963, as she recalled, with the de la Fontaines. Everything she owned, everything and everyone she encountered, was just another Proustian teacake: a repository of memories.

For all that, she wasn't a prisoner of time, she thought, not like so many people her age, who hid in the past like a cave. She kept active, did a certain amount of charity work, worried about The Firm, and continued to visit art galleries, adding to her growing stock of images of Manhattan. She had a whole floor at the Manhattan Storage warehouse now; in 1976, she'd installed racks, had the place painted and climatized and properly lit, so that it was no longer just another windowless floor in a looming brick building, but more like a museum.

She had avoided the obvious traps and temptations. She hadn't made her widowhood into a religion, her life into a shrine, the way so many women she knew had. She did not manufacture busywork to sponge up her days: she did not toy at decorating, or selling apartments, she didn't flee to Palm Beach or Hobe Sound or Newport to lie in wait for a suitable widower. She knew she was something of a local monument, thanks to Chickie, but his natterings to gossip columnists were harmless, and she understood without rancor that C. C. Fenton's access to Lyda Warrington had proved to be a boon to his decorating business.

Not that Chickie wasn't useful to her. Thanks to him, she received early warning of what and who was rising in the city. Keeping in touch was one way of keeping from growing old between the ears. Besides, New York was New York, and there would always be anxious people seeking to rise, some, like Sunny Miles, agreeable, others merely pushy, but it was well to keep them "in inventory," as Andrew described it, against the day she might find a way to put their social anxieties and ambitions to practical use. Look how well Brooke Astor was doing for the library and the zoo.

She walked through the living room, to take a last look at her table. Her eye caught her own reflection in the cheval glass that stood off to one side of the archway that gave on the dining room. She and that mirror had been through a lot together.

She paused to evaluate herself. In her time, she'd bought clothes from all the great designers, from Poiret to Bill Blass and Oscar de la Renta; still, for dressing a woman of a certain age—and seventy-eight (well, for another two months, seventy-seven) had to be considered a "certain age"—there had never been anyone to hold a candle to Alix Grès.

She leaned closer and looked herself in the eye. You were quite right, my dear, she thought, to let your face do what it would. Too many women she knew had let their faces and Heaven knows what else go under the knife. Lyda's regimen was simple: she kept out of the sun and she drank three glasses of milk a day; in two years, she'd be eighty, but she was still straight as a stick.

The table, set for three, looked fine. Most of her things were in storage; two tables of six was now her absolute limit, so she'd only kept what she needed, favorite things, like the Meissen bluebirds she alternated with large Ming bowls as centerpieces. Sunny Miles was mad about those birds.

I'm really developing a soft spot for Sunny, Lyda reflected. Probably just an old woman's crush, but only time will tell.

Sunny made a tremendous fuss over her, and hung on her every word. It was nice to have a protégée, a surrogate daughter, now that Laurel seemed hopeless and Miranda was beyond her mother's comprehension. Sunny was very decorative, with a figure to die over, but she was also a quick study and a good listener, and she had a good eye. Right now, of course, she was still in that stage of development when it was a bit too much just plain shopping and not enough real connoisseurship and dis-crimination, but enough time and tutelage would redress that balance. If you weren't born with them, these things took time and trial and error to acquire. People like Laurel might sniff at the way Sunny snatched things up from the table, turning plates over to examine the makers' marks, wanting to know where this came from, or that. Well, let them sniff! Sunny had more than her share of compensating qualities. Lord knows she seemed to make Morris happy, although as Andrew pointed out, happiness in Morris's case seemed these days to be a relative reduction in grumpiness.

"Is everything all right, Mrs. Warrington?" It was Bruce, the young houseman she'd hired away from her favorite catering firm.

"Just fine, Bruce. Everything looks lovely."

No doubt about it, she thought, one of the few changes in the city since the war that really has been for the better was letting homosexuals out of the closet. They could be difficult and shrill, and the things they got up to, my word, but there were so many things you simply couldn't beat them at. Look at Chickie.

She heard the intercom in the kitchen buzz, and a minute later the doorbell rang. Lyda waved off one of the waiters and went to the door herself.

"Eric, darling."

"Lyda." They embraced, then, still grasping each other by the upper arms, stepped back.

"Can it really have been two years?" he asked.

She thought he looked shorter, with a bit less hair, and all of the crookednesses with which the war had marked him seemed somehow to have become more pronounced. He found her unchanged: marvelous, distinguished, irreproachable.

"It has indeed, you naughty man. Where have you been? Andrew says you don't like us anymore. Come and sit and tell me everything. You don't mind if dinner's a bit on the late side? Andrew's been held up downtown."

She led him into the living room. "Champagne? Two, then, Bruce, thank you."

When they were seated, he looked at her curiously. "I never thought to see you living in a hotel," he said.

"It's just easier, especially at my age. I'm an old lady now, Eric. Seventy-eight come New Year's. Do you think the century and I are carrying the weight of our years well?"

"You better than the century. And I? How do I look, now that I'm an old man?"

"But you're just a baby, just . . . what?"

"Sixty-six last April. Actually, I'm tired. These are difficult times—for Israel, for the Middle East, for the whole world, I fear."

"I know. Isn't it strange? I can remember when everything seemed . . . well, so *fixed*. Then it all started to fall to pieces. When Jack Kennedy was shot, I know I couldn't escape feeling that more than just the life of one young man had ended. I think Jackie sensed it, too; that's why she insisted on such a production for a funeral. It was for all of us, and I have to say that for once her rather showy instincts were entirely correct. Looking back, especially from all this distance, it seems to me that Jack Kennedy and his time was much more of a piece with my old world, the world Howland and I were married in, made our lives in, than anything that's happened since. Back then we seemed so in control, and not just of the world, but of ourselves. Nowadays, everyone seems to be flailing."

She thrashed the air gently to make her point. Then she raised her glass. "To you, dear Eric. Andrew tells me you're going to rusticate yourself in your beloved Alps. He's going to miss you."

" 'Rusticate'? Oh, I suppose so. I have a few years ahead of me, and enough money in the bank, to do what I feel I need to do: spend time at Tarasp—do you know the Unterengadin? No? Oh, you must come and stay with me, it's so beautiful. There are books I need to read, thoughts I need to have the time to think. I have my work for Israel; as time advances and memory recedes, its position becomes more precarious."

"Andrew thinks it's that you don't like Hanover Place anymore."

"I don't think *Andrew* likes Hanover Place anymore. I think he feels alone, encircled, rather like Israel."

Laszlo's comment produced a puzzled expression on his hostess's face, so he added: "It's, as you say, 'the flailing,' Lyda. It's not just Wall Street. America is confused, and if America is, so is the rest of the Western world. The world must have been this way in the fifteenth century, when Copernicus replaced Ptolemy. Not so long ago, America was the center of the universe, the sun, moon, and stars. Not only were you the greatest military power and the greatest financial power, but morally you sat at the right hand of God. Now, between the Viet Cong and OPEC and

Watergate, that trinity's been shattered, and you're having trouble picking
up the pieces."

"Good heavens, Eric, you sound as gloomy as my son-in-law Jerry. He
thinks everything's on the brink. Of course, by his lights, it all has to do
with Vietnam."

"Well, that's what a lot of people his age think."

"Oh, not Jerry! My goodness, no! Jerry thinks we didn't fight hard
enough, that it was God's wish that we save Vietnam from the Communists but that we let God down. He believes everyone who reviled the
war or ran away to Canada is bound straight for Hell! Anyway, this is
all too gloomy, but I must ask you: how do you think things are going at
Hanover Place? I have to warn you, my intention is to persuade you to
stay. Andrew needs you. In a way, you're the only family he has left to
stand up with him."

Laszlo smiled. "You flatter me. From a business point of view, my dear,
I shouldn't worry. We seem to be doing as well as anyone, or better.
Arthur Lubloff is a trading genius, and trading seems to be the wave of
the future. I'm not altogether comfortable with everything that's going
on, but that's quite another matter."

"So what is it that bothers you?"

"Well, if I had to put my finger on it, it's that I don't feel that it's,
well, as much of a *firm* as it was when I first knew it. The *idea* of
Warrington & Co. doesn't seem as strong, do you know what I mean?
Oddly enough, apart from myself and a few other old-timers, and Morris
is, as you know, utterly distracted with marital bliss and conspicuous
consumption, the only ones who really seem to think, well, *institutionally*,
are Andrew and Arthur, and they see things completely differently. To
Andrew, life and work are made up of relationships, which is only natural,
since getting along with people is a particular strength with him. As a
European, of course, my sympathies tend to run with Andrew. Arthur of
course sees life as one transaction after another."

"You haven't mentioned Jay."

Laszlo put a clawlike hand over Lyda's. "Must I? Jay needs help, Lyda.
Desperately."

For a moment they both sat without speaking. Then Laszlo brightened
and said: "I didn't come here to play psychologist. Tell me the gossip,
especially about the new Mrs. Miles, who's on everyone's lips. How did
they ever meet?"

"Through Sunny's sister Lucrece."

"The one who's married to Robert Marryat? A rather thin-lipped
woman with too much hair and a perpetually disappointed manner?"

"That's the one. I've not had her to dine, although if Sunny begged me to, I suppose I'd give in, but Sunny hasn't. I gather there's little love lost between them, rather like Andrew and Jay. In any case, the Marryats invited Max out to meet Sunny—this was a year ago—and he asked if he could bring his father along—poor Morris was still in the dumps after Miriam's death—and before you could say 'Jack Robinson,' it was a true *coup de foudre*."

"I see, and Morris, I gather, is utterly smitten?"

"He is—and a good thing, too, if you ask me. Eric, I've never told you this, indeed I've never told anyone, not even Andrew, but about a year after Howland, after what Morris or probably Miriam—she was still alive then; I've thought ever since that this was her final bit of mischief-making—anyway, after what had obviously been carefully calculated to be the absolute minimum decent interval, Morris came to see me. I was still in Sutton Place then, I remember. He wanted to be named chairman of the board and he wanted my backing."

"I don't believe it!"

"Well, in a way I could understand it. Morris *is* the senior down there. He has made an enormous contribution. Needless to say, he made those arguments himself, in a really quite eloquent and heartfelt manner. Seeing and hearing him now, it's hard to recall what a raw article he was when Howland and I plucked him out of the cage. Anyway, I heard him out, and then I pointed out that it is our name on the door, and that as long as there's a Warrington around to fill the post, although God help us if it comes down to Jay, that is the way things are going to be at Hanover Place. At least while I'm alive."

"All the more reason to be concerned about Andrew's state of mind."

"Absolutely. Of course, if the fates had been kind, I'd have three, possibly four sons down there, and heaps of grandchildren to choose from. But they haven't, and I just have to go from day to day, hoping, like Mr. Micawber, that something will turn up. In any case, that something is not Morris Miles. It was a standoff. I knew he couldn't leave; at his age, where would he go, to work for Billy Salomon or John Weinberg? Hardly. I also know Morris well enough to see that he's not an intriguer. Look how hard Miriam tried, all those years, and to what little effect! Still, it is a blessing to have dear Sunny to keep the old thing's mind elsewhere. You'd rather like her, Eric. She's got spirit enough for six, and is extremely respectful of her elders."

She looked at her guest closely.

"Eric, what's going on?" she asked. "I also know you very well, my dear, and there's something on your mind more than the general morale or the politics at Hanover Place. What is it? Something's bothering you about The Firm. Please—you must be candid."

"Is the name Leo Himelman familiar to you?"

"Indeed it is," said Lyda. "A loathsome little lawyer who was always hanging around the Mileses. Is that the one?"

"Himelman has a client named Lester Vivian. Does his name mean anything to you?"

Lyda shook her head.

"We've been doing business with him for the last five years," said Laszlo. "Bits and pieces of this and that."

"And there's something suspicious about him? Gracious, Eric, there're always new people popping up out of nowhere and making a splash on Wall Street. I thought that was what it was all about. Are you suggesting there's something shady about this man? Is he a con artist?"

"There's just something about him that makes me uneasy, Lyda, very uneasy. On the surface, there's nothing to go on, so that I look at myself in the mirror and see the face of a nervous old fool. But when I've made inquiries in Basel about the man, and in Geneva and Zurich, they've been met with a silence that I recognize from long experience. It has a particular quality: so thick and deferential you feel you can reach out and touch it, yet you can also feel a certain faint tremble of apprehension. It's the special silence the Swiss reserve for large sums of money, *very* large sums of money, of *very* questionable or shady pedigree. Right after the war, my cousin Jürg used to lapse into it whenever I asked him about certain code-named accounts. I rather expect if you mention the names Tshombe or Duvalier or Marcos in a number of banking offices along the Bahnhofstrasse today, you'd achieve the same effect. And yet as far as we at Hanover Place know, Mr. Vivian is merely the proprietor of a number of middling family businesses up and down the East Coast, and a reasonably active trader for his own account. Why are you laughing?"

Lyda was smiling and shaking her head slowly. "Oh, nothing really. It's just that history always seems to repeat itself. When I married Andrew and Jay's father, The Firm was involved in a piece of business with Joe Kennedy, and there were people going around saying Hanover Place might as well be working for Al Capone, and of course he wasn't, he was simply a very bright if ruthless and ambitious young man. Life doesn't change, does it? Have you discussed this with Andrew?"

"I haven't. It's only a suspicion, don't you see, and Andrew has quite enough to worry about without an old man like me raising Cain because the hairs on the back of my neck are tingling."

At that moment, the doorbell rang, and Andy arrived.

The talk over dinner avoided Laszlo's retirement. Within a few minutes of Andy's arrival, he grasped from his mother's tone of voice and something in her face that he would be wasting his breath to bring the subject up.

After Laszlo left, Andy poured himself a second brandy and looked at his mother. "Hopeless, eh?"

Lyda shook her head resignedly. "Certainly for the time being. Tell me, who's Lester Vivian?"

Andy looked puzzled.

"Vivian? Did Laszlo mention Vivian? He's a guy Max brought in, through Himelman. You remember the dreaded—and dreadful—Leo Himelman? Vivian's got a bunch of little businesses we've done work for. A couple of merger letters, a partial liquidation. A small private placement. Nothing earth-shaking. He does some trading through Artie."

"Eric seems to think there's something shady about him."

"If there is, I don't know about it." Andy smiled. "Of course, you could probably say that about any friend of Leo Himelman's."

He drained his snifter, got up as if he was about to pour himself another, thought better of it, and sat down heavily on the sofa. He looked wryly at his mother.

"I was in Chicago the day before yesterday. I decided to take a night off from World War Three and take an overnight at this suite Jay got The Firm to take at the Waldorf. When I arrived, guess what I found? My wife—in bed with another man. The other man was one Junius Morgan Warrington."

"Oh, my God!" Instinctively, Lyda opened her arms, but Andy sat where he was.

"I'm afraid that's the end of it, Mother." His voice sounded dead and factual. "Cleverley's gotten me a lawyer, an Irish guy who makes Himelman look like Learned Hand."

"Where will you live?"

"At the Emerson, for the time being. If it was good enough for the Klopper, it's okay for me."

He shook his head and grinned, but the corners of his mouth were downcast.

"I had a talk with Jay. It was not exactly rich in family feeling. Naturally, it was all Laurel's fault: she called him up; she got *him* drunk; she insisted on . . ." He broke off and looked at Lyda. "There's no point in going into the details. The bottom line is: Jay's taking a leave of absence. Indefinite, which means as long as it takes to detoxify: as the song goes, it may be for years or it may be forever. He's going out to Betty Ford, or Hazel-den—the choice is his—but he's going to be on a plane by tomorrow night. Billy T.'s going along to keep an eye on him. My brother may be entering his Dorian Gray phase, but the old charm's still there, and no one knows how to put the guard dogs to sleep like Jay."

"I had no idea . . ."

"We never do, do we?" said Andy bitterly. "On the other hand, perhaps it's a blessing. 'Good out of evil,' as the school preacher used to say. Can I get you a little something?"

Lyda shook her head dumbly.

"Now, Mother," Andy said calmly, "you and I have to have a talk. Do you by any chance remember an old photo from *Life*? It was taken just after a Japanese raid on Shanghai, I think—and it shows a little Chinese boy sitting naked amid the ruins, bawling his head off?"

Lyda replied with a puzzled nod.

"Well, that's me, except that this Chinese baby is forty-six years old and it's my life, not a bunch of pagodas, that's been reduced to rubble. My wife is sleeping with my brother. When I get to work in the morning, I feel like I should be wielding a chair and a whip instead of an attaché case. Half the stuff that's going on I don't understand, and no one in the shop who's over forty does either. Artie's just done a deal for a guy named Riskind where he bought a company for one hundred fifty million and only had to put up five million in equity. He's got another fish on the line called Herzkow doing what they call 'risk arbitrage,' which also seems to be played with no money down. He's got a kid named Kerry who he trades for that . . ."

"Is that the young man who tore down the old South Mercantile Bank and put up that ghastly building that looks like a lipstick case?"

"The same. Artie introduced him to the Cosmo Life and just for that he wrote us a check for two million for services rendered. I'll say one thing, these people don't mind paying fees; when I think of the way old Gessel used to jew Father down for the last eighth . . ."

He saw his mother's expression.

"Sorry. You're right. With Miranda on the loose, we other Warringtons all better watch our tongues, or we're going to have the Anti-Defamation League on our backs. What's gotten into her, anyway? Doesn't she get the message: half the money she's throwing into that loony church of her husband's is made for her by the likes of Morris Miles and Artie Lubloff?"

"We can discuss that later," said Lyda. "Go on about The Firm."

Andy chuckled. "In a way, it's all of a piece, Mother. Let me see how I can put this." He thought for a moment. Lyda sat silently, waiting.

"Okay," he said finally. "The Street knows what's going on at Hanover Place. They know who our connections are. They know about the kind of horsepower Artie and Jay've put together. Most of all, they know what a franchise we've got. We're still a class act, so whatever the game of the moment is, everybody wants us to play on their team."

He paused to let that sink in. Not that his mother needed any instruction on that score, they both thought.

"Now, what the Street also knows," Andy continued, "is that without the Trust to protect the family interest, The Firm's up for grabs. It's not the force of leadership that keeps things as they are. Jay wakes up in the morning with the equivalent of an ounce of booze or half a line of cocaine already up and about inside him, as it were, so every day he's less and less help. I'm generally thought to be out of touch with the times. We've lost people, mostly through no fault of ours, but there it is. We're a Lehman waiting to happen."

Lyda regarded him coolly, then said in a voice just as cool: "By 'out of touch with the times,' Andrew, I assume you're really saying your heart's no longer in it?"

"Don't get me wrong, Mother, there was a time I loved the business. Loved it so goddamn much it makes me cry just to think of it!" His voice sounded close to breaking.

"Just like I loved my wife!" he added in a desolate tone.

He wigwagged his hands in the air. "No, no, cancel that, forget I said it. Anyway, I loved it! Not because of the people, but because of what it seemed to me we were doing down there. Maybe I was wrong, maybe Father sold me a bill of goods, but it really did seem to my naïve little heart that what the business was about was something more than pushing pieces of paper around! It's like comparing the way J.B. used to talk about the oil business—like it was something precious and alive!—with the way Bobby does."

"Your father and I always worried that it wouldn't hold your attention," Lyda said. "Or your affection," she added faintly.

There was another silence, then she asked: "So, where is this leading, Andrew? Is this preparatory to telling me you wish to quit?"

He shook his head. "No, no, I can't do that, not now, not yet."

He looked across the room at a photograph of his father and shook his head again, slowly, evidently responding to some point his inner voices had raised.

He really is still a little lost boy inside, thought his mother, waiting to hear what he would say next.

Andy took a deep breath, then blew it out, like a weight lifter about to bench-press a thousand pounds.

"I saw Al Gordon in the Downtown Association the other day," he said. He paused. "He said to say hello to you." He paused again, obviously hesitant to raise what was on his mind. Finally, he added: "Al pretty much as said that if we were interested, Kidder would . . ."

"Sell out?" Lyda's voice was disbelieving. "You can't be serious."

"Look, Mother, it's not like I'm talking about doing a deal with a dump like Shearson. That's something else. Kidder; Morgan; Dillon, Read—those're our kind of people."

"I can't be a party to selling out Hanover Place. I won't be. And it shocks me that you might be!"

"Mother, it's just me left now. All alone on the firing line. I'm forty-seven, going gray; I'm tired; my wife has dumped me; I have no children. My brother's on his way to a drying-out tank. In the underbrush I think I hear the hostiles circling. It reminds me of Korea. At night, we used to hear them out there in the dark, getting ready to att . . ."

"How can you say that?"

"I don't know. It's just a feeling. Anyway, if I leave here tonight and a guy lurking in the elevator cuts my throat, you're going to have to sell. You're going to want to sell! I know you pretty well, Mother: you don't fancy the idea of Morris Miles running Hanover Place, do you? Or Max! The sight of them up there on the Platform would kill you!"

"There hasn't been a Platform for thirty years!"

"You know what I mean."

"Well, don't you be ridiculous! Nobody's going to cut your throat! You're just overtired. Jay will be all right, I'm sure of it. Eric assures us *he'll* be no further away than the telephone. You heard him yourself. As for Laurel, I'm sad about you two, but I'm afraid that's just spilt milk we have to live with. I'm sure it's as Jay says: he didn't know what he was doing. You know how he's been the last couple of years!"

She stopped to catch her breath. Andy just stared at her.

"You wouldn't quit either, would you?" she asked. She hated the way her voice sounded, tentative, defensive, pleading.

"It's not just me I'm thinking about," she added unconvincingly. She tried to bolster her argument by gesturing toward the photograph on the nearest table: Howland and Fletcher being presented a golf cup; Watch Hill sometime in the thirties, Lyda recalled; Howland would have been just about the age Andrew was now.

"No," said Andy in a beaten voice. His whole being seemed to slump. "No, no I couldn't do that, could I?"

His surmise had an abstract quality; he seemed to address a third, invisible person.

"Why don't you take a few weeks off?" Lyda said hastily. "You know, dear, anything you want to do with the Trust about changing the way things are downtown, I'm with you all the way." She brightened, her voice took on new life. "You could get away, don't you see? Leave the Laurel business to the lawyers. When it's gone this far, all that's left to fight about is money. Go to France or Italy or even to Double Dune. Somewhere where you can take long walks and think your way through things. Make a plan."

"Like one of your famous lists?" Andy's voice remained weary and gloomy.

"If you wish. Right now you're too close to the situation, and this thing with Jay has to be upsetting . . ."

" 'Upsetting'! Mother, for Christ's sakes! He's my brother, and he was . . . well, he was . . ."

"We both know what he was doing, Andrew, but that was then, and now is now."

Andy had to laugh. "That's a fine sentiment, coming from someone who's using the past like a baseball bat to beat me into line!"

Lyda relaxed. It occurred to her she had been so on edge she'd forgotten to smoke. She took a Marlboro from the cut-glass box on the coffee table and lit it.

Andy grinned at his mother. "While we're dealing with addictions, perhaps you should accompany Jay out west."

"Very amusing," said Lyda. "To return to the serious side of things for a moment, I really do think it wouldn't hurt for you to take a little leave of absence, given all that's happened."

When Andy answered, his voice, too, was grave. "Mother, I hear you, but I just don't dare. If and whenever I take a leave of absence from Hanover Place, you can rest assured it'll be for good."

He looked at his watch. "Jesus!" He jumped up, kissed Lyda, and went off.

She finished smoking her cigarette. What a hand You've dealt me, God, she thought. Two sons dead. The third a drunk and an addict. Sneaky, not stumbling though, the way their sort was taught to be. Jay rarely appeared intoxicated. It was in his thinking and doing that the booze, working on cells and synapses that were forty, no longer eighteen, did its work.

There were people who thought that to hold one's liquor—or whatever—marked a man and a gentleman more truly than anything. How ridiculous! It all started with the ritual of the eighteenth birthday, when with ludicrous solemnity, sons and daughters were invited to take that first drink in the presence and with the approval of their parents—as if they hadn't been stewed a hundred times already. The romantic, religious idea of liquor. How often she had seen her husband or sons cross to the cocktail table; she reflected that what they were doing wasn't so much making a drink as performing a rite, so that she half expected them to elevate the ice-beaded martini glass the way a priest elevated the Host.

And what about Miranda? The child had gone directly from being a raving radical to a raving fascist claiming to do God's work on behalf of the black, the poor, and the disadvantaged. In 1968, Miranda had wanted to string up anyone who had fought in Vietnam; now, ten years later, thanks to her husband, she was raging to lynch anyone who hadn't.

And then there was Andrew. Sad, beleaguered, isolated Andrew.

Her mind turned to a conversation she'd had the week before with Belle Seligsohn when they'd found themselves side by side at a lecture at the Morgan Library.

Belle was old New York Jewish; she liked to joke that she had "two Loeb quarterings." She was very well-informed but also very tactful. She surely knew, everyone in New York did, that Miranda had addressed a neo-Nazi rally in Chicago back in July; even if she hadn't, no one had missed Miranda's recent letter to the *Times* attacking the Camp David accords and the legitimacy of Israel. But Belle had said nothing. Everyone knew what Lyda stood for.

The lecture had been about Edward VIII. "Silly little ass," Belle had said as they were making their way out, "he came to dinner at Mother's back in 1928. Poor Queen Mary; I can imagine just how she felt. Night after night, staring at the ceiling, watching him trying to shirk the family business, wondering if the boy was second-rate to begin with, or whether she and his father either *hadn't* taught him the right things or *had* taught him the wrong ones."

Well, Andrew wasn't the Duke of Windsor. He wasn't silly, he wasn't an ass, but he was alone. How could Jay have done this to his own brother! Still, they had to go on, didn't they? Wasn't that the point of the whole enterprise?

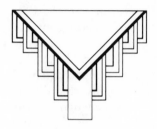

1980
SEPTEMBER

Andy was tired.

He had spent the previous ten days crisscrossing Europe trying to re-finance the Eurodollar debt of one of Hanover Place's proudest connec-tions, Tri-State Agriproducts. Hanover Place had done their first financing, $3 million back in 1947, when Tri-State was still a modest, downhome company called East Nebraska Fertilizer and Farm Supply Company, not an international giant booking sales in the high hundreds of millions.

Tri-State had been one of Hanover Place's stars; its drive and growth had seemed unstoppable until now. Faced with prices for petroleum, its principal raw material, that leaped ahead daily as OPEC continued to turn the screws, it found itself against the wall. Normally Andy wouldn't have gotten personally involved in this sort of thing; the usual form was for London to dispatch a team of its smoothest talkers across the Continent to pacify and conciliate nervous Euro bondholders. But Tri-State was flirting with default; drastic measures were called for, namely to wheel up The Firm's heaviest artillery to put across the ingenious exchange offer Artie Lubloff had devised.

It had been a tough week. At the end, in the sitting room of his suite at the Lotti in Paris, Andy felt pretty certain his efforts had come to naught. Everyone had been brimful of praise for The Firm's probity and technical cleverness. Everyone—the chief executive of Tri-State, his head of International and his top financial guy; the senior VP of Chelsea Trust, Tri-State's lead bank; Andy, Dix Duncan, the number-two partner in Corporations who looked after Tri-State, and Hans-Peter Gernsheimer, who was co-head of Trading and Distribution/Europe—had given it his best shot. Eric Laszlo had been persuaded to leave the Engadine and fly into Frankfurt for the meeting with Commerzbank, where he still had the ear of the executive chairman, and to come on to Paris to see if he could sway the Rothschilds.

The presentations had been lucid, and staged in the most luxurious venues, with fine food and wines intended to soften the most callous lender's heart; the arguments had been convincingly phrased, the exhibits and charts enticing; the plan of modification was equitable and ingenious; Tri-State's prior record was impeccable and its outlook impressive—provided it got through its present rough patch.

Still, Andy was pretty well convinced they hadn't put it over. By now he knew the ominous signs well enough. The steel-rimmed men in Zurich and Geneva and Frankfurt and Dusseldorf and Brussels and Rotterdam and Milan and Vaduz and Paris had all listened impassively. At the end, they all shook hands noncommittally and said things like "Most interesting, but of course we will have to consider the position of our clients," in a way that left no doubt what they considered that position to be.

Funny, thought Andy, when this whole Eurodollar thing got going, everybody on the buy side wanted to show what a player he could be. It had been nothing but "we're in, we'll take, please circle us for . . ." in a half-dozen languages.

Now times had changed; the focus was elsewhere; everyone's eyes were on the Middle East, everyone wanted a piece of the Arab action, or at worst a foothold in the oil business. In the bar of the Richmond in Geneva, the Warrington team had run into a bunch from Lehman and Warburg's that was peddling an issue for a third-tier Canadian oil company. The Lehman guys told Andy the CEO they were squiring had been drunk since his company Gulfstream had left Teterboro, too loaded even to make it off the plane in Milan, but what the hell, they could oversubscribe this deal by a factor of five from a pay phone in the Zurich airport.

Well, that was how it went in this business. Andy tried to put the bravest possible face on things. The night before the Tri-State dog-and-pony show decamped, he took the whole group to dinner at Taillevent and to a show at the Crazy Horse, and—in a Wall Street version of keeping up with the Joneses—Hans-Peter saw to it that those so inclined were ministered to by some of Madame Claude's comeliest minions. The next morning, on a forlorn note of false optimism, the Tri-State people flew back to Omaha, the Chelsea Trust team to New York, and Hans-Peter and his team to London and the English countryside.

Andy decided to remain in Paris for a few days. There was no particular need for him to hurry back to New York. Business was slow; the market was stuck in a trough. He had nothing on the fire personally. To return to New York had no attraction. He was still living at the Emerson Hotel, where he had moved after separating from Laurel, and although hotel life depressed him, he couldn't seem to get himself to take a proper apartment.

The next morning, as he went out to test the day, his eye was caught by a poster in a travel-agency window: a small harbor, boats docked, VISITEZ LA NORMANDIE. It reminded him of his mother's little Boudin. Perfect, he thought. On weekends and in season, Normandy was called "the 21st Arrondissement," so overrun was it by Parisians, but now, in early fall, it would surely be deserted in midweek. He'd go to Deauville. He hadn't been there in twenty years.

He instructed the concierge at the Lotti to book him for three nights at the Hotel Normandie, and to arrange for a rental car. Crossing the rue de Rivoli, on his way to meet Laszlo for lunch, he paused to look back at the old hotel, and remembered the first time he had come here, almost thirty years before, with his mother and Miranda.

Nineteen fifty-two: the summer of Laurel and that pretty girl from Chattanooga. What would have become of her, he wondered. Married, children grown, hips spreading, skin blotched, splendid bosom saggy— the thought pained him. Gone a little shabby with time and age, like himself, like the Lotti: a little worn and out of date, velvets frayed and dusty, paint uneven, gilding dull. Still, there was no place else he would stay in Paris. It wasn't like the places Chickie shepherded his rich new decorating clients, people to whom their ability to pay was the only true validation of self. Chickie was always after Andy to change hotels.

"I know you can't stomach the crowd at the Plaza-Athenée," he'd whine, "but why not the Bristol or the Lancaster, Drew, or even the Ritz, for Lord's sake!"

"Can't do it," Andy would reply sarcastically. "I'm too old, too set in my ways. I leave the height of fashion up to you young chaps."

He was due to meet Laszlo for lunch at L'Ami Louis. Just before Andy left the hotel, Hans-Peter phoned to report that neither the British Coal Board nor the Credit Suisse was prepared to go along on the terms offered. Without either of those bell cows, the deal was dead. Hans-Peter was going to talk to Hanover Place at the New York opening and see what Artie's people could come up with now.

Over lunch, Laszlo listened sympathetically. He signaled the restaurant's owner to bring a second, consolatory bottle of the '61 Corton.

After the meal was finished, along with Andy's tale of woe, cigars, coffee, and armagnac were brought. Laszlo looked closely at Andy. "You really don't like the business anymore, do you, Andrew?"

Andy smiled. "You've been talking to Mother, haven't you?"

"Not really. Oh, I know she worries about you and The Firm. She's very aware of her responsibilities under the Tr . . ."

"I've told her not to worry so much," Andy interrupted. "She's too old to have to carry all that history around. The present's heavy enough as it is."

Now it was Laszlo's turn to smile. "I rather doubt Lyda will ever be too old to do what she thinks has to be done."

"She'd also kill the two of us for mentioning it," said Andy.

"I gather you're going through quite an internal struggle over Rule 415? Does that have something to do with it?"

Andy shook his head slowly, but his downturned mouth gave him away. The proposed "Rule 415" didn't sound like much if you tried to explain it to a layman, he thought: a lot of legalistic blather about how public offerings of corporate securities were henceforth to be registered and dis- tributed. But like "May Day" in 1975, when the Street's commissions were thrown open to negotiation, it drastically tilted the scales away from expertise in corporate finance in favor of the brute power of trading capital. As such, it threatened the very foundations of Wall Street investment banking—at least as Andy, and his father before him, had understood the business.

"Oh, I suppose it's on the edge of my thinking," he told Laszlo after a moment or two. "If 415 passes, they'll be out in Wall Street howling 'the relationship is dead, long live the transaction!' Corporate finance is going to be nothing but a series of block trades. I'm glad my old man isn't around to see it."

"How do you think you'll vote?"

"If I had my druthers, we'd vote with the *ancien régime*, as Max's friend Himelman scornfully calls firms like Morgan and Lehman. Morris feels the same way. Hell, Eric, to hear Morris talk, if 415 passes, it's the end of the American way of life as we know it. I can see his point: guys like Morris, or Dickie Bosworth, whose entire professional lives are invested in their connections and relationships, have got to hate it. I hate it, too, but if Jay and Artie and the Young Turks in the trading room want to go for it, I'm not going to turn The Firm inside out on the issue! You ought to see what's going on at Lehman; they've got a damn civil war on their hands!"

Andy knew he was being disingenuous about his own pragmatism. Sure, Rule 415 might be simply an alteration in the securities registration and offering procedure that brought competitive bidding to corporate finance, but it was more than that. You could see it by the sharp divisions it had aroused on the Street.

On one hand, you had the "relationship bankers" like Morgan, Kuhn

Loeb, and Dillon, Read, houses with longstanding, lucrative connections to blue-chip companies. Ranged against them were the players trying to buy their way in: Salomon Brothers and its ilk, houses short on historical couth and connection but long on money power, guts, and street smarts.

Thanks to the trading capabilities Jay and Artie had built up, Hanover Place could profitably go either way. He felt he owed Laszlo a better answer about his own thinking.

"Right now, Eric, I'm not sure what I think. The game's so different, and so are the people. Guys we thought we'd buried back in the sixties have risen from the dead. Everybody got so desperate in 'seventy-four– 'seventy-five, when things were really bad, so now the refrain is 'never again,' which translates into 'anything for a buck!' "

"What will happen in your opinion if Mr. Reagan is elected?"

"Who knows? You remember Chickie Fenton, my college roommate?"

"Of course."

"He's full of Hollywood horror stories. How Reagan would sell his mother below the bid price, as they say. To hear Chickie talk, if we elect him, we're electing a racist, a liar, an elitist, a homophobe, and a fool. According to Chickie, the guy finked for HUAC . . ."

"HUAC?"

"House Un-American Activities Committee. Back in the late forties, early fifties. The Hollywood blacklist. Chickie also claims Reagan sold out the Screen Actors Guild, where he was president, in order to get a better contract for himself. Mother's the funniest. We were talking about it the other day, and she said to me: 'You know, Andrew, I saw a Ronald Reagan once before, before you were born, before I met your father. He was called Warren Gamaliel Harding then, and he was elected President my next-to-last year at Wellesley. He was handsome; he spoke well; he looked and sounded more American than Buffalo Bill—but he was so shallow it made a thinking body ache! I had seen plenty of vapid, vacant men in my time, but this was shallowness of a transcendent kind. He was playing a part other men had written for him, and he was cheerful and good-looking. Back in 1920 people were depressed, don't forget, they wanted a change that would cheer them up, make them feel better; any-way, when Harding's cronies got their man in the White House, they just sat right down as bold as you please, and started to divide up the country.' "

Both men were silent. Then Andy said: "But what can you do? The prime's going through the roof. Inflation's still out of control. This lunatic in Iran's got our embassy, and the guy in the White House is worrying about who's booked for ten o'clock on the tennis court! What the hell is one to do?"

Another pause while the two men pondered the question. Then Andy grinned and said, "Of course, there are pockets of light relief. You heard J.B. Marryat's running for the Senate?"

"I did."

"He's got religion, J.B. has. Just like my little sister, except J.B.'s deity has the initials R.R. Anyway, he resigned from M-Oil last spring to campaign in the Texas primary, and I don't know if you saw it in the papers, but the first thing Bobby did after taking over as chief executive was to sell the company's reserves."

"Is nothing sacred?"

"Apparently not. Some of those wells have been pumping for thirty years. Still, Bobby got close to thirty dollars a barrel discounted for the oil. He says he's going to keep his powder dry for a while, put the proceeds in T-bills. According to Bobby, over the next few years, it'll be cheaper to find oil on Wall Street than in Texas, smarter to put your drilling budget into oil company stocks than in the ground."

"What do you think?"

"Eric, I really don't know. Bobby may just be right. What I do know is, and perhaps this is the best answer to your original question, the idea kind of turns me off. The whole Street kind of turns me off. I'm finding it hard to keep interested, which in any business is the kiss of death, I guess. I mean, Bobby says he intends to find his new reserves in the financial statements of other oil companies and everyone at Hanover Place gets excited, you can practically see Artie's people sharpening their tom-ahawks, and it sort of leaves me blah. I can't help thinking what it was like back in Texas when I went down there in 'fifty-three. Maybe I should have stayed—or become a schoolteacher!"

Laszlo smiled sympathetically and called for the bill.

There is something irresistibly satisfying about a resort that is only days past its high season. A seductive bittersweet melancholy hangs in the air; faint echoes of the clamor and vitality of the season mingle with foreboding that empty months are on the way, but the shutters have not yet gone up in either minds or shopfronts.

Andy loved Deauville. He relished his solitude, drew it close around him like a blanket. He threw open his windows to the cool, damp breeze off the Channel and slept better than he had in years. He was well taken care of. The hotel was virtually empty; besides, people who wait on other people have an instinct for character—they can tell someone who sees another person standing before him from someone who sees just another cipher dancing to the jingle of coins.

Andy was quickly identified as being of the first category. Warringtons reflected a certain standard of behavior; Andy needed hardly to speak a dozen words to barman, waiter, and chambermaid before the word was out that the genial, square-faced American with the easy smile and the curious white streak running back from his graying left temple, was someone it would repay to serve well. So he was pampered. A barrel of oysters was sorted through in the kitchen to find the half-dozen choicest. When he left the choice of wine to the sommelier, he was brought the best values on the list, not cheap, but not priced to draw the last sou from his wallet.

The morning of his second full day, he awoke (surprisingly late for him) to discover that overnight the weather had turned from faintly hazy to crisp and clear. He decided to walk over to Trouville for lunch; his old wound ached slightly, but it was a matter of only a kilometer, two at most, and an agreeable day for a stroll.

The streets of Deauville were quiet; the branches of the big Paris and London shops were closed and there were few people about. He looked in at a bookshop, bought the *Paris Herald* and *The Financial Times*, examined the books on display, was struck by the elegance of the Pleiade edition of Proust, which reminded him of his old India-paper Oxford Shakespeare, briefly considered, and dismissed, the idea of having a go at *A la recherche* . . . in French, and went on his way.

Wednesday was market day in Trouville. The broad quay between the dockfront and the Boulevard François Moureaux was packed with stalls and carts selling everything from "farmer" Camembert to sneakers. Andy ambled through the market, then crossed the boulevard and found the restaurant.

The restaurant Laszlo had recommended was engagingly elegant: painted shepherds and shepherdesses cavorted around mirrors set in creamy lacquer walls richly yellowed with age. The place wasn't crowded. Andy ordered lunch and a bottle of Sauvigny and scanned the *Trib*. The usual boring stuff: the polls had Reagan well ahead of Carter; a painting by Jasper Johns had sold for $1 million, a number that made Andy shake his head; in Poland, a new workers' movement called "Solidarity" was raising all sorts of hell.

His lunch came. He abandoned the newspaper and devoted himself to his starter: a heap of the tiny gray shrimp for which the region was famous.

He was making his way merrily through the shrimp, idly observing an elderly French couple a few tables over feeding scraps to a small coffee-colored poodle perched on a chair, and thinking to himself that of all the so-called civilized people on earth, the French had the best relationship with their dogs, when the door to the restaurant opened and a couple entered.

The man and woman who were shown to the table next to Andy's were by any standards what one would call a handsome pair. The man was lean and wolfish, very elegantly got up in a tweed suit. From the soft brown trilby in his hand, from his haircut, and from the man's general demeanor as he looked around the room, Andy knew him to be English. A moment later, the man's pale gray eyes settled on Andy for an instant; from the faintly supercilious smile that fleetingly crossed the thin lips, Andy knew he in his turn had been marked as American. He couldn't escape a tiny thrill of antipathy. Instinctively he sensed that the other man automatically disliked all Americans.

The newcomer's wife was a handsome, dark-haired woman whom Andy judged to be in her middle-thirties. She was smartly turned out in a tweed jacket and gray trousers. She had long, sharpish features, not unlike her husband's, with a prominent nose and perfect pale and roselike English skin. Her mouth was broad, and when she smiled at the waiter, she showed a strong set of teeth. In a way, she reminded Andy of his mother, the Lyda of the photographs from the late and middle 1930s, when she was about the same age as he guessed this woman to be. Her face was less resolute, however; her expression seemed tempered by resignation. There came to mind something Chickie had once said of a visiting duchess; Andy could hear his old friend's chirpy, bitchy voice: "It's a look I've seen many, many times before, dear boy. There's only one way a woman can come by it honestly, and that's a minimum of five years' marriage to a genuine, grade-A English shit!"

Andy for some reason couldn't stop looking at her; he examined his plate, the décor, the other diners in the restaurant, but against his will his eyes kept returning to her. Once he thought he caught her looking at him in the mirror. He fidgeted with his book and papers, called the waiter over and ordered mineral water, examined the chandelier, and looked at her again.

It didn't take the Englishman long to notice. "I say, old boy," he said in a stagily languid voice, "if you want her, I'm sure we can work something out. What'll you give me?"

"I beg your pardon?"

"American, is it? One of our beloved transatlantic cousins?"

To uninitiated ears, the Englishman's bantering tone might have sounded agreeable, but Andy heard the nastiness all too clearly. "Whatever makes you happy," he replied, and made a point of directing his warmest smile at the Englishman's lady.

The Englishman grinned. "I call that one up for you, old boy. I say, care to join us for a coffee? Never does to be alone in a place like this, not that a chap can't get into a mess of trouble across the water in Deauville. Been to the casino yet? Of course, it's not Las Vegas, not the tit-and-bum you Yanks fancy, but a damn good shemmy table most times of year, especially when the wogs are about!"

He sat and watched Andy struggle to move his chair around.

"Of course, now it's as dead as dust. What brings you here at this season? Hotels lowered their rates?"

Andy didn't answer. He put out his hand. "I'm Andrew Warrington." He felt as if he had been thrust into a drawing-room comedy and was reading lines.

"And I'm called Simon St. Walden. And this is me lady wife Rachel. I mean that literally, old boy. The lady's a Lady, hah, hah. Lady Rachel St. Walden. Only and best-beloved daughter of Lord and Lady Rieffscher and the center of me universe and the apple of me eye."

St. Walden uttered the last in a mock-Cockney accent; he smirked unpleasantly at his wife.

"How do you do?" said Andy. He felt perfectly at ease. Like most Americans, there had been a time in his life when the mere glance of an Englishman would summon up feelings of the most abject inferiority. No longer.

She let her hand rest in his briefly. She had very long fingers. It seemed to him that when her eyes met his, they lingered for an instant longer than necessary.

Rieffscher . . . Rieffscher, he thought. The name means something. Of course: the founding family of Duke and Green, which had "High Street" stores the length and breadth of Great Britain. A kind of British Macy's.

"*Garçon*," St. Walden called, "*trois cafés, deux calvas*." He turned to smile at Andy, and then said, "And mind you, good calvados now, none of that stuff you serve the bloody Americans!"

Over coffee, they felt each other out. St. Walden was in the horse business, acting as bloodstock adviser to a clientele that included Dubai sheikhs, Greek shipowners, and Texas oilmen. He was in Normandy looking over the yearling crop in anticipation of the October sales. In the course of his disquisition on the state of the French thoroughbred market, he let slip a number of derogatory comments about the clients who were presumably keeping him in the style to which he so obviously felt himself entitled.

His wife said little. It seemed clear to Andy that Rachel St. Walden had come to terms with the life she found herself living, but even so, her serenity in the face of her husband's crude arrogance seemed not only remarkable and admirable to Andy, but downright erotic.

After three calvados, St. Walden lost interest in the subject of himself. Out of the blue, he wheeled on Andy and asked pugnaciously: "You wouldn't be one of the Warrington Warringtons, would you?"

"Depends what you mean by that."

"You know. Top of the Wall Street table. In younger and more foolish days I put in a year at Lucas's in the City. All they ever talked about was Warrington's. Or 'Hanover Place,' that's it. You one of them? Come to think of it, if your name is Warrington, and you're the age you look to be, you must be *the* Warrington. The Warrington of Warringtons, the Warrington of that ilk, heh, heh."

Without waiting for Andy to comment, St. Walden turned to his wife and said, "Think of it, darling, *the* Warrington."

He turned back to Andy.

"I've met your brother Jay, old boy. Grand chap, as I recall; met him at the White's tent at Ascot a few years back. How is he? Quite a naughty one, that lad!" He looked at his wife. "Remember, darling, that American I told you about who kicked up such a bloody fuss at the Clermont?"

"He's fine," said Andy. "He's behaving himself." Which was true. Jay was being a very good boy—three Alcoholics Anonymous meetings a week and never out of the vigilant sight of Billy T.

"Pity," said St. Walden. "Damn few of the old sort left. Everybody's a bloody jogger nowadays!" He gave Andy a large wink. It was clear that henceforward whatever Andy might say, it would be his family's money and position that the Englishman would be hearing.

"You Wall Street boys are all supposed to be very go-ahead," St. Walden continued. "So what brings a busy chap like you to this dull backwater?"

"I need a rest—and I have something to do. Tomorrow I'm going down to St. Laurent, to the American cemetery. I've got a brother buried there."

"I hear it's very beautiful," said Rachel St. Walden. She had a throaty, careful voice.

"So they say," said Andy. "I've never seen it."

"You wouldn't like a passenger, would you?" she continued. She turned to her husband. "You don't mind, do you, darling? You're off at the crack of dawn with Tassos to look at the yearlings, and I really don't fancy sulking about the hotel all day."

"Of course not," said St. Walden.

They separated after lunch, agreeing to reconvene at the Normandie for dinner. The St. Waldens were off to see a *haras* and invited Andy to join them, but he declined. His leg was beginning to hurt, which meant dampness somewhere out over the horizon, and he thought a nap was in order. Andy watched their enormous Daimler vanish down the street and waited on the sidewalk until the taxi the restaurant had summoned appeared to take him back to Deauville. It was only when he stretched out on his bed that he realized he was in the grip of feelings he hadn't felt for a very long time: not since that night, long, long years ago, when in the dark of a shipboard stateroom he'd writhed and ached for love of Laurel Hopewell.

After the powerful feelings of the afternoon, dinner was something of a disappointment to Andy. St. Walden dominated the conversation, talk- ing first about horses, which bored Andy stiff, then disparaging his clients, which Andy found unseemly and unprofessional, punctuating his mon- ologue with loud calls for more wine and snide asides directed at his wife. Eventually, he became quite drunk, and lapsed into a moody silence.

Making his way back upstairs at the end of the evening, Andy stopped in his tracks at the recollection of an instant during dinner, an interval so brief it might have been a hallucination, when he had seen something in Rachel's face. He had been looking at her; in the dim background of his awareness, her husband raged about some injustice that had been done him at Goodwood; she had been unaware of Andy's scrutiny, eyes fixed on her plate. Then it had happened: for a moment, not more, her face lost its usual look of patient resignation, as if a mask had been stripped from it. It gave way to a desperate, lonely vulnerability, an expression made almost unbearably poignant by Andy's sense that he was being invited to share her despair, that she was reaching out to him, for him.

In his life, such moments had occurred two or three times before; he could remember them long afterward, those unseized epiphanies filed un- der "what if . . ." and "if only . . ."

He continued upstairs, but it took him quite a while to get to sleep.

The next morning, he breakfasted in his room, not wanting to run into Simon St. Walden in the hotel dining room. When he came downstairs at the appointed hour, Rachel was waiting near the entrance. The day was overcast, with a freshening damp breeze off the channel. The *huissier* said it looked like rain.

They drove slowly down the Normandy coast. The signs along the coast road bore famous names, but famous for different reasons, making up an odd mixture of fiction and history. Names signifying war, genius, honor, the death of kings. First, Cabourg—Proust's "Balbec." Then Ouistreham, then Arromanches, and finally the invasion beaches: Sword, Juno, Gold, Omaha, beyond them Pointe de Hoc and Utah beach. Arrows pointed to the inland towns: Caen, Bayeux, St. Mère Eglise.

The doorman's apprehensions about the weather seemed ill-founded. By noon, the day had turned bright, only a few scattered whitecaps broke the calm surface of the Channel.

He told Rachel about how Dee came to be buried in the military cemetery.

"The Germans buried him near Hannover; fortunately, they kept meticulous records, but it still took us until nearly 1949 to locate the grave. Then, you know how it is, there was a lot of waffling and red tape, so he lay where he was buried until the middle-fifties. Then, a year or so after I got out of New Haven, Mother heard about the plans for the cemetery here at St. Laurent, so here we are. There's another young man buried here, the grandfather of one of our runners, and I promised him I'd take a picture of the stone."

Nothing had prepared him, either of them, for the impact of the place. When he first passed through the gate, down past the visitors' center, and saw the diagonal rows of white marble crosses interspersed here and there with stars of David, the breath stopped in Andy's throat and he drew up short. Rachel, a half-step behind, put up a hand to avoid bumping into him. It rested on his shoulder. Just as involuntarily he put his other hand over hers, to secure it, to keep it there.

It took them a while to find Dee's grave, but finally here it was: a simple marble cross on which was carved Dee's name and rank, his unit, the date of his death, and state, New York. The boy buried next to Dee on the right was a Jewish infantry corporal from Massachusetts; on the left a captain of Rangers from Idaho, of Norwegian extraction by the sound of the name; behind, an unmistakable name, an airman, also from New York. Andy stared at his brother's monument; the air seemed to tremble with the beating wings of might-have-been and he wondered if the woman standing at his side heard them, too. There was a moment when he almost turned to her and called her "Mother."

After a silent minute or so, he shook his head, and looked over at Rachel and smiled. "Sorry," he said.

She smiled back reassuringly, but he could see her eyes were wet.

"Let's go find the Miraflores boy's marker," he said. For reasons he would never be able to explain to himself, not for the rest of his life, he felt that by coming here he had squared an account on which some small balance remained due, that he was now settled in full for those nights in Korea when Lex and Dee had stood at either side and kept him alive.

"So long, guys," he muttered softly as he turned away, and he swore he could hear spectral voices answer back: "So long, sport."

They lunched at a small inn that turned up on the road inland. They had decided to head for Bayeux to see the tapestry.

Over the meal they told each other their life stories—or part of them. Rachel was one of *those* Rieffschers, all right. Her father wasn't Lord Rieffscher, the head of the group, but he had earned his own knighthood for his work in molecular biology. Her mother was half-Irish, half-Italian, a cellist who had played in the London Symphony.

When she finished, Andy looked at her frankly. "I'm going to ask you something you may find insulting. If you do, don't answer, and I'll drive us back to Deauville in stony silence."

He paused; she looked at him expectantly. This is the moment I ought to notice that her eyes have tiny green flecks, he thought happily. But they don't.

"Your husband doesn't seem very nice to you. I don't get the feeling you're crazy about him. From what you've told me, you have plenty of money. Why don't you leave him?"

She took a contemplative sip of her red wine, wiped her mouth, and smiled at him. "I'm English, don't you see?" she said good-naturedly. "We're not like American women, who pack up one day and leave home and husband to become stockbrokers or estate agents or what have you! That would be very un-English."

She took another sip, then added, with a naughty glint in her eye: "Of course, what we will do in an absolute flash is pack up *for* someone, but these days, when most of the men one meets are pansies, it doesn't seem as easy as it used to be. Why didn't you leave yours?"

"Patience, I expect. Patience and forbearance, my deadly virtues. I stay put; I do what I'm told."

Another bottle was brought, and they took another crack at the cheese tray. Andy talked about himself and his work. She listened patiently, seeming to know what he was talking about. He gathered the ways of the City were not Greek to her.

"I should have tried being a poet," he said, with a soulfulness that surprised him with its genuineness. "I don't know, I got off the track somewhere. Not that I had much choice. Do you remember that old movie *Four Feathers*? The boy on the stairs confronting all those fierce military ancestors staring dourly down from their frames? That's me. Except instead of cutlasses and the like, mine brandished stocks and bonds."

He shook his head, then went on. "Sometimes, it seems to me that my family tradition is like a pawnbroker. It's got my life locked up back there with the fur coats and wristwatches, and I can't seem to raise enough to redeem it."

He drank some wine.

"Not that I knock the past, mind you. Hell, I've become such an old sentimentalist, I can't look at a line of Dante without feeling a wrench. I was in Florence about thirty years ago, and I was in love, and, oh, what a moonish youth I was!"

"With whom?"

"It doesn't matter, does it?"

"No. Do you often read Dante?"

He grinned. "Not as often as I'd like you to think I do," he said.

She smiled back, then suddenly looked at her watch. "Goodness, I think we'd better get going. We're supposed to dine with some Texans tonight, and apparently those people consider dinner at anything later than seven positively obscene."

"I'll ask for the check."

She got up from the table. "I'll just go to the loo, then. See you outside."

When he had paid up, Andy rose and went out into the lobby of the small hotel where they'd stopped for lunch. Rachel was leaning against a pillar, arms crossed on her chest, looking into space. The sight of him seemed to startle her.

"Ready?" he asked.

She looked at him levelly, then came across the room and stood close to him, and said: "I hope you're not going to think me forward, but I asked at the desk if they had a free room and they do. I don't think I can tear myself away from you. Not now, possibly not ever."

He said nothing. He couldn't. He wasn't playing for time or anything. He was simply struck dumb in the face of the feelings that had come unleashed within him, like cargo loosed in the hold of a plunging ship.

"Well?" she said. "You do want me?"

"You know I do."

He felt he ought to say more, and started to, but she cut in. "Please, please don't make a speech. I, we, daren't hesitate, don't you see. I've never done anything like this in my life, but something tells me if I don't now, right now, right here, with you, my chance will never come again. And yours either. Please—before I lose my nerve!"

It was late afternoon of the next day when they got back to Deauville. They spent the night in Caen, in a bigger city in a better hotel than the one in which they had first made love. Like a summer sky after a fierce storm, their first twenty hours together, by turns given up to passion and quiet conversation, had been scrubbed clean of any doubts and misgivings.

When they got back to the hotel, Rachel spurned Andy's offer to come in with her to confront her husband. He saw the car put away, and went for a walk along the seafront. It had turned chilly during the afternoon. The boardwalk was deserted, the restaurants closed. A mist blew in off the water. He felt edgy but lighthearted.

After an hour, he felt it would be all right to go back. When he got up to his room, she was sitting on the bed reading the morning paper.

"And . . . ?" he asked, moving toward her.

"Leopards do not change their spots," she said.

She rose from the bed and embraced him.

"Nor shits their price," she said. "Simon wants a million pounds."

Andy kissed her again.

"A bargain at twice the price," he said to Rachel, beaming like a love-struck schoolboy.

She looked at him with mock severity. "That's exactly what Simon will tell his chums," she said. "I can hear him now in the bar at White's as the congratulatory Bollinger goes around one more time."

She screwed up her face, put on an exaggerated upper-class English accent, and produced an astonishingly accurate visual and vocal imitation of Simon St. Walden. " 'Well, I say, chaps, if you think about it, I got a bloody sight more for the bitch than I damn well would ever have got at Newmarket! Heh, heh, what, what!' "

Then Rachel returned to her normal voice. "There's only one thing I insist on," she said.

"What's that?"

"Well, I feel that I should show myself to be a modern, what you Americans call a 'liberated' woman. I think it's only fair that on this particular matter, therefore, we go 'dutch' as I believe you call it."

And dutch they were. Three months later, in January 1981, on Andy's fiftieth birthday, they were married in a London registry office, attended by her parents and his mother and younger brother and Chickie Fenton. The absent Creedmores sent a telegram and pleaded the press of church business, but Andy told Rachel otherwise.

"Mother tells me Miranda's absolutely mortified that I've gone and married someone Jewish," he told Rachel.

She took the news with equanimity. Her new husband had long since told her all she needed (and wanted) to know about his pentecostal sister and brother-in-law.

For his birthday, Rachel gave Andy a case of '66 Mouton-Rothschild, a half-dozen Charvet shirts, and the news she was two months pregnant. Seven months later, Nathaniel Howland Warrington was born in New York Hospital. Lyda at last had the grandson she craved; Hanover Place finally had its next generation.

JANUARY

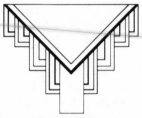

lad only in a pair of black bikini underpants, Sunny Miles sat on the edge of her bed.

"He isn't that bad, really he isn't," she repeated to herself over and over again, like an athlete psyching herself before a big match, except that at this moment, the match at hand for Sunny Miles was her first date with Norton Herzkow.

He really *wasn't* that bad, she thought, not when you considered that according to Max, he was worth $25 maybe $30 million, most of it made in the last two years, since the market exploded back in August '82. Maybe he wasn't the handsomest stud Sunny had ever seen, but there'd been worse, too, and never a one with anything like $25 million.

Why, even her late husband's estate, not that it meant damn-*all* to her, not the way it was set up, had come to barely half that much, after you took out for taxes and hospitals and such. Hard to imagine, Sunny reflected; Norton Herzkow had made twice as much in eight years on Wall Street—although as Max said, anything before '82 pretty much didn't count—as had poor old Morris in the sixty-odd years he'd beavered away downtown.

It had been just over a year now since Sunny's rapt administration of her once-wifely duties had been broken into by the sense that something wasn't quite right.

She had been pumping away on top of Morris, when suddenly she got this chill or something, and she raised up and saw that what she'd thought were an old man's huffs of excitement were in fact groans of pain, and that Morris's eyes were rolled back in his head and his skin was turning gray.

By the time an ambulance could be summoned, Morris was almost gone; he died the next morning, sixty-seven days short of his seventy-eighth birthday. His funeral two days later at Temple Emanu-El was rated by connoisseurs of such things as among the top ten of the last quarter century; the names filling the temple were judged every bit the equal in prominence and aggregate wealth as those who had turned out for such titans as Gustave Levy and Salim Lewis. Calling at the Miles apartment later, Lyda embraced both Sunny and Max and told them how impressed she'd been with both the service and the attendance.

Morris's death should have signaled the opening of a breathtaking new chapter in his widow's life. Instead, when the curtains were drawn aside, the expected golden door proved to be of bronze, at best, and the vistas it disclosed were empty and arid.

For one thing, Morris's will, drafted by Leo Himelman, proved to be, as Himelman snickered to one of his partners, "the modern legal equivalent of a medieval chastity belt."

Sunny had expected to be rich, to be able to move to a chic Fifth Avenue address, which Chickie Fenton would do up for her in a manner befitting the widow of a Wall Street grandee. She had anticipated ample funds to entertain, travel, and accessorize her life with the best the world offered, no matter the cost, to shop the New York, Milan, and Paris couture as aggressively as any woman on earth.

These expectations were shattered by the terms of Morris's will. Sunny had known her husband to be pathologically jealous, as older husbands usually were, and she had watched her step, perhaps subconsciously aware that if the actuarial tables meant anything at all, she'd have a second chance at what she thought of as "real living." Someone as wrapped up in the present as she was could hardly be expected to foresee that there existed legal means for extending jealousy beyond the grave. Morris had seemed so accommodating, so indulgent, and so affectionate. Had someone told Sunny that Morris had actually once dropped his guard so completely as to confess to his bridge table, over five diamonds doubled and vulnerable, that "no Argentine with a stiff penis is going to come along and get my money," she would never have believed it.

Yet that was how it turned out. The terms of Morris's will would not have attracted a Puerto Rican, let alone a dashing Argentine. Sunny was bequeathed a lump sum, but hardly enough to finance her grand Fifth Avenue dreams. The income she would receive from a series of trusts might make her a star at Saks and Bergdorf's, but would not put her in the front row at the Paris and New York showings. The worst part was, if she remarried within ten years, she'd lose every-thing.

A less determined young woman might have done something foolish or hasty. Sunny was made resolute, however, "by her ambition, and by her awareness of her ignorance and her lack of background." These were Lyda's words, uttered to Rachel in a voice periodically filled with kindly amusement and genuine affection.

An intimacy had grown up between Lyda and Andy's new wife, which Sunny resented. Sunny hadn't liked Rachel to begin with. Rachel made her nervous, in the way that people do who seem to take altogether lightly the things for which another person is willing to kill. When the baby came, that only made things worse; Lyda was ga-ga over her grandson. Oh, she still had time for Sunny, but that was all, and on Sunny's terms not enough.

It was worse than losing a mother, Sunny thought. *Archetypal* wasn't a word Sunny would have known to use, but someone who did might have pointed out that to Sunny Lyda was every archetypal figure rolled into one: doting, dependable mother; attentive, reliable schoolmarm; pa-tron, mentor, and guardian. To have her drift away was almost unen-durable, but Sunny was a coper, and her need to get on with life helped stifle the disappointment.

She got up from the bed and went to the window. Across the street she saw a glint in a darkened window and knew that the two young boys who lived over there were peeking at her again. Well, boys, she thought, y'all have you a good look. She fondled one breast and slid her other hand inside her panties, coolly aware of the riot of sensation these gestures would cause across the way.

She turned back into the room and opened her closet. She walked in and inspected the racks. One was entirely devoted to black apparel, wid-ow's weeds by St. Laurent and Chanel, Bill Blass, and Oscar de la Renta. Now that a year's passed, she thought, I can get some real clothes, start to dress up again. She pulled the closet door shut and inspected herself in the full-length, double-width mirror. Like her sister Lucrece, she was on the dark side for a blonde, with big brown eyes and skin that took a tan easily. The big difference, Sunny thought, is that even with what I've been through, I've still got the light of life in my face, while Lucrece is just an old sourpuss who looks like she's sucking on a lemon most of the time.

She hooked her thumbs in her underpants and slid them down, stepped out of them and took stock of the rest of herself. No doubt about it, Lucrece got the short end when these were passed out, she reflected, critically examining breasts and legs; or *this*—turning halfway to check on her behind.

She was pretty sure her date for the evening wouldn't have seen anything like her. Sunny had decided that now that a year had passed, and she was officially out of mourning or whatever, it was time to shit or get off the pot, which meant that unless he turned out to be horned-toad repulsive, Norton Herzkow in the course of the evening was going to be shown some new things, and have some new things done to him, and probably even be shown how to do a few things he didn't know he had in him. If it worked out right, Sunny thought, ol' Norton is going to wake up tomorrow a new man; I'm going to give him the greatest gift a woman can lay on a man, the illusion that when it comes to sex and pleasuring a woman he always had it in him to make Warren Beatty look like chopped liver, but all it took was the right woman to bring it out. From such an illusion, she knew instinctively, significant blessings might flow, in Herzkow's case potentially $30 million worth, which was about at what she budgeted her dreams.

Sunny Miles had met Norton Herzkow ten days earlier, a year and a day to the hour after Morris's death, at the reception Irene Gessel and Max Miles had thrown at 10 East 77th Street following their wedding.

Now there was a marriage made in heaven, thought Sunny. Of course, a lot depended on how you defined the purposes of marriage, which in her view was mainly a question of two people working to help each other rise in life together. In Max and Irene's case, it was kind of a chicken-and-egg thing. Irene was already about the most powerful P.R. and lobbying person in the country, but there wasn't a woman on earth that didn't benefit from making an alliance with a man with the right connections. Irene was sending a lot of business Max's way, Sunny knew, so much so that even Andy Warrington couldn't ignore him anymore and had to put him on The Firm's executive committee. Irene had something like fifty of the top two hundred companies as clients, and thanks to her, a good dozen or so of these were now doing their financing business at Hanover Place. Of course, Sunny had heard Max complain, most people said it was because of Artie Lubloff's reputation as a financial miracle worker, someone who could raise money out of thin air, or get it cheaper, who could instinctively find pollen for exactly whatever financial bee was buzzing around in someone's bonnet. Max liked to think it was his smooth-ness, and Lord knew he had the gift of B.S., especially now with Irene writing his scripts and introducing him around Washington. Back after Morris's death, when she and Lyda were still seeing a fair amount of each other, Sunny had asked the older woman what she thought. "It's just something in the air, dear," Lyda had said. "An age that can take a Ronald Reagan at face value is certainly foolish enough to do the same for a Max Miles."

Irene had put her next to Herzkow, and Sunny had exercised her special powers. This was not the first time in her life that she had seized on the practical possibilities inherent in sex. All her life, people had talked of her as promiscuous, expressed in rather rough East Texas synonyms, and she was perfectly well aware of it, but mostly it was just something she did, most of the time innocently. Men found her sexy. They flattered her, took care of her, and it seemed to be the most natural thing in the world to repay their flattery and attentiveness with the shiniest coin at hand, namely her body and some things she could do with it, things that came as natural to her as kicking a football did to her cousin Heber who got a scholarship to Tech. Sex wasn't something that burned inside her, like some awful itch that had to be scratched.

Men kept after her; she couldn't help it. Why, back a year ago, with Morris not minutes dead, when the doctor had come out to tell her and Max that their husband and father was gone, and she and Max had held each other the way people do at such moments, she'd felt her stepson get hard against her leg.

Of course, Max was famous that way, and for a moment after Him-elman told her about Morris's will, scarcely able to keep the gloating out of his voice, she'd even considered Max as a way out. That would have been too much, even in New York, marrying your own stepson!

Norton Herzkow seemed a good compromise. He might not be glam-orous, never would be, but if he wasn't Robert Redford, he wasn't Leo Himelman either, all scaly and red-faced, with big old ugly blotches; the richer and more important Leo got, the worse he seemed to look. Norton, she was teaching herself to think of him as "Norton," was sort of like a blank blackboard, except instead of chalk she would use all that money to write on it. She could make something of Norton, and not just in bed, although that was where it would have to really get going.

He called a few days after the wedding to ask if maybe she'd like to have dinner sometime, and she said yes, and then he asked where would she like to go, and without thinking she'd said how about Le

Cirque, and then there'd been this pause, and she knew at once that she could have him if she wanted, because here was a man who could bet millions of dollars on a stock without blinking, but was scared shitless of calling a restaurant for a reservation. So she'd said in the next breath, why don't I take care of making the reservation, I'll call Sirio, and she sensed that he was as grateful for that as for anything she might show him later tonight when just the two of them were alone.

Sunny knew most of what there was to know about handling restaurants. Lyda had taught her about that, just as she had tutored her about linens and menus and what jam and bath salts to buy and all those things. From Lyda she learned to distinguish those decorators—like Chickie Fenton—who really had taste, and those who prospered because insecurity loves company, who attracted clients whose own taste might be no worse than their own. Lyda, with Chickie's help, had schooled Sunny in the complex relationship between cost and value, helped her understand when and where inexpensiveness had a special cachet of its own, and when and where it did not. But it had gone further than just sopping up Lyda's lists and little tricks: like when Chickie redid the guest rooms at Double Dune, Lyda insisted on spending two nights in each of them, "Just to see how they 'work,' my dear."

Sunny missed the old intimacy, but she could understand Lyda's involvement with her new daughter-in-law and grandson. And it wasn't as if they weren't still friends, she and Lyda, wasn't as if they didn't talk on the telephone two, three times a week. Lyda hadn't written her out of her life; real ladies and gentlemen didn't do that to people. That was something women like Lucrece, or that model Roger Riskind had married, didn't understand; they were always trading in old friends for new as they scrambled up the ladder.

Sunny's friendship with Lyda had given her a training that now deserved to be exploited. Morris had been sweet and attentive, but set in his ways. Four on Thursdays for dinner and bridge, roast beef on Sundays, occasionally new curtains or a side table: that had been Morris's idea of a life-style. Of course, he liked Sunny to look beautiful, so he'd loaded her up with clothes and jewelry, and liked to show her off in restaurants and at other people's parties, but that was as far as it went.

Sunny was ready to take the big step, to translate her rich grounding in theory into vivid practice. She was trained and ready to deploy a man's wealth at whatever level of discretion or flamboyance seemed appropriate. Had Morris left her a rich widow, that would have been one thing. He hadn't, so now she needed to find a man with real money, and—as a poet with whom Sunny was but faintly familiar had written—now Norton Herzkow had swum into her ken.

She threw open the closet doors, walked nude across the room, pausing to wave gaily at the blank-faced window across the way—I'll miss you boys, she thought—and went into the bathroom to begin her toilette. But two things I won't miss, she thought as she turned on the bath, are this dreary old apartment and this dreary old life.

1984

MAY

As the Executive Committee members took their places, Andy could tell from the atmosphere in the room that he was going to lose. When Jay entered the room, he seemed scarcely able to look his brother in the eye. Jay looked a little bleary. Is he drinking again? Andy wondered. He made a mental note to check with Billy T.

He watched Dick Bosworth grimly shuffle his papers with trembling hands, then look angrily at Max and Artie, who were talking in low voices over by the silver coffee urn on the sideboard. He could tell Bosworth was spoiling for a fight. The trouble is, thought Andy, I'm not—in fact, I really don't give a merry screw.

No, that's not true, he thought in the next breath. I can't let that be true.

Weird, he thought, that trouble should arise out of happiness, but there could be no other explanation for it. If he hadn't been so happy at home, so absorbed in the new life he and Rachel had built around their son, he would have sensed the trouble brewing at Hanover Place.

He knew the traditionalists in Corporations thought he'd let them down, that he should have stood up harder for their side of the business, carried their banner against the upstarts in Trading and Distribution.

Well, for one thing, whatever his sentimental attachments, his rational view of the business told him that the trading side was very much in the ascendant. It wasn't just blocks of stock bought and sold with institutions anymore. Entire deals—mergers and acquisitions involving billions of dollars—were being swung through trading power. Traders wrote big checks on the spot, and that's what it took these days to do deals. Klopper-like cleverness with spreadsheets no longer carried the day; that stuff was mostly window dressing. People like Bobby Marryat, or this fellow Ris-kind, whose proposal to The Firm was the subject of this morning's meet-ing, might style themselves managers or executives, but they were traders at bottom.

Then there was the inescapable fact that most of the really smart people in The Firm were over on Water Street working for Jay and Artie. As Artie had put it, when Andy invited him to address last summer's new hires, "When it's a tie game, with two seconds on the clock, we're the ones calling for the ball." Andy had found that a bit of an overstatement, although essentially correct, but when the Corporations people got wind of it, they were really steamed. Dick Bosworth had marched into Andy's office and with the courage of three lunchtime martinis had demanded to know, "How long are you gonna let these damn Jew traders run wild!" It didn't placate Bosworth when Andy pointed out that among the traders he so rudely characterized was one Junius Morgan Warrington.

He could understand Bosworth's chagrin. Corporations had always been Hanover Place's Holy of Holies. Now the center of the faith was no longer to be found in the old building, but over on the fifty-fifth and fifty-sixth floors of Kerry Riverfront Plaza North, where Trading and Distribution had moved in 1983. No doubt about it, a discernible shift in Hanover Place's internal balance of power had taken place, which the physical relocation of miles of wiring and tons of computer and telecommunications equipment dramatically confirmed.

Given how well his own life was going outside The Firm, this suited Andy just fine. Let someone else worry for a change.

Anyway, business couldn't be better. The Dow continued to roar and the merger business was going crazy. The Firm seemed to be able to raise money for any deal it chose to take on. Jay boasted that Hanover Place could lay its hands within minutes on the best part of a billion dollars, most of it from connections that hadn't existed five years earlier.

No one could quite put his finger on where all the money was coming from. There were many explanations: Volcker had printed too much of the stuff in '81 and '82 to cure the antiinflationary recession; money that normally went into hard-asset investment, mines, factories, inventories, was finding better returns in paper; America's benign political climate and depthless markets had sucked in half the floating capital in the world;

these Reagan deficits didn't hurt. Who cared, anyway? What mattered was that the money was there for the Street to play with.

All well and good: what concerned Andy was that as things seemed to get better, the worse they got. To put it another way, the richer people got, the greedier they seemed to become. For 1983, the thirty-six managing partners of Warrington & Co., Inc., had divided close to forty million dollars of income, or double what The Firm's *capital* had been just five years earlier.

It was a paradox that Andy had confronted before, but he had never made peace with it, and so it was small wonder that events seemed to outstrip him.

"I was trained to manage for survival and teamwork," he told Rachel. "How the hell do you expect someone like that to manage this kind of greed, where everyone's out for himself?" Then he amended his declaration: "No, take that back: the funny thing is, it's the guys making the money who seem to be playing for the team. It's the others who're looking out strictly for number one. Of course, these days guys like Bosworth haven't got a whole lot to do but stir the pot."

Inevitably, turf wars began to erupt, first small conflicts of personality, arising from competing claims for credit or compensation. Thankfully the early months of 1984 brought a brief lull, but by Easter, as things began to pick up, so did The Firm's internal aggravations.

A malign spirit must have seen to it that Dick Bosworth was right in the middle of the first eruption, when Bobby Marryat and M-Oil made a run at Pan-Texas Resources.

The deal itself was trouble enough for Bosworth. Pan-Texas wasn't a connection of The Firm, it banked at Paine Webber, which, as Jay put it, "meant that M-Oil started out no worse than three up," and so the Commitments Committee rejected Bosworth's vehement arguments against Hanover Place getting itself identified as a hostile In'jun in an industry with which it was so closely identified. It wasn't hard to sympathize with Dick; the people Bobby proposed to beat up on were Bosworth's buddies: men with whom he had hunkered down in duck blinds and whored with and swapped tall stories with for decades. But all that hunkering and whoring and swapping seemed to have put precious little in the cash register in the last year, and Bosworth's plea that "I'll never be able to show my face in the Coronado Club again" in the end hadn't counted for much.

Besides, everyone knew the real reason Dick's ass was really red was because Bobby Marryat hadn't gone to Bosworth and Corporations for guidance on a $730 million deal, but to Artie Lubloff and his people in T&D. As Bobby candidly told Andy, it wasn't a matter of taste; Bosworth and his people simply weren't "up to speed." They couldn't grasp the new strategies, techniques, and instruments being spat out by Artie Lubloff's computers and implemented by his cadres of soberly industrious young men and women.

Bosworth drank, and when he drank, he talked, and there were others like him, so by mid-April the word was out on the Street that Hanover Place was going the way of 1 William Street, dividing into two all but armed camps regarding each other with unmixed hostility across a no-man's-land of suspicion. One rumor differed from another only in the specific labels affixed to the belligerents: most of the Street characterized them as "bankers" and "traders"; at the Downtown Association and the Wall Street Club, it was said that the Jews had lined up against the Christians; in the City of London, it was "gentlemen v. players."

Andy himself had played an unwitting part in fanning the flames. Late in March, shortly before he and Rachel and Nat left for a week in Antigua, the question of The Firm's future space needs came up at a meeting of The Firm's Executive Committee.

An expansion into an additional thirty thousand square feet at Kerry Riverfront Plaza North had already been authorized for T&D. There seemed to be no foreseeable halt to the volume The Firm could do. The industry's business was running at three times the rate it had been before the August 1982 breakout, but Jay and Artie's volume had quintupled, thanks mainly to new "financial products" hatched in Trading and Distribution.

In the course of the discussion, Andy made the mistake of letting common sense speak up without reflection. "You know," he remarked, "I sometimes think it would make a lot of sense if we could put everything under one roof."

He could hear the sharp intake of breath around the table and realized he had uttered blasphemy. Still, it made Andy vaguely uncomfortable to have The Firm physically divided. *Out of sight, out of control*: those were words his father had drummed into him.

"I feel the way King George the Third must have felt back in 1775," Andy told Rachel. "I'm trying to rule this huge, unruly, oats-feeling colony across the ocean—in this case T&D over on Water Street. The tail's gotten to be about ten times the size of the dog."

He let it rest at that, as no more than a suggestion, and went off with his family to Mill Reef. On his return, all hell broke loose. A note had appeared in the real estate section of the *Times*, which stated that, "according to highly placed source," Warrington & Co., Inc., was contemplating a move from the location at which it and its predecessors had conducted their business since the end of the War of 1812 to a new financial complex being planned for the tip of Manhattan by developer Kevin Kerry."

The rumor was promptly and forcefully denied, but Andy nevertheless caught hell from all sides. He caught hell from within Hanover Place, he caught hell from his mother, who even at her age had boisterously picketed every one of Kerry's Manhattan sites, he even awoke one night convinced that he'd caught hell from his father and grandfather.

The culprit turned out to be Max Miles, assiduous courtier of journalists and anchormen. Thanks to Max, Warrington & Co., Inc., had the best press on Wall Street, and from that had come a stream of interesting and profitable new business. Max was definitely feeling his oats these days. His wife Irene had done wonders for his standing and his backbone. The time when he could be "taken out to the woodshed," was long past. Now he had a constituency within Hanover Place—"rainmakers" always did, at any firm—that made him immune to the usual disciplines.

Still, there had been nothing for Andy to do but to have a man-to-man talk with Max. Surely Max must agree that The Firm must put forward a united stand, one which had his, Andy's, full blessing as chief executive. Indeed, indeed, said Max, but of course much depended on what that policy was, and there, in view of his responsibility to *his* connections— Kerry Leisure and Development was, after all, the largest single source of revenue to The Firm—he would expect to be consulted.

Listening, Andy wondered whether Max really knew what he was saying. He could hardly believe his own ears. Notionally, Max did have charge of the Kerry connection, and First Penn Financial, and a number of other accounts that had come to Hanover Place in the last few years, but in each case the original contact had been made by or through Artie Lubloff.

Just like this fellow Riskind whose latest deal they were set to review this morning.

Dorothy Darling Foods, which Roger Riskind proposed to take over in a management-supported leveraged buyout, was the fifth-largest grocery-products company in America, exceeded in size and diversity only by P&G, Beatrice, General Foods, and Nabisco. Its revenues, profits, margins, assets, and so on were as intimate a part of the mental baggage of the Street's food analysts as the names of their children. According to *Institutional Investor*, DDF common stock was held by seven out of eight of the most respected investment institutions in the world. It did business in fifty states and a hundred and twelve foreign countries. It was, in a word, a paragon; in sixty years of tough-handed but benevolent manage-ment, it had become as quintessentially American as one of its own Ma Foster's apple pies.

To land Dorothy Darling as a client would have been a plum for any firm. For most of its existence, its outside financial work had been done by one of the Street's oldest and noblest investment banks. In 1983, however, the loss of five of its top executives in a plane crash had neces-sitated the importation of a new CEO, a hotshot divisional executive from P&G.

He made it his business to get to know the company and its top cus-tomers and suppliers. Among the latter were Lugen Trading, Inc., and Conservadores Fincas PLC, which brokered vast quantities of cocoa, sugar, coffee, grains, and vegetable oils to DDF's eighty-two plants around the world. The controlling interest in both of these was held by Sophir S.A., a Swiss holding company, which was in turn a creature of a Lux-embourg shell corporation whose shares were registered to a half dozen Cayman and Bahamas trusts of which the sole trustee was a Netherlands Antilles nominee for Lester Vivian.

A couple of months after the new CEO came on board, in January 1984, he was paid a call by Roger Riskind, for whom Artie had identified Dorothy Darling as a prospective target. In view of the fact that even if a market as riproaring as the present one had failed to value DDF at anything like its real worth, Riskind proposed, might not it make sense to consider a buyout organized around the incumbent management?

Tempted as he was by the sums Riskind dangled in front of him, the CEO was also a realist. Even at a substantial premium to the market, he pointed out, it would still take well over three and a half billion dollars to do the deal. Where could one expect to get that kind of money?

Riskind had smiled knowingly. A week later, DDF's chief executive was his guest in Madison Square Garden at a Ranger game, in a private box registered to South Harlem Federated Savings. While Riskind and the CEO watched the hockey game and chatted of this and that, in the dimly lit rear of the box Artie Lubloff reviewed the detailed financials that the DDF chairman had brought with him, including a half dozen sheets of confidential internal evaluations and projections that any analyst on the Street would have given his eyeteeth to see. At the end of the second period, Artie came forward, spoke to the other two men in low tones, and left. He hated hockey; it was a dipshit sport played by little guys, and if he got home in time, he could catch the Celtics versus the Sonics on ESPN.

Riskind was by now—to the absolute astonishment of anyone who had known him during his early days on the Street—being hailed as one of the coming titans of American finance. Prior to DDF, he had completed close to $10 billion of leveraged buyouts: twenty-two deals, each of which was a roaring success—at least according to the press releases circulated by Irene Gessel and Associates. His buyout profits had been supplemented with a few hundred million in greenmail and "white knight" takings.

Neither Riskind nor The Firm had ever come close to taking on a venture the size of the proposed DDF buyout, which was why it had come before the Executive Committee.

Andy didn't like Riskind. It wasn't that he was slick and boastful; most of the new players were. There was something vindictive about the way he went about his work; in Andy's opinion, people like Riskind were as much about getting even with an old-money establishment that they believed had treated them shabbily as they were about making money.

"The Jewish thing again?" he asked his wife.

"I'm sure that's part of it."

Perhaps that explained why Riskind and his sort put their money on display so aggressively. Ulla Riskind had been on the cover of *Sports Illustrated*'s swimsuit issue when she met her husband; now she was written about in the same tone as the Duchess of Marlborough. The Riskinds and their houses and possessions were inescapable; every time you turned a glossy page, there they were!

Rachel teased Andy about sticking up his nose.

"Don't use the word *vulgar*," she told him, "it makes you sound like every other garden-variety trust-fund snob."

She didn't accept his theory that the Riskinds and people like them were just asking for it by strutting their stuff so baldly. "They know perfectly well that homeless people don't read *Town and Country*," she said.

Andy looked around the room. Everyone was present. Might as well get this over with. He rapped his water glass on the table. "Might as well get going, fellows."

As the others took their seats, Jay came to the head of the table, leaned over, and whispered, "Hey, bro, remember what I told you last night: don't blow it now, you hear?"

On the way uptown the previous evening, Andy had told his brother of his doubts that the DDF deal would fly. On the basis of the summary memorandum Max and Artie had circulated, the numbers didn't appear to support the amount of borrowing that was necessary.

"Hey, bro, no problem," Jay said. "This is a Roger Riskind blue-plate special. His name's more seductive to the money boys than warm pussy to a spade. What Roger wants, Roger gets!"

"I suppose so. Still, where the hell does a guy like Riskind get this kind of dough? Ten years ago, he was peddling municipals for Morgan; today he pulls out his checkbook and writes out markers for fifty, sixty million."

"Liquidity, bro! Liquidity! Between Mr. Volcker and the 'eighty-one tax bill, there's so much money out there you wouldn't believe it. Give Roger a little credit. He got the picture early, made the right connections, if I may use the word, and got in bed with the big players. Hell, he's number-one boy at Bel Air Federated Savings and they're up to damn near eight billion in footings!"

That fact in itself bothered Andy. Somehow it didn't seem right for outfits like Bel Air to be playing the takeover game with federally insured deposits; all that meant was if a couple of these deals cratered, the tax-payers would pick up the pieces, although there was zilch in it for them on the profit side. Still, those were the rules, and you could play within them as long as they remained in effect.

He slumped in his seat and studied the back of Billy T.'s fat neck. He felt contaminated, as if he was being forced to breathe disease-laden air. The late sixties had seemed pretty excessive, and the late seventies—early-eighties, when everyone was chasing after rich Arabs, had been really seedy, but this was starting to verge on anarchy.

"Y'know, bro," Jay said, "if you don't like what's going down on the Street, maybe you ought to run to Momma? Between the two of you, you call the shots, so if you want to turn back the clock, make us into some kind of born-again Clark, Dodge, it's your football."

"I might just do that," Andy replied in a surly voice. I sound just like a goddamn six-year-old, he thought.

"Ah, c'mon," Jay said, "look, let's face facts. The day of the fucking boy scout is over, along with all those dinosaurs who used to hang out at the Racquet Club and talk like they cut their mouths on a beer can. You got to go with the flow, as the man says. For Christ's sake, bro, you're not some fucking candy ass who wants to live out his life tailgating it outside the Yale Bowl—or are you?"

The car slowed and stopped. They had reached Andy's building. He started to clamber out of the back seat. Jay put his hand on his arm.

"Hey, bro, look: everybody knows your mind's not on business. Every-body knows you're apeshit about Rachel and the kid, but, hey, bro, this is our fucking Firm, y'know, so for Christ's sake, don't blow it!"

Andy rapped the table again.

"Okay," he said. "DDF. Dorothy Darling Foods. Max, you want to carry the ball?"

Max took the committee through the memorandum page by page.

"At thirty dollars and change, the current price of Dorothy Darling somewhat underrepresents a consensus of Street estimates of the com-pany's true value," he concluded. "Roger Riskind proposes to pay forty dollars, which is in line with those estimates, as well as offering a thirty-three-percent premium over current market."

"So what's in it for Riskind?" asked Andy.

"Ah," Max replied with a sly smirk. "The fact is, DDF is really worth closer to fifty-five dollars a share, perhaps even as high as sixty."

"Now, wait a minute, Max. Let me clear up my semantic confusion. Apparently there's a difference between 'true value' and 'really worth'? Is that correct?"

"You needn't be supercilious, Andrew. This is a transaction involving several billion dollars—and upwards of one hundred million in fees, all in, to this firm."

"I'm not being supercilious. I am a touch confused. Didn't our invest-ment-research people recently put out a report that said, (a) that at thirty dollars the stock was in line with P&G and General Foods, and (b) that its upside potential was probably around forty dollars, so they were taking it off the 'Buy' list and making it a 'Strong Hold'?"

"Indeed," Max said, looking at Andy as if he was drilling him in the multiplication tables. "But those estimates were based on conventional accounting practices and failed to take into account what a new man-agement might do for the company."

" 'New management'? I thought we were talking about the same guys who've been running DDF for the last year?"

"Quite so," said Max, "but the disciplines enforced by an LBO are different from the conventions of running a normal public corporation."

With that, he launched into a recapitulation of familiar theoretical and conceptual arguments in favor of leveraged buyouts: "incentified" man-agers, operating economies, elimination of marginal operations. Andy had heard them all *ad nauseam*: the financial pages seemed chockablock every day with elaborations on these themes by business-school professors—most of them seeking consulting fees by saying what they knew potential clients liked to hear, or so he guessed.

Max continued in this vein for a few minutes. He's become a good speaker, thought Andy, watching Max make hypnotic little patterns in the air with his hands. Now and then he paused and lifted his eyes from the table to gaze off into space, as if concentrating on what God was whispering in his ear for repetition to lesser mortals.

When he finished, Andy repeated his earlier questions. Max regarded him as if he were a halfwit, and nodded to Artie, who produced a new set of papers conspicuously marked CONFIDENTIAL in red. He placed them on the table in front of him and looked expectantly at his uncle.

"Before we pass these around," Max said, "let me just run through the parameters of the deal again. The stock's selling at thirty dollars, and has been stuck there for some time, since, as is the case with many of these big stocks, the institutions are up to here with it. They're loath to buy more, which at a good price makes them extremely willing sellers, right, Arthur?"

Artie nodded. Well, thought Andy, this is the logical outcome of the
institutional binge we kicked off in the sixties.

"Now, there are, in round figures, ninety million shares of DDF shares
outstanding, is that right, Arthur? Multiply that by forty-two dollars,
which Roger is prepared to pay, and you have, in round figures, three
billion seven. Riskind says they can pull between three and four hundred
million out of working capital and DDF's overfunded benefit plans. He
has commitments from banks and other institutions for a billion, which
leaves a billion five for us to find for him."

"By my reckoning that adds up to three billion nine, Max."

"You'll recall, Andy, I spoke of substantial fees. To us, attorneys, other
firms will be involved on behalf of DDF and its public stockholders. These
will of course be capitalized in the transaction."

"I see." Andy turned to Arthur Lubloff. "And you have no doubts
about your ability to find a billion and a half dollars?"

Artie shook his head in confirmation. Max said: "Indeed, we have a
draft letter in the works advising Riskind that we are, quote, quite positive,
end quote, of our ability to secure financing."

"How much equity is in this deal?" asked Andy.

Max looked at Artie.

"We figure it'll take a five-percent cash equity," said the younger man,
"say two hundred million."

Andy rolled his eyes toward the ceiling in a mock expression of disbelief.
"Two hundred million to support a four-billion deal!" He shook his head.

"Hey, bro," said Jay, "that's all it takes these days, you know."

"The basement money'll come from Riskind," said Artie, "from us, and
we're also gonna get a two-point carry, from the DDF guys and some of
their big suppliers. Herzkow said he'd take twenty mil sight unseen. I
talked to him in Paris this morning."

Andy grinned. "You better button Norton up fast," he said. "My mother
saw him and Sunny in London last week. Whatever isn't nailed down,
she's buying. Plus you know she got him to cough up three million for a
pad at 835 Fifth, and I know what my old friend Mr. Fenton considers
a suitable decorating budget for a residence on that scale. Anyway, Sunny's
a nice woman, and she deserves to have a little fun for a change." With
that, Andy turned and beamed at Max.

Artie didn't appear to have caught the drift of this little sally.

"Okay," he went on, "then I can do easy five hundred big ones in
payment-in-kind paper with the mezzanine crowd, Bel Air Federated,
Prime Professional Life, a couple of guys in Grand Bahama, the Brunei
crowd. We may have to throw in a bunch of warrants, but that'll be
chickenfeed. For the eight hundred million on top of that, I've got commitments from my high-yield players: Tally, Kramer and Boyd, Young-

Dragon Partners, the usual names. Give me the green light, and I can circle this deal in fifteen minutes."

Andy found himself looking at the Shikler portrait of his father that hung over the Sheraton sideboard. What would he have thought about this kind of transaction, involving sums like this? His grandfather's portrait was behind him. Sometimes, when it got hot around the table, Andy imagined the two portraits conversing above the heads below, deciding between themselves what to tell Andy to do.

He returned his attention to the meeting. "Okay," he said, "fine and dandy. I just have a couple of questions which keep nagging at me. What I want to know is, how come Artie can do this deal like falling off a log? The coverages frankly look like shit to me. I don't see how the company can service its debt unless it sells off half its business. That bothers me in itself, because I don't like to think of us as liquidators, but I'm going to try to not let that influence me because I know it's a kind of thinking that's hopelessly out of date. Still, where's the money going to come from to carry this kind of debt?"

"I declare, Andrew," Max said, "you sound exactly like the late, la-mented Klopper. No one talks about 'coverages' anymore."

He looked at his nephew and nodded. Artie picked up the papers in front of him and distributed them. "I'd like these back when we're through," he said quietly.

"These," Max announced in a voice full of pride, "are the real McCoy."

While the men at the table studied the new material, Artie supplied an oral gloss.

"This is the inside game plan. It breaks out assets that can be sold or spun off. Plants to be closed and consolidated. Cash flows adjusted for overhead, operating economies, tax deferrals; they're gonna cut the shit out of the 'corporate' staff. Naturally, we'll be taking advantage of a bunch of tax breaks that only trigger when a company gets sold. The beauty of the 'eighty-one act is that it makes most public businesses worth more dead than alive. See, on line eight, you've got 'mirror subs,' as they call them, that'll shelter an extra thirty million of cash flow. Uncle Sam's in there doing his bit!"

Andy examined the new figures. At a glance he could see that cash flow was fully fifty percent higher than in Max's memorandum, and that the asset write-ups and disposals could support a valuation of close to eighty dollars a share, or twice what the insiders proposed to pay.

He looked around the table, then asked Max: "I assume these haven't been shown to the people being asked to part with their stock at forty dollars, although I have no doubt they were prepared on company time, at company expense, using confidential company information?"

No one said anything.

"This *is* a public company," Andy continued. "Who's going to look out for the stockholders?"

"The DDF board has First Borough Securities all lined up on the fairness letter," Max replied.

First Borough, thought Andy, now who the hell did they used to be? "And is First Borough working off these figures?"

There was an instant's silence, then Max shook his head. "Andrew, these are only *projections*! It would be irresponsible to give these out."

"I see," said Andy. He shrugged and asked: "Didn't I see in DDF's proxy statement that the guy running the company, Riskind's partner in this deal, so to speak, took down nearly five million in compensation last year?"

"Something like that," Max replied.

"And that wasn't enough?"

"Andy, a salary is one thing, entrepreneurial incentives are anoth . . ."

"Oh, fuck 'entrepreneurial incentives,' Max! The bottom line is the stockholders are being invited to fold their hands because the deck is stacked. A deck *they* paid for! Have you run this deal by Cleverley?"

More silence. Then Max said, in a low voice, almost a mumble: "Frankly, Andy, we're not using Auchincloss, Wharton on this one. This kind of deal needs special expertise. Auchincloss is good on indentures, that kind of stuff, Klopper-type problems. Himelman, Plaskow and Gold are representing us. Harvey Gold's on it himself. Riskind requested it."

For the first time, Dick Bosworth spoke up. He looked at Andy and said in a voice full of rage: "Damn it, Andrew, you're not gonna let this firm be represented by those ambulance chasers!"

"I resent that," boomed Max. "Leo Himelman is a close friend of many years' standing. Himelman, Plaskow and Gold is regarded as one of the top law firms in this city, and *the* firm on leveraged buyouts."

Andy looked at Bosworth. "Dick, let's deal with that issue when we come to it. Max, you are doubtless aware I have never been keen to have this firm represented by Leo Himelman, so that will remain on the table. Now, let's cut through all this. Is this a deal we want to do?"

No one said anything.

"Well, let me put it this way, and take first things first. What's in it for us, assuming we can raise the money for Riskind and the insiders to steal DDF from its stockholders?"

"I resent that," Max declared.

"Hey, Drew, c'mon!" It was Jay. "Cut out the 'steal' talk! This is the ballgame today. Everybody's doing it."

Max looked over to Artie. He stared at Andy without feeling, and said: "We get ten million if the deal doesn't go through, ninety-five million if it does. That's counting everything. Plus we get a couple of points on the equity line."

"By 'everything,' I assume you include the sale of our reputation and integrity?"

There was no answer to that. Andy started to say something, then suddenly, feeling awfully tired and out of hope, decided not to. He looked around the table. "We don't come cheap, do we?" he asked rhetorically.

He considered carefully what he should say next. It seemed to him there was only one realistic option. "Well, gentlemen," he said after a pause, "there it is. If I was really the boy scout I know some of you think me to be, I'd go to the SEC and tell them everything, but you've gotten us so entwined, I can see, that the whole ship would probably be dragged under."

"I take exception to that," Max said belligerently. "And as for the Commission, I wouldn't be so sure about how Washington would react. They're tending to leave things up to the markets to resolve, you know."

"Is that what you call it? Anyway, Max, I suspect you're right. You seem to be more in touch with the times than I am. Now, does anyone have anything else to say? Surely one of you must be wanting to warn me that if we pass on this deal, not only will someone like Drexel Burnham be ready, willing, and able to pick up the fallen banner, but we'll be such a laughingstock we might as well go out of business." He looked pointedly around the table.

"No last words? There must be some cliché you haven't thought of, Max." He wanted to sound sarcastic; he feared he only sounded bitter.

"Well, then, let us go forward. I'm going to let this go to a vote, which I will abide by. Obviously, I will reserve my personal options. Now, before you put up your hands, I just want you to look around, at these portraits for openers, think about what this firm has stood for. Max, you might take a second or two to think about Morris and what it meant to him."

He let his gaze come to rest on his brother.

"For Christ's sake, Drew," Jay exclaimed, "this isn't a public trust. This isn't the fucking *New York Times*! This is a business, that's all."

The vote was three-to-two in favor of doing the deal: Jay, Max, and Artie for, Andy and Dick Bosworth against.

After the meeting, Bosworth took Andy aside. "Andy, I'll be seventy-five next year. I stuck around out of respect for your father and your family, which includes you. But I can't handle this, not at my age. If I was twenty years younger, I'd take every one of those damn hebes and throw 'em out the window. They're going to ruin this country, just you wait!"

"Mother, put down the phone!"

Andy's voice was firm. Lyda replaced the receiver.

An instant before, she had announced she was going to call Archer Cleverley and set the wheels in motion for the Trust to take over the governance of The Firm.

"Don't you see, Mother," Andy said, "even if we use the trust to make me dictator, it's a self-defeating proposition? For one thing, I'm sure we'll lose a lot of good people."

Lyda looked at her son, then at his wife.

"Your father always said that was a bluff that had to be called. Has Arthur threatened to quit?"

"Nobody's threatened anything."

"Or Max? Good riddance to bad rubbish!"

"Mother, calm down, damn it!"

Lyda looked helplessly at Rachel.

"That's the trouble with you, Andrew. Always so dismissive."

"Andrew's not dismissing anything, Lyda," said Rachel. "All he's saying is that he needs time off to think things through. I have to say I can't begin to imagine how you expect your businessmen, of all people, to go through life without an occasional sabbatical."

"Mainly, my love," Andy interjected, "because the governing principle of American office politics is, 'out of sight, out of a job.'"

"That may be," said Rachel, "but I think it's a jolly good idea. Lyda, Andrew's *only* talking about nine months. Surely nothing drastic will happen at Hanover Place in that short a time."

"Oh, all right," said Lyda. "I suppose I'm being selfish. The three of you *will* be at Double Dune this summer?"

"Of course," said Rachel. "It'll give Andy a chance to know his son better."

"If he gets any closer to that little boy," Lyda said, "they're going to become one person. By the way, did I tell you Sunny Herzkow telephoned from Paris this morning? She was full of news. She was at the Duc de Blois' last night for dinner. So was Mrs. Riskind, apparently. Odd, how small the world is. According to Sunny, the highlight of the evening, or the low, depending on how you look at it, came after dinner, when, in front of *le tout Paris*, Mrs. Riskind asked the Duc how much he'd take for his famous ensemble of Palissy dishes, the ones his great-great-what-ever-it-is-grandfather was given by Catherine de Medici! Can you be-lieve it?"

"These days, I can believe anything," said Andy.

Lyda lit a cigarette and blew out the smoke contemplatively. She looked at her son and said: "You promise you'll come back?"

"I promise," said Andy. He looked at the two women. "Cross my heart and hope to die. Nine months, mother, that's all. Just to get my head clear. Now, how about some more of that champagne?"

Sixteen blocks to the south, Lester Vivian and Artie Lubloff shared a bench near the entrance to the zoo. It was a pleasant, breezy evening; at a quarter to eight, the western sky was still bright, slashed with heavy, deep pinks and oranges softened here and there by fingers of cirrus. To the south, a jazz band had set up shop in Grand Army Plaza and was pumping away at an amateurish reworking of Thelonious Monk. The upper stories of the Plaza, cream and oxidized copper green, reflected the dying light.

"I really think he's gonna quit this time," said Artie.

Vivian nodded; he stared up at the sky.

"He was steaming when he left," Artie added. "Really pissed. Andy never says much, but after a while, you get to know. He's not coming back."

"You really think so?" Vivian asked.

"I'll lay you eleven to five. It's a lock." Artie pondered for a moment. "He's sick of the Street, you know. Plus, he's totally browned off at Jay."

"Jay back on the sauce?" Vivian asked casually.

"Looks that way." Artie nodded sadly. "He's been pretty uncool on a couple of things the last week or so."

"I see," said Vivian. "How's the old lady going to react?"

"She won't do anything," said Artie. "You know these people, Lester. They don't even fight for what they already own! They could downsize The Firm and still make out like bandits. This kind of market, there's money for everyone." He shook his head. "It's really weird!"

"What is?"

"You and I, we won't play without a marked deck. These people, it's like they've pushed all their chips into the middle of the table without bothering to look at the cards."

"Perhaps they also think the deck's stacked," said Vivian.

Artie grinned. "Coming from you, Lester, I think that's very funny. Yeah, that's a real gas!"

The two men chuckled, then rose. Next to Artie's towering lankiness, the slender Vivian seemed almost tiny. They shook hands and separated. Vivian watched Artie make his way toward Fifth Avenue, right leg imperceptibly dragging. An amazing young man, he thought.

The pieces were all coming together. Working control of Hanover Place was the final, necessary element in the puzzle. Now he had nine months to utterly corrupt it, to cause it to change so completely that even if Andrew Warrington should try to come back with all the king's horses and all the king's men, he wouldn't be able to put it back to what it had been.

Lester Vivian was thinking his way through what Arthur Lubloff would have called "a high-grade problem." He was suddenly faced with the prospect of having to put a vastly greater sum of money to work in the world's legitimate streams of commerce and finance. By a multiple of two or three. Fortunately, the big accommodative outlets, the securities markets, cash-and-carry retail and food service, New York and Hong Kong real estate, were growing exponentially themselves.

The disparate enterprises for which Lester Vivian worked as *de facto* global coordinator of finance had recently introduced a new product. In four or five years, they were projecting it to account for close to fifty percent of its broad market classification, perhaps as much as $60 billion a year worldwide. It was as commercial a product as man's mind had ever hit upon. It sold for cash, had low manufacturing costs—which offset a somewhat antiquated distribution system—and required zero investment in marketing and advertising. The regulation to which it was notionally subject was hopelessly inefficient. Its demand demographics seemed virtually perfect.

Introduced on a limited basis earlier in the year, it had achieved consumer acceptance beyond anyone's wildest imaginings. Of course, it wasn't a conventional product, not a new type of cola, toothpaste, disposable diaper—more of a sensation, really. Unlike conventional market introductions, its promoters hadn't tried it out in conventional test markets like Portland, Oregon, or Hornell, New York. Its early test markets and focus groups were in Bedford-Stuyvesant, East St. Louis, and the Chicago projects, and in these it had in no time achieved unprecedented market penetration. It had been originally offered under a number of different, regional names, but the one that seemed to be emerging as the clear consumer preference was "crack."

The trouble, thought Lester Vivian, looking approvingly at the bright façade of the Plaza, is that with great commercial success came the heavy responsibility of investing the profits in a productive and legitimate manner. The thought made him smile.

Lester Vivian considered himself a technocrat of finance, a money manager faced with the same problems that confronted any man obliged to deploy large cash flows prudently and systematically. Had anyone confronted him with the proposition that he was merely the latest in a line of what the sensationalist press called "crimeworld comptrollers," that his ancestral line was not that of Graham and Dodd but of "Greasy Thumb" Guzik and "Abbadabba" Berman, that he was merely an up-to-date version of the latter, differentiated from those vocational forebears only by an increment of zeros, he would have been deeply offended.

Well, he had his scheme, and Artie Lubloff would be its linchpin. DDF was only the first step. Vivian envisioned a series of breathtaking deals, breathtaking in size and financial audacity and ingenuity, baited with breathtaking fees. In the thrill no one would think to ask where the money was coming from, how it was that a member of formerly obscure or marginal institutions was empowered to take $10- and $20-million chunks of highly speculative paper. With the sweet aroma of big profits in its nostrils, Wall Street wouldn't think to ask where all this wealth derived, because it wouldn't want to know.

Once DDF and a couple of other big deals were closed, the game would be afoot. Everyone would want in, would be calling Warrington's asking for a piece: pension and mutual funds, insurance companies, investment trusts, all strictly legit. A huge torrent of clean money would pour in, a universe of virginal cash so vast that the sums under Lester Vivian's management, enormous as they might be in the absolute, would seem no more than a handful of stars in a galaxy.

1984

SEPTEMBER

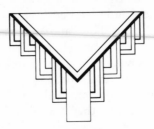

The poking in his ribs became persistent. Andy groaned and opened an eye to the sun streaming into the bedroom. He raised his arm over his head and looked up at his watch; J.B. Marryat's old Navy Hamilton read six forty-seven.

"Daddy!" Poke, poke. "Daddy!"

Andy examined his son standing by the bed. "Why, if it isn't good old reliable Nathan: Nathan, Nathan, Nathan Detroit! How are you? Did you have a good sleep?"

He reached out and hauled his son up on the bed. "Ooof! You are getting to be a very heavy little boy."

"Hey, Momma," said Nathaniel Warrington, age three and a half. The little boy reached across his father and speared his mother in the cheek with a forefinger, to remind her of his presence. Rachel—no morning person—moaned, shifted away from her son's probings, and slipped back into sleep.

Andy lowered his son back onto the floor and put his finger to his lips. He swung his feet over the edge of the bed; the stiffness in his lower back reminded him that he was fifty-three, no matter how youthful the song in his heart. He shrugged into a robe, took his son by the hand, and led him out the bedroom door.

"Go tell Maria that you and I are going to drive into town for the

papers and a real man's breakfast, and then we'll go look at the beach."
He patted Nat's bottom and sent him scampering down the stairs.

Thank God the weather's changed, he thought as he shaved. A big,
unseasonable nor'easter had howled in three days earlier; until last night,
there'd been no electricity at Double Dune except for the generator.
Branches and power lines were down everywhere; the lashing rains had
flooded the low-lying areas inland; closer to the ocean, Georgica Pond
had overflowed its banks and run up onto the Montauk Highway.

But they were okay, and Double Dune seemed not to have been seriously
damaged—only one big tree in front had gone down—and the beauty of
the morning seemed to make up for all the bother. As was in the nature
of storms, this one's violent passage seemed to have sucked every last
impurity and imperfection from sky and sea. Outside the bathroom window, the air was a bright, deep blue; beyond the dunes, the sea, once
violent and gray, ran steady and green and smooth.

Labor Day had come and gone, and Andy felt he could go to town
again. In August, when the summer crowds were at their thickest and
worst, he'd stayed away from East Hampton, not wanting to run into
anyone from Wall Street. East Hampton was stockbroker country; someone at dinner a few weeks ago had said that over twenty Shearson Lehman
partners had bought houses there in the last year.

Shearson Lehman: wow, Andy thought. Hard to imagine Lehman Brothers, a house once counted among the Street's most elite, being peddled to
a crummy firm like Shearson because its partners couldn't get along.

He washed his face with cold water and looked at himself in the mirror.
Amazing what just ten weeks away from Hanover Place could do, he
thought. The face looking back at him seemed essentially the same one,
in most particulars, that he remembered looking at for the last fifty years.
An intelligent face, cheerful withal, more optimistic than skeptical. A bit
worn—that was inevitable—but not dissolute like Jay's. The hair might
be all gray now, but at least there was still plenty of it. He fingered the
skin at his throat; the once-angulate lines of chin and jaw were now soft,
but the overall effect, he concluded, was "agreeably mature," and definitely not "run to fat."

As he turned away, he sneaked a final peek over his shoulder, and
reflexively sucked in his stomach.

Ten weeks. Could it only have been that long? Hanover Place seemed
part of another life.

Thank God it had gone as smoothly as it had. The Street and, more
importantly, The Firm's connections seemed to have taken the announcement of Andy's sabbatical at face value. As he told *The Wall Street Journal*,
"I need some time off to recharge my batteries and do some thinking about
our future down here." His administrative and executive duties would

be allocated to a *pro tem* office of the Chief Executive consisting of Jay, Max, and Artie Lubloff. He didn't need to add what everyone knew: that watching the proceedings, like an old hawk perched on a high limb, would be Lyda. To those connections who called, he assured them he would be available to consult, and that seemed to satisfy them; in the last ten weeks, the telephone had not rung once.

He guessed there were people at Hanover Place prepared to book a large wager that Andrew Warrington would never darken the premises again. He couldn't blame them. He had certainly given them that impression.

Well, they were all in for a terrible surprise. He realized now that he had made a mistake, that he should have stood his ground, fought on the spot, used the Trust and every other weapon to blow the sons of bitches out of the water. He had made the mistake, usually fatal on the Street, of gearing his own actions to surmises about other people's reactions. That was one of the things that had killed Lehman; after Bobby Lehman died, they all sat around trying to figure out "what Bobby would have wanted us to do." You might as well try to run a business with a Ouija board.

Ironically, it had been Jay who'd given Andy the clue. What exactly was *wrong* with places like Dillon, Read and Alex, Brown and Brown Brothers? Nothing. They'd found niches and exploited them. So long as you didn't care about getting your face on the cover of *Time* or your wife didn't need your business as a stepping-stone to a front-row seat at the fashion shows, the universe of money was now so big that there was plenty to go around. Whatever capital The Firm might lose by paying off people who left or were fired could easily be replaced. That was one blessing that this stampeding bull market brought with it.

It was a matter of "playing within yourself," which was the analogy Andy's father often drew between good golf and good business.

"Your grandfather never saw that," Howland used to tell his son. "He was always going for the pin, trying to carry the trees, attempting the impossible shot. Of course, that sort of thing's easier now if now and then you get to tee it up in the rough."

First and foremost, this business ought to be fun, thought Andy. The fees ought to be secondary. Whether Drexel was doing this, or Morgan Stanley that, or Bear Stearns something else should have no bearing on Warrington & Co.'s decisions. Competitiveness was all to the good, a necessary part of the process, but not an end in itself. Let it even be pervasive, but yet stop it short of becoming all-consuming. The urge to win had a way of turning into a kind of paranoia, a terror of being bested, which brought with it a terrific compulsion to cheat.

You could see it in the faces of the Wall Street types he hadn't been able to avoid this past summer. Anxious tanned faces arriving at parties and silently asking who's here, is this the right party to be at, am I too early or too late, are we overdressed or under? Petty social calibrations fraught with cosmic insecurity.

Well, he reflected, hard cheese for them, and no more of that for Hanover Place. We'll reestablish the distinction between adventurousness and outright thrill-seeking, take the heat off, let our people have some time to build lives of their own.

It would not go down easy with some, he knew. There would be some bleeding. Artie Lubloff might walk, and take some productive people with him, but you never knew what Artie would do. It wouldn't be all that easy for someone like Artie to move sideways.

Well, people would simply have to make up their own minds whether they would live with the new deal or not. Some would undoubtedly want a livelier atmosphere, something more in tune with the prevailing action. Some of Artie's people were pretty combative; they might flutter to the hot and gaudy flames of places like Drexel Burnham or Bear Stearns.

The main thing Andy intended was a precipitate withdrawal from certain types of business; he would winnow the list of connections, expunge the Riskinds and the Herzkows, resign as Kevin Kerry's investment banker.

Of course, Max Miles would have to go. Max was simply too identified with Riskind and the rest.

There would have been a time, thought Andy, when I would have thought twice about cutting someone like Max loose, not for old times' sake, but simply because I'd worry how he'd take care of himself. With Irene looking out for him now, there was no need to worry about Max.

Andy felt he could count on Jay. For practically the first time in their lives, Andy felt that he and Jay were part of the same family, that it was real between them, not just lip service.

Jay was full of remorse about what had happened. He'd even apologized, which wasn't easy for Jay, and said he'd give anything to have that vote back.

"Fuck the excitement of the chase," Jay had declared, "the thrill of victory, the agony of defeat. Hey, bro, let's not forget you and I weren't exactly small-time B.A."

" 'B.A.'?"

"Before Artie."

A noise interrupted his thoughts.

"Turn off that goddamn TV!" he called down the stairs, but his mood gave the lie to his voice. The September sun washed the room with warmth. He was in love with life again.

He found his son staring at the set. Garrick Utley was giving more details about Beirut. The body count was over 230 and rising.

Christ! thought Andy. He stopped to watch. These were Marines, these were his own!

When the news had come in the day before, he'd called the Pentagon, got through to the Corps Commander's office, and asked if there was anything he could do to help the families of these poor kids. They promised to let him know.

What the hell were the Marines doing there in the first place? Another one of Reagan's goddamn posturings, that was what. And Andy was sure when they started to bring the bodies home, Reagan would turn it into a photo event, pose beside tall stacks of coffins, weep silver-screen tears.

Maybe this bull market *was* Reagan's doing, as J.B. claimed it was. Of course, talking to him about Reagan was like talking to Miranda and Jerry about Jesus. When Andy had broached some pretty sharp criticisms of the administration's fiscal policies, said that it looked to him like the country was going broke, the senator had grinned, but his eyes had narrowed as if to say, Now listen up, 'cause what I'm about to tell you is God's own truth.

"Hell, boy," he'd boomed, "don't you know you ain't busted as long as there's someone out there'll lend you the money to keep goin'?" And as long as we keep 'merica the way it is, with free markets and stable politics, they ain't goin' to be no shortage of such folks, no way!"

Well, thought Andy, we shall see. He snapped off the television.

"Come on, sport," he said to his son. Nathaniel bounded toward the door.

Andy followed, full of love. The sight, even just the thought of the little boy, often made him shiver with affection. There were times he couldn't help wondering if, well, if he and Laurel had been able to have a Nat, might things have worked out differently? He didn't let such thoughts linger; the very notion was so manifestly unfair to his wife that it made him feel guilty.

As always, the local coffee shop was full at seven thirty. The place was a morning schooling ground: for the local movers and shakers, and for the pickup crowd, the guys that built the houses, put out the fires, laid the pipe, and filled the oil tanks. Andy picked up the papers, greeted Gus behind the counter and Bob at the register, and led Nat to a booth.

When his son set to work clankily sawing away at a sausage, Andy reflexively checked the "Business and Finance" briefs on the front page of the *Journal*.

The lead item was that "M-Oil Acquisition Holdings" was offering $4.7 billion for all of the voting stock of Pan Northern Petroleum in a hostile takeover bid. Damn, Andy thought, since Dorothy Darling Foods, these guys haven't drawn breath.

He followed the story into the inside pages. Pan Northern's incumbent management, it reported, had announced its intention to fight the bid vigorously. M-Oil's offer was expected to be financed through a placement of securities arranged by Warrington & Co., Inc. A Pan Northern representative had disparaged the M-Oil bid as "dreamtalk," declaring the securities being used to finance the offer were "junk which no self-respecting investor would put into a portfolio." M-Oil was relying on a letter from Warrington & Co., Inc., stating The Firm was "quite positive" about arranging satisfactory financing. The article concluded with a note that the Pan Northern offer was the third such hostile offer since the Fourth of July in which Warrington & Co. had taken the lead in advising the bidder and arranging financing. The writer recorded "the surprise of many on Wall Street that an old-line firm, known mainly for its conservatism and avoidance of the limelight, continues to participate so aggressively in high-visibility transactions which the financial and business community view with decidedly mixed feelings. Spokesmen for Warrington & Co., Inc., were unavailable for comment on the M-Oil–Pan Northern transaction or on any matters relating to firm policy."

"Can we go to the beach now, Daddy?" Nathaniel had made short work of his breakfast.

They drove leisurely down Keene Lane toward the ocean. It's hard, Andy thought, to square Bobby Marryat, the squat toad of those bygone days in the dingy Fort Worth offices, with "Bust-Up Bob," the feared raider of the oil patch. But that was what money did. If you got in the way of enough of it, it made you a new man, turned frogs into princes.

Andy remembered meeting the guy who ran Pan Northern. A pleasant, sixtyish guy a couple of years short of retirement. He probably went to work right out of school for Pan Northern, with a G.I. Bill degree in engineering, and never worked anywhere else. Put in his time in the outfit, years in the field in places like Tulsa, Kuala Lumpur, and Oman, moving around, learning the business from wellhead to gas tank. Then coming back to headquarters as a senior VP in Refining and Marketing, or Production, or whatever, and then being elected to the board, and finally moving up to president and, a year or so ago, being given the big corner office overlooking Lake Michigan, and the keys to the duck camp and the Gulfstream and the membership at Augusta National. An honorable career, ending not only in a bunch of perks but in the ultimate responsibility for billions in assets and tens of thousands of people. How must it seem to a fellow like that, Andy wondered, to wake up one morning and find the way of the world was such that a Bobby Marryat could covet his company, and an Artie Lubloff could, just like that, raise enough money for Bobby to buy it?

Morgan Stanley had sure as hell thrown open Pandora's box when they did the ESB deal, he thought. Jay had a friend at Morgan who said it was 'cause they had a real gung-ho guy, one of those clenched-fist Marine ROTC types who'd fallen in the crack between Korea and Vietnam and who was looking for a real war to fight when ESB came along. "Guys like that," Jay told Andy, "just go crazy. If they can't find a beachhead to fight on, they settle for a balance sheet."

They arrived at the end of the road. It was hard to imagine that the green sea, still cloudy with sand tossed up by the passing storm and running with a discernible but gentle east-west set, could have been the foaming gray monster of the day before.

They walked down the beach. He helped Nat take off his shirt, disentangling the small St. Christopher medal that had been a christening present from Grandma. Hand in hand they walked to the water's edge. Except for two dots in the far distance, they were alone.

The water that lapped over their ankles was surprisingly warm. With an exaggerated movement Andy shielded his eyes and peered out to sea. There was still white water a good ways offshore; the churning of the storm had evidently created a sandbar.

"Watcha looking for?" asked his son.

"Just checking to make sure Jaws isn't around," he said. "C'mon."

He hoisted the boy on his shoulders and waded in, pausing to let his nerves get used to the first shock of coolness. The temperature must be close to seventy, he thought. The sand felt smooth under his feet.

He could not have known, of course, nor could anyone, that the perverse action of the currents had cut a deep channel some yards offshore, a hole in the sea into which he stepped and plunged straight down, as if a trapdoor had been sprung.

As his head went under, he heard Nat laugh at this great new trick of Daddy's, and then they were both down, sinking, the water suddenly cooler, the child jerking and pulling away as his reaction turned from delight to panic. At that moment the riptide grabbed them like a giant fist, hauling them deeper, dragging them away from shore.

Andy tried to adjust, to shift his son so he could use an arm; the tide had him; it felt like they were being pulled out to sea at a high speed; the water was colder, the light dimmer, there was nothing under his feet. He opened his eyes, tried to get Nat under his arm so he could try to get to the surface with the other. The current pulling him down was horribly strong, and the child was in a frenzy now, desperate. Andy thought he could hear his son screaming over the rush of the ocean, and he felt panic rising in his own gut.

He remembered faintly that one was supposed to swim to the edge of a rip, not fight it. It seemed there were too many things to do at once, and not enough arms and legs, not enough strength.

Then, suddenly, his son squirmed and broke from his grasp. Andy looked around, saw him being carried away, reached for him. The sand was dense in the water, it was dark. There was a momentary glint, sunlight on a gold chain, and then the little boy was swept out of sight. Breathless, Andy gave a mighty kick, the sea loosened its grip for an instant, and he rose to the surface. In all directions around him, the sea was empty. The sun hung in the sky, but it was a cold, dull, impassive eye; it glowered pale and heartless, and it seemed there was no color left in anything. He heard the waves vaguely, and a dog barking with obscene happiness on the beach.

He plunged back beneath the water, forced himself down, looking around. The tide got him again, held and tugged him. He was faintly aware of the dull light from the surface. In a moment, he was out of breath again.

He gathered himself to try for the surface, then an immense weight of resignation overcame him, as if the blood in his veins had turned to lead. Gripped by a helplessness too powerful to fight against, even if he had any will left, he gave himself up to the sea and his terrible, sad desolation. There's a long way to go, he thought in that last second, a long and difficult journey. Time would cease to be a dimension where he was bound, but there was not a second to lose. The light overhead faded. He heard a roaring somewhere. In his last wink of awareness, Andy begged God, Death, Neptune—whoever was in charge—to command the merciless waters to take him wherever it was that they had borne his little boy.

BOOK

IX

HORSEMEN OF THE APOCALYPSE

MAY

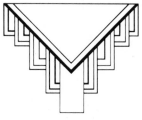

hen Max's secretary advised him that Mrs. Warrington was on the phone, he was very pleased. It was about time she called. He hadn't seen or spoken to Lyda since the day after poor Andy's drowning.

Considering what an old friend he was of Andy's, Max thought himself to have been treated pretty shabbily by the Warringtons. He hadn't been an usher at the memorial service, he hadn't even been assigned a seat in a front pew, and afterward when he'd come to Double Dune, Miranda had accosted him at the front door and said such vile things that the only choice had been simply to climb back into his limousine and return to the city.

He picked up the phone. "Lyda, my love," he said expansively, "how good to hear from you. What can I do for you?"

"I wonder, dear, if you might come to see me. I have something quite urgent to discuss with you," Lyda said.

The voice on the other end sounded strong and assured. Good, thought Max, she's over Andrew at last. Poor old dear, to have that happen, and Miranda crazy, and on top of it all for Rachel to run out on her like that. No wonder she'd withdrawn from everything.

"I'll be happy to," he said. "What would your pleasure be, my dear? Perhaps you'd let Irene and myself give you dinner. Next week? We've become rather fond of this new place Arcadia, on Sixty-second Street. Would that suit you?"

"It's really quite urgent, Max. Actually, it's more of a business matter. I don't suppose you could come by the Carlyle after the close today? I know it's the other direction from Sutton Place, but I seem to have done something to my aging hip, otherwise I'd come to Hanover Place."

Damn, thought Max, she wants to talk about Jay.

"No problem at all, dear," he said. He leaned forward and ran a finger down the current day's page in the large leather agenda that Ulla and Roger Riskind had given him for Christmas. Crocodile, from Hermès, very good stuff.

"Now, let's see, yes, how about six thirty, Lyda? That ought to leave me time to get home and change for Dotty Gesternblatt's dinner for Henry Kissinger."

"Six thirty will be fine, Max. Oh, and given the circumstances, I think it might be appropriate for you to bring Mr. Himelman."

When he hung up, Max frowned and leaned back. Damn, he thought! Why should she want him to bring Leo along? It must be about Jay. God, he speculated, she'd gone off her rocker and decided to invoke the Trust! No, she wouldn't be foolish enough to do that; Leo would tie her up in the courts until the cows came home, and, second, they'd all quit if she did, so what would that leave her with? An empty building, that's what.

She must want to work out a final settlement regarding Jay, he reflected. Technically, Jay was still on temporary leave of absence, but everyone around the shop knew he wouldn't be coming back, not after what had happened.

Not that you could blame Jay entirely, considering what he and his family had been through. He seemed to blame himself for the tragedy, and that had started him drinking again.

Still, there were some things for which there could be no excuses. Billy T., the thug that still drove Jay—Max reminded himself to double-check that *he* was no longer on the payroll—had been given strict orders not to let Jay come to Hanover Place unless he was sober, and Artie was supposed to keep a weather eye on him, too. But somehow Jay had given Billy T. the slip, and on the day of the incident Artie was in Cleveland on a road show.

When Jay turned up in the main dining room, he had obviously been drinking. On any other day allowances might have been made, but on this day, Roger Riskind and Leo Himelman had brought the new ambassador to Israel to lunch at The Firm. He was seated to Max's right at the head of the long table.

As had been expected, the conversation at lunch turned to the burning issue of President Reagan's forthcoming trip to Germany, and the scheduled visit to the Nazi cemetery at Bitburg. No one at the table approved of the President's action.

Jay appeared to doze through much of the discussion, chin on chest, food ignored. He might as well not have been there.

In the course of one of Leo's more forthright protestations, however, Jay came awake with a start. "Hey, Leo," he called from the end of the table, halting the lawyer in midsentence, "got an idea for you."

Before anyone could do or say anything, Jay was on his feet waggling a finger at the men at the head of the table. "Got a great fuckin' idea," he said. "Help you guys, help solve the fuckin' balance of payments, too, maybe. So listen to this. What you Jews do, see, is you tell the fuckin' Germans that unless *they* get Reagan to call off the trip, *no*, that's *n-o*, no American Jew is gonna buy another fuckin' Mercedes or BMW! Never, never, never!"

Jay thrashed the air for emphasis.

"Hey, you think that'll ever happen? Hah!" He slapped his thigh like a vaudeville comedian.

"Hah! Hah! Get it, Leo? Who ever heard of a Jew without a Mercedes! Hah! Hey, Leo. What're you drivin' these days, anyway? Hah, hah, hah!"

He roared with laughter, until the effort seemed too much, and he subsided into his chair. When two waiters helped him to his feet, it was discovered that he had urinated in his pants.

Max had tried to put a light face to it, and somehow they got through the rest of lunch, but afterward Jay was suspended by action of the Executive Committee.

Well, Max thought, as far as Jay is concerned, we will be as generous in victory as the Warringtons have been graceful in defeat, no more, no less. He buzzed his secretary to tell Mr. Himelman to meet him at the Carlyle at six fifteen.

When they arrived at Lyda's, they found Archer Cleverley with her. She offered them drinks, which they refused, and then she got right to the point. "I have decided to sell the Trust's interest in Warrington and Company, as well as the shares held by the estates of my late husband and my son Andrew. Together with various other family holdings, which will join in the sale, that comes to . . . how much, Archer?"

"Sixty-four-point-two-three percent of the voting stock, Mrs. Warring-ton."

"My asking price is four hundred twenty-five million," said Lyda.

"My word," said Max.

"Outrageous!" said Himelman.

Lyda turned her head slowly, looked at Himelman with an expression more of curiosity than anything else, then returned her regard to Max, and continued. "The Chelsea Trust has been kind enough to prepare data on the recent sales of both Salomon Brothers and Lehman Brothers. When you do the same, Max, I am certain you will agree that my price is very much 'in the ballpark,' as they say."

"Now, Mrs. Warrington . . ." said Himelman.

"Please let me finish, Mr. Himelman. Let me caution you that any assumption on your part that my position is in any way negotiable would be sadly mistaken. I should advise you that I have had feelers put out to Parker Gilbert at Morgan Stanley, and while on the whole I should be more comfortable to place Warrington & Company in his hands—both his father and stepfather were friends of my late husband and mine—I feel that since I have more to sell *you* than I do him, in a manner of speaking, fiduciary duty compels me to pursue it with you first. Isn't that right, Archer?"

The attorney nodded.

" 'More'?" asked Max. "I'm not quite sure I follow you."

"If I sell to Morgan, or any other house, I cannot guarantee whom they might retain on staff and whom not."

Lyda paused and smiled at the two men. "And of course," she concluded, "Morgan Stanley's legal representation has, as long as Archer and I can recall, been entrusted to the capable hands of Messrs. Davis Polk, which I expect would continue to be the case."

"And your other terms?" asked Max quickly.

"I will retain all rights to the name Warrington, in whatever form. I will sell you our business, but I will not sell you our good name—or what's left of it. There remain at Hanover Place a number of family memorabilia of no conceivable business value to you, but of great sentimental importance to myself and my family. I wish to have those; Archer will present you with a list."

She turned to her lawyer. "Can you think of anything I've forgotten?"

Cleverley shook his head.

Lyda looked expectantly at Max and smiled. He pursed his lips, gathered a knee in both hands and massaged it, then looked at the ceiling. It was not nerves or indecision that he was showing, but exultation. Sure, her price was high, but really not so much in this day and age. Artie could lay his hands on that kind of money with four or five phone calls.

He uncrossed his legs and looked at Lyda with a wide smile. "When would you like to close?" he asked in the voice of one born to command.

Max insisted on holding the closing in the fourth-floor conference room in the old building, beneath the portraits of three generations of Warringtons. It went smoothly, up until the moment when Max explained, in a voice lubricated by unctuous embarrassment, that in the course of several moves within The Firm, Andrew's Navy Cross had somehow been misplaced. All the other items on Cleverley's list had been located, packed by Grosso Brothers, and would that very afternoon be delivered to Lyda's warehouse, as she requested.

She nodded resignedly at this bit of news. Such things happen, she said, and Max assured her that the place would be turned upside down until the missing medal was found.

When she received the checks, $125 million drawn on the account of Warmile Holdings S.A., and $150 million each from Warmile Acquisition Corporation, Inc., and Warmile Euclid Partners, her face seemed to brighten.

"Goodness," she said to the officer from Chelsea Trust who, along with Cleverley, had accompanied her to the closing, "so that's what people mean when they speak of 'medium nine digits.' " She handed the three checks to the banker.

"Yes, indeed, my dear Lyda, that's what real money looks like," said Max.

He couldn't keep the gloating out of his voice. From where he was sitting, Artie saw the old woman look up sharply. Cut it short, Max, he thought.

But Max had his head. "You know," he said pompously, "it's really a pity Drew couldn't be with us today . . ."

For Christ's sakes, thought Artie.

"Yes," said Max, "he'd be a very rich man."

He shook his thick, gray tonsure, unconsciously raising a hand to touch the juncture of hair and shiny pate. "A very rich man," he repeated, and beamed around the table.

Lyda said nothing for a moment. Then she turned to Cleverley and her banker. "Well," she said, "I suppose that's that. It makes me really quite giddy. I suppose we should let these busy men get back to work."

She rose and was helped into her dark fur coat by Max. She went around the table and shook hands. When it came Max's turn, he took hers in both of his, and bent to kiss her, but she drew back, and stared at him as if seeing him plain for the first time.

"Poor Max," she said in a sad voice. "Poor, poor Max Miles. I've known you since you were a babe in Miriam's arms. You always had an extraordinary talent for the *mot gauche*. Well, at least you had enough taste, or would it be 'sense,' not to try to tell me that Andrew and the twins didn't die in vain, that what's happened here today somehow made their sacrifice worthwhile.

"You know, I rather expected to have sad feelings about this, but now, dear Max, I find them tempered by the realization that at long last I am free of the Mileses. You may well feel the same way about us. Now, at long last, I am under no further obligation to look out for you, or your family, or anyone connected with you. Indeed, I have no desire ever to see or hear from you again, or anyone who will remind me of this place."

She paused and looked at him. He smiled patiently at her; his face invited applause from those present for the kindliness and forbearance with which he was handling this petulant old woman.

"You know, dear," Lyda said, "it's a pity . . ."

"*What* is a pity, dear Lyda?" asked Max, in a deep, confident voice.

"That you never learned the greatest lesson people like us need to teach people like you."

"And what is that lesson?"

"Just this. That knowing how much you are worth isn't the same thing as knowing who you are."

She looked at the men who had accompanied her. "Archer, Tom, shall we be going?"

In the doorway, she stopped, obviously struck with another thought. "No," she said. "I take that back. If that's all there is to a person, how can that person be expected to know anything more about himself?"

Outside on the curb, Lyda thanked the young man from Chelsea Trust. Archer Cleverley saw her into her car.

"Well, Archer," she said, "I don't suppose I shall ever come here again."

"I *know* I won't," said the attorney. "We were advised this morning that Himelman, Plaskow will be taking over The Firm's legal affairs, effective the close of business today. As we speak, the computer files are being downloaded, as they say."

He looked up at the building. "Odd, isn't it, to have been Hanover Place's lawyers for over one hundred fifty years, and then to have the association go phfft just like that!"

Lyda looked out the limousine window and smiled at him. "Don't give it a second thought. The Firm you and I knew ceased to exist a half hour ago." She tapped Billy T. on the shoulder and Cleverley watched the heavy black car slide out of Hanover Place into Water Street.

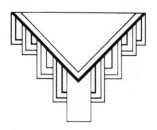

1987

NOVEMBER

When he got to Lyda's, Eric Laszlo was surprised, and not pleased, to find Miranda there. He had business to discuss with Lyda, and Miranda had a way of wearing her mother out.

As she showed him into the living room, Lyda whispered: "Nothing I could do about it, Eric. She just popped up."

"Hello, Mr. Laszlo."

Miranda Warrington Creedmore rose gracefully from the couch where she had been chatting with her mother and came across the room, hand extended.

At forty-five, she was as taut and severe as a saint in a Spanish painting. Laszlo could still see elements of her mother in Miranda: a faint swarthiness of skin, the upright posture that made her seem taller than she was. But her face was ascetic and down-mouthed, lit by the unwavering cold fire of zealotry. Her mind was studiously attentive to voices no one else could hear.

"It's nice to see you again, Miranda," said Laszlo. "What brings you to New York? I thought you were pretty much in California these days."

"We're preaching our Tri-State crusade tomorrow at the Meadowlands."

"Your 'crusade'?" asked Laszlo. His question was disingenuous. He

knew perfectly well about the Reverend Jerry Creedmore's "crusades."
He had read reports of the reverend's exhortations in Cleveland and
Detroit the previous week. This was one reason he was here: to watch
and listen.

"A Crusade for Christian Capitalism," said Miranda. There was venom
in her voice. "We—my husband, that is—have been called by God to
lead a rededication. To put an end to the selling-out of millions of hard-
working men and women to Mammon, so that a few, um, *people* on Wall
Street can get rich."

"I see," said Laszlo.

"Would you like some champagne, Eric?" Lyda asked. "Lunch won't
be a minute. Oh, I *am* glad to see you."

"Mother and I were just discussing the latest Wall Street scandal,"
said Miranda, looking at Laszlo challengingly. "Amazing, isn't it?"

"I'm not sure I follow you, Miranda."

"That they're all Jewish. Dennis Levine, Ilan Reich, Ivan Boesky, Martin Siegel, Ira Sokolow."

Lyda could say nothing. This was what was so unsettling about Miranda. One moment she could be talking perfectly rationally; the next
she'd be over the edge. I should have tried to intercept Eric, she thought.

"I wonder," said Miranda, "if you think that's wholly coincidental,
Mr. Laszlo?"

"Miranda, really!" said Lyda. "I will not have this discussion over lunch.
Eric and I have so much else to talk about. If you're going to spoil things,
I must insist that you leave."

Miranda appeared not to hear. She started to say something, but fortunately at that moment Bruce appeared, to say that lunch was ready.

To some extent, Lyda understood Miranda's attitude. She blamed the
loss of Andrew and little Nat entirely on Max Miles. Lyda herself was
not free from such feelings; when she went back over the sequence of
events that had culminated in Andrew's being on the beach on a day
when he would normally have been at work, vicious thoughts and words
came into Lyda's mind; she had to suppress them the way one chokes
back a sudden uprush of nausea in the gullet.

This Miranda seemed unable to do. There had been an ugly scene after
the memorial service, when Max had tried to call at Double Dune and
Miranda had barred the way. Lyda, too weak with sorrow to have intervened on the spot, remonstrated with her daughter afterward.

Miranda had spat at her: "Oh, come on, Mother! Use your eyes! Admit
it! We'd all be better off if Peter Stuyvesant had gone through with it,
and kicked the Jews out of New York. We'd be better off, and Drew and
Nat would still be alive!"

All Lyda could do was murmur, "That's ridiculous."

Since then, it had simply gotten worse. Lyda was mortified when she read press accounts of her son-in-law's "crusades." The message being preached by Jerry Creedmore was clear, even if not couched in so many words.

"You have no right to project your own angry feelings about a family matter onto the public stage," Lyda had said angrily to Miranda over the phone. She was furious. Furious and mortified.

The trouble was, the news kept providing Miranda with aid and comfort. Lyda tried not to think of it that way, but it was hard sometimes. It seemed almost vengeful: the way these people were going after fine old companies, turning them inside out.

"Well, ya gotta unnerstan', Mrs. W.," Billy T. observed one day when he was driving Lyda while her own car was being serviced, "these Jewish guys, they got a chip on their shoulder as big as a baseball bat, so when they get an edge, which to them don't have to be better'n even money, and maybe don't happen too often, they like to whack the other guys around pretty good."

And now all these scandals—and, just as Miranda said, all the people being paraded into court did seem to be Jewish. Even Lyda wondered: insider trading, was that "even money"? She intended to ask Billy T. the next time she saw him.

Any hopes for a peaceful lunch were soon dashed. After they were seated, and the soufflé was served, Miranda picked up where she had left off. As she listened, it struck Lyda that there was something dull and catatonic in her daughter's voice, as if Miranda was repeating phrases hissed to her from somewhere out of sight.

"Why is it, Mr. Laszlo, that if I point out in public that five out of six violent crimes are committed by blacks, even black people will concede I'm simply making an interesting sociological observation with an apparent basis in fact. But if I point out that nine out of ten of those indicted for insider trading and the like are Jewish, and that maybe there's a connection there, too, the world blows up in my face! Why is the one a mere statistic, but the other an act of bigotry! Why is it that the police can beat a black youth half to death, and no one says boo, but give a Jew a parking ticket, and he screams 'Holocaust!'?"

"Miranda, stop it!" said Lyda. "Stop it at once! No wonder Christianity is in trouble, when it's represented by the likes of you!"

"May I remind you, Mother, that the likes of me are the likes of you."

Lyda started to reply to that, but Laszlo cut in. He spoke calmly and pleasantly. "It's all right, Lyda. I think what Miranda fails to grasp is that Jews are especially sensitive to any persecution. You may describe it in terms of parking tickets, Miranda, but for six million of us, what were at first parking tickets became something much worse."

He watched as Miranda considered his words. It seemed to him that her answer was being transmitted from somewhere beyond this pretty room.

He was right, although no one could have guessed, from her cool exterior, the rapture of perfect, pure, orgasmic hatred that convulsed Miranda and filled her with a sense of mission. Her hatred had become her best friend, closer to her even than her husband, whom she was determined to draw into its embrace, where, like Tristan and Isolde, they would rise to a common blazing apotheosis. Her hatred spoke to her with the chilly little voice in which madness often instructs its adherents. It taught her to mimic its own rational tones, coached her what words to use, what ones to be careful to avoid. It helped her read the newspapers and look at television, sharpened her perceptions so that a name, an accent, a physiognomy asserted itself to her as if incised in the sky by an angel's sword.

Miranda apparently had her answer. She put down her knife and fork and smiled at Laszlo. Watching, Lyda understood what men meant by the seductiveness of evil.

"Well, then, since you want to talk about the war, Mr. Laszlo, let's do just that. I gather what you're saying is that because of the Holocaust, as you call it, there's one rule for Jews and another for everyone else?"

Laszlo said nothing.

"And of course, because of the Holocaust, the Jews are owed compensation by all mankind, which is why we are stuck with Israel?"

"Come again?" asked Laszlo mildly.

"Let's see if I can put it another way, then. Perhaps you'll answer me this. Why did this country send Marines to Lebanon?"

"Obviously: to preserve peace there."

"Exactly. But to preserve peace for whom? Whenever we mess around in the Middle East, it *does* always seem to be for Israel's benefit, doesn't it?"

"There are diplomatic and military undertakings between the two nations, Miranda, you understand that."

"By which I assume you mean the two hundred and thirty young lives that were lost there?"

Laszlo said nothing.

"Speaking of which, and, Mother, this should interest you, can you tell me, Mr. Laszlo, just how many of those two hundred and thirty Marines were Jews?"

Laszlo said nothing. Miranda looked at him triumphantly, then at Lyda.

"Well, let me tell you. Among those two hundred and thirty Marines killed in Beirut, preserving Israel, Eric, there wasn't one Jew! Would you like to know how many Jewish names there are out of the forty-seven

thousand on the Vietnam Memorial? Would you like to hear that interesting statistic? Of course, the Jews have better things to do. Like getting
rich selling this country to the Japanese!"

"Miranda, please!"

"The same Japanese who killed my brother Alexander, naturally. Oh,
Mother, stop it! Don't give me your 'you wicked girl' voice! And don't
look at me like I've got three heads! Mother, the real war is here!"

She gestured toward the window. "Out there! Mother, you've read
that speech of Max's, where he talked about 'restructuring America.'
Mother, this isn't a restructuring, it's a revolution! A revolution . . ."

She paused. A curious thing happened. Her voice turned dull and
expressionless. "A revolution brought about and underwritten by people
whose only object is to disorganize the way we live," she continued,
almost robotlike, "because there's money in instability, provided they can
call it 'change.' People whose object isn't to build, but to . . ."

"Plunder."

Laszlo's one-word interruption stopped Miranda short. He looked at
her with infinite sadness, and said:

"Perhaps I can finish it for you, Miranda. Let's see. Ah, yes, I remember
now: 'Ihre Parole hies nicht: Ordnung und Ausbau, als vielmehr: Aus-
plunderung derselben. Der wirkliche Organisator der Revolution und ihr
tatsachlicher Drahtzieher, der internationale Jude, hatte damals die Situation richtig abgeschazt.' "

"What on earth are you talking about, Eric?" asked Lyda. "My word,
it must be thirty years since I've spoken a word of German."

"It's not important," said Laszlo. He looked at Miranda, sitting there
sullenly. "Or is it, Miranda?"

She didn't answer, just sat there studying the wall behind her mother
with unseeing eyes.

"Well, what is important, Miranda, is that your behavior has been
perfectly monstrous." Lyda turned to Laszlo. "Eric, I apologize."

"Apologize!" Miranda came out of her brief trance with a vengeance.
"Apologize to who? For what!" she demanded furiously. "It's not enough
they're rich and powerful. Not enough that they buy anything they want,
that they rub their money in our faces! They also want us to think they're
mistreated, so they can whine their way to another few billion!"

"Miranda, stop it! I forbid you to say another word!"

The younger woman looked at her mother pityingly. "Mother, people
like you are such fools! Thank God you're a vanishing breed! You handed
this country over to them and let them turn it into a temple for the money
changers just the way they've turned Hanover Place into a synagogue!
Well, some of us aren't going to roll over and play dead! Mother, Mr.
Laszlo, I have some exciting news for you . . ."

She stood up and looked at them contemptuously. "Mr. Laszlo, everyone tells me you're a very important Jew. Well, you better tell some of your friends downtown to go easy. There's a world out there beyond the Hudson which isn't about to stand for being torn to pieces while a bunch of New York Jews quarrel over the scraps. There are angry people your friends don't see out of the window of their fifty-thousand-dollar Mercedes Benzes, people whose poverty . . ."

Miranda's voice trembled, and she halted in midsentence, momentarily silenced by the sheer violence of her rage. Lyda and Laszlo looked at each other.

At last, in an ominous cold voice, she concluded: "If this keeps up, what the people with the black *skins* are likely to do to you will make your crowd miss the people with the black *shirts!*"

She dropped her napkin on her plate and strode out of the room.

After she was gone, Laszlo and Lyda sat silently, contemplating the empty doorway, as if some ectoplasmic remnant lingered. Finally, Lyda turned to her guest. "Oh, Eric, I am so sorry."

He appeared not to hear her at first. Then he said: "Actually, in a way that's why I came to see you. The activities of Miranda and her husband are not exactly unknown to me."

Over coffee, he told Lyda, "I guessed by your expression when I started spouting German at your daughter that you've never read *Mein Kampf.* Am I correct?"

"Is that what it was? My goodness! I suppose like everyone else I tried to read it when we first started hearing about this silly man with a mustache whose palm the Germans seemed to be eating out of."

"A tragic underestimation of a man and a national mood. What Hitler says in that passage is that the man who organized the 'revolution,' who actually pulled the strings, was what he called 'the international Jew.' That's who Miranda's talking about."

Lyda shook her head. "Eric, I am speechless. How . . . I mean, why? Where did I go wrong with Miranda? Why, I never . . ."

"Lyda, no one ever quite knows, at least until it's too late. Anti-Semitism is like a gas beneath the ground, as old as the earth. It's highly volatile and inflammable, always pressing upward to break out in the open air where it will burst into flame. Most of the time it's contained by the weight of the soil—by which I mean human decency, and—since the Holocaust and thanks to it—by a mixture of shame and memory. Now and then, however, a storm comes along which is so violent that the topsoil, no matter how thick, is blown or washed away; perhaps over time it simply erodes, until it's little more than dust. It's been forty years since the war, after all. People forget. New generations rise—to whom the burning memories of their elders are just so much babble by the fireside.

The ironic part is, it's usually the children who find themselves in the middle."

"Oh, I know," sighed Lyda. "Years ago, I remember Andrew made a squash date with Max and without thinking—well, they were just boys, twelve or so, took him to the Gorse to play. Howland got a very sharp letter from the club."

"And what did Howland do?"

"If you're asking, did he resign, no, he didn't. But he didn't apologize to the club either. Didn't we have this conversation years ago?"

Laszlo nodded. "You're absolutely right. It was in Paris. None of us knew what to expect then, but the years since have been a wonderful time for Jews in this country, in most of the world. We are clever, studious, adaptable people; given half the chance, we'll do well. People resent that, however. I'm not going to go into all the reasons, I can't begin to, because everyone is quite capable of inventing his or her own.

"Anyway, Miranda is not alone in her concern—if I may call it that. A great many Jewish people have been increasingly concerned by the recent scandals . . ."

"I know," said Lyda. "You should hear Belle Seligsohn on the subject! And old Marvin Lederbinder! Marvin even wrote a letter to the *Times* the other day, he's so upset! He practically turned blue at the opera the other night when someone brought up this man Boesky's name at inter-mission."

"Quite so. And may I say I think they have a right to be concerned, since Miranda's 'statistics' are regrettably correct. I wish they weren't, and I wish I could find a rational explanation for the correlation, but there we are."

"I do sometimes wonder how Morris would have felt if he'd lived to see this, especially since Max and Arthur seem to be right in the middle of it all!"

"Well, my dear Lyda, that is exactly why I have come to see you. There are some of us who feel that something must be done."

Lyda looked at him with evident puzzlement.

"There isn't much we can do," he said. "But what we can do, is to try to be in a position to foretell, and thus forestall, anything that might be construed as so provocative or controversial or ill-timed as to make trouble that none of us need or want."

He saw that Lyda still wasn't following him.

"Intelligence," he said. "We need better intelligence. We need to pen-etrate, if you will, the two or three cadres, for lack of a better word, which seem to be the center of things. There are only about a dozen people making these things happen; the others are just followers. We need to know what those dozen are up to."

"Goodness," laughed Lyda. "How terribly James Bond!"

"Ordinarily, I'd laugh, too, but this could be serious. Up to now, it seemed possible to plead a certain industrial rationale for these enormous takeovers. In the light of Mr. Boesky's revelations, that strikes me as questionable. If it goes too far, and perhaps it already is too late, a wave of revulsion could be touched off that could be very nasty for everyone."

"I'm sorry, Eric, I didn't mean to giggle. About James Bond, I mean. Are you suggesting, seriously suggesting, that something like what happened with the Nazis might happen here, just because a few Jewish men cheated in the stock market? You can't be serious?"

"One careless match can touch off a forest fire, Lyda. You know that."

"I suppose I do. Of course, I'll do whatever you feel might be helpful. Provided it's not violent, of course. At my age ..."

"Perish the thought." Laszlo smiled. "All I need you to do is make a certain introduction."

"Of course I'll do that."

"Don't answer that so quickly." Laszlo shook his forefinger. "You are a person of principle, Lyda. You seldom go back on your word, least of all if you've given it to yourself. I'm going to ask you to do that, to reinstate a friendship you yourself terminated when you sold The Firm."

"With Max? Oh, Eric, anything but that!"

Laszlo grinned. He looked more cunning than Lyda could ever remember seeing him.

"Not Max, Lyda—although that may come. Tell me, what do you hear these days about your former friend Mrs. Norton Herzkow?"

"Sunny? All I know is what Chickie Fenton tells me. He says she's bored to tears."

Laszlo told her what he had in mind.

After her guest left, Lyda stood at the window and smoked a cigarette. He had explained exactly what he wanted her to do; according to him, it had been tested, it had been done at least once before.

She wasn't sure she entirely approved, although perhaps this was a clear-cut case of the end justifying the means.

In any case, given Miranda's atrocious behavior, how could she refuse Eric Laszlo?

Outside, a few flakes of snow drifted down, then more. Damn, she thought. She had planned to walk down to the Frick Collection. The Frick was where she was getting the best ideas for her own museum. So far only Chickie was privy to her plans. Had he kept her secret, she wondered? Probably not, she thought; everyone knew how pansies were with secrets; they traded them for dinner invitations and rides on people's airplanes. On the other hand, not a whisper had come back to her, so maybe Chickie *had* kept his mouth shut.

She couldn't get her mind off Miranda's deportment. Where, oh where, had she and Howland gone wrong? Church—that had to be it. For a long time after she and Howland were married, they had gone to church regularly, usually with his parents, to Trinity or to St. Thomas, if the music was particularly good. She could remember going on Christmas Eve to St. Thomas; she and Ariadne in long gowns, the men in white tie. When the children were old enough, she sent them around the corner to Sunday school at St. James; Fletcher hadn't approved; the congregation there was too flashy, he said. But then they started going to Double Dune on weekends, and somehow got out of the habit, and by the time the war started, Lyda and Howland found themselves in church only for weddings and funerals and christenings, and the children never. Perhaps if she'd had a good dose of Episcopal piety instilled in her, Miranda wouldn't have been so susceptible to Jerry's Southern California extremism.

The snow didn't seem too bad. She decided to walk. Billy T. could follow her down Fifth Avenue, in case she tired. What with Jay in and out of Smithers all the time, and her own driver having retired, it seemed more sensible to share Billy T. than to try to break in someone new.

While her maid was helping her into her coat, the doorbell rang. A bellboy handed the maid a book.

Lyda took it. *Childhood and Society* by Erik Erikson. Laszlo had inserted his business card between two pages. "You may find this enlightening," he had scrawled on it.

"Ring for the elevator, Marie," she instructed the maid. Holding her glasses in her right hand, Lyda examined the passage Laszlo had marked with a stroke of his pen.

"Strong eras and strong countries," she read, "assimilate the contributions of strong Jews because their sense of identity is enhanced by progressive redefinitions. In times of collective anxiety, however, the very suggestion of relativity is resented, and this especially by those classes which are about to lose stature and self-esteem . . . It is at this point that paranoid antisemitism is aroused by agitators of many descriptions and purposes, who exploit mass cowardice and mass cruelty."

Gracious, she thought. She handed the book to the maid and told her she wouldn't be more than a couple of hours.

Outside, the air was bracing. She crossed 77th Street to Fifth, Billy T. crawling behind her in the sluglike black Lincoln. The fresh wintry air made her think of St. Moritz. I haven't been there in twenty years, she thought; it will be amusing to go back, especially on a top-secret mission. Poor dear Howland, she reflected, he'd be thrilled, he did so love spy stories. The thought made her quite weepy.

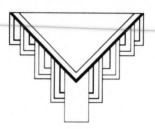

1988

FEBRUARY

Although wives were welcome to attend the working sessions, Sunny decided to skip the morning panel on "The 1988 Investment Outlook for the Common Market." The subject bored her; too general, nothing specific to get her teeth into. As Norton said, the real money was in trades, not theories.

She decided to take a long walk. Down toward the lake, she thought, and then back into town by the road above the Cresta run and up to the cog railway that ran up the Corviglia, where she would meet the rest of the group for lunch at the famous Marmite restaurant.

Sunny and Norton Herzkow had come to St. Moritz for the annual five-day investment "seminar" staged by Vicomte Guy de Balzac, who the year before had left Prudential-Bache's Paris office, where he was the top-producing broker, and opened up his own London firm. It was a very tony affair: only a dozen invitees (and wives or consorts) and everything on the house, from Concorde tickets to suites in the Palace Hotel to private ski instructors on call.

Sunny hadn't been all that keen to come, not after she'd heard that Ulla and Roger Riskind *and* the Bobby Marryats would also be attending. On the other hand, it *was* St. Moritz, and as Norton said, considering the commissions he routed through Guy de Balzac, why not get some of them back?

In the lobby, she pecked Norton's cheek and watched him stride off toward the private suite where the seminars were held. She had fixed a lot of things about Norton, but she hadn't been able to cure him of his bouncing, graceless lope. That walk was the despair of her and Chickie's existence; Chickie, to whom Sunny told everything—well, almost, they *never* talked about Norton's business—said that Norton walked the way "weenies" did back when Chickie was at Yale. From Chickie's tone, Sunny could get a pretty good idea of what a "weenie" was, and the thought made her wince.

Outside it was a fine morning, the air sparkling, an inch of new snow not yet slushed by the busy hotel traffic. A driver from one of the three Rolls-Royces put at the conferees' disposal approached; no thank you, she told him, I'm just going to take a walk, and dazzled him with a flirtatious smile.

There were few people about at this hour. The early skiers had already made for the surrounding mountains. The shoppers were not yet up and at it.

She walked quickly up the hill toward the Kulm, cut around the old hotel, reminding herself that next week Sotheby's was holding some jewelry sales there, which might be worth scouting, and set off on the path that twined back and forth from the heights down to the snow-covered lake that lay at the valley's base like a giant white lozenge. Even at this elevation, in the still air, the hotel flags hung limply in the sunlight, Sunny could make out the bells of a horse-drawn carriage making its stately way across the frozen lake toward St. Moritz-Bad.

Halfway down, she came across a bench that surveyed a splendid prospect of lake, valley, and mountains. She sat down, nursing and trying to make sense of the vague discontent that had been troubling her for several months now.

By most people's measure, she had everything. In Norton Herzkow, she had chosen wisely. He adored her and indulged her in any whim that took her fancy. She was a supportive wife, who had made for him a high-visibility social life, much celebrated in the press, which he seemed to enjoy as much as any business coup. She listened gravely to his plans and problems—he told her *everything!*—and the advice she gave had been surprisingly useful. Just weeks earlier, in an article that had caused both Ulla Riskind and Lucrece Marryat to gnash their teeth, a Manhattan paper had described Sunny and Norton Herzkow's marriage as "the epitome of an '80s High-Style partnership."

Something was missing in her life, however. It wasn't just the low regard in which she knew people held Norton's work. Sunny was pressing her husband hard to move out of arbitrage and high-stakes currency and securities trading and into mergers and acquisitions and leveraged buyouts.

What he did was extravagantly profitable, and he was probably worth every bit as much as his running mates Roger Riskind or Kevin Kerry, and twice what Bobby Marryat was, but ever since Ivan Boesky, well, when you said you were an arbitrageur, or a trader, people just sort of sniffed. It was like the difference between a horse doctor and a brain surgeon, thought Sunny. Norton knew he was every bit as smart as Roger or Kevin; as he said, all they did was borrow money and buy things, while he dealt in the most complex equations of global finance, but they were the ones to whom the glamor attached.

Still, he was a devoted and indulgent husband, who let Sunny remake him sartorially and tonsorially, and fashion a stylish, modish existence for the two of them with Chickie Fenton's help. If he wasn't quite the sexual athlete he thought he was, there had been a few times when Sunny had actually been able to let herself go in his embrace.

Sunny believed she knew what was lacking in her life. She was increasingly aware how often these days, when she observed something or someone in the circles in which she moved, the first word that popped into her head was "*déclassé*."

It was a word she'd picked up from Chickie. Of course, to him, everything these days was *déclassé*. Unclassy.

She was beginning to understand what he meant, and from that to infer what was missing from her life: real class—which meant Lyda Warrington. She now realized there was more to Lyda's "life-style" than lists and tricks. There were qualities which, once experienced, stayed with one and spoiled the taste of everything else.

Lyda was the real thing, as was the way she lived and went about her days. The Lyda-less world to which Sunny had been banished by her beloved mentor after Andy's death and the sale of The Firm was not the real thing. There was no lack of money; everything was the finest and costliest that wish could want or money could buy, from clothes and jewels to friends and entertainment, but something was lacking, an invisible ingredient without which all her endowments were mere expenditure.

She rose from the bench and looked down the valley toward Sils Maria. High overhead, the sky was bisected by the contrail of a streaking jet.

Damn, thought Sunny, kicking a pebble, and resuming her promenade.

She wished she hadn't come to St. Moritz. It was all very well for Ulla and Lucrece, they didn't know any better and so they could be happy going fur-to-fur, diamond-to-diamond with people like those attending Guy de Balzac's conference. Sure, there was a kind of satisfaction from sitting in a room with eleven other couples and guessing there wasn't one there worth less than half a billion dollars, but that was as far as it went. Sunny knew better.

She knew, for example, that while the conferees oohed and aahed over the silver-dished delicacies offered up in the hotel dining room or at the nearby Chesa Veglia, and danced and guzzled Dom Perignon in one or the other of the palace's discotheques, there was a whole other life going on in St. Moritz. She knew it because, each afternoon, the New York gossip columns clicked in on Norton Herzkow's portable facsimile machine, and Sunny had read yesterday that just two nights earlier there had been a big dance at Villa Poppi, the Fretta villa over in Suvretta, and that among the revelers, as reported by "Suzy," had been Count and Countess Guy de Balzac. That had been the night Guy had begged off dinner, saying his wife wasn't feeling well, and he needed to sit up with her.

Sunny knew all about the Corviglia Club, too. That was where the "in" crowd went. Now that she was wise to Guy de Balzac's tricks, she was pretty sure that was where he sneaked off for lunch. Those were *his* "real people." It was all very well, she realized, for Norton and people like Norton to pay Guy de Balzac the millions in commissions a year that paid for a Paris *hôtel de ville* and a Normandy stud farm. In the eyes of a Guy de Balzac, that's what the Norton Herzkows and Roger Riskinds were for. People one bought off with $2,000-a-day suites, oceans of Dom Perignon, and hogsheads of caviar, because they didn't know any better.

Sunny knew better. She understood the Balzacs' viewpoint completely. Insulting? In a way, she supposed, but she also recognized that, in Guy and Sylvie de Balzac's position, she would have behaved the same way.

By the time she got back into town, the day had turned decidedly warm, too hot for the long sable coat, and she decided to dart into the hotel and change. The concierge informed her the conference was still in progress. Upstairs, she found the coat she wanted, a medium-length lynx, briefly considered waiting around the room for Norton, and decided against it, the day being as nice as it was.

The elevator, to her exasperation, passed the lobby floor and descended to the lower story where the Palace's pool and health club were located. When the elevator doors parted, she found herself face to face with Lyda Warrington, and, on Lyda's arm, the most gorgeous, glamorous human being Sunny had ever seen.

For an instant, the two women stared at each other. The elevator doors started to close, and Lyda's companion reached out and held them open.

"My goodness!" said Lyda. "Sunny!" She was evidently flustered. How unlike her, thought Sunny.

There was a pause, then Lyda added, "Well, we mustn't keep the entire hotel waiting." She and her companion followed Sunny into the elevator, the doors closed, and it rose toward the lobby. The man on Lyda's arm regarded Sunny and smiled. She felt stripped stark naked and atingle.

"Sunny, this is Marchese Fretta, Carlo Fretta. I'm staying with him and his enchanting wife Vergogna. They have the most beautiful villa. You can look practically all the way up the Engadine into Italy. Oh, my goodness, my manners! Carlo, this is Sunny Mi—I'm sorry, Sunny Herz-kow. Mrs. Norman Herzkow, isn't it?"

"Norton," said Sunny in a small voice. The man extended his hand. Sunny took it and wondered whether she should curtsy.

"Enchanted," he said. The elevator doors opened and the three of them stepped into the lobby.

It had been almost three years since Sunny and Lyda had spoken. They had seen each other from time to time, New York was too small to prevent that, but those encounters, sightings in restaurants, glimpses from rival boxes at the opera, had always been distant. Once or twice, Sunny had considered calling Lyda, but something told her not to.

"And what brings you to St. Moritz, Mrs. Herzkow?" asked the mar-chese.

"I'm with my husband," she said. "He's on a conference." As she usually did in the presence of the Old World, Sunny tried to sound European.

"Ah, of course," the man said. "Guy de Balzac's." He gave a great, merry chuckle; Sunny had never seen teeth like that; she wanted them to tear a piece out of her then and there. "Dear Guy, such a success he's made!"

"And how long are you and Norton here for, my dear?" asked Lyda.

"Just another two days, I'm afraid."

"Ah," said Lyda, "pity. Carlo, perhaps we should be going. I do think the massage helped." She turned to Sunny. "I gave my ankle rather a nasty little twist the other day, walking down from Chantarella." She extended a hand; the gesture was imperious. "Well, dear," she said, "per-haps we'll run into each other on the mountain."

She turned away. The marchese took Sunny's hand and kissed it.

"We shall see each other soon again, I hope, Mrs. Herzkow," he said. He glanced round at Lyda, who was talking with Andrea Badrutt, the hotel's proprietor, then back at Sunny, and winked. "I was a diplomat for many years," he said in a very low voice. "Perhaps I can be of service in healing old wounds."

Two hours later, while Sunny was lunching up the mountain, a liveried footman arrived at the Palace in a Range Rover. The Herzkows returned to find a thick, creamy, discreetly crested envelope in their box, bidding them to dinner that very evening at Villa Poppi.

The next day, Sunny awoke with a singing heart. She and Lyda had had a long girl-to-girl talk before dinner and if they weren't yet the best of friends again, they would surely soon be so by the end of lunch—at the Corviglia Club, where they were to join the Frettas.

Norton himself was bowled over. After dinner, the marchese had taken him aside, and, over an ancient *grappa* ordinarily bottled for Garibaldi, searchingly solicited the American's views on the outlook for interest rates.

The marchese's interest in the subject was understandable. Along with Gianni Agnelli, Carlo Fretta was one of the two most successful and aristocratic businessmen in Italy, and possibly even wealthier than the former. Just as Agnelli was universally known simply as "L'Avvocato," the lawyer, Fretta was "Il Cavaliere," in recognition of the gold medal he had carried off for Italy in equitation in the 1960 Rome Olympics.

When Sunny met him, he was approaching seventy, but still a dashing, splendid specimen, with wavy gray hair, the eyes of a war bird, and a nose that would have done honor to the Capitoline. He was immensely rich, with a fortune based on agriculture in the South and electronics in the North, not to mention the four hectares in the very center of Rome that a wise ancestor's connection to a Borgia pope had produced. By 1988, his investment and industrial empire spanned a half-dozen countries.

He took his pleasure as he liked from a world he had been raised to believe was his personal oyster. Gratification was not merely a hobby in pursuit of which he raced ceaselessly around the world in his fleet of jets and helicopters, high-performance automobiles, and world-class power-boats. The world might mark down Carlo Fretta's unflinching self-indulgence as his true vocation, but to Il Cavaliere, it was merely the screen behind which to conceal his intelligence and seriousness, as befitted a man of his station. He admitted the life-style press to his yacht, but not his library and laboratory; he let the *paparazzi* follow him on the ski slopes and *plages*, but not into the boardroom.

Of course, he loved women. It was a simple matter of connoisseurship. In his scheme of things, a lively, attractive woman—of any age—was as worthy of study and appreciation as a Titian or a Lamborghini, a perfectly prepared dish of *penne* or a snowy dawn in the Dolomites. His wife knew this, and was understanding and patient. To cage a tiger, she once told Lyda, would deprive the animal of its distinction.

He was surely the most sophisticated, charming man Sunny had ever met. He might as well have been from another planet. Sunny was wise by now in many of the ways of the world, but among the Frettas and their set, people who talked of the sixteenth century as if it were yesterday, she reverted to the tongue-tied girl who'd grown up thirty miles south of Thalia, Texas, on a farm road that meandered between Buffalo Springs and Vashti, where the nearest movie theater was fifteen miles away and there was only one TV station.

Chickie was thrilled when she called to report her exciting news. He knew all about Fretta, including, as he told Sunny, that Il Cavaliere was said to be "hung on a scale that makes Porfirio Rubirosa look like a cocktail sausage."

Two days after meeting him, with good relations restored between herself and Lyda, the telephone rang early in the Herzkows' suite. The conference had ended the evening before; Sunny and Norton were due to fly that afternoon to Geneva, where Norton had business.

Il Cavaliere himself came on the phone. With charming apologies for the last-minute urgency, Fretta asked if Norton could find it in his heart—it would only be for the day—to consult tomorrow in Zurich with the managers of the Fretta accounts at PrivatBank on timely matters of investment and finance. He could fly down on the Fretta jet; Il Cavaliere himself, alas, was required in Milano, but they would regroup in the evening, where all had been invited to Eliane and Tony Paige's dinner at the Chesa that evening. Then, if they could manage, there was Theo Rossi's the next night and on Sunday, George and Lita Livanos were entertaining in honor of Sunny and Rosita Marlborough. The Herzkows should have no concern about retaining their suite; Il Cavaliere had spoken to Andrea Badrutt personally, and although the rooms were booked to some Arabs, the sheikhs could be shifted to the Kulm. After all, joshed Fretta, Arabs are no longer what they once were.

Norton was hardly out the door when the phone rang again. It was Donna Vergogna—to invite Sunny to join herself and Lyda at the Corviglia Club for "just a girls' lunch." When Sunny went downstairs, a lad in the Fretta livery awaited. He handed her a note instructing her to be outside Hanselmann's tea-shop at three thirty.

When her husband returned from Zurich that evening, he found Sunny abrim with high spirits. "Lyda's asked me to be chairman of her opening gala at her museum!"

"What museum?"

"Oh, I'll tell you all about it! Hurry now—we're due at Stefan Klein's for drinks and I promised Tino and Lily we'd look in on our way to the Chesa."

Sunny's recital of her day was selective. She had lunched at the club with Vergogna Fretta and Lyda, and Lyda had discussed "the Museum of Manhattan" with her. After lunch, however, she had declined their invitation to walk back down the mountain from Chantarella. An hour later, in an unprepossessing house in the neighboring village of Celerina, she fell into Carlo Fretta's embrace.

It had been, well, *fantastico!*

The Herzkows ended up remaining in St. Moritz for another five days; it was an idyll, a dazzling parade of dukes and duchesses, *Fursten u. Furstinen, principi e principesse.* There were dinners formal and informal, evenings devoted to kegeling or private screenings, sleighrides, lunches, teas. Heaps of Glattfelter's best Russian caviar; gushing torrents of Roederer Cristal and Lafite Rothschild. The most exclusive doors in St. Moritz were thrown open to them. Sunny charmed and Norton was sought after. When she came in a room, men's eyes lit up; when her husband spoke, they stroked their chins and nodded in grave agreement with his views on the deficit and the forthcoming election. She spent her afternoons in Carlo Fretta's arms, truly in love for the first time with a man for whom she would do anything, risk all, so hugely did he thrill her with his lovemaking, so completely did he incarnate every quality of which Sunny had ever daydreamed. This man truly is, she thought, writhing on top of Carlo, exercising the unique muscular control and dexterity that had once driven half the graduating class of Thalia High crazy, the real, real thing.

Only Lyda seemed to guess what was going on. "You've got quite a crush on Carlo, dear, don't you?"

Sunny blushed. "Such a thing to say!" she exclaimed, looking around, although there was no one within three tables of them. "Does it show?"

Lyda didn't seem to hear.

"Not that I blame you," said Lyda. "Carlo's enchanting. He really is what Chaucer must have had in mind when he wrote of 'a very perfect gentle Christian knight.' "

Lyda was not being totally forthcoming with this quotation. She knew perfectly well what Laszlo had told her. That the only scar in Carlo Fretta's life had been the loss of his parents, in the war; they had been lined up against the wall of the family *castello* outside Ferrara and shot, while their son watched trembling from a nearby copse. The crime for which they were executed by Mussolini's men was that they were Jewish.

1989

APRIL

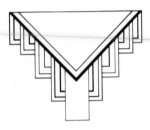

The polite young woman behind the EXECUTIVE RECEPTIONIST sign advised Eric Laszlo that Mr. Miles would be with him in a few minutes. He wandered over to the windows. From the sixty-fifth floor, the view was surreal; the day was overcast so that to the west, the uppermost floors of the World Trade Center disappeared into sultry low-hanging clouds like needles into dirty cotton. To his left, New York harbor stretched dully away; if the sun were out, it would have been possible to look all the way out to the ocean.

Laszlo looked around. None of the charm of Hanover Place, he thought. A large, rather mediocre abstract painting stretched the length of a curtain wall; its label identified it as belonging to "The Permanent Collection of the Warmile Financial Group." Beneath it was a long, glass-topped display cabinet. Laszlo expected to find memorabilia from the old building, but all the case housed were souvenirs of Hanover Place's more recent triumphs: Lucite-enclosed newspaper clippings, magazine covers, and tombstone advertisements for completed deals.

I am on a fool's errand, he thought. The past is dead here; it has no meaning for this place and these people. Still, he had promised himself to try.

One last attempt at "jawboning," as they called it. It certainly hadn't worked so far. In the wake of the Milken indictments, his group had

402

discreetly put the word out on Wall Street that it wouldn't be a bad idea to "cool it" for a bit. But the new breed were pugnacious with success. They were young. What memories they had were instructed, not visceral. If they awoke screaming in the night, the chimeras that wakened them were not those that visited men like Eric Laszlo.

They seemed oblivious to currents of feeling that were beginning to run deeper and faster in the rest of the country; Wall Street seemed sealed off in a capsule of self-regard. Lip service was paid to the conventional wisdoms: too much debt was being created, and yet the leveraging went on; a gulf was being dug between Wall Street's interest and that of the rest of the land, and yet the digging went on; the game was rigged, and yet the game went on, and presumably the rigging.

Men Laszlo's age had seen it all before. Economic disruption was economic disruption, whether measured in Reichsmarks, dollars, or any other currency. In those parts of America where true disruption existed, no matter where the game could rationally and reasonably be fixed, the fearful, familiar personifications were again being muttered. In Texas, turned topsy-turvy financially, its economy shredded by recklessness and chicanery, the phrase "Jew York" wasn't a joke anymore. When the Pennzoil-Texaco dispute finally came to trial in a Houston courtroom in 1987 there were not a few moments in the course of the testimony when it seemed that what was at issue was less a tortuous dispute between two oil companies but more whether decent, hard-working oil patchers should go down the tubes to satisfy the money lust of a bunch of New York Jews.

In 1988, when two major bank reorganizations were stalled by bond arbitrageurs pressing for a better deal, the word in River Oaks and Turtle Creek was that "we're gonna be killed on account of a bunch of New York Jews," although in fact the arbitrage group included some of the whitest shoes on Wall Street and its biggest player was believed to be a Quaker.

In other parts of the country, the words "New York investment banker" were pronounced in a certain ethnically resonant way, and people knew whom and what was meant.

Eric Laszlo was one of a group that "stood watch" around the world. Some of these monitored various radical elements in American life, ranging from Crypto-Aryan youth gangs to pentecostal fundamentalists, clots of disaffection and fanaticism of the sort that in other times and other places had transformed prejudices into pandemics of hysterical evil. That was why, having vowed never again to set foot at The Firm, he had come here today.

"Eric," said a bumptious, deep voice behind him, and a hand clapped him heavily on the shoulder, "how grand to see you, old man."

"Max." The two men shook hands.

"Please," said Max, gesturing for Laszlo to follow. He led him down a short hall.

They passed through a second foyer off a private elevator, then through an anteroom in which three secretaries were lodged, and finally into a grand corner office in which two men were waiting.

Max gestured Laszlo to a chair.

"Please, Eric. You know Arthur Lubloff, of course? Artie's our *gaon* around here, heh, heh."

"Of course. It's been a long time. How are you, Arthur?"

"And you remember Leo Himelman? Our outside counsel."

Laszlo was taken aback by the attorney's appearance. It was as if Himelman's skin had been savagely blistered by the sun and then varnished. The hand that Laszlo now shook felt scaly and swollen. The little black eyes glared from beneath red and crusted rims.

The four men settled down at a round, leather-topped Georgian rent table. Did Laszlo remember it from the old building; he couldn't say.

"Tell me," he asked, "what's become of Hanover Place?"

"Just as it always was," said Max pensively. "Of course, the size we are now, we use it mainly for functions. Perhaps when we're through, I'll walk you over there. I've got some time before my trustees' meeting at Sloan-Kettering. You'll find it just as it was, Eric."

"I'd enjoy that, Max."

Max looked at Laszlo, and said jovially: "Now, Eric, what can we do for you? I must say, it's grand to see an old friend looking so well. You don't look a day over seventy, heh, heh. Switzerland must be agreeing with you."

"It is very agreeable." Laszlo looked around the table. "Gentlemen, what I have to say is very delicate and obviously mustn't leave this room."

Max looked curious; Himelman contentious; Artie doodled on a yellow pad.

"If I may," Laszlo continued, "I should like to speak with you Jew to Jew."

"As you wish," said Max.

"I am old enough, gentlemen, to have had an experience of the worst consequences of anti-Semitism there will ever be. I—and others like me —am thus understandably concerned with seeing that anti-Semitism not expand beyond its normal condition . . ."

"May I ask what you mean by 'normal,' Mr. Laszlo?" interrupted Himelman. "I think I resent that. There is no such thing as 'normal anti-Semitism'!"

"And I think you know perfectly well what I mean, Mr. Himelman," said Laszlo coldly. He returned his gaze to Max. "We may not like it, but it's there. What concerns me are the existence today of inflammatory elements which, given certain conditions, might actively promote it into something worse."

"What do you mean by 'worse,' Eric?" asked Max.

"A backlash, a hunt for scapegoats, a witchhunt."

"I see," said Max, "you're referring to the Palestine question. Well, I think your point's well taken. This is doing precious little good for Israel. I take it then that you're raising funds for a public-relations counterattack? I must say that makes sense. You can certainly put this firm down for one hundred thousand."

"Not quite, Max." Again Laszlo examined each of the other three. "To be specific, it is my understanding that you are contemplating acting for a man called Norton Herzkow in connection with a hostile tender offer for Global Airways—or InterModal Corporation, as I understand it is now known. My purpose in coming here, Max, is to dissuade you from so doing. With any other company, it might not matter, but Global is special. In its way, it is a national corporate icon, a symbol of what America was in its great postwar hegemony. There are few enough of those left. You should also consider Global's blood ties to Reverend Jerry Creedmore."

There was a long moment's silence. Max looked questioningly at his colleagues, then started to say something. Before he could get a word out, however, Himelman broke in: "I can tell you right off, Mr. Laszlo, that your request is rejected out of hand, and that you can go back to that groveling pack of court Jews you obviously represent and tell them so! I am shocked, sir, shocked! Does the memory of the six million mean noth . . ."

"Mr. Himelman," interrupted Laszlo in a calm voice, "there are many, many interpretations as to what end the six million died. Some of us, who have seen Auschwitz, sometimes doubt that a horror so great could have served any purpose, but if it did, I doubt it was in furtherance of making more money. If there is an overdue bill that history owes us, it will be to show men of good will a way in which hated and hater alike can work to put an end to hatred itself. I can tell you, Mr. Himelman, that people like me are as disturbed by Jews who use the six million as an opportunity to obtain special treatment, as we are by gentiles who regard the Holocaust as a mere historical curiosity."

"I might add, however," he said during the silence that followed, "that the current situation in Israel does, as Max has inferred, bear on my visit here today."

"I thought so," said Max. "Still, Eric, I don't see how this can be allowed to affect us as a firm. Around here, support of Israel, while deeply felt, I can assure you, has been mandated as a matter of individual conscience."

He brightened suddenly. "Why don't you talk to Norton Herzkow? Global is his deal. We're only his bankers." Max raised his hands palms-upward in a stage gesture of helplessness. "You know how powerless bankers are. We're just hired guns, heh, heh."

"That may be," said Laszlo, "but this firm, along with one or two others, has acquired a reputation as a moving force in these kinds of transactions. I, and the people I work with, believe this is a potentially incendiary situation."

"No more incendiary than if this firm backs out on a valued connection." This was Himelman. Arthur Lubloff continued to doodle; he was obviously working out a problem. So far he had said nothing. "Such a transaction—may I say we can neither confirm nor deny your allegation that such a transaction is even contemplated—would be very important to a connection like Mr. Herzkow."

"How important?" asked Laszlo. "I saw in the latest *Forbes* poll that Mr. Herzkow's personal fortune is rated at close to five hundred million. How much more does he need?"

"That is utterly beside the point," said Himelman contemptuously.

Max rose. "Eric, would you mind if we went into executive session for a minute? Just to speak among ourselves."

"Not at all."

Max and the others withdrew to the adjoining private dining room. When the door closed, Artie asked: "How the hell does this guy know Norton's gonna take a run at InterModal?"

"What difference does it make?" said Himelman. "These people have their ways. You can't keep something like this quiet forever."

"I don't like it," said Artie. He sat down heavily and resumed his calculations.

"I don't either," said Max. "I haven't liked it from day one. Global has been with this firm a long time."

"*Was* with this firm a long time," corrected Himelman. "I might remind you that the day after we closed with Mrs. Warrington, the business was moved to Dillon, Read. I should think that in itself would inspire you to stand firm, Max, or are you like your father, so anxious to be assimilated by these people, that when one of them looks at you sideways you turn into a cipher!"

"Cut it out, Leo," murmured Artie.

"Leo *does* have a point," said Max. "And Eric *did* say he was speaking Jew to Jew, which I find rather offensive."

"Quite so," said Himelman.

"Still, I have worried all along whether Global—whether InterModal could carry the debt Norton's plan envisages."

"Who cares," said Himelman, "as long as Arthur can raise the financing? There's no problem with that, is there, Arthur?"

Artie didn't look up, but he shook his head. He drew a line through a column of equations and began again.

"Max," said Himelman in his most ingratiatingly sympathetic tone, "how long will it take you to get out of your head those old wives' tales of Foster Klopp's about debt? Those are horror stories designed to discourage adventurousness, peddled by their sort to keep our sort in our place."

"I suppose you're right," said Max, but he sounded dubious. "Shall we go back in?"

"Eric," he said, when they were seated, in a voice plummy with condescension, "Do you know who Arthur Krock was, the great columnist for the *Times?*"

Max pointed at a large wall completely covered with certificates, underwriting tombstones, and important-looking photographs. "That's him over there with Father and Mother and Mr. and Mrs. Ochs."

"I do," said Laszlo.

"Well, Mr. Krock once told Father that the greatest good fortune in his life had been that he had been an employee of gentlemen."

"Yes?"

"Eric, this is a firm of gentlemen. Our clients expect it of us. We expect it of ourselves. Some may say that we're in this for the money, but let me assure you that for us, the size fee we would expect to earn in a hypothetical transaction of this size is *bupkis*. It's the principle of the thing. We are not some *schmatte* house like Drexel Burnham. We have given our word as gentlemen, Eric, and it is as gentlemen that we shall keep it. I regret to have to reject an old friend, but what can I do?"

Leo Himelman smiled in triumph. With those words, his lifetime investment in Max Miles had been repaid many times over.

"That's really too bad," said Laszlo quietly. "The consequences may be grave. Are you quite certain you won't reconsider? If not for yourselves, then for Israel?"

Before Max could answer, Leo Himelman broke in: "I think you miss the point, Mr. Laszlo," he said.

"Which is what, Mr. Himelman?"

"Simply this, sir: when we have New York, do we really need Israel?"

1989

MAY

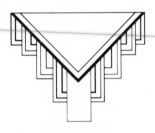

When Jay came into her living room, Lyda was watching the nightly business news. On screen, Myron Kandel was saying, "Well, Lou, the day's big story is arbitrageur-turned-LBO artist Norton Herzkow's six-billion-dollar hostile offer for Inter-Modal Corporation, which most people probably still think of as the old Global Air Transport."

"The Four Horsemen ride again, eh, Mike," said Lou Dobbs to his coanchor.

"You heard, huh?" Jay asked his mother. "I was at the Racquet Club when it came over Reuters. Thought I'd better hurry up and break the news."

He slumped heavily into a chair. Lyda clicked off the television.

"Hey, thanks, Bruce," Jay said. Lyda's houseman had appeared with a tray that held glasses, ice, and a bottle of seltzer. Her son's on-again, off-again attempts at temperance were on at the moment, thought Lyda.

Jay poured himself a glass and took a healthy swig. He belched loudly, like a small boy showing off, and said: "Hanover Place making an un-friendly run at Global. Jesus, Ma, who'd'a thunk it!"

"I think it's very sad," she said.

"Boyohboy," said Jay, "when Jerry and Miranda get the good news they're gonna shit a brick!"

"While I wouldn't put it quite so colorfully," Lyda said with a smile, "I'm not at all sad that they happen to be in Japan at this moment."

"Teaching the Yellow Peril to hate the Chosen People, eh, Ma?"

Lyda's silence was answer enough for Jay; he abandoned this tack. "This gonna cause any problem between you and Sunny?" he asked. "About the museum, I mean?"

"I don't see that it should."

"I hope you're right." Jay took another big belt of the seltzer, and blew out his cheeks.

"Phooey," he said, "this stuff is awful." He shook his head sadly. "Christ, Ma, I just don't get it. At first it was kinda funny. You know, some old fart running a big public company like it was his personal property, and then, bingo!, one day six young guys who look and talk like Alan King zip in on a G2 and blow him out of the water. I mean, there was a kind of justice, you know. But now—I don't know. Hey, yesterday, I went downtown and had lunch at Harry's, figured I'd see some of the guys, catch up, and afterward, I just walked around down there, had Billy tail me in the car, you know, the way you do sometimes. Hey, Ma, it was eerie! All these places. One Willie, used to be Lehman Brothers? It's a guinea bank now, although the rumor is the wops're getting set to sell it to the chinks. Then there's Thirty Wall, used to be KL—gone! Thirty-six Wall was Bache—gone! Forty-two was Loeb Rhoades, same thing. Forty-eight Wall was Dillon, Read, which sold out to the Travelers. Ten Exchange Place was Clark, Dodge—gone! Kidder was across the way at One Exchange Place—they're part of GE now."

Jay's words surprised Lyda. In his entire life, she had never once heard him speak of the past. In his scheme of things, time had only two dimensions: today and tomorrow. When she was with Jay, she always thought of him as six and herself as a young mother. He had a kind of talismanic youthfulness. Now she looked at him and saw a shrunken-eyed, graying man of fifty-seven, the light in his face gone out, the spark of life dying. She felt a hundred years old.

"Oh, sure. They've got a couple of big bronze plaques stuck up on the columns. 'Warmile Financial Group.'" Jay shook his head. "Humph," he said, "weird, isn't it? What'd the guy call it in *Forbes*? 'The most hated and feared address on Wall Street?' Jesus, Ma, who'd've fuckin' believed it!"

Anyone made remotely familiar with the business world would have known at once whom Lou Dobbs meant by "the Four Horsemen." By

1989, they had become an imperishable part of the iconography of "the Roaring Eighties."

Norton Herzkow, Roger Riskind, Kevin Kerry, Arthur Lubloff, "The Four Horsemen of the Apocalypse."

The sobriquet had been affixed to them in 1988 by a senior editor at *Forbes*. By then, they had laid waste to tens of billions' worth of industrial America. They were at the forefront of the nation's commercial consciousness; it was natural that the magazine decided to do an article on them.

At the weekly editorial conference, the writer assigned to the piece observed: "I hear Kerry told a guy at *Time* that he and Herzkow and Riskind think of themselves as the Three Musketeers, with Arthur Lubloff as d'Artagnan."

" 'Three Musketeers,' my ass!" snorted the senior editor. "More like the goddamn Four Horsemen of the Apocalypse, if you ask me!"

Three issues later, when the story appeared, the cover of the magazine stamped the image indelibly into the awareness of corporate America.

The artist had hit on the ingenious idea of adapting Albert Dürer's 1498 woodcut of *The Horsemen of the Apocalypse*. He stuck close to the original, but the four dread riders were no longer War, Famine, Pestilence, and Death. Famine, the skeletal old man astride the gaunt horse in the foreground, no longer wore tattered robes, but a dark pinstriped suit; in place of a trident, he carried a rolled-up prospectus; his face was unmistakably that of Roger Riskind.

The other three riders ranged alongside had also exchanged their traditional habiliments and attributes. In place of the scales of justice, the sword, the bow and arrow, they brandished wands tipped with dollar signs, and could be identified without difficulty as Norton Herzkow, Kevin Kerry, and Arthur Lubloff. Perched behind Kerry, like an update of Sancho Panza, the artist had placed "Lucky," the ubiquitous carrot-topped cartoon leprechaun who symbolized "Kerryland," the sprawling theme park/casino/convention centers in California, Nevada, the Bahamas, France and—largest of all—Fort Lee, New Jersey.

The artist had taken other liberties with the Dürer original. The figures being trampled underfoot, men in three-piece suits, could be identified by the corporate logos on their lapels as the chief executives of companies recently taken over or "greenmailed" by one or a combination of the Horsemen. The fearsome beast consuming the mitred prelate was given the face of Nicholas Palinga, chief of the New York City pension funds and chairman of the Council of Institutional Investors and considered by many the Horsemen's principal accessory after the fact. The angel overhead sounding the last trump was obviously Irene Gessel-Miles, who handled their public relations. The Antichrist looking on from above was clearly S. Maximilian Miles, chief executive of Warmile Financial Group, an admired and vocal advocate for "the restructuring of American industry," which was how the Horsemen's advocates described their work. The squat, Bosch-like toad in the foreground, from whose mouth protruded several pairs of trousered legs, could be identified by his thick spectacles as Robert "Bust-Up Bobby" Marryat, chief executive of M-Oil Corp. and M-Oil Energy Partners. In the background, composed so that the ferocious four seemed to have emerged from it, appeared the façade of Hanover Place; on its portico, the artist had lettered the famous legend from Dante's Hell: ABANDON HOPE, ALL YE WHO ENTER HERE.

Finally, in the right-hand background, there could be discerned a rabble armed with pikestaffs and cutlasses; these were identified in the text of the accompanying article as "the Horsemen's camp followers": propagandists posing as financial journalists; favor-seeking business-school professors spouting Schumpeter and braying about "efficient market theory," and other miscellaneous ideological crumb-snatchers.

As with their symbolic predecessors, each of these modern horsemen represented a particular form of destruction. Norton Herzkow's game was arbitrage and greenmail. His was a hit-and-run business. Technically, he described what he did as "risk arbitrage," although after a 1983 misadventure involving Cities Service in which he had come close to going to the wall, the risks he claimed to take seemed negligible relative to his ratio of profit and rate of success.

Roger Riskind was the leveraged-takeover specialist. His special acumen was for value-spotting and the acquisition of companies for far less than they turned out to be worth. By 1989, The Riskind Partnership had spearheaded a dozen such deals, collectively valued at close to $75 billion.

Kevin Kerry, who had staked out media, entertainment, and real estate for himself, was the most highly visible of the four. He was as well known to the readers of *People* as to those of *Real Estate Week* or *Advertising Times*. To many, he symbolized the age itself. When naysayers and gloom-spreaders claimed America had lost its grit or was being led down the primrose path, one needed only to point to Kevin Kerry, the "Kan Do Kid."

Kerry had an ego as large and flamboyant as his theme parks. When the *Forbes* cover appeared, he declared it "utterly obnoxious," complained to Malcolm and Steve Forbes, attempted to instigate an advertising boycott, and had Leonard Plaskow threaten litigation. A lawsuit, if pursued, would have brought the total of Kerry's legal entanglements to an even three hundred. A deluge of letters, from corporate chiefs, mayors, governors, even the cardinal, pelted down on *Forbes*. These pointed out how much Kerry had contributed to the regional economy, and how the new "Kerryland Palisades" would bring many additional billions into the area.

It was amazing how the "Kan Do Kid" had prevailed over the opposition of everyone from the Port Authority to the big Atlantic City casinos. To knock off the conservationists, the Palisades Preservation Society, the Port Authority, and the Tri-State Commission was a considerable achievement in itself, but to whip the construction unions into line, and to successfully take on the hard guys lurking in the neon-edged shadows of Atlantic City who controlled gambling in New Jersey, that was really something!

Finally, there was Artie Lubloff. Even before the *Forbes* cover appeared, he had acquired his own symbolic trappings. More than one cartoonist had dredged up the hoary image of a man-faced spider at the epicenter of a web. In its sticky toils struggled insects labeled with corporate names, victims of takeovers financed by his firm. There had been other graphic depictions: on *Adam Smith's Money World*, a popular television program that grew out of the big bull market, one Lubloff-orchestrated takeover had been given a medieval context: the company was shown as a castle under assault, with its besiegers deploying "Bridge Loans" and "Junk Bonds" in lieu of catapults and battering rams, and the defenders dumping boiling oil, here labeled "Litigation" and "By-Law Changes," and pelting them with boulders titled "Poison Pills."

Reams of paper had been exhausted analyzing, criticizing, and apostrophizing Artie. Depending where one stood, he was "a dealaholic," "a threat to the American way," "the greatest financier since Vanderbilt," "a pathological trader," or any of a score of other epithets or plaudits.

Artie was personally uninterested in publicity. He didn't cultivate the company of celebrities—it was Frank Sinatra who had asked to be introduced to *him* one night at "21." He stayed away from the press. He gave only one speech a year—the keynote address of the annual gathering of the "Club of 100," the Caribbean get-together of Hanover Place's biggest players. These were not meetings at which the big hitters boasted to each other during the day and in the evening were feted, feasted, and fellated at the sponsor's expense. Like Artie, the annual sessions were all business.

He wasn't even listed as an officer of Warmile Financial Group, Inc., merely as a vice-president of Warmile Dealers Inc., the subsidiary formed in 1987 to carry on the traditional business of T&D. "Dealers" was universally acknowledged to be the tail that wagged the dog.

Next to nothing was known of Artie's private life. He lived alone in a small apartment at the Sherry-Netherland, and was now and then spotted in one of the city's best restaurants, usually in the company of old friends and business associates like the Riskinds and the Herzkows. He participated in a weekly poker game with a small circle of friends, men like Nicholas Palinga, the deputy mayor for investment affairs, Leonard Plaskow the attorney, and Irene Gessel-Miles the publicist, his aunt by marriage. His only known hobby was watching professional basketball; he was an avid fan of the Boston Celtics, and two or three nights a week during the season, he would charter a jet and fly to wherever they were playing.

What was universally acknowledged was that Artie was the straw that stirred the drink. Without him, the Horsemen would be walking.

Fuck, thought Artie, as he clicked the remote and the television screen went black. I do not like this deal—but now there was nothing to do but plunge ahead.

He was lying naked on top of the mussed bed in his hotel apartment. To one side, a young woman was getting dressed silently. She was quite pretty, in her mid-twenties, with a slim build, small breasts, and an amazingly thick reddish-brown bush.

"Over there on the dresser," he said, gesturing with a thumb. I do not like this deal, he thought again. He watched the girl finish hooking her brassiere, cross to the bureau, and take three $100 bills from the folded sheaf.

"Hey," he said, "that was really great. Take another—but don't tell the boss."

"I won't." She blew him a kiss and left.

That's the great thing about New York, Artie thought as he heard the door close. Take-out City. You pay for it, it's yours: sushi, a blow job, anything you want, delivered right to your door. No fuss, no problems. Strictly business. Kerry was always trying to fix him up with broads, girls from the casino, even the daytime anchor on Kerry News Network, but who needed that kind of trouble?

His mind returned to the Global deal. What was this about? Was Vivian on some kind of an ego trip? Taking his eye off the ball?

Herzkow I can understand, thought Artie. Boesky had spoiled the arbs' image. Plus Sunny was on Norton's case about "trading up"; the ink was in LBOs, and so was the respect of the society types the Herzkows hung around with. Roger Riskind got written up like he was a goddamn industrialist, but arbitrageurs were lowlifes.

Fine—what the fuck did Norton Herzkow know about running an airline! Norton's thinking with his dick, Artie reflected, he was doing this for reasons other than money, and that was an automatic recipe for trouble.

On paper, of course, Herzkow's game plan walked. He planned to sell Global's computerized reservations system for $450 million; get rid of a half dozen, maybe eight slots at L.A. International, LaGuardia, and Washington National: that'd be another $200 million; then there was probably $100–$125 million of coverage in the pension funds, say $800 million in total, which would reduce the bank debt. Sell a bunch of airplanes for another $300, $400 million. That would leave a little over a billion outstanding with the banks, and $3 billion in PIK junk. So you go back into the banks for a $500-million line, for "contingencies," and you dividend $200 million up to NH Holdings, which was eighty percent Herzkow and twenty percent Warmile, and you essentially owned the world's third-largest airline for zero cash.

You could probably pop the unions hard—Herzkow was talking concessions that would save $80 million a year—to help meet debt service. Let 'em choose between a pay cut or no job. Every man his own economist. That was the advantage of these takeovers. You came in cold, unencumbered by forty years in the outfit or a lot of warm human feelings, not caring whose ass you kicked, just as long as you "maximized stockholder value" for a lot of pricks in the institutions who would have sold their children for a twenty percent premium over market.

No, thought Artie: on paper, the deal played. It might not be plain vanilla, the Klopper never would have gone for it, but you could see the light at the end of the tunnel. What bothered him was why Lester Vivian was letting Norton Herzkow do it at all.

For one thing, Riskind would be pissed off. LBOs were his territory. Guys who got pissed off about other guys' deals sometimes did stupid things trying to get even.

Herzkow's move on Global messed up what had been a nice, orderly universe. At the beginning, Riskind had been virtually alone doing big LBOs, but once people saw how big the fees and profits were, others came in, guys on whom Vivian had no due bills, pushing up prices and making deals more rickety and difficult. You couldn't help what guys outside the charmed circle would do, but Riskind and Herzkow were part of a team, with assigned roles. Herzkow took huge stock positions that set up the target, Riskind came in and did the deals. Two months ago, when they'd jumped North Pacific Petroleum, taking advantage of loopholes Himelman, Plaskow had sedulously woven into the "standstill agreement" negotiated a year earlier when Bobby Marryat had greenmailed NPP for $350 million, Herzkow had loaded up stock in a dozen accounts around the world, Artie had put the financing in place, and then Riskind pounced. When the smoke cleared, between selling off the pieces, and Kerry taking NPP's downtown L.A. real estate in a partnership he set up with Warmile, they'd cut up a billion six on a $200 million investment. That was the way it was supposed to work.

Maybe it wasn't only Herzkow who was on an ego trip. Maybe Vivian was on one, too. Artie had noticed Vivian starting to talk crap, like that bullshit about "the alchemical properties" of money.

Back in January, when Vivian and Artie met in Seville for their annual "planning session," and he and Vivian had been sitting in the square one afternoon, out of the blue Vivian had said, "You know, Arthur, money's a wonderful thing. You take someone who's a real schmuck, and will always be one but for us, and you and I come along and wave our magic wand, and overnight he's a financial genius."

Then he'd gone off about what "alchemy" meant, how it changed lead into gold, stuff like that.

Maybe so, thought Artie, but with the kind of money Vivian had to play with, who needed philosopher's stones and the rest of that crap?

Artie was under no illusions about Lester Vivian. Everyone at Warmile continued to buy the story that Vivian was a wholesaler who leveraged himself to his armpits and caught the big post-OPEC commodity boom just right, and then shifted into the financial markets just in time to catch the Reagan bull market. He hardly ever came around to Hanover Place. His key business with Artie was settled at an annual January meeting, just the two of them, always in some remote, secure place—before Seville it had been the North Island of New Zealand. At these meetings, Vivian would lay the number that would be available for investment over the next three years, the sum Artie could count on playing with. It was averaging $5 billion a year! And that could be leveraged to $30–$40 billion! Vivian was like one of those guys you saw in TV documentaries, up in a glass-enclosed, air-conditioned booth, looking at an electronic display board and pushing buttons. Except that, instead of a subway system or a chemical plant or a hydroelectric grid, what Lester Vivian had put together was a wonderful machine that was fed very dirty dollar bills at one end and turned out clean and shiny ones at the other. It was like one of those oil refineries that turned crude oil into all sorts of different end products, except instead of filter and valves and catalysts, Vivian's system was made up of Panamanian banks and Lichtenstein trusts and Texas thrifts and Ohio insurance companies.

It was "technology" responding to rising volume. The business had once consisted of Mustache Petes lugging satchels of used bills up to bank windows, but when you were talking maybe five hundred big ones a year out of the New York City gasoline tax scam alone, you had to build up the same kind of electronic daisy-chain the big New York banks had deployed at the turn of the eighties to handle the flight capital streaming out of places like Mexico and Nigeria. With the kind of cash flow the rackets were throwing off now, there weren't enough pizza parlors, trash haulers, building materials wholesalers, heating-oil distributors to handle

the money pouring in. Instead of beat-up valises, you were talking 747
cargo jets flying paper money by the ton into Panama or Liberia, where
a couple of key strokes transformed the green stuff into an electronic blip
and shuttled it into Zurich and wherever. Money had acquired electronic
anonymity. The sums that flashed across the settlement and transfer wires
might represent the economic distillate of goods and services that benefited
all mankind, or of a few thousand blighted lives in Watts or the South
Bronx. What did it matter?

The thrifts would take the dough, and lend it out or buy into Artie's
deals, and thus it would not only get into the legitimate financial blood-
stream, but be backed with the full faith and credit of Uncle Sam, which
was a super irony! Artie could also see variations: a dozen ways of passing
it through the insurance industry. Big single premium annuities bought
for benefit plans that would never have to pay off; product liability insurance purchases for products that didn't exist. Money for deals, Artie's
deals. The world volume in financial transactions was $90 trillion a year,
trillion! and that left plenty of room to hide a measly ten billion or so.

Vivian's machine had many parts, and Artie could only guess at a few
of them. Certainly it was much more sophisticated than the LIFO-FIFO
switchbacks in a bunch of Seven-Elevens that Vivian was doing when
Artie was introduced to him by Leo Himelman. Take Riskind. Back in
'83, when Herzkow bet the house arbitraging Cities Service and almost
went down the toilet, he had been bailed out by an infusion of $75 million
circulated by Vivian through various limited partnerships. That money
may well have begun life as a field of coca plants on some high Andean
plateau. The $137 million of "mezzanine loans" that had gotten Kerryland
Florida off the ground had probably fallen off the back of a thousand
trucks somewhere between customs sheds and final destinations.

The weird thing was, nobody asked. All these smart guys on the Street,
and nobody seemed curious as to how come an obscure savings and loan
or the pension fund of a chickenshit chain of Louisiana convenience stores
could come up with $25, $50, $100 million in subordinated money deal
after deal after deal. There could be only one reason. Nobody asked because
nobody wanted to know, not with the kind of money there was in mid-
dlemanning deals!

Artie certainly didn't give a damn. He read the same tabloid stories as
anyone, saw the same TV clips of sixteen-year-old black kids blowing
each other away in Queens for crack money, and now and then he felt
the same twinges as any other normal human being. It helped that he
didn't actually *know*—that he only suspected—where Vivian's seemingly
unlimited resources came from. But even if he had known, moral qualms
would have had to take second place to his compulsion to be Number

One. For Artie, second place was worse than hell. It was just as Lester
Vivian said: "There's no such thing as a good loser because there's no
such thing as a good loss." And between winning and losing, in the end
there was just this difference: $90 beat $80, $91 beat $90, $100 beat
$99.99. Getting the $100 was the genius part, and the best kind of genius
was to know a guy who'd write out a check. Artie was under no illusions
about himself. His "genius," the talent that made him the biggest player
in the history of the Street was, plain and simply, that he knew a guy
with money. Without the money, brains were nothing. Money talked.
Money won, and winning was the thing!

Artie knew he was hooked on winning. The fact that Warmile was
about to pick up a $50 million fee for its role in the Global takeover was
of only passing interest to him. Let guys like Uncle Max get a hard-on
over the money; for Artie, getting the deal done was the thing. Like a
poker hand, your chances were in the numbers. Emotions, people-type
considerations, had to be kept out of it. Artie's giant takeover equations
were based on a buy-sell calculus intentionally leached of all human feelings.

There was only one human being Artie Lubloff truly, deeply, revered
and admired: Larry Bird, the great Celtics basketball star. Artie thought
of himself and Bird as two of a kind.

It wasn't just that they could do it all: knock it down from outside, go
baseline, play in the paint, pass off, move without the ball or make the
great steal, or the Wall Street equivalents of those. People said Bird could
will the goddamn ball into the hoop! People said that Artie had gotten
the Allied Merchants LBO done by sheer force of willpower. Different
game, same talent.

Bird sure as hell wasn't playing for the money. He didn't get off on the
million or whatever a year the Celtics paid him. It was the game and the
winning. Hell, the guy had played maybe a thousand games in the NBA
since he came out of Indiana State, and never dogged a one, never went
less than one hundred percent flat-out. Anybody with a little talent or
luck could get hot for a game or two. Even a bunch of assholes like E. F.
Hutton—or, when Artie was just starting out on the Street, even a Kuhn
Loeb—could once in a while swing a deal you wished you'd done yourself.
But night after night, year after year, there was Bird—and there was
Artie. And to do that you had to love what you did almost more than
life itself. Well, what was life without the game? The night before you
played it in your head, then you went out and played it, and afterward
you played it over in your mind, and each time you learned something.

What it came down to in the end was being Number One: on the team,
in the league, in the entire goddamn game! Because when the game was

on the line, it was Numero Uno who wanted the ball and Numero Uno who got it. Numero Uno. Bird got the ball; Artie Lubloff got first call on the biggest deals and the toughest deals.

Of course, without the dough, nothing got done. That was where Vivian came in. What the hell was Vivian thinking about, letting Herz- kow run with the ball like this?

If you come to play, you play, he thought. Artie picked up a sheet of paper, crumpled it into a ball, and hooked it gracefully into the wastebasket across the room. In his inner ear, the crowd exploded.

1989

OCTOBER

achel's flight from London landed at Cork just after twelve noon, and by quarter past two, she was driving by the pretty painted shopfronts of the little port of Sneem, almost home. It was a warm day—here in the south of Ireland the offshore current provided a moderate climate right through the year—and she bowled along with the windows open.

To her left, the Kenmare estuary stretched blue and friendly toward the Atlantic; the day was so clear she could look across the water to the mounds of Slieve Miskish purpling in the afternoon light. It was good to be able to look at open water again. For quite a time after the drownings, she hadn't been able to make herself look at the ocean. If there were errands to be done in Sneem or Kenmare, she would send Gilhooley her groundsman, to shop, and when business took her to Cork, she used the long way round, the inland route up and over through Killarney and Mallow. Gradually, however, her new life took over, and one day, without thinking, she'd simply turned the Rover right at the end of the driveway and driven south; and when the first gray-green sliver of open water had appeared between the trees, her heart hadn't stopped and her breath hadn't caught, and after that, it was all right.

She'd lived in Ireland five years now. In the beginning, her people had worried that she'd go daft with loneliness.

But she hadn't. Her life was quiet, hived off from the rest of the busy world, which was just as she wanted it. She didn't lack for companionship. Once or twice a week she would send the car over to Muckross to fetch Father Hogan. The good padre liked his dram, but the whiskey hadn't completely dulled his fingers, and before supper they would play duets, the cello sonatas of Beethoven and Schubert and Debussy. Their playing wouldn't have lit up Wigmore Hall, they agreed, but it was good for the soul, and, if you please, Miss Rachel, I'll just have the one more glass of this splendid claret.

She spent most evenings reading, and listening to the English music she'd taught Andy to enjoy: Holst, Elgar, Delius, Bridge. Music that spoke gently of soft summer evenings on willow-banked streams, of great lawns under a full sun, of mellow twilights. Sometimes, on a clear night, she would walk out into the fields and sit for hours on one of the rough, low stone walls and study the great curving plates of the sky, hoping to catch sight of the two stars she was sure were up there circling the constellations, seeking reunion.

She seldom thought of Lyda any longer. At first she'd felt guilty about "deserting" the old woman. Those first few nights after the drownings, she and her mother-in-law had sat up late on the veranda of Double Dune, keeping a wordless vigil, as if the waves might part and Andy and Nat, perched on his father's shoulder as always, would stride up the beach and everything would be as it was.

On the fourth day, when Andy's corpse washed up near Shinnecock, the faint few hopes that remained were finished. She had not wanted to see her husband's remains, although the sheriff was kind and returned to her Andy's watch, that old Hamilton of J.B. Marryat's he always insisted on wearing, and his St. Christopher medal. People had been considerate. The Senator had flown up from Washington and sat with her and Lyda, trying to dull their sorrow with old and futile anecdotes; Eric Laszlo had flown in from Switzerland, and Chickie had of course been there within hours, and it was on his shoulder that Rachel had finally broken down. There had been many calls, and Jay, his old trading-room decisiveness momentarily restored, had dealt with the arrangements, fielded the telegrams, deflected all the well-meant but intrusive gestures of sympathy, and organized the brief oceanside ceremony in which, with only his family and a few old friends as witnesses, Andy's ashes were returned to the sea to rejoin his brothers and his son.

Rachel had tried to keep a handle on her own feelings, and everyone marveled at her fortitude. Of course, she had a motive. If she gave in to the grief and recriminations that clawed at her and let herself go, she feared, those talons of emotion might tear loose the new life growing within her.

Should she have told Andy that she was pregnant? Would it have made a difference? How could it?

So she kept her secret, and tiptoed on eggshells until she could in decency flee Double Dune and the Warringtons and all their troubles.

When she left, she promised to return, but she knew, and suspected Lyda did as well, that she wouldn't. As the Concorde broke through the clouds over JFK and settled on its course for London, she breathed good-bye to the country where she had known such happiness and such sorrow; shortly afterward she fell into a deep sleep, and for the first time dreamed that Andy appeared, sparkling like a star, a phosphorescent messenger, part creature of the sea, part creature of the night. In the dream, he said to her: "I had to go after him, you see. He was so small and the night is so big."

Her mother and father had been waiting at Heathrow. They had im-mediately driven up to Oxfordshire, where she had told them everything.

She remained in the country until it was time for her confinement. For the first few weeks either her mother or father lingered nearby, but when they saw they had nothing to fear, they gradually resumed their busy London lives. Rachel had completely lost her appetite for cities and she declined their invitations to come up to town. She grew large and rosy, ruddy with long winter walks. She felt at ease. Something told her that no harm would come to this baby.

On April 3, 1985, in a hospital off Marylebone High Street, Andrew Eric Warrington was born. When she came out from under the anesthetic, through the film of pain and relief she saw her parents standing beside her bed, along with a third figure, bent and bald but with the old merry light in his eyes.

"Not a word, Eric," she'd sighed, just before drowsing off, "not one word to her, never!"

She was resolved to keep her new son out of the clutches of his late father's family, and she had. Little Andy was four now, a bright and gracious child with the world of his namesake in him.

Outside of Sneem, she turned right onto a road that rose toward the high hills called McGillicuddy's Reeks. Her farm—fortress as she thought of it—lay nestled in a fold of the lower slopes. It had come into her mother's family as an accident, a casual, impetuous byproduct of Victorian prosperity, and though Rachel had been brought there often enough as a girl, the novelty of "an Irish season" had soon enough worn off and her parents stopped coming.

Rachel cherished it, and her parents in their fastidious way had seen that it was kept in a good state against the day when some nostalgic whim might send them there again, so when she asked for it, after little Andy's birth, they had been only too happy to give it to her.

She lived there, with her small son, Miss Coggins the nanny, Eileen the cook, and Gilhooley, the keeper, in his outlying cottage. In a slanting field above the stone house, a few fat sheep grazed idly. A stream ran in front, bridged by an arch barely wide enough to allow passage to the vans that from time to time came to the house. According to Gilhooley, there had once been trout in the stream, but no longer, although little Andy would sit for hours—with his father's same patient good humor—watching his line bulge and eddy in vain.

Except for delivery vans, and Father Hogan, and a small circle of friends to whom little Andy's existence was a sworn secret, the outside world didn't come to call. There was a telephone, "ex-directory," unlisted; a television for the servants; the local papers and, on Tuesdays, the London Sunday papers—by that time the news was no longer a matter for reaction but merely for reflection.

Rachel seldom left Kilkennen. At Christmas and in late summer, she took little Andy to England to see her parents, and twice a year she went to London; in March, she and the boy visited Laszlo in the Lower Engadine. Two or three times a year she traveled to London by herself, staying overnight, to shop for clothes and review her accounts with the men at Lucas Brothers.

Laszlo had been named Andy's executor and he watched her accounts as carefully as if they had been his own. So far, thought Rachel, watching for the sneaky sharp turn into the twisting quarter-mile path up to the house, 1989 had been every bit as difficult a year as Eric had predicted. He had not been fooled by the serene aftermath of the 1987 convulsion, now all but forgotten. He was extremely cautious. He had a joke he liked to repeat. He'd cup a hand behind his ear and ask, "Hear that?"

"What?"

"It's the wingbeat of giant chickens coming home to roost. Here, in New York, Tokyo, Buenos Aires, everywhere."

Her American connections were by now completely severed. In 1984 and '85, her Dublin bank had forwarded letters from Lyda and Chickie, but she hadn't answered them, and for the last two years, there had been nothing. They obviously had gotten the message.

A hundred yards past the sign for Killarney, she swung the Range Rover onto a narrow road, clattered between the stone gateposts over the loose and rusty cattleguard, and bounced up the rocky driveway. She crested a last small rise, and jolted down into the cobblestoned courtyard, tooting the horn to let her son know she was home.

And then her heart sank. An unfamiliar Ford sedan was parked off to one side of the stableyard, with a capped driver reading The Irish Times in the front seat. The license plates told her the car was a Shannon-based rental.

"Mother!" Little Andy burst from the house. She bent to kiss him, and became aware of someone standing in the open doorway. She looked up and saw that it was Chickie Fenton.

"Oh, my God!" she sighed so deeply it made her shudder, shook her head, and leaned on the hood of the Range Rover. "Oh, Chickie. Oh, no, no, no."

"What's this, no kiss?" said Chickie, waddling out onto the cobble-stones, arms outstretched. In the years since she'd seen him, most of his hair had gone, just a scraggly gray tonsure remained, although his voice was as buoyant as ever, and the bright buttons of eyes had given up none of their old mischievous sparkle. My lord, she thought, Chickie must be almost sixty now!

He hugged her again, then stepped back. "Well, aren't you pleased to see me? Say it: you know you are!"

"I suppose so," she said with resignation, and put out her own arms. For a minute they just stood there, holding each other. Then he drew away, looked at her, winked, and put a hand on little Andy's tousled head.

"And this, I expect, is 'the man in your life' Eric Laszlo told Lyda about? Oh, don't look so shocked, I can assure you that's all he told Lyda, in just those words, and indeed Lyda quite imagines you've hunkered down with a braw young lad from the village, dousing your grief with wild Celtic abandon of the most lascivious sort."

"Mother, is he really my uncle?" asked her son.

Rachel looked at little Andy, then at Chickie, then at her son again. Finally, she said: "Oh, why not? Why not indeed? Yes, Andy, that is. Now come inside, you two, and I'll give you tea."

In the house, the first thing that caught her eye was a large, battered Gucci suitcase sitting on the floor of the front hall.

She wheeled on Chickie. "Tea is one thing, my friend, but if you think you're staying . . ."

He held up a pudgy little hand. "You wouldn't send me off just like that, darling, would you? Knowing what I know now?"

He looked meaningfully at little Andy, standing by Rachel's side. "Besides," he added cheerfully, "I've looked round, and you need me. Who is your decorator?"

"What I need is for you to stay in New York and mind your own business."

"Pish tosh! For one thing, you've always had the best manners in the world, so you wouldn't begin to know how to send me off, no matter what you say. For another, my honorary nephew, young Master Andrew here, has kindly shown me the house, and what do you think: there's the most exquisite guest room upstairs—well, that is, it could be, if you got rid of that dresser, and those ghastly curtains—in which I shall be entirely comfortable. Tomorrow, we'll go to Kenmare. Desmond FitzGerald—I'm sure you know Desmond, the Knight of Glin, and his lovely Olda?—tells me you can still get perfectly decent Irish Georgian things there for not too much money. And of course we have a great, great deal to talk about. You haven't even had the decency to ask me what brought me here. You can hardly imagine I went out to pick up a quart of milk at the local Korean's and took a wrong turn."

"What Korean?"

"Korean Koreans, naturally. Of course, you've not been to New York in a coon's age, have you? My dear, nowadays all the greengrocers come from Seoul and you can hardly buy a newspaper unless you speak Hindi."

"How very interesting. All right, Chickie, I'll bite. What brings you here? To spy on me for Lyda?"

"Not exactly. I've been sent by Lyda to bring you back to New York. Don't look so horrified. Only for three or four days, for the opening of her museum in December. That's right, *her* museum, the Museum of Manhattan, I'll tell you all about it later. And don't worry—the bright and joyful secret of Drew Two is safe with his Uncle Chickie."

And somehow Rachel thought it was.

Chickie stayed for four days. She made it clear that it was out of the question for her to come to New York, but he continued to press her. It would only be for a few days, after all.

"My dear, she's going to be ninety on New Year's Day! Imagine! Born with the century!"

"Tell me about the museum."

"Well, I don't know if she ever told you, but for years, it must be fifty at least, she's been piling up paintings, models, you name it, an entire record of life in New York *de l'antiquité à nos jours*, as they say. So after An·. . . well, after she sold The Firm and found herself with all this money on her hands, I persuaded her to take all this stuff, I mean, darling, it's just been sitting in this great dreary room in the Morgan Manhattan warehouse, and do a proper museum. More to keep her mind off . . . well, you know what I mean. Anyway, you won't believe this, but the house on Park Avenue she and Howland lived in just after they were married, apparently it was *built* for them, can you imagine, well, anyway it came on the market—belonged to a Filipino who went bust—and then so did the houses next door and around the corner, and all of a sudden there you are. Now it's set to open in December, with this great smashing gala. Sunny Herzkow, you remember her, old Morris Miles's dishy young wife who then married a ghastly little—little *man* named Norton Herzkow, who's trying to take over Global Airlines or whatever it's called now, which keeps him busy while his lady wife is having a walkout with a very important and very glamorous Italian gentleman, anyway, Sunny's going to be chairperson of the opening gala, yours truly is doing the décor, natch, and Lyda wants all her family to be there, except Miranda, of course."

"Why do you say 'except Miranda, of course'?"

"My dear, have you been on Mars? If mortification could kill, poor Lyda'd be dead thirty times over! Miranda's turned into a cross between Aimee Semple McPherson and Josef Goebbels."

"Who's Aimee Semple McPherson?"

"Do you know who Billy Graham is? Jerry Falwell? You know, Elmer Gantry types. Well, she and her husband Jerry have gone off on a Jew-baiting rampage, right on television, they have their own satellite station or something, and this big white jet they call 'The Arrow of God,' with a gold cross painted on the tail, can you imagine, and they go around the country telling anyone who'll listen, which seems to be a growing number, that it's all the fault of you-know-who."

"In so many words?"

"Well, not exactly, that's their trick. But nobody's under any illusions who they're talking about. I mean, darling, the other night I happened to see Miranda on one of these shows where people swear and spit at each other, I don't suppose you have them here but right now they're all the rage, and they were talking about how America seems to lack gumption, I mean first this Rushdie business, you must have heard about *that*, and then how if we eat anything we like it'll kill us, I mean *grapes*, can you believe it, but there was Miranda bold as brass shouting at this nice old rabbi 'How can you wonder that we've become a nation of cowards when it's your people we've turned this country over to, people who only care about making money on the backs of the rest, and won't fight in our wars, and kill innocent Arab babies,' and so on! Darling, I couldn't believe my ears! You can imagine how Lyda must have felt. So you see, she needs all the support we can give her!"

Against her own instincts, Rachel began to feel glad that Chickie had come. It wasn't just the invigoration and amusement that flowed from his lively small talk. He made her realize that this burrowing away from the world was just another form of selling out, of avoiding realities that needed to be faced in order to be conquered.

Still, she held back from saying she'd come to Lyda's gala. The prospect of New York appalled her, and Chickie's gossip didn't help. New York, he told her, had become a place she'd scarcely recognize.

"You can't believe the money people are throwing about. And the way others have got their backs up. It's the old story: new money versus no money."

"Good for you decorators, I should think."

" 'Good!' My dear, my little man at Chelsea Trust stands up straight as a sergeant-major when C. C. Fenton enters the room. Of course, I do everything now."

"Everything?"

"Not just chintz and rickrack, darling, I do entire lives for these people! I get them into restaurants, into the columns, put new friends in their drawing rooms and at their dining-room tables, get their ghastly children into schools, choose their clothes for them, you name it! And, in certain cases, and only if I am so disposed, or it will produce a minimum of a million dollars for her museum, I arrange for them to orbit in Lyda's outer circles."

"And that's important?"

"That, my dear, is 'of the most important,' as the French say. To these people, Lyda Warrington is Mt. Rushmore, the Parthenon, and Buckingham Palace combined, socially speaking of course. And I am the keeper of the keys!"

"I'm surprised Lyda lets herself be used like that," said Rachel. "I would have thought she had more dignity. She *must* be getting old."

"Old! Not on your life, young lady. She can still charm the birds out of the trees. Just last week she got a dreadful man named Kevin Kerry to ante up two and a half million at Sotheby's for a very grand Childe Hassam of Gramercy Park."

"Who, may I ask, is Kevin Kerry?"

"Who, may I ask, are you: Robinson Crusoe? This doesn't look like a desert island. Aren't those telephone wires I see out my window? You don't know who Kevin Kerry is?"

"Very amusing. I don't believe you answered my question."

"Kevin Kerry, my dear child, is the man who's torn down half of Manhattan and replaced it with the architectural equivalent of sequins and rhinestones. He owns these enormous amusement parks where everything's plastic except the customers' money. All financed through Hanover Place. He and his wife are right out of *The Gilded Age*. Knee deep in second-rate Renoirs and more Louis Quinze than Versailles. An antique-dealer friend of mine sold them a pair of fifty-thousand-dollar Boulle *tabourets* for a ski house! You can't take ten steps anywhere without his name screaming at you in neon!"

"And he's making amends to posterity by buying a painting for Lyda's museum?"

"Good heavens, no! These people don't know how to spell 'posterity,' let alone what it means. It's consumption—the more conspicuous the better—in which they shall find deliverance. The object is to spend, spend, spend." Chickie rubbed his hands together in mock avarice. "And a very good object it is, too—for some of us. As long as it looks like it came out of *Brideshead Revisited*. Or the 'Springtime of America.' You wouldn't believe how many indifferent American Impressionist paintings of pretty girls in white dresses I've ushered into Fifth Avenue co-ops just in the last year!"

He had other gossip. Bobby Marryat, whom Rachel remembered well —he had been a great disappointment to Andy—had apparently walked out on his wife for a chorus girl. According to Chickie, Mrs. Marryat was very, very angry and it was rumored that she had threatened that, unless she received a satisfactory settlement, she would disclose to the authorities various interesting aspects of her estranged husband's business practices and associations.

"It's all too dime novel," Chickie reported. "Apparently, there's even a little black notebook."

It wasn't just gossip that Chickie brought. He tended to drink too much over dinner, and once or twice turned morose.

"Lyda was really hurt when you left," he told Rachel at the shank of one claret-soaked evening.

"Surely, knowing what you know now, you can see why I felt I had no choice?"

"I suppose so. Anyway, she has Sunny. You know—no, I don't suppose you do—that she actually banished Sunny after . . . well, you know. But then they got back together again, in St. Moritz of all places, and now they're as thick as a pair of schoolgirls."

One drizzly morning, she fitted Chickie with Wellingtons and a Macintosh, and they took a long walk through the violet hills, with little Andy wandering ahead, a doughty figure in yellow oilskin. Chickie was flushed and hung over, and he stopped frequently to catch his breath. Halfway up, they halted and sat down on a moldering old wall, its stones made soft with moss and lichen. Chickie gazed out at the vista of soft purples and ochers. It seemed to make him sad.

"It really is over, I guess," he said.

"What is?"

"Oh, just a way of life. You know how sometimes you feel you're in on the end of a chapter of history. Well, I can't help feeling this is the end of an entire volume, maybe even something as big as the Encyclopedia Britannica. Or maybe it's just what Drew used to say it was: an illusion, that we were all fooling ourselves."

"I don't follow you."

"You're too young. Drew and I grew up, you see, thinking that the world we knew, the forties and fifties, the America of the war and afterward, and the Marshall Plan and things like that, was the real America. But I think Drew changed his mind, I know he did, and began to feel toward the end of the seventies that the real America was what he saw now, that our world after the war had just been a lovely dream, an interlude of time, an illusion. He used to say he'd been fooled by history. I disagreed at the time, but now I think he was right."

"Come on," said Rachel, getting up. "The day's too fine for such depressing thoughts."

Chickie pounded a clump of bracken with his stick, then shook his head, and sighed assent. "I suppose so."

They climbed still higher, where the landscape grew rockier and only the hardiest vegetation clung to the stones. After fifteen minutes, Chickie was breathing hard; he sat down heavily on the ground and wiped his brow with a giant pink handkerchief.

"I must ask you this," he said. "Do you blame Max Miles for what happened? Lyda does, you know."

"Of course not! It was no one's fault. At first, I blamed myself, but you know Andy was the happiest I ever saw him that summer. If anything, he was grateful to the Mileses, because he was looking for an excuse to get out and they gave it to him. They opened the door a crack, and he dashed right through it! It let him quit with honor, on a matter of principle, on a basis his father would have understood."

"Lyda thinks he might have gone back."

"He was never going to go back! Chickie, he couldn't have dealt with it. He had all the wrong instincts."

They sat there, not speaking. The rain had stopped. The sun was breaking up the clouds. A rainbow arched over a cleft in the distant Reeks. Rachel felt extremely happy. The coastward view was spectacular, a long, easy downward slope several times folded, its mélange of autumn russet and green tinged with violet and lingering yellow. The far end of a distant meadow was punctuated by the ruin of an old Celtic circular fort and the fat white blobs of grazing sheep, and beyond was the estuary.

"Beautiful, isn't it?" she asked.

Chickie nodded. "Sublime." He got up and looked around in all directions. "Absolutely sublime. It makes you think."

He sighed. "It's terrible to be crushed by one's own virtues, you know. And yet, think about it, can you imagine any attitudes more self-destructive than the ones our sort were brought up to venerate? It's like being born with a fatal disease. *Noblesse oblige*—there's a real killer! Good sportsmanship! That true happiness is something money can't buy! That character matters! That the other fellow counts! That there's something called shame! How can you have shame, I ask you, in an utterly shameless world? We were brought up to think we were the American norm. What fools we were! The American norm is a Kevin Kerry or a Norton Herzkow: someone who thinks a social compact's something you carry makeup in."

"I hate to hear you talk that way." Rachel drew her son to her and nodded at him. "What about this one? How shall I bring him up? Full of the same illusions?"

"You bet!" declared Chickie. "Because they're the right illusions, don't you see?"

He grinned, reached out, and hugged the boy. "Rachel Warrington," he then said with mock ferocity, "if you bring him up any other way, I will hunt you down and kill you!"

On Chickie's last evening, Rachel knew her resistance had been worn down. They killed the last two bottles of her late father's '61 Haut-Brion, and then she told Chickie he could report to Lyda that Rachel would be there for her gala. It seemed the least she could do.

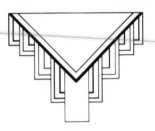

1989

NOVEMBER

At twelve thirty, the decision of the Delaware court came in; the last of InterModal Corp.'s anti-takeover defenses had been reduced to rubble.

"Well, Norton," said Lester Vivian, "it would appear that you've bought yourself an airline. Here."

From a paper shopping-bag at his feet, he produced a Global pilot's cap, and he slid it across the table to Norton Herzkow. Herzkow snatched it up. It was obvious he was in a state of near-hysterical excitement.

"When you get hold of yourself," said Vivian, "you might call Leonard Plaskow in Wilmington and congratulate him on a job well done."

Vivian picked up the phone. He called room service for a celebratory bottle of champagne and then dialed Arthur Lubloff's number. If Norton's going to have his fun, he thought, we might as well pay for it now and get it over with.

When Artie came on the line, Vivian said, "It's a go on Global. Yeah, Plaskow just called from Wilmington. All we have to do is decide how many prisoners to take, if any. Lenny did tell me one funny thing . . ."

At the other end, Artie, as he listened, beckoned to Tony Gargiulo, who was in charge of the section that handled merger-and-acquisition placements.

When Gargiulo came over, Artie put a hand over the mouthpiece and said: "You can hit the wires on InterModal. It's a done deal. Another win for the good guys. One thing I want to do is . . ."

He broke off in midsentence, apparently at what he was hearing from Vivian at the other end. A big smile broke out on Artie's face. "No shit?" he said to Vivian. He gestured to Gargiulo to stick around a minute. His expression said: Hey, this is really good.

Gargiulo watched his boss listen, heard him say, "He did what? He couldn't've! He got down on the goddamn floor! No shit!"

When he hung up, Artie looked at Gargiulo and said, "Tony, you're not gonna believe this! You remember Creedmore, the Jesus freak who's married to Jay's sister? His old man started Global, you know, and he's still on the board. Anyway, when Wilmington threw out their final motion, the son of a bitch got down on the floor on his fucking knees and prayed that if the fucking lord God of Hosts couldn't deliver them from the heathen, which means us, he'd at least bring down His fucking wrath on our heads! How about that for fucking balls!"

"Crazy," said Gargiulo, "'course I'm exempt, being a good and faithful son of my Holy Mother and the Blessed Church of Rome, but *you* are scheduled for the deep shit."

"Whatever. Anyway, circle it up. Don't forget to run a couple of million bonds through Jay. Just for old times' sake."

"No problem. Hey, Artie, you think Herzkow knows diddleysquat about running an airline?"

"Does anyone?" asked Artie by way of reply. "Anyway, who cares?"

He felt tired all of a sudden. When you got close on a deal this size, with fees this big, a kind of hysterical momentum took over, born out of exhilaration and fatigue. Guys went fifty, sixty hours without sleep when one this size was going down.

The Creedmores must be a real pair of squirrels, he thought. He reached over and yanked off a sheet of paper that was Scotch-taped to one of his video screens. It was a photocopy of a cartoon that had appeared in *The Orange County Christian Reporter*, the weekly paper of the Creedmore Ministry. It showed an airliner sinking in the ocean, the Global marking clearly visible, and to one side a raft full of survivors nervously eying a giant dorsal fin coming at them. The fin carried a star of David. The cartoon was simply captioned "J-WS."

Fucking squirrels, he thought; he crumpled the sheet and flipped it into the wastebasket.

The command post at which Artie sat was an octagonal waist-high booth raised on a two-foot-high platform smack in the middle of the hundred-foot-square, double-storied trading room. At what would have been the sixty-fourth floor of Kerry Riverfront Plaza North, a gallery ran around three sides of the room. It had been built at Max's urging; he liked to bring important visitors there and dazzle them with the telecommunications and manpower deployed below.

When Artie stood in his booth, talking on his cordless headset, flicking the switches that controlled the array of video screens banked on the shelf that ran around the booth's circumference, there was no part of his domain he could not see. He had an old Eames chair, but during the trading day, Artie never sat down or left the room, except to take a crap. He had a private office up on sixty-five, down the hall from Max, and a desk in the partners' room of the old building, but he was almost never in either of those places.

Now and then, after the close, he'd steal an hour and go over to Hanover Place and browse in the Archive. He was about the only one who ever did. After five o'clock, Hanover Place was like a graveyard.

The old building was just a showplace now, a sort of museum to impress people who flipped for leather furniture and wood paneling and Currier and Ives. It was where Warmile housed the "Formerlys," as Artie called them, Max's carefully recruited ex-thises and ex-thats, men whose value to Warmile lay almost entirely in what they'd been, whose résumés read "formerly" Deputy Secretary of Defense, "formerly" vice chairman, Bank of America, "formerly" chairman of the Executive Committee of Coca-Cola.

Max seemed to think this impressed people; he was always wheeling one of the "Formerlys" into meetings. The people who seemed to fall for this crock in a big way were the Japs. Show them a heavy résumé and they'd buy the Brooklyn Bridge ten times over, just as long as the recommendation came from a guy in a vest who was "*formerly* Undersecretary of State for Asian Affairs."

The action was here in the trading room. It looked no different from any other such facility, only twice as large with twice as much. Rows and clumps of consoles stacked and banked with quote screens and computers; world clocks overhead in an air-conditioned, coolly fluoresced ozone; everywhere papers, paraphernalia, agitation, and clamor.

The room was divided into several domains. In the southeast corner, hedged off behind sound-deadening panels, with its own inner conference room, was "Cape Canaveral," the stomping ground of Warmile's "quants" and "rocket scientists," MIT and Cal Tech types lured from high science—as Artie had been—by the big money and ferocious action of high finance. They devised calculus-based, computer-driven trading programs that Warmile sold and managed on a proprietary basis.

Next to them was "Top Gun," where the "jet jockeys" operated; these were the men and women who traded for Warmile's own account, leveraging a quarter of a billion of Warmile capital. Artie had to keep a close eye on his flyboys; they tended to get overstimulated and try to fight the tape.

Across the room was "Santa's Workshop," where the elves also had Ph.D.s and invented toys that could be peddled for hard or soft dollars. A lot of it was bullshit, Artie thought, but there was always some jerk at Teachers' or MONY or Batterymarch who came in his pants when a Stanford Ph.D. described the oldest fact of finance, the time value of money, as "multifactor duration matching." Usually, if the elves could sell a new toy, he let them unless it was just too much bullshit. At the end of '86, they'd lobbied to get The Firm involved in a big way in "portfolio insurance," which was that year's buzzword. Artie heard them out, thought it over for a day, and told them no. Portfolio insurance was nothing but a pile of limit orders the height of the Eiffel Tower, and when the market tanked in October '87, they did just what margin calls had done back in '29. Forced stock onto the market in unmanageable quantities, which drove prices down, which triggered more sales, which drove the Dow south by five hundred points.

Of course, thought Artie, it helped to have some sense of 1929, which took place one whole depression and one whole war before ninety-nine percent of the people in the room had even been born, including himself.

The difference was: when he was a kid, he'd had the Klopper beating on him about '29 and some of the Klopper's teachings had stuck. "Research, research, research, Arthur. The only basis for judgment!" In his mind, Artie could hear it still. Truer words had never been spoken, either. Compared to a computer, the Klopper might have lacked a few megahertz in calculating speed, but he made up for it in common sense.

He sometimes wondered what the Klopper would have made of Wall Street twenty years after his death. He liked to put people in their place, the Klopper did, and he was pretty sharp at calling to people's attention the valuable distinction between genius and good fortune.

Even someone as smart as Riskind didn't get the picture: Roger thought the difference was himself; he couldn't make himself admit that the tidal wave of liquidity made everyone surfing on it look like a genius.

"No tree grows to the sky, Arthur!" He could hear Klopper now. "Protect the credit estate."

Boy was that a laugh! The guys in the institutions were howling now because they'd bought bonds whose protective covenants were nil; you could load 'em up with a ton of debt that kicked the shit out of the coverages and consequently the quality ratings and the insurance companies couldn't say boo. What a bunch of assholes!

He looked over to his left, to a cluster of work stations manned by a half dozen young men and women incongruously wearing overalls and straw hats. That was "The Old Country Swap and Barter Shop," open twenty-four hours a day to do interest-rate swaps, transactions in which you traded the interest payments but not the debt itself.

Artie had moved that business, which had been invented in London, stateside. Hans-Peter, in London, was an empire-builder, but Artie had refused to let him go apeshit the way Salomon Brothers had. Solly had moved into a facility the size of a hockey rink on top of Victoria Station and almost immediately the Euromarkets had cratered, starting with the crash of the "perp"—perpetual floating-rate notes—bandwagon. Now Gutfreund was having to can half of Solly's London staff. Not Warmile. Hans-Peter had nice offices and a first-class chef in Bishopsgate, and got to remain in his splendid Belgravia apartment with his sturdy young Welsh catamite, and he technically remained in charge of Euroswaps, but the dealing was done under Artie's eyes out of New York.

That was the way it had to work. Artie's guess was that if the feds ever made good on their big mouth and actually nailed Milken, it would be because of the off-the-book partnerships Drexel had let him organize.

It might sound like a whole new ballgame, but once you cut through the language, you were generally back to basics. Buy and sell, sell and buy, differences of opinion as to the worth and prospects of pieces of paper, that's what it came down to. The thing was not to stretch too far, or to push your luck. Not financially, to where, say, if the Deutschmark dropped another pfennig against the dollar that was tap city. Not ethically, either. There was plenty of room within the rules to do all the deals in the world, just as long as you could find the capital. As the Klopper used to say: "The point, gentlemen, is to shoot the fish, not the barrel."

"Hey, Artie!"

A woman's voice interrupted his reverie.

It was Dolly Dewveall, "Dolly Dimples," the massive black woman who was head of "the Department of Sanitation." That was where they dealt in "garbage," as the guy who'd gone down fighting at Morrison Tire called the high-yield subordinated bonds with which they'd buried him. He'd been a scrapper, but he was also a prick, one of those Gorse Club types who looked down his nose at Artie and Riskind when they called on him to tell him what they were about to do with his company. He was the only guy Artie had ever dealt with who got nasty at the end.

"You goddamn people may think you own the world right now," the guy had said, "but all you are, are a bunch of ragpickers peddling junk!" His voice was spooky, ice cold with hatred; not just an extended kind of mad, but the real thing, a killing sort of hate. It was choked, like if he let go, he'd explode. It was obvious he was just this side of breaking down.

"Just ... you ... wait ... your ... turn ... will ... come," he told them, as if his choice of words was like walking on hot coals. Afterward,

Artie wondered what the guy would've thought if he'd gotten a look at Dolly Dimples; he'd have shit his pants in the country-club men's room if he'd known it was a two-hundred-pound spade with a high-school degree who'd clinched the takeover of his billion-dollar company.

"Yeah, Dolly?"

"Mercator's on six. Sully's seeing three hundred thousand Paul Revere. I can get short the bonds in L.A. What d'you wanna do? Think Milord's gonna chicken out on us?"

"No way, honey. London tells me he wants to be a member of White's Club so he'll leave his bid in so people'll think he's a fucking gentleman. Take the stock for Pacific Combined. Put an extra eighth on the tab for services rendered."

"Okay." She retreated, slabs of ebony weight shifting tectonically under her custom-made Givenchy shift. Last year Dolly had taken down just under a cool $4 million.

"Hey, Artie!" It was Marty Mocasco, who looked out for Warmile's "soft dollar" business.

"I gotta see the guys from Cotswold at Harry's after the close. They want to talk some kind of a deal, we give 'em first call on the Nifty Fifty, anything we see over a hundred thousand shares."

"How many first-call setups have you got already?"

"Six maybe, maybe seven."

"Ah, a guy can never have enough first calls. But not less than three mil a year soft, okay?"

"Gotcha."

"And, hey, Marty, check with Tony. I want to throw some stuff Jay's way, okay?"

"You got it."

Jay had set up a little shop up town, "Warrington & Co.," just like the old days. He had a couple of go-getters working for him, and Jay had a lot of good will around the Street, so Artie guessed he was making out all right. It wasn't as if he needed the money. For reasons Artie couldn't explain to himself, he got a good feeling knowing the old name was back in business.

"Now hear this! Now hear this!"

The loudspeaker erupted with the deep southern voice of Buddy Grusson, head of Government Agencies and Mortgage-Backeds. Buddy had captained a patrolboat in 'Nam and he was still running a tight ship.

"First Boston is gonna strip four hundred million Ginnie Mae 9s of '05. Let's clear for action!"

A phone buzzed. Artie picked it up. It was his secretary upstairs. "Mr. Grand Prix" wanted to come in and re-review the projections.

"When's he want to come?"

Grand Prix was the code name for a deal being put together to buy GM's Pontiac division.

He saw the door at the far end of the trading room open. Max Miles entered and made for Artie's command post, smiling as he went, as if he was a president reviewing the troops of another nation.

"Yeah, yeah, okay," Artie said. "Tell him I can give him a half hour Tuesday morning. Here—six thirty, okay?"

"Well, Arthur," said Max, "I gather the Global matter is satisfactorily resolved."

"Yeah."

"I thought you might also like to know that Mrs. Marryat has decided to remain silent. I just heard."

Max was grinning.

At approximately the same time that her husband was capering around the sitting room of Lester Vivian's suite at the Pierre, and Max Miles was conveying his exciting information to Artie, Sunny Herzkow was lunching with Carlo Fretta at Le Velo, a smart midtown restaurant. They were seated at Il Cavaliere's special table, in a mirrored ell that commanded a view of the rest of the room, but was itself visible only from a few other tables.

Fretta was animatedly arguing with Licio, the restaurant's owner, as to the relative merits of Agnelli's Juventus soccer team and Fretta's own *Camici Verdi*, the green-shirted Ferrara Dynamo. The two men accentuated their rapid-fire, jocose exchange with dramatic gestures; only a faint twitching at the corner of Il Cavaliere's jaw indicated the excruciating pleasure being created for him out of sight beneath the tablecloth—where he was being slowly, exquisitely masturbated by his luncheon companion.

Nor was one likely to have guessed from Sunny's expression how busy her right hand was, almost as if it had taken on a life of its own. She had composed her face to create the impression that she was keenly following the men's conversation. From time to time she nodded and pursed her succulent lips gravely, as if in solemn agreement as to the point being made about this striker or that goaltender.

In fact, she understood not a single word. Not that it mattered. Behind the mask adopted for public consumption, she was herself in the grip of an excitement as intense as if Il Cavaliere had been inside her—which was where, God willing, he would be in an hour or so. It was so typical

of him, this! As soon as they'd been seated, and the waiter had brought
Il Cavaliere's usual buffalo mozzarella and the olive oil from his own
Tuscan vineyards, Carlo had seized the cruet.

"*Extra vergine*," he said, with that *condottiere's* grin with which his
ancestors had conquered half the hill towns between Modena and the
Adriatic. He'd poured a bit in her hand and guided it under the table.

"*Ah, mi scusa, Cavaliere.*"

In the mirror behind the table, Il Velo's proprietor caught sight of an
important patron entering the restaurant. "*Momento, per favore.*" He
turned away from the table just as Sunny felt her lover begin to come,
and in the next instant felt him cover her hand and himself with a discreet
napkin. He sighed deeply, once, and turned toward her, fixing her with
those eagle-gray eyes that never failed to turn her to sexual jelly.

"*Fantastica*," he murmured, and traced the line of her cheek with the
tip of a finger. She could swear tiny sparks flew up where he touched her.

"Pardon, sir," a waiter appeared with a silver tray on which rested a
single sheet of paper, folded.

Fretta took it, read it, smiled, and said to the waiter, "I think this calls
for more champagne. Licio knows my preference."

He turned to Sunny.

"*Brava, carissima*, it's official. Norton has won Global. You must be
very proud. I salute you!" He lifted his glass, then said: "You will of
course tell Norton how grateful I was, I am, for the information?"

"Of course."

He leaned closer to her.

"You did tell Norton to buy United Pharmachemical, didn't you?"

"I did. He and Guy Balzac worked out some deal on doing it through
Lugano."

"*Ah, bene.* You might suggest to Norton it would be a good idea to
buy some more. I spoke yesterday to my friend the minister. He tells me
the government is prepared to increase its offer from seventy to seventy-
seven dollars. I intend to take a considerable position myself."

He smiled, and his gray eyes on hers were like probing fingers between
Sunny's thighs. She felt light-headed with sexiness. He poured her more
champagne.

Lyda was dozing in the back of the car when she felt Billy T.'s hand on
her shoulder.

"Hey, Mrs. Warrington!"

She awoke with a start and saw that the car was stopped, parked in front of the General Motors Building on Madison Avenue.

"Goodness, Billy," said Lyda, "what's happened?"

She had been downtown at Chelsea Trust for a quarterly meeting on the museum endowment. As usual, they had insisted on giving her lunch, and a glass of quite decent red wine, which had made her sleepy.

"I guess you'd wanta see this," said Billy. "I heard it on the radio, so I figured get a paper, huh, make sure it's true, before bothering you?" He thrust a copy of the early afternoon edition of the *Post* at her. The headline read SOCIALITE DIES IN EAST SIDE PLUNGE.

Billy got back into the driver's seat and started up the car. Lyda absentmindedly studied the rolls of fat at the back of his neck. He had grown enormously fat and could barely squeeze behind the wheel. According to Jay, he'd recently eaten an entire tin washtub of linguine to win a thousand-dollar bet.

She took out her glasses and studied the paper. The story began: "Texas-born Manhattan socialite Lucrece Chisum Marryat, 47, leaped or fell to her death from the sixteenth story of her luxury Upper East Side apartment early this morning. Said to be despondent over the breakup of her marriage, . . . etc., etc., . . ." Lyda scanned the rest of the story, ". . . Estranged husband, oil multimillionaire Robert Marryat, 51, in Midland at the time etc., etc. . . . Body was discovered by maintenance man Homero Cruz, 37 etc., etc., etc."

Poor sour Lucrece, thought Lyda. I would never have thought her capable of such a thing.

Then she had another, troubling thought. A few days earlier, Jay had told her that it was all over the Street that Lucrece Marryat was "blowing the whistle to the feds" about some of her husband's dealings.

"I suppose you're too young to remember Mr. Abe 'Kid Twist' Reles, Billy?" Lyda asked.

" 'Kid' who, Mrs. W.?"

"In 1940, when something called Murder Inc. was being investigated by the district attorney, Mr. Reles offered to provide the prosecution with important evidence. Before he was able to do so, he fell to his death from the window of a Brooklyn hotel room in which he was being guarded by several federal marshals."

"You sayin' maybe Mrs. Marryat was pushed?"

"Stranger things have happened."

"Hey," said Billy T. cheerfully, "how about that! Well, you know what they say, Mrs. W.: it ain't all that far from getting your picture on the cover of *Time* to gettin' it on the wall of the post office."

They drove along in silence for a few blocks, then Billy said: "Say, Mrs. W. . . ." He sounded abashed, almost embarrassed.

"Yes, Billy?"

"Well, I guess you oughta know. It was on the radio, too. It seems Mr. Herzkow's taken over the Creedmores' airline. Some court handed him the okay."

"Billy, that wasn't unexpected." Lyda was surprised the people at the trust company hadn't told her, but then they always treated her like Meissen.

"Well, what happened was, just after I heard that, while you was napping, Mrs. Creedmore called on the car phone. Hey, Mrs. W., she sounded kind of crazy, so I told her you were still upstairs at the bank. I figured it was better she calls when she calms down, you know. Mrs. W., that is one very angry woman, if I do say so myself!"

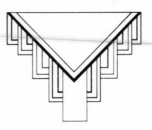

1989

DECEMBER

hen Rachel came out of the customs hall, Lyda was standing there, absolutely erect, her only concession to age a gold-headed walking-stick. Her mother-in-law's appearance astounded Rachel. It was hard to imagine that Lyda was eighty-nine; she looked twenty years younger.

She seemed fretful and preoccupied, however. It was the museum opening, she told Rachel apologetically, but Rachel sensed there was more to it than that.

"You're right, of course," said Chickie, as he and Rachel strolled across 72nd Street one day after lunch at Mortimer's. Chickie had been appointed to look out for Rachel, whom Lyda had installed in a very comfortable room two floors below in the Carlyle.

"It's Miranda and Jerry, don't you see?" he continued as they waited in the middle of Park Avenue. "Lyda's dying inside at what they're up to, with this 'Crusade for Christian Capitalism' they just kicked off."

Reverend Creedmore had proclaimed his "crusade" from his Long Beach pulpit the Sunday after Norton Herzkow had won control of InterModal/Global. To his adherents, it was the equivalent of the Second Crusade preached by St. Bernard of Clairvaux in the twelfth century, calling down the wrath of God and his archangels on the infidel. He had preached the crusade in Seattle, Minneapolis, Canton and Peoria, Dallas and Houston,

Des Moines and Milwaukee, Pontiac, and Birmingham, whistle-stopping the country in his gleaming white jet with the golden cross on the stabilizer. As with all of the Creedmore exhortatory enterprises, it was smoothly professional, with flawless advance work and follow-up techniques as meticulous as they were intense. Some of the same people whose advice had given the 1988 presidential campaign its particular flavor were now said to be advising Jerry Creedmore.

Typically, a few days before Reverend Jerry's appearance in a given city, his "Christian Action Cadres" would move in. These were quiet-voiced, earnest men and women—men, mostly—who spoke of being dispossessed by the takeover mania then still raging: decent Christian middle-level executives whose jobs and lives' work had been "restructured" out of existence "so that a bunch of New York investment bankers could turn a quick buck." Everyone knew who was meant by "New York investment bankers." Everyone knew who the "infidel" was.

The message was tailored to the venue: in Peoria, headquarters of Caterpillar, Reverend Jerry railed the money changers' manipulation of exchange rates, which had cost exports, which had lost jobs; in Dallas, those nailed to "the New York investment bankers' " cross were bank tellers and shipping clerks; in Winston-Salem, food- and tobacco-manufacturing workers.

The message was simplistic. The Reverend and those who followed him were for Christ, and against Mammon. He made it clear—not very subtly—that Mammon was simply another name for the god of Abraham. The words *Jew* and *Jewish* never passed his lips. It was always *They*, or *Them*, as in: "*They* say they're chosen by God, but whose god? Who gave *them* the right to destroy the jobs of decent American workers with their thirty-pieces-of-silver mergers?"

Mammon's seat was New York. Everyone knew *they* controlled New York.

In Dallas, at Thanksgiving, he spoke of "the Four Horsemen" for the first time. "We think of the Horsemen as they were seen by St. John," he told a huge, excited crowd in Texas Stadium, "but how many of your brothers and sisters in Christ know that according to *their* Old Testament, *Zachariah* six, verses one through eight, the Four Horsemen were sent by *their* god to scourge *their* enemies?"

The message struck home. A week earlier, Roger Riskind had announced that he had bought four-point-nine percent of Texas Instruments and intended to see that the company undertook the steps necessary to maximize shareholder value.

The whole world was talking about the Creedmores. There were elements in England, haters of what they called "the rapacious materialism of Nanny Thatcher," who had urged the Reverend Creedmore to extend his crusade to the British Isles. One Sunday paper, which was fond of referring to the Prime Minister as "the Queen of the Jews," had called on the Labour Party to tender an invitation to address its annual autumn conference at Blackpool. A crusade in Japan was already scheduled, and there were rumbles of a "ministry" to West Germany and Austria in preparation.

"I must say," Rachel said, as the light changed, "Mr. Creedmore certainly seems to attract the most extraordinary collection of people under his umbrella."

"Every sicko in America," said Chickie. "Skinheads, blacks, neo-Nazis, any lion or lamb full of hate."

"It rather makes one think of Hitler, doesn't it?"

"That's what Lyda thinks. It's one reason she's so mortified. According to her, most of Jerry's stuff isn't coming from the Bible, but straight out of *Mein Kampf*, as rewritten by Miranda, who's the *eminence grise* in all of this, or perhaps I should say, *eminence* in a black shirt. Anyway, you can see how Lyda feels. Here she is, about to open the museum, the final, I should think, triumph in a life lived foursquare on the side of decency, and here's her only daughter running around the country, practically foaming at the mouth."

"Honor and optimism," murmured Rachel to herself.

"What's that?"

"Oh, nothing, just a thought."

As Rachel started to say something else, Chickie seized her arm and pulled her to a halt.

When she reacted, he explained: "I don't suppose you noticed that large man standing outside this store, obviously a salesman on his cigarette break from here?" He pointed up at the store they were passing.

"I can't say I did."

"Well, my dear, he was at Princeton about the time Drew and I were at Yale. He's called Nugget Newton. We used to see him at all the debutante parties in that dear, dead world we grew up in and he was quite famous for picking fights with doormen. Then he went down to Wall Street—people of his sort mostly did back then—he may even have owned a seat on the Exchange. I heard he married quite well, but I suppose she left him and took her money with her. Now it would appear he's selling ties or socks or whatever to the sort of people who shop in places like this."

Rachel looked up at the imposing building. "My God," she said, "what is *this* place?"

"Well, on one level of reality," said Chickie, "it's the old Rhinelander mansion. On another, it's a costume shop. People come here thinking they can transform themselves from what they really are by buying copies of other people's old clothes. I mean, darling, have you ever seen anything more ridiculous than those ghillie shoes! And look at all that tatty old fishing tackle."

"It looks as if someone's gone out the length of one side of the Pimlico Road with a giant vacuum cleaner and come back the other."

"Precisely. You can imagine how Lyda feels when she sees it. I gather she was passing by the other day and there in the window, shilling for a lot of ersatz polo gear, were a bunch of old family photographs that one of Howland's sister Alice's husbands—probably that ghastly Milo Mitchell—obviously pinched when they were divorced. It really makes one feel sorry for Lyda."

Lyda said as much to Rachel at dinner the next evening, the night before the museum gala.

"There are days I feel like one of those grizzly bears they're always showing on Channel Thirteen, the ones whose habitat is being overrun by the very people who insist on coming to observe them. Of course, my dear, at my age, I've become something like the Statue of Liberty. When someone moves to town, or makes his first hundred or so million, whatever people consider real money these days, they insist on coming to call on me, as if I were some kind of talisman, like that statue of Buddha down at India House whose stomach everyone rubs for luck. They seem to think I can do something for them, and if they're willing to pay for it, so be it, because it all goes to charity. Of course, I leave the administrative functions, the weeding-out and so on, to Chickie and dear Sunny Herzkow; I think of them as my forest rangers, if you will. I certainly understand how poor old Goethe felt in his old age. Just trying to live out his days quietly in Weimar, and yet every Tom, Dick, and Harry who arrived in town felt compelled to drop by."

"Chickie says you've adapted very well to the way the city's changed."

"Does he now? I'm not so sure. Chickie has an ability to separate the compromises he makes for money from what he really thinks. It's an art I've tried to master, but as I've never had to do anything for money, don't you see, I'm afraid so far I've been a hopeless failure."

"Isn't that hypocritical?"

"Possibly, but how is one expected to get through life without a little hypocrisy, especially in New York?"

"It really must have changed."

"New York? Oh, I think it has, yes, but sometimes I just don't know. Maybe change is in the nature of the beast. Go back and read the diaries of George Templeton Strong, who was a friend of Andrew's great-grandfather, or Phillip Hone's diary before him, or read anyone from Henry James and Mrs. Wharton to dear Louis Auchincloss. Complaints, complaints, complaints—all about change! Change for the dirtier, and the

noisier, for the more crass and less humane! New York is New York. If
you can't bear it, you probably ought to do what you've done, rusticate
yourself, go live on a desert island."

She looked closely at Rachel.

"Now don't get me wrong, my dear. I think it *has* changed, and very
much for the worse. It's not just the poverty and the dirt, the people in
doorways. The rich behave so badly nowadays. All sleek and barbered
and reeking of cologne, and inside so coarse and insensitive. Everyone
running pell-mell to get what they want. This was always a swift city,
God knows, but in the old days, no matter how great a hurry we were
in, we at least went *around* each other, not *over!*"

"That's what Andy couldn't stand about it," said Rachel. She didn't
add what she was thinking: and it killed him.

"Of course, he couldn't," said Lyda. "Andrew was a misfit here. His
father and I always knew that, I suppose, although we never discussed
it, because what could we do? There was The Firm to think of. And
now . . ."

She halted in midphrase. Rachel watched the old woman get hold of
herself. When Lyda again spoke, her voice was closer to cracking with
emotion than Rachel had ever heard; not even during the awful days
following Andy and Nat's death had Lyda seemed so vulnerable to her
feelings.

"Oh, we were all such fools, weren't we! Of course, our life seemed
wonderful. Before the war, even in the bad years, we had money and
nothing cost anything. After the war, we were the lords of creation, rulers
of the earth! But it wasn't just contentment that made us quiet. We were
at peace with ourselves because we were exhausted, don't you see? We'd
been through a crash, then a depression, and then the war. Life needed
a rest; things had to stand still for a time. It was tiring enough just getting
Humpty-Dumpty back together again without trying to create Franken-
stein. No wonder it all seems so peaceful, looking back, but the truth is,
dear, New York wasn't itself then. To be peaceful and generous and
courteous isn't its natural condition. So you see, Rachel, the New York
I miss and love in memory wasn't really New York!"

Rachel nodded. No one could love this city. She had always hated it,
loathed its tendency to confuse commotion with energy, its pathological,
thuggish impatience. She couldn't wait to return to Ireland and her son.

Lyda looked at her daughter-in-law and smiled. "Of course," she said,
"it was much more than just that, you know. One could *feel* the good
will, the altruism; it seemed to hang in the air like morning mist. Soon to
burn off, of course."

She looked at the floor quickly, shook her head at some inner musing,
then returned her gaze to Rachel.

"There was a wonderful poem by Phyllis McGinley. You wouldn't know who she is, of course; nowadays I don't suppose anyone would, we forget people so quickly. Oh, but she was a good poetess, though—although *poetess* isn't a word I suppose one's allowed to use today. Anyway, I always had a good memory for verse, and what we've been talking about has put it back in my head just like that. Let's see, how did it go? Oh, yes: 'That was an island in time, secure and candid,/When we seemed to walk in freedom as in the sun,/With a promise kept, with the dangers of battle ended,/And the fearful perils of peace not yet begun.' "

On December 18, 1989, the Museum of Manhattan opened with a special benefit dinner dance chaired by Mrs. Norton Herzkow.

It was expected to be the culminating gala of a year that had already seen its share of extravagant parties, including the Riskind's seventh-anniversary ball in the Wrightsman Rooms of the Metropolitan Museum, for which the caviar bill alone was reported to have been in excess of $100,000. There had been no press previews, no privileged peeks for the *Times*, and the details of the party itself were held in the closest confidence, so much so that *W* reported that "discretion" was definitely the "in" attitude for 1990.

It was Sunny's intention to stage an evening both exclusive and grand. Lyda gave her her head, although she had considerable reservations about letting the museum be identified with a party that was publicly predicted to be the most stratospheric in its social exclusivity since the Gilded Age.

For one thing, it was all in a good cause. For another, Lyda felt faint twinges of guilt about her part in involving Sunny in whatever Eric Laszlo was up to. It was truly, by the definition of the day, a forbiddingly exclusive affair. There were only twenty-five tables of ten, at $250,000 the table, or $25,000 the seat. The decision as to who was to be permitted to fork over a quarter of a million dollars or multiples, and for how good a table, was left entirely to Sunny.

Mrs. Herzkow's triumph was complete, not least because she repaid many an old grudge or slight. With the exception of Sylvie and Guy de Balzac, who canceled at the last minute, all her European friends rose to the occasion. Carlo and Vergogna Fretta took two tables, and announced they were flying in the Belgian Minister of Industry and the head of the Bank of Italy. Net, net, net, declared Norton Herzkow, with justifiable pride in his wife, the twenty-five tables in the Grand Gallery would include approximately ninety-nine-point-four percent, excluding Iron Curtain countries, of the top people in the entire world. It would be an evening that would establish Sunny beyond cavil as heir to the symbolic ermine mantle of Lyda Warrington.

With so much energy, expenditure, and anxiety invested, it was no surprise that the cloud that darkened the dawn of the day of the gala was not allowed to affect, at least not visibly, the spirits of the celebrants.

That morning's *Washington Post* had reported that the Securities and Exchange Commission and the Department of Justice, "with the full co-operation of Belgian, Italian, and Swiss authorities, and certain overseas investors," were investigating "alleged trading irregularities and possible criminal fraud" in connection with two recent corporate takeovers. The origin of the story was identified only as "a highly-placed source" familiar with the investigation.

The story failed to make the New York papers or *The Wall Street Journal*, but by the opening bell, the Street had established that the deals being investigated were Norton Herzkow's successful hostile bid for InterModal Corporation, and the pending acquisition, for $15.3 billion, of United Pharmachemicals Inc. by Brussels-based Gaz et Chimie Fla-mand, an energy and chemical conglomerate fifty percent controlled by the Belgian government. Neither the Justice Department, nor the chief of the SEC's Enforcement Division, nor any of those involved in the two transactions, including Norton Herzkow or various principals at Warmile Financial Group, which had acted as advisers to both Herzkow and United Pharmachemicals, had been "available for comment."

The news hit an already queasy stock market in the solar plexus and sent it to a loss of 146 points on the day. It might be expected that among those being barbered and primped for the evening's festivities, one or two pulses beat more rapidly than normal. By late afternoon, wild rumor was feeding on rumor still wilder. The final edition of the *Post* reported that, prior to her death, Lucrece Marryat had furnished the government with damaging information, and that the investigation extended much wider than anyone had thought.

But no unease could be read in the faces of those whom limousine after limousine disgorged on the carpeted pavement outside the museum, where the flaring of fifty photographers' strobe lights created the impression of an artillery barrage. These were not concerned men and women who made their way up the trench dug through the in-pressing crowd by sweating police. On their faces was written the armoring certitude of vast wealth. To such, how could it matter that the market had sustained its greatest loss since the '87 crash? The amount of money these people had made in the previous five or six years had placed them as far beyond the reach of personal financial crisis as Pluto was from Earth. They had, in effect, moved themselves to a new financial galaxy.

Each of the women presiding at the twenty-five tables had come as a famous New York hostess of her choice; disputes, such as who would come as *the* Mrs. Astor, were settled by lot; in this instance, the winner was Ulla Riskind, who came in a Worth gown borrowed from the Costume Institute and altered to her own exceptional dimensions.

"Actually," Lyda told the reporter covering the event for *Women's Wear Daily*, "the only confusion this evening is that we have quite a few Mrs. Astors. There's Brooke over there—she's come as herself, of course—and then Mrs. Riskind as Mrs. William Astor, and even though Mrs. Kerry's technically come as Mrs. Lytle Hull, one mustn't forget that *she* was once a Mrs. Astor, too."

A few of the men got in the spirit as well. Chickie, unable to decide between Ward McAllister and Truman Capote, came as an extraordinary combination of the two, and Max Miles was got up as the famous dandy E. Barry Wall.

Lyda came as herself, wearing the gown Alix Grès had designed for her back in 1960, for the fiftieth-birthday party that never had been. She and Sunny, glorious as Mrs. John Jay in gathered and ruffled opal silk by Givenchy, greeted the guests at the top of the stairs that led from the foyer up to the Grand Gallery.

Although the brilliant company was much less concerned with inspecting the fruits of Lyda's six-decade whirlwind of acquisition than studying itself, everyone agreed that the collections were splendid in their variety.

Centering the opposing long walls of the Grand Gallery, in which the dining tables were set up, were the famous pair of Eastman Johnson conversation pieces: *Erasmus Warrington and His Family*, and *Erasmus Warrington and His Partners*, the latter on extended loan from Warmile Financial Group. Surrounding them were a big Edward Hopper, *Office: Wall Street*, a gift from S. Maximilian Miles and Irene Gessel-Miles; a grand Bellows of the Sheep Meadow in Central Park, the large Childe Hassam donated by Kevin Kerry, and a suite of four huge Georgia O'Keeffe *Manhattan Nocturnes*.

Upstairs, in a series of galleries opening off a domed rotunda, were a wide range of works: prints, in splendid states, by Currier and Ives, paintings by Cropsey and Healy, a Copley of a British Governor-General and his wife; photographs by Steiglitz and Berenice Abbott and Weegee and Kertesz and fifty others; paintings by Hassam, the Ashcan School, Glackens, Reginald Marsh, Stella and Lozowick, works by artists both well known and obscure. One whole room was given over to architectural ornament rescued from the wrecker's ball; another, understandably, to Hanover Place and its role in the life of Manhattan: it began with the Healy portrait of Samuel Warrington and concluded with a group portrait painted by John Koch in 1968, which showed Howland and Morris Miles talking in the foreground; in the middle distance, Andrew Warrington was shown gesturing at the big windows overlooking Old William Slip to his brother Jay, seated at one of the big partners' desks. Both of these paintings were gifts of Warmile Financial Group.

In other galleries were city views and harbor views, costumes, furniture, framed documents, and dioramas that depicted the island's evolution.

Finally, in the westernmost gallery, illuminated in a fashion that suggested the light of an autumn afternoon, was the exhibit that soon commanded the most enthusiastic attention of the glittering throng, and provided the evening's greatest excitement.

It was a forty-foot-long polychrome model of Manhattan itself that had been built in Taiwan. Each structure was cast to scale and exquisitely, accurately detailed.

Among the oohing-and-aahing crowd that soon collected around it during the cocktail hour, Kevin Kerry was, characteristically, the first to comment. "Hey, what's the Polo Grounds doing here?" he asked loudly.

He examined the model more closely. His mouth compacted into a pout; he looked like a three-year-old about to have a tantrum.

"Hey, goddamn it!" he said loudly.

His wife, reddening, tugged at his sleeve to shush him. "Goddamn it!" he repeated. "Where's *my* buildings!"

He quickly circumambulated the model, pushing people aside, cursing as he went. Then he stopped and looked angrily around the room.

"Goddamn! Where's Lyda? This is a big fat goddamn ripoff! I gave five goddamn million bucks to buy that goddamn picture downstairs, and I've been goddamn well fucked over!" As usual, he doubled the amount of money he had actually contributed.

His wife shrank back, face in her hands.

"Get on the goddamn phone," shouted Kerry over his shoulder to one of the dinner-jacketed bodyguards. "Get me Lenny Plaskow, I don't give a damn where he is!"

One of the men produced a cellular handset and began to punch out numbers.

"I'm gonna get the goddamn tax-exemption lifted from this place," Kerry swore to the room at large. "I've been goddamn ripped off, and nobody rips off Kevin Kerry!"

It took several minutes to locate Leonard Plaskow on St. Bart's, but the voice of reason prevailed, and the innate high tone of the occasion reasserted itself. Joelle Kerry fled weeping to the ladies room and remained there until her personal hairdresser and *maquillagiste* arrived to put her back together again.

Whether Kerry had been defrauded was arguable. He was right about the model. It did not include "The Ring of Kerry," as his clusters of midtown buildings were known, or the Kerry Riverside Plazas, but he wasn't the only one left out. The World Trade Center was missing, and the World Financial Center and Battery Park City; the Pan Am Building wasn't there, hunched behind Grand Central, nor was the air over Tiffany's filled by the glistening bulk of Trump Tower. Pennsylvania Station was the classic temple of yore. The gross tuberosities of Madison Square Garden were absent, as was Lincoln Center. Great liners were berthed at the model piers jutting into the Hudson at the island's waist. All in all, it was a vision of Manhattan that was more spacious and less looming than most of those at the gala had ever known or cared about. Pleasing to nostalgists, perhaps, but as a calmer Kevin Kerry was quoted in the *Post* the next morning: "Pure B.S., bottom-line-wise."

Lyda saw nothing perverse in what she had done. "A museum need not always go with the flow," she told the *Times*'s Paul Goldberger in an interview the following Sunday. The present generation and those to come, she continued, deserved to have a living reminder of the city as it had been during its best times, as it would doubtless want to be remembered if it could speak. "When I want to see America as I prefer to imagine it," she told the interviewer, "I always go to the Metropolitan or over to the Brooklyn Museum and look at those great green-and-golden paintings of the land, the Coles and the Cropseys and the others. It's the same here with our Hassams and Sloans. And the model. I stopped with President Kennedy's assassination: that more than ever seems to me to have marked the break between the world I grew up in, and into which my children were born, and the world we live in now. I really think that way of life deserves a better monument and more respect than it has been given so far, that's all."

Two days before Christmas, "The Arrow of God" brought Miranda to New York at Lyda's request.

"All right, Mother," she asked irritably, as soon as she arrived, "what's up your sleeve this time? I can't tell you how inconvenient this is. Jerry's had to fly back to California commercial, thanks to you, and I absolutely must be there tomorrow for the Christmas Eve Message."

"Sit down, dear," Lyda said calmly. "We have a great deal to discuss. Do tell me what Jerry's message of peace and goodwill is going to be. A call for the massacre of the innocents? Would you like some tea? Ah, thank you, Bruce."

When the houseman had disappeared, Miranda glared at her mother and said, "That's very amusing. In fact I wouldn't be surprised if quite a few people weren't amused half to death. Anyway, you should talk! I read the gossip accounts of the opening. From the guest list, it sounded like a Hadassah meeting!"

"You must see the museum," said Lyda. "It's really very beautiful. Richard Meier's masterpiece—at least he thinks so. I am sorry not to have invited you to my opening, but I know you'd have found some way of spoiling it—or at least you'd have tried."

She poured out the tea.

"Now dear," she said, looking closely at Miranda, "I think it is time for this current foolishness of yours and Jerry's to end, before it becomes dangerous. No, don't say anything . . ." She held up a hand.

"What you are doing is a desecration of everything our family has stood for. Or this nation, for that matter. At first I was inclined to dismiss it as mere mischief, but I'm afraid these are troubled times . . ."

"You bet they are!" Miranda spat out the words. "Especially now that half your new friends are about to be indicted for stealing. You read the U.S. Attorney's statement yesterday. You know what I mean! Some of those people were at your opening, Mother! And you talk about 'values'! The cream of New York society, hah! The cream of Jewry, that's what they were! The very people our sort sold this country out to!"

As she spoke, Miranda's voice rose and fell, like a radio signal in a turbulent atmosphere; Lyda couldn't help thinking that her daughter was slipping in and out of madness.

"Calm down, dear," she said firmly. "As I recall, you told me not so long ago that my sort was your sort. Or was it the other way round?"

"Oh, come on, Mother, you know what I mean!"

"Do I? Yes, I suppose I do. But does it matter, really? What does is that this must stop, do you understand that?"

"And what's to stop us? You don't understand, Mother. We are doing God's work. He speaks to us. We are reconquering America for Christ, reclaiming it from the money changers into whose hands it has fallen!"

"How eloquently put, my dear. I must tell you, when I hear that sort of thing from you, it really *does* make me feel like Hitler's mother, although whether Frau Hitler felt as dreadful about her son's ravings as I do about yours, I can't say. But that's really neither here nor there, is it, although when I think of all the books you could have taken as your text for life, all the books I tried to interest you in, that you should settle on Herr Hitler's filthy screed as your lesson for the day is a terrible comment on me as a mother. I have something to tell you that I think may come as a terrible shock."

"And what is that, Mother?" Miranda asked. Her tone was supercilious, detached, manic.

"My dear, I want you to listen very carefully to what I am about to relate, because when I am through, I am certain you will wish to discuss the matter with God, especially if you're as close to Him as you claim to be. He will certainly want to be in possession of all the facts before advising you what to do. More tea?"

Miranda's eyes were bright, her gaze transfixed; it was difficult for Lyda to tell whether she was hearing her, or some inner voice. She plunged ahead.

"It is clear that you have not the slightest sense of the force of my feelings, Miranda. You have disgraced me. So much so that if my own death could somehow put a stop to what you are doing, I would lay down my life gladly. I don't suppose you know Macaulay, 'Horatius at the Bridge'? I suspect no one reads him anymore; he was a great favorite of my father's. Anyway, he has a lovely line: 'For how can man die better, than facing fearful odds, for the ashes of his fathers and the temples of his gods.' "

"Very cute, Mother," said Miranda, her voice businesslike again. She looked at her watch. "If you've brought me here to listen to you recite poems of your girlhood, I really must be going."

"Well, actually, one reason I've invited you here was that I briefly had a crazy idea I might push you out the window, or shoot you, or put strychnine in your tea, although I doubt the nice man at the chemist's downstairs would sell me any."

"Mother, don't be ridiculous."

"Now," Lyda said, "you listen and you listen carefully, young woman. I don't suppose you know T. S. Eliot's verse, no one your age seems to know anything, although that's quite beside the point. He was all the rage when I was young, though, and there's a line I remember from one of the poems, is it 'Prufrock'? It speaks of 'the awful daring of a moment's surrender which an age of prudence can never retract.' I can't tell you how often that line has buzzed in my head over the last year or so, as I've watched you turn into a monster."

"Mother, get on with it!"

"In 1942, dear, a young man came to visit me in New York. He came at your fath⁻ . . . at Howland's suggestion. It happened that I took him down to Double Dune for the day. While we were there, we made love. Don't ask me why. People do strange things in wartime. I was lonely, distracted, I felt left out, Howland was so busy in Washington. I was never unfaithful again, never considered it for a moment, but this happened, I missed my next period, and nine months later, there you were."

"In other words, you're trying to tell me that Daddy wasn't my real father?" Miranda's question was tempered with uninterest.

"He was not. I pretended that it might have been possible, but I can assure you it wasn't, not with Howland. I was quite determined after Jay that I didn't want any more children, and I was unfailingly careful."

"So—who was he?"

"Someone you've come to know quite well. Eric Laszlo."

She watched the implications of her words sink into Miranda. For an instant, the indulgent smirk remained in place, then, as if she had been sprayed with corrosive compound, she seemed to dissolve.

"I see it hasn't taken you long to sort it out," said Lyda. She knew she was being cruel, but cruelty, even to her own daughter, seemed a terribly small price relative to the stakes.

"Yes, dear," she added in as motherly a voice as she could muster. "It means exactly what you think: you are a Jew."

She saw her daughter fight for control.

"Oh, Mother," Miranda said in an unconvincing way, "don't try that tired ploy on me!"

"I can assure you, my dear, it is no ploy."

"Besides, even if it is true, that doesn't make me Jewish! You have to have a Jewish mother!"

"Really?" Lyda said. She put every ounce of sarcasm she could draw up into her words. "I somehow doubt such an interesting technicality would carry much weight with the sort of people to whom you and Jerry seem to be beaming your message. On the whole, they strike me as rather a simplistic lot, to whom life is essentially a matter of black and white— I believe the technical term is 'Manichean.' "

Miranda said nothing. Lyda went on: "Let me repeat, just so you understand, your real father was Jewish, indeed he is one of the most prominent Jews in the world, someone of whom a decent human being would be proud. Yes, my darling girl, you *are* Jewish."

Miranda looked quickly over her shoulder.

"For God's sakes, Mother, keep your voice down! Bruce might be listening!"

"Why should that make a difference?" asked Lyda in a mild voice. Miranda didn't answer.

"I want you to understand my terms," Lyda said. "I have written letters to the *Times* and to that nice Mr. Hewitt who does '60 Minutes' for Bill Paley. The letters outline the facts just as I've recounted them to you. I have also written to Eric in Switzerland, telling him the whole story, including some surmises about our little chat today which, I must say, have proven really quite accurate. Those three letters are in the possession of young Fritz Stenton, whom you know has succeeded poor Archer as our attorney. Unless Fritz hears to the contrary from me in the next forty-eight hours, that is, by the day after Christmas, he is instructed to see that they are delivered. Naturally, this means I shall be most interested in whatever words you put in Jerry's mouth tomorrow night."

"Only God tells Jerry what to say!"

"Then perhaps you should have a word with Him." Lyda took a long, sad look at her daughter, canvassing her face for a reading of her thoughts.

"I should have told you earlier," she finally said in a soft voice. "Perhaps it would have helped you understand yourself better, understand the nature of this rage that seems to consume you. On the other hand, perhaps not: perhaps all that would have happened is that you'd hate me, and yourself, and the entire world, even more than you do already."

Miranda rose. Her movements were shaky, like those of an old, drained woman, and her voice quavered as she spoke to her mother. "You will burn in hell for this, Mother," she said. But the words had a dead ring, and there was no fire in her face.

"I rather think not," said Lyda. "Do you remember that little painting in the Metropolitan, the little Sienese picture? Surely you do, darling; it was one of the few things I can ever recall you liking that didn't have an edge of violence or anger or vindictiveness to it. Remember? All those nicely dressed people hugging each other among the orange trees. A very pretty notion of heaven, I always thought. I *do* hope that's where I'm bound. Perhaps you'll join us there some day. You know what they say, darling? That it's never too late to make amends. In any case, I can hardly wait. It's been a very long life."

The sequence of events was simple enough to reconstruct. "The Arrow of God" had been "wheels up" out of Teterboro at 7:26 Eastern Standard Time on December 23. Once airborne, Miranda Warrington Creedmore had spoken briefly to her husband in Long Beach. She had then gone aft, to the sleeping compartment, to rest, leaving orders not to disturb her until they were an hour out of Orange County/John Wayne Airport.

At 8:17 Pacific Standard Time, the flight attendant had rapped on the compartment door, received no answer, and gone in. According to the Orange County coroner, she would have been dead by then for at least three hours. The contents of the empty Seconal bottle on the floor had done their work quickly.

She had left a letter to her husband. Grief-stricken, the Reverend Jerry Creedmore had canceled his Christmas Eve "ministry" and all public appearances for the following sixty days.

The morning after Christmas, Lyda telephoned Fritz Stenton and requested the return of the letters she had entrusted to him for safekeeping. He offered her his best wishes for the coming new year, and many happy returns, and said that the envelope would be messengered to her promptly.

Miranda was buried with great ceremony from her husband's soaring glass-and-stainless steel "cathedral." Reverend Jerry was himself too grief-stricken to preach over his dead wife, but the other orators, a United States senator, prominent middle-western and southern industrialists, a clutch of fire-breathing ministers from various pentecostal faiths and, as the star eulogist, a retired President of the United States, all made it clear that Miranda's death, even though self-induced, was an act of martyrdom for the glory of the faith and the cause.

Lyda did not attend her daughter's funeral. It was just as well, she thought, that Jerry had made it clear she would not be welcome. In his rantings, he had also made it clear that, even though Miranda had indicated her deep depression was attributable to a quarrel with Lyda, she had not disclosed the big ancestral fact that had come out in the dead woman's final confrontation with her mother.

On the day Miranda was buried, in Southern California gray and drizzling, in New York bitter cold and brilliant, Lyda walked down Madison Avenue to St. James'. The back of the church was filled with homeless men and women; she put a hundred-dollar bill in the poor box, and then proceeded to a pew near the altar where she prayed briefly for the repose of her daughter's angry soul and for God's forgiveness for herself. That evening, Jay—who had flown west—called to report that "every right-wing crazy" in America had seemed to be there.

In the weeks following, Lyda busied herself putting her life in order.

"Things have gotten too messy," she told Bruce. "We've got to get things sorted out. I have too many possessions in my life!"

As Bruce told his friend Kenn, it was like a yard sale, only without money. She cleaned out the warehouses—a good Duncan Phyfe suite went to the Museum of the City of New York, whose institutional nose was out of joint over Lyda's museum, along with a check for a million dollars—and winnowed her bric-a-brac and closets mercilessly. Startled friends came home to find parcels containing objects they might have admired years before. Chickie was given a Matisse drawing and an old photograph he'd long coveted, a stuffy picture of Lyda and Howland and his parents taken at the time of Lyda's engagement, although he was told the latter should be until final notice considered a loan.

She didn't go out, and declined invitations to go south, to Hobe Sound and Jamaica and Lyford Key, for warm weeks with old friends. In the evenings, she stayed at home, working on her wall full of scrapbooks, playing old records, sometimes over and over to the point that Jay, who came to dine twice a week, shouted over coffee that if he had to hear that goddamn Piaf record one more time, he'd jump out the window.

She read the papers, stayed on top of things—the law's vise seemed to be closing on Norton Herzkow—and got her life in order. I am waiting, she knew, just waiting; that is all. Soon it must surely be time.

Jay noticed. He tried to chaff and chivvy her, but as he told Billy T., "My old lady just sits there like the fat lady's done sung, and now it's time for the curtain to fall."

There seemed so little to show for so long a life. She had done her best, and all she had to show for it was stuff—and the veneration of a lot of people whose respect she didn't particularly covet.

So much had changed. Little things: "21" had been ruined. There didn't seem to be such a season as spring; winter plunged right into summer. There were no true neighborhoods left, built around a dry cleaners and a newsstand and a bad French restaurant for servants' night out. Even Hanover Place wasn't at Hanover Place anymore!

Worst of all, there seemed to be no young people. Once, it occurred to her, the city had rung with their laughter, but now even the young all seemed grim and avaricious.

She tried to console herself with self-examination. She *had* done her best. She *had* attended to what it said in the Constitution: to "ourselves and our posterity."

She wrote letters, read and waited. She turned her back on things she knew or could guess at: the cause of Miranda's suicide; the way in which Eric Laszlo and Carlo Fretta and, yes, herself, had used Sunny Herzkow.

On a Friday late in February 1990, after the close of a market now thoroughly convulsed by crescendo after crescendo of bad economic news, the Attorney-General of the United States announced that the government intended to seek indictments for numerous counts of criminal securities fraud against Norton Herzkow, Roger Riskind, Warmile Financial Group, and certain of its employees and other persons to be named. The nightly news showed Max Miles heatedly denying any wrongdoing on behalf of Hanover Place and vowing to fight the charges to the bitter end.

That night, Lyda had trouble sleeping. She got up a little after two and went into the library and began going through her scrapbooks. There were sixty-one of them now, sixty for the years from her marriage through Andrew's death, and then just one for the years since. The photos ranged from a yellowed sepia snapshot of a young intense woman peering into a friend's old box Brownie, to a photo showing her outside Le Cirque with Sunny Herzkow's arm wound through hers.

All those faces, she thought, turning the pages, putting one volume back on the shelf, taking another down. All those men in dinner jackets, women in evening dresses, in nightclubs and restaurants—that's what she seemed not to be able to get out of her mind, nightclubs and restaurants; how silly could you be! All those places and pictures. All those hats! What kind of a life did five hundred hats add up to?

Here were Howland and his father on a first tee somewhere: the National/Newport? Seminole? Gulph Mills? Sometime in the thirties, neckties tucked inside their shirts. A formal Bachrach photograph of Ariadne Warrington on the occasion of her investiture as president of the Colony Club. Here were she and Howland, with Eddy Duchin—was that Hollywood, back before the war? Then Lex and Dee in their Exeter baseball uniforms; then their flight-school pictures; then Dee posing proudly by his fighter at an English airfield and Lex under the wing of his Hellcat on the *Essex*; herself and Howland the year they went to Ascot with Tom and Jessica Creedmore, standing outside Claridge's with the men looking ridiculous in their gray toppers. Jerry Zerbe clowning with Howland at Belmont Park. Andrew and Jay sticking their heads through the holes of a funhouse photo: fat bathing beauties with boys' heads. Taken where? Palisades? Coney Island? Rye? Another one of Jay, wearing a terrible hand-painted Countess Mara tie one of Howland's connections had sent him for Christmas. Children on beaches, tennis courts, steps of famous museums, graduating from schools, on horseback, with fishing rods, in gondolas, on ski lifts. Miranda's Junior Assembly photo: typical Bachrach, although grave, hinting at *terribilita*. Howland and Jay, tipsy, posed next to the Corvette they bought at the Bond Club auction-raffle; the gauzy stiff photograph of Howland that Pach Brothers took in 1958 when he went on the United Milling board; another of him breaking ground for a plant The Firm had financed; another on the Floor, at the listing of some company; others shaking hands with Franklin, Ike, Hap Arnold, Foster Dulles, Jack Dempsey, Joe Dimaggio. Herself and Howland in Paris, Tokyo, Beirut, Cannes; at Sun Valley, LaGuardia, Malibu, Churchill Downs; in El Morocco, the Stork Club, the White Elephant, the 400; at Maxim's, Quaglino's, the Savoy, Harry's Bar, Romanoff's. On the steps of airliners and the fantails of yachts and the observation platforms of private railway cars. Hundreds and hundreds of photographs, certificates, matchbook covers, sheet music, children's drawings: an archive of shared fun and caring, memories of no earthly use to anyone except a family that was dying out.

It was close to five when she closed the last volume. She went over to the window and lit a cigarette. Shouldn't smoke, she thought—Ben Miles was threatening to send her over to Sloan-Kettering for some tests. She and the doctor had worked it out together: 70 years times 365 made 25,550 days which, times, say, 40, equaled 1,022,000 cigarettes she'd smoked in her life. It didn't really seem so many.

Into her head came the old Piaf song: *"Avec mes souvenirs, j'ai allumé le feu, mes chagrins, mes plaisirs, je n'ai plus besoin d'eux."* She gazed out over the dark city; in the western distance there was a glow, probably from the grotesque battlements and parapets of Kerryland on the Jersey banks of the Hudson; the place stayed open twenty-four hours a day. She recalled taking Andrew and Jay to the old Palisades Park, remembered how Jay got the radio jingle in his head, repeated it, as was his habit as a boy, over and over again until she and Howland had threatened to send him off to summer camp. She could hear him now, high little voice stressing the syncopation: "Skip the bo-ther and skip the fuss, take a Pub-lic Ser-vice Bus!"

It was the halfway hour between dark and dawn. In the silent park below, the lights were still orange, haloed by mist; in another hour they would turn pale in the early light, become whitish-yellow. The radio had spoken of possible snow.

She felt sleepy and returned to bed. She lay down and gazed up into the dark. It seemed to her she was light-headed, and that her feet, now her legs, were already asleep. In the next instant, she realized what it was: the rising of the same tide which in its other seasons had carried off her men. She started to push herself, up, to reach for the telephone, but a second later, matters were decided for her. With only an infinitesimal flash of pain to signal the moment of passage, her heart stopped, and the long life of Lyda Warrington was over.

BOOK

X

THE FIRE
THIS TIME

MARCH

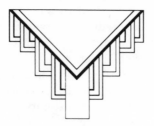

s Billy T. said, what the guy
didn't know wouldn't hurt him.

Jay's driver had scouted out that the latest owner of Double Dune had
gone to Barbados for the winter, and so on the Saturday a week after
Lyda's death, Billy T. drove Jay and Chickie and the houseman Bruce to
East Hampton. They parked the Lincoln at the lot of the public beach
and walked down the sand through the blustering wind and up onto the
bluff and, there in front of the sprawling house, they scattered Lyda's
ashes in the dune grass.

They each prayed silently, but as Chickie later told Rachel, perhaps
the most fitting epitaph was pronounced by Billy T. As they made ready
to leave, he said to the others, "Hey, how 'bout a last look," and walked
quickly up the boardwalk over the dunes, up the lawn and onto the
veranda. Producing a fearsome switchblade, he pried loose a board from
the shutters that had been installed against the depredations of winter
and peered in.

"Jesus," he exclaimed. "Hey, Mr. Fenton, check this shit!"

Chickie joined him, scrutinized the drawing room, and said to Jay:
"Really, I mean, some people! Mahogany paneling in *this* house! Really!"

"Yeah," said Billy T. enthusiastically, "boy, Mrs. W. woulda hated
that shit, huh, Boss? Maybe she was right to check out when she did!"

At Lyda's request, no memorial service was held. As she had written Fritz Stenton, she refused to have people at her urn that she would never have had at her dinner table. She directed that her ashes be scattered—Jay and Chickie would know where—and that people so inclined make contributions to the museum. She could not know that, in her memory, a tree would be planted in the Garden of the Righteous Gentiles at Yad Vashem, the Holocaust memorial near Jerusalem, but if she had, as Eric Laszlo told his friend Carlo Fretta, she surely would have been pleased.

It soon began to seem that she had picked a wise time to die. By mid-March, financial markets were in disarray. The recession was proving to be deeper than anyone had predicted. Economic concerns were now making way for graver worries; there was an unmistakable political restiveness in the country as the unemployment number went back over ten percent and tales of economic and financial woe multiplied.

In Manhattan, the grand jury's deliberations on the Herzkow indictments dragged on, adding to the uncertainty and the rumors.

Warmile had decided to hang tough. At Max's insistence, The Firm's annual investment conference was held as scheduled on the island of St. Columba.

It was not a complete success. The old joviality and bonhomie were there, but, to experienced ears, too loud this time, forced, nervous. The aura of implacable, all-conquering confidence was lacking. When Arthur Lubloff addressed the conference on its final night, he spoke bravely and coolly; at the conclusion of his remarks, his audience leaped to its feet and clapped its hands raw; the reaction was all out of proportion to the tenor and hard matter of Artie's remarks, a level of acclamation that was, as more than one of those present surely felt, more appropriate to the passing of an era than to a half-hour speech.

As it turned out, Artie had in fact pronounced his own eulogy. Warmile G4 Gulfstream N1HP crashed shortly after takeoff, killing all aboard: Artie, Max Miles and his wife Irene Gessel-Miles, Leo Himelman, and the flight crew of three.

The plane crash created panic to the markets. Arthur Lubloff was the linchpin of a complex interleaved structure of debt-creation and interaction that only he understood, and to which he was universally regarded as indispensable. The flames of panic were fed by rumor. Obviously, the crash had been someone's work, and fingers were pointed in every direction, senselessly this way and that, like the needle of a magnetically deranged compass.

Inevitably, as the markets' problems multiplied, curiosity about the whys and wherefores of the crash of N1HP ebbed in the face of larger disasters, and the incident joined such other unsolved mysteries of finance as the 1975 disappearance over Mexico of the jet carrying rogue financier

David Graiver, the murder-suicides of Calvi and Sindona, and the shooting in an Oklahoma parking lot of the chairman of Telex. Within months, all that was permanent in the memory of N1HP could be found on the small island of St. Columba. For a number of years afterward, the attention of passengers being driven to the luxury resorts down the coast was drawn to a shack on the outskirts of Port Margaret Town. The ramshackle shed, which housed a bilious goat, was notable for its color, a rich chocolate brown that even the streaming Caribbean sunlight failed to fade, on which was superimposed a yellow decorative scheme. On close inspection, the lean-to's roof and sides proved to be carpentered from the salvagings of a set of extremely expensive Louis Vuitton luggage.

Around the neck of a Port Margaret fisherman hung the other remnant of the last flight of the Warmile jet. The force of the crash had thrown Max clear; a day later, his body, still intact and strapped in its seat, washed ashore down the coast. His hand was in his pocket clenched tightly. When his fingers were pried apart, Max—a notoriously nervous flier—was found to be gripping what was obviously a good-luck piece, a smallish bronze cross incised with anchors and a tiny sailing ship, with a shred of dark blue ribbon divided by a frayed white stripe.

By Memorial Day, 1990, the world financial system had been plunged into the worst turmoil since the Phoenicians invented money. Every crash, Fletcher Warrington had once noted, was the obverse of the glories of the bull market that had preceded it. Right through the eighties, the "globalization" of the financial markets had been cause for celebration; if New York caught cold, went the saying, Tokyo or London would be there with the aspirin. The global markets were asserted to be so vast, diverse, and commodious that any potential for real catastrophe had been all but eliminated.

Not so. It was soon evident that what had been praised as a wholly efficient series of market linkages providing checks, balances, and hedges, could prove to be an equally efficient equation describing a financially fissionable chain reaction. As the economy slackened, and voices that a year earlier had been dismissive of the likelihood of a recession now spoke respectfully of the prospect of a depression, cracks appeared along long-identified fault lines.

Mid-June thus brought the realization that the so-called "junk financing" market was in grievous difficulty. The death of Arthur Lubloff had deprived the system of its bidder of last resort. General uncertainty about the dollar had driven interest rates skyward. Worsening economic conditions were being reflected at the corporate cash register. As summer began, three of the largest leveraged buyouts of the recent past were rumored to be in trouble. Over the July 4th holiday, two went into default and things really began to collapse.

It had been widely put about that lenders to major LBOs had insisted the deals be hedged against cash-flow problems and increases in interest rates. Now the writers of those hedges, called to put up, defaulted, reneged, sought refuge in bankruptcy, or simply could not be found.

A pattern familiar to students of the 1929 crash now reasserted itself. The linkages in which the great men of finance had rejoiced turned on the celebrants. A cascade of financial and economic disasters ensued. Whatever could go wrong, did; whatever should have been done, was not; whatever should not have been done, was.

It is possible that if events could have been confined to the merely financial, the largest horrors would not have resulted. In mid-summer, however, a Global 747 carrying 380 people from Dallas-Forth Worth to Los Angeles plunged to earth in a crowded shopping mall five miles from the airport, killing another 193 people on the ground, and Wall Street found itself in a whole new, utterly terrifying ball game.

Within a fortnight after the crash, it was all over the newspapers that the Global crash had been the consequence of essential maintenance deferred in order to conserve the airline's shrinking cash flow—so that debt service payments could be met on the huge debts Norton Herzkow had placed on Global in taking it over. On June 17, the Federal Aviation Administration, moving to forestall Herzkow's own anticipated legal actions, placed Global Airlines in receivership and ordered an immediate diversion of all cash flow into the airline's maintenance requirements. It was pointed out on the editorial page of *The Wall Street Journal* that this amounted to *de facto* nationalization of a flagship of the free-enterprise system, but in view of the public outcry, such opinions carried no weight. In addition, criminal indictments for reckless endangerment were obtained against Herzkow personally in seven states—he would subsequently be arraigned in Manhattan Criminal Court—and full-scale hearings were launched in Washington.

Now the "junk bond" market collapsed completely; the late Arthur Lubloff's "Department of Sanitation" was caught with $8 billion of LBO-related obligations on its hands; three other leading houses were frozen with over $13 billion in so-called "bridge loans" awaiting refinancing. On August 16, the New York Stock Exchange declared Warmile Securities in violation of capital requirements, and took it over. Shortly thereafter two other big LBOs filed for bankruptcy protection.

By then the stock markets were in headlong retreat. On the Friday before Labor Day, the Dow-Jones lost 303 points and change before the governors of the Stock Exchange, summoned hastily to the Exchange president's office, voted to suspend trading; by then, the Dow-Jones Industrial Average had lost nearly forty percent of its value at the beginning of the summer, and stood at barely over 1,100.

Half-day trading sessions were now in effect, as well as a series of "collars" and "trigger-points" designed to ensure, mathematically at least, that the leading indices would not go to absolute zero.

The panic had spread to other markets, to London, Milan, Hong Kong, Tokyo; the Nikkei Index of Japanese shares had in the last nine months fallen from 37,000 to 17,630.

It was inevitable, because such had always been the case throughout history, that a financial crisis of this magnitude took on an ominous political dimension. Washington was looking for scapegoats.

In October, the Revenue Stabilization and Fiscal Integrity Act of 1990 was rushed through Congress, vetoed by the President, and passed over his veto. The bill effectively removed all tax privileges from merger, take-over, and buyout debt, and did so retroactive to 1988. As a grinning senator from Iowa told CBS: "Those who lived by junk are now going to die by it!" At the same time, in almost twenty state legislatures, and in half again as many state and federal courtrooms, law was either enacted or—under the overpowering weight of public opinion—judgment obtained prohibiting corporations and the shadowy Wall Streeters now seen lurking behind every toppling tree from reducing payrolls in order to meet debt payments. In November, the Special Bankruptcy Act of 1990 created a Title 14 of the Bankruptcy Code, which effectively canceled all rights of the holders of takeover debt in favor of the ongoing interest and welfare of communities and employees.

None of this was lost on the rest of the world. By November, the dollar had fallen to ninety-eight yen and in Zurich one dollar could be exchanged for eight-tenths of a Swiss franc. The Federal Reserve was trapped, unable to defend the currency by raising interest rates in an economy that was now perceived rapidly to be sliding into recession or worse.

Now, inevitably, ensued a repeat of the fiscal xenophobia that had thrown the world into depression sixty years earlier. For the first time in its history, the United States was seen as no better than politically uncertain, and perhaps politically unstable, from an investor's point of view. In September, the Japanese had been notable by their absence from the Treasury offering, which had the effect of raising the government's effective borrowing cost by almost seventy-five basis points, which ratcheted rates upward right through the system, from the borrowing costs of General Motors to what a Kansas coed paid on her VISA card.

In early November, Tokyo made it official. Pending stabilization of the dollar at not less than one hundred yen or the indexation of Treasury debt to that price level, all Japanese investment would be essentially limited to rollovers of existing positions. The day after the Bank of Japan's announcement, the Dow-Jones fell three hundred points, to 665, before trading was halted at noon.

Two weeks later, it was announced that the Empire of Japan and the Union of Soviet Socialist Republics had entered into a ten-year Economic Assistance and Military Cooperation Pact, committing Japan to $300 billion in development and other investments. The New York Stock Exchange did not open that day, nor did it a week later, when a similar pact was announced between the USSR and the soon-to-be-unified European Economic Community.

Around the world, the consensus grew that America was finished. One by one, the South American debts, scenting that the shambling, wounded giant to the north was no longer a threat, defaulted. Furious, frustrated, in great pain, it was natural that America lash back; shortly after the turn of the new year, Congress passed unanimously, and this time the President signed without cavil, The Economic Autonomy and Asset Repatriation Act of 1991, which isolated the nation from world financial flows as effectively as the Smoot-Hawley tariff of 1931 had shut down its trade with the rest of the globe. Asked to comment, the British Chancellor of the Exchequer could only quote Carlyle: "All outward, all inward things are fallen into one general wreck of madness."

Nineteen ninety-one dawned miserably. Troubles everywhere, so numerous it seemed pointless to try to list them all. Mired in economic gloom, few people took much account of other, more ominous forces now openly at work in American life and politics, forces that historians of Wall Street were manifestly less equipped to recognize than would be historians of the Weimar Republic.

This threnody, a counterpoint to the events unfolding on the exchanges around the world, had begun in earnest at the beginning of the summer of the previous year, with the opening of "The Marryat Hearings," the hearings of the Senate Subcommittee on Capital Markets (Sen. J.B. Marryat, R.-Tex. presiding).

Some called them "The Washington Show Trials." It was not an altogether unapt description. As had State Prosecutor Andrei Vishinsky fifty-odd years earlier in Moscow, and Pujo and Pecora in America in their time, the subcommittee's chairman had made it clear from day one of the hearings that he was looking for villains and scapegoats. "The average working 'merican didn't get us into this mess," he told "Face the Nation" on the morning that light Saudi crude hit twenty-six dollars a barrel F.O.B. Jedda, "folks on Wall Street did. You don't hang the horse, boys, you hang the rustler."

The Marryat hearings dovetailed with the conclusion of the FAA's Global enquiry, which had produced a litany of tales of repairs being substituted for mandated replacements, of unairworthy aircraft sent aloft with regularity, of subminimum pilot training and supervision, of the funds that might have cured these deficiencies not being reinvested in Global but funneled upstream to Herzkow's holding company. It was a supreme stroke of stagecraft, then, when Jack Marryat opened his hearings with Norton Herzkow as his first witness.

The opening witness often sets the tone for an entire, months-long process, and Herzkow was no exception. With his sleek, overtailored appearance, noisy New York voice and pugnacious, knowing manner, he was benchmade to be a focus of a troubled nation's animus. In the weeks following his appearance, it seemed to the Hearings' growing television audience, which increasingly consisted of men laid off from middle man-agement and other jobs that didn't keep the goods and services flowing into the diminishing economy, that they were seeing one Norton Herzkow after another: men who looked alike, dressed alike, sounded alike, and seemed utterly unrepentant.

As the hearings proceeded, however, it became clear that their real star would be a man who would never be called to testify, one Lester Vivian. In early August, like two exploring parties who have cut their way through heavy underbrush from opposite sides of a thick jungle and now come face-to-face in a clearing, a working party from the United States Treasury and several other agencies, which was looking into the connection between a Toronto penny-stock scheme and certain Bahamas-Miami financial net-works, and a special team from Scotland Yard backtracking a money-laundering arrangement originating in the Isle of Wight and running through a dummy Luxembourg trust to three defunct federally-insured savings-and-loans in Jacksonville, bumped into each other. Each had a number of pieces of a picture puzzle, so to speak. When put together, there were the narrow features of Lester Vivian.

By then, Vivian was gone, however, fled to Switzerland, ensconced in a well-guarded villa outside Zug, secure behind the impenetrable barrier of Swiss law. He had, it seemed, committed no crime that Switzerland regarded as extraditable, although the U.S. Attorney for New York's Southern District did enter an unenthusiastic pleading charging Vivian with "destruction of railroad property," and asking for him to be remanded in U.S. custody. For not the first time in the Helvetic Confederation's history, Berne was apologetic, but obdurate. Its hands were tied by a law in force since 1291, a period three times as long as the whole history of America.

Nevertheless, Vivian *in absentia* became as powerful a presence as any of the witnesses who paraded to the stand from September 1990 nearly up to the end of the following January. Standing in for him physically was a large signboard behind Senator Marryat's head. With each witness, the chart grew in both size and complexity. By the end of the hearings, the chart, which Senator Marryat described as "more complicated than an engineering diagram of the Humble cat cracker at Bay City," involved no less than eighty-three boxes joined by a tracery that had taken the SEC mainframe computer four passes to get right. These entities were domiciled in a dozen jurisdictions including the Bahamas, Panama, Grand Cayman, Switzerland, the Channel Islands, Luxembourg, Lichtenstein, Liberia, and Monaco.

It was an impressive display, but it was made clear that behind these boxes, behind even Vivian, were ranged dread and violent powers, a loose community of interest, often at war within itself, made up of Italo-Americans, Afro-Americans, Jamaicans, Panamanians, Colombians, and Cubans, who were faced with the problem of investing the greatest, fastest-flowing torrent of money the world of private capital had ever known. Much of it had found its way to Wall Street, it became clear, under the auspices, conscious or otherwise, of men and women who had up to now been acclaimed as the heroes and heroines of the brave new Financial Order. The sickening revelations culminated in the disclosure that one of the most acclaimed bankers of the day had roomed at Yale with a young man who was now one of the kingpins of the Medellin cocaine cartel.

The tale unfolded by the subcommittee's witnesses was sordid, even if a good deal of the time it was beyond the grasp of all but the most expert observers of the world of high finance. The revelation that, at his death, Arthur Lubloff had been working on the takeover and dissection of General Motors by an Asiatic consortium, though hardly criminous, at least as far as it had been carried, came as a tremendous shock. Was there no limit to the effrontery of these people! It set the emotional stage for the disclosures that followed, as one by one, the rats turned on each other, proving conclusively that there was, indeed, no honor among thieves. They detailed episodes of gross insider trading, phony buybacks, front-running, stock parking and warehousing, of "soft dollar" abuses, payoffs —book cooking and market fiddling of the most manipulative sort.

In the early stages of the hearings, it was sometimes difficult to tell whether the disclosures being made were more effective in provoking the public's outrage or in capturing its fancy. All of this changed when it became clear that New York criminal elements, working through front men and elaborate corporate screens, had effectively controlled a number of failed "thrift" institutions now being made whole with the taxpayers' money. As with most major frauds, the operation was breathtaking both in its simplicity and its effrontery. The cash takings from street narcotics sales were weighed—the money was coming in at too great a rate to be counted!—packaged and transported by chartered cargo jet to half a dozen overseas jurisdictions where it was credited to bank accounts, and the wealth transformed from crumpled bills, which would be returned by the jurisdictions' central banks to the U.S. Treasury to be burned, into book-keeping entries and electronic blips.

These blips were circuited back into the U.S., broken down into $100,000 (the maximum insurable amount) particles, and placed on deposit with the "friendly" savings and loans. These institutions had used these deposits to make loans to certain favored parties, essentially to entities controlled by the very same depositors; most of the sums loaned had simply vanished into thin air, leaving the federal government to cover the short-fall. One witness testified that he deposited $1,000,000 in ten pieces, using ten different money brokers, at Bel Air Federated Savings, then got it loaned back to himself, through a shell corporation that he looted, so that in the end he had $100,000 cash and Uncle Sam's insurance company was on the hook for his original deposit, a two-for-one return and safe as a church! Those New York boys, he said, you hadda give 'em credit!

An ancient perception, dormant for the previous decade, reawoke and tried its wings: Manhattan as Babylon, as Sodom and Gomorrah, as the Temple of the Money Changers, stinking, striving, concupiscent; wild and wasteful, innately evil, a hive of thieves, humming with a wicked current alternating between a luxury class pirouetting on the backs of the poor and homeless, and the gunshot-punctuated howlings of a dope-sucking underclass that drugs and violence had rendered beyond redemption. As a noted New York liberal columnist wrote apropos of the testimony of Kevin Kerry: "In my day, the guardian angels were called Matthew, Mark, Luke, and John, but it would appear today they have names like Angelo, Carmine, Luis, and Jose."

The most dramatic moment in the hearings came when brother faced brother. Bobby Marryat came to talk. He had been confronted with a tape of his wife's testimony and had agreed to plea-bargain. While in protective custody, just to make certain he suffered no change of mind or sudden amnesia during his appearance, his guardians had, two nights earlier, driven him north, on his own recognizance, to spend a night alone in an unoccupied cell in the maximum-security block at Sing-Sing. What Bobby Marryat had heard in the course of that short but inter-minable stretch of time, those sighs, shrieks, slitherings, moans, and grunts barely distinguishable from the sounds of the jungle, ensured his cooperation.

He told the committee everything he knew: about secret profit-sharing arrangements with Roger Riskind respecting the maximization of the profit potential in certain takeover bids and greenmail ploys initiated in 1985, '86, '87 in the oil business. About "the Black Knight" strategy devised by Arthur Lubloff and Norton Herzkow to dupe threatened takeover targets into flying into certain welcoming arms that turned into carniv-orous jaws. And he told the committee what he knew, especially about a meeting held years before in the Pierre Hotel. His testimony respecting that evening was vivid. What he seemed to be describing was a sinister conspiracy to unravel the very fabric of American commercial life, all for thirty pieces of silver.

When he finished, there was a thoughtful silence in the committee room. Then Senator Wilkes (R.-Miss.) asked a question that suddenly gave flesh to a ghost of an idea that had haunted the proceedings for some weeks now, that had in fact been moving slowly and ominously toward the forefront of the nation's awareness. The senator was an ambitious man. He had studied the career of Joseph McCarthy, identified the critical errors committed by the late senator from Wisconsin, and thought he knew a hot issue when he saw one. A parochial man, he was a favorite of the Hill press corps, whom he kept entertained with decent bourbon whiskey and a string of pithy backwoods apothegms. Like many of his kind, he was also sly, vicious, and bigoted. Now something Bobby Marryat had said was revealed to him as a hook on which to hang as glorious and powerful a career as any American legislator had ever enjoyed.

"Jus' one las' thing, Mr. Marryat," asked the senator. " 'Bout this meetin' back in June of 1974 at the Hotel Pierre: could you tell me, sir, in your recollection, exactly how many of the people there at the time were, um, uh, of the Hebrew persuasion?"

Three weeks later, on Halloween night, 1990, Jerry Creedmore preached a ministry to two hundred fifty thousand people gathered in the stands and infield of the Indianapolis Speedway; some of them had come from a thousand miles away to hear him. His message was magnetic; it drew the nation's disaffected, its alienated, its angry, its disenfranchised, its vengeful.

America had been plunged into this nightmare, he cried, by the greed of a few. To all these people out there in the dark, huddled in the cold around loudspeakers, Jerry's point seemed clear and irrefutable, and he offered them a banner around which to rally.

"The right to life," he shouted to the thousands out there in the dark, "is more than the right just to be born. It's the right to live and work and not feel that any minute one of them will come along with a checkbook full of junk bonds and buy your life out from under you! They are the enemy. It must be our struggle to seize our nation from them."

Our struggle. *Unser Kampf.*

"It's just like Vienna after World War One," he told "ABC Newsmakers" in November: "*They* control the media. *They* control the money market. *They* control real estate. Before this nation can be great again, we must seize it back from *them!*"

Jerry was scheduled to speak at Winston-Salem the following week, but the night before, as he came out of his hotel into the glare of the television lights, looking into the cameras with his angelic, handsome features refined by passion into something terrifying and hypnotic, a girl burst from the crowd and shot him dead.

The young woman, a seminarian named Heba Greenspin, was terribly beaten by Jerry's bodyguards, a contingent from the local chapter of the White Aryan Resistance Movement; she died in a hospital before regaining consciousness. No charges were brought. As the ambulance pulled away, rumor spread in the crowd, and eventually found its way around the nation, that she had been an undercover agent of Mossad, an assassin in the pay of B'nai B'rith.

"Not content with building their Zion on the ashes of the rest of us," raved an editorial in a South Carolina paper, "they now seek blood! Well, those who teach bloody instructions, shall receive them!"

The paper was published in a small city whose once-thriving textile mills had been "restructured" by Wall Street into darkness and silence.

Two nights later, in Encino, a predominantly Jewish suburb of Los Angeles, a dozen L.A. street gangs converged and ran rampant in the streets. The Los Angeles police seemed unusually dilatory in responding to the situation. Speaking on television, the Los Angeles police chief noted a curious phenomenon. "About half of the perpetrators," he said, "were white skinheads, and about half blacks and Hispanics. I can't figure it. Usually these guys get along like oil and water, but this was kind of like a military operation, real disciplined. I've got fourteen officers in the hospital, two of them critical." That same week, similar desecrations occurred in Woodmere, Long Island, and on Chicago's West Devon Street.

The political effect was immediate. In March 1991, the Congress passed, by a six-to-one margin, a bill to suspend military aid to the state of Israel. The bill went to the White House and was signed without comment. Later that afternoon, the White House press office announced that the President, as a former naval officer, had for the first time accepted an invitation to the annual ceremony commemorating the dedication of a monument to the U.S.S. *Liberty*, which had been sunk some years earlier by the mistaken action of Israeli forces. When the monument had first been proposed, the outcry from organizations in the Israeli/Jewish interest had been enormous. Now, strangely, there was none.

Shortly before Thanksgiving 1990, Rachel flew to New York. People warned her against it, this was not a good time for Jews to visit America, but she felt she had no choice.

Jay sent Billy T. to meet her at Kennedy. He looked more battered than usual—forty years of double Bushmills was obviously taking its toll—but he was in his customary high spirits. The Boss, he reported, was back in business; "Mrs. W." had left Jay the lifetime use of the Warrington name, and his business was growing nicely.

" 'Course," said Billy T., "this boycott of them Jewish houses hasn't exactly hurt."

They drove directly to Memorial Hospital. When she entered Chickie's room, Rachel hesitated in the doorway.

"Oh, don't be such a silly Irish cow," he called. "You don't have to shy away. It's just an ordinary, run-of-the-mill leukemia."

Rachel crossed the room and kissed his cheek. He shook his head petulantly.

"I don't know why it is that everyone thinks it has to be AIDS. Honestly! I haven't had a bite out of *that* apple for twenty years—but that's another story. So, darling, how are you?"

"I'm all right," said Rachel. "It's you I'm worried about."

"Well, don't!" Chickie made a pout. "Soon I shall be one with my dear Lyda, which is what I've always wanted. Now don't *you* be ridiculous and start crying."

He made a little waving gesture that took in the room. "Have you ever seen anything like this? Do you know, dear, at first I thought this décor was God's way of punishing me!"

"Don't be silly. Jay told me the doctor says you're coming along fine." Rachel smiled through her white lie.

"Well, that's all very well for *him* to say! But I can tell, my dear, for blood this tired, there's not enough Geritol in the whole wide world."

Neither of them was fooled. Death was roosting in Chickie's hospital room. They could sense its moldering presence, hear the impatient ruffling of its invisible feathers.

"Well," he said, "let that be the end of the graves-worms-and-epitaphs department of our little chat. As that great philosopher Doris Day said: 'Che sera, sera.' Now—what news of the Rialto? How's the lad? Did you visit the museum? How does it look? That was a fabulous idea of Lyda's, wasn't it. You feel so sorry for new money; it doesn't have any old friends. How is it out in the mean streets?"

"I find it scary."

Rachel felt uneasier than ever in New York. There was something distinctly evil in the air. Just a few more hours, she told herself, and I'll be gone.

"Reach over there," said Chickie, "and hand me those books."

Rachel got up and went across to the metal dresser. There were four slim green volumes piled in a neat stack. She carried them back to the bed.

"I want little Andy to have these," he said. "They were Lyda's. She left them to me in her will."

He passed across one of the books. It was elegantly bound in well-preserved morocco; the gilt stamping was still bright; the title on the spine read: "*Old New York*," and underneath, "*False Dawn*."

"Read the inscription," said Chickie.

On the flyleaf was written in a firm hand: "For Lyda Vanderlyn and Howland Warrington on the occasion of their marriage, with the affectionate good wishes of Edith Wharton, November 16, 1924."

"Isn't that something?" said Chickie. "Now, did you get the albums? Oh, come on, wipe that disapproving frown off your beautiful mouth. You can't be angry with me for telling her!"

"I should be, but I'm not."

Three months after Lyda's death, the doorbell at Kilkennen had clanged. Rachel had opened it to find a perspiring, red-faced lorry driver. He had three packing crates for Mrs. Warrington, Kilkennen House, County Kerry.

His truck was too wide to pass over the narrow bridge at the foot of the drive so he had to break open the larger crate and trundle the contents up to the house on a handcart. It took him four trips, after which Rachel rewarded him with a bottle of Guinness and a twenty-pound note.

There were twenty large oblong parcels, wrapped in thick brown paper and strongly sealed with plastic tape, stacked in Rachel's front hall. The bill of lading accompanying them identified the consigner as Lyda's New York law firm. The parcels contained sixty-one photograph albums, obviously brand new, of dark green linen edged with red leather trim, each numbered, dated, and stamped with little Andy's initials. There were also some old books, in particular a copy of *Stuart Little*. On the flyleaf Rachel recognized an early, youthful version of her late husband's upright spokey scrawl. Attached was a square card stamped with the familiar LFW monogram on which was written "For Andrew Jr., from his doting grandmother."

In the other long box was something for Rachel: a tall Empire cheval glass, which she knew had been a favorite possession of Lyda's. Along with it was a note, dated the previous November. "I wanted you and young Andrew to have these things," Lyda had written. "We should all know where we came from, although by now it seems sadly clear to me that it has little or no bearing on where life takes us."

"Eric Laszlo called last week," said Chickie, breaking into Rachel's thoughts. "He sounds very well, although he's terribly worried about what's going on. With the Jews, I mean. Who'd have thought J.B. Marryat would turn out to be such a *gauleiter* at heart? Of course, Drew always said that was the one thing he didn't like about Texans—they were so bloodthirsty!"

"I think Eric should be worried," said Rachel. "I know I am."

"I gather the Limbergs have decided to remain year 'round at Lyford, at least until things get better," Chickie added. "And Buddy Grosser's counting his lucky stars he's got a Swiss wife. Speaking of Switzerland, my dear, I gather the eerie Mr. Vivian is all the social rage over there. What a sinister piece of work he must be. I must say, I never would have dreamed that Hanover Place was fronting for the Mob."

"Maybe they didn't think of it that way," said Rachel.

"Perhaps, perhaps. Nothing seems to make sense. It's glad I'll be to be taking my leave of a world that's turning out the way this one is. I mean, my dear, bombs! Have you ever?"

The week before, a Manhattan brokerage office had been firebombed. The bombing was the latest in a series of outrages: car-burnings, defacings, not to mention an epidemic of small, selective discourtesies in restaurants and hotels. Discriminatory advertising cutbacks and boycotts had been applied here and there in the media. Similar actions had broken out in England after the fall of the Thatcher government the previous autumn. More troubling still was what was happening in Washington. The latest rumor was that Congress was considering a range of special new taxes—targeting capital and finance and the income of such well-paid service industries as law, accounting, and investment banking.

Rachel could see her visit was beginning to tell on Chickie. He lay back on his pillow, closed his eyes for an instant as if gathering strength to go on, then opened them again and said: "You heard Sunny's moved to Paris?"

"I hadn't."

"Yep. Filed for divorce the day after they indicted Norton. Now there's a girl who's a survivor."

He lapsed into silence again. Rachel said nothing.

"Odd, isn't it," he said next, looking pensive. "All this that's going on? Yet I suppose someone—we, our lot—should have seen it coming. I never liked the Japanese. All those dreary little yellow men in gray suits bowing and nodding and buying everything. Do you suppose they think that writing out a check for the Empire State Building gets them even for Hiroshima?"

"A little of both, I should think."

"Eric told me he planted a tree in the Garden of the Righteous Gentiles at the Yad-whatever-they-call-it."

"He did—an olive tree."

"How nice of him. I expect Lyda rather thought of herself as an oak, but frankly I think it would be rather grim, don't you, to have to go through eternity being something as foursquare as an oak?"

He screwed his mouth up ruefully, and said: "It's sad, isn't it? We were a righteous decent lot—and look where it's gotten us. All those Sunday-school ideas people like us are born with and brought up to: the Golden Rule, fair play, *noblesse oblige*. Cheer the winner, cheer the loser, be a good sport no matter what. We're taught that self-sacrifice is more virtuous than survival, that losing gracefully's almost as good as winning. Ridiculous, isn't it! And the Jews think they have a monopoly on self-hatred!"

He spread his hands palms-up on the spread, and shrugged to suggest the hopelessness of it all.

"And of course: never, never, *never* show the slightest enthusiasm for making money! You know, darling, I'm beginning to think that maybe, in the end, that kind of thinking's just as destructive as this thing that's got me by the corpuscles. Yet in a way, we have no choice, do we? Lyda used to harp on that. 'Chickie,' she'd say, 'you can't buy what's not for sale.' Her premise was sound, but her application faulty, I think.

"Drew used to say—oh, I think of him so much, but soon enough I'll be seeing him face to face, I imagine . . . oh, anyway, maybe Drew was right. He told me once that the pattern of our lives is fixed in our character, and to blame it on life in general is stupid. If the world seems to move away from us, or we from it, it's just an illusion—or a delusion—to make us feel better. Our kind uses nostalgia the way other people take aspirin—as a cure for moral neuralgia."

Chickie lay back on the pillow. "Goodness, all this philosophizing has quite worn me out. I think I'll just get some sleep." He closed his eyes. "Ta-ta, my lovely Rose of Sharon, take care of everyone." He opened his eyes slowly and looked at Rachel, and his smile made him look ten years old.

"No last kiss for naughty little Chickie?" he asked.

"Of course." She bent and kissed him. Before she took her lips away he seemed to have fallen asleep. At the door, she looked back. From that short distance, it was impossible to tell if he was still breathing.

As Rachel left Chickie's hospital room, it was ten at night in Switzerland.

In his study, Lester Vivian studied the bank of screens. The New York Stock Exchange had stopped trading at 10:13 Eastern Standard Time that day, a loss on the Dow of 22.07, or just at five percent of its opening value of 442 and change. Thirteen minutes was a briefer session than usual, but the money-velocity statistics released that morning had been disastrous.

The dull green glow from the screens lent a dead, unearthly cast to his thin, cynical features. He flicked a switch, and the bank of screens went dark. He got up from the black leather recliner. Without the light from the screens, the room was in almost total darkness. He went to the window and drew the draperies aside. A beautiful night. The full moon danced on the surface of the lake. He looked at his watch. Time for a last turn around the garden.

Before going outside, he went quickly to his desk and checked the electronic display board that showed the status of the electric eyes and electrified fencing that guarded the Villa Leggia. He punched a quick number and spoke to the guard at the gatehouse.

It was cool outside. As he walked toward the lake, a guard with an Uzi under his arm and a big, snuffling Rottweiler on a tight lead emerged from the darkness, saluted, and passed on. At the water's edge, he sat down on a stone bench and looked back up at the house. On the hillside above, he had caused vineyards to be planted. If everything went as planned, in a year or two they might be making quite a decent Fendant.

Vivian's villa was already the talk of Switzerland. Last weekend, at the Faroukhs in Gstaad, more then one hint had been dropped that an invitation chez Vivian would be most welcome. Perhaps he should consider giving a reception; build a platform out on the lake, with a chamber orchestra; have Fauchon take care of the catering. Odd, wasn't it, how life worked out. In New York, he would be behind bars. Here, he was a star of the Gstaad–St. Moritz circuit.

Yes, thought Lester Vivian, to everything there is a season. The devil didn't sleep—you might close the New York Stock Exchange, but in Astoria, fifteen-year-olds still killed their grandmothers for crack money, and in turn that pittance, together with a hundred million other such pittances, would have to be put to work.

Well, so be it, he thought. The winds of enterprise blew fierce and changeable. The devil didn't sleep, and wherever he was, there was Mammon, and wherever Mammon was, there would Lester Vivian be. It was too bad about America, he thought; now that had been a market as spacious as a man could dream of. But the Americans lacked the will, and so it went. A man must move on. These people he was talking to in Leningrad and Moscow sounded promising: aggressive types who knew how to do business, how to get things done.

He leaned his head against the back of the tall bench and closed his eyes; he hated these interim hours, when the markets were shut down. But already the eastern rim of the world was turning toward the sun, soon morning's rays would set afire the spires of the Ginza and Kowloon, and the great game would begin again. He could hardly wait; he would take a sleeping pill tonight, to make the dead hours pass more rapidly, until the screens in his study could come alight again, and the numbers would again move to that relentless tempo of buying and selling and seeking advantage, a rhythm as ancient and innate to man as the very beating of his heart.

Billy T. fetched Rachel early. With two of the bridges out, traffic had a way of turning bad very quickly, he told her, and he wanted to get her to JFK in plenty of time. Sure, the Concorde only flew twice a week now, there were hassles about tickets and reservations all the time, he heard, and it was better to be an early bird.

The best way to go was to cut over the West Side at 66th Street, then go straight down Broadway to Wall Street—the financial district would truly be a ghost town at this hour—and then go out via the Brooklyn Battery tunnel.

At a light, Billy T. turned suddenly and said: "Hey, Mrs. Warrington, I almost forgot. I was over to see Mr. Fenton last night. I don't think he's doin' too good. He said he forgot to give you this." He passed back a manila envelope.

"Funny," said Billy, as Rachel opened the envelope, "there's no people anywhere. Mrs. W. used to say it was this way back during the Depression. You could blow off a twelve gauge in Times Square at high noon and not hit nobody. Wonder what Mrs. W. would think if she could see how it is now? Well, as they say—what goes round, comes round, huh, Mrs. Warrington?"

She examined the photograph. It was an old sepia photograph, now almost umber with age; the bitumen had in some places been completely absorbed by the paper, and the edges were crumbling. Rachel knew it at once: it had been Lyda's engagement picture. Taken in 1924. She studied the faces closely. There had been something of his parents when young in the Andrew she'd known, and there was something of them now in the grandson neither had lived to see.

"Hey, Mrs. Warrington," said Billy, "you know where we are? You wanna stop and take a look at the old place? Hey, c'mon."

He turned the car off Wall Street, took a quick left, and they were in Hanover Place.

Rachel got out. In the Warmile Securities Corp. liquidation in the previous year, the building had been sold, but the new owners had never taken possession. On the entablature, gilded letters read: BANK OF TAIPEI AND OKINAWA. The T in TAIPEI had become detached, and hung at an angle that gave the whole façade a decidedly seedy air. A sullen young black man in the uniform of a private security service lounged sulkily on the bottom step; on his lapel was the familiar white button with the little gold cross: the Crusade for Christian Capitalism. He looked Rachel over without interest and returned to his contemplations. A poster stuck to one of the flanking columns announced that the building was subject to a lien under the sequestration provisions of the Alien Assets Repatriation Act.

"Boy," said Billy, "if them stones could talk."

Indeed, thought Rachel.

She stepped back, to take the whole thing in. The old gargoyle still ruled his summit, keeping a watchful eye on the harbor traffic. The letters of HONOR AND OPTIMISM were all but worn away from the high cartouche.

Above the cornice line, the sky was bright blue; puffy clouds made their stately way toward the harbor and out to sea.

Rachel remembered the first time Andy'd brought her here. They'd toured the building from top to bottom. Then Andy had taken her up to the top floor and up a short flight of iron stairs and out onto the roof. In those days, Kerry Riverside Plaza North was still just a huge excavation, and they could look out over the East River Drive to the river.

"I used to come here all the time to think," Andy had told her. "I feel relaxed up here. It's about the only place I do."

Rachel could still hear his voice.

"Sometimes," he said, "I like to close my eyes and try to imagine it the way it must have been when Verrazano and Henry Hudson first sailed into the harbor. I try to imagine I'm a gull, soaring over the harbor, seeing it just as it was hundreds and hundreds of years ago, when there was no one living here but the Indians. You try it. It does wonders for the soul. Just use your imagination."

Rachel, looking up at the building, closed her eyes and heard his voice and imagined the world as he had.

She saw it clearly. Saw the brown headlands, the pale yellow marshes, and the fresh, green water meadows stretching away from white beaches. The sky bright blue, and the air so pure and clear you wanted to drink it. The dark smear of the forests, and here and there a plume of smoke from an Indian village.

It's as if I were a gull, she thought, cast free from earth and earth's cares, floating and flying, drifting with the soft winds, riding the currents of the sky.

Billy touched her arm gently, and murmured they'd best be going.

Just one last instant, she thought, keeping her eyes shut; just one last tiny, tiny interval to be free, to fly: to travel back, back, across the immemorial centuries to the end of the ocean, the beginning of the world, when everything was green and innocent and time itself was young.

Bridgehampton, 1986–1989